WILLI

Willis, Connie.

The winds of Marble
Arch and other
stories.

$40.00                        01/03/2008

WITHDRAWN

| | | DATE | |
|---|---|---|---|
| | | | |
| | | | |
| | | | |
| | | | |
| | | | |
| | | | |
| | | | |
| | | | |
| | | | |
| | | | |
| | | | |

BAKER & TAYLOR

# The Winds of Marble Arch

## And Other Stories

# The Winds of Marble Arch

### And Other Stories

## A Connie Willis Compendium

In Which May be Found
Personal Correspondence,
Travel Guides, References
to Royalty, Weather Reports,
Parking Fines, and Other Violations,
including Matters of Life and Death
(and Afterwards), an Epiphany or Two,
and an Appendix.

## CONNIE WILLIS

Subterranean Press • 2007

*The Winds of Marble Arch and Other Stories*

**Second Printing**

**ISBN**
978-1-59606-110-1

Subterranean Press
PO Box 190106
Burton, MI 48519

# Table of Contents

# An Introduction to This Book,

## or

# "These Are a Few of My Favorite Things"

Actually, writers have no business writing about their own works. They either wax conceited, saying things like: "My brilliance is possibly most apparent in my dazzling short story, "The Cookiepants Hypoteneuse." Or else they get unbearably cutesy: "My cat Ootsywootums has given me all my best ideas, hasn't oo, squeezums?"

Or they tell us things we DO NOT want to know about how and under what circumstances they got the idea for the story—"Late one January night in the throes of food poisoning, I found myself on the cold tile floor of my bathroom, thinking..."

This has brought me to the conclusion that writers should only be allowed to talk about other authors' books, not their own. They're hardly ever good judges of their own stuff. Mark Twain thought *Tom Sawyer* was his best novel. Wrong. (Though the scene where Huck and Tom go to their own funeral is pretty good.)

And the places most stories come from aren't that interesting. I've had stories come from walking to the post office and from misreading a billboard and from being stuck behind an RV going five miles an hour. And from listening, or rather, *not* listening to boring sermons. I am not alone in this. P.G. Wodehouse's "The Great Sermon Handicap" was obviously inspired by a particularly long and numbing sermon, and who knows how many other great works of literature have been spawned in this way? *The Scarlet Letter*? *Remembrance of Things Past*? *Lolita*?

Once I even got a story idea while watching *General Hospital*. It was during the glory days of Luke and Laura, and everyone thought Luke

9

was dead. They were having a funeral for him at the disco (don't ask) and Luke had sneaked back to get something and was listening to his own eulogy, and I thought, "Why, they stole that from *Tom Sawyer*," and then, "Well, if they can steal it, I can steal it."

But none of that really tells you anything about where the idea really came from—somewhere deep in the temporal lobe, I suspect, or the amygdala—or why an overheard conversation or the sight of a flock of geese being snowed on or a headline will suddenly strike the writer as hilarious (I read an article this morning about a high school principal who'd issued rules for dancing at the prom which included, "Both feet must remain on the floor at all times") or troubling or ironic or appalling (or all of the above), and will trigger something in them that compels them to write a story.

And it tells you nothing at all about how the story got from Idea to Finished Product. (The General Hospital/Tom Sawyer idea took a sharp left turn and became a ghost story.) And you *really* don't want to know that, any more than you want to know how Houdini escaped from that locked trunk. As one of my Clarion West students said after I'd explained a plotting technique I'd used, "I thought you were a good writer, but it's just a lot of tricks."

So I won't tell you any of that. And I definitely won't talk about my career. No one in their right mind wants to hear it. Which doesn't leave much in the way of topics. But we are both too far into this introduction to back out now. So how about if I tell you about some of the things I find interesting and/or love and which may or may not have influenced the stories you are about to read? Like:

## SCIENCE FICTION (Well, duh!)

I stumbled on Robert A. Heinlein's *Have Space Suit, Will Travel* when I was thirteen and have never recovered. I promptly read all of Heinlein's books and then everything else in my public library with a spaceship-and-atom symbol on the spine, which, luckily for me, included a complete collection of *The Year's Best from Fantasy and Science Fiction*, which were even more amazing than Heinlein. I was able to read stories by Kit Reed and Theodore Sturgeon and Zenna Henderson and Fredric Brown, "Vintage Season" and "Flowers for Algernon" and "The Veldt" all in one volume, fairy tales and imaginative high-tech futures and nightmares (political, social, and literal) and bittersweet love stories and knock-your-socks-off pyrotechnical experiments in styles and ideas. They gave me a glimpse of science fiction's incredible range of tone and ideas and techniques, from Philip K. Dick's mind-twisting "I Hope We Shall Arrive Soon" to Bob Shaw's heartbreaking, "The Light of Other Days," from William Tenn's funny "Bernie the Faust" to John Collier's haunting "Evening Primrose" to Ward Moore's terrifying "Lot."

It seemed interested in anything and everything—science, psychology, stars (both astronomical and Hollywoodian), ghosts, robots, aliens, dodoes, illuminated manuscripts, Martians, merry-go-rounds, nuclear war, spaceships, curious little shops... There was nothing that fell outside its boundaries. And since I was interested in everything, too—from campus parking to signing apes to mistakes that can't be rectified—I fell hopelessly in love with the field. I've been in love ever since.


**THREE MEN IN A BOAT**

On the very first page of *Have Space Suit, Will Travel*, Kip's father is reading Jerome K. Jerome's classic *Three Men in a Boat* while Kip is trying to talk to him about going to the moon. His dad tells Kip his situation is similar to that of J, Harris, and George when they discover they've forgotten the can opener. (Why he suggests this is beyond me. The three men nearly put George's eye out in their efforts to get the tin of pineapple open and never do succeed.) Well, anyway, as soon as I finished reading *Have Space Suit*, I found a copy of *Three Men* and read it and joined that lucky group of people who laugh aloud at the mere mention of large smelly cheeses, small sarcastic dogs, and killer swans. My favorite part of the book is the chapter where they get lost in the Hampton Court maze...no, wait, the part about the comic songs...no, wait, the packing scene...no, wait...

This gave me an early taste for humorous authors, of which there were—and are—far too few (though there are *lots* who labor under the misapprehension that they're funny.) Among the *truly* funny I've found and hoarded over the years are P.G. Wodehouse (I love the golf stories best, followed closely by Bertie and Jeeves, the Empress of Blandings, and assorted bulldogs), E.F. Benson's *Mapp and Lucia* books, Calvin Trillin, Helen Fielding's *Bridget Jones's Diary*, Stella Gibbons' *Cold Comfort Farm*, Anita Loos' *Gentlemen Prefer* Blondes, Dorothy Parker, and, of course, Mark Twain. And Shakespeare. (See next section.) They all (except maybe Dorothy) share a tremendous affection for humanity and a delight in demolishing the pompous, the smug, the self-righteous, and the willfully stupid.

One of the things that I like best about science fiction is that it has so many wonderfully funny writers and stories—Ron Goulart, Fredric Brown, Howard Waldrop, Shirley Jackson's "One Ordinary Day with Peanuts," Gordon Dickson's "Computers Don't Argue." And that it provides me a place for writing the romantic comedies I love. "At the Rialto" was probably the most fun, though "Ado" runs a close second, since it gave me a chance to write about Shakespeare, whom I adore even when he isn't being played by Joseph Fiennes. Which brings us to:

## SHAKESPEARE

I know, I know, everybody loves Shakespeare. But how can you *not* love him? I mean, Mercutio and Bottom and "It is the nightingale," and Birnam Wood and "We band of brothers!" and *The Mousetrap* and "A horse! A horse! My kingdom for a horse!" and Dogberry and "Come, kiss me, Kate," and poor hanged Cordelia. What's not to love? My favorite play is *Twelfth Night*, which manages to be hilarious and heartbreaking at the same time. (I recommend the Imogen Stubbs and Ben Kingsley version.) Tom Stoppard's right. Viola's the best heroine ever written.

I also hate Shakespeare. He is *so* good at everything: character, plot, dialogue, comedy, tragedy, suspense, variety, romance, snappy banter, irony. It's obvious every single one of the good fairies was present at his christening. (The bad fairy's curse obviously went something like, "No one will believe a boy from Stratford-on-Avon could write this stuff, and they'll drive you crazy by claiming your plays were written by Christopher Marlowe, Queen Elizabeth, or a committee.")

Most of us writers limp along with one or two gifts, or none, or are stuck telling the same story over and over, like F. Scott Fitzgerald with Zelda, or only have one book in them, like Margaret Mitchell or Harper Lee. But Shakespeare wrote tons of stuff, and it's all great. He can do slapstick and sword fights and love scenes and philosophy. His supporting characters are terrific—Feste and Puck and Polonius and Falstaff—and his women are the best in the business—Beatrice and Portia and Helena and Lady Macbeth and Rosalind. His story structure's dazzling, his death scenes are unforgettable—Lear saying, "For (as I am a man) I think this lady to be my child Cordelia," and "Never, never, never, never, never." He could take the exact same story of star-crossed lovers and do it as tragedy (*Romeo and Juliet*) and then farce (the Pyramus and Thisbe play in *A Midsummer Night's Dream*) and romantic comedy (*Much Ado About Nothing*) and ironic tragicomedy (*A Winter's Tale*) and say something new and original every time. And, as if that weren't enough, he invented the entire language the rest of us use, from "the witching hour" to "Westward, ho!" It is so totally unfair.

He's even good at screwball comedy. Which brings us to:

## SCREWBALL COMEDIES

I am addicted to movies of all kinds, from *A Beautiful Mind* to *The Searchers* to *The Others*. But my absolute favorite genre is the romantic comedy. I love the snappy bantering movies of the thirties and forties—*It Happened One Night*, and *My Favorite Wife* and *Bachelor Mother* and *The Miracle of Morgan's Creek*. *His Girl Friday* is my favorite. Cary Grant's line, "Maybe Bruce will let us stay with him," is the funniest thing in any comedy ever, though the loon calling in *Bringing Up Baby* and the nightclub scene in *The Bachelor and the Bobbysoxer* are close seconds.

But I'm not a purist. I also love the new stuff: *While You Were Sleeping* and *Notting Hill* and *French Kiss* and *Return to Me* and *Love, Actually*. I even like the remake of Sabrina better than the original. (I know, heresy.) And, of course, I love *Father Goose* and *Walk, Don't Run* and *How to Steal a Million*.

What I love about them (besides the fact that they occasionally seem to mirror my own life) is that they manage to be inventive and fun within a highly-structured form. They're like sonnets, sort of, with happy endings, and I only wish there were more of them.

Since there aren't, I've had to write my own, and luckily, science fiction's the perfect genre for screwball comedies. That's because they're both very cutting-edge and very old-fashioned. (And Shakespearean—he invented the genre with Beatrice and Benedick in *Much Ado About Nothing*.) The screwball comedy takes place in a very modern world (gyroplanes, online dating, corporate committee meetings, L-5 space colonies), there's lots of social commentary, *lots* of unintended consequences, and a general air of craziness that seems to fit the future, but at its heart, it's an old-fashioned love story. The first story I sold (except for some confessions stories and "The Secret of Santa Titicaca," a story so bad no genre would willingly claim it) was a screwball comedy titled, fittingly enough, "Capra Corn," and I've been writing (and living) them ever since. Which brings us to:

## MY OWN BIZARRE LIFE

Writers are supposed to live exciting lives, and I have: in the wilds of suburbia. I have sat on bleachers during gymnastics meets, attended Tupperware parties, made casseroles for potluck suppers, and sung in church choirs. The entire range of human experiences is present in a church choir, including but not restricted to jealousy, revenge, horror, pride, incompetence (the tenors have never been on the right note in the entire history of church choirs, and the basses have never been on the right page), wrath, lust, and existential despair.

I have taken cats to the vet, watched my friends have their colors done, changed diapers, and chaperoned junior proms. All of this has given me a definite advantage when writing stories about strange worlds and alien intelligences. And everything else I got from:

## AGATHA CHRISTIE

I learned everything I know about plot from Dame Agatha. She's the master of misdirection, red, green, and blue herrings, making you feel like a complete idiot that you didn't see who the murderer was, and, most of all, making you underestimate her. The reason *The Murder of Roger Ackroyd* works is not that she brilliantly plants her clues in plain sight (which she does) or plays on our assumptions about detective novels (which she also does, and not only in that book), but that she makes us think we're reading a harmless English country house mystery, complete with a rich squire, a sinister butler, a nosy old maid, and an eccentric detective. In other words, we underestimate the book the same way her characters underestimate fussy Hercule Poirot or sweet old Miss Marple. Or Agatha herself.

My first introduction to her was through the movie, *Murder on the Orient Express*, at which I disgraced myself by saying disgustedly about halfway through, "Oh, for heaven's sake, they can't all have done it!" I then raced to the library to read *The ABC Murders, Death on the Nile, After the Funeral, The Moving Finger, 4:50 from Paddington,* and the one that made everybody so mad: *The Murder of Roger Ackroyd.* Critics, authors, and readers declared that she'd cheated (she hadn't) and that she'd broken all the rules of civilized mystery writing (she had.) S.S. Van Dine was so incensed, he wrote up a list of rules, including "There shall be no romance," and "Only one person shall have committed the murder," rules which I believe Agatha tacked up above her desk and then proceeded to break, one after the other.

And yet, in spite of that little episode, in spite of being knighted and writing the longest-running play in the history of the theater and making it onto the bestseller list even after she was dead (twice) and being involved in a personal mystery (she vanished without a trace and then turned up two weeks later at a hotel in Harrogate) which has never been solved, she remains underestimated.

A good trick and one, like all of her tricks, that should be emulated whenever possible.

Note: I also love Dorothy Sayers' Lord Peter Wimsey mysteries, particularly *Nine Tailors* and the Harriet Vane books: *Strong Poison, Have His Carcase, Gaudy Night,* and *Busman's Honeymoon* (to be read in that order), but Dorothy's doing something totally different from Agatha. Her mystery plots are hopeless, bogging down in train schedules, circumcisions, and omelets, but that's because she's no more interested in them than Agatha is in doing characters. What Dorothy's interested in is writing comedies of manners and chronicling one of the great love stories of literature.

I was on a walking tour of Oxford colleges once with a group of bored and unimpressable tourists. They yawned at Balliol's quad, T.E. Lawrence's and Churchill's portraits, and the blackboard Einstein wrote his $E=mc^2$ on. Then the tour guide said, "And this is the Bridge of Sighs, where Lord Peter proposed (in Latin) to Harriet," and everyone suddenly came to life and began snapping pictures. Such is the power of books.

Finally, my biggest and most important influence has been:

## THE PUBLIC LIBRARY

I was born into a family that didn't read and that didn't own many books. My mother had a movie edition of *Gone with the Wind,* my grandmother subscribed to *Redbook* and *The Saturday Evening Post*, and the girl across the street had a copy of *A Little Princess*, and that was about it. Consequently, pretty much everything I read came from the public library, and I spent as much time there as I could.

It was there that I discovered science fiction and *Anne of Green Gables* and Lenora Mattingly Weber and H.V. Morton's *London*, which was where I first read about the St. Paul's fire watch in World War II sleeping in the crypts of the cathedral during the day and putting out incendiaries on the roofs at night. I wrote *Doomsday Book* in the public library, and "Chance" and "A Letter from the Clearys," and I researched *Passage* and "Fire Watch" and "Just Like the Ones We Used to Know" there. The public library was where I read about the Hindenburg and Emily Dickinson and the curse of Tutankhamen.

When I was eleven, I decided to read my way through the library alphabetically just like Francie in *A Tree Grows in Brooklyn*, and, in doing so, found James Agee's *A Death in the Family* and Jane Austen and Peter Beagle's *A Fine and Private Place* before stumbling onto science fiction. And it was in the library that I found all sorts of things I wasn't looking for at all—books on chaos theory and literary criticism, an article on body sniffers in the Blitz and one about Aberfan in Wales, where all the children had been killed when the coal tip slid down on the school, and scientific articles about the EPR paradox and the effect of large particulates on the color of the stratosphere.

I couldn't have become a writer—or anything—without the public library, and it appears in some guise or other in every one of my stories. And quite a few of those stories are in this book. I hope you enjoy them.

Connie Willis
March 3, 2007

# Weather Reports

# The Winds of Marble Arch

Cath refused to take the tube.

"You loved it the last time we were here," I said, rummaging through my suitcase for a tie.

"Correction. *You* loved it," she said, brushing her short hair. "*I* thought it was dirty and smelly and dangerous."

"You're thinking of the New York subway. This is the London Underground." The tie wasn't there. I unzipped the side pocket and jammed my hand down it. "You rode the tube the last time we were here."

"I also carried my suitcase up five flights of stairs at that awful bed and breakfast we stayed at. I have no intention of doing that either."

She wouldn't have to. The Connaught had a lift *and* a bellman.

"I *hated* the tube," she said. "I only took it because we couldn't afford taxis. And now we can."

We certainly could. We could also afford a hotel with carpet on the floor and a bathroom in our room instead of down the hall. A far cry from the—what was it called? It had had brown linoleum floors you hadn't wanted to walk on in your bare feet, and you had to put coins in a meter above the bathtub to get hot water.

"What was the name of that place we stayed at?" I asked Cath.

"I've repressed it," she said. "All I remember is that the tube station had the name of a cemetery."

"Marble Arch," I said, "and it wasn't named after a cemetery. It was named after the copy of the Roman arch of Constantine in Hyde Park."

"Well, it sounded like a cemetery."

"The Royal Hernia!" I said, suddenly remembering.

Cath grinned. "The Royal *Heritage*."

"The Royal Hernia of Marble Arch," I said. "We should go visit it, just for old times' sake."

"I doubt if it's still there," she said, putting on her earrings. "It's been twenty years."

"Of course it's still there," I said. "Scummy showers and all. Do you remember those narrow beds? They were just like coffins, only at least coffins have sides so you don't roll off." The tie wasn't there. I started taking shirts out of the suitcase and piling them on the bed. "These aren't much better. It makes you wonder how the British have managed to reproduce all these years."

"We seemed to manage all right," Cath said, putting on her shoes. "What time does the conference start?"

"Ten," I said, dumping socks and underwear onto the bed. "What time are you meeting Sara?"

"Nine-thirty," she said, looking at her watch. "Will you have time to pick up the tickets for the play?"

"Sure," I said. "The Old Man won't show up before eleven."

"Good," she said. "Sara and Elliott can only go Saturday. They've got something tomorrow night, and we've got dinner with Milford Hughes's widow and her sons Friday night. Is Arthur going with us to the play? Did you get in touch with him?"

"No, but I know the Old Man'll want to go. What are we seeing?" I asked, giving up on the tie.

"*Ragtime*, if we can get tickets. It's at the Adelphi. If not, try to get *The Tempest* or *Sunset Boulevard*, and if they're sold out, *Endgames*. Hayley Mills is in it."

"*Kismet* isn't playing?"

She grinned again. "*Kismet* isn't playing."

"Which tube stop does it say for the Adelphi?"

"Charing Cross," she said, consulting the map. "*Sunset Boulevard's* at the Old Vic, and *The Tempest's* at the Duke of York. On Shaftesbury Avenue. You could get the tickets through a ticket agent. It would be a lot faster than going to the theaters."

"Not on the tube, it won't," I said. "It's a snap to go anywhere. And ticket agents are for tourists."

She looked skeptical. "Get third row if you can, but not on the sides. And no farther back than the dress circle."

"Not the balcony?" I asked. The farthest, highest seats had been all we could afford the first time we were here, so high up all you could see was the tops of the actors' heads. When we'd gone to *Kismet*, the Old Man had spent the entire time leaning forward to look down the well-endowed Lalume's Arabian costume through a pair of rental binoculars.

"*Not* the balcony," Cath said, sticking an umbrella and the guidebook in her bag. "Put it on the American Express, if they'll take it. If not, the Visa."

"Are you sure the third row's a good idea?" I said. "Remember, the Old Man nearly got us thrown out of the upper balcony the last time, and there wasn't even anybody else up there."

Cath stopped putting things in her bag. "Tom," she said, looking worried. "It's been twenty years, and you haven't seen Arthur in over five."

"And you think the Old Man will have grown up in the meantime?" I said. "Not a chance. This is the guy who got us thrown out of Graceland five years ago. He'll still be the same."

Cath looked like she was going to say something else, and then began putting stuff in her bag again. "What time is the cocktail party tonight?"

"Sherry party," I said. "They have sherry parties here. Six. I'll meet you back here, okay? Or is that enough time for you and Sara to buy out the town and catch up on—what is it?—three years' gossip?"

I'd seen Elliott and Sara last year in Atlanta and the year before that in Barcelona, but Cath hadn't come with me to either conference. "Where are you doing all this shopping?" I asked.

"Harrods," she said. "Remember the tea set I bought the first time we were here? I'm going to buy the matching china. And a scarf at Liberty's and a cashmere cardigan, all the things we couldn't afford last time." She looked at her watch again. "And I'd better get going. The traffic's going to be bad in this rain."

"The tube would be faster," I said. "And drier. You take the Piccadilly line to Knightsbridge, and you're right there. You don't even have to go outside. There's an entrance to Harrods right in the tube station."

"I am not maneuvering shopping bags up and down those awful escalators," she said. "They're broken half the time. Besides, there are rats."

"You saw *one* mouse in Piccadilly Circus *one* time, and it was down on the tracks," I said.

"It's been twenty years," she said, coming over to the bed and deftly pulling my tie out of the mess. "There are probably thousands of rats down there now." She kissed me on the cheek. "Good luck presenting your paper." She grabbed up an umbrella. "*You* take the tube," she said, going out the door. "You're the one who's crazy about it."

"I intend to," I called after her, but the lift had already closed.

⊣ • • • ⊢

In spite of Cath's dire predictions, the tube was exactly the same as it had been twenty years ago. Well, maybe not exactly. There were ticket machines now, and automated stiles that sucked up my five-day pass and spit it out to me again. And the escalators were metal now instead of wooden. But they were as steep as ever, and the posters for musicals and plays that lined them had hardly changed at all. *Kismet* and *Cats* had been playing then. Now it was *Showboat* and *Cats*.

Cath was right—I did love the tube. It's the best underground system in the world. Boston's T is old and decrepit, Tokyo's subway system is a sardine can, and Washington's Metro looks like it was designed as a bomb shelter. The Metro's not bad, but it has the handicap of being in Paris. BART's in San Francisco, but it doesn't go anywhere.

The tube goes everywhere, all the way to Heathrow and Hampton Court and beyond, to obscure suburban stops like Cockfosters and Mudchute. There's a stop at every tourist attraction, and it's impossible to get lost.

But it isn't just an efficient way of getting from the Tower to Westminster Abbey to Buckingham Palace. It's a place in itself, a wonderful underground warren of tunnels and stairs and corridors, as colorful as the billboard-sized theater posters on the walls of the platforms, as the maps posted on every pillar and wall and forking of the tunnels.

I stopped in front of one, studying the crisscrossing green and blue and red lines. Charing Cross. I needed the gray line. What was that? Jubilee.

I followed the signs down a curving platform and out onto the eastbound platform.

A train was pulling out. An LED sign above the tracks said NEXT TRAIN 6 MIN. The train started into the narrow tunnel, and I waited for the blast of wind that would follow it, pushing the air in front of it as the train disappeared.

It came, smelling faintly of diesel and dust, ruffling the hair of the woman standing next to me, rippling her skirt. NEXT TRAIN 5 MIN., the sign said.

I filled the time by watching a pair of newlyweds holding hands and reading the posters on the tunnel walls for *Sunset Boulevard* and *Sliding Doors* and Harrods. "A Blast from the Past," the one on the end said. "Experience the London Blitz at the Imperial War Museum. Elephant and Castle Tube Station."

"Train approaching," a voice said from nowhere, and I stepped forward to the yellow line.

The familiar MIND THE GAP sign was still painted on the edge of the platform. Cath had always refused to stand anywhere near the edge. She had stood nervously against the tiled wall as if she expected the train to suddenly leap off the tracks and plow into us.

The train pulled in. Right on time, shining chrome and plastic, no gum on the floor, no unknown substances on the orange plush seats.

"I beg your pardon," the woman next to me said, shifting her shopping bag so I could sit down.

Even the people who rode the tube were more polite than people on any other subway. And better read. The man opposite me was reading Dickens' *Bleak House*.

The train slowed. "Regent's Park," the flat voice announced.

Regent's Park. The last time we were here, the Old Man had shouted "To the head!" and vaulted off the train at this station.

He had been taking us on a riotous tour of Sir Thomas More's body. We had gone to the Tower of London to see the Crown Jewels, and Cath, reading her Frommer's *England on $40 a Day* while we stood in line, had said, "Sir Thomas More is buried in the church here. You know, *A Man for All Seasons*," and we had all trooped over to see his grave.

"Want to see the rest of him?" the Old Man had said.

"The rest of him?" Sara had asked.

"Only his body's buried there," the Old Man had said. "You need to see his head!" and had led us off to London Bridge, where More's head had been stuck on a pike, and the Chelsea garden where his daughter Margaret had buried it after she took it down, and then off to Canterbury, with the Old Man turned around and talking to us as he drove, to the small church where the head was buried now.

"Thomas More's Remains: The World Tour," he had said, driving us back at breakneck speed.

"Except for Lake Havasu," Elliott had said. "Isn't that where the original London Bridge is?" And when the annual conference was in San Diego, the Old Man had roared up in a rental car and highjacked us all to Arizona to see it.

I couldn't wait to see him. There was no telling what wild sightseeing he had in mind this time. This was, after all, the man who had gotten us thrown out of Alcatraz.

He hadn't been at the last four conferences—he'd been off in Nepal for the first one and finishing a book the last three—and I was eager to hear what he'd been up to.

"Oxford Circus," the flat voice said. Two more stops to Charing Cross.

I leaned out to look at the station as we stopped. Each station has its own distinctive design, its own identifying color: St. Pancras green edged with navy, Euston Square black and orange, Bond Street red. Oxford Circus had a blue chutes and ladders design that was new since the first time we'd been here.

The train pulled out, picked up speed. I would be there in five minutes and to the Adelphi in ten, a lot faster than Cath in her taxi, and at least as comfortable.

I was there in eight, up the escalators and out in the rain, up the Strand to the Adelphi in twenty. It would have been fifteen, but I had to wait ten (huddled under an awning and wishing I'd taken Cath's advice about an umbrella) to cross the Strand. Black London taxis, bumper to bumper, and double-decker buses, and minis, all going nowhere fast.

*Ragtime* was sold out. I got a theater map from the rack in the lobby and looked to see where the Duke of York was. It was over on Shaftesbury, with the nearest tube stop Leicester Square. I went back to Charing Cross, and went down the escalator and into the passage that led to the Northern Line. I still had half an hour, which would be cutting it close, but not impossible.

I started down the left-hand tunnel toward the trains, keeping pace with the crowd, straining to hear the rumble of a train pulling in over the muffled din of voices, the crisp clatter of high heels.

People began to walk faster. The high heels beat a quicker tattoo. I got the tube map out of my back pocket. I could take the Piccadilly Line to South Kensington and change to the District and—

The wind hit me like the blast from an explosion. I reeled back, nearly losing my balance. My head snapped back sharply like I'd been punched in the jaw. I groped wildly for the tiled wall.

"The IRA's blown up a train!" I thought.

But there was no sound accompanying the sudden blast of searing air, only a dank, horrible smell.

Sarin gas, I thought, and reflexively put my hand over my nose and mouth, but I could still smell it. Sulfur and a wet earthy smell, and something else. Gunpowder? Dynamite? I sniffed at the air, trying to identify it.

But whatever it was, it was already over. The wind had stopped as abruptly as it had hit me, and so had the smell. Not even a trace of it lingered in the dry, stuffy air.

And it must not have been an explosion, or poison gas, because no one else had even slackened their steps. The sound of high heels retained its brisk, even clatter down the tiled passage. Two German teenagers with backpacks hurried past, giggling, and a businessman in a gray topcoat, the *Times* tucked under his arm, and a young woman in floppy sandals, all of them oblivious.

Hadn't any of them felt it? Or was it a usual occurrence in Charing Cross Station and they were used to it?

How could anybody possibly get used to a blast like that? They must not have felt it.

Had *I* felt it?

It was like an earthquake back home in California, a jolt, and then before you could even register it, it was over, and you weren't sure it had really happened. The only way you could tell for sure was by asking Cath or the kids, "Did you feel that?" or by the picture tilted on the wall.

The only pictures on the walls down here were pasted on, and the German students, the businessman had already told me the answer to "Did you feel that?"

But I felt it, I thought, and tried to reconstruct it. Heat, and the sharp tang of sulfur and wet dirt. But that wasn't what had made me lose my balance, what had sent me staggering against the wall. It was the smell of panic and people screaming, of a bomb going off.

But it couldn't be a bomb. The IRA was in peace negotiations with the British, there hadn't been an incident for over a year, and bombs didn't stop in mid-blast. There had been bombs in the tube before—the mechanical voice would be saying, "Please exit up the escalator immediately," not, "Mind the gap."

But if it wasn't a bomb, what was it? And where had it come from? I looked up at the roof of the passage, but there wasn't a grate or a vent, no water pipes running along the ceiling. I walked along the tunnel, sniffing the air, but there were only the usual smells—dust and damp wool and cigarette smoke, and, where the passage went up a short flight of stairs, a strong smell of oil.

A train rumbled in somewhere down the passage. The train. There had been one pulling in when it hit. It must be causing the wind somehow.

I went out onto the platform and stood there looking down the tunnel, half-hoping, half-dreading it would happen again.

The train pulled in and stopped, and a handful of people got off. "Mind the gap!" the computerized voice said. The doors whooshed shut, and the train pulled out. A wind picked up the scraps of paper on the track and whirled them into the side walls, and I braced myself, my feet apart, but it was just an ordinary breeze, smelling of nothing in particular.

I went back out in the passage and examined the walls for doors, felt along the tiles for drafts, stood in the same place as before, waiting for another train to come in.

But there was nothing, and I was in the way. People going around me murmured, "Sorry," over and over, which I have never been able to get used to, even though I know it's merely the British equivalent of "excuse me." It still sounded like they were apologizing, when I was the one blocking traffic. And I needed to get to the conference.

And whatever had caused the wind, it was probably just a fluke. The passages connecting the trains and the different lines and levels were like a rabbit warren. The wind could have come from anywhere. Maybe somebody on the Jubilee Line had been transporting a carton of rotten eggs. Or blood samples. Or both.

I went up to the Northern Line, caught a train that had just pulled in, and made it to the conference in time for the eleven o'clock session, but the episode must have unnerved me more than I'd admitted to myself. Standing in the lobby and pinning on my registration badge, the outside door opened, letting in a blast of air.

I flinched away from it, and then stood there, staring blindly at the door, until the woman at the registration table asked, "Are you all right?"

I nodded. "Have the Old Man or Elliott Templeton registered yet?"

"An old man?" the woman said, bewilderedly.

"Not *an* old man, *the* Old Man," I said impatiently. "Arthur Birdsall."

"The morning session's already started," she said, looking through the ranked badges. "Have you looked in the ballroom?"

The Old Man had never attended a session in his life.

"Mr. Templeton's here," she said, still looking. "No, Mr. Birdsall hasn't registered yet."

"Daniel Drecker's here," Marjorie O'Donnell said, descending on me. "You heard about his daughter, didn't you?"

28

"No," I said, scanning the room for Elliott.

"She's in an institution," she said. "Schizophrenia."

I wondered if she was telling me this because she thought I was acting unbalanced, too, but she added, "So, for heaven's sake, don't ask him about her. And don't ask Peter Jamieson if Leslie's here. They're separated."

"I won't," I said and escaped to the first session. Elliott wasn't in the audience, or at lunch. I sat down next to John McCord, who lived in London, and said, without preamble, "I was in the tube this morning."

"Wretched, isn't it?" McCord said. "And *so* expensive. What's a day pass now? Two pounds fifty?"

"While I was in Charing Cross Station, there was this strange wind."

McCord nodded knowingly. "The trains cause them. When they pull out of a station, they push the air in front of them," he said, illustrating the pushing with his hands, "and because they fill the tunnel, it creates a slight vacuum in the train's wake, and air rushes in behind to fill the vacuum, and it creates a wind. The same thing happens in reverse as trains pull into the station."

"I know," I said impatiently. "But this one was like an explosion, and it smelled—"

"It's all the dirt down there. And the beggars. They sleep in the passages, you know. Some of them even urinate on the walls. I'm afraid the Underground's deteriorated considerably in the past few years."

"Everything in London has," the woman across the table said. "Did you know there's a Disney store in Regent Street?"

"And a Gap," McCord said.

"Mind the Gap," I said, but they were off on the subject of the Decline and Fall of London. I said I needed to go look for Elliott.

He was nowhere to be found. The afternoon session was starting. I sat down next to John and Irene Watson.

"You haven't seen Arthur Birdsall or Elliott Templeton, have you?" I said, scanning the ballroom.

"Elliott was here before the morning session," John said. "Stewart's here."

Irene leaned across John. "You heard about his surgery, didn't you? Colon cancer."

"The doctors say they got it all," John said.

"I hate coming to these things anymore," Irene said, leaning confidingly across John again. "Everybody's either gotten old or sick or divorced. You heard Hari Srinivasau died, didn't you? Heart attack."

"I see somebody over there I need to talk to," I said. "I'll be right back." I started up the aisle.

And ran straight into Stewart.

"Tom!" he said, "How have you been?"

"How have *you* been?" I said. "I heard you've been ill."

"I'm fine. The doctors tell me they caught it in time, that they got it all," he said. "It isn't so much the cancer coming back that worries me as knowing this is the kind of thing in store for us as we get older. You heard about Paul Wurman?"

"No," I said. "Look, I have to go make a phone call before the session starts." And before he could fill me in on the Decline and Fall of Everybody.

I took off for the lobby. "Where have you been?" Elliott said, clapping a hand on my shoulder. "I've been looking all over for you."

"Where have *I* been?" I said, like a shipwreck victim who'd been on a raft for days. "You have no idea how glad I am to see you," I said, looking happily at him. He looked just the same as ever, tall, in shape, his hairline not even receding. "Everyone else is falling apart."

"Including you," he said, grinning. "You look like you need a drink."

"Is the Old Man with you?" I asked, looking around for him.

"No," he said. "Do you have any notion where the bar is in this place?"

"In there," I pointed.

"Lead the way," he said. "I've got all sorts of things to tell you. I've just talked Evers and Associates into a new project. I'll tell you all about it over a couple of pints."

He did, and then told me about what he and Sara had been doing since the last conference.

"I thought the Old Man would be here today," I said. "He'll be here tonight, though?"

"I think so," Elliott said. "Or tomorrow."

"He's all right isn't he?" I said, looking across the bar to where Stewart stood talking. "He's not sick or anything?"

"I don't think so," Elliott said, looking reassuringly surprised. "He lives in Cambridge now, you know. And Sara and I won't be there either. Evers and Associates are taking us out to dinner to celebrate. We'll stop by for a few minutes on our way, though. Sara insisted. She wants to see you. She's been so excited about your visit. She's talked of nothing else for weeks. She couldn't wait to go shopping with Cath." He went over to the bar and got us two more pints. "Speaking of which, Sara said I'm to tell you we're definitely on for the play and supper Saturday. What are we going to see? Please tell me it's not *Sunset Boulevard*."

"Oh, my God!" I said. "It's not anything. I forgot to get the tickets." I glanced hastily at my watch. 3:45. "Do you think the box offices will be open now?"

He nodded.

"Good." I snatched up my coat and started for the lobby.

"And not *Cats*!" Elliott called after me.

I would be lucky if I got anything, I thought, sprinting down to the tube station and pushing my way through the turnstile, including a train at this hour. The escalators were so jammed I had trouble getting the list of theatres out of my pocket. *The Tempest* was at the Duke of York. Leicester Square. I pulled my tube map out—Piccadilly Line. The passage to the Piccadilly Line was even more crowded than the escalator, and slower. The elderly woman ahead of me, in a gray headscarf and an ancient brown coat, was shuffling at a snail's pace, clutching her coat collar to her throat with a blue-veined hand, her head down and her body hunched forward as if she were struggling against a hurricane.

I tried to get around her, but the way was blocked by more teenagers with backpacks, Spanish this time, walking four abreast and discussing "El Tour de Londres."

I missed the train and had to wait for the next one, checking the "Next train 4 Min." sign every fifteen seconds and listening to the American couple behind me bitterly arguing.

"I *told* you it started at four," the woman said. "Now we'll be late."

"Who was the one who had to take one more picture?" the man said. "You've already taken five hundred pictures, but, oh, no, you had to take one more."

"I wanted to have something to remember our vacation by," she said bitterly. "Our happy, happy vacation."

The train came in, and I mashed my way on and grabbed a pole, and then stood there, squashed, reading my list. The Wyndham was near Leicester Square, too. What was at the Wyndham? *Cats*.

No good. But *Death of a Salesman* was at the Prince Edward, which was only a few blocks over. And there was a whole row of theatres on Shaftesbury.

"Leicester Square," the automated voice said, and I forced my way off the train, down the passage, and up the escalators and into Leicester Square.

The traffic up top was even worse, and it took me nearly twenty minutes to get to the Duke of York, only to find that its box office was closed until six. The Prince Edward was open, but it only had two sets of single seats fifteen rows apart for *Death of a Salesman*. "The soonest I can get you five seats all together," the black-lipsticked girl said, tapping keys on a computer, "is March fifteenth."

The Ides of March, I thought. How fitting, since Cath would kill me if I came home without the tickets.

"Where's the nearest ticket agent?" I asked the girl.

"There's one on Cannon Street," she said vaguely.

Cannon Street. That was the name of a tube station. I consulted my tube map. District and Circle Line. I could take the Northern Line down to Embankment and catch the District and Circle from there.

I looked at my watch. It was already four-thirty. We were supposed to be at the sherry party at six. I would be cutting it close. I sprinted back to Leicester Square, down to the Northern Line, and onto a train. It was even more jammed, but everyone was still polite. They held their books above the fray and continued to read in spite of the crush. *Madame Bovary* and Geoffrey Ryman's *253* and Charles Williams' *Descent into Hell*.

"Cannon Street," the computer voice said, and I pushed my way off and headed for the exit.

I was halfway down the passage when it hit again, the same violent blast as before, the same smell.

No, not the same, I thought, regaining my footing, watching unconcerned commuters walk past. There had been the same sharp smell of sulfur and explosives, but no musty wetness. And this time there was the smell of smoke.

But no fire alarms had gone off, no sprinkler system been activated. No one had even noticed it.

Maybe it's one of those things where it's so common the locals don't even notice it, I thought, they can't even smell it anymore. Like a lumber mill or chemical plant. We had gone to see Cath's uncle in Nebraska one time, and I'd asked him if he minded the smell from the feed lots.

"What smell?" he'd said.

But manure didn't smell like violence, like panic. And it was everywhere. If this was a persistent, pervasive smell, why hadn't I smelled it in Piccadilly Circus or Leicester Square?

I was all the way to South Kensington before I realized I had gone back down the passage without even being aware of it, boarded a train, ridden seven stops. And not gotten the tickets.

I got off the train, half-intending to go back, and then stood there on the platform uncertainly. This was no carton of rotten eggs, or blood samples, no localized phenomenon of Charing Cross. So what was it?

A woman got off the train, glancing irritatedly at her watch. I looked at mine. Five-thirty. It was too late to go back to the ticket agent's, too late to do anything but figure out which line to take to get home.

I felt a rush of relief that I wouldn't have to go back to Cannon Street, wouldn't have to face that wind again. What were they, I wondered, pulling out my tube map, that they produced such a feeling of fear?

I thought about it all the way back to the hotel, wondering if I should tell Cath. It would only confirm her in her opinion of the tube, and she would hardly be in the mood for wild stories about winds in the tube, not if she'd been waiting for me to show up. Cath hated being late to things, and it was already after six. By the time I made it back to the hotel it would be nearly six-thirty.

It was six forty-five. I pushed unavailingly on the lift button for five minutes and then took the stairs. Maybe she was running late, too. When she and Sara started shopping, they lost all track of time. I fished the room key out of my pants pocket.

Cath opened the door.

"I'm late, I know," I said, unpinning my nametag and peeling my jacket off. "Give me five minutes. Are you ready?"

"Yes," she said. She walked over and sat down on the bed, watching me.

"How was Harrods?" I said, unbuttoning my shirt. "Did you get your china?"

"No," she said, looking down at her folded hands.

I grabbed a clean shirt out of my suitcase and pulled it on. "But you and Sara had a good time?" I said, buttoning it. "What did you buy? Elliott said he was afraid you'd clean out Harrods between the two of you." I stopped, looking at her. "What's wrong?" I said. "Did the kids call? Has something happened?"

"The kids are fine," she said.

"But something happened," I said. "The taxi you and Sara took had an accident."

She shook her head. "Nothing happened," and then, still looking down at her hands. "Sara's having an affair."

33

"What?" I said stupidly.

"She's having an affair."

"*Sara?*" I said, disbelieving. Not Sara, affectionate, loyal Sara.

Cath nodded, still looking at her hands.

I sat down on my bed. "Did she tell you she was?"

"No, of course not," Cath said, standing up and walking over to the mirror.

"Then how do you know?" I asked, but I knew how. The same way she had known that the kids were getting chicken pox, that her sister was engaged, that her father was worried about his business. Cath had always noticed things before anybody else—she was equipped with some kind of super-sensitive radar that picked up on subliminal signs or vibrations in the air or something. And she was always right.

But Sara and Elliott had been married as long as we had. They were the couple at the top of our "Marriage is Still a Viable Institution" list.

"Are you sure?" I said.

"I'm sure."

I wanted to ask her how she knew, but there wasn't any point. When Ashley had gotten the chicken pox, she'd said, "Her eyes always look bright when she has a fever, and, besides, Lindsay had them two weeks ago," but most of the time she could only shake her short blonde hair, unable to say how she'd reached her conclusion, but always right. Always right.

"But—I saw Elliott today," I said. "He was fine. He didn't—" I thought back over everything he had said, wondering if there had been some indication in it that he was worried or unhappy. He had said Sara and Cath would spend a lot of money, but he always said that. "He sounded fine."

"Put your tie on," she said.

"But if she—we don't have to go if you don't want to," I said.

"No," she said, shaking her head. "No. No, we have to go."

"Maybe you misinterpreted—"

"I didn't," she said and went into the bathroom and shut the door.

We had trouble getting a taxi. The Connaught's doorman seemed to have disappeared, and all of the black boxy London cabs ignored my frantic waving. Even when one finally stopped, it took us forever to get to the party. "Theatergoers," the cabbie explained cheerfully of the traffic. "You two plan to see any plays while you're here?"

I wondered if Cath would still want to go to a play, convinced as she was that Sara was having an affair, but as we passed the Savoy, its neon sign for *Miss Saigon* blazing, she asked, "What play did you get tickets for?"

"I didn't," I said. "I ran out of time." I started to say that I intended to get them tomorrow, but she wasn't listening.

"Harrods didn't have my china," she said, and her tone sounded as hopeless as it had telling me about Sara. "They discontinued the pattern four years ago."

We were nearly an hour and a half late for the party. Elliott and Sara have probably long since left for dinner, I thought, and was secretly relieved.

"Cath!" Marjorie said as we walked in the door and hurried over with her nametag. "You look wonderful! I have so much to tell you!"

"I'm going to go look for the Old Man," I said. "I'll see if he wants to go to dinner afterwards." He would probably drag us off to Soho or Hampstead Heath. He always knew some out-of-the-way place that had eel pie or authentic English stout.

I set off through the crowd. You could usually locate the Old Man by the crowd of people gathered around, and the laughter. And the proximity to the bar, I thought, spotting a huddle of people in that direction.

I waded toward them through the crush, grabbing glass of wine off a tray as I went, but it wasn't the Old Man. It was the people who'd been at lunch. They were discussing, of all things, the Beatles, but at least it wasn't the Decline and Fall.

"The three of them were talking about a reunion tour," McCord was saying. "I suppose that's all off now."

"The Old Man took us on a Beatles tour," I said. "Has anybody seen him? He insisted we recreate all the album covers. We nearly got killed crossing Abbey Road."

"I don't think he's coming down from Cambridge till tomorrow," McCord said. "It's a long drive."

The Old Man had driven us four hundred miles to see London Bridge. I peered over their heads, trying to spot the Old Man. I couldn't see him, but I did spot Evers, which meant Sara and Elliott were still here. Cath was over by the door with Marjorie.

"It was just so *sad* about Linda McCartney," the Gap woman said.

I took a swig of my wine and remembered too late this was a sherry party.

"How old was she?" McCord was asking.

"Fifty-three."

"I know three women who've been diagnosed with breast cancer," the Gap woman said. "*Three.* It's dreadful."

"One keeps wondering who's next," the other woman said.

"Or *what's* next," McCord said. "You heard about Stewart, didn't you?"

I handed my sherry glass to the gap woman, who looked at me, annoyed, and started through the crowd toward Cath, but now I couldn't see her either. I stopped, craning my neck to see over the crowd.

"*There* you are, you handsome thing!" Sara said, coming up behind me and putting her arm around my waist. "We've been looking all over for you!"

She kissed me on the cheek. "Elliott's been fretting that you were going to make us all go see *Cats*. He *loathes Cats*, and everyone who comes to visit drags us to it. And you know how he frets over things. You didn't, did you? Get tickets for *Cats*?"

"No," I said, staring at her. She looked the same as always—her dark hair still tucked behind her ears, her eyebrows still arched mischievously. This was the same old Sara who'd gone with us to *Kismet*, to Lake Havasu, to Abbey Road.

Cath was wrong. She might pick up subliminal signals about other people, but this time she was wrong. Sara wasn't acting guilty or uneasy, wasn't avoiding my eyes, wasn't avoiding Cath.

"Where *is* Cath?" she asked, standing on tiptoe to peer over the crowd. "I have something I've got to tell her."

"What?"

"About her china. We couldn't find it today, did she tell you? Well, after I got home, I thought, 'I'll wager they have it at Selfridge's.' They're always years behind the times. Oh, there she is." She waved frantically. "I want to tell her before we leave," she said and took off through the crowd. "Find Elliott and tell him I'll only be a sec. And tell him we aren't seeing *Cats*," she called back to me. "I don't want him stewing all night. He's over there somewhere." She waved vaguely in the direction of the door, and I pushed my way between people till I found him, standing by the front door.

"You haven't seen Sara, have you?" he said. "Evers is bringing his car round."

"She's talking to Cath," I said. "She said she'll be here in a minute."

"Are you kidding? When those two get together—" He shook his head indulgently. "Sara said they had a wonderful time today."

"Is the Old Man here yet?" I said.

"He called and said he couldn't make it tonight. He said to tell you he'll see us tomorrow. I'm looking forward to it. We've scarcely seen him since he moved to Cambridge. We're down in Wimbledon, you know."

"And he hasn't swooped down and kidnapped you to go see Dickens' elbow or something?"

"Not lately. Oh, God, do you remember that time Sara mentioned Arthur Conan Doyle, and he dragged us up and down Baker Street, looking for Sherlock Holmes's missing flat?"

I laughed, remembering him knocking on doors, demanding, "What have you done with 221B, madam?" deciding we needed to call in Scotland Yard.

"And then demanding to know what they'd done with the yard," Elliott said, laughing.

"Did you tell him we're all going to a play together Saturday?"

"Yes. You didn't get tickets for *Cats*, did you?"

"I didn't get tickets for anything," I said. "I ran out of time."

"Well, *don't* get tickets for *Cats*. Or *Phantom*."

Sara came running up, flushed and breathless. "I'm sorry. Cath and I got to talking," she said. She gave me a smacking kiss on the lips. "Goodbye, you adorable hunk. See you Saturday."

"Come *on*," Elliott said. "You can kiss him all you like on Saturday." He hustled her out the door. "And not *Les Miz*!" he shouted back to me.

I stood, smiling after them. You're wrong, Cath, I thought. Look at them. Not only would Sara never have kissed me like that if she were having an affair, but Elliott wouldn't have looked on complacently like that, and neither of them would have been talking about china, about *Cats*.

Cath had made a mistake. Her radar, usually so infallible, had messed up this time. Sara and Elliott's marriage was fine. Nobody was having an affair, and we'd all have a great time Saturday night.

The mood persisted through the rest of the evening, in spite of Marjorie's latching onto me and telling me all about the Decline and Fall of her father, who she was going to have to put in a nursing home, and our finding out that the pub that had had such great fish and chips the first time we'd been here had burned down.

"It doesn't matter," Cath said, standing on the corner where it had been. "Let's go to the Lamb and Crown. I know it's still there. I saw it on the way to Harrods this morning."

"That's on Wilton Place, isn't it?" I said, pulling out my tube map. "That's right across from Hyde Park Corner Station. We can take—"

"A taxi," Cath said.

⊣•••⊢

Cath didn't say anything else about the affair she thought Sara was having, except to tell me they were going shopping again the next day. "Selfridge's first, and then Reject China—" and I wondered if she had realized, seeing Sara at the party, that she'd made a mistake.

But in the morning, as I was leaving, she said, "Sara called and cancelled while you were in the shower."

"They can't go to the play with us Saturday?"

"No," Cath said. "She isn't going shopping with me today. She said she had a headache."

"She must have drunk some of that awful sherry," I said. "So what are you going to do? Do you want to come have lunch with me?"

"I think it's someone at the conference."

"Who?" I said, lost.

"The man Sara's having an affair with," she said, picking up her guidebook. "If it was someone who lived here, she wouldn't risk seeing him while we're here."

"She's *not* having an affair," I said. "I saw her. I saw Elliott. He—"

"Elliott doesn't know." She jammed the guidebook savagely into her bag. "Men never notice anything."

She began stuffing things into her bag—her sunglasses, her umbrella. "We're having dinner with the Hugheses tonight at seven. I'll meet you back here at five-thirty." She picked up her umbrella.

"You're wrong," I said. "They've been married longer than we have. She's crazy about Elliott. Why would somebody with that much to lose risk it all by having an affair?"

She turned and looked at me, still holding the umbrella. "I don't know," she said bleakly.

"Look," I said, suddenly sorry for her, "why don't you come and have lunch with the Old Man and me? He'll probably get us thrown out like he did at that Indian restaurant. It'll be fun."

She shook her head. "You and Arthur will want to catch up, and I don't want to wait on Selfridge's." She looked up at me. "When you see Arthur—" she paused, looking like she did when she was thinking about Sara.

"You think he's having an affair, too, oh, Madame Knows-All, Sees-All?"

"No," she said. "He was older than us."

"Which was why we called him the Old Man," I said, "and you think he'll have gotten a cane and grown a long white beard?"

"No," she said, and slung her bag over her shoulder. "I think if they have my china at Selfridge's, I'll buy twelve place settings."

She was wrong, and I would prove it to her. We would have a great time at the play, and she would realize Sara couldn't be having an affair. If I could get the tickets. *Ragtime* had been sold out, which meant *The Tempest* was likely to be, too, and there weren't a lot of other choices, since Elliott had said no to *Sunset Boulevard*. And *Cats*, I thought, looking at the theater posters as I went down the escalator. And *Les Miz*.

*The Tempest* and the Hayley Mills thing, *Endgames*, were both at theatres close to Leicester Square. If I couldn't get tickets at either, there was a ticket agent in Lisle Street.

*The Tempest* was sold out, as I'd expected. I walked over to the Albery.

*Endgames* had five seats in the third row center of the orchestra. "Great," I said, and slapped down my American Express, thinking how much things had changed.

In the old days I would have been asking if they didn't have anything in the sherpa section, seats so steep we had to clutch the arms of our seats to keep from plummeting to our deaths and we had to rent binoculars to even see the stage.

And in the old days, I thought grimly, Cath would have been at my side, making rapid calculations to see if our budget could afford even the cheap seats. And now I was getting tickets in third row center, and not even asking the price, and Cath was on her way to Selfridge's in a taxi.

The girl handed me the tickets. "What's the nearest tube station?" I asked.

"Tottenham Court Road," she said.

I looked at my tube map. I could take the Central Line over to Holborn and then a train straight to South Kensington. "How do I get there?"

She waved an arm full of bracelets vaguely north. "You go up St. Martin's Lane."

I went up St. Martin's Lane, and up Monmouth, and up Mercer and Shaftesbury and New Oxford. There clearly had to be closer stations than Tottenham Court Road, but it was too late to do anything about it now. And I wasn't about to take a taxi.

It took me half an hour to make the trek, and another ten to reach Holborn, during which I figured out that the Lyric had been less than four blocks from Piccadilly Circus. I'd forgotten how deep the station was, how long the escalators were. They seemed to go down for miles. I rattled down the slatted wooden steps and down the passage, glancing at my watch as I walked.

Nine-thirty. I'd make it to the conference in plenty of time. I wondered when the Old Man would get there. He had to drive down from Cambridge, I thought, going down a short flight of steps behind a man in a tweed jacket, which was an hour and a—

I was on the bottom step when the wind hit. This time it was not so much a blast as a sensation of a door opening onto a cold room.

A cellar, I thought, groping for the metal railing. No. Colder. Deathly cold. A meat locker. A frozen food storage vault. With a sharp, unpleasant chemical edge, like disinfectant. A sickening smell.

No, not a refrigerated vault, I thought, a biology lab, and recognized the smell as formaldehyde. And something under it. I shut my mouth, held my breath, but the sweet, sickening stench was already in my nostrils, in my throat. Not a biology lab, I thought in horror. A charnelhouse.

It was over, the door shutting as suddenly as it had opened, but the bite of the icy air was still in my nostrils, the nasty taste of formaldehyde still in my mouth. Of corruption and death and decay.

I stood there on the bottom step taking shallow, swallowing breaths, while people walked around me. I could see the man in the tweed jacket, rounding the corner in the passage ahead. He *must* have felt it, I thought. He was right in front of me. I started after him, dodging around a pair of children, an Indian woman in a sari, a housewife with a string bag, finally catching up to him as he turned out onto the crowded platform.

"Did you feel that wind?" I asked, taking hold of his sleeve. "Just now, in the tunnel?"

He looked alarmed, and then, as I spoke, tolerant. "You're from the States, aren't you? There's always a slight rush of air as a train enters one of the tunnels. It's perfectly ordinary. Nothing to be alarmed about." He looked pointedly at my hand on his sleeve.

"But this one was ice-cold," I persisted. It—"

"Ah, yes, well, we're very near the river here," he said, looking less tolerant. "If you'll excuse me." He freed his arm. "Have a pleasant holiday," he said and walked away through the crowd to the farthest end of the platform.

I let him go. He clearly hadn't felt it. But he had to, I thought. He was right in front of me.

Unless it wasn't real, and I was experiencing some bizarre form of hallucination.

"Finally," a woman said, looking down the track, and I saw a train was approaching. Wind fluttered a flyer stuck on the wall and then the blonde hair of the woman standing closest to the edge. She turned unconcernedly toward the man next to her, saying something to him, shifting the leather strap of the bag on her shoulder.

It hit again, an onslaught of cold and chemicals and corruption, a stench of decay.

He has to have felt that, I thought, looking down the platform, but he was unconcernedly boarding the train, the tourists next to him were looking up at the train and back down at their tube maps, unaware.

They have to have felt it, I thought, and saw the elderly black man. He was halfway down the platform, wearing a plaid jacket. He shuddered as the wind hit, and then hunched his gray grizzled head into his shoulders like a turtle withdrawing into its shell.

*He* felt it, I thought, and started toward him, but he was already getting on the train, the doors were already starting to close. Even running, I wouldn't reach him.

I bounded onto the nearest car as the doors whooshed shut and stood there just inside the door, waiting for the next station. As soon as the doors opened I jumped out, holding onto the edge of the door, to see if he got off. He didn't, or at the next station, and Bond Street was easy. Nobody got off.

"Marble Arch," the disembodied voice said, and the train pulled into the tiled station.

What the hell was at Marble Arch? There had never been this many people when Cath and I stayed at the Royal Hernia. Everybody on the train was getting off.

But was the old man? I leaned out from the door, trying to see if he'd gotten off.

I couldn't see him for the crowd. I stepped forward and was immediately elbowed aside by an equally large herd of people getting on.

I headed down the platform toward his car, craning my neck to spot his plaid jacket, his grizzled head in the exodus.

"The doors are closing," the voice of the tube said, and I turned just in time to see the train pull out, and the old man sitting inside, looking out at me.

And now what? I thought, standing on the abruptly deserted platform. Go back to Holborn and see if it happened again and somebody else felt it? Somebody who wasn't getting on a train.

Certainly nothing was going to happen here. This was our station, the one we had set out from every morning, come home to every night, the first time we were here, and there hadn't been any strange winds. The Royal Hernia was only three blocks away, and we had run up the drafty stairs, holding hands, laughing about what the Old Man had said to the verger in Canterbury when he had shown us Thomas More's grave—

The Old Man. He would know what was causing the winds, or how to find out. He loved mysteries. He had dragged us to Greenwich, the British Museum, and down into the crypt of St. Paul's, trying to find out what had happened to the arm Nelson lost in one of his naval battles. If anybody could, he'd find out what was causing these winds.

And he should be here by now, I thought, looking at my watch. Good God. It was nearly one. I went over to the tube map on the wall to find the best way over to the conference. Go to Notting Hill Gate and take the District and Circle Line. I looked up at the sign above the platform to see how long it would be till the next train, so that when the wind hit, I didn't have time to hunch down the way the old man had, to flinch away from the blow. My neck was fully extended, like Sir Thomas More's on the block.

And it was like a blade, slicing through the platform with killing force. No charnelhouse smell this time, no heat. Nothing but blast and the smell of salt and iron. The scent of terror and blood and sudden death.

What *is* it? I thought, clutching blindly for the tiled wall. What *are* they?

The Old Man, I thought again. I have to find the Old Man.

I took the tube to South Kensington and ran all the way to the conference, half-afraid he wouldn't be there, but he was. I could hear his voice when I came in. The usual admiring group was clustered around him. I started across the lobby toward them.

Elliott detached himself from the group and came over to me.

"I need to see the Old Man," I said.

He put a restraining hand on my arm. "Tom—" he said.

He looked like Cath had, sitting on the bed, telling me Sara was having an affair.

"What's wrong?" I asked, dreading the answer.

"Nothing," he said, glancing back toward the lounge. "Arthur—nothing." He let go of my arm. "He'll be overjoyed to see you. He's been asking for you."

The Old Man was sitting in an easy chair, holding court. He looked exactly the same as he had twenty years ago, his frame still lanky, his light hair still falling boyishly over his forehead.

See, Cath, I thought. No long white beard. No cane.

He broke off as soon as he saw us and stood up. "Tom, you young reprobate!" he said, and his voice sounded as strong as ever. "I've been waiting for you to get here all morning. Where were you?"

"In the tube," I said. "Something happened. I—"

"In the *tube*? What were you doing down in the tube?"

"I was—"

"Never use the tube anymore," he said. "It's gone completely to hell ever since Tony Blair got into office. Like everything else."

"I want you to come with me," I said. "I want to show you something."

"Come where?" he said. "Down in the tube? Not on your life." He sat back down. "I *loathe* the tube. Smelly, dirty—"

He sounded like Cath.

"Look," I said, wishing there weren't all these people around. "Something peculiar happened to me in Charing Cross Station yesterday. You know the winds that blow through the tunnels when the trains come in?"

"I certainly do. Dreadful drafty places—"

"Exactly," I said. "It's the drafts I want you to see. Feel. They—"

"And catch my death of cold? No, thank you."

"You don't understand," I said. "These weren't ordinary drafts. I was heading for the Northern Line platform, and—"

"You can tell me about it at lunch." He turned back to the others. "Where shall we go?"

He had never, ever, in all the years I'd known him, asked anybody where to go for lunch. I blinked stupidly at him.

"How about the Bangkok House?" Elliott said.

The Old Man shook his head. "Their food's too spicy. It always makes me bloat."

"There's a sushi place round the corner," one of the admiring circle volunteered.

"*Sushi!*" he said, in a tone that put an end to the discussion.

I tried again. "Yesterday I was in Charing Cross Station, and this wind, this *blast* hit me that smelled like sulfur. It—"

"It's the damned smog," the Old Man said. "Too many cars. Too many people. It's got nearly as bad as it was in the old days, when there were coal fires."

Coal, I thought. Could that have been the smell I couldn't identify? Coal smelled of sulfur.

"The inversion layer makes it worse," the admirer who'd suggested sushi said.

"Inversion layer?" I said.

"Yes," he said, pleased to have been noticed. "London's in a shallow depression that causes inversion layers. That's when a layer of warm air above the ground traps the surface air under it, so the smoke and particulates collect—"

"I thought we were going to lunch," the Old Man said petulantly.

"Remember the time we tried to find out what had happened to Sherlock Holmes' address?" I said. "This is an even stranger mystery."

"That's *right*," he said. "221B Baker Street. I'd forgotten that. Do you remember the time I took you on a tour of Sir Thomas More's head? Elliott, tell them what Sara said in Canterbury."

Elliott told them, and they roared with laughter, the Old Man included. I half expected somebody to say, "Those were the days."

"Tom, tell everybody about that time we went to see *Kismet*," the Old Man said.

"We've got tickets for *Endgames* for the five of us for tomorrow night," I said, even though I knew what was coming.

He was already shaking his head. "I never go to plays anymore. The theatre's gone to hell like everything else. Lot of modernist nonsense." he smacked his hands on the arms of the easy chair. "Lunch! Did we decide where we're going?"

"What about the New Delhi Palace?" Elliott said.

"Can't handle Indian food," the Old Man, who had once gotten us thrown out of the New Delhi Palace by dancing with the Tandoori chicken, said. "Isn't there anywhere that serves plain, ordinary food?"

"Wherever we're going, we need to make up our minds," the admirer said. "The afternoon session starts at two."

"We can't miss that," the Old Man said. He looked around the circle. "So where are we going? Tom, are you coming to lunch with us?"

"I can't," I said. "I wish you'd come with me. It would be like old times."

"Speaking of old times," the Old Man said, turning back to the group, "I still haven't told you about the time I got thrown out of *Kismet*. What was that harem girl's name, Elliott?"

"Lalume," Elliott said, turning to look at the Old Man, and I made my escape.

—|•••|—

An inversion layer. Holding the air down so it couldn't escape, trapping it belowground so that smoke and particulates, and smells, became concentrated, intensified.

I took the tube back to Holborn and went down to the Central Line to look at the ventilation system. I found a couple of wall grates no larger than the size of a theatre handbill and a louvered vent two-thirds of the way down the west-bound passage, but no fans, nothing that moved the air or connected it with the outside.

There had to be one. The deep stations went down hundreds of feet. They couldn't rely on nature recirculating the air, especially with diesel fumes and carbon monoxide from the traffic up above. There must be ventilation. But some of these tube stations had been built as long ago as 1880s, and Holborn looked like it hadn't been repaired since then.

I went out into the large room containing the escalators and stood, looking up. It was open all the way to the ticket machines at the top, and the station had wide doors on three sides, all open to the outside.

Even without ventilation, the air would eventually make its way up and out onto the streets of London. Wind would blow in from outside, and rain, and the movement of the people hurrying through the station, up the escalators, down the passages, would circulate it. But if there was an inversion layer, trapping the air close to the ground, keeping it from escaping—

Pockets of carbon monoxide and deadly methane accumulated in coal mines. The tube was a lot like a mine, with its complicated bendings and turnings of its tunnels. Could pockets of air have accumulated in the train tunnels, becoming more concentrated, more lethal as time went by?

The inversion layer would explain why there were winds but not what had caused them in the first place. An IRA bombing, like I had thought when I felt the first one? That would explain the blast and the smell of explosives, but not the formaldehyde. Or the stifling smell of dirt in Charing Cross.

A collapse of one of the tunnels? Or a train accident?

I made the long trek back up to the station and asked the guard next to the ticket machines, "Do these tunnels ever collapse?"

"Oh, no, sir, they're quite safe." He smiled reassuringly. "There's no need to worry."

"But there must be accidents occasionally," I said.

"I assure you, sir, the London Underground is the safest in the world."

"What about bombings?" I asked. "The IRA—"

"The IRA has signed the peace agreement," he said, looking at me suspiciously.

A few more questions, and I was likely to find myself arrested as an IRA bomber. I would have to ask the Old—Elliott. And in the meantime, I could try to find out if there were winds in all the stations or just a few.

"Can you show me how to get to the Tower of London?" I asked him, extending my tube map like a tourist.

"Yes, sir, you take the Central Line, that's this red line, to Bank," he said, tracing his finger along the map, "and then change to the District and Circle. And don't worry. The London Underground is perfectly safe."

Except for the winds, I thought, getting on the escalator. I got out a pen and marked an X on the stations I'd been to as I rode down. Marble Arch, Charing Cross, Sloane Square.

I hadn't been to Russell Square. I rode there and waited in the passages and then on both platforms through two trains. There wasn't anything at Russell Square, but on the Metropolitan Line at St. Pancras there was the same shattering blast as at Charing Cross—heat and the acrid smells of sulfur and violent destruction.

There wasn't anything at Barbican, or Aldgate, and I thought I knew why. At both of them the tracks were above-ground, with the platform open to the air. The winds would disperse naturally instead of being trapped, which meant I could eliminate most of the suburban stations.

But St. Paul's and Chancery Lane were both underground, with deep, drafty tunnels, and there was nothing in either of them except a faint scent of diesel and mildew. There must be some other factor at work.

It isn't the line they're on, I thought, riding toward Warren Street. Marble Arch and Holborn were on the Central Line, but Charing Cross wasn't, and neither was St. Pancras. Maybe it was the conversion of them. Chancery Lane, St. Paul's, and Russell Square all had only one line. Holborn had two lines, and Charing Cross had three. St. Pancras had five.

Those are the stations I should be checking, I thought, the ones where multiple lines meet, the ones honeycombed with tunnels and passages and turns. Monument, I thought, looking at the circles where green and purple and red lines converged. Baker Street and Moorgate.

Baker Street was closest, but hard to get to. Even though I was only two stops away, I'd have to switch over at Euston, take the Northern going the other way back to St. Pancras, and catch the Bakerloo. I was glad Cath wasn't here to say, "I thought you said it was easy to get anywhere on the tube."

Cath! I'd forgotten all about meeting her at the hotel so we could go to dinner with the Hughes.

What time was it? Only five, thank God. I looked hastily at the map. Good. Northern down to Leicester Square and then the Piccadilly Line, and who says it isn't easy to get anywhere on the tube? I'd be to the Connaught in less than half an hour.

And when I got there I'd tell Cath about the winds, even if she did hate the tube. I'd tell her about all of it, the Old Man and the charnel-house smell and the old man in the plaid jacket.

But she wasn't there. She'd left a note on the pillow of my bed. "Meet you at Grimaldi's. 7 p.m."

No explanation. Not even a signature, and the note looked hasty, scribbled. What if Sara called? I wondered, a thought as chilly as the wind in Marble Arch. What if Cath had been right about her, the way she'd been right about the Old Man?

But when I got to Grimaldi's, it turned out she'd only been shopping. "The woman in the china department at Fortnum and Mason's told me about a place in Bond Street that specialized in discontinued patterns."

Bond Street. It was a wonder we hadn't run into each other. But she wasn't in the tube station, I thought with a flash of resentment. She was safely above-ground in a taxi.

"They didn't have it either," she said, "but the clerk suggested I try a shop next door to the Portmerion store which was clear out in Kensington. It took the rest of the day. How was the conference? Was Arthur there?"

You know he was, I thought. She had foreseen his having gotten old, she'd tried to warn me that first morning in the hotel, and I hadn't believed her.

"How was he?" Cath asked.

You already know, I thought bitterly. Your antennae pick up vibrations from everybody. Except your husband.

And even if I tried to tell her, she'd be too wrapped up in her precious china pattern to even hear me.

"He's fine," I said. "We had lunch and then spent the whole afternoon together. He hadn't changed a bit."

"Is he going to the play with us?"

"No," I said and was saved by the Hugheses coming in right then, Mrs. Hughes, looking frail and elderly, and her strapping sons Milford Junior and Paul and their wives.

Introductions all around, and it developed that the blonde with Milford Junior wasn't his wife, it was his fiance. "Barbara and I just couldn't talk to each other anymore," he confided to me over cocktails. "All she was interested in was buying things, clothes, jewelry, furniture."

China, I thought, looking across the room at Cath.

⊢•••⊢

At dinner I was seated between Paul and Milford Jr., who spent the meal discussing the Decline and Fall of the British Empire.

"And now Scotland wants to separate," Milford said. "Who's next? Sussex? The City of London?"

"At least perhaps then we'd see decent governmental services. The current state of the streets and the transportation system—"

"I was in the tube today," I said, seizing the opening. "Do either of you know if Charing Cross has ever been the site of a train accident?"

"I shouldn't wonder," Milford said. "The entire system's a disgrace. Dirty, dangerous—the last time I rode the tube, a thief tried to pick my pocket on the escalator."

"I never go down in the tube anymore," Mrs. Hughes put in from the end of the table where she and Cath were deep in a discussion of china shops in Chelsea. "I haven't since Milford died."

"There are beggars everywhere," Paul said. "Sleeping on the platforms, sprawled in the passages. It's nearly as bad as it was during the Blitz."

The Blitz. Air raids and incendiaries and fires. Smoke and sulfur and death.

"The Blitz?" I said.

"During Hitler's bombing of London in World War II, masses of people sheltered in the tubes," Milford said. "Along the tracks, on the platforms, even on the escalators."

"Not that it was any safer than staying above-ground," Paul said.

"The shelters were hit?" I said eagerly.

Paul nodded. "Paddington. And Marble Arch. Forty people were killed in Marble Arch."

Marble Arch. Blast and blood and terror.

"What about Charing Cross?" I asked.

"I've no idea," Milford said, losing interest. "They should pass legislation keeping beggars out of the Underground. And requiring cabbies to speak understandable English."

The Blitz. Of course. That would explain the smell of gunpowder or whatever it was. And the blast. A high-explosive bomb.

But the Blitz had been over fifty years ago. Could the air from a bomb blast have stayed down in the tube all those years without dissipating?

There was one way to find out. The next morning I took the tube to Tottenham Court Road, where there was a whole street of bookstores, and asked for a book about the history of the Underground in the Blitz.

"The Underground?" the girl at Foyle's, the third place I tried, said vaguely. "The Tube Museum might have something."

"Where's that?" I asked.

She didn't know, and neither did the ticket vendor back at the tube station, but I remembered seeing a poster for it on the platform at Oxford Circus during my travels yesterday. I consulted my tube map, took the train to Victoria, and changed for Oxford Circus, where I checked five platforms before I found it.

Covent Garden. The London Transport Museum. I checked the map again, took the Central Line across to Holborn, transferred to the Piccadilly Line, and went to Covent Garden.

And apparently it had been hit, too, because a gust of face-singeing heat struck me before I was a third of the way down the tunnel. There was no smell of explosives, though, or of sulfur or dust. Just ash and fire and hopeless desperation that it was all, all burning down.

The scent of it was still with me as I hurried upstairs and out into the market, through the rows of carts selling T-shirts and postcards and toy double-decker buses, to the Transport Museum.

It was full of T-shirts and postcards, too, all sporting the Underground symbol or replicas of the tube map. "I need a book on the tube during the Blitz," I asked a boy across a counter stacked with "Mind the Gap" placemats and playing cards.

"The Blitz?" he said vaguely.

"World War II," I said, which didn't evoke any recognition either.

He waved a hand loosely to the left. "The books are over there."

They weren't. They were on the far wall, past a rack of posters of tube ads from the Twenties and Thirties, and most of what books they had were about trains, but I finally found two histories of the tube and a paperback called *London in Wartime*. I bought them all and a notebook with a tube map on the cover.

The Transport Museum had a snack bar. I sat down at one of the plastic tables and began taking notes. Nearly all the tube stations had been used as shelters, and a lot of them had been hit—Euston Station, Aldwych, Monument. "In the aftermath of the bombing, the acrid smell of brick dust and cordite was everywhere," the paperback said. Cordite. That was what I had smelled.

Marble Arch had taken a direct hit, the bomb bursting like a grenade in one of the passages, ripping tiles off the walls as it exploded, sending them slicing through the people sheltered there. Which explained the smell of blood. And the lack of heat. It had been pure blast.

I looked up Holborn. There were several references to its having been used as a shelter, but nothing in any of the books that said it had taken a hit.

Charing Cross had, twice. It had been hit by a high-explosive bomb, and then by a V-2 rocket. The bomb had broken water mains and loosed an avalanche of dirt down onto the room containing the escalators. That was the damp earthiness I'd smelled—mud from the roof collapsing.

Nearly a dozen stations had been hit the night of May tenth, 1941: Cannon Street, Paddington, Blackfriars, Liverpool Street—

Covent Garden wasn't on the list. I looked it up in the paperback. The station hadn't been hit, but incendiaries had fallen all around Covent Garden, and the whole area had been on fire. Which meant that Holborn wouldn't have to have taken a direct hit either. There could have been a bombing nearby, with lots of deaths, that was responsible for Holborn's charnelhouse smell. And the fact that there had been fires all around Covent Garden fit with the fact that there hadn't been sulfur, or concussion.

It all fit—the smell of mud and cordite in Charing Cross, of smoke in Cannon Street, of blast and blood in Marble Arch. The winds I was feeling were the winds of the Blitz, trapped there by London's inversion layer, caught belowground with no way out, nowhere to go, held and recirculated and intensified through the years in the mazelike tunnels and passages and pockets of the tube. It all fit.

And there was a way to test it. I copied a list of all the stations I hadn't been to that had been hit—Blackfriars, Monument, Paddington, Liverpool Street. Praed Street, Bounds Green, Trafalgar Square and Balham had taken direct hits. If my theory was correct, the winds should definitely be there.

I started looking for them, using the tube map on the cover of my notebook. Bounds Green was far north on the Piccadilly Line, nearly to the legendary Cockfosters, and Balham was nearly as far south on the Northern Line. I couldn't find either Praed Street or Trafalgar Square. I wondered if those stations had been closed or given other names. The Blitz had, after all, been fifty years ago.

Monument was the closest. I could get there by way of the Central Line and then follow the Circle Line around to Liverpool Street and from there go on up to Bounds Green. Monument had been down near the docks—it should smell like smoke, too, and the river water they'd sprayed on the fire, and burning cotton and rubber and spices. A warehouse full of pepper had burned. That odor would be unmistakable.

—|•••|—

But I didn't smell it. I wandered up and down the passages of the Central and Northern and District Lines, stood on each of the platforms, waited in the corners near the stairways for over an hour, and nothing.

51

It doesn't happen all the time, I thought, taking the Circle Line to Liverpool Street. There's some other factor—the time of day or the temperature or the weather. Maybe the winds only blew when London was experiencing an inversion layer. I should have checked the weather this morning, I thought.

Whatever the factor was, there was nothing at Liverpool Street, either, but at Euston the wind hit me full force a minute I had stepped off the train—a violent blast of soot and dread and charred wood. Even though I knew what it was now, I had to lean against the cold tiled wall a minute, till my heart stopped pounding, and the dry taste of fear in my mouth subsided.

I waited for the next train and the next, but the wind didn't repeat itself, and I went down to the Victoria Line, thought a minute, and went back up to the surface to ask the ticket seller if the tracks at Bounds Green were above-ground.

"I believe they are, sir," he said in a thick Scottish brogue.

"What about Balham?"

He looked alarmed. "Balham's the other way. It's not on the same line either."

"I know," I said. "Are they? Above-ground?"

He shook his head. "I'm afraid I don't know, sir. Sorry. If you're going to Balham, you go down to the Northern Line and take the train to Tooting Bec and Morden. Not the one to Elephant and Castle."

I nodded. Balham was even farther out in the suburbs than Bounds Green. The tracks were almost certain to be above-ground, but it was still worth a try.

Balham had taken the worst hit of any of the stations. The bomb had fallen just short of the station, but in the worst possible place. It had plunged the station into darkness, smashed the water and sewer pipes and the gas mains. Filthy water had rushed into the station in torrents, flooding the pitch-black passages, pouring down the stairs and into the tunnels. Three hundred people had drowned. And how could that not still be there, even if Balham was above-ground? And if it was there, the smell of sewage and gas and darkness would be unmistakable.

I didn't follow the ticket vendor's directions. I detoured to Blackfriars, since it was nearly on the way, and stood around its yellow-tiled platforms for half an hour with no result before going on to Balham.

The train was nearly deserted for most of the long trip. From London

52

Bridge out there were only two people in my car, a middle-aged woman reading a book and, at the far end, a young girl, crying.

She had spiked hair and a pierced eyebrow, and she cried helplessly, obliviously, making no attempt to wipe her mascaraed cheeks, or even turn her head toward the window.

I wondered if I should go ask her what was wrong or if the woman with the book would think I was hitting on her. I wasn't even sure she would be aware of me if I did go over—there was a complete absorption to her sorrow that reminded me of Cath, intent on finding her china. I wondered if that was what had broken this girl's heart, that they had discontinued her pattern? Or had her friends betrayed her, had affairs, gotten old?

"Borough," the automated voice said, and she seemed to come to herself with a jerk, swiped at her cheeks, grabbed up her knapsack, and got off.

The middle-aged woman stayed on all the way to Balham, never once looking up from her book. When the train pulled in, I went over and stood next to her at the door so I could see what classic of literature she found so fascinating. It was *Gone With the Wind*.

But the winds aren't gone, I thought, leaning against the wall of Balham's platform, listening for the occasional sound of an incoming train, futilely waiting for a blast of sewage and methane and darkness. The winds of the Blitz are still here, endlessly blowing through the tunnels and passages of the tube like ghosts, wandering reminders of fire and flood and destruction.

If that was what they were. Because there was no smell of filthy water at Balham, or any indication that any had ever been there. The air in the passages was dry and dusty. There wasn't even a hint of mildew.

And even if there had been, it still wouldn't explain Holborn. I waited through three more trains on each side and then caught a train for Elephant and Castle and the Imperial War Museum.

"Experience the London Blitz," the poster had said, but the exhibit didn't have anything about which tube stations had been hit. Its gift shop yielded three more books, though. I scoured them from cover to cover, but there was no mention at all of Holborn or of any bombings near there.

And if the winds were leftover breezes from the Blitz, why hadn't I felt them the first time we were here? We had been in the tube all the time, going to the conference, going to plays, going off on the Old Man's wild hares, and there hadn't been even a breath of smoke, of sulfur?

53

What was different that time? The weather? It had rained nearly non-stop that first time. Could that have affected the inversion layer? Or was it something that had happened since then? Some change in the routing of the trains or the connections between stations?

I walked back to Elephant and Castle in a light rain. A man in a clerical collar and two boys with white surplices over their arms were coming out of the station. There must be a church nearby, I thought, and realized that could be the solution for Holborn.

The crypts of churches had been used as shelters during the Blitz. Maybe they had also been used as temporary morgues.

I looked up "morgue" and then, when that didn't work, "body disposal."

I was right. They had used churches, warehouses, even swimming pools after some of the worst air raids to store bodies. I doubted if there were any swimming pools near Holborn, but there might be a church.

There was only one way to find out—go back to Holborn and look. I looked at my tube map. Good. I could catch a train straight to Holborn from here. I went down to the Bakerloo Line and got on a northbound train. It was nearly as empty as the one I'd come out on, but when the doors opened at Waterloo, a huge crowd of people surged onto the train.

It can't be rush hour yet, I thought, and glanced at my watch. Six-fifteen. Good God. I was supposed to meet Cath at the theater at seven. And I was how many stops from the theater? I pulled out my tube map and clung to the overhead pole, trying to count. Embankment and then Charing Cross and Piccadilly Circus. Five minutes each, and another five to get out of the station in this crush. I'd make it. Barely.

"Service on the Bakerloo Line has been disrupted from Embankment north," the automated voice said as we pulled in. "Please seek alternate routes."

Not now! I thought, grabbing for my map. Alternate routes. I could take the Northern Line to Leicester Square and then change for Piccadilly Circus. No, it would be faster to get off at Leicester Square and run the extra blocks.

I raced off the train the minute the doors open and down the corridor to the Northern Line. Five to seven, and I was still two stops away from Leicester Square, and four blocks from the theater. A train was coming in. I could hear its rumble down the corridor. I darted around people, shouting, "Sorry, sorry, sorry," and burst onto the packed north-bound platform.

The train must have been on the southbound tracks. "Next train 4 min.," the overhead sign said.

Great, I thought, hearing it start up, pushing the air in front of it, creating a vacuum in its wake. Embankment had been hit. And that was all I needed right now, a blast from the Blitz.

I'd no sooner said it than it hit, whipping my hair and my coat lapels back, rattling the unglued edges of a poster for *Showboat*. There was no blast, no heat, even though Embankment was right on the river, where the fires had been the worst. It was cold, cold, but there was no smell of formaldehyde with it, no stench of decay. Only the icy chill and a smothering smell of dryness and of dust.

It should have been better than the other ones, but it wasn't. It was worse. I had to lean against the back wall of the platform for support, my eyes closed, before I could get on the train.

What *are* they? I thought, even though this proved they were the residue of the Blitz. Because Embankment had been hit. And people must have died, I thought. Because it was death I'd smelled. Death and terror and despair.

I stumbled onto the train. It was jammed tight, and the closeness, the knowledge that any wind, any air, couldn't reach me through this mass of people, revived me, calmed me, and by the time I pulled in to Leicester Square, I had recovered and was thinking only of how late I was.

Seven-ten. I could still make it, but just barely. At least Cath had the tickets, and with luck Elliott and Sara would get there in the meantime and they'd all be busy saying hello.

Maybe the Old Man changed his mind, I thought, and decided to come. Maybe yesterday he'd been under the weather, and tonight he'd be his old self.

The train pulled in. I raced down the passage, up the escalator, and out onto Shaftesbury. It was raining, but I didn't have time to worry about it.

"Tom! Tom!" a breathless voice shouted behind me.

I turned. Sara was frantically waving at me from half a block away.

"Didn't you hear me?" she said breathlessly, catching up to me. "I've been calling you ever since the tube."

She'd obviously been running. Her hair was mussed, and one end of her scarf dangled nearly to the ground.

"I know we're late," she said, pulling at my arm, "but I *must* catch my breath. You're not one of those dreadful men who've taken up marathon-running in old age, are you?"

"No," I said, moving over in front of a shop and out of the path of traffic.

55

"Elliott's always talking about getting a Stairmaster." She pulled her dangling scarf off and wrapped it carelessly around her neck. "I have *no* desire to get in shape."

Cath was wrong. That was all there was to it. Her radar had failed her and she was misinterpreting the whole situation.

I must have been staring. Sara put a defensive hand up to her hair. "I know I look a mess," she said, putting up her umbrella. "Oh, well. How late are we?"

"We'll make it," I said, taking her arm, and setting off toward the Lyric. "Where's Elliott?"

"He's meeting us at the theater. Did Cath get her china?"

"I don't know. I haven't seen her since this morning," I said.

"Oh, look, there she is," Sara said, and began waving.

Cath was standing in front of the Lyric, next to the water-spotted sign that said, "Tonight's Performance Sold Out," looking numb and cold.

"Why didn't you wait inside out of the rain?" I said, leading them both into the lobby.

"We ran into each other coming out of the tube," Sara said, pulling off her scarf. "Or, rather, I saw Tom. I had to *scream* to get his attention. "Isn't Elliott here yet?"

"No," Cath said.

"He and Mr. Evers came back after lunch. The day was *not* a success, so don't bring up the subject. Mrs. Evers insisted on buying everything in the entire gift shop, and then we couldn't find a taxi. Apparently there are no taxis down in Kew. I had to take the tube, and it was *blocks* to the station." She put her hand up to her hair. "I got blown to pieces."

"Did you change trains at Embankment?" I asked, trying to remember which line went out to Kew Gardens. Maybe she'd felt the wind, too. "Were you on the Bakerloo Line platform?"

"I don't remember," Sara said impatiently. "Is that the line for Kew? You're the tube expert."

"Do you want me to check your coats?" I said hastily.

Sara handed me hers, jamming her long scarf into one sleeve, but Cath shook her head. "I'm cold."

"You should have waited in the lobby," I said.

"Should I?" she said, and I looked at her, surprised. Was she mad I was late? Why? We still had fifteen minutes, and Elliott wasn't even here yet.

"What's the matter?" I started to say, but Sara was asking, "Did you get your china?"

"No," she said, still with that edge of anger in her voice. "Nobody has it."

"Did you try Selfridge's?" Sara asked, and I went off to check Sara's coat. When I came back, Elliott was there.

"Sorry I'm late," he said. He turned to me. "What happened to you this—"

"We were all late," I said, "except Cath, who, luckily, was the one with the tickets. You *do* have the tickets?"

Cath nodded and pulled them out of her evening bag. She handed them to me, and we went in. "Right-hand aisle and down to your right," the usher said. "Row three."

"No stairs to climb?" Elliott said. "No ladders?"

"No rock-axes and pitons," I said. "No binoculars."

"You're kidding," Elliott said. "I won't know how to act."

I stopped to buy programs from the usher. By the time we got to Row 3, Cath and Sara were already in their seats. "Good God," Elliott said as we sidled past the people on the aisle. "I'll bet you can actually *see* from here."

"Do you want to sit next to Sara?" I said.

"Good God, no," Elliott joked. "I want to be able to ogle the chorus girls without her smacking me with her program."

"I don't think it's that kind of play," I said.

"Cath, what's this play about?" Elliott said.

She leaned across Sara. "Hayley Mills is in it," she told him.

"Hayley Mills," he said reminiscently, leaning back, his hands behind his head. "I thought she was truly sexy when I was ten years old. Especially that dance number in *Bye-Bye, Birdie*."

"You're thinking of Ann-Margaret, you fool," Sara said, reaching across me to smack him with her program. "Hayley Mills was in that one where she's the little girl who always saw the positive side of things—what was it called?"

I looked across at Cath, surprised she hadn't chimed in with the answer—she was the Hayley Mills fan. She was sitting with her coat pulled around her shoulders. Her face looked pinched with cold.

"*You* know Hayley Mills," Sara said to Elliott. "We watched her in *The Flame Trees of Thika*."

Elliott nodded. "I always admired her chest. Or am I thinking of Annette?"

"I don't think this is that kind of play," Sara said.

It wasn't that kind of play. Everyone wore high-necked costumes, including Hayley Mills who swept in swathed in a bulky coat. "I'm *so* sorry I'm late, dear," she said, taking off her coat to reveal a turtleneck sweater and going over to stand in front of a stage fire. "It's so cold out. And the air's so strange."

Whoever was playing her husband said, "'Into my heart an air that kills from yon far country blows,'" and Elliott leaned over and whispered, "Oh, God, a *literary* play."

I'd missed the rest of the husband's line, but he must have asked Hayley why she was late because she said, "My assistant cut her hand, and I had to take her to hospital. It took forever for her to get stitched up."

A hospital. I hadn't considered that. Their morgues would have been full during the Blitz. Was there a hospital close to Holborn? I would have to ask Elliott at intermission.

A sudden rattle of applause brought me out of my reverie.

The stage was dark. I'd missed Scene I. When the lights went back up, I tried to focus on the play, so I could discuss it at least halfway intelligibly at the intermission.

"The wind is rising," Hayley Mills said, looking out an imaginary window.

"Storm brewing," a man, not her husband, said.

"That's what I fear," she said, rubbing her hands along her arms to warm them. "Oh, Derek, what if he finds out about us?"

I glanced sideways across Sara at Cath, but couldn't see her face in the darkened theater. She obviously hadn't known what this play was about, or she'd never have chosen it.

But Hayley wasn't acting anything like Sara. She chain-smoked, she paced, she hung up the phone hastily when her husband came into the room and was so obviously guilty no one, least of all her husband, could have failed to miss it.

Elliott certainly didn't. "The husband's got to be a complete moron," he said as soon as the curtain went down for the intermission. "Even the *dog* could deduce that she's having an affair. Why is it characters in plays never act any way remotely resembling real life?"

"Maybe because people in real life don't look like Hayley Mills," Cath said. "She *does* look wonderful, doesn't she, Sara? She hasn't aged a day."

"You're joking, right?" Elliott said. "All right, I know people kid themselves about their spouses having affairs, but—"

"I *have* to go to the bathroom," Cath said. "I suppose there'll be a horrible line. Come with me, Sara, and I'll tell you the saga of my china." They edged past us.

"Get us a glass of white wine," Sara called back from the aisle, and Elliott and I shouldered our way to the bar, which took ten minutes, and another five to get served. Sara and Cath still weren't back.

"So where were you all day?" Elliott asked me, sipping Sara's wine. "I looked for you at lunch."

"I was researching something," I said. "Holborn Tube station is in Bloomsbury, isn't it?"

"I think so," he said. "I rarely take the tube."

"Are there any hospitals near the tube station?"

"Hospitals?" he said bewilderedly. "I don't know. I don't think so."

"Or churches?"

"I don't know. What's this all about?"

"Have you ever heard of a thing called an inversion layer?" I said. "It's when air is trapped—"

"They simply must do something about the women's bathroom situation," Sara said, grabbing her wine and taking a sip. "I thought we were going to be in there the entire third act."

"Sounds like an excellent idea," Elliott said. "I don't mean to sound like the Old Man, but if this is any indication, plays truly have gone to hell! I mean, we're expected to believe that Hayley Mills' husband is so blind that he can't see his wife's in love with—the other one—what's his name—?"

"*Pollyanna*," Cath said. "I've been trying to remember it all through the first two acts. The name of the little girl who always saw the positive side of things."

"Sara," I said, "are there any hospitals near Holborn?"

"The Great Ormond Street Hospital for Sick Children. That's the one James Barrie left all the money to," she said. "Why?"

The Great Ormond Street Hospital. That had to be it. They had used it as a temporary morgue, and the air—

"It's so *obvious*," Elliott said, still on the subject of infidelity. "The excuses Hayley Mills's character makes for where she's been—"

"She looks wonderful, doesn't she?" Cath said. "How old do you suppose she is? She looks so young!"

The end-of-intermission bell chimed.

"Let's go," Cath said, setting her wine down. "I don't want to have to crawl over all those people again."

Sara swallowed her wine at one gulp, and we went back down the aisle. We were too late. The people on the end had to stand up and let us past.

"But don't you agree," Elliott said, sitting down, "that any normal person—?"

"Shhh," Cath said, leaning all the way across Sara and me to shut him up. "The lights are going down."

They did, and I felt an odd sense of relief, as if we'd just avoided something terrible. The curtain began to go up.

"I still say," Elliott said in a stage whisper, "that nobody could have that many clues thrown at him and not realize his wife's having an affair."

"Why not?" Sara said, "You didn't," and Hayley Mills came onstage.

Beside me, in the dark, Elliott was applauding like everyone else, and I thought, it's as if nothing happened. Elliott will think he didn't really hear it, like the wind in the tube, over so fast you wonder if it was really real, and he'll decide it wasn't, he'll lean across me and say, "What do you mean? You're not having an affair, are you?" and Sara will whisper, "Of course not, you idiot. I just meant you never notice anything," and it won't all have blown up, it won't all—

"Who is it?" Elliott said.

His voice echoed in the space between two of Hayley Mills and her husband's lines, and a man in front of us turned around and glared.

"Who is it?" Elliott said again, louder. "Who are you having an affair with?"

Cath said, in a strangled voice, "Don't—"

"No, you're right," Elliott said, standing up. "What the hell difference does it make?" and pushed his way out over the people on the aisle.

Sara sat an endless minute, and then she plunged past us too, tripping over my foot and nearly falling as she did.

I looked over at Cath, wondering if I should go after Sara. I had the ticket for her coat and scarf in my pocket. Cath was staring stiffly up at the stage, her coat clutched tightly around her.

"This can't go on," Hayley Mills said, looking now fully as old as she was, but still going gamely on with her lines, "I want a divorce," and Cath stood up and pushed past me, me following clumsily after her, muttering, "Sorry, sorry," over and over to the people on the aisle.

"It's *over*," Hayley said from the stage. "Can't you *see* that?"

⊣ • • • ├─

I didn't catch up to Cath till she was halfway through the lobby.

"Wait," I said, reaching for her arm. "Cath."

Her face was white and set. She pushed unseeingly through the glass doors and out onto the pavement, and then stood there, looking bewildered.

"I'll get a taxi," I said, thinking, At least we don't have to compete with the end-of-the-play crowd.

Wrong. People were streaming out of the Apollo, and farther down the street, *Miss Saigon*, and God knew what else. There were swarms of people on the curb and at the corner, shouting and whistling for taxis.

"Wait here," I said, pushing Cath back under the Lyric's marquee, and plunged out into the meleé, my arm thrust out. A taxi pulled toward the curb, but it was only avoiding a clot of people, newspapers over their heads, ducking across the street. The driver put his arm out and gestured toward the "in use" light on top of the taxi.

I stepped off the curb, scanning the mess for a taxi that didn't have its light on, jerking back again as a motorbike splashed by.

Cath tugged on the back of my jacket. "It's no use," she said. "*Phantom* just let out. We'll never get a taxi."

"I'll go to one of the hotels," I said, gesturing up the street, "and have the doorman get one. You stay here."

"No, it's all right," she said. "We can take the tube. Piccadilly Circus is close, isn't it?"

"Right down there," I said, pointing.

She nodded and put her purse uselessly over her head against the rain, and we darted out onto the sidewalk, through the crowd, and down the steps into Piccadilly Circus.

"At least it's dry in here," I said, fishing for change for a ticket for her.

She nodded again, shaking the skirt of her coat out.

There was a huge crush at the machines and an even bigger one at the turnstiles. I handed her her ticket, and she put it gingerly in the slot and yanked her hand back before the machine could suck it away.

None of the down escalators were working. People clomped awkwardly down the steps. Two punkers with shaved heads and bad skin shoved their way past, muttering obscenities.

At the bottom there was a nasty-looking puddle under the tube map. "We need the Piccadilly Line," I said, taking her arm and leading her down the tunnel and out onto the jammed platform. The LED sign over-head said, "Next train 2 min."

A train rumbled through on the other side and people poured onto the platform behind us, pushing us forward. Cath stiffened, staring down at the "Mind the Gap" sign, and I thought, all we need now is a rat. Or a knifing.

A train pulled in, and we pushed onto it, crammed together like sardines. "It'll thin out in a couple of stops," I said, and she nodded. She looked dazed, shell-shocked.

Like Elliott, staring blindly at the stage, saying in a flat voice, "Who are you having the affair with?," stumbling blindly over people's feet, people's knees, trying to get out of the row, looking like he'd been hit by a blast of sulfurous, deadly wind. Everything fine one minute, sipping wine and discussing Hayley Mills, and the next, a bomb ripping the world apart and everything in ruins.

"Green Park," the loudspeaker said, and the door opened and more people pushed on. "You better watch out!" a woman with matted hair said, shaking a finger in Cath's face. Her fingertip was stained blue-black. "You better! I mean it!"

"That's it," I said, pushing Cath behind me. "We're getting off at the next stop." I put my hand on her back and began propelling her through the mass of people toward the door.

"Hyde Park Corner," the loudspeaker said.

We got off, the door whooshed shut, and the train began to pull out.

"We'll go up top and get a taxi," I said tightly. "You were right. The tube's gone to hell."

It's all gone to hell, I thought bitterly, starting down the empty tunnel, Cath behind me. Sara and Elliott and London and Hayley Mills. All of it. The Old Man and Regent Street and us.

The wind caught me full in the face. Not from the train we had just gotten off of, from ahead of us somewhere, farther down the tunnel. And worse, worse, worse than before. I staggered back against the wall, doubling up like I'd been punched in the stomach. Disaster and death and devastation.

I straightened up, clutching my stomach, unable to catch my breath, and looked across the tunnel. Cath was standing with her back against the op-posite wall, her hands flattened against the tiles, her face pinched and pale.

"You felt it," I said, and felt a vast relief.

"Yes."

Of course she felt it. This was Cath, who sensed things nobody else noticed, who had known Sara was having an affair, that the Old Man had turned into an old man. I should have gone and gotten her the first time it happened, dragged her down here, made her stand in the tunnels with me.

"Nobody else felt them," I said. "I thought I was crazy."

"No," she said, and there was something in her voice, in the way she stood huddled against the green-tiled wall, that told me what should have been obvious all along.

"You felt them that first time we were here," I said, amazed. "That's why you hate the tube. Because of the winds."

She nodded.

"That's why you wanted to take a taxi to Harrods," I said. "Why didn't you say something that first time?"

"We didn't have enough money for taxis," she said, "and you didn't seem to be aware of them."

I wasn't aware of anything, I thought, not Cath's obvious reluctance to go down into the tube stations, nor her flinching back from the incoming trains. She was watching for the next wind, I thought, remembering her peering nervously into the tunnel. She was waiting for it to hit.

"You should have told me," I said. "If you'd told me, I could have helped you figure out what they were so they wouldn't frighten you anymore."

She looked up. "What they were?" she repeated blankly.

"Yes. I've figured out what's causing them. It's because of the inversion layer. The air gets trapped down here, and there's no way out. Like gas pockets in a mine. So it just stays here, year after year," I said, unbelievably glad I could talk to her, tell her.

"People used these tube stations as shelters during the Blitz," I said eagerly. "Balham was hit, and so was Charing Cross. That's why you can smell smoke and cordite. Because of the high-explosive bombs. And people were killed by flying tiles at Marble Arch. That's what we're feeling—the winds from those events. They're winds from the past. I don't know what this one was caused by. A tunnel collapse, maybe, or a V-2—" I stopped.

She was looking the way she had sitting on the narrow bed in our hotel room, right before she told me Sara was having an affair.

I stared at her.

"You know what's causing the winds," I said finally. Of course she knew. This was Cath, who knew everything. Cath, who had had twenty years to think about this.

I said, "What's causing them, Cath?"

"Don't—" she said, and looked down the passageway, as if hoping somebody would come, a sudden rush of people, hurrying for the trains, pushing between us, cutting her off before she could answer, but the tunnel remained empty, still, no air moving at all.

"Cath," I said.

She took a deep breath, and then said, "They're what's coming."

"What's *coming*?" I repeated stupidly.

"What's waiting for us," she said, and then, bitterly, "Divorce and death and decay. The ends of things."

"They can't be," I said. "Marble Arch took a direct hit. And Charing Cross—"

But this was Cath, who was always right. And what if the scent wasn't of smoke but of fear, not of ashes but of despair? What if the formaldehyde wasn't the charnelhouse odor of a temporary morgue but of a permanent one, Death itself, the marble arch that waited for us all? No wonder it had reminded Cath of a cemetery.

What if the direct hits, shrapnel flying everywhere, slashing through youth and marriage and happiness, weren't V-2s, but death and devastation and decline?

The winds all, all smelled of death, and the Blitz hardly had a monopoly on that. Look at Hari Srinivasau. And the pub with the great fish and chips.

"But all of the stations where there are winds were hit," I said. "And in Charing Cross there was a smell of water and dirt. It has to be the Blitz."

Cath shook her head. "I've felt them on BART, too."

"But that's in San Francisco. It might be the earthquake. Or the fire."

"And on the Metro in D.C. And once, at home, in the middle of Main Street," she said, staring at the floor. "I think you're right about the inversion layer. It must concentrate them down here, make them stronger and more—"

She paused, and I thought she was going to say "lethal."

"More noticeable," she said.

But I hadn't noticed. Nobody had noticed except Cath, who noticed everything.

And the old, I thought, remembering the white-haired woman in South Kensington Station, her coat collar clutched closed with a blue-veined hand, the stooped old black man on the platform in Holborn. The old feel them all the time, I thought. They walked bent nearly double against a wind which blew all the time.

Or stayed out of the tube. I thought of the Old Man saying, "I *loathe* the Underground." The Old Man, who had run us merrily all over London on the tube after adventure, on at Baker Street and off at Tower Hill, up escalators, down stairs, shouting stories over his shoulder the whole time. "Horrible place," he had said, shuddering, yesterday. "Filthy, smelly, drafty." Drafty.

He felt the winds, and so did Mrs. Hughes. "I never go down in the tube anymore," she had said at dinner. Not, 'I never take the tube.' I never *go down* in the tube. And it wasn't just the stairs or the long distances she had to walk. It was the winds, reeking of separation and loss and sorrow.

And Cath had to be right. They had to be the winds of mortality. What else would blow so steadily, so inexorably, on the old and no one else?

But then why had I noticed them? Maybe the convention was an inversion layer of another kind, bringing me face-to-face with old friends and old places. With cancer and the Gap and the Old Man, railing about newfangled plays and spicy food. Bringing me face-to-face early with death and old age and change.

And a feeling of time running out, that made you go shoving down escalators and racing through corridors, frantic to catch the train before it pulled out. A feeling of panic, that it might be the last one. "The doors are closing."

I thought of Sara, running up out of Piccadilly Station, her hair windblown, her cheeks unnaturally red, of her pushing past my knees in the theater, desperate, pursued.

"Sara felt them," I said.

"Did she?" Cath said, her voice flat.

I looked at her, standing there against the far wall, braced for the next wind, waiting for it to hit.

It was funny. This very passage, this very station had been used as a shelter during the Blitz. But there weren't any shelters that could protect you from this kind of raid.

And no matter what train you caught, no matter which line you took, they all went to the same station. Marble Arch. End of the line.

"So what do we do?" I said.

She didn't answer. She stood there looking at the floor as if it had "Mind the Gap" written on it. Mind the Gap.

"I don't know," she said finally.

And what had I thought she would say? That it wouldn't be so bad as long as we had each other? That love conquers all? That was the whole point, wasn't it, that it didn't? That it was no match for divorce and destruction and death? Look at Milford Hughes Senior. Look at Daniel Drecker's daughter.

"They didn't have my china at any of the shops in Chelsea," she said bleakly. "It never occurred to me it might be discontinued. All those years, I—it never occurred to me it wouldn't still be there." Her voice broke. "It was such a pretty pattern."

And the Old Man was so funny and so full of life, the pub was always jam-packed, Sara and Elliott had a great marriage. But even that couldn't save them. Divorce and destruction and decay.

And what could anybody do about any of it? Button up your overcoat? Stay above-ground?

But that was the problem, staying above-ground. And somehow getting through the days, knowing the doors were closing and it was all going to go smash. Knowing that everything you ever loved or liked or even thought was pretty were all going to be torn down, burned up, blown away. "Gone with the wind," I said, thinking of the woman on the train.

"What?" Cath said, still in that numb, hopeless voice.

"The novel," I said ruefully. "*Gone With the Wind*. There was a woman on the train to Balham today reading it. When I was tracking down the winds, trying to find out which stations had them, if they were stations that had been hit during the Blitz."

"You went to Balham?" she demanded. "Today?"

"And Blackfriars. And Embankment. And Elephant and Castle. I went to the Transport Museum to find which stations had been hit, and then to Monument and Balham, trying to see if they had winds." I shook my head. "I spent the whole day, trying to figure out the pattern of the—what is it?"

Cath had put her hand up to her mouth as if she were in pain.

"What is it?"

She said, "Sara cancelled again today. After you left. I thought maybe we could have lunch." She looked across at me. "Nobody knew where you were."

"I didn't want anybody to know I was running around London chasing winds nobody else could feel," I said.

"Elliott told me you'd disappeared the day before, too," she said, and there was still something I wasn't getting here. "He said he and Arthur wanted you to have lunch with them, but you left."

"I went back to Holborn, to try to see what was causing the winds. And then to Marble Arch."

"Sara told me she and Elliott had to go take Evers and his wife sightseeing, that they wanted to see Kew Gardens."

"Elliott? I thought you said he was at the conference?"

"He was. He said Sara had a doctor's appointment she'd forgotten about," she said. "Nobody knew where you were. And then at the theatre, you and Sara—"

Had shown up together, late, out of breath, Sara's cheeks flaming. And the day before I had lied about lunch, about the afternoon session. To Cath, who could sense when people were lying, who could sense when something was wrong.

"You thought *I* was the one who was having an affair with Sara," I said.

She nodded numbly.

"You thought I was having an affair with *Sara?*" I said. "How could you think that? I *love* you."

"And Sara loved Elliott. People cheat on their spouses, they leave each other. Things…"

"…fall apart," I murmured.

And the air down here registered it all, trapped it below-ground, distilled it into an essence of death and destruction and decay.

Cath was wrong. It was the Blitz, after all. And the girl crying on the train to Balham, and the arguing American couple. Estrangement and disaster and despair. I wondered if it would record this, too, Cath's fear and our unhappiness, and send it blowing through the tunnels and tracks and passages of the tube to hit some poor unsuspecting tourist in the face next week. Or fifty years from now.

I looked at Cath, still standing against the opposite wall, impossibly far away.

"I'm not having an affair with Sara," I said, and Cath leaned weakly against the tiles and started to cry.

"I love you," I said and crossed the passage in one stride and put my arms around her, and for a moment everything was all right. We were together, and safe. Love conquers all.

But only till the next wind—the results of the X-ray, the call in the middle of the night, the surgeon looking down at his hands, not wanting to tell you the bad news. And we were still down in the tube tunnels, still in its direct path.

"Come on," I said, and took her arm. I couldn't protect her from the winds, but I could get her out of the tube tunnels. I could keep her out of the inversion layer. For a few years. Or months. Or minutes.

"Where are we going?" she asked as I propelled her along the passage.

"Up," I said. "Out."

"We're miles from our hotel," she said.

"We'll get a taxi," I said. I led her up the stairs, around a curve, listening as we went for the sound of a train rumbling in, for a tinny voice announcing, "Mind the Gap."

"We'll take taxis exclusively from now on," I said.

Down another passage, down another set of stairs, trying not to hurry, as if hurrying might bring another one on. Through the arch to the escalators. Almost there. Another minute, and I'd have her on the escalator and headed up out of the inversion layer. Out of the wind. Safe for the moment.

A clot of people emerged abruptly from the Circle Line tunnel opposite and jammed up in front of the escalator, chattering in French. Teenagers on holiday, lugging enormous backpacks and a duffel too wide for the escalator steps, stopping, maddeningly, to consult their tube maps at the foot of the escalator.

"Excuse me," I said, "*Pardonnez moi*," and they looked up, and, instead of moving aside, tried to get on the escalator, jamming the too-wide duffel between the rubber handholds, mashing it down onto the full width of the escalator steps so no one could get past.

Behind us, in the Piccadilly Line tunnel, I could hear the faint sound of a train approaching.

The French kids finally, finally, got the bag onto the escalator, and I pushed Cath onto the bottom step, and stepped on the one below her.

Come on. Up, up. Past a poster for *Remains of the Day* and *Forever, Patsy Cline* and *Death of a Salesman*. Below us, the rumble of the train grew louder, closer.

"What do you say we forget going back to our hotel? We're not far from Marble Arch," I said to cover the sound. "What say we call the Royal Hernia and see if they've got an extra bed?"

THE WINDS OF MARBLE ARCH

Come on, come on. Up. *King Lear. The Mousetrap.*

"What if it's not still there?" Cath said, looking down at the depths below us. We'd come almost three floors. The sound of the train was only a murmur, drowned out by the giggling students and the dull roar of the station hall above us.

"It's still there," I said positively.

Come on, up, up.

"It'll be just like it was," I said. "Steep stairs and the smells of mildew and rotting cabbage. Nice wholesome smells."

"Oh, no," Cath said. She pointed across at the down escalators, suddenly jammed with people in evening dress, shaking the rain from their fur coats and theater programs. "*Cats* just got out. We'll never find a taxi."

"We'll walk," I said.

"It's raining," Cath said.

Better the rain than the wind, I thought. Come on. Up.

We were nearly to the top. The students were already heaving their backpacks onto their shoulders. We would walk to a phone booth and call a taxi. And what then? Keep our heads down. Stay out of drafts. Turn into the Old Man.

It won't work, I thought bleakly. The winds are everywhere. But I had to try to protect Cath from them, having failed to protect her for the last twenty years, I had to try now to keep her out of their deadly path.

Three steps from the top. The French students were yanking on the wedged duffel, shouting, "*Allons! Allons! Vite!*"

I turned to look back, straining to hear the sound of the train over their voices. And saw the wind catch the gray hair of the old woman just stepping onto the top step of the down escalator. She hunched down, ducking her head as it blew down on her from above. From above! It flipped the hair back from the oblivious young faces of the French students above us, lifted their collars, their shirttails.

"Cath!" I shouted and reached for her with one hand, digging the fingers of my other one into the rubber railing as if I could stop the escalator, keep it from carrying us inexorably forward, forward into its path.

My grabbing for her had knocked her off-balance. She half-fell off her step and into me. I turned her toward me, pulled her against my chest, wrapped my arms around her, but it was too late.

"I love you," Cath said, as if it was her last chance.

"Don't—" I said, but it was already upon us, and there was no protecting her, no stopping it. It hit us full-blast, forcing Cath's hair across her cheeks, blowing us nearly back off the step, hitting me full in the face with its smell. I caught my breath in surprise.

The old lady was still standing poised at the top of the escalator, her head back, her eyes closed. People jammed up behind her, saying irritatedly, "Sorry!" and "May I get past, please!" She didn't hear them. Head tilted back, she sniffed deeply at the air.

"Oh," Cath said, and tilted her head back, too.

I breathed it in deeply. A scent of lilacs and rain and expectation. Of years of tourists reading *London on $40 a Day* and newlyweds holding hands on the platform. Of Elliott and Sara and Cath and I, tumbling laughingly after the Old Man, off the train and through the beckoning passages to the District Line and the Tower of London. The scent of spring and the All-Clear and things to come.

Caught in the winding tunnels along with the despair and the terror and the grief. Caught in the maze of passages and stairs and platforms, trapped and magnified and held in the inversion layer.

We were at the top. "May I get past, please?" the man behind us said.

"We'll find your china, Cath," I said. "There's a second-hand market at Portobello Road that has everything under the sun."

"Does the tube go there?" she said.

"I *beg* your pardon," the man said. "*Sorry.*"

"Ladbroke Grove Station. The Hammersmith and City Line," I said and bent to kiss her.

"You're blocking the way," the man said. "People are trying to get through."

"We're improving the atmosphere," I said and kissed her again.

We stood there a moment, breathing it in—leaves and lilacs and love.

Then we got on the down escalator, holding hands and went down to the eastbound platform and took the tube to Marble Arch.

# Blued Moon

FOR IMMEDIATE RELEASE: Mowen Chemical today announced implementation of an innovative waste emissions installation at its experimental facility in Chugwater, Wyoming. According to project directors Bradley McAfee and Lynn Saunders, nonutilizable hydrocarbonaceous substances will be propulsively transferred to stratospheric altitudinal locations, where photochemical decomposition will result in triatomic allotropism and formation of benign bicarbonaceous precipitates. Preliminary predictive data-basing indicates positive ozonation yields without statistically significant shifts in lateral ecosystem equilibria.

"Do you suppose Walter Hunt would have invented the safety pin if he had known that punk rockers would stick them through their cheeks?" Mr. Mowen said. He was looking gloomily out the window at the distant six hundred-foot-high smokestacks.

"I don't know, Mr. Mowen," Janice said. She sighed. "Do you want me to tell them to wait again?"

The sigh was supposed to mean, it's after four o'clock and it's getting dark, and you've already asked Research to wait three times, and when are you going to make up your mind? but Mr. Mowen ignored it.

"On the other hand," he said, "what about diapers? And all those babies that would have been stuck with straight pins if it hadn't been for the safety pin?"

"It is supposed to help restore the ozone layer, Mr. Mowen," Janice said. "And according to Research, there won't be any harmful side effects."

"You shoot a bunch of hydrocarbons into the stratosphere, and there won't be any harmful side effects. According to Research." Mr. Mowen swiveled his chair around to look at Janice, nearly knocking over the picture of his daughter Sally that sat on his desk. "I stuck Sally once. With a safety pin. She screamed for an hour. How's that for a harmful side effect? And what about the stuff that's left over after all this ozone is formed? Bicarbonate of soda, Research says. Perfectly harmless. How do they know that? Have they ever dumped bicarbonate of soda on people before? Call Research..." he started to say, but Janice had already picked up the phone and tapped the number. She didn't even sigh. "Call Research and ask them to figure out what effect a bicarbonate of soda rain would have."

"Yes, Mr. Mowen," Janice said. She put the phone up to her ear and listened for a moment. "Mr. Mowen..." she said hesitantly.

"I suppose Research says it'll neutralize the sulfuric acid that's killing the statues and sweeten and deodorize at the same time."

"No, sir," Janice said. "Research says they've already started the temperature-differential kilns, and you should be seeing something in a few minutes. They say they couldn't wait any longer."

Mr. Mowen whipped back around in his chair to look out the window. The picture of Sally teetered again, and Mr. Mowen wondered if she were home from college yet. Nothing was coming out of the smokestacks. He couldn't see the candlestick-base kilns through the maze of fast-food places and trailer parks. A McDonald's sign directly in front of the smokestacks blinked on suddenly, and Mr. Mowen jumped. The smokestacks themselves remained silent and still except for their blinding strobe aircraft lights. He could see sagebrush-covered hills in the space between the stacks, and the whole scene, except for the McDonald's sign, looked unbelievably serene and harmless.

"Research says the kilns are fired to full capacity," Janice said, holding the phone against her chest.

Mr. Mowen braced himself for the coming explosion. There was a low rumbling like distant fire, then a puff of whitish smoke, and finally a deep, whooshing sound like one of Janice's sighs, and two columns of blue shot straight up into the darkening sky.

"Why is it blue?" Mr. Mowen said.

"I already asked," Janice said. "Research says visible spectrum diffraction is occurring because of the point eight micron radii of the hydrocarbons being propelled—"

"That sounds like that damned press release," Mr. Mowen said. "Tell them to speak English."

After a minute of talking into the phone she said, "It's the same effect that causes the sunsets after a volcanic eruption. Scattering. Research wants to know what staff members you'd like to have at the press conference tomorrow."

"The directors of the project," Mr. Mowen said grumpily, "and anyone over at Research who can speak English."

Janice looked at the press release. "Bradley McAfee and Lynn Saunders are the directors," she said.

"Why does the name McAfee sound familiar?"

"He's Ulric Henry's roommate. The company linguist you hired to—"

"I know why I hired him. Invite Henry, too. And tell Sally as soon as she gets home that I expect her there. Tell her to dress up." He looked at his watch. "Well," he said. "It's been going five minutes, and there haven't been any harmful side effects yet."

The phone rang. Mr. Mowen jumped. "I knew it was too good to last," he said. "Who is it? The EPA?"

"No," Janice said, and sighed. "It's your ex-wife."

"I'm shut of that," Brad said when Ulric came in the door. He was sitting in the dark, the green glow of the monitor lighting his face. He tapped at the terminal keys for a minute more and then turned around. "All done. Slicker'n goose grease."

Ulric turned on the light. "The waste emissions project?" he said.

"Nope. We turned that on this afternoon. Works prettier than a spotted pony. No, I been spending the last hour erasing my fiancée Lynn's name from the project records."

"Won't Lynn object to that?" Ulric said, fairly calmly, mostly because he did not have a very clear idea of which one Lynn was. He never could tell Brad's fiancées apart. They all sounded exactly the same.

"She won't hear tell of it till it's too late," Brad said. "She's on her way to Cheyenne to catch a plane back east. Her mother's all het up about getting a divorce. Caught her husband Adam 'n' Evein'."

If there was anything harder to put up with than Brad's rottenness, it was his incredibly good luck. While Ulric was sure Brad was low enough to engineer a sudden family crisis to get Lynn out of Chugwater, he was just as sure that he had had no need to. It was a lucky coincidence that Lynn's mother was getting a divorce just now, and lucky coincidences were Brad's specialty. How else could he have kept three fiancées from ever meeting each other in the small confines of Chugwater and Mowen Chemical?

"Lynn?" Ulric said. "Which one is that? The redhead in programming?"

"Nope, that's Sue. Lynn's little and yellow-haired and smart as a whip about chemical engineering. Kind of a dodunk about everythin' else."

"Dodunk, " Ulric said to himself. He should make a note to look that up. It probably meant "one so foolish as to associate with Brad McAfee." That definitely included him. He had agreed to room with Brad because he was so surprised at being hired that it had not occurred to him to ask for an apartment of his own.

He had graduated with an English degree that everyone had told him was worse than useless in Wyoming, and which he very soon found out was. In desperation, he had applied for a factory job at Mowen Chemical and been hired on as company linguist at an amazing salary for reasons that had not yet become clear, though he had been at Mowen for over three months. What had become clear was that Brad McAfee was, to use his own colorful language, a thimblerigger, a pigeon plucker, a hornswoggler. He was steadily working his way toward the boss's daughter and the ownership of Mowen Chemical, leaving a trail of young women behind him who all apparently believed that a man who pronounced fiancée 'fee-an-see' couldn't possibly have more than one. It was an interesting linguistic phenomenon.

At first Ulric had been taken in by Brad's homespun talk, too, even though it didn't seem to match his sophisticated abilities on the computer. Then one day he had gotten up early and caught Brad working on a program called Project Sally.

"I'm gonna be the president of Mowen Chemical in two shakes of a sheep's tail," Brad had said. "This little dingclinker is my master plan. What do you think of it?"

What Ulric thought of it could not be expressed in words. It outlined a plan for getting close to Sally Mowen and impressing her father based almost entirely on the seduction and abandonment of young women in key positions at Mowen Chemical. Three-quarters of the way down he had seen Lynn's name.

"What if Mr. Mowen gets hold of this program?" Ulric had said finally.

"Not a look-in chance that that'd happen. I got this program locked up tighter than a hog's eye. And if anybody else tried to copy it, they'd be sorrier than a coon romancin' a polecat."

Since then Ulric had put in six requests for an apartment, all of which had been turned down "due to restrictive areal housing availability," which Ulric supposed meant there weren't any empty apartments in Chugwater. All of the turndowns were initialed by Mr. Mowen's secretary, and there were moments when Ulric thought that Mr. Mowen knew about Project Sally after all and had hired Ulric to keep Brad away from his daughter.

"According to my program, it's time to go to work on Sally," Brad said now. "Tomorrow at this press conference. I'm enough of a rumbustigator with this waste emissions project to dazzlefy Old Man Mowen. Sally's going to be there. I got my fiancée Gail in publicity to invite her."

"I'm going to be there, too," Ulric said belligerently.

"Now, that's right lucky," Brad said. "You can do a little honeyfuggling for me. Work on old Sally while I give Pappy Mowen the glad hand. Do you know what she looks like?"

"I have no intention of honeyfuggling Sally Mowen for you," Ulric said, and wondered again where Brad managed to pick up all these slang expressions. He had caught Brad watching Judy Canova movies on TV a couple of times, but some of these words weren't even in Mencken. He probably had a computer program that generated them. "In fact, I intend to tell her you're engaged to more than one person already."

"Boy, you're sure wadgetty," Brad said. "And you know why? Because you don't have a gal of your own. Tell you what, you pick out one of mine, and I'll give her to you. How about Sue?"

Ulric walked over to the window. "I don't want her," he said.

"I bet you don't even know which one she is," Brad said.

I don't, Ulric thought. They all sound exactly alike. They use interface as a verb and support as an adjective. One of them had called for Brad and when Ulric told her he was over at Research, she had said, "Sorry. My wetware's nonfunctional this morning." Ulric felt as if he were living in a foreign country.

"What difference does it make?" Ulric said angrily. "Not one of them speaks English, which is probably why they're all dumb enough to think they're engaged to you."

"How about if I get you a gal who speaks English and you honeyfuggle Sally Mowen for me?" Brad said. He turned to the terminal and began typing furiously. "What exactly do you want?"

Ulric clenched his fists and looked out the window. The dead cottonwood under the window had a kite or something caught in its branches.

He debated climbing down the tree and walking over to Mr. Mowen's office to demand an apartment.

"Makes no never mind," Brad said when he didn't answer. "I've heard you oratin' often enough on the subject." He typed a minute more and hit the print button. "There," he said.

Ulric turned around.

Brad read from the monitor, "'Wanted: Young woman who can generate enthusiasm for the Queen's English, needs to use correct grammar and syntax, no gobbledygook, no slang, respect for the language. Signed, Ulric Henry.' What do you think of that? It's the spittin' image of the way you talk."

"I can find my own 'gals,'" Ulric said. He yanked the sheet of paper as it was still coming out of the printer, ripping over half the sheet in a long ragged diagonal. Now it read, "Wanted: Young woman who can generate language. Ulric H."

"I'll swop you horses," Brad said. "If this don't rope you in a nice little filly, I'll give you Lynn when she gets back. It'll cheer her up, after getting her name taken off the project and all. What do you think of that?"

Ulric put the scrap of paper down carefully on the table, trying to resist the impulse to wad it up and cram it down Brad's throat. He slammed the window up. There was a sudden burst of chilly wind, and the paper on the table balanced uneasily and then drifted onto the windowsill.

"What if Lynn misses her plane in Cheyenne?" Ulric said. "What if she comes back here and runs into one of your other fiancées?"

"No chance on the map," Brad said cheerfully "I got me a program for that, too." He tore the rest of the paper out of the printer and wadded it up. "Two of my fiancées come callin' at the same time, they have to come up in the elevators, and there's only two of them. They work on the same signals, so I made me up a program that stops the elevators between floors if my security code gets read in more than once in an hour. It makes an override beep go off on my terminal, too, so's I can soft-shoe the first gal down the back stairs." He stood up. "I gotta go over to Research and check on the waste emissions project again. You better find yourself a gal right quick. You're givin' me the flit-flats with all this unfriendly talk."

He grabbed his coat off the back of the chair and went out. He slammed the door, perhaps because he had the flit-flats, and the resultant breeze hit the scrap of paper on the windowsill and sailed it neatly out the window.

"Flit-flats," Ulric mumbled to himself, and tried to call Mowen's office. The line was busy.

⊣ • • • ⊢

Sally Mowen called her father as soon as she got home. "Hi, Janice," she said. "Is Dad there?"

"He just left," Janice said. "But I have a feeling he might stop by Research. He's worried about the new stratospheric waste emissions project."

"I'll walk over and meet him."

"Your father said to tell you there's a press conference tomorrow at eleven. Are you at your terminal?"

"Yes," Sally said, and flicked the power on.

"I'll send the press releases for you so you'll know what's going on."

Sally was going to say that she had already received an invitation to the press conference and the accompanying PR material from someone named Gail, but changed her mind when she saw what was being printed out on the printer. "You didn't send me the press releases," she said. "You sent me a bio on somebody named Ulric Henry. Who's he?"

"I did?" Janice said, sounding flustered. "I'll try it again."

Sally held up the tail of the printout sheet as it came rolling out of the computer. "Now I've got a picture of him." The picture showed a dark-haired young man with an expression somewhere between dismay and displeasure. I'll bet someone just told him she thought they could have a viable relationship, Sally thought. "Who is he?"

Janice sighed, a quick, flustered kind of sigh. "I didn't mean to send that to you. He's the company linguist. I think your father invited him to the press conference to write press releases."

I thought the press releases were already done and you were sending them to me, Sally thought, but she said, "When did my father hire a linguist?"

"Last summer," Janice said, sounding even more flustered. "How's school?"

"Fine," Sally said. "And no, I'm not getting married. I'm not even having a viable relationship, whatever that is."

"Your mother called today. She's in Cheyenne at a NOW rally," Janice said, which sounded like a non sequitur, but wasn't. With a mother like

Sally's, it was no wonder her father worried himself sick over who Sally might marry. Sometimes Sally worried, too. Viable relationship.

"How did Charlotte sound?" Sally said. "No, wait. I already know. Look, don't worry about the press conference stuff. I already know all about it. Gail somebody in publicity sent me an invitation. That's why I came home for Thanksgiving a day early."

"She did?" Janice said. "Your father didn't mention it. He probably forgot. He's been a little worried about this project," she said, which must be the understatement of the year, Sally thought, if he'd managed to rattle Janice. "So you haven't met anyone nice?"

"No," Sally said. "Yes. I'll tell you tomorrow." She hung up. They're all nice, she thought. That isn't the problem. They're nice, but they're incoherent. A viable relationship. What on earth was that? And what was "respecting your personal space"? Or "fulfilling each other's socioeconomic needs"? I have no idea what they are talking about, Sally thought. I have been going out with a bunch of foreigners.

She put her coat and her hat back on and started down in the elevator to find her father. Poor man. He knew what it was like to be married to someone who didn't speak English. She could imagine what the conversation with her mother had been like. All sisters and sexist pigs. She hadn't been speaking ERA very long. The last time she called, she had been speaking est and the time before that California. It was no wonder Sally's father had hired a secretary that communicated almost entirely through sighs, and that Sally had majored in English.

Tomorrow at the press conference would be dreadful. She would be surrounded by nice young men who spoke Big Business or Computer or Bachelor on the Make, and she would not understand a word they said.

It suddenly occurred to her that the company linguist, Ulric Something, might speak English, and she punched in her security code all over again and went back up in the elevator to get the printout with his address on it. She decided to go through the oriental gardens to get to Research instead of taking the car. She told herself it was shorter, which was true, but she was really thinking that if she went through them, she would go past the housing unit where Ulric Henry lived.

The oriental gardens had originally been designed as a shortcut through the maze of fast-food places that had sprung up around Mowen Chemical, making it impossible to get anywhere quickly. Her father had purposely stuck Mowen Chemical on the outskirts of Chugwater so the plant wouldn't disturb the natives, trying to make the original buildings and housing blend in to the Wyoming landscape. The natives had promptly disturbed Mowen Chemical, so that by the time they built the Research complex and computer center, the only land not covered with Kentucky Fried Chickens and Arbys was in the older part of town and very far from the original buildings. Mr. Mowen had given up trying not to disturb the natives. He had built the oriental gardens so that at least people could get from home to work and back again without being run over by the Chugwaterians. Actually, he had intended just to put in a brick path that would wind through the original Mowen buildings and connect them with the new ones, but at the time Charlotte had been speaking Zen. She had insisted on bonsais and a curving bridge over the irrigation ditch. Before the landscaping was finished, she had switched to an anti-Watt dialect that had put an end to the marriage and sent Sally flying off east to school. During that same period her mother had campaigned to save the dead cottonwood she was standing under now, picketing her husband's office with signs that read TREE MURDERER!

Sally stood under the dead cottonwood tree, counting the windows so she could figure out which was Ulric Henry's apartment. There were three windows on the sixth floor with lights in all three, and the middle window was open for some unknown reason, but it would require an incredible coincidence to have Ulric Henry come and stand at one of the windows while Sally was standing there so she could shout up to him, "Do you speak English?"

I wasn't looking for him anyway, she told herself stubbornly. I'm on my way to meet my father, and I stopped to look at the moon. My, it certainly is a peculiar blue color tonight. She stood a few minutes longer under the tree, pretending to look at the moon but it was getting very cold, the moon did not seem to be getting any bluer, and even if it were, it did not seem like an adequate reason for freezing to death, so she pulled her hat down farther over her ears and walked past the bonsais and over the curved bridge towards Research.

As soon as she was across the bridge, Ulric Henry came to the middle window and shut it. The movement of pulling the window shut made a little breeze. The torn piece of printout paper that had been resting on the ledge fluttered to a place closer to the edge and then went over, drifting down in the bluish moonlight past the kite, and coming to rest on the second lowest branch of the cottonwood tree.

⊣•••⊢

Wednesday morning Mr. Mowen got up early so he could get some work done at the office before the press conference. Sally wasn't up yet, so he put the coffee on and went into the bathroom to shave. He plugged his electric razor into the outlet above the sink, and the light over the mirror promptly went out. He took the cord out of the outlet and un-screwed the blackened bulb. Then he pattered into the kitchen in his bare feet to look for another light bulb.

He put the burned-out bulb gently in the wastebasket next to the sink and began opening cupboards. He picked up the syrup bottle to look be-hind it. The lid was not screwed on tightly, and the syrup bottle dropped with a thud onto its side and began oozing syrup all over the cupboard. Mr. Mowen grabbed a paper towel, which tore in a ragged, useless diag-onal, and tried to mop it up. He knocked the salt shaker over into the pool of syrup. He grabbed the other half of the paper towel and turned on the hot water faucet to wet it. The water came out in a steaming blast.

Mr. Mowen jumped sideways to get out of the path of the boiling water and knocked over the wastebasket. The light bulb bounced out and smashed onto the kitchen floor. Mr. Mowen stepped on a large ragged piece. He tore off more paper towels to stanch the blood and limped back to the bathroom walking on the side of his bleeding foot, to get a bandaid.

He had forgotten about the light in the bathroom being burned out. Mr. Mowen felt his way to the medicine cabinet, knocking the shampoo and a box of Q-Tips into the sink before he found the bandaids. The shampoo lid wasn't screwed on tightly either. He took the metal box of bandaids back to the kitchen.

It was bent, and Mr. Mowen got a dent in his thumb trying to pry the lid off. As he was pushing on it, the lid suddenly sprang free, spraying bandaids all over the kitchen floor. Mr. Mowen picked one up, being careful to avoid the pieces of light bulb, ripped the end off the wrapper, and pulled on the orange string. The string came out. Mr. Mowen looked at the string for a long minute and then tried to open the bandaid from the back.

When Sally came into the kitchen, Mr. Mowen was sitting on a kitchen chair sucking his bleeding thumb and holding a piece of paper towel to his other foot. "What happened?" she said.

"I cut myself on a broken light bulb," Mr. Mowen said. "It went out while I was trying to shave."

She grabbed for a piece of paper toweling. It tore off cleanly at the perforation, and Sally wrapped Mr. Mowen's thumb in it. "You know better than to try to pick up a broken light bulb," she said. "You should have gotten a broom."

"I did not try to pick up the light bulb," he said. "I cut my thumb on a bandaid . I cut my *feet* on the light bulb."

"Oh, I see," Sally said. "Don't you know better than to try to pick up a light bulb with your feet?"

"This isn't funny," Mr. Mowen said indignantly. "I am in a lot of pain."

"I know it isn't funny," Sally said. She picked a bandaid up off the floor, tore off the end, and pulled the string neatly along the edge of the wrapping. "Are you going to be able to make it to your press conference?"

"Of course I'm going to be able to make it. And I expect you to be there, too."

"I will," Sally said, peeling another bandaid and applying it to the bottom of his foot. "I'm going to leave as soon as I get this mess cleaned up so I can walk over. Or would you like me to drive you?"

"I can drive myself," Mr. Mowen said, starting to get up.

"You stay right there until I get your slippers," Sally said, and darted out of the kitchen. The phone rang. "I'll get it," Sally called from the bedroom. "You don't budge out of that chair."

Mr. Mowen picked a bandaid up off the floor, tore the end off of it and peeled the string along the side, which made him feel considerably better. My luck must be starting to change, he thought. "Who's on the phone?" he said cheerfully as Sally came back into the kitchen carrying his slippers and the phone.

She plugged the phone cord into the wall and handed him the receiver. "It's Mother," she said. "She wants to talk to the sexist pig."

⊣ • • • ⊢

Ulric was getting dressed for the press conference when the phone rang. He let Brad answer it. When he walked into the living room, Brad was hanging up the phone.

"Lynn missed her plane," Brad said.

Ulric looked up hopefully. "She did?"

"Yes. She's taking one out this afternoon. While she was shooting the breeze, she let fall she'd signed her name on the press release that was sent out on the computer."

"And Mowen's already read it," Ulric said. "So he'll know you stole the project away from her." He was in no mood to mince words. He had lain awake most of the night trying to decide what to say to Sally Mowen. What if he told her about Project Sally and she looked blankly at him and said, "Sorry. My wetware is inoperable?"

"I didn't steal the project," Brad said amiably. "I just sort of skyugled it away from her when she wasn't looking. And I already got it back. I called Gail as soon as Lynn hung up and asked her to take Lynn's name of the press releases before Old Man Mowen saw them. It was right lucky Lynn missing her plane and all."

Ulric put his down parka on over his sports coat.

"Are you heading for the press conference?" Brad said. "Wait till I rig myself out, and I'll ride over with you."

"I'm walking," Ulric said, and opened the door.

The phone rang. Brad answered it. "No, I wasn't watching the morning movie," Brad said, "but I'd take it big if you'd let me gander a guess anyway. I'll say the movie is *Carolina Cannonball* and the jackpot is six hundred and fifty-one dollars. That's right? Well, bust my buttons. That was a right lucky guess."

Ulric slammed the door behind him.

—| • • |—

When Mr. Mowen still wasn't in the office by ten, Janice called him at home. She got a busy signal. She sighed, waited a minute, and tried again. The line was still busy. Before she could hang up, the phone flashed an incoming call. She punched the button. "Mr. Mowen's office," she said.

"Hi," the voice on the phone said. "This is Gail over in publicity. The press releases contain an inoperable statement. You haven't sent any out, have you?"

I tried. Janice thought with a little sigh. "No," she said.

"Good. I wanted to confirm nonrelease before I effected the deletion."

"What deletion?" Janice said. She tried to call up the press release but got a picture of Ulric Henry instead.

"The release catalogs Lynn Saunders as co-designer of the project."

"I thought she *was* co-designer."

"Oh, no," Gail said. "My fiancé Brad McAfee designed the whole project. I'm glad the number of printouts is nonsignificant."

After Gail hung up, Janice tried Mr. Mowen again. The line was still busy. Janice called up the company directory on her terminal, got a resume on Ulric Henry instead, and called the Chugwater operator on the phone. The operator gave her Lynn Saunders' number. Janice called Lynn and got her roommate.

"She's not here," the roommate said. "She had to leave for back east as soon as she was done with the waste emissions thing. Her mother was doing head trips on her. She was really bummed out by it."

"Do you have a number where I could reach her?" Janice asked.

"I sure don't," the roommate said. "She wasn't with it at all when she left. Her fiancé might have a number."

"Her fiancé?"

"Yeah. Brad McAfee."

"I think if she calls you'd better have her call me. Priority." Janice hung up the phone. She called up the company directory on her terminal again and got the press release for the new emissions project. Lynn's name was nowhere on it. She sighed, an odd, angry sigh, and tried Mr. Mowen's number again. It was still busy.

On Sally's way past Ulric Henry's housing unit, she noticed something fluttering high up in the dead cottonwood tree. The remains of a kite were tangled at the very top, and just out of reach, on the second lowest branch, there was a piece of white paper. She tried a couple of halfhearted jumps, swiping at the paper with her hand, but she succeeded only in blowing the paper farther out of reach. If she could get the paper down, she could take it up to Ulric Henry's apartment and ask him if it had fallen out of his window. She looked around for a stick and then stood still, feeling foolish. There was no more reason to go after the paper than to attempt to get the ruined kite down, she told herself, but even as she thought that, she was measuring the height of the branches to see if she could get a foot up and reach the paper from there. One branch wouldn't do it, but two might. There was no one in the gardens. This is ridiculous, she told herself, and swung up into the crotch of the tree.

She climbed swiftly up to the third branch, stretched out across it, and reached for the paper. Her fingers did not quite reach, so she straightened up again, hanging onto the trunk to get her balance, and made a kind of downsweeping lunge toward the piece of paper. She lost her balance and nearly missed the branch, and the wind she had created by her sudden movement blew the paper all the way to the end of the branch, where it teetered precariously but did not fall off.

Someone was coming across the curving bridge. She blew a couple of times on the paper and then stopped. She was going to have to go out on the branch. Maybe the paper is blank, she thought. I can hardly take a blank piece of paper to Ulric Henry, but she was already testing the weight of the branch with her hand. It seemed firm enough, and she began to edge out onto the dead branch, holding onto the trunk until the last possible moment and then dropping into an inching crawl that brought her directly over the sidewalk. From there she was able to reach the paper easily.

The paper was part of a printout from a computer, torn raggedly at an angle. It read, "Wanted: Young woman who can generate language. Ulric. H." The *ge* in "language" was missing, but otherwise the message made perfect sense, which she would have thought was peculiar if she had not been so surprised at the message. Her area of special study was language generation. She had spent all last week in class doing it, using all the rules of linguistic change on existing words: generalization and specialization of meaning, change in part of speech, shortening, prepositional verb clustering, to create a new-sounding language. It had been almost impossible to do at first, but by the end of the week, she had greeted her professor with, "Good aft. I readed up my book taskings," without even thinking about it. She could certainly do the same thing with Ulric Henry, whom she had been wanting to meet anyway.

She had forgotten about the man she had seen coming across the bridge. He was almost to the tree now. In approximately ten more steps he would look up and see her crouched there like an insane vulture. How will I explain this to my father if anyone sees me? she thought, and put a cautious foot behind her. She was still wondering when the branch gave way.

Mr. Mowen did not leave for the press conference until a quarter to eleven. He had still been on the phone with Charlotte when Sally left, and when he had asked Charlotte to wait a minute so he could tell Sally to wait and he'd drive her over, Charlotte had called him a sexist tyrant and accused him of stifling Sally's dominant traits by repressive male psychological intimidation. Mr. Mowen had had no idea what she was talking about.

Sally had swept up the glass and put a new light bulb in the bathroom before she left, but Mr. Mowen had decided not to tempt fate. He had shaved with a disposable razor instead. Leaning over to get a piece of toilet paper to put on the cut on his chin, he had cracked his head on the medicine cabinet door. After that, he had sat very still on the edge of the tub for nearly half an hour, wishing Sally were home so she could help him get dressed.

At the end of the half hour, Mr. Mowen decided that stress was the cause of the series of coincidences that had plagued him all morning (Charlotte had spoken Biofeedback for a couple of weeks), and that if he just relaxed, everything would be all right. He took several deep, calming breaths and stood up. The medicine cabinet was still open.

By moving very carefully and looking for hazards everywhere, Mr. Mowen managed to get dressed and out to the car. He had not been able to find any socks that matched, and the elevator had taken him all the way to the roof, but Mr. Mowen breathed deeply and calmly each time, and he was even beginning to feel relaxed by the time he opened the door to the car.

He got into the car and shut the door. It caught the tail of his coat. He opened the door again and leaned over to pull the coat out of the way. One of his gloves fell out of his pocket onto the ground. He leaned over farther to rescue the glove and cracked his head on the armrest of the door.

He took a deep, rather ragged breath, snagged the glove, and pulled the door shut. He took the keys out of his pocket and inserted the car key in the ignition. The key chain snapped open and scattered the rest of his keys all over the floor of the front seat. When he bent over to pick them up, being very careful not to hit his head on the steering wheel, his other glove fell out of his pocket. He left the keys where they were and straightened up again, watching out for the turn signals and the sun visor. He turned the key with its still dangling key chain. The car wouldn't start.

Very slowly and carefully he got out of the car and went back up to the apartment to call Janice and tell her to cancel the press conference. The phone was busy.

⊣ • • • ⊢

Ulric didn't see the young woman until she was nearly on top of him. He had been walking with his head down and his hands jammed into the pockets of his parka, thinking about the press conference. He had left the apartment without his watch and walked very rapidly over to Research. He had been over an hour early, and no one had been there except one of Brad's fiancées whose name he couldn't remember. She had said, "Your biological clock is nonfunctional. Your biorhythms must be low today," and he had told her they were, even though he had no idea what they were talking about.

He had walked back across the oriental gardens, feeling desperate. He was not sure he could stand the press conference, even to warn Sally Mowen. Maybe he should forget about going and walk all over Chugwater instead, grabbing young women by the arm and saying, "Do you speak English?"

While he was considering this idea, there was a loud snap overhead, and the young woman fell on him. He tried to get his hands out of his pockets to catch her, but it took him a moment to realize that he was under the cottonwood tree and that the snap was the sound of a branch breaking, so he didn't succeed. He did get one hand out of his pocket and he did take one bracing step back, but it wasn't enough. She landed on him full force, and they rolled off the sidewalk and onto the leaves. When they came to a stop, Ulric was on top of her, with one arm under her and the other one flung above her head. Her wool hat had come off and her hair was spread out nicely against the frost-rimed leaves. His hand was tangled in her hair. She was looking up at him as if she knew him. It did not even occur to him to ask her if she spoke English.

After a while it did occur to him that he was going to be late to the press conference. The hell with the press conference, he thought. The hell with Sally Mowen, and kissed her again. After a few more minutes of that, his arm began to go numb, and he disengaged his hand from her hair and put his weight on it to pull himself up.

She didn't move, even when he got onto his knees beside her and extended a hand to help her up. She lay there, looking up at him as if she were thinking hard about something. Then she seemed to come to a decision because she took his hand and let him pull her up. She pointed above and behind him. "The moon blues," she said.

"What?" he said. He wondered if the branch had cracked her on the head.

She was still pointing. "The moon blues," she said again. "It blued up some last dark, but now it blues moreishly, "

He turned to look in the direction she was pointing, and sure enough, the three-quarters moon was a bright blue in the morning sky, which explained what she was talking about, but not the way she was talking. "Are you all right?" he said. "You're not hurt, are you?" She shook her head. You never ask someone with a concussion if they are all right, he thought. "Does your head hurt?"

She shook her head again. Maybe she wasn't hurt. Maybe she was a foreign exchange consultant in Research. "Where are you from?" he said.

She looked surprised. "I falled down of the tree. You catched me with your face." She brushed the cottonwood leaves out of her hair and put her wool hat back on.

She understood everything he said, and she was definitely speaking English words even though the effect wasn't much like English. You catched me with your face. Irregular verb into regular. The moon blues. Adjective becomes verb. Those were both ways language evolved. "What were you doing in the tree?" he said, so she would talk some more.

"I hidinged in the tree for cause people point you with their faces when you English oddishly "

English oddishly "You're generating language, aren't you?" Ulric said. "Do you know Brad McAfee?"

She looked blank, and a little surprised, the way Brad had probably told her to when he put her up to this. He wondered which one of Brad's fiancées this was. Probably the one in programming. They had had to come up with all this generated language somewhere. "I'm late for a press conference," he said sharply, "as you well know. I've got to talk to Sally Mowen." He didn't put out his hand to help her up. "You can go tell Brad his little honeyfuggling scheme didn't work."

She stood up without his help and walked across the sidewalk, past the fallen branch. She knelt down and picked up a scrap of paper and looked at it for a long time. He considered yanking it out of her hand and looking at it since it was probably Brad's language generation program, but he didn't. She folded it and put it in her pocket.

"You can tell him your kissing me didn't work," he said, which was a lie. He wanted to kiss her again as he said it, and that made him angrier than ever. Brad had probably told her he was wadgetty, that what he needed was a half hour in the leaves with her. "I'm still going to tell Sally." She looked at him from the other side of the sidewalk.

"And don't get any ideas about trying to stop me." He was shouting now. "Because they won't work."

His anger got him over the curving bridge. Then it occurred to him that even if she was one of Brad's fiancées, even if she had been hired to kiss him in the leaves and keep him from going to the press conference, he was in love with her, and he went tearing back, but she was nowhere in sight.

At a little after eleven Janice got a call from Gail in publicity. "Where is Mr. Mowen? He hasn't shown up, and my media credibility is effectively nonfunctional."

"I'll try to call him at home," Janice said. She put Gail on hold and dialed Mr. Mowen's apartment. The line was busy. When she punched up the hold button to tell Gail that, the line went dead. Janice tried to call her back. The line was busy.

She typed in the code for a priority that would override whatever was on Mr. Mowen's home terminal. After the code, she typed, "Call Janice at once." She looked at it for a minute, then back-erased and typed, "Press conference. Research. Eleven A.M.," and pressed RUN. The screen clicked once and displayed the preliminary test results of side effects on the waste emissions project. At the bottom of the screen, she read, "Tangential consequences statistically negligible."

"You want to bet?" Janice said.

She called programming. "There's something wrong with my terminal," she said to the woman on the line.

"This is Sue in peripherals rectification. Is your problem in implementation or hardware?"

She sounded just like Gail in publicity. "You wouldn't know Brad McAfee, would you?" she said.

"He's my fiancé," Sue said. "Why?"

Janice sighed. "I keep getting readouts that have nothing to do with what I punch in," Janice said.

"Oh, then you want hardware repair. The number's in your terminal directory," she said, and hung up.

Janice called up the terminal directory. At first nothing happened. Then the screen clicked once and displayed something titled Project Sally. Janice noticed Lynn Saunders' name three-quarters of the way down the screen, and Sally Mowen's at the bottom. She started at the top and read it all the way through. Then she typed in PRINT and read it again as it came rolling out of the printer. When it was done, she tore off the sheet carefully, put it in a file folder, and put the file folder in her desk.

"I found your glove in the elevator," Sally said when she came in. She looked terrible, as if the experience of finding Mr. Mowen's glove had been too much for her. "Is the press conference over?"

"I didn't go," Mr. Mowen said. "I was afraid I'd run into a tree. Could you drive me over to the office? I told Janice I'd be there by nine and it's two-thirty."

"Tree?" Sally said. "I fell out of a tree today. On a linguist."

Mr. Mowen put on his overcoat and fished around in the pockets. "I've lost my other glove," he said. "That makes fifty-eight instances of bad luck I've had already this morning, and I've been sitting stock-still for the last two hours. I made a list. The pencil broke, and the eraser, and I erased a hole right through the paper, and I didn't even count those." He put the single glove in his coat pocket.

Sally opened the door for him, and they went down the hall to the elevator. "I never should have said that about the moon," she said. "I should have said hello. Just a simple hello. So what if the note said he wanted someone who could generate language? That didn't mean I had to do it right then, before I even told him who I was."

Mr. Mowen punched his security code into the elevator. The REJECT light came on. "Fifty-nine," Mr. Mowen said. "That's too many coincidences to just be a coincidence. And all bad. If I didn't know better, I'd say someone was trying to kill me."

Sally punched in her security code. The elevator slid open. "I've been walking around for hours, trying to figure out how I could have been so stupid," Sally said. "He was on his way to meet me. At the press conference. He had something to tell me. If I'd just stood up after I fell on him and said, 'Hello, I'm Sally Mowen, and I've found this note. Do you really want someone who can generate language?' but oh, no, I have to say,

'The moon blues.' I should have just kept kissing him and never said anything. But oh, no, I couldn't let well enough alone."

Mr. Mowen let Sally push the floor button in the elevator so no more warning lights would flash on. He also let her open the door of the apartment building. On the way out to the car, he stepped in some gum.

"Sixty. If I didn't know better, I'd say your mother was behind this," Mr. Mowen said. "She's coming up here this afternoon. To see if I'm minimizing your self-realization potential with my chauvinistic role expectations. That should count for a dozen bad coincidences all by itself." He got in the car, hunching far back in the seat so he wouldn't crack his head on the sun visor. He peered out the window at the gray sky. "Maybe there'll be a blizzard and she won't be able to get up from Cheyenne."

Sally reached for something under the driver's seat. "Here's your other glove," she said, handed it over to him, and started the car. "That note was torn in half. Why didn't I think about the words that were missing instead of deciding the message was all there? He probably wanted somebody who could generate electricity and speak a foreign language. Just because I liked his picture and I thought he might speak English I had to go and make a complete fool out of myself."

It started to snow halfway to the office. Sally turned on the windshield wipers. "With my luck," Mr. Mowen said, "there'll be a blizzard, and I'll be snowed in with Charlotte." He looked out the side window at the smokestacks. They were shooting another wavery blue blast into the air. "It's the waste emissions project. Somehow it's causing all these damn coincidences."

Sally said, "I look and look for someone who speaks decent English, and when I finally meet him, what do I say? You catched me with your face. And now he thinks somebody named Brad McAfee put me up to it to keep him from getting to a press conference, and he'll never speak to me again. Stupid! How could I have been so stupid?"

"I never should have let them start the project without more testing," Mr. Mowen said. "What if we're putting too much ozone into the ozone layer? What if this bicarbonate of soda fallout is doing something to people's digestion? No measurable side effects, they said. Well, how do you measure bad luck? By the fatality rates?"

Sally had pulled into a parking space directly in front of Mr. Mowen's office. It was snowing hard now. Mr. Mowen pulled on the glove Sally had handed him. He fished in his pocket for the other one. "Sixty-one," he said. "Sally, will you go in with me? I'll never get the elevator to work."

Sally walked with him into the building. On the way up in the elevator, she said, "If you're so convinced the waste emissions project is causing your bad luck, why don't you tell Research to turn it off?"

"They'd never believe me. Whoever heard of coincidences as a side effect of trash?"

They went into the outer office. Janice said, "Hello!" as if they had returned from an arctic expedition. Mr. Mowen said, "Thanks, Sally. I think I can make it from here." He patted her on the shoulder. "Why don't you go explain what happened to this young man and tell him you're sorry?"

"I don't think that would work," Sally said. She kissed him on the cheek. "We're in bad shape, aren't we?"

Mr. Mowen turned to Janice. "Get me Research, and don't let my wife in," he said, went into his office, and shut the door. There was a crash and the muffled sound of Mr. Mowen swearing.

Janice sighed. "This young man of yours," she said to Sally. "His name wouldn't be Brad McAfee, would it?"

"No," Sally said, "but he thinks it is." On the way to the elevator she stopped and picked up Mr. Mowen's glove and put it in her pocket.

⊣ • • ⊢

After Mr. Mowen's secretary hung up, Sue called Brad. She wasn't sure what the connection was between Brad and Mr. Mowen's secretary's terminal not working, but she thought she'd better let him know that Mr. Mowen's secretary knew his name.

There was no answer. She tried again at lunch and again on her afternoon break. The third time the line was busy. At a quarter of three her supervisor came in and told Sue she could leave early, since heavy snow was predicted for rush hour. Sue tried Brad's number one more time to make sure he was there. It was still busy.

It was a good thing she was getting off early. She had only worn a sweater to work, and it was already snowing so hard she could hardly see out the window. She had worn sandals, too. Somebody had left a pair of bright blue moon boots in the coatroom, so she pulled those on over her sandals and went out to the parking lot. She wiped the snow off the windshield with the sleeve of her sweater, and started over to Brad's apartment.

⊣ • • ⊢

"You didn't meander on over to the press conference," Brad said when Ulric came in.

"No," Ulric said. He didn't take off his coat.

"Old Man Mowen didn't either. Which was right lucky, because I got to jaw with all those reporters instead of him. Where did you go off to? You look colder than an otter on a snowslide."

"I was with the 'gal' you found for me. The one you had jump me so I wouldn't go to the press conference and ruin your chances with Sally Mowen."

Brad was sitting at his terminal. "Sally wasn't there, which turned out to be right lucky because I met this reporter name of Jill who…" He turned around and looked at Ulric. "What gal are you talking about?"

"The one you had conveniently fall out of a tree on me. I take it she was one of your spare fiancées. What did you do? Make her climb out of the apartment window?"

"Now let me get this straight. Some gal fell out of that old cottonwood on top of you? And you think I did it?"

"Well, if you didn't, it was an amazing coincidence that the branch broke just as I was passing under it and an even more amazing coincidence that she generated language, which was just what that printout you came up with read. But the most amazing coincidence of all is the punch in the nose you're going to get right now."

"Now, don't get so dudfoozled. I didn't drop no gal on you, and if I'm lyin', let me be kicked to death by grasshoppers. If I was going to do something like that, I'd have gotten you one who could speak good English, like you wanted, not—what did you say she did? Generated language?"

"You expect me to believe it's all some kind of coincidence?" Ulric shouted. "What kind of—of—dodunk do you take me for?"

"I'll admit it is a pretty seldom thing to have happen," Brad said thoughtfully. "This morning I found me a hundred-dollar bill on the way to the press conference. Then I meet this reporter Jill and we get to talking and we have a whole lot in common like her favorite movie is *Lay That Rifle Down* with Judy Canova in it, and then it turns out she's Sally Mowen's roommate last year in college."

The phone rang. Brad picked it up. "Well, ginger peachy. Come on over. It's the big housing unit next to the oriental gardens. Apartment 6B." He hung up the phone. "Now that's just what I been talking about. That was that gal reporter on the phone. I asked her to come over so's I could honeyfuggle her into introducing me to Sally, and she says she can't cause she's gotta catch a plane outta Cheyenne. But now she says the highway's closed, and she's stuck here in Chugwater. Now that kind of good luck doesn't happen once in a blue moon."

"What?" Ulric said, and unclenched his fists for the first time since he'd come into the room. He went over to look out the window. He couldn't see the moon that had been in the sky earlier. He supposed it had long since set, and anyway it was starting to snow. "The moon blues," he said softly to himself.

"Since she is coming over here, maybe you should skedaddle so as not to spoil this run of good luck I am having."

Ulric pulled *Collected American Slang* out of the bookcase and looked up, "moon, blue" in the index. The entry read, "Once in a blue moon: rare, as an unusual coincidence, orig. rare as a blue moon; based on the rare occurrence of a blue-tinted moon from aerosol particulates in upper atmosphere; see Superstitions." He looked out the window again. The smokestacks sent another blast up through the gray clouds.

"Brad," he said, "is your waste emissions project putting aerosols into the upper atmosphere?"

"That's the whole idea," Brad said. "Now I don't mean to be bodacious, but that gal reporter's going to be coming up here any minute."

Ulric looked up "Superstitions." The entry for "moon, blue" read, "Once in a blue moon; folk saying attrib. SE America; local superstition linked occurrence of blue moon and unusual coincidental happenings; origin unknown."

He shut the book. "Unusual coincidental happenings," he said. "Branches breaking, people falling on people, people finding hundred-dollar bills. All of those are coincidental happenings." He looked up at Brad. "You wouldn't happen to know how that saying got started, would you?"

"Bodacious? It probably was made up by some feller who was waiting on a gal and this other guy wouldn't hotfoot it out of there so's they could be alone."

Ulric opened the book again. "But if the coincidences were bad ones, they would be dangerous, wouldn't they? Somebody might get hurt."

Brad took the book out of his hands and shoved Ulric out the door. "Now git!" he said. "You're givin' me the flit-flats again."

"We've got to tell Mr. Mowen. We've got to shut it off," Ulric said, but Brad had already shut the door.

—|•••|—

"Hello, Janice," Charlotte said. "Still an oppressed female in a dehumanizing male-dominated job, I see."

Janice hung up the phone. "Hello, Charlotte," she said. "Is it snowing yet?"

"Yes," Charlotte said, and took off her coat. It had a red button pinned to the lapel. It read "NOW…or else!" "We just heard on the radio they've closed the highway. Where's your reactionary chauvinist employer?"

"Mr. Mowen is busy," Janice said, and stood up in case she needed to flatten herself against Mr. Mowen's door to keep Charlotte out.

"I have no desire to see that last fortress of sadistic male dominance," Charlotte said. She took off her gloves and rubbed her hands together. "We practically froze on the way up. Lynn Saunders rode back up with me. Her mother isn't getting a divorce after all. Her bid for independence crumbled at the first sign of societal disapproval, I'm afraid. Lynn had a message on her terminal to call you, but she couldn't get through. She said for me to tell you she'd be over as soon as she checks in with her fiancé."

"Brad McAfee," Janice said.

"Yes," Charlotte said. She sat down in the chair opposite Janice's desk and took off her boots. "I had to listen to her sing his praises all the way from Cheyenne. Poor brainwashed victim of male oppressionist propaganda. I tried to tell her she was only playing into the hands of the entrenched male socio-sexual establishment by getting engaged, but she wouldn't listen." She stopped massaging her stockinged foot. "What do you mean, he's busy? Tell that arrogant sexist pig I'm here and I want to see him."

Janice sat back down and took the file folder with Project Sally in it out of her desk drawer. "Charlotte," she said, "before I do that, I was wondering if you'd give me your opinion of something."

Charlotte padded over to the desk in her stockinged feet. "Certainly," she said. "What is it?"

—|•••|—

Sally wiped the snow off the back window with her bare hands and got in the car. She had forgotten about the side mirror. It was caked with snow. She rolled down the window and swiped at it with her hand. The snow landed in her lap. She shivered and rolled the window back up, and then sat there a minute, waiting for the defroster to work and blowing on her cold, wet hands. She had lost her gloves somewhere.

No air at all was coming out of the defroster. She rubbed a small space clean so she could see to pull out of the parking space and edged forward. At the last minute she saw the ghostlike form of a man through the heavy curtain of snow and stamped on the brake. The motor died. The man she had almost hit came around to the window and motioned to her to roll the window down. It was Ulric.

She rolled the window down. More snow fell in her lap. "I was afraid I'd never see you again," Ulric said.

"I—" Sally said, but he waved her silent with his hand.

"I haven't got much time. I'm sorry I shouted at you this morning. I thought—anyway, now I know that isn't true, that it was a lot of coincidences that—anyway I've got to go do something right now that can't wait, but I want you to wait right here for me. Will you do that?"

She nodded.

He shivered and stuck his hands in his pockets, "You'll freeze to death out here. Do you know where the housing unit by the oriental gardens is? I live on the sixth floor, apartment B. I want you to wait for me there. Will you do that? Do you have a piece of paper?"

Sally dug in her pocket and pulled out the folded scrap of paper with "Wanted: Young woman" on it. She looked at it a minute and then handed it to Ulric. He didn't even unfold it. He scribbled some numbers on it and handed it back to her.

"This is my security code," he said. "You have to use it for the elevator. My roommate will let you into the apartment." He stopped and looked hard at her. "On second thought, you'd better wait for me in the hall. I'll be back as soon as I can." He bent and kissed her through the window. "I don't want to lose you again."

"I—" Sally said, but he had already disappeared into the snow. Sally rolled the window up. The windshield was covered with snow again. She put her hand up to the defroster. There was still no air coming out. She turned on the windshield wipers. Nothing happened.

—|•••|—

Gail didn't get back to her office until after two. Reporters had hung around after the press conference asking her questions about Mr. Mowen's absence and the waste emissions project. When she did make it back to the office, they began calling, and she didn't get started on her press conference publicity releases until nearly three. She almost immediately ran into a problem. Her notes mentioned particulates, and she knew Brad had said what kind, but she hadn't written it down. She couldn't let the report go without specifying which particulates or the press would jump to all kinds of alarming conclusions. She called Brad. The line was busy. She stuffed everything into a large manila envelope and started over to his apartment to ask him.

"Did you get Research yet?" Mr. Mowen said when Janice came into his office.

"No, sir," Janice said. "The line is still busy. Ulric Henry is here to see you."

Mr. Mowen pushed against his desk and stood up. The movement knocked over Sally's picture and a pencilholder full of pencils. "You might as well send him in. With my luck, he's probably found out why I hired him and is here to quit. "

Janice went out, and Mr. Mowen tried to gather up the pencils that had scattered all over his desk and get them back in the pencil holder. One rolled toward the edge, and Mr. Mowen leaned over the desk to catch it. Sally's picture fell over again. When Mr. Mowen looked up, Ulric Henry was watching him. He reached for the last pencil and knocked the receiver off the phone with his elbow.

"How long has it been like this?" Ulric said.

Mr. Mowen straightened up. "It started this morning. I'm not sure I'm going to live through the day."

"That's what I was afraid of," Ulric said, and took a deep breath. "Look, Mr. Mowen, I know you hired me to be a linguist, and I probably don't have any business interfering with Research, but I think I know why all these things are happening to you."

I hired you to marry Sally and be vice-president in charge of saying what you mean, Mr. Mowen thought, and you can interfere in anything you like if you can stop the ridiculous things that have been happening to me all day.

Ulric pointed out the window. "You can't see it out there because of the snow, but the moon is blue. It's been blue ever since you turned on your waste emissions project. 'Once in a blue moon' is an old saying used to describe rare occurrences. I think the saying may have gotten started because the number of coincidences increased every time there was a blue moon. I think it may have something to do with the particulates in the stratosphere doing something to the laws of probability. Your waste emissions project is pumping particulates into the stratosphere right now. I think these coincidences are a side effect."

"I *knew* it," Mr. Mowen said. "It's Walter Hunt and the safety pin all over again. I'm going to call Research." He reached for the phone. The receiver cord caught on the edge of the desk. When he yanked it, the phone went clattering over the edge, taking the pencil holder and Sally's picture with it. "Will you call Research for me?"

"Sure," Ulric said. He punched in the number and then handed the receiver to Mr. Mowen.

Mr. Mowen thundered, "Turn off the waste emissions project. Now. And get everyone connected with the project over here immediately." He hung up the phone and peered out the window. "Okay. They've turned it off," he said, turning back to Ulric. "Now what?"

"I don't know," Ulric said from the floor where he was picking up pencils. "I suppose as soon as the moon starts to lose its blue color, the laws of probability will go back to normal. Or maybe they'll rebalance themselves, and you'll have all good luck for a day or two." He put the pencil holder back on the desk and picked up Sally's picture.

"I hope it changes before my ex-wife gets back," Mr. Mowen said. "She's been here once already, but Janice got rid of her. I knew she was a side effect of some kind."

Ulric didn't say anything. He was looking at the picture of Sally.

"That's my daughter," Mr. Mowen said. "She's an English major."

Ulric stood the picture on the desk. It fell over, knocking the pencil holder onto the floor again. Ulric dived for the pencils.

"Never mind about the pencils," Mr. Mowen said. "I'll pick them up after the moon gets back to normal. She's home for Thanksgiving vacation. You might run into her. Her area of special study is language generation."

Ulric straightened up and cracked his head on the desk. "Language generation," he said, and walked out of the office.

Mr. Mowen went out to tell Janice to send the Research people in as soon as they got there. One of Ulric's gloves was lying on the floor next

to Janice's desk. Mr. Mowen picked it up. "I hope he's right about putting a stop to these coincidences by turning off the stacks," he said. "I
think this thing is catching."

Lynn called Brad as soon as Charlotte dropped her off. Maybe he
knew why Mr. Mowen's secretary wanted to see her. The line was
busy. She took off her parka, put her suitcase in the bedroom, and
then tried again. It was still busy She put her parka back on, pulled on
a pair of red mittens, and started across the oriental gardens to Brad's
apartment.

"Are those nincompoops from Research here?" Mr. Mowen
asked Janice.

"Yes, sir. All but Brad McAfee. His line is busy."

"Well, put an override on his terminal. And send them in."

"Yes, sir," Janice said. She went back to her desk and called up a directory on her terminal. To her surprise, she got it. She wrote down Brad's
code and punched in an override. The computer printed ERROR. I knew
it was too good to last, Janice thought. She punched the code again. This
time the computer printed OVERRIDE IN PLACE. Janice thought a
minute, then decided that whatever the override was, it couldn't be more
important than Mr. Mowen's. She punched the code for a priority override and typed, "Mr. Mowen wants to see you immediately." The computer immediately confirmed it.

Exhilarated by her success, Janice called Brad's number again. He answered the phone. "Mr. Mowen would like to see you immediately," she said.

"I'll be there faster than blue blazes," Brad said, and hung up.

Janice went in and told Mr. Mowen Brad McAfee was on the way.
Then she herded the Research people into his office. When Mr. Mowen
stood up to greet them, he didn't knock over anything, but one of the
Research people managed to knock over the pencils again. Janice helped
him pick them up.

When she got back to her desk she remembered that she had super-
seded an override on Brad's terminal. She wondered what it was. Maybe

Charlotte had gone to his apartment and poisoned him and then put an override on so he couldn't call for help. It was a comforting thought somehow, but the override might be something important, and now that she had gotten him on the phone there was really no reason to leave the priority override in place. Janice sighed and typed in a cancellation. The computer immediately confirmed it.

Jill opened the door to Brad's apartment building and stood there for a minute trying to get her breath. She was supposed to have driven back to Cheyenne tonight, and she had barely made it across Chugwater. Her car had slid sideways in the street and gotten stuck, and she had finally left it there and come over here to see if Brad could help her put her chains on. She fished clumsily in her purse for the numbers Brad had written down for her so she could use the elevator. She should have taken her gloves off.

A young woman with no gloves on pushed open the door and headed for one of the two elevators, punched some numbers, and disappeared into the nearer elevator. The doors shut. She should have gone up with her. Jill fished some more and came up with several folded scraps of paper. She tried to unfold the first one, gave up, and balanced them all on one hand while she tried to pull her other glove off with her teeth.

The outside door opened, and a gust of snowy air blew the papers out of her hand and out the door. She dived for them, but they whirled away in the snow. The man who had opened the door was already in the other elevator. The doors slid shut. Oh, for heaven's sake.

She looked around for a phone so she could call Brad and tell him she was stranded down here. There was one on the far wall. The first elevator was on its way down, between four and three. The second one was on six. She walked over to the phone, took both her gloves off and jammed them in her coat pocket, and picked up the phone.

A young woman in a parka and red mittens came in the front door, but she didn't go over to the elevators. She stood in the middle of the lobby brushing snow off her coat. Jill rummaged through her purse for a quarter. There was no change in her wallet but she thought there might be a couple of dimes in the bottom of her purse. The second elevator's doors slid open, and the mittened woman hurried in.

She found a quarter in the bottom of her purse and dialed Brad. The line was busy. The first elevator was on six now. The second one was down in the parking garage. She dialed Brad's number again.

The second elevator's doors slid open. "Wait!" she said, and dropped the phone. The receiver hit her purse and knocked its contents all over the floor. The outside door opened again, and snow whirled in. "Push the hold button," the middle-aged woman who had just come in from outside. She had a red, "NOW...or else!" button pinned to her coat, and she was clutching a folder to her chest. She knelt down and picked up a comb, two pencils, and Jill's checkbook.

"Thank you," Jill said gratefully

"We sisters have to stick together," the woman said grimly. She stood up and handed the things to Jill. They got into the elevator. The woman with the mittens was holding the door. There was another young woman inside, wearing a sweater and blue moon boots.

"Six, please," Jill said breathlessly trying to jam everything back into her purse. "Thanks for waiting. I'm just not all together today." The doors started to close.

"Wait!" a voice said, and a young woman in a suit and high heels, with a large manila envelope under her arm, squeezed in just as the door shut. "Six, please," she said. "The wind chill factor out there has to be twenty below. I don't know where my head was to try to come over and see Brad in weather like this."

"Brad?" the young woman in the red mittens said.

"Brad?" Jill said.

"Brad?" the young woman in the blue moon boots said.

"Brad McAfee," the woman with the "NOW...or else!" button said grimly

"Yes," the young woman in high heels said, surprised. "Do you all know him? He's my fiancé."

Sally punched in her security code, stepped in the elevator, and pushed the button for the sixth floor. "Ulric, I want to explain what happened this morning," she said as soon as the door closed. She had practiced her speech all the way over to Ulric's housing unit. It had taken her forever to get here. The windshield wipers were frozen and two cars had slid sideways in the snow and created a traffic jam. She had had to park the car and trudge through the snow across the oriental gardens, but she still hadn't thought of what to say.

"My name is Sally Mowen, and I don't generate language." That was out of the question. She couldn't tell him who she was. The minute he heard she was the boss's daughter, he would stop listening.

"I speak English, but I read your note, and it said you wanted someone who could generate language." No good. He would ask, "What note?" and she would haul it out of her pocket, and he would say, "Where did you find this?" and she would have to explain what she was doing up in the tree. She might also have to explain how she knew he was Ulric Henry and what she was doing with his file and his picture, and he would never believe it was all a coincidence.

Number six blinked on, and the door of the elevator opened. "I can't," Sally thought and pushed the lobby button. Halfway down she decided to say what she should have said in the first place. She pushed six again.

"Ulric, I love you," she recited. "Ulric, I love you." Six blinked. The door opened. "Ulric," she said. He was standing in front of the elevator, glaring at her.

"Aren't you going to say something?" he said. "Like 'I withspeak myself?' That's a nice example of Germanic compounding. But of course you know that. Language generation is your area of special study, isn't that right, Sally?"

"Ulric," Sally said. She took a step forward and put her hand on the elevator door so it wouldn't close.

"You were home for Thanksgiving vacation and you were afraid you'd get out of practice, is that it? So you thought you'd jump out of a tree on the company linguist just to keep your hand in."

"If you'd shut up a minute, I'd explain," Sally said.

"No, that's not right," Ulric said. "It should be 'quiet up' or maybe 'mouth-close you.' More compounding."

"Why did I ever think I could talk to you?" Sally said. "Why did I ever waste my time trying to generate language for you?"

"For me?" Ulric said. "Why in the hell did you think I wanted you to generate language?"

"Because...oh forget it," Sally said. She punched the lobby button. The door started to shut. Ulric stuck his hand in the closing doors and then snatched them free and pressed the hold button. Nothing happened.

He jammed in four numbers and pressed the hold button again. It gave an odd click and began beeping, but the doors opened again.

"Damn it," Ulric said. "Now you've made me punch in Brad's security code, and I've set off his stupid override."

"That's right," Sally said, jamming her hands in her pockets. "Blame everything on me. I suppose I'm the one who left that note in the tree saying you wanted somebody who could generate language?"

The beeping stopped. "What note?" Ulric said, and let go of the hold button.

Sally pulled her hand out of her pocket to press the lobby button again. A piece of paper fell out of her pocket. Ulric stepped inside as the doors started to close and picked up the piece of paper. After a minute, he said, "Look, I think I can explain how all this happened."

"You'd better make it snappy," Sally said. "I'm getting out when we get to the lobby."

As soon as Janice hung up the phone Brad grabbed his coat. He had a good idea of what Old Man Mowen wanted him for. After Ulric had left, Brad had gotten a call from *Time*. They'd talkified for over half an hour about a photographer and a four-page layout on the waste emissions project. He figured they'd call Old Man Mowen and tell him about the article, too, and sure enough, his terminal had started beeping an override before he even hung up. It stopped as he turned toward the terminal, and the screen went blank, and then it started beeping again, double-quick, and sure enough, it was his pappy-in-law to be. Before he could even begin reading the message, Janice called. He told her he'd be there faster than blue blazes, grabbed his coat, and started out the door.

One of the elevators was on six and just starting down. The other one was on five and coming up. He punched his security code in and put his arm in the sleeve of his overcoat. The lining tore, and his arm went down inside it. He wrestled it free and tried to pull the lining back up to where it belonged. It tore some more.

"Well, dadfetch it!" he said loudly. The elevator door opened. Brad got in, still trying to get his arm in the sleeve. The door closed behind him.

The panel in the door started beeping. That meant an override. Maybe Mowen was trying to call him back. He pushed the "door open" button, but nothing happened. The elevator started down. "Dagnab it all," he said.

"Hi, Brad," Lynn said. He turned around.

"You look a mite wadgetty " Sue said. "Doesn't he, Jill?"

"Right peaked," Jill said.

"Maybe he's got the flit-flats," Gail said.

Charlotte didn't say anything. She clutched the file folder to her chest and growled. Overhead, the lights flickered, and the elevator ground to a halt.

FOR IMMEDIATE RELEASE: Mowen Chemical today announced temporary finalization of its pyrolitic stratospheric waste emissions program pending implementation of an environmental impact verification process. Lynn Saunders, director of the project, indicated that facilities will be temporarily deactivized during reorientation of predictive assessment criteria. In an unrelated communication, P B. Mowen, president of Mowen Chemical, announced the upcoming nuptials of his daughter Sally Mowen and Ulric Henry, vice-president in charge of language effectiveness documentation.

# Just Like the Ones
# We Used to Know

The snow started at 12:01 a.m. Eastern Standard Time just outside of Branford, Connecticut. Noah and Terry Blake, on their way home from a party at the Whittiers' at which Miranda Whittier had said, "I guess you could call this our Christmas Eve Eve party!" at least fifty times, noticed a few stray flakes as they turned onto Canoe Brook Road, and by the time they reached home, the snow was coming down hard.

"Oh, good," Tess said, leaning forward to peer through the windshield. "I've been hoping we'd have a white Christmas this year."

—|•••|—

At 1:37 A.M. Central Standard Time, Billy Grogan, filling in for KYZT's late-night radio request show out of Duluth, said, "This just in from the National Weather Service. Snow advisory for the Great Lakes region tonight and tomorrow morning. Two to four inches expected," and then went back to discussing the callers' least favorite Christmas songs.

"I'll tell you the one I hate," a caller from Wauwatosa said. "'White Christmas.' I musta heard that thing five hundred times this month."

"Actually," Billy said, "according to the St. Cloud *Evening News,* Bing Crosby's version of 'White Christmas' will be played 2150 times during the month of December, and other artists' renditions of it will be played an additional 1890 times."

The caller snorted. "One time's too many for me. Who the heck wants a white Christmas anyway? I sure don't."

"Well, unfortunately, it looks like you're going to get one," Billy said. "And, in that spirit, here's Destiny's Child, singing 'White Christmas.'"

At 1:45 A.M., a number of geese in the city park in Bowling Green, Kentucky, woke up to a low, overcast sky and flew, flapping and honking loudly, over the city center, as if they had suddenly decided to fly farther south for the winter. The noise woke Maureen Reynolds, who couldn't get back to sleep. She turned on KYOU, which was playing "Holly Jolly Oldies," including "Rockin' Around the Christmas Tree" and Brenda Lee's rendition of "White Christmas."

—|•••|—

At 2:15 A.M. Mountain Standard Time, Paula Devereaux arrived at DIA for the red-eye flight to Springfield, Illinois. It was beginning to snow, and as she waited in line at the express check-in (she was carrying on her maid-of-honor dress and the bag with her shoes and slip and makeup—the last time she'd been in a wedding, her luggage had gotten lost and caused a major crisis) and in line at security and in line at the gate and in line to be de-iced, she began to hope they might not be able to take off, but no such luck.

Of course not, Paula thought, looking out the window at the snow swirling around the wing, because Stacey wants me at her wedding.

"I want a Christmas Eve wedding," Stacey'd told Paula after she'd informed her she was going to be her maid of honor, "all candlelight and evergreens. And I want snow falling outside the windows."

"What if the weather doesn't cooperate?" Paula'd asked.

"It will," Stacey'd said. And here it was, snowing. She wondered if it was snowing in Springfield, too. Of course it is, she thought. Whatever Stacey wants, Stacey gets, Paula thought. Even Jim.

Don't think about that, she told herself. Don't think about anything. Just concentrate on getting through the wedding. With luck, Jim won't even be there except for the ceremony, and you won't have to spend any time with him at all.

She picked up the in-flight magazine and tried to read and then plugged in her headphones and listened to Channel 4, "Seasonal Favorites." The first song was "White Christmas" by the Statler Brothers.

—|•••|—

At 3:38 A.M., it began to snow in Bowling Green, Kentucky. The geese circling the city flew back to the park, landed, and hunkered down to sit it out on their island in the lake. Snow began to collect on their backs, but they didn't care, protected as they were by down and a thick layer of subcutaneous fat designed to keep them warm even in sub-zero temperatures.

⊣•••⊢

At 3:39 A.M., Luke Lafferty woke up, convinced he'd forgotten to set the goose his mother had talked him into having for Christmas Eve dinner out to thaw. He went and checked. He *had* set it out. On his way back to bed, he looked out the window and saw it was snowing, which didn't worry him. The news had said isolated snow showers for Wichita, ending by mid-morning, and none of his relatives lived more than an hour and a half away, except Aunt Lulla, and if she couldn't make it, it wouldn't exactly put a crimp in the conversation. His mom and Aunt Madge talked so much it was hard for anybody else to get a word in edgewise, especially Aunt Lulla. "She was always the shy one," Luke's mother said, and it was true, Luke couldn't remember her saying anything other than "Please pass the potatoes," at their family get-togethers.

What did worry him was the goose. He should never have let his mother talk him into having one. It was bad enough her having talked him into having the family dinner at his place. He had no idea how to cook a goose.

"What if something goes wrong?" he'd protested. "Butterball doesn't have a goose hotline."

"You won't need a hotline," his mother had said. "It's just like cooking a turkey, and it's not as if you had to cook it. I'll be there in time to put it in the oven and everything. All you have to do is set it out to thaw. Do you have a roasting pan?"

"Yes," Luke had said, but lying there, he couldn't remember if he did. When he got up at 4:14 A.M. to check—he did—it was still snowing.

⊣•••⊢

At 4:16 Mountain Standard Time, Slade Henry, filling in on WRYT's late-night talk show out of Boise, said, "For all you folks who wanted a white Christmas, it looks like you're going to get your wish. Three to six inches forecast for western Idaho." He played several bars of Johnny Cash's "White Christmas," and then went back to discussing JFK's assassination with a caller who was convinced Clinton was somehow involved.

"Little Rock isn't all that far from Dallas, you know," the caller said. "You could drive it in four and a half hours."

Actually, you couldn't, because I-30 was icing up badly, due to freezing rain that had started just after midnight and then turned to snow. The treacherous driving conditions did not slow Monty Luffer down as he had a Ford Explorer. Shortly after five, he reached to change stations on the radio so he didn't have to listen to "those damn Backstreet Boys" singing "White Christmas," and slid out of control just west of Texarkana. He crossed the median, causing the semi in the left-hand eastbound lane to jam on his brakes and jackknife, and resulting in a thirty-seven-car pileup that closed the road for the rest of the night and all the next day.

—|•••|—

At 5:21 A.M. Pacific Standard Time, four-year-old Miguel Gutierrez jumped on his mother, shouting, "Is it Christmas yet?"

"Not on Mommy's stomach, honey," Pilar murmured and rolled over.

Miguel crawled over her and repeated his question directly into her ear. *"Is it Christmas yet?"*

"No," she said groggily. "Tomorrow's Christmas. Go watch cartoons for a few minutes, okay, and then Mommy'll get up," and pulled the pillow over her head.

Miguel was back again immediately. He can't find the remote, she thought wearily, but that couldn't be it, because he jabbed her in the ribs with it. "What's the matter, honey?" she said.

"Santa isn't gonna come," he said tearfully, which brought her fully awake.

He thinks Santa won't be able to find him, she thought. This is all Joe's fault. According to the original custody agreement, she had Miguel for Christmas and Joe had him for New Year's, but he'd gotten the judge to change it so they split Christmas Eve and Christmas Day, and then, after she'd told Miguel, Joe had announced he needed to switch.

When Pilar had said no, he'd threatened to take her back to court, so she'd agreed, after which he'd informed her that "Christmas Day" meant her delivering Miguel on Christmas Eve so he could wake up and open his presents at Joe's.

"He can open your presents to him before you come," he'd said, knowing full well Miguel still believed in Santa Claus. So after supper she was delivering both Miguel *and* his presents to Joe's in Escondido, where she would not get to see Miguel open them.

"I can't go to Daddy's," Miguel had said when she'd explained the arrangements, "Santa's gonna bring my presents *here*."

"No, he won't," she'd said. "I sent Santa a letter and told him you'd be at your daddy's on Christmas Eve, and he's going to take your presents there."

"You sent it to the North Pole?" he'd demanded.

"To the North Pole. I took it to the post office this morning," and he'd seemed contented with that answer. Till now.

"Santa's going to come," she said, cuddling him to her. "He's coming to Daddy's, remember?"

"No, he's not," Miguel sniffled.

Damn Joe. I shouldn't have given in, she thought, but every time they went back to court, Joe and his snake of a lawyer managed to wangle new concessions out of the judge, even though until the divorce was final, Joe had never paid any attention to Miguel at all. And she just couldn't afford any more court costs right now.

"Are you worried about Daddy living in Escondido?" she asked Miguel. "Because Santa's magic. He can travel all over California in one night. He can travel all over the *world* in one night."

Miguel, snuggled against her, shook his head violently. "No, he can't!"

"Why not?"

"Because it isn't *snowing!* I want it to snow. Santa can't come in his sleigh if it doesn't."

Paula's flight landed in Springfield at 7:48 A.M. Central Standard Time, twenty minutes late. Jim met her at the airport. "Stacey's having her hair done," he said. "I was afraid I wouldn't get here in time. It was a good thing your flight was a few minutes late."

"There was snow in Denver," Paula said, trying not to look at him. He was as cute as ever, with the same knee-weakening smile.

"It just started to snow here," he said.

How does she do it? Paula thought. You had to admire Stacey. Whatever she wanted, she got. I wouldn't have had to mess with carrying this stuff on, Paula thought, handing Jim the hanging bag with her dress in it. There's no way my luggage would have gotten lost. Stacey wanted it here.

"The roads are already starting to get slick," Jim was saying. "I hope my parents get here okay. They're driving down from Chicago."

They will, Paula thought. Stacey wants them to.

Jim got Paula's bags off the carousel and then said, "Hang on, I promised Stacey I'd tell her as soon as you got here." He flipped open his cell phone and put it to his ear. "Stacey? She's here. Yeah, I will. Okay, I'll pick them up on our way. Yeah. Okay."

He flipped the phone shut. "She wants us to pick up the evergreen garlands on our way," he said, "and then I have to come back and get Kindra and David. We need to check on their flights before we leave."

He led the way upstairs to ticketing so they could look at the arrival board. Outside the terminal windows snow was falling, large, perfect, lacy flakes.

"Kindra's on the two-nineteen from Houston," Jim said, scanning the board, "and David's on the eleven-forty from Newark. Oh, good, they're both on time."

Of course they are, Paula thought, looking at the board. The snow in Denver must be getting worse. All the Denver flights had "delayed" next to them, and so did a bunch of others: Cheyenne and Portland and Richmond. As she watched, Boston and then Chicago changed from "on time" to "delayed" and Rapid City went from "delayed" to "cancelled." She looked at Kindra's and David's flights again. They were still on time.

⊣•••⊢

Ski areas in Aspen, Lake Placid, Squaw Valley, Stowe, Lake Tahoe, and Jackson Hole woke to several inches of fresh powder. The snow was greeted with relief by the people who had paid ninety dollars for their lift tickets, with irritation by the ski resort owners, who didn't see why it couldn't have come two weeks earlier when people were making their Christmas reservations, and with whoops of delight by snowboarders Kent Slakken and Bodine Cromps. They promptly set out from Breckenridge without maps, matches, helmets, avalanche beacons, avalanche probes, or telling anyone where they were going, for an off-limits backcountry area with "totally extreme slopes."

⊣ • • • ⊢

At 7:05, Miguel came in and jumped on Pilar again, this time on her bladder, shouting, "It's snowing! Now Santa can come! Now Santa can come!"

"Snowing?" she said blearily. In L.A.? "Snowing? Where?"

"On TV. Can I make myself some cereal?"

"No," she said, remembering the last time. She reached for her robe. "You go watch TV some more and Mommy'll make pancakes."

⊣ • • • ⊢

When she brought the pancakes and syrup in, Miguel was sitting, absorbed, in front of the TV, watching a man in a green parka standing in the snow in front of an ambulance with flashing lights, saying, "—third weather-related fatality in Dodge City so far this morning—"

"Let's find some cartoons to watch," Pilar said, clicking the remote.

"—outside Knoxville, Tennessee, where snow and icy conditions have caused a multi-car accident—"

She clicked the remote again.

"—to Columbia, South Carolina, where a surprise snowstorm has shut off power to—"

Click.

"—problem seems to be a low-pressure area covering Canada and the northern two-thirds of the United States, bringing snow to the entire Midwest and Mid-Atlantic States and—"

Click.

"—snowing here in Bozeman—"

"I told you it was snowing," Miguel said happily, eating his pancakes, "just like I wanted it to. After breakfast can we make a snowman?"

"Honey, it isn't snowing here in California," Pilar said. "That's the national weather, it's not here. That reporter's in Montana, not California."

Miguel grabbed the remote and clicked to a reporter standing in the snow in front of a giant redwood tree. "The snow started about four this morning here in Monterey, California. As you can see," she said, indicating her raincoat and umbrella, "it caught everybody by surprise."

"*She's* in California," Miguel said.

"She's in northern California," Pilar said, "which gets a lot colder than it does here in L.A. L.A.'s too warm for it to snow."

"No, it's not," Miguel said and pointed out the window, where big white flakes were drifting down onto the palm trees across the street.

At 9:40 Central Standard Time the cell phone Nathan Andrews thought he'd turned off rang in the middle of a grant money meeting that was already going badly. Scheduling the meeting in Omaha on the day before Christmas had seemed like a good idea at the time—businessmen had hardly any appointments that day and the spirit of the season was supposed to make them more willing to open their pocketbooks—but instead they were merely distracted, anxious to do their last-minute Mercedes-Benz shopping or get the Christmas office party started or whatever it was businessmen did, and worried about the snow that had started during rush hour this morning.

Plus, they were morons. "So you're saying you want a grant to study global warming, but then you talk about wanting to measure snow levels," one of them had said. "What does snow have to do with global warming?"

Nathan had tried to explain *again* how warming could lead to increased amounts of moisture in the atmosphere and thus increased precipitation in the form of rain and snow, and how that increased snowfall could lead to increased albedo and surface cooling.

"If it's getting cooler, it's not getting warmer," another one of the businessmen had said. "It can't be both."

"As a matter of fact, it can," he'd said and launched into his explanation of how polar melting could lead to an increase in freshwater in the North Atlantic, which would float on top of the Gulf Stream, preventing its warm water from sinking and cooling, and effectively shutting the current down. "Europe would freeze," he'd said.

"Well, then, global warming would be a good thing, wouldn't it?" yet another one had said. "Heat the place up."

He had patiently tried to explain how the world would grow both hotter and colder, with widespread droughts, flooding, and a sharp increase in severe weather. "And these changes may happen extremely quickly," he'd said. "Rather than temperatures gradually increasing and sea levels rising, there may be a sudden, unexpected event—a discontinuity. It may take the form of an abrupt, catastrophic temperature increase or a superhurricane or other form of megastorm, occurring without any warning. That's why this project is so critical. By setting up a comprehensive climate data base, we'll be able to create more accurate computer models, from which we'll be able to—"

"Computer models!" one of them had snorted. "They're wrong more often than they're right!"

"Because they don't include enough factors," Nathan said. "Climate is an incredibly complicated system, with literally thousands of factors interacting in intricate ways—weather patterns, clouds, precipitation, ocean currents, manmade activities, crops. Thus far computer models have only been able to chart a handful of factors. This project will chart over two hundred of them and will enable the models to be exponentially more accurate. We'll be able to predict a discontinuity before it happens—"

It was at that point that his cell phone rang. It was his graduate assistant Chin Sung, from the lab. "Where *are* you?" Chin demanded.

"In a grant meeting," Nathan whispered. "Can I call you back in a few minutes?"

"Not if you still want the Nobel Prize," Chin said. "You know that hare-brained theory of yours about global warming producing a sudden discontinuity? Well, I think you'd better get over here. Today may be the day you turn out to be right."

"Why?" Nathan asked, gripping the phone excitedly. "What's happened? Have the Gulf Stream temp readings dropped?"

"No, it's not the currents. It's what's happening here."

"Which is what?"

Instead of answering, Chin asked, "Is it snowing where you are?"

Nathan looked out the conference room window. "Yes."

"I thought so. It's snowing here, too."

"And that's what you called me about?" Nathan whispered. "Because it's snowing in Nebraska in December? In case you haven't looked at a calendar lately, winter started three days ago. It's *supposed* to be snowing."

"You don't understand," Chin said. "It isn't just snowing in Nebraska. It's snowing everywhere."

"What do you mean, everywhere?"

"I mean everywhere. Seattle, Salt Lake City, Minneapolis, Providence, Chattanooga. All over Canada and the U.S. as far south as—" there was a pause and the sound of computer keys clicking "—Abilene and Shreveport and Savannah. No, wait, Tallahassee's reporting light snow. As far south as Tallahassee."

The jet stream must have dipped radically south. "Where's the center of the low pressure system?"

"That's just it," Chin said. "There doesn't seem to be one."

"I'll be right there," Nathan said.

A mile from the highway snowboarders Kent Slakken and Bodine Cromps, unable to see the road in heavily falling snow, drove their car into a ditch. "Shit," Bodine said, and attempted to get out of it by revving the engine and then flooring it, a technique that only succeeded in digging them in to the point where they couldn't open either car door.

It took Jim and Paula nearly two hours to pick up the evergreen garlands and get out to the church. The lacy flakes fell steadily faster and thicker, and it was so slick Jim had to crawl the last few miles. "I hope this doesn't get any worse," he said worriedly, "or people are going to have a hard time getting out here."

But Stacey wasn't worried at all. "Isn't it beautiful? I wanted it to snow for my wedding more than anything," she said, meeting them at the door of the church. "Come here, Paula, you've got to see how the snow looks through the sanctuary windows. It's going to be perfect."

Jim left immediately to go pick up Kindra and David, which Paula was grateful for. Being that close to him in the car had made her start entertaining the ridiculous hopes about him she'd had when they first met. And they were ridiculous. One look at Stacey had shown her that.

The bride-to-be looked beautiful even in a sweater and jeans, her makeup exquisite, her blonde hair upswept into glittery snowflake-sprinkled curls. Every time Paula had had her hair done to be in a wedding, she had come out looking like someone in a bad 1950s movie. How does she do it? Paula wondered. You watch, the snow will stop and start up again just in time for the ceremony.

But it didn't. It continued to come down steadily, and when the minister arrived for the rehearsal, she said, "I don't know. It took me half an hour to get out of my driveway. You may want to think about canceling."

"Don't be silly. We can't cancel. It's a Christmas Eve wedding," Stacey said, and made Paula start tying the evergreen garlands to the pews with white satin ribbon.

It was sprinkling in Santa Fe when Bev Carey arrived at her hotel, and by the time she'd checked in and ventured out into the plaza, it had turned into an icy, driving rain that went right through the light coat and thin gloves she'd brought with her. She had planned to spend the morning shopping, but the shops had signs on them saying "Closed Christmas Eve and Christmas Day," and the sidewalk in front of the Governor's Palace, where, according to her guidebook, Zunis and Navajos sat to sell authentic silver-and-turquoise jewelry, was deserted.

But at least it's not snowing, she told herself, trudging, shivering, back to the hotel. And the shop windows were decorated with *ristras* and lights in the shape of chili peppers, and the Christmas tree in the hotel lobby was decorated with kachina dolls.

Her friend Janice had already called and left a message with the hotel clerk. And if I don't call her back, she'll be convinced I've taken a bottle of sleeping pills, Bev thought, going up to her room. On the way to the airport, Janice had asked anxiously, "You haven't been having suicidal thoughts, have you?" and when her friend Louise had found out what Bev was planning, she'd said, "I saw this piece on *Dateline* the other night about suicides at Christmas, and how people who've lost a spouse are especially vulnerable. You wouldn't do anything like that, would you?"

They none of them understood that she was doing this to save her life, not end it, that it was Christmas at home, with its lighted trees and evergreen wreaths and candles, that would kill her. And its snow.

"I know you miss Howard," Janice had said, "and that with Christmas coming, you're feeling sad."

Sad? She felt flayed, battered, beaten. Every memory, every thought of her husband, every use of the past tense, even "Howard liked...," "Howard knew...," "Howard was...,"was like a deadly blow. The grief-counseling books all talked about "the pain of losing a loved one," but she had had no idea the pain could be this bad. It was like being stabbed over and over, and her only hope had been to get away. She hadn't "decided to go to Santa Fe for Christmas." She had run there like a victim fleeing a murderer.

She took off her drenched coat and gloves and called Janice. "You promised you'd call as soon as you got there," Janice said reproachfully. "Are you all right?"

"I'm fine," Bev said. "I was out walking around the Plaza." She didn't say anything about its raining. She didn't want Janice saying *I told you so.* "It's beautiful here."

"I should have come with you," Janice said. "It's snowing like crazy here. Ten inches so far. I suppose you're sitting on a patio drinking a margarita right now."

"Sangria," Bev lied. "I'm going sightseeing this afternoon. The houses here are all pink and tan adobe with bright blue and red and yellow doors. And right now the whole town's decorated with *luminarias.* You should see them."

"I wish I could," Janice sighed. "All I can see is snow. I have no idea how I'm going to get to the store. Oh, well, at least we'll have a white Christmas. It's so sad Howard can't be here to see this. He always loved white Christmases, didn't he?"

Howard, consulting the *Farmer's Almanac,* reading the weather forecast out loud to her, calling her over to the picture window to watch the snow beginning to fall, saying, "Looks like we're going to get a white Christmas this year," as if it were a present under the tree, putting his arm around her—

"Yes," Bev managed to say through the sudden, searing stab of pain. "He did."

It was spitting snow when Warren Nesvick checked into the Marriott in Baltimore. As soon as he got Shara up to the suite, he told her he had to make a business call, "and then I'll be all yours, honey." He went down to the lobby. The TV in the corner was showing a weather map. He looked at it for a minute and then got out his cell phone.

"Where *are* you?" his wife Marjean said when she answered.

"In St. Louis," he said. "Our flight got rerouted here because of snow at O'Hare. What's the weather like there?"

"It's snowing," she said. "When do you think you'll be able to get a flight out?"

"I don't know. Everything's booked because of it being Christmas Eve. I'm waiting to see if I can get on standby. I'll call you as soon as I know something," and hung up before she could ask him which flight.

It took Nathan an hour and a half to drive the fifteen miles to the lab. During the ride he considered the likelihood that this was really a discontinuity and not just a major snowstorm. Global warming proponents (and opponents) confused the two all the time. Every hurricane, tornado, heat wave, or dry spell was attributed to global warming, even though nearly all of them fell well within the range of normal weather patterns.

And there had been big December snowstorms before. The blizzard of 1888, for instance, and the Christmas Eve storm of 2002. And Chin was probably wrong about there being no center to the low pressure system. The likely explanation was that there was more than one system involved—one centered in the Great Lakes and another just east of the Rockies, colliding with warm, moist air from the Gulf Coast to create unusually widespread snow.

And it *was* widespread. The car radio was reporting snow all across the Midwest and the entire East Coast—Topeka, Tulsa, Peoria, northern Virginia, Hartford, Montpelier, Reno, Spokane. No, Reno and Spokane were west of the Rockies. There must be a third system, coming down from the Northwest. But it was still hardly a discontinuity.

The lab parking lot hadn't been plowed. He left the car on the street and struggled through the already knee-deep snow to the door, remembering when he was halfway across the expanse that Nebraska was famous for pioneers who got lost going out to the barn in a blizzard and whose frozen bodies weren't found till the following spring.

He reached the door, opened it, and stood there a moment blowing on his frozen hands and looking at the TV Chin had stuck on a cart in the corner of the lab. On it, a pretty reporter in a parka and a Mickey Mouse hat was standing in heavy snow in front of what seemed to be a giant snowman. "The snow has really caused problems here at Disney

World," she said over the sound of a marching band playing "White Christmas." "Their annual Christmas Eve Parade has—"

"Well, it's about time," Chin said, coming in from the fax room with a handful of printouts. "What took you so long?" Nathan ignored that. "Have you got the IPOC data?" he asked.

Chin nodded. He sat down at his terminal and started typing. The upper left-hand screen lit up with columns of numbers.

"Let me see the National Weather Service map," Nathan said, unzipping his coat and sitting down at the main console.

Chin called up a U.S. map nearly half-covered with blue, from western Oregon and Nevada east all the way to the Atlantic and up through New England and south to the Oklahoma panhandle, northern Mississippi, Alabama, and most of Georgia.

"Good Lord, that's even bigger than Marina in '92," Nathan said. "Have you got a satellite photo?"

Chin nodded and called it up. "And this is a real-time composite of all the data coming in, including weather stations, towns, and spotters reporting in. The white's snow," he added unnecessarily.

The white covered even more territory than the blue on the NWS map, with jagged fingers stretching down into Arizona and Louisiana and west into Oregon and California. Surrounding them were wide uneven pink bands. "Is the pink rain?" Nathan asked.

"Sleet," Chin said. "So what do you think? It's a discontinuity, isn't it?"

"I don't know," Nathan said, calling up the barometric readings and starting through them.

"What else could it be? It's snowing in Orlando. And San Diego."

"It's snowed both of those places before," Nathan said. "It's even snowed in Death Valley. The only place in the U.S. where it's never snowed is the Florida Keys. And Hawaii, of course. Everything on this map right now is within the range of normal weather events. You don't have to start worrying till it starts snowing in the Florida Keys."

"What about other places?" Chin asked, looking at the center right-hand screen.

"What do you mean, other places?"

"I mean, it isn't just snowing in the U.S. I'm getting reports from Cancun. And Jerusalem."

⊣•••⊢

At eleven-thirty Pilar gave up trying to explain that there wasn't enough snow to make a snowman and took Miguel outside, bundled up in a sweatshirt, a sweater, and his warm jacket, with a pair of Pilar's tube socks for mittens. He lasted about five minutes.

When they came back in, Pilar settled him at the kitchen table with crayons and paper so he could draw a picture of a snowman and went into the living room to check the weather forecast. It was really snowing hard out there, and she was getting a little worried about taking Miguel down to Escondido. Los Angelenos didn't know how to drive in snow, and Pilar's tires weren't that good.

"—snowing here in Hollywood," said a reporter standing in front of the nearly invisible Hollywood sign, "and this isn't soapflakes, folks, it's the real thing."

She switched channels. "—snowing in Santa Monica," a reporter standing on the beach was saying, "but that isn't stopping the surfers...."

Click. "—*para la primera vez en ciencuenta años en* Marina del Rey—"

Click. "—snowing here in L.A. for the first time in nearly fifty years. We're here on the set of *XXX II* with Vin Diesel. What do you think of the snow, Vin?"

She gave up and went back in the kitchen where Miguel announced he was ready to go outside again. She talked him into listening to Alvin and the Chipmunks instead. "Okay," he said, and she left him warbling "White Christmas" along with Alvin and went in to check the weather again. The Santa Monica reporter briefly mentioned the roads were wet before moving on to interview a psychic who claimed to have predicted the snowstorm, and on a Spanish-language channel she caught a glimpse of the 405 moving along at its usual congested pace.

The roads must not be too bad, she thought, or they'd all be talking about it, but she still wondered if she hadn't better take Miguel down to Escondido early. She hated to give up her day with him, but his safety was the important thing, and the snow wasn't letting up at all.

When Miguel came into the living room and asked when they could go outside, she said, "After we pack your suitcase, okay? Do you want to take your Pokemon jammies or your Spidermans?" and began gathering up his things.

—| • • |—

By noon Eastern Standard Time, it was snowing in every state in the lower forty-eight. Elko, Nevada, had over two feet of snow, Cincinnati was reporting thirty-eight inches at the airport, and it was spitting snow in Miami.

On talk radio, JFK's assassination had given way to the topic of the snow. "You mark my words, the terrorists are behind this," a caller from Terre Haute said. "They want to destroy our economy, and what better way to do it than by keeping us from doing our last-minute Christmas shopping? To say nothing of what this snow's going to do to my relationship with my wife. How am I supposed to go buy her something in this weather? I tell you, this has got Al Qaeda's name written all over it."

During lunch, Warren Nesvick told Shara he needed to go try his business call again. "The guy I was trying to get in touch with wasn't in the office before. Because of the snow," he said and went out to the lobby to call Marjean again. On the TV in the corner, there were shots of snow-covered runways and jammed ticket counters. A blonde reporter in a tight red sweater was saying, "Here in Cincinnati, the snow just keeps on falling. The airport's still open, but officials indicate it may have to close. Snow is building up on the runways—"

He called Marjean. "I'm in Cincinnati," he told her. "I managed to get a flight at the last minute. There's a three-hour layover till my connecting flight, but at least I've got a seat."

"But isn't it snowing in Cincinnati?" she asked. "I was just watching the TV and…"

"It's supposed to let up here in an hour or so. I'm really sorry about this, honey. You know I'd be there for Christmas Eve if I could."

"I know," she said, sounding disappointed. "It's okay, Warren. You can't control the weather."

⊣ • • • ⊢

The television was on in the hotel lobby when Bev came down to lunch. "—snowing in Albuquerque," she heard the announcer say, "Raton, Santa Rosa, and Wagon Mound."

But not in Santa Fe, she told herself firmly, going into the dining room. "It hardly ever snows there," the travel agent had said, "New Mexico's a desert. And when it does snow, it never sticks."

"There's already four inches in Espanola," a plump waitress in a ruffled blouse and full red skirt was saying to the busboy. "I'm worried about getting home."

"I'd rather it didn't snow for Christmas," Bev had teased Howard last year, "all those people trying to get home."

"Heresy, woman, heresy! What would Currier and Ives think to hear you talk that way?" he'd said, clutching his chest.

Like she was clutching hers now. The plump waitress was looking at her worriedly. "Are you all right, *señora?*"

"Yes," Bev said. "One for lunch, please."

The waitress led her to a table, still looking concerned, and handed her a menu, and she clung to it like a life raft, concentrating fiercely on the unfamiliar terms, the exotic ingredients: blue corn tortillas, quesadillas, chipotle—

"Can I get you something to drink?" the waitress asked.

"Yes," Bev said brightly, looking at the waitress's name tag. "I'd like some sangria, Carmelita."

Carmelita nodded and left, and Bev looked around the room, thinking, I'll drink my sangria and watch the other diners, eavesdrop on their conversations, but she was the only person in the broad tiled room. It faced the patio, and through the glass doors the rain, sleet now, drove sharply against the terracotta pots of cactus outside, the stacked tables and chairs, the collapsed umbrellas.

She had envisioned herself having lunch out on the patio, sitting in the sun under one of those umbrellas, looking out at the desert and listening to a mariachi band. The music coming over the loudspeakers was Christmas carols. As she listened, "Let It Snow" came to an end, and the Supremes began to sing "White Christmas."

"What would cloud-seeding be listed under?" Howard had asked her one year when there was still no snow by the twenty-second, coming into the dining room, where she was wrapping presents, with the phone book.

"You are *not* hiring a cloud seeder," she had laughed.

"Would it be under 'clouds' or 'rainmaker'?" he'd asked mock-seriously. "Or 'seeds'?" And when it had finally snowed on the twenty-fourth, he had acted like he was personally responsible.

"You did *not* cause this, Howard," she had told him.

"How do you know?" He'd laughed, catching her into his arms.

I can't stand this, Bev thought, looking frantically around the dining room for Carmelita and her sangria. How do other people do it? She knew lots of widows, and they all seemed fine. When people mentioned their husbands, when they talked about them in the past tense, they were able to stand there, to smile back, to talk about them. Doreen Matthews had even said, "Now that Bill's gone, I can finally have all pink ornaments on the Christmas tree. I've always wanted to have a pink tree, but he wouldn't hear of it."

"Here's your sangria," Carmelita said, still looking concerned. "Would you like some tortilla chips and salsa?"

"Yes, thank you," Bev said brightly. "And I think I'll have the chicken enchiladas."

Carmelita nodded and disappeared again. Bev took a gulp of her sangria and got her guidebook out of her bag. She would have a nice lunch and then go sightseeing. She opened the book to Area Attractions. "Pueblo de San Ildefonso." No, that would involve a lot of walking around outdoors, and it was still sleeting outside the window.

"Petroglyphs National Monument." No, that was down near Albuquerque, where it was snowing. "El Santuario de Chimayo. 28 mi. north of Santa Fe on Hwy. 76. Historic weaving center, shops, chapel dubbed 'American Lourdes.' The dirt in the anteroom beside the altar is reputed to have healing powers when rubbed on the afflicted part of the body."

But I hurt all over, she thought.

"Other attractions include five nineteenth-century reredos, a carving of Santo Niño de Atocha, carved wooden altarpiece. (See also Lagrima, p. 98.)"

She turned the page to ninety-eight. "Chapel of Our Lady of Perpetual Sorrow, Lagrima, 28 mi. SE of Santa Fe on Hwy 41. Sixteenth-century adobe mission church. In 1968 the statue of the Virgin Mary in the transept was reported to shed healing tears."

Healing tears, holy dirt, and wasn't there supposed to be a miraculous staircase right here in town? Yes, there it was. The Loretto Chapel. "Open 10-5 Apr-Oct, closed Nov-Mar."

It would have to be Chimayo. She got out the road map the car rental place had given her, and when Carmelita came with the chips and salsa, she said, "I'm thinking of driving up to Chimayo. What's the best route?"

"Today?" Carmelita said, dismayed. "That's not a good idea. The road's pretty curvy, and we just got a call from Taos that it's really snowing hard up there."

"How about one of the pueblos then?"

She shook her head. "You have to take dirt roads to get there, and it's getting very icy. You're better off doing something here in town. There's a Christmas Eve mass at the cathedral at midnight," she added helpfully.

But I need something to do this afternoon, Bev thought, bending over the guidebook again. Indian Research Center—open weekends only. El Rancho de las Golondrinas—closed Nov-Mar. Santa Fe Historical Museum—closed Dec 24-Jan 1.

The Georgia O'Keeffe Museum-open daily.

Perfect, Bev thought, reading the entry: "Houses world's largest permanent collection of O'Keeffe's work. A major American artist, O'Keeffe lived in the Santa Fe area for many years. When she first arrived in 1929, she was physically and psychologically ill, but the dry, hot New Mexico climate healed and inspired her, and she painted much of her finest work here."

Perfect. Sun-baked paintings of cow skulls and giant tropical flowers and desert buttes. "Open daily. 10 A.M.-6 P.M. 217 Johnson St."

She looked up the address on her map. Only three blocks off the Plaza, within easy walking distance even in this weather. Perfect. When Carmelita brought her enchiladas, she attacked them eagerly.

"Did you find somewhere to go in town?" Carmelita asked curiously.

"Yes, the Georgia O'Keeffe Museum."

"Oh," Carmelita said and vanished again. She was back almost immediately. "I'm sorry, *señora,* but they're closed."

"Closed? It said in the guidebook the museum's open daily."

"It's because of the snow."

"Snow?" Bev said and looked past her to the patio where the sleet had turned to a heavy, slashing white.

—|•••|—

At 1:20, Jim called from the airport to tell them Kindra's and David's planes had both been delayed, and a few minutes later the bakery delivered the wedding cake. "No, no," Stacey said, "that's supposed to go to the country club. That's where the reception is."

"We tried," the driver said. "We couldn't get through. We can either leave it here or take it back to the bakery, take your pick. If we can *get* back to the bakery. Which I doubt."

"Leave it here," Stacey said. "Jim can take it over when he gets here."

"But you just heard him," Paula said. "If the truck can't get through, Jim won't be able to—" The phone rang.

It was the florist, calling to say they weren't going to be able to deliver the flowers. "But you have to," Stacey said. "The wedding's at five. Tell them they have to, Paula," and handed the phone to her.

"Isn't there any way you can get here?" Paula asked.

"Not unless there's a miracle," the florist said. "Our truck's in a ditch out at Pawnee, and there's no telling how long it'll take a tow truck to get to it. It's a skating rink out there."

"Jim will have to go pick up the flowers when he gets back with Kindra and David," Stacey said blithely when Paula told her the bad news. "He can do it on his way to the country club. Is the string quartet here yet?"

"No, and I'm not sure they'll be able to get here. The florist said the roads are really icy," Paula said, and the viola player walked in.

"I told you," Stacey said happily, "it'll all work out. Did I tell you, they're going to play Boccherini's 'Minuet No. 8' for the wedding march?" and went to get the candles for the altar stands.

Paula went over to the viola player, a lanky young guy. He was brushing snow off his viola case. "Where's the rest of the quartet?"

"They're not here yet?" he said, surprised. "I had a lesson to give in town and told 'em I'd catch up with them." He sat down to take off his snow-crusted boots. "And then my car ended up in a snowbank, and I had to walk the last mile and a half." He grinned up at her, panting. "It's times like these I wish I played the piccolo. Although," he said, looking her up and down, "there are compensations. Please tell me you're not the bride."

"I'm not the bride," she said. Even though I wish I was.

"Great!" he said and grinned at her again. "What are you doing after the wedding?"

"I'm not sure there's going to be one. Do you think the other musicians got stuck on the way here, too?"

He shook his head. "I would have seen them." He pulled out a cell phone and punched buttons. "Shep? Yeah, where are you?" There was a pause. "That's what I was afraid of. What about Leif?" Another pause. "Well, if you find him, call me back." He clipped the phone shut. "Bad news. The violins were in a fender bender and are waiting for the cops. They don't know where the cello is. How do you feel about a viola solo of 'Minuet No. 8'?"

124

Paula went to inform Stacey. "The police can bring them out," Stacey said blithely and handed Paula the white candles for the altar stands. "The candlelight on the snow's going to be just beautiful."

—|•••|—

At 1:48 P.M. Eastern Standard Time, snow flurries were reported at Sunset Point in the Florida Keys.

"I get to officially freak out now, right?" Chin asked Nathan. "Jeez, it really *is* the discontinuity you said would happen!"

"We don't know that yet," Nathan said, looking at the National Weather Service map, which was now entirely blue, except for a small spot near Fargo and another one in north-central Texas that Nathan thought was Waco and Chin was convinced was the president's ranch in Crawford.

"What do you mean, we don't know that yet? It's snowing in Barcelona. It's snowing in Moscow."

"It's supposed to be snowing in Moscow. Remember Napoleon? It's not unusual for it to be snowing in over two-thirds of these places reporting in: Oslo, Kathmandu, Buffalo—"

"Well, it's sure as hell unusual for it to be snowing in Beirut," Chin said, pointing to the snow reports coming in, "and Honolulu. I don't care what you say, I'm freaking out."

"You can't," Nathan said, superimposing an isobaric grid over the map. "I need you to feed me the temp readings."

Chin started over to his terminal and then came back. "What do you think?" he asked seriously. "Do you think it's a discontinuity?"

There was nothing else it could be. Winter storms were frequently very large, the February 1994 European storm had been huge, and the one in December 2002 had covered over a third of the U.S., but there'd never been one that covered the entire continental United States. And Mexico and Manitoba and Belize, he thought, watching the snowfall reports coming in.

In addition, snow was falling in six locations where it had never fallen before, and in twenty-eight like Yuma, Arizona, where it had snowed only once or twice in the last hundred years. New Orleans had a foot of snow, for God's sake. And it was snowing in Guatemala.

And it wasn't behaving like any storm he'd ever seen. According to the charts, snow had started simultaneously in Springfield, Illinois; Hoodoo, Tennessee; Park City, Utah; and Branford, Connecticut; and spread in a completely random pattern. There was no center to the storm, no leading edge, no front.

And no let-up. No station had reported the snow stopping, or even diminishing, and new stations were reporting in all the time. At this rate, it would be snowing everywhere by—he made a rapid calculation— five o'clock.

"Well?" Chin said. "Is it?" He looked really frightened.

And him freaking out is the last thing I need with all this data to feed in, Nathan thought. "We don't have enough data to make a determination yet," he said.

"But you think it might be," Chin persisted. "Don't you? You think all the signs are there?"

Yes, Nathan thought. "Definitely not," he said. "Look at the TV."

"What about it?"

"There's one sign that's not present." He gestured at the screen. "No logo."

"No what?"

"No logo. Nothing qualifies as a full-fledged crisis until the cable newschannels give it a logo of its own, preferably with a colon. You know, *OJ: Trial of the Century* or *Sniper at Large* or *Attack: Iraq.* He pointed at Dan Rather standing in thickly falling snow in front of the White House. "Look, it says *Breaking News,* but there's no logo. So it can't be a discontinuity. So feed me those temps. And then go see if you can scare up a couple more TVs. I want to get a look at exactly what's going on out there. Maybe that'll give us some kind of clue."

Chin nodded, looking reassured, and went to get the temp readings. They were all over the place, too, from eighteen below in Saskatoon to thirty-one above in Ft. Lauderdale. Nathan ran them against average temps for mid-December and then highs and lows for the twenty-fourth, looking for patterns, anomalies.

Chin wheeled in a big-screen TV on an AV cart, along with Professor Adler's portable, and plugged them in. "What do you want these on?" he asked.

"CNN, the Weather Channel, Fox—" Nathan began.

"Oh, no," Chin said.

"What? What is it?"

"Look," Chin said and pointed to Professor Adler's portable. Wolf Blitzer was standing in the snow in front of the Empire State Building. At the lower right-hand corner was the CNN symbol. And in the upper left-hand corner: *Storm of the Century.*

⊣•••⊢

As soon as Pilar had Miguel's things packed, she checked on the TV again.

"—resulting in terrible road conditions," the reporter was saying. "Police are reporting accidents at the intersection of Sepulveda and Figueroa, the intersection of San Pedro and Whittier, the intersection of Hollywood and Vine," while accident alerts crawled across the bottom of the screen. "We're getting reports of a problem on the Santa Monica Freeway just past the Culver City exit and…this just in, the northbound lanes of the 110 are closed due to a five-car accident. Travelers are advised to take alternate routes."

The phone rang. Miguel ran into the kitchen to answer it. "Hi, Daddy, it's snowing," he shouted into the receiver. "We're going outside and make a snowman," and then said, "Okay," and handed it to Pilar.

"Go watch cartoons and let Mommy talk to Daddy," she said and handed him the remote. "Hello, Joe."

"I want you to bring Miguel down now," her ex-husband said without preamble, "before the snow gets bad."

"It's already bad," Pilar said, standing in the door of the kitchen watching Miguel flip through the channels:

"—really slick out here—"

"—advised to stay home. If you don't have to go someplace, folks, don't."

"—treacherous conditions—"

"I'm not sure taking him out in this is a good idea," Pilar said. "The TV's saying the roads are really slick, and—"

"And I'm saying bring him down here now," Joe said nastily. "I know what you're doing. You think you can use a little snow as an excuse to keep my son away from me on Christmas."

"I am not," she protested. "I'm just thinking about Miguel's safety. I don't have snow tires—"

"Like hell you're thinking about the kid! You're thinking this is a way to do me out of my rights. Well, we'll see what my lawyer has to say about that. I'm calling him *and* the judge and telling them what you're up to, and that I'm sick of this crap, I want full custody. And then I'm coming up there myself to get him. Have him ready when I get there!" he shouted and hung up the phone.

—|•••|—

At 2:22 P.M., Luke's mother called on her cell phone to say she was going to be late and to go ahead and start the goose. "The roads are terrible, and people do *not* know how to drive. This red Subaru ahead of me just *swerved* into my lane and—"

"Mom, Mom," Luke cut in. "The goose. What do you mean, start the goose? What do I have to do?"

"Just put it in the oven. Shorty and Madge should be there soon, and she can take over. All you have to do is get it started. Take the bag of giblets out first. Put an aluminum foil tent over it."

"An aluminum-foil what?"

"Tent. Fold a piece of foil in half and lay it over the goose. It keeps it from browning too fast."

"How big a piece?"

"Big enough to cover the goose. And don't tuck in the edges."

"Of the oven?"

"Of the tent. You're making this much harder than it is. You wouldn't *believe* how many cars there are off the road, and every one of them's an SUV. It serves them right. They think just because they've got four-wheel drive, they can go ninety miles an hour in a *blizzard*—"

"Mom, Mom, what about stuffing? Don't I have to stuff the goose?"

"No. Nobody does stuffing inside the bird anymore. Salmonella. Just put the goose in the roasting pan and stick it in the oven. At 350 degrees."

I can do that, Luke thought, and did. Ten minutes later he realized he'd forgotten to put the aluminum foil tent on. It took him three tries to get a piece the right size, and his mother hadn't said whether the shiny or the dull side should be facing out, but when he checked the goose twenty minutes later, it seemed to be doing okay. It smelled good, and there were already juices forming in the pan.

—|•••|—

After Pilar hung up with Joe, she sat at the kitchen table a long time, trying to think which was worse, letting Joe take Miguel out into this snowstorm or having Miguel witness the fight that would ensue if she tried to stop him. "Please, please…" she murmured, without even knowing what she was praying for.

Miguel came into the kitchen and climbed into her lap. She wiped hastily at her eyes. "Guess what, honey?" she said brightly. "Daddy's going to come get you in a little bit. You need to go pick out which toys you want to take."

"Hunh-unh," Miguel said, shaking his head.

"I know you wanted to make a snowman," she said, "but guess what? It's snowing in Escondido, too. You can make a snowman with Daddy."

"Hunh-*unh*," he said, climbing down off her lap and tugging on her hand. He led her into the living room.

"What, honey?" she said, and he pointed at the TV. On it, the Santa Monica reporter was saying, "—the following road closures: I-5 from Chula Vista to Santa Ana, I-15 from San Diego to Barstow, Highway 78 from Oceanside to Escondido—"

Thank you, she murmured silently, thank you. Miguel ran out to the kitchen and came back with a piece of construction paper and a red crayon. "Here," he said, thrusting them at Pilar. "You have to write Santa. So he'll know to bring my presents here and not Daddy's."

By ordering sopapillas and then Mexican coffee, Bev managed to make lunch last till nearly two o'clock. When Carmelita brought the coffee, she looked anxiously out at the snow piling up on the patio and then back at Bev, so Bev asked for her check and signed it so Carmelita could leave, and then went back up to her room for her coat and gloves.

Even if the shops were closed, she could window-shop, she told herself, she could look at the Navajo rugs and Santa Clara pots and Indian jewelry displayed in the shops, but the snowstorm was getting worse. The luminarias that lined the walls were heaped with snow, the paper bags which held the candles sagging under the soggy weight.

They'll never get them lit, Bev thought, turning into the Plaza.

By the time she had walked down one side of it, the snow had become a blizzard, it was coming down so hard you couldn't see across the Plaza, and there was a cutting wind. She gave up and went back to the hotel.

In the lobby, the staff, including the front desk clerk and Carmelita in her coat and boots, was gathered in front of the TV looking at a weather map of New Mexico. "...currently snowing in most of New Mexico," the announcer was saying, "including Gallup, Carlsbad, Ruidoso, and Roswell. Travel advisories out for central, western, and southern New Mexico, including Lordsburg, Las Cruces, and Truth or Consequences. It looks like a white Christmas for most of New Mexico, folks."

"You have two messages," the front desk clerk said when he saw her. They were both from Janice, and she phoned again while Bev was taking her coat off.

"I just saw on TV that it's snowing in Santa Fe, and you said you were going sightseeing," Janice said. "I just wondered if you were okay."

"I'm here at the hotel," Bev said. "I'm not going anywhere."

"*Good*," Janice said, relieved. "Are you watching TV? The weathermen are saying this isn't an ordinary storm. It's some kind of extreme mega-storm. We've got three feet here. The power's out all over town, and the airport just closed. I hope you're able to get home. Oops, the lights just flickered. I'd better go hunt up some candles before the lights go off," she said, and hung up.

Bev turned on the TV The local channel was listing closings: "The First United Methodist Church Christmas pageant has been cancelled and there will be no *Posadas* tonight at Our Lady of Guadalupe. Canyon Day Care Center will close at 3:00 P.M...."

She clicked the remote. CNBC was discussing earlier Christmas Eve snowstorms, and on CNN, Daryn Kagan was standing in the middle of Fifth Avenue in a snowdrift. "This is usually the busiest shopping day of the year," she said, "but as you can see—"

She clicked the remote, looking for a movie to watch. Howard would have loved this, she thought involuntarily. He would have been in his element.

She clicked quickly through the other channels, trying to find a film, but they were all discussing the weather. "It looks like the whole country's going to get a white Christmas this year," Peter Jennings was saying, "whether they want it or not."

You'd think there'd be a Christmas movie on, Bev thought grimly, flipping through the channels again. It's Christmas Eve. *Christmas in Connecticut* or *Holiday Inn*. Or *White Christmas*.

Howard had insisted on watching it every time he came across it with the remote, even if it was nearly over. "Why are you watching that?" she'd ask, coming in to find him glued to the next-to-the-last scene. "We own the video."

"Shh," he'd say. "It's just getting to the good part," and he'd lean forward to watch Bing Crosby push open the barn doors to reveal fake-looking snow falling on the equally fake-looking set.

When he came into the kitchen afterward, she'd say sarcastically, "How'd it end this time? Did Bing and Rosemary Clooney get back together? Did they save the General's inn and all live happily ever after?"

But Howard would refuse to be baited. "They got a white Christmas," he'd say happily and go off to look out the windows at the clouds.

Except for news about the storm, there was nothing at all on except an infomercial selling a set of Ginsu knives. How appropriate, she thought, and sat back on the bed to watch it.

At 2:08, the weight of the new loose snow triggered a huge avalanche in the "awesome slopes" area near Breckenridge, knocking down huge numbers of Ponderosa pines and burying everything in its path, but not Kent and Bodine, who were still in their Honda, trying to keep warm and survive on a box of Tic-Tacs and an old donut found in the glove compartment.

By two-thirty, Madge and Shorty still weren't there, so Luke checked the goose. It seemed to be cooking okay, but there was an awful lot of juice in the pan. When he checked it again half an hour later, there was over an inch of the stuff.

That couldn't be right. The last time he'd gotten stuck with having the Christmas Eve dinner, the turkey had only produced a few tablespoons of juice. He remembered his mom pouring them off to make the gravy.

He tried his mom. Her cell phone said, "Caller unavailable," which meant her batteries had run down, or she'd turned it off. He tried Aunt Madge's. No answer.

He dug the plastic and net wrapping the goose had come in out of the trash, flattened it out, and read the instructions: "Roast uncovered at 350 degrees for twenty-five minutes per pound."

Uncovered. That must be the problem, the aluminum foil tent. It wasn't allowing the extra juice to evaporate. He opened the oven and removed it. When he checked the goose again fifteen minutes later, it was sitting in two inches of grease, and even though, according to the wrapping, it still had three hours to go, the goose was getting brown and crispy on top.

—|•••|—

At 2:51 P.M., Joe Gutierrez slammed out of his house and started up to get Miguel. He'd been trying to get his goddamned lawyer on the phone ever since he'd hung up on Pilar, but the lawyer wasn't answering.

The streets were a real mess, and when Joe got to the I-15 entrance ramp, there was a barricade across it. He roared back down the street to take Highway 78, but it was blocked, too. He stormed back home and called Pilar's lawyer, but he didn't answer either. He then called the judge, using the unlisted cell phone number he'd seen on his lawyer's palm pilot.

The judge, who had been stuck waiting for AAA in a Starbuck's at the Bakersfield exit, listening to Harry Connick, Jr., destroy "White Christmas" for the last three hours, was not particularly sympathetic, especially when Joe started swearing at him.

Words were exchanged, and the judge made a note to himself to have Joe declared in contempt of court. Then he called AAA to see what was taking so long, and when the operator told him he was nineteenth in line, and it would be at least another four hours, he decided to revisit the entire custody agreement.

—|•••|—

By three o'clock, all the networks and cable newschannels had logos. ABC had *Winter Wonderland,* NBC had *Super Storm,* and Fox News had *Winter Wallop.* CBS and MSNBC had both gone with *White Christmas,* flanked by a photo of Bing Crosby (MSNBC's wearing the Santa Claus hat from the movie.)

The Weather Channel's logo was a changing world map that was now two-thirds white, and snow was being reported in Karachi, Seoul, the Solomon Islands, and Bethlehem, where Christmas Eve services (usually cancelled due to Israeli-Palestinian violence) had been cancelled due to the weather.

—|•••|—

At 3:15 P.M., Jim called Paula from the airport to report that Kindra and David's flights had both been delayed indefinitely. "And the US Air guy says they're shutting the airport in Houston down. Dallas International's already closed, and so are JFK and O'Hare. How's Stacey?"

Incorrigible, Paula thought. "Fine," she said. "Do you want to talk to her?"

"No. Listen, tell her I'm still hoping, but it doesn't look good."

Paula told her, but it didn't have any effect. "Go get your dress on," Stacey ordered her, "so the minister can run through the service with you, and then you can show Kindra and David where to stand when they get here."

Paula went and put on her bridesmaid dress, wishing it wasn't sleeveless, and they went through the rehearsal with the viola player, who had changed into his tux to get out of his snow-damp clothes, acting as best man. As soon as they were done, Paula went into the vestry to get a sweater out of her suitcase. The minister came in and shut the door. "I've been trying to talk to Stacey," she said. "You're going to have to cancel the wedding. The roads are getting really dangerous, and I just heard on the radio they've closed the interstate."

"I know," Paula said.

"Well, she doesn't. She's convinced everything's going to work out."

And it might, Paula thought. After all, this is Stacey.

The viola player poked his head in the door. "Good news," he said.

"The string quartet's here?" the minister said.

"Jim's here?" Paula said.

"No, but Shep and Leif found the cello player. He's got frostbite, but otherwise he's okay. They're taking him to the hospital." He gestured toward the sanctuary. "Do you want to tell the Queen of Denial, or shall I?"

"I will," Paula said and went back into the sanctuary. "Stacey—"

"Your dress looks beautiful!" Stacey cried and dragged her over to the windows. "Look how it goes with the snow!"

─┤•••├─

When the bell rang at a quarter to four, Luke thought, Finally! Mom! and literally ran to answer the door. It was Aunt Lulla. He looked hopefully past her, but there was no one else pulling into the driveway or coming up the street. "You don't know anything about cooking a goose, do you?" he asked.

She looked at him a long, silent moment and then handed him the plate of olives she'd brought and took off her hat, scarf, gloves, plastic boots, and old-lady coat. "Your mother and Madge were always the domestic ones," she said, "I was the theatrical one," and while he was digesting that odd piece of information, "Why did you ask? Is your goose cooked?"

"Yes," he said and led her into the kitchen and showed her the goose, which was now swimming in a sea of fat.

"Good God!" Aunt Lulla said, "where did all that grease come from?"

"I don't know," he said.

"Well, the first thing to do is pour some of it off before the poor thing drowns."

"I already did," Luke said. He took the lid off the saucepan he'd poured the drippings into earlier.

"Well you need to pour off some more," she said practically, "and you'll need a larger pan. Or maybe we should just pour it down the sink and get rid of the evidence."

"It's for the gravy," he said, rummaging in the cupboard under the sink for the big pot his mother had given him to cook spaghetti in.

"Oh, of course," she said, and then thoughtfully, "I *do* know how to make gravy. Alec Guinness taught me."

Luke stuck his head out of the cupboard. "Alec Guinness taught you to make *gravy?*"

"It's not really all that difficult," she said, opening the oven door and looking speculatively at the goose. "You wouldn't happen to have any wine on hand, would you?"

"Yes." He emerged with the pot. "Why? Will wine counteract the grease?"

"I have no idea," she said. "But one of the things I learned when I was playing off-Broadway was that when you're facing a flop or an opening night curtain, it helps to be a little sloshed."

"You played off-Broadway?" Luke said. "Mom never told me you were an actress."

"I wasn't," she said, opening cupboard doors. She pulled out two wine glasses. "You should have seen my reviews."

By 4:00 P.M., all the networks and cable newschannels had changed their logos to reflect the worsening situation. ABC had *Mega-Blizzard,* NBC had *MacroBlizzard,* and CNN had *Perfect Storm,* with a graphic of a boat being swamped by a gigantic wave. CBS and MSNBC had both gone with *Ice Age,* CBS's with a question mark, MSNBC's with an exclamation point and a drawing of the Abominable Snowman. And Fox, ever the responsible news network, was proclaiming, *End of the World!*

"*Now* can I freak out?" Chin asked.

"No," Nathan said, feeding in snowfall rates. "In the first place, it's Fox. In the second place, a discontinuity does not necessarily mean the end of the wo—"

The lights flickered. They both stopped and stared at the overhead fluorescents. They flickered again.

"Backup!" Nathan shouted, and they both dived for their terminals, shoved in zip drives, and began frantically typing, looking anxiously up at the lights now and then.

Chin popped the zip disk out of the drive. "You were saying that a discontinuity isn't necessarily the end of the world?"

"Yes, but losing this data would be. From now on we back up every fifteen minutes."

The lights flickered again, went out for an endless ten seconds, and came back on again to Peter Jennings saying, "—Huntsville, Alabama, where thousands are without power. I'm here at Byrd Middle School, which is serving as a temporary shelter." He stuck the microphone under the nose of a woman holding a candle. "When did the power go off?" he asked.

"About noon," she said. "The lights flickered a couple of times before that, but both times the lights came back on, and I thought we were okay, and then I went to fix lunch, and they went off, like that—" she snapped her fingers. "Without any warning."

"We back up every five minutes," Nathan said, and to Chin, who was pulling on his parka, "Where are you going?"

"Out to my car to get a flashlight."

He came back in ten minutes later, caked in snow, his ears and cheeks bright red. "It's four feet deep out there. Tell me again why I shouldn't freak out," he said, handing the flashlight to Nathan.

"Because I don't think this is a discontinuity," Nathan said. "I think it's just a snowstorm."

"Just a snowstorm?" Chin said, pointing at the TVs, where red-eared, red-cheeked reporters were standing in front of, respectively, a phalanx of snowplows on the Boardwalk in Atlantic City, a derailed train in Casper, and a collapsed Wal-Mart in Biloxi, "—from the weight of a record fifty-eight inches of snow," Brit Hume was saying. "Luckily, there were no injuries here. In Cincinnati, however—"

"*Fifty-eight* inches," Chin said. "In *Mississippi*. What if it keeps on snowing and snowing forever till the whole world...?"

"It can't," Nathan said. "There isn't enough moisture in the atmosphere, and no low pressure system over the Gulf to keep pumping moisture up across the lower United States. There's no low pressure system at all, and no ridge of high pressure to push against it, no colliding air masses, nothing. Look at this. It started in four different places hundreds of miles from each other, in different latitudes, different altitudes, none of them along a ridge of high pressure. This storm isn't following any of the rules."

"But doesn't that prove it's a discontinuity?" Chin asked nervously. "Isn't that one of the signs, that it's completely different from what came before?"

"The *climate* would be completely different, the *weather* would be completely different, not the laws of physics." He pointed to the world map on the mid-right-hand screen. "If this were a discontinuity, you'd see a change in ocean current temps, a shift in the jet stream, changes in wind patterns. There's none of that. The jet stream hasn't moved, the rate of melting in the Antarctic is unchanged, the Gulf Stream's still there. El Niño's still there. *Venice* is still there."

"Yeah, but it's snowing on the Grand Canal," Chin said. "So what's causing the mega-storm?"

"That's just it. It's not a mega-storm. If it were, there'd be accompanying ice-storms, hurricane-force winds, microbursts, tornadoes, none of

136

which has shown up on the data. As near as I can tell, all it's doing is snowing." He shook his head. "No, something else is going on."

"What?"

"I have no idea." He stared glumly at the screens. "Weather's a remarkably complex system. Hundreds, thousands of factors we haven't figured in could be having an effect: cloud dynamics, localized temperature variations, pollution, solar activity. Or it could be something we haven't even considered: the effects of de-icers on highway albedo, beach erosion, the migratory patterns of geese. Or the effect on electromagnetic fields of playing 'White Christmas' hundreds of times on the radio this week."

"Four thousand nine hundred and thirty-three," Chin said.

"What?"

"That's how many times Bing Crosby's 'White Christmas' is played the two weeks before Christmas, with an additional nine thousand and sixty-two times by other artists. Including Otis Redding, U2, Peggy Lee, the Three Tenors, and the Flaming Lips. I read it on the internet."

"Nine thousand and sixty-two," Nathan said. "That's certainly enough to affect something, all right."

"I know what you mean," Chin said. "Have you heard Eminem's new rap version?"

⊣ • • • ⊢

By 4:15 P.M., the spaghetti pot was two-thirds full of goose grease, Luke's mother and Madge and Shorty still weren't there, and the goose was nearly done. Luke and Lulla had decided after their third glass of wine apiece to make the gravy.

"And put the tent back on," Lulla said, sifting flour into a bowl. "One of the things I learned when I was playing the West End is that uncovered is not necessarily better." She added a cup of water. "Particularly when you're doing Shakespeare."

She shook in some salt and pepper. "I remember a particularly ill-conceived nude *Macbeth* I did with Larry Olivier." She thrust her hand out dramatically. "'Is that a dagger that I see before me?' should not be a laugh line. Richard taught me how to do this," she said, stirring the mixture briskly with a fork, "It gets the lumps out."

"Richard? Richard *Burton?*"

"Yes. Adorable man. Of course he drank like a fish when he was depressed—this was after Liz left him for the second time—but it never seemed to affect his performance in bed *or* in the kitchen. Not like Peter."

"Peter? Peter Ustinov?"

"O'Toole. Here we go." Lulla poured the flour mixture into the hot drippings. It disappeared. "It takes a moment to thicken up," she said hopefully, but after several minutes of combined staring into the pot, it was no thicker.

"I think we need more flour," she said, "and a larger bowl. A much larger bowl. And another glass of wine."

Luke fetched them, and after a good deal of stirring, she added the mixture to the drippings, which immediately began to thicken up. "Oh, good," she said, stirring. "As John Gielgud used to say, 'If at first you don't succeed...' Oh, dear."

"What did he say that for?—oh, dear," Luke said, peering into the pot where the drippings had abruptly thickened into a solid, globular mass.

"That's not what gravy's supposed to look like," Aunt Lulla said.

"No," Luke said. "We seem to have made a lard ball."

They both looked at it awhile.

"I don't suppose we could pass it off as a very large dumpling," Aunt Lulla suggested.

"No," Luke said, trying to chop at it with the fork.

"And I don't suppose it'll go down the garbage disposal. Could we stick sesame seeds on it and hang it on a tree and pretend it was a suet ball for the birds?"

"Not unless we want PETA and the Humane Society after us. Besides, wouldn't that be cannibalism?"

"You're right," Aunt Lulla said. "But we've got to do something with it before your mother gets here. I suppose Yucca Mountain's too far away," she said thoughtfully. "You wouldn't have any acid on hand, would you?"

⊣•••⊢

At 4:23 P.M., Slim Rushmore, on KFLG out of Flagstaff, Arizona, made a valiant effort to change the subject on his talk radio show to school vouchers, usually a sure-fire issue, but his callers weren't having any of it. "This snow is a clear sign the Apocalypse is near," a woman from Colorado Springs informed him. "In the Book of Daniel, it says that

God will send snow 'to purge and to make them white, even to the time of the end,' and the Book of Psalms promises us 'snow and vapours, stormy wind fulfilling his word,' and in the Book of Isaiah..."

After the fourth Scripture (from Job: "For God saith to the snow, Be thou on the earth") Slim cut her off and took a call from Dwayne in Poplar Bluffs.

"You know what started all this, don't you?" Dwayne said belligerently. "When the commies put fluoride in the water back in the fifties."

─┤ • • • ├─

At 4:25 P.M., the country club called the church to say they were closing, none of the food and only two of the staff could get there, and anybody who was still trying to have a wedding in this weather was crazy. "I'll tell her," Paula said and went to find Stacey.

"She's in putting on her wedding dress," the viola player said.

Paula moaned.

"Yeah, I know," he said. "I tried to explain to her that the rest of the quartet was *not* coming, but I didn't get anywhere." He looked at her quizzically. "I'm not getting anywhere with you either, am I?" he asked, and Jim walked in.

He was covered in snow. "The car got stuck," he said.

"Where are Kindra and David?"

"They closed Houston," he said, pulling Paula aside, "and Newark. And I just talked to Stacey's mom. She's stuck in Lavoy. They just closed the highway. There's no way she can get here. What are we going to do?"

"You have to tell her the wedding has to be called off," Paula said. "You don't have any other option. And you have to do it now, before the guests try to come to the church."

"You obviously haven't been out there lately," he said. "Trust me, nobody's going to come out in that."

"Then you obviously have to cancel."

"I know," he said worriedly. "It's just...she'll be so disappointed."

Disappointed is not the word that springs to mind, Paula thought, and realized she had no idea how Stacey would react. She'd never seen her not get her way. I wonder what she'll do, she thought curiously, and started back into the vestry to change out of her bridesmaid dress.

"Wait," Jim said, grabbing her hand. "You have to help me tell her."

This is asking way too much, Paula thought. I want you to marry me, not her. "I—" she said.

"I can't do this without you," he said. "Please?"

She extricated her hand. "Okay," she said, and they went into the changing room, where Stacey was in her wedding dress, looking at herself in the mirror.

"Stacey, we have to talk," Jim said, after a glance at Paula. "I just heard from your mother. She's not going to be able to get here. She's stuck at a truck stop outside Lavoy."

"She can't be," Stacey said to her reflection. "She's bringing my veil." She turned to smile at Paula. "It was my great-grandmother's. It's lace, with this snowflake pattern."

"Kindra and David can't get here either," Jim said. He glanced at Paula and then plunged ahead. "We're going to have to reschedule the wedding."

"Reschedule?" Stacey said as if she'd never heard the word before. Which she probably hasn't, Paula thought. "We can't reschedule. A Christmas Eve wedding has to be on Christmas Eve."

"I know, honey, but—"

"Nobody's going to be able to get here," Paula said. "They've closed the roads."

The minister came in. "The governor's declared a snow emergency and a ban on unnecessary travel. You've decided to cancel?" she said hopefully.

"*Cancel?*" Stacey said, adjusting her train. "What are you talking about? Everything will be fine."

And for one mad moment, Paula could almost see Stacey pulling it off, the weather magically clearing, the rest of the string quartet showing up, the flowers and Kindra and David and the veil all arriving in the next thirty-five minutes. She looked over at the windows. The snow, reflected softly in the candlelight, was coming down harder than ever.

"We don't have any other choice than to reschedule," Jim said. "Your mother can't get here, your maid of honor and my best man can't get here—"

"Tell them to take a different flight," Stacey said.

Paula tried. "Stacey, I don't think you realize, this is a major snowstorm. Airports all over the country are closed—"

"Including here," the viola player said, poking his head in. "It was just on the news."

"Well, then, go get them," Stacey said, adjusting the drape of her skirt. Paula'd lost the thread of this conversation. "Who?"

"Kindra and David." She adjusted the neckline of her gown.

"To *Houston?*" Jim said, looking helplessly at Paula.

"Listen, Stacey," Paula said, taking her firmly by the shoulders. "I know how much you wanted a Christmas Eve wedding, but it's just not going to work. The roads are impassable. Your flowers are in a ditch, your mother's trapped at a truck stop—"

"The cello player's in the hospital with frostbite," the viola player put in.

Paula nodded. "And you don't want anyone else to end up there. You have to face facts. You can't have a Christmas Eve wedding."

"You could reschedule for Valentine's Day," the minister said brightly. "Valentine weddings are very nice. I've got two weddings that day, but I could move one up. It could still be in the evening," but Paula could tell Stacey had stopped listening at "you can't have—"

"*You* did this," Stacey snapped at Paula. "You've always been jealous of me, and now you're taking it out on me by ruining my wedding."

"Nobody's ruining anything, Stacey," Jim said, stepping between them. "It's a snowstorm."

"Oh, so I suppose it's *my* fault!" Stacey said. "Just because I wanted a winter wedding with snow—"

"It's nobody's fault," Jim said sternly. "Listen, I don't want to wait either, and we don't have to. We can get married right here, right now."

"Yeah," the viola player said. "You've got a minister." He grinned at Paula. "You've got two witnesses."

"He's right," Jim said. "We've got everything we need right here. You're here, *I'm* here, and that's all that really matters, isn't it, not some fancy wedding?" He took her hands in his. "Will you marry me?"

And what woman could resist an offer like that? Paula thought. Oh, well, you knew when you got on the plane that he was going to marry her.

"Marry you," Stacey repeated blankly, and the minister hurried out, saying, "I'll get my book. And my robe."

"Marry you?" Stacey said. "*Marry you?*" She wrenched free of his grasp. "Why on earth would I marry a *loser* who won't even do one simple thing for me? I *want* Kindra and David here. I *want* my flowers.

I *want* my veil. What is the *point* of *marrying* you if I can't have what I want?"

"I thought you wanted me," Jim said dangerously.

"*You?*" Stacey said in a tone that made both Paula and the viola player wince. "I *wanted* to walk down the aisle at twilight on Christmas Eve," she waved her arm in the direction of the windows, "with candlelight reflecting off the windowpanes and snow falling outside." She turned, snatching up her train, and looked at him. "Will I *marry* you? Are you *kidding?*"

There was a short silence. Jim turned and looked seriously at Paula. "How about you?" he said.

At six o'clock on the dot, Madge and Shorty, Uncle Don, Cousin Denny, and Luke's mom all arrived. "You poor darling," she whispered to Luke, handing him the green bean casserole and the sweet potatoes, "stuck all afternoon with Aunt Lulla. Did she talk your ear off?"

"No," he said. "We made a snowman. Why didn't you tell me Aunt Lulla had been an actress?"

"An *actress?*" she said, handing him the cranberry sauce. "Is that what she told you? Don't tip it, it'll spill. Did you have any trouble with the goose?" She opened the oven and looked at it, sitting in its pan, brown and crispy and done to a turn. "They tend to be a little juicy."

"Not a bit," he said, looking past her out the window at the snowman in the backyard. The snow he and Aunt Lulla had packed around it and on top of it was melting. He'd have to sneak out during dinner and pile more snow on.

"Here," his mom said, handing him the mashed potatoes. "Heat these up in the microwave while I make the gravy."

"It's made," he said, lifting the lid off the saucepan to show her the gently bubbling gravy. It had taken them four tries, but as Aunt Lulla had pointed out, they had more than enough drippings to experiment with, and, as she had also pointed out, three lardballs made a more realistic snowman.

"The top one's too big," Luke had said, scooping up snow to cover it with.

"I may have gotten a little carried away with the flour," Aunt Lulla had admitted. "On the other hand, it looks exactly like Orson."

She stuck two olives in for eyes. "And so appropriate. He always was a fathead."

"The gravy smells delicious," Luke's mother said, looking surprised. "*You* didn't make it, did you?"

"No. Aunt Lulla."

"Well, I think you're a saint for putting up with her and her wild tales all afternoon, she said, ladling gravy into a bowl and handing it to Luke.

"You mean she made all that stuff up?" Luke said.

"Do you have a gravy boat?" his mother asked, opening cupboards.

"No," he said. "Aunt Lulla wasn't really an actress?"

"*No.*" She took a bowl out of the cupboard. "Do you have a ladle."

"No."

She got a dipper out of the silverware drawer. "Lulla was never in a single play," she said, ladling the gravy into a bowl and handing it to Luke, "where she hadn't gotten the part by sleeping with somebody. Lionel Barrymore, Ralph Richardson, Kenneth Branagh…" She opened the oven to look at the goose. "And that's not even counting Alfred."

"Alfred *Lunt?*" Luke asked.

"Hitchcock. I think this is just about done."

"But I thought you said she was the shy one."

"She was. That's why she went out for drama in high school, to over-come her shyness. Do you have a platter?"

⊣ • • • ⊢

At 6:35 P.M., a member of the Breckenridge ski patrol, out looking for four missing cross-country skiers, spotted a taillight (the only part of Kent and Bodine's Honda not covered by snow). He had a collapsible shovel with him, and a GPS, a satellite phone, a walkie-talkie, Mylar blankets, insta-heat packs, energy bars, a thermos of hot cocoa, and a stern lecture on winter safety, which he delivered after he had dug Kent and Bodine out and which they really resented. "Who did that fascist geek think he was, shaking his finger at us like that?" Bodine asked Kent after several tequila slammers at the Laughing Moose.

"Yeah," Kent said eloquently, and they settled down to the serious business of how to take advantage of the fresh powder that had fallen while they were in their car.

"You know what'd be totally extreme?" Bodine said. "Snowboarding at night!"

Shara was quite a girl. Warren didn't have a chance to call Marjean again until after seven. When Shara went in the bathroom, he took the opportunity to dial home. "Where *are* you?" MarJean said, practically crying. "I've been worried sick! Are you all right?"

"I'm still in Cincinnati at the airport," he said, "and it looks like I'll be here all night. They just closed the airport."

"Closed the airport..." she echoed.

"I *know*," he said, his voice full of regret. "I'd really counted o n being home with you for Christmas Eve, but what can you do? It's snowing like crazy here. No flights out till tomorrow afternoon at the earliest. I'm in line at the airline counter right now, rebooking, and then I'm going to try to find a place to stay, but I don't know if I'll have much luck." He paused to give her a chance to commiserate. "They're supposed to put us up for the night, but I wouldn't be surprised if I end up sleeping on the floor."

"At the airport," she said, "in Cincinnati."

"Yeah." He laughed. "Great place to spend Christmas Eve, huh?" He paused to give her a chance to commiserate, but all she said was, "You didn't make it home last year either."

"Honey, you know I'd get there if I could," he said. "I tried to rent a car and drive home, but the snow's so bad they're not even sure they can get a shuttle out here to take us to a hotel. I don't know how much snow they've had here—"

"Forty-six inches," she said.

Good, he thought. From her voice he'd been worried it might not be snowing in Cincinnati after all. "And it's still coming down hard. Oh, they just called my name. I'd better go."

"You do that," she said.

"All right. I love you, honey," he said, "I'll be home as soon as I can," and hung up the phone.

"You're married," Shara said, standing in the door of the bathroom. "You sonofabitch."

⊣ • • • ⊢

Paula didn't say yes to Jim's proposal after all. She'd intended to, but before she could, the viola player had cut in. "Hey, wait a minute!" he'd said. "I saw her first!"

"You did not," Jim said.

"Well, no, not technically," he admitted, "but when I did see her, I had the good sense to flirt with her, not get engaged to Vampira like you did."

"It wasn't Jim's fault," Paula said. "Stacey always gets what she wants."

"Not this time," the viola player said. "And not me."

"Only because she doesn't want you," Paula said. "If she did—"

"Wanna bet? You underestimate us musicians. And yourself. At least give me a chance to make my pitch before you commit to this guy. You can't get married tonight anyway."

"Why not?" Jim asked.

"Because you need two witnesses, and I have no intention of help-ing you," he pointed at Jim, "get the woman I want. I doubt if Stacey's in the mood to be a witness either," he said as Stacey stormed back in the sanctuary, with the minister in pursuit. Stacey had on her wedding dress, a parka, and boots.

"You can't go out in this," the minister was saying. "It's too dangerous!"

"I have no intention of staying here with him," Stacey said, shooting Jim a venomous glance. "I want to go home now." She flung the door open on the thickly falling snow. "And I want it to stop *snowing!*"

At that exact moment, a snowplow's flashing yellow lights had ap-peared through the snow, and Stacey had run out. Paula and Jim went over to the door and watched Stacey wave it down and get in. The plow continued on its way.

"Oh, good, now we'll be able to get out," the minister said, and went to get her car keys.

"You didn't answer my question, Paula," Jim said, standing very close.

The plow turned and came back. As it passed, it plowed a huge mass of snow across the end of the driveway.

"I mean it," Jim murmured. "How about it?"

"Look what I found," the viola player said, appearing at Paula's elbow. He handed her a piece of wedding cake.

"You can't eat that. It's—" Jim said.

"—not bad," the viola player said. "I prefer chocolate, though. What kind of cake shall we have at our wedding, Paula?"

"Oh, look," the minister said, coming back in with her car keys and looking out the window. "It's stopped snowing."

⊣ • • • ⊢

"It's stopped snowing," Chin said.

"It has?" Nathan looked up from his keyboard. "Here?"

"No. In Oceanside, Oregon. And in Springfield, Illinois."

Nathan found them on the map. Two thousand miles apart. He checked their barometer readings, temperatures, snowfall amounts. No similarity. Springfield had thirty-two inches, Oceanside an inch and a half. And in every single town around them, it was still snowing hard. In Tillamook, six miles away, it was coming down at the rate of five inches an hour.

But ten minutes later, Chin reported the snow stopping in Gillette, Wyoming; Roulette, Massachusetts; and Saginaw, Michigan; and within half an hour the number of stations reporting in was over thirty, though they seemed just as randomly scattered all over the map as the storm's beginning had been.

"Maybe it has to do with their names," Chin said.

"Their names?" Nathan said.

"Yeah. Look at this. It's stopped in Joker, West Virginia; Bluff, Utah; and Blackjack, Georgia."

⊣ • • • ⊢

At 7:22 P.M., the snow began to taper off in Wendover, Utah. Neither the Lucky Lady Casino nor the Big Nugget had any windows, so the event went unnoticed until Barbara Gomez, playing the quarter slots, ran out of money at 9:05 P.M. and had to go out to her car to get the emergency twenty she kept taped under the dashboard. By this time, the snow had nearly stopped. Barbara told the change girl, who said, "Oh, good. I was worried about driving to Battle Mountain tomorrow. Were the plows out?"

Barbara said she didn't know and asked for four rolls of nickels, which she promptly lost playing video poker.

⊣ • • • ⊢

By 7:30 P.M. CNBC had replaced its logo with *Digging Out,* and ABC had retreated to Bing and *White Christmas,* though CNN still had side-by-side experts discussing the possibility of a new ice age, and on Fox News, Geraldo Rivera was intoning, "In his classic poem, 'Fire and Ice,' Robert Frost speculated that the world might end in ice. Today we are seeing the coming true of that dire prediction—"

The rest had obviously gotten the word, though, and CBS and the WB had both gone back to their regular programming. The movie *White Christmas* was on AMC.

"Whatever this was, it's stopping," Nathan said, watching "I-80 now open from Lincoln to Ogalallah," scroll across the bottom of NBC's screen.

"Well, whatever you do, don't tell those corporate guys," Chin said, and, as if on cue, one of the businessmen Nathan had met with that morning called.

"I just wanted you to know we've voted to approve your grant," he said.

"Really? Thank you," Nathan said, trying to ignore Chin, who was mouthing, "Are they giving us the money?"

"Yes," he mouthed back.

Chin scribbled down something and shoved it in front of Nathan. "Get it in writing," it said.

"We all agreed this discontinuity thing is worth studying," the businessman said, then, shakily, "They've been talking on TV about the end of the world. You don't think this discontinuity thing is that bad, do you?"

"No," Nathan said, "in fact—"

"Ix-nay, ix-nay," Chin mouthed, wildly crossing his arms.

Nathan glared at him. "—we're not even sure yet if it is a discontinuity. It doesn't—"

"Well, we're not taking any chances," the businessman said. "What's your fax number? I want to send you that confirmation before the power goes out over here. We want you to get started working on this thing as soon as you can."

Nathan gave him the number. "There's really no need—" he said.

Chin jabbed his finger violently at the logo *False Alarm* on the screen of Adler's TV.

"Consider it a Christmas present," the businessman said, and the fax machine began to whir. "There *is* going to be a Christmas, isn't there?"

Chin yanked the fax out of the machine with a whoop.

"Definitely," Nathan said. "Merry Christmas," but the businessman had already hung up.

Chin was still looking at the fax. "How much did you ask them for?"

"Fifty thousand," Nathan said.

Chin slapped the grant approval down in front of him. "And a merry Christmas to you, too," he said.

At 7:30 P. M., after watching infomercials for NordicTrack, a combination egg poacher and waffle iron, and the revolutionary new DuckBed, Bev put on her thin coat and her still-damp gloves and went downstairs. There had to be a restaurant open somewhere in Santa Fe. She would find one and have a margarita and a beef chimichanga, sitting in a room decorated with sombreros or piñatas with striped curtains pulled across the windows to shut the snow out.

And if they were all closed, she would come back and order from room service. Or starve. But she was *not* going to ask at the desk and have them phone ahead and tell her the El Charito had closed early because of the weather, she was not going to let them cut off all avenues of escape, like Carmelita. She walked determinedly past the registration desk toward the double doors.

"Mrs. Carey!" the clerk called to her, and when she kept walking, he hurried around the desk and across the lobby to her. "I have a message for you from Carmelita. She wanted me to tell you midnight mass at the cathedral has been cancelled," he said. "The bishop was worried about people driving home on the icy roads. But Carmelita said to tell you they're having mass at eight o'clock, if you'd like to come to that. The cathedral's right up the street at the end of the plaza. If you go out the north door," he pointed, "it's only two blocks. It's a very pretty service, with the luminarias and all."

And it's somewhere to go, Bev thought, letting him lead her to the north door. It's something to do. "Tell Carmelita thank you for me," she said at the door. "And *Feliz Navidad.*"

"Merry Christmas." He opened the door. "You go down this street, turn left, and it's right there," he said and ducked back inside, out of the snow.

It was inches deep on the sidewalk as she hurried along the narrow street, head down, and snowing hard. By morning it would look just like back home. It's not fair, she thought. She turned the corner and looked up at the sound of an organ.

The cathedral stood at the head of the Plaza, its windows glowing like flames, and she had been wrong about the luminarias being ruined—they stood in rows leading up the walk, up the steps to the wide doors, lining the adobe walls and the roofs and the towers, burning steadily in the descending snow.

It fell silently, in great, spangled flakes, glittering in the light of the street lamps, covering the wooden-posted porches, the pots of cactus, the pink adobe buildings. The sky above the cathedral was pink, too, and the whole scene had an unreal quality, like a movie set.

"Oh, Howard," Bev said, as if she had just opened a present, and then flinched away from the thought of him, waiting for the thrust of the knife; but it didn't come. She felt only regret that he couldn't be here to see this and amusement that the sequined snowflakes sifting down on her hair, on her coat sleeve, looked just like the fake snow at the end of White Christmas. And, arching over it all, like the pink sky, she felt affection—for the snow, for the moment, for Howard.

"You did this," she said, and started to cry.

The tears didn't trickle down her cheeks, they poured out, drenching her face, her coat, melting the snowflakes instantly where they fell. Healing tears, she thought, and realized suddenly that when she had asked Howard how the movie ended, he hadn't said, "They lived happily ever after." He had said, "They got a white Christmas."

"Oh, Howard."

The bells for the service began to ring. I need to stop crying and go in, she thought, fumbling for a tissue, but she couldn't. The tears kept coming, as if someone had opened a spigot.

A black-shawled woman carrying a prayer book put her hand on Bev's shoulder and said, "Are you all right, *señora?*"

"Yes," Bev said, "I'll be fine," and something in her voice must have reassured the woman because she patted Bev's arm and went on into the cathedral.

The bells stopped ringing and the organ began again, but Bev continued to stand there until long after the mass had started, looking up at the falling snow.

"I don't know how you did this, Howard," she said, "but I know you're responsible."

At eight P.M., after anxiously checking the news to make sure the roads were still closed, Pilar put Miguel to bed. "Now go to sleep," she said, kissing him good-night. "Santa's coming soon." "Hunh-unh," he said, looking like he was going to cry. "It's snowing too hard."

He's worried about the roads being closed, she thought. "Santa doesn't need roads," she said. "Remember, he has a magic sleigh that flies through the air even if it's snowing."

"Hunh-*unh*," he said, getting out of bed to get his Rudolph book. He showed her the illustration of the whirling blizzard and Santa shaking his head, and then stood up on his bed, pulled back the curtain, and pointed through the window. She had to admit it did look just like the picture.

"But he had Rudolph to show the way " she said. "See?" and turned the page, but Miguel continued to look skeptical until she had read the book all the way through twice.

At 10:15 P.M. Warren Nesvick went down to the hotel's bar. He had tried to explain to Shara that Marjean was his five-year-old niece, but she had gotten completely unreasonable. "So I'm a cancelled flight out of Cincinnati, am I?" she'd shouted. "Well, I'm canceling you, you bastard!" and slammed out, leaving him high and dry. On Christmas Eve, for Christ's sake.

He'd spent the next hour and a half on the phone. He'd called some women he knew from previous trips but none of them had answered. He'd then tried to call Marjean to tell her the snow was letting up and United thought they could get him on standby early tomorrow morning and to try to patch things up—she'd seemed kind of upset—but she hadn't answered either. She'd probably gone to bed.

He'd hung up and gone down to the bar. There wasn't a soul in the place except the bartender. "How come the place is so dead?" Warren asked him.

"Where the hell have you been?" the bartender said and turned on the TV above the bar.

"Most widespread snowstorm in recorded history," Dan Abrams was saying. "Although there are signs of the snow beginning to let up here in Baltimore, in other parts of the country they weren't so lucky. We take you now to Cincinnati, where emergency crews are still digging victims out of the rubble." It cut to a reporter standing in front of a sign that read *Cincinnati International Airport*. "A record forty-six inches of snow caused the roof of the main terminal to collapse this afternoon. Over two hundred passengers were injured, and forty are still missing."

The goose was a huge hit, crispy and tender and done to a turn, and everyone raved about the gravy. "Luke made it," Aunt Lulla said, but Madge and his mom were talking about people not knowing how to drive in snow and didn't hear her.

It stopped snowing midway through dessert, and Luke began to worry about the snowman but didn't have a chance to duck out and check on it till nearly eleven, when everyone was putting on their coats.

It had melted (sort of), leaving a round greasy smear in the snow. "Getting rid of the evidence?" Aunt Lulla asked, coming up behind him in her old-lady coat, scarf, gloves, and plastic boots. She poked at the smear with the toe of her boot. "I hope it doesn't kill the grass."

"I hope it doesn't affect the environment," Luke said.

Luke's mother appeared in the back door. "What are you two doing out there in the dark?" she called to them. "Come in. We're trying to decide who's going to have the dinner next Christmas. Madge and Shorty think it's Uncle Don's turn, but—"

"I'll have it," Luke said and winked at Lulla.

"Oh," his mother said, surprised, and went back inside to tell Madge and Shorty and the others.

"But not goose," Luke said to Lulla. "Something easy. And nonfat."

"Ian had a wonderful recipe for duck a l'orange Alsacienne, as I remember," Lulla mused.

"Ian McKellen?"

"No, of course not, Ian Holm. Ian McKellen's a terrible cook," she said. "Or—I've got an idea. How about Japanese blowfish?"

By 11:15 P.M. Eastern Standard Time, the snow had stopped in New England, the Middle East, the Texas panhandle, most of Canada, and Nooseneck, Rhode Island.

"The storm of the century definitely seems to be winding clown," Wolf Blitzer was saying in front of CNN's new logo: *The Sun'll Come Out Tomorrow,* "leaving in its wake a white Christmas for nearly every-one—"

"Hey," Chin said, handing Nathan the latest batch of temp readings. "I just thought of what it was."

"What what was?"

"The factor. You said there were thousands of factors contributing to global warming, and that any one of them, even something really small, could have been what caused this."

He hadn't really said that, but never mind. "And you've figured out what this critical factor is?"

"Yeah," Chin said. "A white Christmas."

"A white Christmas," Nathan repeated.

"Yeah! You know how everybody wants it to snow for Christmas, little kids especially, but lots of adults, too. They have this Currier-and-Ives thing of what Christmas should look like, and the songs reinforce it: 'White Christmas' and 'Winter Wonderland' and that one that goes, 'The weather outside is frightful,' I never can remember the name—"

"'Let It Snow,'" Nathan said.

"Exactly," Chin said. "Well, suppose all those people and all those little kids wished for a white Christmas at the same time—"

"They *wished* this snowstorm into being?" Nathan said.

"No. They *thought* about it, and their—I don't know, their brain chemicals or synapses or something—created some kind of electrochem-ical field or something, and that's the factor."

"That everybody was dreaming of a white Christmas."

"Yeah. It's a possibility, right?"

"Maybe," Nathan said. Maybe there was some critical factor that had caused this. Not wishing for a white Christmas, of course, but some-thing seemingly unconnected to weather patterns, like tiny variations in the earth's orbit. Or the migratory patterns of geese.

Or an assortment of factors working in combination. And maybe the storm was an isolated incident, an aberration caused by a confluence of these unidentified factors, and would never happen again.

Or maybe his discontinuity theory was wrong. A discontinuity was by definition an abrupt, unexpected event. But that didn't mean there might not be advance indicators, like the warning flickers of electric lights before the power goes off for good. In which case—

"What are you doing?" Chin said, coming in from scraping his windshield. "Aren't you going home?"

"Not yet. I want to run a couple more extrapolation sets. It's still snowing in L.A."

Chin looked immediately alarmed. "You don't think it's going to start snowing everywhere again, do you?"

"No," Nathan said. Not yet.

At 11:43 P.M., after singing several karaoke numbers at the Laughing Moose, including "White Christmas," and telling the bartender they were going on "a moonlight ride down this totally killer chute," Kent Slakken and Bodine Cromps set out with their snowboards for an off-limits, high-avalanche-danger area near Vail and were never heard from again.

At 11:52 P.M., Miguel jumped on his sound-asleep mother, shouting, "It's Christmas! It's Christmas!"

It can't be morning yet, Pilar thought groggily, fumbling to look at the clock. "Miguel, honey, it's still nighttime. If you're not in bed when Santa comes, he won't leave you any presents," she said, hustling him back to bed. She tucked him in. "Now go to sleep. Santa and Rudolph will be here soon."

"Hunh-unh," he said and stood up on his bed. He pulled the curtain back. "He doesn't need Rudolph. The snow stopped, just like I wanted, and now Santa can come all by himself." He pointed out the window. Only a few isolated flakes were still sifting down.

Oh, no, Pilar thought. After she was sure he was asleep, she crept out to the living room and turned on the TV very low, hoping against hope.

"—roads will remain closed until noon tomorrow," an exhausted-looking reporter said, "to allow time for the snow plows to clear them: I-15, State Highway 56, I-15 from Chula Vista to Murrietta Hot Springs, Highway 78 from Vista to Escondido—"

Thank you, she murmured silently. Thank you.

—|•••|—

At 11:59 P.M. Pacific Standard Time, Sam "Hoot'n'Holler" Farley's voice gave out completely. The only person who'd been able to make it to the station, he'd been broadcasting continuously on KTTS, "Seattle's talk 24/7" since 5:36 A.M. when he'd come in to do the morning show, even though he had a bad cold. He'd gotten steadily hoarser all day, and during the 9:00 P.M. newsbreak, he'd had a bad coughing fit.

"The National Weather Service reports that that big snowstorm's finally letting up," he croaked, "and we'll have nice weather tomorrow. Oh, this just in from NORAD, for all you kids who're up way too late. Santa's sleigh's just been sighted on radar over Vancouver and is headed this way."

He then attempted to say, "In local news, the snow—" but nothing came out.

He tried again. Nothing.

After the third try, he gave up, whispered, "That's all, folks," into the mike, and put on a tape of Louis Armstrong singing "White Christmas."

# Daisy, in the Sun

N one of the others were any help. Daisy's brother, when she knelt beside him on the kitchen floor and said, "Do you remember when we lived at Grandma's house, just the three of us, nobody else?" looked at her blankly over the pages of his book, his face closed and uninterested. "What is your book about?" she asked kindly. "Is it about the sun? You always used to read your books out loud to me at Grandma's. All about the sun."

He stood up and went to the windows of the kitchen and looked out at the snow, tracing patterns on the dry window. The book, when Daisy looked at it, was about something else altogether.

"It didn't always snow like this at home, did it?" Daisy would ask her grandmother. "It couldn't have snowed all the time, not even in Canada, could it?"

It was the train this time, not the kitchen, but her grandmother went on measuring for the curtains as if she didn't notice. "How can the trains run if it snows all the time?" Her grandmother didn't answer her. She went on measuring the wide curved train windows with her long yellow tape measure. She wrote the measurements on little slips of paper, and they drifted from her pockets like the snow outside, without sound.

Daisy waited until it was the kitchen again. The red cafe curtains hung streaked and limp across the bottom half of the square windows. "The sun faded the curtains, didn't it?" she asked slyly, but her grandmother would not be tricked. She measured and wrote and dropped the measurements like ash around her.

Daisy looked from her grandmother to the rest of them, shambling up and down the length of her grandmother's kitchen. She would not ask them. Talking to them would be like admitting they belonged here, muddling clumsily around the room, bumping into each other.

Daisy stood up. "It *was* the sun that faded them," she said. "I remember," and went into her room and shut the door.

The room was always her own room, no matter what happened outside. It stayed the same, yellow ruffled muslin on the bed, yellow priscillas at the window. She had refused to let her mother put blinds up in her room. She remembered that quite clearly. She had stayed in her room the whole day with her door barricaded. But she could not remember why her mother had wanted to put them up or what had happened afterward.

Daisy sat down cross-legged in the middle of the bed, hugging the yellow ruffled pillow from her bed against her chest. Her mother constantly reminded her that a young lady sat with her legs together. "You're fifteen, Daisy. You're a young lady whether you like it or not."

Why could she remember things like that and not how they had gotten here and where her mother was and why it snowed all the time yet was never cold? She hugged the pillow tightly against her and tried, tried to remember.

It was like pushing against something, something both yielding and unyielding. It was herself, trying to push her breasts flat against her chest after her mother had told her she was growing up, that she would need to wear a bra. She had tried to push through to the little girl she had been before, but even though she pressed them into herself with the flats of her hands, they were still there. A barrier, impossible to get through.

Daisy clutched at the yielding pillow, her eyes squeezed shut. "Grandma came in," she said out loud, reaching for the one memory she could get to, "Grandma came in and said…"

She was looking at one of her brother's books. She had been holding it, looking at it, one of her brother's books about the sun, and as the door opened he reached out and took it away from her. He was angry—about the book? Her grandmother came in, looking hot and excited, and he took the book away from her. Her grandmother said, "They got the material in. I bought enough for all the windows." She had a sack full of folded cloth, red-and-white gingham. "I bought almost the whole bolt," her grandmother said. She was flushed. "Isn't it pretty?" Daisy reached out to touch the thin pretty cloth. And…Daisy clutched at the pillow, wrinkling the ruled edge. She had reached out to touch the thin pretty cloth and then…

It was no use. She could not get any further. She had never been able to get any further. Sometimes she sat on her bed for days. Sometimes she started at the end and worked back through the memory and it was still the same. She could not remember any more on either side. Only the book and her grandmother coming in and reaching out her hand.

Daisy opened her eyes. She put the pillow back on the bed and uncrossed her legs and took a deep breath. She was going to have to ask the others. There was nothing else to do.

She stood a minute by the door before she opened it, wondering which of the places it would be. It was her mother's living room, the walls a cool blue and the windows covered with venetian blinds. Her brother sat on the gray-blue carpet reading. Her grandmother had taken down one of the blinds. She was measuring the tall window. Outside the snow fell.

The strangers moved up and down on the blue carpet. Sometimes Daisy thought she recognized them, that they were friends of her parents or people she had seen at school, but she could not be sure. They did not speak to each other in their endless, patient wanderings. They did not even seem to see each other. Sometimes, passing down the long aisle of the train or circling her grandmother's kitchen or pacing the blue living room, they bumped into each other. They did not stop and say excuse me. They bumped into each other as if they did not know they did it, and moved on. They collided without sound or feeling, and each time they did, they seemed less and less like people Daisy knew and more and more like strangers. She looked at them anxiously, trying to recognize them so she could ask them.

The young man had come in from outside. Daisy was sure of it, though there was no draft of cold air to convince her, no snow for the young man to shrug from his hair and shoulders. He moved with easy direction through the others, and they looked up at him as he passed. He sat down on the blue couch and smiled at Daisy's brother. Her brother looked up from his book and smiled back. He has come in from outside, Daisy thought. He will know.

She sat down near him, on the end of the couch, her arms crossed in front of her. "Has something happened to the sun?" she asked him in a whisper.

He looked up. His face was as young as hers, tanned and smiling. Daisy felt, far down, a little quiver of fear, a faint alien feeling like that which had signaled the coming of her first period. She stood up and backed away from him, only a step, and nearly collided with one of the strangers.

"Well, hello," the boy said. "If it isn't little Daisy!"

Her hands knotted into fists. She did not see how she could not have recognized him before: the easy confidence, the casual smile. He would not help her. He knew, of course he knew, he had always known everything, but he wouldn't tell her. He would laugh at her. She must not let him laugh at her.

"Hi, Ron," she was going to say, but the last consonant drifted away into uncertainty. She had never been sure what his name was.

He laughed. "What makes you think something's happened to the sun, Daisy-Daisy?" He had his arm over the back of the couch. "Sit down and tell me all about it." If she sat down next to him he could easily put his arm around her.

"Has something happened to the sun?" she repeated more loudly from where she stood. "It never shines anymore."

"Are you sure?" he said, and laughed again. He was looking at her breasts. She crossed her arms in front of her.

"Has it?" she said stubbornly, like a child.

"What do you think?"

"I think maybe everybody was wrong about the sun." She stopped, surprised at what she had said, at what she was remembering now. Then she went on, forgetting to keep her arms in front of her, listening to what she said next. "They all thought it was going to blow up. They said it would swallow the whole earth up. But maybe it didn't. Maybe it just burned out, like a match or something, and it doesn't shine anymore and that's why it snows all the time and—"

"Cold," Ron said.

"What?"

"Cold," he said. "Wouldn't it be cold if that had happened?"

"What?" she said stupidly.

"Daisy," he said, and smiled at her. She reeled a little. The tugging fear was further down and more definite.

"Oh," she said, and ran veering around the others milling up and down, up and down, into her own room. She slammed the door behind her and lay down on the bed, holding her stomach and remembering.

⊣•••⊢

Her father had called them all together in the living room. Her mother perched on the edge of the blue couch, already looking frightened. Her brother had brought a book in with him, but he stared blindly at the page.

It was cold in the living room. Daisy moved into the one patch of sunlight, and waited. She had already been frightened for a year. And in a minute, she thought, I'm going to hear something that will make me more afraid.

She felt a sudden stunning hatred of her parents, able to pull her in out of the sun and into darkness, able to make her frightened just by talking to her. She had been sitting on the porch today. That other day she had been lying in the sun in her old yellow bathing suit when her mother called her in.

"You're a big girl now," her mother had said once they were in her room. She was looking at the outgrown yellow suit that was tight across the chest and pulled up on the legs. "There are things you need to know."

Daisy's heart had begun to pound. "I wanted to tell you so you wouldn't hear a lot of rumors." She had had a booklet with her, pink and white and terrifying. "I want you to read this, Daisy. You're changing, even though you may not notice it. Your breasts are developing and soon you'll be starting your period. That means—"

Daisy knew what it meant. The girls at school had told her. Darkness and blood. Boys wanting to touch her breasts, wanting to penetrate her darkness. And then more blood.

"No," Daisy said. "No. I don't want to."

"I know it seems frightening to you now, but someday soon you'll meet a nice boy and then you'll understand…"

No, I won't. Never. I know what boys do to you.

"Five years from now you won't feel this way, Daisy. You'll see…"

Not in five years. Not in a hundred. No.

"I won't have breasts," Daisy shouted, and threw the pillow off her bed at her mother. "I won't have a period. I won't let it happen. No!"

Her mother had looked at her pityingly. "Why, Daisy, it's already started." She had put her arms around her. "There's nothing to be afraid of, honey."

Daisy had been afraid ever since. And now she would be more afraid, as soon as her father spoke.

"I wanted to tell you all together," her father said, "so you would not hear some other way. I wanted you to know what is really happening and not just rumors." He paused and took a ragged breath. They even started their speeches alike.

"I think you should hear it from me," her father said. "The sun is going to go nova."

Her mother gasped, a long, easy intake of breath like a sigh, the last easy breath her mother would take. Her brother closed his book. Is that all? Daisy thought, surprised.

"The sun has used up all the hydrogen in its core. It's starting to burn itself up, and when it does, it will expand and—" he stumbled over the word.

"It's going to swallow us up," her brother said. "I read it in a book. The sun will just explode, all the way out to Mars. It'll swallow up Mercury and Venus and Earth and Mars and we'll all be dead."

Her father nodded. "Yes," he said, as if he was relieved that the worst was out.

"No," her mother said. And Daisy thought, This is nothing. Nothing. Her mother's talks were worse than this. Blood and darkness.

"There have been changes in the sun," her father said. "There have been more solar storms, too many. And the sun is releasing unusual bursts of neutrinos. Those are signs that it will—"

"How long?" her mother asked.

"A year. Five years at the most. They don't know."

"We have to stop it!" Daisy's mother shrieked, and Daisy looked up from her place in the sun, amazed at her mother's fear.

"There's nothing we can do," her father said. "It's already started."

"I won't let it," her mother said. "Not to my children. I won't let it happen. Not to my Daisy. She's always loved the sun."

At her mother's words, Daisy remembered something. An old photograph her mother had written on, scrawling across the bottom of the picture in white ink. The picture was herself as a toddler in a yellow sunsuit, concave little girl's chest and pooching toddler's stomach. Bucket and shovel and toes dug into the hot sand, squinting up into the sunlight. And her mother's writing across the bottom: "Daisy, in the sun."

Her father had taken her mother's hand and was holding it. He had put his arm around her brother's shoulders. Their heads were ducked, prepared for a blow, as if they thought a bomb was going to fall on them.

Daisy thought, All of us, in a year or maybe five, surely five at the most, all of us children again, warm and happy, in the sun. She could not make herself be afraid.

—|•••|—

It was the train again. The strangers moved up and down the long aisle of the dining car, knocking against each other randomly. Her grandmother measured the little window in the door at the end of the car. She did not look out the window at the ashen snow. Daisy could not see her brother.

Ron was sitting at one of the tables that were covered with the heavy worn white damask of dining cars. The vase and dull silver on the table were heavy so they would not fall off with the movement of the train. Ron leaned back in his chair and looked out the window at the snow.

Daisy sat down across the table from him. Her heart was beating painfully in her chest. "Hi," she said. She was afraid to add his name for fear the word would trail away as it had before and he would know how frightened she was.

He turned and smiled at her. "Hello, Daisy-Daisy," he said.

She hated him with the same sudden intensity she had felt for her parents, hated him for his ability to make her afraid.

"What are you doing here?" she asked.

He turned slightly in the seat and grinned at her.

"You don't belong here," she said belligerently. "I went to Canada to live with my grandmother." Her eyes widened. She had not known that before she said it. "I didn't even know you. You worked in the grocery store when we lived in California." She was suddenly overwhelmed by what she was saying. "You don't belong here," she murmured.

"Maybe it's all a dream, Daisy."

She looked at him, still angry, her chest heaving with the shock of remembering. "What?"

"I said, maybe you're just dreaming all this." He put his elbows on the table and leaned toward her. "You always had the most incredible dreams, Daisy-Daisy."

She shook her head. "Not like this. They weren't like this. I always had good dreams." The memory was coming now, faster this time, a throbbing in her sides where the pink and white book said her ovaries were. She was not sure she could make it to her room. She stood up, clutching at the white tablecloth. "They weren't like this." She stumbled through the milling people toward her room.

"Oh, and Daisy," Ron said. She stopped, her hand on the door of her room, the memory almost there. "You're still cold."

"What?" she said blankly.

"Still cold. You're getting warmer, though."

She wanted to ask him what he meant, but the memory was upon her. She shut the door behind her, breathing heavily, and groped for the bed.

—|•••|—

All her family had had nightmares. The three of them sat at breakfast with drawn, tired faces, their eyes looking bruised. The lead-backed curtains for the kitchen hadn't come yet, so they had to eat breakfast in the living room where they could close the venetian blinds. Her mother and father sat on the blue couch with their knees against the crowded coffee table. Daisy and her brother sat on the floor.

Her mother said, staring at the closed blinds, "I dreamed I was full of holes, tiny little holes, like dotted Swiss."

"Now, Evelyn," her father said.

Her brother said, "I dreamed the house was on fire and the fire trucks came and put it out, but then the fire trucks caught on fire and the fire men and the trees and—"

"That's enough," her father said. "Eat your breakfast." To his wife he said gently, "Neutrinos pass through all of us all the time. They pass right through the earth. They're completely harmless. They don't make holes at all. It's nothing, Evelyn. Don't worry about the neutrinos. They can't hurt you."

"Daisy, you had a dotted Swiss dress once, didn't you?" her mother said still looking at the blinds. "It was yellow. All those little dots, like holes."

"May I be excused?" her brother asked, holding a book with a photo of the sun on the cover.

Her father nodded and her brother went outside, already reading. "Wear your hat!" Daisy's mother said, her voice rising perilously on the last word. She watched him until he was out of the room, then she turned and looked at Daisy with her bruised eyes. "You had a nightmare too, didn't you, Daisy?"

Daisy shook her head, looking down at her bowl of cereal. She had been looking out between the venetian blinds before breakfast, looking out at the forbidden sun. The stiff plastic blinds had caught open, and now there was a little triangle of sunlight on Daisy's bowl of cereal. She and her mother were both looking at it. Daisy put her hand over the light.

"Did you have a nice dream, then, Daisy, or don't you remember?" She sounded accusing.

"I remember," Daisy said, watching the sunlight on her hand. She had dreamed of a bear. A massive golden bear with shining fur. Daisy was playing ball with the bear. She had in her two hands a little blue-green ball. The bear reached out lazily with his wide golden arm and swatted the blue ball out of Daisy's hands and away. The wide, gentle sweep of his great paw was the most beautiful thing she had ever seen. Daisy smiled to herself at the memory of it.

"Tell me your dream, Daisy," her mother said.

"All right," Daisy said angrily "It was about a big yellow bear and a little blue ball that he swatted." She swung her arm toward her mother.

Her mother winced.

"Swatted us all to kingdom come, Mother!" she shouted and flung herself out of the dark living room into the bright morning sun.

"Wear your hat," her mother called after her, and this time the last word rose almost to a scream.

Daisy stood against the door for a long time watching him. He was talking to her grandmother. She had put down her yellow tape measure with the black coal numbers and was nodding and smiling at what he said. After a very long time he reached out his hand and covered hers, patting it kindly.

Her grandmother stood up slowly and went to the window, where the faded red curtains did not shut out the snow, but she did not look at the curtains. She stood and looked out at the snow, smiling faintly and without anxiety.

Daisy edged her way through the crowd in the kitchen, frowning, and sat down across from Ron. His hands still rested flat on the red linoleum-topped table. Daisy put her hands on the table, too, almost touching his. She turned them palm up, in a gesture of helplessness.

"It isn't a dream, is it?" she asked him.

His fingers were almost touching hers. "What makes you think I'd know? I don't belong here, remember? I work in a grocery store, remember?"

"You know everything," she said simply.

"Not everything."

The cramp hit her. Her hands, still palm up, shook a little and then groped for the metal edge of the red table as she tried to straighten up.

"Warmer all the time, Daisy-Daisy," he said.

She did not make it to her room. She leaned helplessly against the door and watched her grandmother, measuring and writing and dropping the little slips of paper around her. And remembered.

—|•••|—

Her mother did not even know him. She had seen him at the grocery store. Her mother, who never went out, who wore sunglasses and long-sleeved shirts and a sun hat, even inside the darkened blue living room—her mother had met him at the grocery store and brought him home. She had taken off her hat and her ridiculous gardening gloves and gone to the grocery store to find him. It must have taken incredible courage.

"He said he'd seen you at school and wanted to ask you out himself, but he was afraid I'd say you were too young, isn't that right, Ron?" Her mother spoke in a rapid, nervous voice. Daisy was not sure whether she had said Ron or Rob or Rod. "So I said why don't you just come on home with me right now and meet her? There's no time like the present, I say. Isn't that right, Ron?"

He was not embarrassed by her at all. "Would you like to go get a Coke, Daisy? I've got my car here."

"Of course she wants to go. Don't you, Daisy?"

No. She wished the sun would reach out lazily, the great golden bear, and swat them all away. Right now.

"Daisy," her mother said, hastily brushing at her hair with her fingers. "There's so little time left. I wanted you to have..." Darkness and blood. You wanted me to be as frightened as you are. Well, I'm not, Mother. It's too late. We're almost there now.

But when she went outside with him, she saw his convertible parked at the curb, and she felt the first faint flutter of fear. It had the top down. She looked up at his tanned, smiling face, and thought, He isn't afraid.

"Where do you want to go, Daisy?" he asked. He had his bare arm across the back of the seat. He could easily move it from there to around her shoulders. Daisy sat against the door, her arms wrapped around her chest.

"I'd like to go for a ride. With the top down. I love the sun," she said to frighten him, to see the same expression she could see on her mother's face when Daisy told her lies about the dreams.

"Me, too," he said. "It sounds like you don't believe all that garbage they feed us about the sun, either. It's a lot of scare talk, that's all. You don't see me getting skin cancer, do you?" He moved his golden-tanned arm lazily around her shoulder to show her. "A lot of people getting hysterical for nothing. My physics teacher says the sun could emit neutrinos at the present rate for five thousand years before the sun would collapse.

All this stuff about the aurora borealis. Geez, you'd think these people had never seen a solar flare before. There's nothing to be afraid of, Daisy-Daisy."

He moved his arm dangerously close to her breast.

"Do you have nightmares?" she asked him, desperate to frighten him.

"No. All my dreams are about you." His fingers traced a pattern, casually, easily on her blouse. "What do you dream about?"

She thought she would frighten him like she frightened her mother. Her dreams always seemed so beautiful, but when she began to tell them to her mother, her mother's eyes became wide and dark with fear. And then Daisy would change the dream, make it sound worse than it was, ruin its beauty to make it frighten her mother.

"I dreamed I was rolling a golden hoop. It was hot. It burned my hand whenever I touched it. I was wearing earrings, little golden hoops in my ears that spun like the hoop when I ran. And a golden bracelet." She watched his face as she told him, to see the fear. He traced the pattern aimlessly with his finger, closer and closer to the nipple of her breast.

"I rolled the hoop down a hill and it started rolling faster and faster. I couldn't keep up with it. It rolled on by itself, like a wheel, a golden wheel, rolling over everything."

She had forgotten her purpose. She had told the dream as she remembered it, with the little secret smile at the memory. His hand had closed over her breast and rested there, warm as the sun on her face.

He looked as if he didn't know it was there. "Boy, my psych teacher would have a ball with that one! Who would think a kid like you could have a sexy dream like that? Wow! Talk about Freudian! My psych teacher says—"

"You think you know everything, don't you?" Daisy said.

His fingers traced the nipple through her thin blouse, tracing a burning circle, a tiny burning hoop.

"Not quite," he said, and bent close to her face. Darkness and blood. "I don't know quite how to take you."

She wrenched free of his face, free of his arm. "You won't take me at all. Not ever. You'll be dead. We'll all be dead in the sun," she said, and flung herself out of the convertible and back into the darkened house.

⊣•••⊢

Daisy lay doubled up on the bed for a long time after the memory was gone. She would not talk to him anymore. She could not remember anything without him, but she did not care. It was all a dream anyway. What did it matter? She hugged her arms to her.

It was not a dream. It was worse than a dream. She sat very straight on the edge of the bed, her head up and her arms at her side, her feet together on the floor, the way a young lady was supposed to sit. When she stood up, there was no hesitation in her manner. She walked straight to the door and opened it. She did not stop to see what room it was. She did not even glance at the strangers milling up and down. She went straight to Ron and put her hand on his shoulder.

"This is hell, isn't it?"

He turned, and there was something like hope on his face. "Why, Daisy!" he said, and took her hands and pulled her down to sit beside him. It was the train. Their folded hands rested on the white damask tablecloth. She looked at the hands. There was no use trying to pull away.

Her voice did not shake. "I was very unkind to my mother. I used to tell her my dreams just to make her frightened. I used to go out without a hat, just because it scared her so much. She couldn't help it. She was so afraid the sun would explode." She stopped and stared at her hands. "I think it did explode and everybody died, like my father said. I think...I should have lied to her about the dreams. I should have told her I dreamed about boys, about growing up, about things that didn't frighten her. I could have made up nightmares like my brother did."

"Daisy," he said. "I'm afraid confessions aren't quite in my line. I don't—"

"She killed herself," Daisy said. "She sent us to my grandmother's in Canada and then she killed herself. And so I think that if we are all dead, then I went to hell. That's what hell is, isn't it? Coming face to face with what you're most afraid of."

"Or what you love. Oh, Daisy," he said, holding her fingers tightly, "whatever made you think that this was hell?"

In her surprise, she looked straight into his eyes. "Because there isn't any sun," she said.

His eyes burned her, burned her. She felt blindly for the white-covered table, but the room had changed. She could not find it. He pulled her down beside him on the blue couch. With him still clinging to her hands, still holding onto her, she remembered.

—|•••|—

They were being sent away, to protect them from the sun. Daisy was just as glad to go. Her mother was angry with her all the time. She forced Daisy to tell her her dreams every morning at breakfast in the dark living room. Her mother had put blackout curtains up over the blinds so that no light got in at all, and in the blue twilight not even the little summer slants of light from the blinds fell on her mother's frightened face.

There was nobody on the beaches. Her mother would not let her go out, even to the grocery store, without a hat and sunglasses. She would not let them fly to Canada. She was afraid of magnetic storms. They sometimes interrupted the radio signals from the towers. Her mother was afraid the plane would crash.

She sent them on the train, kissing them goodbye at the train station, for the moment oblivious to the long dusty streaks of light from the vaulted train-station windows. Her brother went ahead of them out to the platform, and her mother pulled Daisy suddenly into a dark shadowed corner. "What I told you before, about your period, that won't happen now. The radiation—I called the doctor and he said not to worry. It's happening to everyone."

Again Daisy felt the faint pull of fear. Her period had started months ago, dark and bloody as she had imagined. She had not told anyone. "I won't worry," she said.

"Oh, my Daisy," her mother said suddenly. "My Daisy in the sun," and seemed to shrink back into the darkness. But as they pulled out of the station, she came out into the direct sun and waved goodbye to them.

It was wonderful on the train. The few passengers stayed in their cabins with the shades drawn. There were no shades in the dining car, no people to tell Daisy to get out of the sunlight. She sat in the deserted dining car and looked out the wide windows. The train flew through forests, thin branchy forests of spindly pines and aspens. The sun flickered in on Daisy—sun and then shadows and then sun, running across her face. She and her brother ordered an orgy of milkshakes and desserts and nobody said anything to them.

Her brother read his books about the sun out loud to her. "Do you know what it's like in the middle of the sun?" he asked her. Yes. You stand with a bucket and a shovel and your bare toes digging into the sand, a child again, not afraid, squinting up into the yellow light.

"No," she said.

"Atoms can't even hold together in the middle of the sun. It's so crowded they bump into each other all the time, bump bump bump, like that, and their electrons fly off and run around free. Sometimes when there's a collision, it lets off an X-ray that goes whoosh, all the way out at the speed of light, like a ball in a pinball machine. Bing-bang-bing, all the way to the surface."

"Why do you read those books anyway? To scare yourself?"

"No. To scare Mom." That was a daring piece of honesty, suitable not even for the freedom of Grandma's, suitable only for the train. She smiled at him.

"You're not even scared, are you?"

She felt obliged to answer him with equal honesty. "No," she said, "not at all."

"Why not?"

Because it won't hurt. Because I won't remember afterwards. Because I'll stand in the sun with my bucket and shovel and look up and not be frightened. "I don't know," Daisy said. "I'm just not."

"I am. I dream about burning all the time. I think about how much it hurts when I burn my finger and then I dream about it hurting like that all over forever." He had been lying to their mother about his dreams, too.

"It won't be like that," Daisy said. "We won't even know it's happened. We won't remember a thing."

"When the sun goes nova, it'll start using itself up. The core will start filling up with atomic ash, and that'll make the sun start using up all its own fuel. Do you know it's pitch-dark in the middle of the sun? See, the radiations are X-rays, and they're too short to see. They're invisible. Pitch-dark and ashes falling around you. Can you imagine that?"

"It doesn't matter." They were passing a meadow and Daisy's face was full in the sun. "We won't be there. We'll be dead. We won't remember anything."

Daisy had not realized how relieved she would be to see her grandmother, narrow face sunburned, arms bare. She was not even wearing a hat. "Daisy, dear, you're growing up," she said. She did not make it sound like a death sentence. "And David, you still have your nose in a book, I see."

It was nearly dark when they got to her little house. "What's that?" David asked, standing on the porch.

Her grandmother's voice did not rise dangerously at all. "The aurora borealis. I tell you, we've had some shows up here lately. It's like the Fourth of July."

Daisy had not realized how hungry she had been to hear someone who was not afraid. She looked up. Great red curtains of light billowed almost to the zenith, fluttering in some solar wind. "It's beautiful," Daisy whispered, but her grandmother was holding the door open for her to go in, and so happy was she to see the clear light in her grandmothers eyes, she followed her into the little kitchen with its red linoleum table and the red curtains hanging at the windows.

"It is so nice to have company," her grandmother said, climbing onto a chair. "Daisy, hold this end, will you?" She dangled the long end of a yellow plastic ribbon down to Daisy. Daisy took it, looking anxiously at her grandmother. "What are you doing?" she asked.

"Measuring for new curtains, dear," she said, reaching into her pocket for a slip of paper and a pencil. "What's the length, Daisy?"

"Why do you need new curtains?" Daisy asked. "These look fine to me."

"They don't keep the sun out," her grandmother said. Her eyes had gone coal-black with fear. Her voice was rising with every word. "We have to have new curtains, Daisy, and there's no cloth. Not in the whole town, Daisy. Can you imagine that? We had to send to Ottawa. They bought up all the cloth in town. Can you imagine that, Daisy?"

"Yes," Daisy said, and wished she could be afraid.

Ron still held her hands tightly. She looked steadily at him. "Warmer, Daisy," he said. "Almost here."

"Yes," she said.

He untwined their fingers and rose from the couch. He walked through the crowd in the blue living room and went out the door into the snow. She did not try to go to her room. She watched them all, the strangers in their endless, random movement, her brother walking while he read, her grandmother standing on a chair, and the memory came quite easily and without pain.

"You wanta see something?" her brother asked.

Daisy was looking out the window. All day long the lights had been flickering, even though it was calm and silent outside. Their grandmother had gone to town to see if the fabric for the curtains had come in. Daisy did not answer him.

He shoved the book in front of her face. "That's a prominence," he said. The pictures were in black and white, like old-fashioned snapshots, only under them instead of her mother's scrawled white ink, it said, "High Altitude Observatory, Boulder, Colorado."

"That's an eruption of hot gas hundreds of thousands of feet high."

"No," Daisy said, taking the book into her own lap. "That's my golden hoop. I saw it in my dream."

She turned the page.

David leaned over her shoulder and pointed. "That was the big eruption in 1946 when it first started to go wrong only they didn't know it yet. It weighed a billion tons. The gas went out a million miles."

Daisy held the book like a snapshot of a loved one.

"It just went bash, and knocked all this gas out into space. There were all kinds of—"

"It's my golden bear," she said. The great paw of flame reached lazily out from the sun's black surface in the picture, the wild silky paw of flaming gas.

"This is the stuff you've been dreaming?" her brother asked. "This is the stuff you've been telling me about?" His voice went higher and higher. "I thought you said the dreams were nice."

"They were," Daisy said.

He pulled the book away from her and flipped angrily through the pages to a colored diagram on a black ground. It showed a glowing red ball with concentric circles drawn inside it. "There," he said, shoving it at Daisy. "That's what's going to happen to us." He jabbed angrily at one of the circles inside the red ball. "That's us. That's us! Inside the sun! Dream about that, why don't you?"

He slammed the book shut.

"But we'll all be dead, so it won't matter," Daisy said. "It won't hurt. We won't remember anything."

"That's what you think! You think you know everything. Well, you don't know what anything is. I read a book about it, and you know what it said? They don't even know what memory is. They think maybe it isn't even in the brain cells. That it's in the atoms somewhere, and even if we're blown apart, that memory stays. What if we do get burned by the sun and we still remember? What if we go on burning and burning and remembering and remembering forever?"

Daisy said quietly, "He wouldn't do that. He wouldn't hurt us." There had been no fear as she stood digging her toes into the sand and looking up at him, only wonder. He—"

"You're crazy!" her brother shouted. "You know that? You're crazy! You talk about him like he's your boyfriend or something! It's the sun, the wonderful sun that's going to kill us all!" He yanked the book away from her. He was crying.

"I'm sorry," Daisy was about to say, but their grandmother came in just then, hatless, with her hair blowing around her thin, sunburned face.

"They got the material in," she said jubilantly. "I bought enough for all the windows." She spilled out two sacks of red gingham. It billowed out across the table like the northern lights, red over red. "I thought it would never get here."

Daisy reached out to touch it.

She waited for him, sitting at the white-damask table of the dining car. He hesitated at the door, standing framed by the snow of ash behind him, and then came gaily in, singing.

"Daisy, Daisy, give me your theory do," he sang. He carried in his arms a bolt of red cloth. It billowed out from the bolt as he handed it to her grandmother—she standing on the chair, transfixed by joy, the pieces of paper, the yellow tape measure fallen from her forever.

Daisy came and stood in front of him.

"Daisy, Daisy," he said gaily. "Tell me—"

She put her hand on his chest. "No theory," she said. "I know."

"Everything, Daisy?" He smiled the easy, lopsided smile, and she thought sadly that even knowing, she would not be able to see him as he was, but only as the boy who had worked at the grocery store, the boy who had known everything.

"No, but I think I know." She held her hand firmly against his chest, over the flaming hoop of his breast. "I don't think we are people anymore. I don't know what we are—atoms stripped of our electrons maybe, colliding endlessly against each other in the center of the sun while it burns itself to ash in the endless snowstorm at its heart."

He gave her no clue. His smile was still confident, easy. "What about me, Daisy?" he asked.

"I think you are my golden bear, my flaming hoop, I think you are Ra, with no end to your name at all, Ra who knows everything."

"And who are you?"

"I am Daisy, who loved the sun."

He did not smile, did not change his mocking expression. But his tanned hand closed over hers, still pushing against his chest.

"What will I be now, an X-ray zigzagging all the way to the surface till I turn into light? Where will you take me after you have taken me? To Saturn, where the sun shines on the cold rings till they melt into happiness? Is that where you shine now, on Saturn? Will you take me there? Or will we stand forever like this, me with my bucket and shovel, squinting up at you?"

Slowly he gave her hand back to her. "Where do you want to go, Daisy?"

Her grandmother still stood on the chair, holding the cloth as if it were a benediction. Daisy reached out and touched the cloth, as she had in the moment when the sun went nova. She smiled up at her grandmother. "It's beautiful," she said. "I'm so glad it's come."

She bent suddenly to the window and pulled the faded curtains aside as if she thought because she knew she might be granted some sort of vision, might see for some small moment the little girl that was herself, with her little girl's chest and toddler's stomach;…might see herself as she really was: Daisy, in the sun. But all she could see was the endless snow.

Her brother was reading on the blue couch in her mother's living room. She stood over him, watching him read. "I'm afraid now," Daisy said, but it wasn't her brother's face that looked back at her.

All right, then, Daisy thought. None of them are any help. It doesn't matter. I have come face to face with what I fear and what I love and they are the same thing.

"All right, then," Daisy said, and turned back to Ron. "I'd like to go for a ride. With the top down." She stopped and squinted up at him. "I love the sun," she said.

When he put his arm around her shoulder, she did not move away. His hand closed on her breast and he bent down to kiss her.

# Personal Correspondence

# A Letter from the Clearys

There was a letter from the Clearys at the post office. I put it in my backpack along with Mrs. Talbot's magazine and went outside to untie Stitch.

He had pulled his leash out as far as it would go and was sitting around the corner, half strangled, watching a robin. Stitch never barks, not even at birds. He didn't even yip when Dad stitched up his paw. He just sat there the way we found him on the front porch, shivering a little and holding his paw up for Dad to look at. Mrs. Talbot says he's a terrible watchdog, but I'm glad he doesn't bark. Rusty barked all the time and look where it got him.

I had to pull Stitch back around the corner to where I could get enough slack to untie him. That took some doing because he really liked that robin. "It's a sign of spring, isn't it, fella?" I said, trying to get at the knot with my fingernails. I didn't loosen the knot, but I managed to break one of my fingernails off to the quick. Great. Mom will demand to know if I've noticed any other fingernails breaking.

My hands are a real mess. This winter I've gotten about a hundred burns on the back of my hands from that stupid wood stove of ours. One spot, just above my wrist, I keep burning over and over so it never has a chance to heal. The stove isn't big enough and when I try to jam a log in that's too long the same spot hits the inside of the stove every time. My stupid brother David won't saw them off to the right length. I've asked him and asked him to please cut them shorter, but he doesn't pay any attention to me.

I asked Mom if she would please tell him not to saw the logs so long, but she didn't. She never criticizes David. As far as she's concerned he can't do anything wrong just because he's twenty-three and was married.

"He does it on purpose," I told her. "He's hoping I'll burn to death."

"Paranoia is the number one killer of fourteen-year-old girls," Mom said. She always says that. It makes me so mad I feel like killing her. "He doesn't do it on purpose. You need to be more careful with the stove, that's all," but all the time she was holding my hand and looking at the big burn that won't heal like it was a time bomb set to go off.

"We need a bigger stove," I said, and yanked my hand away. We do need a bigger one. Dad closed up the fireplace and put the woodstove in when the gas bill was getting out of sight, but it's just a little one because Mom didn't want one that would stick way out in the living room. Anyway, we were only going to use it in the evenings.

We won't get a new one. They are all too busy working on the stupid greenhouse. Maybe spring will come early, and my hand will have half a chance to heal. I know better. Last winter the snow kept up till the middle of June and this is only March. Stitch's robin is going to freeze his little tail if he doesn't head back south. Dad says that last year was unusual, that the weather will be back to normal this year, but he doesn't believe it either or he wouldn't be building the greenhouse.

As soon as I let go of Stitch's leash, he backed around the corner like a good boy and sat there waiting for me to stop sucking my finger and untie him. "We'd better get a move on," I told him. "Mom'll have a fit." I was supposed to go by the general store to try and get some tomato seeds, but the sun was already pretty far west, and I had at least a half hour's walk home. If I got home after dark I'd get sent to bed without supper and then I wouldn't get to read the letter. Besides, if I didn't go to the general store today they would have to let me go tomorrow and I wouldn't have to work on the stupid greenhouse.

Sometimes I feel like blowing it up. There's sawdust and mud on everything, and David dropped one of the pieces of plastic on the stove while they were cutting it and it melted onto the stove and stinks to high heaven. But nobody else even notices the mess, they're so busy talking about how wonderful it's going to be to have homegrown watermelon and corn and tomatoes next summer.

I don't see how it's going to be any different from last summer. The only things that came up at all were the lettuce and the potatoes. The lettuce was about as tall as my broken fingernail and the potatoes were as hard as rocks. Mrs. Talbot said it was the altitude, but Dad said it was the funny weather and this crummy Pike's Peak granite that passes for soil around here and he went up to the little library in the back of the general store and got a do-it-yourself book on greenhouses and started tearing everything up and now even Mrs. Talbot is crazy about the idea.

The other day I told them, "Paranoia is the number one killer of people at this *altitude*," but they were too busy cutting slats and stapling plastic to even pay any attention to me.

Stitch walked along ahead of me, straining at his leash, and as soon as we were across the highway I took it off. He never runs away like Rusty used to. Anyway, it's impossible to keep him out of the road, and the times I've tried keeping him on his leash, he dragged me out into the middle and I got in trouble with Dad over leaving footprints. So I keep to the frozen edges of the road, and he moseys along, stopping to sniff at potholes, and when he gets behind I whistle at him and he comes running right up.

I walked pretty fast. It was getting chilly out, and I'd only worn my sweater. I stopped at the top of the hill and whistled at Stitch. We still had a mile to go. I could see the Peak from where I was standing. Maybe Dad is right about spring coming. There was hardly any snow on the Peak, and the burned part didn't look quite as dark as it did last fall, like maybe the trees are coming back.

Last year at this time the whole Peak was solid white. I remember because that was when Dad and David and Mr. Talbot went hunting and it snowed every day and they didn't get back for almost a month. Mom just about went crazy before they got back. She kept going up to the road to watch for them even though the snow was five feet deep and she was leaving footprints as big as the Abominable Snowman's. She took Rusty with her even though he hated the snow about as much as Stitch hates the dark. And she took a gun. One time she tripped over a branch and fell down in the snow. She sprained her ankle and was frozen stiff by the time she made it back to the house. I felt like saying, "Paranoia is the number one killer of mothers," but Mrs. Talbot butted in and said the next time I had to go with her and how this was what happened when people were allowed to go places by themselves, which meant me going to the post office. And I said I could take care of myself and Mom told me not to be rude to Mrs. Talbot and Mrs. Talbot was right, I should go with her the next time.

She wouldn't wait till her ankle was better. She bandaged it up and we went the very next day. She wouldn't say a word the whole trip, just limped through the snow. She never even looked up till we got to the road. The snow had stopped for a little while and the clouds had lifted enough so you could see the Peak. It was really neat, like a black-and-white photograph, the gray sky and the black trees and the white mountain. The Peak was completely covered with snow. You couldn't make out the toll road at all. We were supposed to hike up the Peak with the Clearys.

When we got back to the house, I said, "The summer before last the Clearys never came."

—|•••|—

Mom took off her mittens and stood by the stove, pulling off chunks of frozen snow. "Of course they didn't come, Lynn," she said.

Snow from my coat was dripping onto the stove and sizzling. "I didn't mean that," I said. "They were supposed to come the first week in June. Right after Rick graduated. So what happened? Did they just decide not to come or what?"

"I don't know," she said, pulling off her hat and shaking her hair out. Her bangs were all wet.

"Maybe they wrote to tell you they'd changed their plans," Mrs. Talbot said. "Maybe the post office lost the letter."

"It doesn't matter," Mom said.

"You'd think they'd have written or something," I said.

"Maybe the post office put the letter in somebody else's box," Mrs. Talbot said.

"It doesn't matter," Mom said, and went to hang her coat over the line in the kitchen. She wouldn't say another word about them. When Dad got home I asked him about the Clearys, too, but he was too busy telling about the trip to pay any attention to me.

Stitch didn't come. I whistled again and then started back after him. He was all the way at the bottom of the hill, his nose buried in something. "Come *on*," I said, and he turned around and then I could see why he hadn't come. He'd gotten himself tangled up in one of the electric wires that was down. He'd managed to get the cable wound around his legs like he does his leash sometimes, and the harder he tried to get out, the more he got tangled up.

He was right in the middle of the road. I stood on the edge of the road, trying to figure out a way to get to him without leaving footprints. The road was pretty much frozen at the top of the hill, but down here snow was still melting and running across the road in big rivers. I put my toe out into the mud, and my sneaker sank in a good half inch, so I backed up, rubbed out the toe print with my hand, and wiped my hand on my jeans. I tried to think what to do. Dad is as paranoiac about foot-prints as Mom is about my hands, but he is even worse about my being out after dark. If I didn't make it back in time he might even tell me I couldn't go to the post office anymore.

Stitch was coming as close as he ever would to barking. He'd gotten the wire around his neck and was choking himself. "All right," I said, "I'm coming." I jumped out as far as I could into one of the rivers and then waded the rest of the way to Stitch, looking back a couple of times to make sure the water was washing away the footprints.

I unwound Stitch like you would a spool of thread, and threw the loose end of the wire over to the side of the road, where it dangled from the pole, all ready to hang Stitch next time he comes along.

"You stupid dog," I said. "Now hurry!" and I sprinted back to the side of the road and up the hill in my sopping wet sneakers. He ran about five steps and stopped to sniff at a tree. "Come on!" I said. "It's getting dark. Dark!"

He was past me like a shot and halfway down the hill. Stitch is afraid of the dark. I know, there's no such thing in dogs. But Stitch really is. Usually I tell him, "Paranoia is the number one killer of dogs," but right now I wanted him to hurry before my feet started to freeze. I started run-ning, and we got to the bottom of the hill about the same time.

Stitch stopped at the driveway of the Talbots' house. Our house wasn't more than a few hundred feet from where I was standing, on the other side of the hill. Our house is down in kind of a well formed by hills on all sides. It's so deep and hidden you'd never even know it's there. You can't even see the smoke from our wood stove over the top of the Talbots' hill. There's a shortcut through the Talbots' property and down through the woods to our back door, but I don't take it anymore. "Dark, Stitch," I said sharply, and started running again. Stitch kept right at my heels.

The Peak was turning pink by the time I got to our driveway. Stitch peed on the spruce tree about a hundred times before I got it dragged back across the dirt driveway. It's a real big tree. Last summer Dad and David chopped it down and then made it look like it had fallen across the road. It completely covers up where the driveway meets the road, but the trunk is full of splinters, and I scraped my hand right in the same place as always. Great.

I made sure Stitch and I hadn't left any marks on the road (except for the marks he always leaves—another dog could find us in a minute. That's probably how Stitch showed up on our front porch, he smelled Rusty) and then got under cover of the hill as fast as I could. Stitch isn't the only one who gets nervous after dark. And besides, my feet were starting to hurt. Stitch was really paranoiac tonight. He didn't even take off running after we were in sight of the house.

David was outside, bringing in a load of wood. I could tell just by looking at it that they were all the wrong length. "Cutting it kind of close, aren't you?" he said. "Did you get the tomato seeds?"

"No," I said. "I brought you something else, though. I brought everybody something."

I went on in. Dad was rolling out plastic on the living room floor. Mrs. Talbot was holding one end for him. Mom was holding the card table, still folded up, waiting for them to finish so she could set it up in front of the stove for supper. Nobody even looked up. I unslung my backpack and took out Mrs. Talbot's magazine and the letter.

"There was a letter at the post office," I said. "From the Clearys."

They all looked up.

"Where did you find it?" Dad asked.

"On the floor, mixed in with all the third-class stuff. I was looking for Mrs. Talbot's magazine."

Mom leaned the card table against the couch and sat down. Mrs. Talbot looked blank.

"The Clearys were our best friends," I said. "From Illinois. They were supposed to come see us the summer before last. We were going to hike up Pike's Peak and everything."

David banged in the door. He looked at Mom sitting on the couch and Dad and Mrs. Talbot still standing there holding the plastic like a couple of statues. "What's wrong?" he said.

"Lynn says she found a letter from the Clearys today," Dad said.

David dumped the logs on the hearth. One of them rolled onto the carpet and stopped at Mom's feet. Neither of them bent over to pick it up.

"Shall I read it out loud?" I said, looking at Mrs. Talbot. I was still holding her magazine. I opened up the envelope and took out the letter.

"'Dear Janice and Todd and everybody,'" I read. "'How are things in the glorious west? We're raring to come out and see you, though we may not make it quite as soon as we hoped. How are Carla and David and the baby? I can't wait to see little David. Is he walking yet? I bet Grandma Janice is so proud she's busting her britches. Is that right? Do you westerners wear britches or have you all gone to designer jeans?'"

David was standing by the fireplace. He put his head down across his arms on the mantelpiece.

"'I'm sorry I haven't written, but we were very busy with Rick's graduation and anyway I thought we would beat the letter out to Colorado, but now it looks like there's going to be a slight change in plans. Rick has definitely decided to join the Army. Richard and I have talked ourselves blue in the face, but I guess we've just made matters worse. We can't even get him to wait to join until after the trip to Colorado. He says we'd spend the whole trip trying to talk him out of it, which is true, I guess. I'm just so worried about him. The Army! Rick says I worry too much, which is true too, I guess, but what if there was a war?'"

Mom bent over and picked up the log that David had dropped and laid it on the couch beside her.

"'If it's okay with you out there in the Golden West, we'll wait until Rick is done with basic the first week in July and then all come out. Please write and let us know if this is okay. I'm sorry to switch plans on you like this at the last minute, but look at it this way: you have a whole extra month to get into shape for hiking up Pike's Peak. I don't know about you, but I sure can use it.'"

Mrs. Talbot had dropped her end of the plastic. It didn't land on the stove this time, but it was so close to it it was curling from the heat. Dad just stood there watching it. He didn't even try to pick it up.

"'How are the girls? Sonja is growing like a weed. She's out for track this year and bringing home lots of medals and dirty sweat socks. And you should see her knees! They're so banged up I almost took her to the doctor. She says she scrapes them on the hurdles, and her coach says there's nothing to worry about, but it does worry me a little. They just don't seem to heal. Do you ever have problems like that with Lynn and Melissa?

"'I know, I know. I worry too much. Sonja's fine. Rick's fine. Nothing awful's going to happen between now and the first week in July, and we'll see you then. Love, the Clearys. P.S. Has anybody ever fallen off Pikes Peak?'"

Nobody said anything. I folded up the letter and put it back in the envelope.

"I should have written them," Mom said. "I should have told them, 'Come now.' Then they would have been here."

"And we would probably have climbed up Pike's Peak that day and gotten to see it all go blooie and us with it," David said, lifting his head up. He laughed and his voice caught on the laugh and kind of cracked. "I guess we should be glad they didn't come."

"Glad?" Mom said. She was rubbing her hands on the legs of her jeans. "I suppose we should be glad Carla took Melissa and the baby to Colorado Springs that day so we didn't have so many mouths to feed." She was rubbing her jeans so hard she was going to rub a hole right through them. "I suppose we should be glad those looters shot Mr. Talbot."

"No," Dad said. "But we should be glad the looters didn't shoot the rest of us. We should be glad they only took the canned goods and not the seeds. We should be glad the fires didn't get this far. We should be glad—"

"That we still have mail delivery?" David said. "Should we be glad about that too, Dad?" He went outside and shut the door behind him.

"When I didn't hear from them I should have called or something," Mom said.

Dad was still looking at the ruined plastic. I took the letter over to him. "Do you want to keep it or what?" I said.

"I think it's served its purpose," he said. He wadded it up, tossed it in the stove, and slammed the door shut. He didn't even get burned. "Come help me on the greenhouse, Lynn," he said.

It was pitch-dark outside and really getting cold. My sneakers were starting to get stiff. Dad held the flashlight and pulled the plastic tight over the wooden slats. I stapled the plastic every two inches all the way around the frame and my finger about every other time. After we finished one frame I asked Dad if I could go back in and put on my boots.

"Did you get the seeds for the tomatoes?" he said, like he hadn't even heard me. "Or were you too busy looking for the letter?"

"I didn't look for it," I said. "I found it. I thought you'd be glad to get the letter and know what happened to the Clearys."

Dad was pulling the plastic across the next frame, so hard it was getting little puckers in it. "We already knew," he said.

He handed me the flashlight and took the staple gun out of my hand. "You want me to say it?" he said. "You want me to tell you exactly what happened to them? All right. I would imagine they were close enough to Chicago to have been vaporized when the bombs hit. If they were, they were lucky. Because there aren't any mountains like ours around Chicago.

So they got caught in the fire storm or they died of flash burns or radiation sickness or else some looter shot them."

"Or their own family," I said.

"Or their own family." He put the staple gun against the wood and pulled the trigger. "I have a theory about what happened the summer before last," he said. He moved the gun down and shot another staple into the wood. "I don't think the Russians started it or the United States either. I think it was some little terrorist group somewhere or maybe just one person. I don't think they had any idea what would happen when they dropped their bomb. I think they were just so hurt and angry and frightened by the way things were that they just lashed out. With a bomb." He stapled the frame clear to the bottom and straightened up to start on the other side. "What do you think of that theory, Lynn?"

"I told you," I said. "I found the letter while I was looking for Mrs. Talbot's magazine."

He turned and pointed the staple gun at me. "But whatever reason they did it for, they brought the whole world crashing down on their heads. Whether they meant it or not, they had to live with the consequences."

"If they lived," I said. "If somebody didn't shoot them."

"I can't let you go to the post office anymore," he said. "It's too dangerous."

"What about Mrs. Talbot's magazines?"

"Go check on the fire," he said.

I went back inside. David had come back and was standing by the fireplace again, looking at the wall. Mom had set up the card table and the folding chairs in front of the fireplace. Mrs. Talbot was in the kitchen cutting up potatoes, only it looked like it was onions the way she was crying.

The fire had practically gone out. I stuck a couple of wadded-up magazine pages in to get it going again. The fire flared up with a brilliant blue and green. I tossed a couple of pine cones and some sticks onto the burning paper. One of the pine cones rolled off to the side and lay there in the ashes. I grabbed for it and hit my hand on the door of the stove.

Right in the same place. Great. The blister would pull the old scab off and we could start all over again. And of course Mom was standing right there, holding the pan of potato soup. She put it on the top of the stove and grabbed up my hand like it was evidence in a crime or something. She didn't say anything, she just stood there holding it and blinking.

"I burned it," I said. "I just burned it."

She touched the edges of the old scab, like she was afraid of catching something.

"It's a burn!" I shouted, snatching my hand back and cramming David's stupid logs into the stove. "It isn't radiation sickness. It's a burn."

"Do you know where your father is, Lynn?" she said as if she hadn't even heard me.

"He's out on the back porch," I said, "building his fucking greenhouse."

"He's gone," she said. "He took Stitch with him."

"He can't have taken Stitch," I said. "He's afraid of the dark." She didn't say anything. "Do you *know* how dark it is out there?'

"Yes," she said, and went and looked out the window. "I know how dark it is."

I got my parka off the hook by the fireplace and started out the door. David grabbed my arm. "Where the hell do you think you're going?"

I wrenched away from him. "To find Stitch. He's afraid of the dark."

"It's too dark," he said. "You'll get lost."

"So what? It's safer than hanging around this place," I said and slammed the door shut on his hand.

I made it halfway to the woodpile before he grabbed me again, this time with his other hand. I should have gotten them both with the door.

"Let me go," I said. "I'm leaving. I'm going to go find some other people to live with."

"There aren't any other people! For Christ's sake, we went all the way to South Park last winter. There wasn't anybody. We didn't even see those looters. And what if you run into them, the looters that shot Mr. Talbot?"

"What if I do? The worst they could do is shoot me. I've been shot at before."

"You're acting crazy, you know that, don't you?" he said. "Comin' in here out of the clear blue, taking potshots at everybody with that crazy letter!"

"Potshots!" I said, so mad I was afraid I was going to start crying. "Potshots! What about last summer? Who was taking potshots then?"

"You didn't have any business taking the shortcut," David said. "Dad told you never to come that way."

"Was that any reason to try and *shoot* me? Was that any reason to *kill* Rusty?"

David was squeezing my arm so hard I thought he was going to snap it right in two. "The looters had a dog with them. We found its tracks all around Mr. Talbot. When you took the shortcut and we heard Rusty barking, we thought you were the looters." He looked at me. "Mom's right. Paranoia's the number one killer. We were all a little crazy last summer. We're all a little crazy all the time, I guess, and then you pull a stunt like bringing that letter home, reminding everybody of everything that's happened, of everybody we've lost..." He let go of my arm and looked down at his hand like he didn't even know he'd practically broken my arm.

"I told you," I said. "I found it while I was looking for a magazine. I thought you'd all be glad I found it."

"Yeah," he said. "I'll bet."

He went inside and I stayed out a long time, waiting for Dad and Stitch. When I came in, nobody even looked up. Mom was still standing at the window. I could see a star over her head. Mrs. Talbot had stopped crying and was setting the table. Mom dished up the soup and we all sat down. While we were eating, Dad came in.

He had Stitch with him. And all the magazines. "I'm sorry, Mrs. Talbot," he said. "If you'd like, I'll put them under the house and you can send Lynn for them one at a time."

"It doesn't matter," she said. "I don't feel like reading them anymore."

Dad put the magazines on the couch and sat down at the card table. Mom dished him up a bowl of soup. "I got the seeds," he said. "The tomato seeds had gotten watersoaked, but the corn and squash were okay." He looked at me. "I had to board up the post office, Lynn," he said. "You understand that, don't you, that I can't let you go there anymore? It's just too dangerous."

"I told you," I said. "I found it. While I was looking for a magazine."

"The fire's going out," he said.

After they shot Rusty I wasn't allowed to go anywhere for a month for fear they'd shoot me when I came home, not even when I promised to take the long way around. But then Stitch showed up and nothing happened and they let me start going again. I went every day till the end of summer and after that whenever they'd let me. I must have looked through every pile of mail a hundred times before I found the letter from the Clearys. Mrs. Talbot was right about the post office. The letter was in somebody else's box.

# Newsletter

Later examination of weather reports and newspapers showed that it may have started as early as October nineteenth, but the first indication I had that something unusual was going on was at Thanksgiving.

I went to Mom's for dinner (as usual), and was feeding cranberries and cut-up oranges into Mom's old-fashioned meat grinder for the cranberry relish and listening to my sister-in-law Allison talk about her Christmas newsletter (also as usual).

"Which of Cheyenne's accomplishments do you think I should write about first, Nan?" she said, spreading cheese on celery sticks. "Her playing lead snowflake in *The Nutcracker* or her hitting a home run in Peewee Soccer?"

"I'd list the Nobel Peace Prize first," I murmured, under cover of the crunch of an apple being put through the grinder.

"There just isn't room to put in all the girls' accomplishments," she said, oblivious. "Mitch insists I keep it to one page."

"That's because of Aunt Lydia's newsletters," I said. "Eight pages single-spaced."

"I know," she said. "And in that tiny print you can barely read." She waved a celery stick thoughtfully. "That's an idea."

"Eight pages single-spaced?"

"No. I could get the computer to do a smaller font. That way I'd have room for Dakota's Sunshine Scout merit badges. I got the cutest paper for my newsletters this year. Little angels holding bunches of mistletoe."

Christmas newsletters are *very* big in my family, in case you couldn't tell. Everybody—uncles, grandparents, second cousins, my sister Sueann—sends the Xeroxed monstrosities to family, coworkers, old friends from high school, and people they met on their cruise to the Caribbean (which they wrote about at length in their newsletter the year before). Even my Aunt Irene, who writes a handwritten letter on every one of her Christmas cards, sticks a newsletter in with it.

My second cousin Lucille's are the worst, although there are a lot of contenders. Last year hers started:

*"Another year has hurried past*
*And, here I am, asking, 'Where did the time go so fast?'*
*A trip in February, a bladder operation in July,*
*Too many activities, not enough time, no matter how hard I try."*

At least Allison doesn't put Dakota and Cheyenne's accomplishments into verse.

"I don't think I'm going to send a Christmas newsletter this year," I said.

Allison stopped, cheese-filled knife in hand. "Why not?"

"Because I don't have any news. I don't have a new job, I didn't go on a vacation to the Bahamas, I didn't win any awards. I don't have anything to tell."

"Don't be ridiculous," my mother said, sweeping in carrying a foil-covered casserole dish. "Of course you do, Nan. What about that sky-diving class you took?"

"That was last year, Mom," I said. And I had only taken it so I'd have something to write about in my Christmas newsletter.

"Well, then, tell about your social life. Have you met anybody lately at work?"

Mom asks me this every Thanksgiving. Also Christmas, the Fourth of July, and every time I see her.

"There's nobody to meet," I said, grinding cranberries. "Nobody new ever gets hired, because nobody ever quits. Everybody who works there's been there for years. Nobody even gets fired. Bob Hunziger hasn't been to work on time in eight years, and *he's* still there."

"What about...what was his name?" Allison said, arranging the celery sticks in a cut-glass dish. "The guy you liked who had just gotten divorced?"

"Gary," I said. "He's still hung up on his ex-wife."

"I thought you said she was a real shrew."

"She is," I said. "Marcie the Menace. She calls him twice a week complaining about how unfair the divorce settlement is, even though she got virtually everything. Last week it was the house. She claimed she'd been too upset by the divorce to get the mortgage refinanced and he owed her twenty thousand dollars because now interest rates have gone up. But it doesn't matter. Gary still keeps hoping they'll get back together. He almost didn't fly to Connecticut to his parents' for Thanksgiving because he thought she might change her mind about a reconciliation."

"You could write about Sueann's new boyfriend," Mom said, sticking marshmallows on the sweet potatoes. "She's bringing him today."

This was as usual, too. Sueann always brings a new boyfriend to Thanksgiving dinner. Last year it was a biker. And no, I don't mean one of those nice guys who wear a beard and black Harley T-shirt on weekends and work as accountants between trips to Sturgis. I mean a Hell's Angel.

My sister Sueann has the worst taste in men of anyone I have ever known. Before the biker, she dated a member of a militia group and, after the ATF arrested him, a bigamist wanted in three states.

"If this boyfriend spits on the floor, I'm leaving," Allison said, counting out silverware. "Have you met him?" she asked Mom.

"No," Mom said, "but Sueann says he used to work where you do. Nan. So *somebody* must quit once in a while."

I racked my brain, trying to think of any criminal types who'd worked in my company. "What's his name?"

"David something," Mom said, and Cheyenne and Dakota raced into the kitchen, screaming, "Aunt Sueann's here. Aunt Sueann's here! Can we eat now?"

Allison leaned over the sink and pulled the curtains back to look out the window.

"What does he look like?" I asked, sprinkling sugar on the cranberry relish.

"Clean-cut," she said, sounding surprised. "Short blond hair, slacks, white shirt, tie."

Oh, no, that meant he was a neo-Nazi. Or married and planning to get a divorce as soon as the kids graduated from college—which would turn out to be in twenty-three years, since he'd just gotten his wife pregnant again.

"Is he handsome?" I asked, sticking a spoon into the cranberry relish.

"No," Allison said, even more surprised. "He's actually kind of ordinary-looking."

I came over to the window to look. He was helping Sueann out of the car. She was dressed up, too, in a dress and a denim slouch hat. "Good heavens," I said. "It's David Carrington. He worked up on fifth in Computing."

"Was he a womanizer?" Allison asked.

"No," I said, bewildered. "He's a very nice guy. He's unmarried, he doesn't drink, and he left to go get a degree in medicine."

"Why didn't *you* ever meet him?" Mom said.

⊣ • • • ⊢

David shook hands with Mitch, regaled Cheyenne and Dakota with a knock-knock joke, and told Mom his favorite kind of sweet potatoes were the ones with the marshmallows on top.

"He must be a serial killer," I whispered to Allison.

"Come on, everybody, let's sit down," Mom said. "Cheyenne and Dakota, you sit here by Grandma. David, you sit here, next to Sueann. Sueann, take off your hat. You know hats aren't allowed at the table."

"Hats for *men* aren't allowed at the table," Sueann said, patting her denim hat. "Women's hats are." She sat down. "Hats are coming back in style, did you know that? *Cosmopolitan*'s latest issue said this is the Year of the Hat."

"I don't care what it is," Mom said. "Your father would never have allowed hats at the table."

"I'll take it off if you'll turn off the TV," Sueann said, complacently opening out her napkin.

They had reached an impasse. Mom always has the TV on during meals. "I like to have it on in case something happens," she said stubbornly.

"Like what?" Mitch said. "Aliens landing from outer space?"

"For your information, there was a UFO sighting two weeks ago. It was on CNN."

"Everything looks delicious," David said. "Is that homemade cranberry relish? I *love* that. My grandmother used to make it."

He had to be a serial killer.

For half an hour, we concentrated on turkey, stuffing, mashed potatoes, green-bean casserole, scalloped corn casserole, marshmallow-topped sweet potatoes, cranberry relish, pumpkin pie, and the news on CNN.

"Can't you at least turn it down, Mom?" Mitch said. "We can't even hear to talk."

"I want to see the weather in Washington," Mom said. "For your flight."

"You're leaving tonight?" Sueann said. "But you just got here. I haven't even seen Cheyenne and Dakota."

"Mitch has to fly back tonight," Allison said. "But the girls and I are staying till Wednesday."

"I don't see why you can't stay at least until tomorrow," Mom said.

"Don't tell me this is homemade whipped cream on the pumpkin pie," David said. "I haven't had homemade whipped cream in years."

"You used to work in computers, didn't you?" I asked him. "There's a lot of computer crime around these days, isn't there?"

"Computers!" Allison said. "I forgot all the awards Cheyenne won at computer camp." She turned to Mitch. "The newsletter's going to have to be at least two pages. The girls just have too many awards—T ball, tadpole swimming, Bible-school attendance."

"Do you send Christmas newsletters in your family?" my mother asked David.

He nodded. "I love hearing from everybody."

"You see?" Mom said to me. "People *like* getting newsletters at Christmas."

"I don't have anything against Christmas newsletters," I said. "I just don't think they should be deadly dull. Mary had a root canal, Bootsy seems to be getting over her ringworm, we got new gutters on the house. Why doesn't anyone ever write about anything *interesting* in their newsletters?"

"Like what?" Sueann said.

"I don't know. An alligator biting their arm off. A meteor falling on their house. A murder. Something interesting to read."

"Probably because they didn't happen," Sueann said.

"Then they should make something up," I said, "so we don't have to hear about their trip to Nebraska and their gallbladder operation."

"You'd do that?" Allison said, appalled. "You'd make something up?"

"People make things up in their newsletters all the time, and you know it," I said. "Look at the way Aunt Laura and Uncle Phil brag about their vacations and their stock options and their cars. If you're going to lie, they might as well be lies that are interesting for other people to read."

"You have plenty of things to tell without making up lies, Nan," Mom said reprovingly. "Maybe you should do something like your cousin Celia. She writes her newsletter all year long, day by day" she explained to David. "Nan, you might have more news than you think if you kept track of it day by day like Celia. She always has a lot to tell."

Yes, indeed. Her newsletters were nearly as long as Aunt Lydia's. They read like a diary, except she wasn't in junior high, where at least there were pop quizzes and zits and your locker combination to give it a little zing. Celia's newsletters had no zing whatsoever:

"Wed. Jan. 1. Froze to death going out to get the paper. Snow got in the plastic bag thing the paper comes in. Editorial section all wet. Had to dry it out on the radiator. Bran flakes for breakfast. Watched *Good Morning America*."

"Thurs. Jan. 2. Cleaned closets. Cold and cloudy."

"If you'd write a little every day," Mom said, "you'd be surprised at how much you'd have to tell by Christmas."

Sure. With my life, I wouldn't even have to write it every day. I could do Monday's right now. "Mon. Nov. 28. Froze to death on the way to work. Bob Hunziger not in yet. Penny putting up Christmas decorations. Solveig told me she's sure the baby is going to be a boy. Asked me which name I liked, Albuquerque or Dallas. Said hi to Gary, but he was too depressed to talk to me. Thanksgiving reminds him of ex-wife's giblets. Cold and cloudy."

I was wrong. It was snowing, and Solveig's ultrasound had showed the baby was a girl. "What do you think of Trinidad as a name?" she asked me. Penny wasn't putting up Christmas decorations either. She was passing out slips of paper with our Secret Santas' names on them. "The decorations aren't here yet," she said excitedly. "I'm getting something special from a farmer upstate."

"Does it involve feathers?" I asked her. Last year the decorations had been angels with thousands of chicken feathers glued onto cardboard for their wings. We were still picking them out of our computers.

"No," she said happily "It's a surprise. I love Christmas, don't you?"

"Is Hunziger in?" I asked her, brushing snow out of my hair. Hats always mash my hair down, so I hadn't worn one.

"Are you kidding?" she said. She handed me a Secret Santa slip. "It's the Monday after Thanksgiving. He probably won't be in till sometime Wednesday."

Gary came in, his ears bright red from the cold and a harried expression on his face. His ex-wife must not have wanted a reconciliation.

"Hi, Gary," I said, and turned to hang up my coat without waiting for him to answer.

And he didn't, but when I turned back around, he was still standing there, staring at me. I put a hand up to my hair, wishing I'd worn a hat.

"Can I talk to you a minute?" he said, looking anxiously at Penny.

"Sure," I said, trying not to get my hopes up. He probably wanted to ask me something about the Secret Santas.

He leaned farther over my desk. "Did anything unusual happen to you over Thanksgiving?"

"My sister didn't bring home a biker to Thanksgiving dinner," I said.

He waved that away dismissively. "No, I mean anything odd, peculiar, out of the ordinary."

"That is out of the ordinary."

He leaned even closer. "I flew out to my parents' for Thanksgiving, and on the flight home—you know how people always carry on luggage that won't fit in the overhead compartments and then try to cram it in?"

"Yes," I said, thinking of a bridesmaid's bouquet I had made the mistake of putting in the overhead compartment one time.

"Well, nobody did that on my flight. They didn't carry on hanging bags or enormous shopping bags full of Christmas presents. Some people didn't even have a carry-on. And that isn't all. Our flight was half an hour late, and the flight attendant said, 'Those of you who do not have connecting flights, please remain seated until those with connections have deplaned.' And they did." He looked at me expectantly.

"Maybe everybody was just in the Christmas spirit."

He shook his head. "All four babies on the flight slept the whole way, and the toddler behind me didn't kick the seat."

That *was* unusual.

"Not only that, the guy next to me was reading *The Way of All Flesh* by Samuel Butler. When's the last time you saw anybody on an airplane reading anything but John Grisham or Danielle Steele? I tell you, there's something funny going on."

"What?" I asked curiously.

"I don't know," he said. "You're sure you haven't noticed anything?"

"Nothing except for my sister. She always dates these losers, but the guy she brought to Thanksgiving was really nice. He even helped with the dishes."

"You didn't notice anything else?"

"No," I said, wishing I had. This was the longest he'd ever talked to me about anything besides his ex-wife. "Maybe it's something in the air at DIA. I have to take my sister-in-law and her little girls to the airport Wednesday: I'll keep an eye out."

He nodded. "Don't say anything about this, okay?" he said, and hurried off to Accounting.

"What was that all about?" Penny asked, coming over.

"His ex-wife," I said. "When do we have to exchange Secret Santa gifts?"

"Every Friday and Christmas Eve."

I opened up my slip. Good, I'd gotten Hunziger. With luck I wouldn't have to buy any Secret Santa gifts at all.

⊣•••⊢

Tuesday I got Aunt Laura and Uncle Phil's Christmas newsletter. It was in gold ink on cream-colored paper, with large gold bells in the corners. "Joyeux Noel," it began. "That's French for Merry Christmas. We're sending our newsletter out early this year because we're spending Christmas in Cannes to celebrate Phil's promotion to assistant CEO and my wonderful new career! Yes, I'm starting my own business—Laura's Floral Creations—and orders are pouring in! It's already been written up in *House Beautiful*, and you will never guess who called last week—Martha Stewart!" Et cetera.

I didn't see Gary. Or anything unusual, although the waiter who took my lunch order actually got it right for a change. But he got Tonya's (who works up on third) wrong.

"I told him tomato and lettuce only," she said, picking pickles off her sandwich. "I heard Gary talked to you yesterday. Did he ask you out?"

"What's that?" I said, pointing to the folder Tonya'd brought with her to change the subject. "The Harbrace file?"

"No," she said. "Do you want my pickles? It's our Christmas schedule. Never marry anybody who has kids from a previous marriage. Especially when you have kids from a previous marriage. Tom's ex-wife, Janine, my ex-husband, John, and four sets of grandparents all want the kids, and they all want them on Christmas morning. It's like trying to schedule the D-Day invasion."

"At least your husband isn't still hung up on his ex-wife," I said glumly.

"So Gary didn't ask you out, huh?" She bit into her sandwich, frowned, and extracted another pickle. "I'm sure he will. Okay, if we take the kids to Tom's parents at four on Christmas Eve, Janine could pick them up at eight....No, that won't work." She switched her sandwich to her other hand and began erasing. "Janine's not speaking to Tom's parents."

She sighed. "At least John's being reasonable. He called yesterday and said he'd be willing to wait till New Year's to have the kids. I don't know what got into him."

⊣ • • • ⊢

When I got back to work, there was a folded copy of the morning newspaper on my desk.

I opened it up. The headline read "City Hall Christmas Display to Be Turned On," which wasn't unusual. And neither was tomorrow's headline, which would be "City Hall Christmas Display Protested."

Either the Freedom Against Faith people protest the Nativity scene or the fundamentalists protest the elves or the environmental people protest cutting down Christmas trees or all of them protest the whole thing. It happens every year.

I turned to the inside pages. Several articles were circled in red, and there was a note next to them which read "See what I mean? Gary."

I looked at the circled articles. "Christmas Shoplifting Down," the first one read. "Mall stores report incidences of shoplifting are down for the first week of the Christmas season. Usually prevalent this time of—"

"What are you doing?" Penny said, looking over my shoulder.

I shut the paper with a rustle. "Nothing," I said. I folded it back up and stuck it into a drawer. "Did you need something?"

"Here." she said, handing me a slip of paper.

"I already got my Secret Santa name," I said.

"This is for Holiday Goodies," she said. "Everybody takes turns bringing in coffee cake or tarts or cake."

I opened up my slip. It read "Friday Dec. 20. Four dozen cookies."

"I saw you and Gary talking yesterday," Penny said. "What about?"

"His ex-wife," I said. "What kind of cookies do you want me to bring?"

"Chocolate chip," she said. "Everybody loves chocolate."

As soon as she was gone, I got the newspaper out again and took it into Hunziger's office to read. "Legislature Passes Balanced Budget," the other articles read. "Escaped Convict Turns Self In," "Christmas Food Bank Donations Up."

I read through them and then threw the paper into the wastebasket. Halfway out the door I thought better of it and took it out, folded it up, and took it back to my desk with me.

While I was putting it into my purse, Hunziger wandered in. "If anybody asks where I am, tell them I'm in the men's room," he said, and wandered out again.

—|•••|—

Wednesday afternoon I took the girls and Allison to the airport. She was still fretting over her newsletter.

"Do you think a greeting is absolutely necessary?" she said in the baggage check-in line. "You know, like 'Dear Friends and Family'?"

"Probably not," I said absently. I was watching the people in line ahead of us, trying to spot this unusual behavior Gary had talked about, but so far I hadn't seen any. People were looking at their watches and complaining about the length of the line, the ticket agents were calling, "Next. Next!" to the person at the head of the line, who, after having stood impatiently in line for forty-five minutes waiting for this moment, was now staring blankly into space, and an unattended toddler was methodically pulling the elastic strings off a stack of luggage tags.

"They'll still know it's a Christmas newsletter, won't they?" Allison said. "Even without a greeting at the beginning of it?"

With a border of angels holding bunches of mistletoe, what else could it be? I thought.

"*Next!*" the ticket agent shouted.

The man in front of us had forgotten his photo ID, the girl in front of us in line for the security check was wearing heavy metal, and on the train out to the concourse a woman stepped on my foot and then glared at me as if it were my fault. Apparently all the nice people had traveled the day Gary came home.

And that was probably what it was—some kind of statistical clump where all the considerate, intelligent people had ended up on the same flight.

I knew they existed. My sister Sueann had had an insurance actuary for a boyfriend once (he was also an embezzler, which is why Sueann was dating him) and he had said events weren't evenly distributed, that there were peaks and valleys. Gary must just have hit a peak.

Which was too bad, I thought, lugging Cheyenne, who had demanded to be carried the minute we got off the train, down the concourse. Because the only reason he had approached me was because he thought there was something strange going on.

"Here's Gate 55," Allison said, setting Dakota down and getting out French-language tapes for the girls. "If I left off the 'Dear Friends and Family,' I'd have room to include Dakota's violin recital. She played 'The Gypsy Dance.'"

She settled the girls in adjoining chairs and put on their headphones. "But Mitch says it's a letter, so it has to have a greeting."

"What if you used something short?" I said. "Like 'Greetings' or something. Then you'd have room to start the letter on the same line."

"Not 'Greetings.'" She made a face. "Uncle Frank started his letter that way last year, and it scared me half to death. I thought Mitch had been *drafted.*"

I had been alarmed when I'd gotten mine, too, but at least it had given me a temporary rush of adrenaline, which was more than Uncle Frank's letters usually did, concerned as they were with prostate problems and disputes over property taxes.

"I suppose I could use 'Holiday Greetings,'" Allison said. "Or 'Christmas Greetings,' but that's almost as long as 'Dear Friends and Family.' If only there were something shorter."

"How about 'Hi'?"

"That might work." She got out paper and a pen and started writing. "How do you spell 'outstanding'?"

"O-u-t-s-t-a-n-d-i-n-g," I said absently. I was watching the moving sidewalks in the middle of the concourse. People were standing on the right like they were supposed to, and walking on the left. No people were standing four abreast or blocking the entire sidewalk with their luggage. No kids were running in the opposite direction of the sidewalk's movement, screaming and running their hands along the rubber railing.

"How do you spell 'fabulous'?" Allison asked.

"Flight 2216 to Spokane is now ready for boarding," the flight attendant at the desk said. "Those passengers traveling with small children or those who require additional time for boarding may now board."

A single old lady with a walker stood up and got in line. Allison unhooked the girls' headphones, and we began the ritual of hugging and gathering up belongings.

"We'll see you at Christmas," she said.

"Good luck with your newsletter," I said, handing Dakota her teddy bear, "and don't worry about the heading. It doesn't need one."

They started down the passageway. I stood there, waving, till they were out of sight, and then turned to go.

"We are now ready for regular boarding of rows 25 through 33," the flight attendant said, and everybody in the gate area stood up. Nothing unusual here, I thought, and started for the concourse.

"What rows did she call?" a woman in a red beret asked a teenaged boy.

"25 through 33," he said.

"Oh, I'm Row 14," the woman said, and sat back down.

So did I.

"We are now ready to board rows 15 through 24 " the flight attendant said, and a dozen people looked carefully at their tickets and then stepped back from the door, patiently waiting their turn. One of them pulled a paperback out of her tote bag and began to read. It was *Kidnapped* by Robert Louis Stevenson. Only when the flight attendant said, "We are now boarding all rows," did the rest of them stand up and get in line.

Which didn't prove anything, and neither did the standing on the right of the moving sidewalk. Maybe people were just being nice because it was Christmas.

Don't be ridiculous, I told myself. People aren't nicer at Christmas. They're ruder and pushier and crabbier than ever. You've seen them at the mall and in line for the post office. They act worse at Christmas than any other time.

"This is your final boarding call for Flight 2216 to Spokane," the flight attendant said to the empty waiting area. She called to me "Are you flying to Spokane, ma'am?"

"No." I stood up. "I was seeing friends off."

"I just wanted to make sure you didn't miss your flight," she said, and turned to shut the door.

I started for the moving sidewalk and nearly collided with a young man running for the gate. He raced up to the desk and flung his ticket down.

"I'm sorry, sir," the flight attendant said, leaning slightly away from the young man as if expecting an explosion. "Your flight has already left. I'm really terribly sor—"

"Oh, it's okay," he said. "It serves me right. I didn't allow enough time for parking and everything, that's all. I should have started for the airport earlier."

The flight attendant was tapping busily on the computer. "I'm afraid the only other open flight to Spokane for today isn't until 11:05 this evening."

"Oh, well," he said, smiling. "It'll give me a chance to catch up on my reading." He reached down into his attaché case and pulled out a paperback. It was W. Somerset Maugham's *Of Human Bondage*.

⊣ • • • ⊢

"Well?" Gary said as soon as I got back to work Thursday morning. He was standing by my desk, waiting for me.

"There's definitely something going on," I said, and told him about the moving sidewalks and the guy who'd missed his plane. "But what?"

"Is there somewhere we can talk?" he said, looking anxiously around.

"Hunziger's office," I said, "but I don't know if he's in yet."

"He's not," he said, led me into the office, and shut the door behind him.

"Sit down," he said, indicating Hunziger's chair. "Now, I know this is going to sound crazy, but I think all these people have been possessed by some kind of alien intelligence. Have you ever seen *Invasion of the Body Snatchers?*"

"What?" I said.

"*Invasion of the Body Snatchers,*" he said. "It's about these parasites from outer space who take over people's bodies and—"

"I *know* what it's about," I said, "and it's *science fiction.* You think the man who missed his plane was some kind of pod-person? You're right," I said, reaching for the doorknob. "I do think you're crazy."

"That's what Donald Sutherland said in *Leechmen from Mars.* Nobody ever believes it's happening, until it's too late."

He pulled a folded newspaper out of his back pocket. "Look at this," he said, waving it in front of me. "Holiday credit-card fraud down twenty percent. Holiday suicides down thirty percent. Charitable giving up sixty percent."

"They're coincidences." I explained about the statistical peaks and valleys. "Look," I said, taking the paper from him and turning to the front page. "People Against Cruelty to Our Furry Friends Protests City Hall Christmas Display. Animal Rights Group Objects to Exploitation of Reindeer."

"What about your sister?" he said. "You said she only dates losers. Why would she suddenly start dating a nice guy? Why would an escaped convict suddenly turn himself in? Why would people suddenly start reading the classics? Because they've been taken over."

"By aliens from outer space?" I said incredulously.

"Did he have a hat?"

"Who?" I said, wondering if he really was crazy. Could his being hung up on his horrible ex-wife have finally made him crack?

"The man who missed his plane," he said. "Was he wearing a hat?"

"I don't remember," I said, and felt suddenly cold. Sueann had worn a hat to Thanksgiving dinner. She'd refused to take it off at the table. And the woman whose ticket said Row 14 had been wearing a beret.

"What do hats have to do with it?" I asked.

"The man on the plane next to me was wearing a hat. So were most of the other people on the flight. Did you ever see *The Puppet Masters?* The parasites attached themselves to the spinal cord and took over the nervous system," he said. "This morning here at work I counted nineteen people wearing hats. Les Sawtelle, Rodney Jones, Jim Bridgeman—"

"Jim Bridgeman always wears a hat," I said. "It's to hide his bald spot. Besides, he's a computer programmer. All the computer people wear baseball caps."

"DeeDee Crawford," he said. "Vera McDermott, Janet Hall—"

"Women's hats are supposed to be making a comeback," I said.

"George Frazelli, the entire Documentation section—"

"I'm sure there's a logical explanation," I said. "It's been freezing in here all week. There's probably something wrong with the heating system."

"The thermostat's turned down to fifty," he said, "which is something else peculiar. The thermostat's been turned down on all floors."

"Well, that's probably Management. You know how they're always trying to cut costs—"

"They're giving us a Christmas bonus. And they fired Hunziger."

"They fired Hunziger?" I said. Management never fires anybody.

"This morning. That's how I knew he wouldn't be in his office."

"They actually fired Hunziger?"

"And one of the janitors. The one who drank. How do you explain that?"

"I—I don't know," I stammered. "But there has to be some other explanation than aliens. Maybe they took a management course or got the Christmas spirit or their therapists told them to do good deeds or something. Something besides leechmen. Aliens coming from outer space and taking over our brains is impossible!"

"That's what Dana Wynter said in *Invasion of the Body Snatchers.* But it's not impossible. It's happening right here, and we've got to stop it before they take over everybody and we're the only ones left. They—"

There was a knock on the door. "Sorry to bother you, Gary," Carol Zaliski said, leaning in the door, "but you've got an urgent phone call. It's your ex-wife."

"Coming," he said, looking at me. "Think about what I said, okay?" He went out.

I stood looking after him and frowning.

"What was that all about?" Carol said, coming into the office. She was wearing a white fur hat.

"He wanted to know what to buy his Secret Santa person," I said.

⊣•••⊢

Friday Gary wasn't there. "He had to go talk to his ex-wife this morning," Tonya told me at lunch, picking pickles off her sandwich. "He'll be back this afternoon. Marcie's demanding he pay for her therapy. She's seeing this psychiatrist, and she claims Gary's the one who made her crazy, so he should pick up the bill for her Prozac. Why is he still hung up on her?"

"I don't know," I said, scraping mustard off my burger.

"Carol Zaliski said the two of you were talking in Hunziger's office yesterday. What about? Did he ask you out? Nan?"

"Tonya, has Gary talked to you since Thanksgiving? Did he ask you about whether you'd noticed anything unusual happening?"

"He asked me if I'd noticed anything bizarre or abnormal about my family. I told him, in my family bizarre is normal. You won't believe what's happened now. Tom's parents are getting a divorce, which means five sets of parents. Why couldn't they have waited till after Christmas to do this? It's throwing my whole schedule off."

She bit into her sandwich. "I'm sure Gary's going to ask you out. He's probably just working up to it."

If he was, he had the strangest line I'd ever heard. Aliens from outer space. Hiding under hats!

Though, now that he'd mentioned it, there were an awful lot of people wearing hats. Nearly all the men in Data Analysis had baseball caps on, Jerrilyn Wells was wearing a wool stocking cap, and Ms. Jacobson's secretary looked like she was dressed for a wedding in a white thing with a veil. But Sueann had said this was the Year of the Hat.

Sueann, who dated only gigolos and Mafia dons. But she had been bound to hit a nice boyfriend sooner or later, she dated so many guys.

And there weren't any signs of alien possession when I tried to get somebody in the steno pool to make some copies for me. "We're *busy,*" Paula Grandy snapped. "It's Christmas, you know!"

I went back to my desk, feeling better. There was an enormous dish made of pine cones on it, filled with candy canes and red and green foil-wrapped chocolate kisses. "Is this part of the Christmas decorations?" I asked Penny.

"No. They aren't ready yet," she said. "This is just a little something to brighten the holidays. I made one for everyone's desk."

I felt even better. I pushed the dish over to one side and started through my mail. There was a green envelope from Allison and Mitch. She must have mailed her newsletters as soon as she got off the plane. I wonder if she decided to forgo the heading or Dakota's Most Improved Practicing Piano Award, I thought, slicing it open with the letter opener.

"Dear Nan," it began, several spaces down from the angels-and-mistletoe border. "Nothing much new this year. We're all okay, though Mitch is worried about downsizing, and I always seem to be running from behind. The girls are growing like weeds and doing okay in school, though Cheyenne's been having some problems with her reading and Dakota's still wetting the bed. Mitch and I decided we've been pushing them too hard, and we're working on trying not to overschedule them for activities and just letting them be normal, average little girls."

I jammed the letter back into the envelope and ran up to fourth to look for Gary.

"All right," I said when I found him. "I believe you. What do we do now?"

⊣ • • • ⊢

We rented movies. Actually, we rented only some of the movies. *Attack of the Soul Killers* and *Invasion from Betelgeuse* were both checked out.

"Which means somebody else has figured it out, too," Gary said. "If only we knew who."

"We could ask the clerk," I suggested.

He shook his head violently. "We can't do anything to make them suspicious. For all we know, they may have taken them off the shelves themselves, in which case we're on the right track. What else shall we rent?"

"What?" I said blankly.

"So it won't look like we're just renting alien invasion movies."

"Oh," I said, and picked up *Ordinary People* and a black-and-white version of *A Christmas Carol*.

It didn't work. *"The Puppet Masters,"* the kid at the rental desk, wearing a blue-and-yellow Blockbuster hat, said inquiringly. "Is that a good movie?"

"I haven't seen it," Gary said nervously.

"We're renting it because it has Donald Sutherland in it," I said. "We're having a Donald Sutherland film festival. *The Puppet Masters, Ordinary People, Invasion of the Body Snatchers*—"

"Is Donald Sutherland in this?" he asked, holding up *A Christmas Carol.*

"He plays Tiny Tim," I said. "It was his first screen appearance."

⊣•••⊢

"You were great in there," Gary said, leading me down to the other end of the mall to Suncoast to buy *Attack of the Soul Killers.* "You're a very good liar."

"Thanks," I said, pulling my coat closer and looking around the mall. It was freezing in here, and there were hats everywhere, on people and in window displays, Panamas and porkpies and picture hats.

"We're surrounded. Look at that," he said, nodding in the direction of Santa Claus's North Pole.

"Santa Claus has always worn a hat," I said.

"I meant the line," he said.

He was right. The kids in line were waiting patiently, cheerfully. Not a single one was screaming or announcing she had to go to the bathroom. "I want a Masters of Earth," a little boy in a felt beanie was saying eagerly to his mother.

"Well, we'll ask Santa," the mother said, "but he may not be able to get it for you. All the stores are sold out."

"Okay," he said. "Then I want a wagon."

Suncoast was sold out of *Attack of the Soul Killers,* but we bought *Invasion from Betelgeuse* and *Infiltrators from Space* and went back to his apartment to screen them.

"Well?" Gary said after we'd watched three of them. "Did you notice how they start slowly and then spread through the population?"

Actually, what I'd noticed was how dumb all the people in these movies were. "The brain-suckers attack when we're asleep," the hero would say, and promptly lie down for a nap. Or the hero's girlfriend would say, "They're on to us. We've got to get out of here. Right now," and then go back to her apartment to pack.

And, just like in every horror movie, they were always splitting up instead of sticking together. And going down dark alleys. They deserved to be turned into pod-people.

"Our first order of business is to pool what we know about the aliens," Gary said. "It's obvious the purpose of the hats is to conceal the parasites' presence from those who haven't been taken over yet," he said, "and that they're attached to the brain."

"Or the spinal column," I said, "like in *The Puppet Masters*."

He shook his head. "If that were the case, they could attach themselves to the neck or the back, which would be much less conspicuous. Why would they take the risk of hiding under hats, which are so noticeable, if they aren't attached to the top of the head?"

"Maybe the hats serve some other purpose."

The phone rang.

"Yes?" Gary answered it. His face lit up and then fell.

His ex-wife, I thought, and started watching *Infiltrators from Space*.

"You've got to believe me," the hero's girlfriend said to the psychiatrist. "There are aliens here among us. They look just like you or me. You have to believe me."

"I do believe you," the psychiatrist said, and raised his finger to point at her. "Ahhhggghhh!" he screeched, his eyes glowing bright green.

"Marcie," Gary said. There was a long pause. "A friend." Longer pause. "No."

The hero's girlfriend ran down a dark alley, wearing high heels. Halfway through, she twisted her ankle and fell.

"You know that isn't true," Gary said.

I fast-forwarded. The hero was in his apartment, on the phone. "Hello, Police Department?" he said. "You have to help me. We've been invaded by aliens who take over your body!"

"We'll be right there, Mr. Daly," the voice on the phone said. "Stay there."

"How do you know my name?" the hero shouted. "I didn't tell you my address."

"We're on our way," the voice said.

"We'll talk about it tomorrow," Gary said, and hung up.

"Sorry," he said, coming over to the couch. "Okay, I downloaded a bunch of stuff about parasites and aliens from the Internet," he said, handing me a sheaf of stapled papers. "We need to discover what it is they're doing to the people they take over, what their weaknesses are, and how we can fight them. We need to know when and where it started," Gary went on, "how and where it's spreading, and what it's doing to people. We need to find out as much as we can about the nature of the aliens so we can figure out a way to eliminate them. How do they communicate with each other? Are they telepathic, like in *Village of the Damned,* or do they use some other form of communication? If they're telepathic, can they read our minds as well as each other's?"

"If they could, wouldn't they know we're on to them?" I said.

The phone rang again.

"It's probably my ex-wife again," he said.

I picked up the remote and flicked on *Infiltrators from Space* again.

Gary answered the phone. "Yes?" he said, and then warily, "How did you get my number?"

The hero slammed down the phone and ran to the window. Dozens of police cars were pulling up, lights flashing.

"Sure," Gary said. He grinned. "No, I won't forget."

He hung up. "That was Penny. She forgot to give me my Holiday Goodies slip. I'm supposed to take in four dozen sugar cookies next Monday." He shook his head wonderingly. "Now, *there's* somebody I'd like to see taken over by the aliens."

He sat down on the couch and started making a list. "Okay, methods of fighting them. Diseases. Poison. Dynamite. Nuclear weapons. What else?"

I didn't answer. I was thinking about what he'd said about wishing Penny would be taken over.

"The problem with all of those solutions is that they kill the people too," Gary said. "What we need is something like the virus they used in *Invasion.* Or the ultrasonic pulses only the aliens could hear in *War with the Slugmen.* If we're going to stop them, we've got to find something that kills the parasite but not the host."

"Do we have to stop them?"

"What?" he said. "Of course we have to stop them. What do you mean?"

"All the aliens in these movies turn people into zombies or monsters," I said. "They shuffle around, attacking people and killing them and trying to take over the world. Nobody's done anything like that. People are standing on the right and walking on the left, the suicide rate's down, my sister's dating a very nice guy. Everybody who's been taken over is nicer, happier, more polite. Maybe the parasites are a good influence, and we shouldn't interfere."

"And maybe that's what they want us to think. What if they're acting nice to trick us, to keep us from trying to stop them? Remember *Attack of the Soul Killers?* What if it's all an act, and they're only acting nice till the takeover's complete?"

If it was an act it was a great one. Over the next few days, Solveig, in a red straw hat, announced she was naming her baby Jane, Jim Bridgeman nodded at me in the elevator, my cousin Celia's newsletter/diary was short and funny, and the waiter, sporting a soda jerk's hat, got both Tonya's and my orders right.

"No pickles!" Tonya said delightedly, picking up her sandwich. "Ow! Can you get carpal tunnel syndrome from wrapping Christmas presents? My hand's been hurting all morning."

She opened her file folder. There was a new diagram inside, a rectangle with names written all around the sides.

"Is that your Christmas schedule?" I asked.

"No," she said, showing it to me. "It's a seating arrangement for Christmas dinner. It was crazy, running the kids from house to house like that, so we decided to just have everybody at our house."

I took a startled look at her, but she was still hatless.

"I thought Tom's ex-wife couldn't stand his parents."

"Everybody's agreed we all need to get along for the kids' sake. After all, it's Christmas."

I was still staring at her.

She put her hand up to her hair. "Do you like it? It's a wig. Eric got it for me for Christmas. For being such a great mother to the boys through the divorce. I couldn't believe it." She patted her hair. "Isn't it great?"

"They're hiding their aliens under wigs," I told Gary.

"I know," he said. "Paul Gunden got a new toupee. We can't trust anyone." He handed me a folder full of clippings.

Employment rates were up. Thefts of packages from cars, usually prevalent at this time of year, were down. A woman in Minnesota had brought back a library book that was twenty-two years overdue. "Groups Praise City Hall Christmas Display," one of the clippings read, and the accompanying picture showed the People for a Non-Commercial Christmas, the Holy Spirit Southern Baptists, and the Equal Rights for Ethnics activists holding hands and singing Christmas carols around the crèche.

On the ninth, Mom called. "Have you written your newsletter yet?"

"I've been busy," I said, and waited for her to ask me if I'd met anyone lately at work.

"I got Jackie Peterson's newsletter this morning," she said.

"So did I." The invasion apparently hadn't reached Miami. Jackie's newsletter, which is usually terminally cute, had reached new heights:

> "M *is for our trip to Mexico*
> E *is for Every place else we'd like to go*
> R *is for the RV that takes us there....*"

And straight through MERRY CHRISTMAS, A HAPPY NEW YEAR, and both her first and last names.

"I do wish she wouldn't try to put her letters in verse," Mom said. "They never scan."

"Mom," I said. "Are you okay?"

"I'm fine," she said. "My arthritis has been kicking up the last couple of days, but otherwise I've never felt better. I've been thinking, there's no reason for you to send out newsletters if you don't want to."

"Mom," I said, "did Sueann give you a hat for Christmas?"

"Oh, she told you," Mom said. "You know, I don't usually like hats, but I'm going to need one for the wedding, and—"

"Wedding?"

"Oh, didn't she tell you? She and David are getting married right after Christmas. I am so relieved. I thought she was never going to meet anyone decent."

I reported that to Gary. "I know," he said glumly. "I just got a raise."

"I haven't found a single bad effect," I said. "No signs of violence or antisocial behavior. Not even any irritability."

"There you are," Penny said crabbily, coming up with a huge poinsettia under each arm. "Can you help me put these on everybody's desks?"

"Are these the Christmas decorations?" I asked.

"No, I'm still waiting on that farmer," she said, handing me one of the poinsettias. "This is just a little something to brighten up everyone's desk." She reached down to move the pine-cone dish on Gary's desk. "You didn't eat your candy canes," she said.

"I don't like peppermint."

"Nobody ate their candy canes," she said disgustedly. "They all ate the chocolate kisses and left the candy canes."

"People like chocolate," Gary said, and whispered to me, "When is she going to be taken over?"

"Meet me in Hunziger's office right away," I whispered back, and said to Penny, "Where does this poinsettia go?"

"Jim Bridgeman's desk."

I took the poinsettia up to Computing on fifth. Jim was wearing his baseball cap backward. "A little something to brighten your desk," I said, handing it to him, and started back toward the stairs.

"Can I talk to you a minute?" he said, following me out into the stairwell.

"Sure," I said, trying to sound calm. "What about?"

He leaned toward me. "Have you noticed anything unusual going on?"

"You mean the poinsettia?" I said. "Penny does tend to go a little overboard for Christmas, but—"

"No," he said, putting his hand awkwardly to his cap, "people who are acting funny, people who aren't themselves?"

"No," I said, smiling. "I haven't noticed a thing."

⊣•••⊢

I waited for Gary in Hunziger's office for nearly half an hour. "Sorry I took so long," he said when he finally got there. "My ex-wife called. What were you saying?"

"I was saying that even you have to admit it would be a good thing if Penny was taken over," I said. "What if the parasites aren't evil? What if they're those—what are those parasites that benefit the host called? You know, like the bacteria that help cows produce milk? Or those birds that pick insects off of rhinoceroses?"

"You mean symbiotes?" Gary said.

"Yes," I said eagerly. "What if this is some kind of symbiotic relationship? What if they're raising everyone's IQ or enhancing their emotional maturity; and it's having a good effect on us?"

"Things that sound too good to be true usually are. No," he said, shaking his head. "They're up to something, I know it. And we've got to find out what it is."

On the tenth when I came to work, Penny was putting up the Christmas decorations. They were as she had promised, something special: wide swags of red velvet ribbons running all around the walls with red velvet bows and large bunches of mistletoe every few feet. In between were gold-calligraphic scrolls reading "And kiss me 'neath the mistletoe, For Christmas comes but once a year."

"What do you think?" Penny said climbing down from her stepladder. "Every floor has a different quotation." She reached into a large cardboard box. "Accounting's is 'Sweetest the kiss that's stolen under the mistletoe.'"

I came over and looked into the box. "Where did you get all the mistletoe?" I asked.

"This apple farmer I know," she said, moving the ladder.

I picked up a big branch of the green leaves and white berries. "It must have cost a fortune." I had bought a sprig of it last year that had cost six dollars.

Penny, climbing the ladder, shook her head. "It didn't cost anything. He was glad to get rid of it." She tied the bunch of mistletoe to the red velvet ribbon. "It's a parasite, you know. It kills the trees."

"Kills the trees?" I said blankly, staring at the white berries.

"Or deforms them," she said. "It steals nutrients from the tree's sap, and the tree gets these swellings and galls and things. The farmer told me all about it."

As soon as I had the chance, I took the material Gary had downloaded on parasites into Hunziger's office and read through it.

Mistletoe caused grotesque swellings wherever its rootlets attached themselves to the tree. Anthracnose caused cracks and then spots of dead bark called cankers. Blight wilted trees' leaves. Witches' broom weakened limbs. Bacteria caused tumorlike growths on the trunk, called galls.

We had been focusing on the mental and psychological effects when we should have been looking at the physical ones. The heightened intelligence, the increase in civility and common sense, must simply be side effects of the parasites' stealing nutrients. And damaging the host.

I stuck the papers back into the file folder, went back to my desk, and called my sister Sueann.

"Sueann, hi," I said. "I'm working on my Christmas newsletter, and I wanted to make sure I spelled David's name right. Is Carrington spelled C-A-R-R or C-E-R-R?"

"C-A-R-R. Oh, Nan, he's so wonderful! So different from the losers I usually date! He's considerate and sensitive and—"

"And how are you?" I said. "Everybody at work's been down with the flu."

"Really?" she said. "No, I'm fine."

What did I do now? I couldn't ask "Are you sure?" without making her suspicious. "C-A-R-R," I said, trying to think of another way to approach the subject.

Sueann saved me the trouble. "You won't believe what he did yesterday. Showed up at work to take me home. He knew my ankles had been hurting, and he brought me a tube of Ben-Gay and a dozen pink roses. He is so thoughtful."

"Your ankles have been hurting?" I said, trying not to sound anxious.

"Like crazy. It's this weather or something. I could hardly walk on them this morning."

I jammed the parasite papers back into the file folder, made sure I hadn't left any on the desk like the hero in *Parasite People from Planet X*, and went up to see Gary.

He was on the phone.

"I've got to talk to you," I whispered.

"I'd like that," he said into the phone, an odd look on his face.

"What is it?" I said. "Have they found out we're on to them?"

"Shh," he said. "You know I do," he said into the phone.

"You don't understand," I said. "I've figured out what it's doing to people."

He held up a finger, motioning me to wait. "Can you hang on a minute?" he said into the phone, and put his hand over the receiver. "I'll meet you in Hunziger's office in five minutes," he said.

"No," I said. "It's not safe. Meet me at the post office."

He nodded and went back to his conversation, still with that odd look on his face.

I ran back down to second for my purse and went to the post office. I had intended to wait on the corner, but it was crowded with people jockeying to drop money into the Salvation Army Santa Claus's kettle.

I looked down the sidewalk. Where was Gary? I went up the steps and scanned the street. There was no sign of him.

"Merry Christmas!" a man said, half-tipping a fedora and holding the door for me.

"Oh no, I'm—" I began, and saw Tonya coming down the street. "Thank you," I said, and ducked inside.

It was freezing inside, and the line for the postal clerks wound out into the lobby. I got in it. It would take an hour at least to work my way to the front, which meant I could wait for Gary without looking suspicious.

Except that I was the only one not wearing a hat. Every single person in line had one on, and the clerks behind the counter were wearing mail carriers' caps. And broad smiles.

"Packages going overseas should really have been mailed by November fifteenth," the middle clerk was saying, not at all disgruntledly, to a little Japanese woman in a red cap, "but don't worry, we'll figure out a way to get your presents there on time."

"The line's only about forty-five minutes long," the woman in front of me confided cheerfully. She was wearing a small black hat with a feather and carrying four enormous packages. I wondered if they were full of pods. "Which isn't bad at all, considering it's Christmas."

I nodded, looking toward the door. Where was he?

"Why are you here?" the woman said, smiling.

"What?" I said, whirling back around, my heart pounding.

"What are you here to mail?" she said. "I see you don't have any packages."

"S-stamps," I stammered.

"You can go ahead of me," she said. "If all you're buying is stamps. I've got all these packages to send. You don't want to wait for that."

I *do* want to wait, I thought. "No, that's all right. I'm buying a lot of stamps," I said. "I'm buying several sheets. For my Christmas newsletter."

She shook her head, balancing the packages. "Don't be silly. You don't want to wait while they weigh all these." She tapped the man in front of her. "This young lady's only buying stamps," she said. "Why don't we let her go ahead of us?"

"Certainly," the man, who was wearing a Russian karakul hat, said, and bowed slightly, stepping back.

"No, really," I began, but it was too late. The line had parted like the Red Sea.

"Thank you," I said, and walked up to the counter. "Merry Christmas."

The line closed behind me. They know, I thought. They know I was looking up plant parasites. I glanced desperately toward the door.

"Holly and ivy?" the clerk said, beaming at me.

"What?" I said.

"Your stamps." He held up two sheets. "Holly and ivy or Madonna and Child?"

"Holly and ivy," I said weakly. "Three sheets, please."

I paid for the sheets, thanked the mob again, and went back out into the freezing-cold lobby. And now what? Pretend I had a box and fiddle with the combination? Where was he?

I went over to the bulletin board, trying not to seem suspicious, and looked at the Wanted posters. They had probably all turned themselves in by now and were being model prisoners. And it really was a pity the parasites were going to have to be stopped. *If* they could be stopped.

It had been easy in the movies (in the movies, that is, in which they had managed to defeat them, which wasn't all that many. Over half the movies had ended with the whole world being turned into glowing green eyes). And in the ones where they did defeat them, there had been an awful lot of explosions and hanging precariously from helicopters. I hoped whatever we came up with didn't involve skydiving.

Or a virus or ultrasonic sound, because even if I knew a doctor or scientist to ask, I couldn't confide in them. "We can't trust anybody," Gary had said, and he was right. We couldn't risk it. There was too much at stake. And we couldn't call the police. "It's all in your imagination, Miss Johnson," they would say. "Stay right there. We're on our way."

We would have to do this on our own. And *where* was Gary?

I looked at the Wanted posters some more. I was sure the one in the middle looked like one of Sueann's old boyfriends. He—

"I'm sorry I'm late," Gary said breathlessly. His ears were red from the cold and his hair was ruffled from running. "I had this phone call and—"

"Come on," I said, and hustled him out of the post office, down the steps, and past the Santa and his mob of donors.

"Keep walking," I said. "You were right about the parasites, but not because they turn people into zombies."

I hurriedly told him about the galls and Tonya's carpal tunnel syndrome. "My sister was infected at Thanksgiving, and now she can hardly walk," I said. "You were right. We've got to stop them."

"But you don't have any proof of this," he said. "It could be arthritis or something, couldn't it?"

I stopped walking. "What?"

"You don't have any proof that it's the aliens that are causing it. It's cold. People's arthritis always acts up when it's cold out. And even if the aliens are causing it, a few aches and pains is a small price to pay for all the benefits. You said yourself—"

I stared at his hair.

"Don't look at me like that," he said. "I haven't been taken over. I've just been thinking about what you said about your sister's engagement and—"

"Who was on the phone?"

He looked uncomfortable. "The thing is—"

"It was your ex-wife," I said. "She's been taken over, and now she's nice, and you want to get back together with her. That's it, isn't it?"

"You know how I've always felt about Marcie," he said guiltily. "She says she never stopped loving me."

When something sounds too good to be true, it probably is, I thought.

"She thinks I should move back in and see if we can't work things out. But that isn't the only reason," he said, grabbing my arm. "I've been looking at all those clippings—dropouts going back to school, escaped convicts turning themselves in—"

"People returning overdue library books," I said.

"Are we willing to be responsible for ruining all that? I think we should think about this before we do anything."

I pulled my arm away from him.

"I just think we should consider all the factors before we decide what to do. Waiting a few days can't hurt."

"You're right," I said, and started walking. "There's a lot we don't know about them."

"I just think we should do a little more research," he said, opening the door of our building.

"You're right," I said, and started up the stairs.

"I'll talk to you tomorrow; okay?" he said when we got to second.

I nodded and went back to my desk and put my head in my hands.

He was willing to let parasites take over the planet so he could get his ex-wife back, but were my motives any better than his? Why had I believed in an alien invasion in the first place and spent all that time watching science-fiction movies and having huddled conversations? So I could spend time with him.

He was right. A few aches and pains were worth it to have Sueann married to someone nice and postal workers nondisgruntled and passengers remaining seated till those people with connecting flights had deplaned.

"Are you okay?" Tonya said, leaning over my desk.

"I'm fine," I said. "How's your arm?"

"Fine," she said, rotating the elbow to show me. "It must have been a cramp or something."

I didn't *know* these parasites were like mistletoe. They might cause only temporary aches and pains. Gary was right. We needed to do more research. Waiting a few days couldn't hurt.

The phone rang. "I've been trying to get hold of you," Mom said. "Dakota's in the hospital. They don't know what it is. It's something wrong with her legs. You need to call Allison."

"I will," I said, and hung up the phone.

I logged on to my computer, called up the file I'd been working on and scrolled halfway through it so it would look like I was away from my desk for just a minute, took off my high heels and changed into my sneakers, stuck the high heels into my desk drawer, grabbed my purse and coat, and took off.

The best place to look for information on how to get rid of the parasites was the library, but the card file was on-line, and you had to use your library card to get access. The next best was a bookstore. Not the independent on Sixteenth. Their clerks were far too helpful. And knowledgeable.

I went to the Barnes & Noble on Eighth, taking the back way (but no alleys). It was jammed, and there was some kind of book signing going on up front, but nobody paid any attention to me. Even so, I didn't go straight to the gardening section. I wandered casually through the aisles, looking at T-shirts and mugs and stopping to thumb through a copy of *How Irrational Fears Can Ruin Your Life,* gradually working my way back to the gardening section.

They had only two books on parasites: *Common Garden Parasites and Diseases* and *Organic Weed and Pest Control.* I grabbed them both, retreated to the literature section, and began to read.

"Fungicides such as Benomyl and Ferbam are effective against certain rusts," *Common Garden Parasites* said. "Streptomycin is effective against some viruses."

But which was this, if either? "Spraying with Diazinon or Malathion can be effective in most cases. Note: These are dangerous chemicals. Avoid all contact with skin. Do not breathe fumes."

That was out. I put down *Common Garden Parasites* and picked up *Organic Weed and Pest Control.* At least it didn't recommend spraying with deadly chemicals, but what it did recommend wasn't much more useful. Prune affected limbs. Remove and destroy berries. Cover branches with black plastic.

Too often it said simply: Destroy all infected plants.

"The main difficulty in the case of parasites is to destroy the parasite without also destroying the host." That sounded more like it. "It is therefore necessary to find a substance that the host can tolerate that is intolerable to the parasite. Some rusts, for instance, cannot tolerate a vinegar and ginger solution, which can be sprayed on the leaves of the host plant. Red mites, which infest honeybees, are allergic to peppermint. Frosting made with oil of peppermint can be fed to the bees. As it permeates the bees' systems, the red mites drop off harmlessly. Other parasites respond variously to spearmint, citrus oil, oil of garlic, and powdered aloe vera."

But which? And how could I find out? Wear a garlic necklace? Stick an orange under Tonya's nose? There was no way to find out without their figuring out what I was doing.

I kept reading. "Some parasites can be destroyed by rendering the environment unfavorable. For moisture-dependent rusts, draining the soil can be beneficial. For temperature-susceptible pests, freezing and/or use of smudge pots can kill the invader. For light-sensitive parasites, exposure to light can kill the parasite."

Temperature-sensitive. I thought about the hats. Were they to hide the parasites or to protect them from the cold? No, that couldn't be it. The temperature in the building had been turned down to freezing for two weeks, and if they needed heat, why hadn't they landed in Florida?

I thought about Jackie Peterson's newsletter. She hadn't been affected. And neither had Uncle Marty, whose newsletter had come this morning. Or, rather, Uncle Marty's dog, who ostensibly dictated them. "Woof, woof!" the newsletter had read. "I'm lying here under a Christmas saguaro out on the desert, chewing on a bone and hoping Santa brings me a nice new flea collar."

So they hadn't landed in Arizona or Miami, and none of the newspaper articles Gary had circled had been from Mexico or California. They had all been datelined Minnesota and Michigan and Illinois. Places where it was cold. Cold and cloudy, I thought, thinking of Cousin Celia's Christmas newsletters. Cold and cloudy.

I flipped back through the pages, looking for the reference to light-sensitive parasites.

"It's right back here," a voice said.

I shut the book, jammed it in among Shakespeare's plays, and snatched up a copy of *Hamlet*.

"It's for my daughter," the customer, who was, thankfully, hatless, said, appearing at the end of the aisle. "That's what she said she wanted for Christmas when I called her. I was so surprised. She hardly ever reads."

The clerk was right behind her, wearing a mobcap with red and green ribbons. "Everybody's reading Shakespeare right now," she said, smiling. "We can hardly keep it on the shelves."

I ducked my head and pretended to read the *Hamlet*. "O villain, villain, smiling, damned villain!" Hamlet said. "I set it down, that one may smile, and smile, and be a villain."

The clerk started along the shelves, looking for the book. "*King Lear, King Lear*...let's see."

"Here it is," I said, handing it to her before she reached *Common Garden Parasites*.

"Thank you," she said, smiling. She handed it to the customer. "Have you been to our book signing yet? Darla Sheridan, the fashion designer, is in the store today, signing her new book, *In Your Easter Bonnet*. Hats are coming back, you know."

"Really?" the customer said.

"She's giving away a free hat with every copy of the book," the clerk said.

"*Really?*" the customer said. "Where, did you say?"

"I'll show you," the clerk said, still smiling, and led the customer away like a lamb to the slaughter.

As soon as they were gone, I pulled out *Organic Gardening* and looked up "light-sensitive" in the index. Page 264. "Pruning branches above the infection and cutting away surrounding leaves to expose the source to sunlight or artificial light will usually kill light-sensitive parasites."

I closed the book and hid it behind the Shakespeare plays, laying it on its side so it wouldn't show, and pulled out *Common Garden Pests.*

"Hi," Gary said, and I nearly dropped the book. "What are you doing here?"

"What are *you* doing here?" I said, cautiously closing the book.

He was looking at the title. I stuck it on the shelf between *Othello* and *The Riddle of Shakespeare's Identity.*

"I realized you were right." He looked cautiously around. "We've got to destroy them."

"I thought you said they were symbiotes, that they were beneficial," I said, watching him warily.

"You think I've been taken over by the aliens, don't you?" he said. He ran his hand through his hair. "See? No hat, no toupee."

But in *The Puppet Masters* the parasites had been able to attach themselves anywhere along the spine.

"I thought you said the benefits outweighed a few aches and pains," I said.

"I wanted to believe that," he said ruefully. "I guess what I really wanted to believe was that my ex-wife and I would get back together."

"What changed your mind?" I said, trying not to look at the bookshelf.

"You did," he said. "I realized somewhere along the way what a dope I'd been, mooning over her when you were right there in front of me. I was standing there, listening to her talk about how great it was going to be to get back together, and all of a sudden I realized that I didn't want to, that I'd found somebody nicer, prettier, someone I could trust. And that someone was you, Nan." He smiled at me. "So what have you found out? Something we can use to destroy them?"

I took a long, deep breath, and looked at him, deciding.

"Yes," I said, and pulled out the book. I handed it to him. "The section on bees. It says in here that introducing allergens into the bloodstream of the host can kill the parasite."

"Like in *Infiltrators from Space*."

"Yes." I told him about the red mites and the honeybees. "Oil of wintergreen, citrus oil, garlic, and powdered aloe vera are all used on various pests. So if we can introduce peppermint into the food of the affected people, it—"

"Peppermint?" he said blankly.

"Yes. Remember how Penny said nobody ate any of the candy canes she put out? I think it's because they're allergic to peppermint," I said, watching him.

"Peppermint," he said thoughtfully "They didn't eat any of the ribbon candy Jan Gundell had on her desk either. I think you've hit it. So how are you going to get them to ingest it? Put it in the water cooler?"

"No," I said. "In cookies. Chocolate chip cookies. Everybody loves chocolate." I pushed the books into place on the shelf and started for the front. "It's my turn to bring Holiday Goodies tomorrow. I'll go to the grocery store and get the cookie ingredients—"

"I'll go with you," he said.

"No," I said. "I need you to buy the oil of peppermint. They should have it at a drugstore or a health food store. Buy the most concentrated form you can get, and make sure you buy it from somebody who hasn't been taken over. I'll meet you back at my apartment, and we'll make the cookies there."

"Great," he said.

"We'd better leave separately," I said. I handed him the *Othello*. "Here. Go buy this. It'll give you a bag to carry the oil of peppermint in."

He nodded and started for the checkout line. I walked out of Barnes & Noble, went down Eighth to the grocery store, ducked out the side door, and went back to the office. I stopped at my desk for a metal ruler, and ran up to fifth. Jim Bridgeman, in his backward baseball cap, glanced up at me and then back down at his keyboard.

I went over to the thermostat.

And this was the moment when everyone surrounded you, pointing and squawking an unearthly screech at you. Or turned and stared at you with their glowing green eyes. I twisted the thermostat dial as far up as it would go, to ninety-five.

Nothing happened.

Nobody even looked up from their computers. Jim Bridgeman was typing intently.

I pried the dial and casing off with the metal ruler and stuck them into my coat pocket, bent the metal nub back so it couldn't be moved, and walked back out to the stairwell.

And now, please let it warm up fast enough to work before everybody goes home, I thought, clattering down the stairs to fourth. Let everybody start sweating and take off their hats. Let the aliens be light-sensitive. Let them not be telepathic.

I jammed the thermostats on fourth and third, and clattered down to second. Our thermostat was on the far side, next to Hunziger's office. I grabbed up a stack of memos from my desk, walked purposefully across the floor, dismantled the thermostat, and started back toward the stairs.

"Where do you think you're going?" Solveig said, planting herself firmly in front of me.

"To a meeting," I said, trying not to look as lame and frightened as the hero's girlfriend in the movies always did. She looked down at my sneakers. "Across town."

"You're not going anywhere," she said.

"Why not?" I said weakly.

"Because I've got to show you what I bought Jane for Christmas."

She reached for a shopping bag under her desk. "I know I'm not due till May, but I couldn't resist this," she said, rummaging in the bag. "It is so cute!"

She pulled out a tiny pink bonnet with white daisies on it. "Isn't it adorable?" she said. "It's newborn size. She can wear it home from the hospital. Oh, and I got her the cutest—"

"I lied," I said, and Solveig looked up alertly. "Don't tell anybody, but I completely forgot to buy a Secret Santa gift. Penny'll kill me if she finds out. If anybody asks where I've gone, tell them the ladies' room," I said, and took off down to first.

The thermostat was right by the door. I disabled it and the one in the basement, got my car (looking in the backseat first, unlike the people in the movies) and drove to the courthouse and the hospital and McDonald's, and then called my mother and invited myself to dinner. "I'll bring dessert," I said, drove out to the mall, and hit the bakery, the Gap, the video-rental place, and the theater multiplex on the way.

⊣ • • • ⊢

Mom didn't have the TV on. She did have the hat on that Sueann had given her. "Don't you think it's adorable?" she said.

"I brought cheesecake," I said. "Have you heard from Allison and Mitch? How's Dakota?"

"Worse," she said. "She has these swellings on her knees and ankles. The doctors don't know what's causing them." She took the cheesecake into the kitchen, limping slightly. "I'm so worried."

I turned up the thermostats in the living room and the bedroom and was plugging the space heater in when she brought in the soup. "I got chilled on the way over," I said, turning the space heater up to high. "It's freezing out. I think it's going to snow."

We ate our soup, and Mom told me about Sueann's wedding. "She wants you to be her maid of honor," she said, fanning herself. "Aren't you warm yet?"

"No," I said, rubbing my arms.

"I'll get you a sweater," she said, and went into the bedroom, turning the space heater off as she went.

I turned it back on and went into the living room to build a fire in the fireplace.

"Have you met anyone at work lately?" she called in from the bedroom.

"What?" I said, sitting back on my knees.

She came back in without the sweater. Her hat was gone, and her hair was mussed up, as if something had thrashed around in it. "I hope you're not still refusing to write a Christmas newsletter," she said, going into the kitchen and coming out again with two plates of cheesecake. "Come sit down and eat your dessert," she said.

I did, still watching her warily.

"Making up things!" she said. "What an idea! Aunt Margaret wrote me just the other day to tell me how much she loves hearing from you girls and how interesting your newsletters always are." She cleared the table. "You can stay for a while, can't you? I hate waiting here alone for news about Dakota."

"No, I've got to go," I said, and stood up. "I've got to…"

I've got to…what? I thought, feeling suddenly overwhelmed. Fly to Spokane? And then, as soon as Dakota was okay, fly back and run wildly around town turning up thermostats until I fell over from exhaustion?

And then what? It was when people fell asleep in the movies that the aliens took them over. And there was no way I could stay awake until every parasite was exposed to the light, even if they didn't catch me and turn me into one of them. Even if I didn't turn my ankle.

The phone rang.

"Tell them I'm not here," I said.

"Who?" Mom asked, picking it up. "Oh, dear, I hope it's not Mitch with bad news. Hello?" Pause. "It's Sueann," she said, putting her hand over the receiver, and listened for a long interval. "She broke up with her boyfriend."

"With David?" I said. "Give me the phone."

"I thought you said you weren't here," she said, handing the phone over.

"Sueann?" I said. "Why did you break up with David?"

"Because he's so deadly dull," she said. "He's always calling me and sending me flowers and being nice. He even wants to get married. And tonight at dinner, I just thought, '*Why* am I dating him?' and we broke up."

Mom went over and turned on the TV. "In local news," the CNN guy said, "special-interest groups banded together to donate fifteen thousand dollars to City Hall's Christmas display."

"Where were you having dinner?" I asked Sueann. "At McDonald's?"

"No, at this pizza place, which is another thing. All he ever wants is to go to dinner or the movies. We never do anything *interesting*."

"Did you go to a movie tonight?" She might have been in the multi-plex at the mall.

"*No.* I *told* you, I broke up with him."

This made no sense. I hadn't hit any pizza places.

"Weather is next," the guy on CNN said.

"Mom, can you turn that down?" I said. "Sueann, this is important. Tell me what you're wearing."

"Jeans and my blue top and my zodiac necklace. What does that have to do with my breaking up with David?"

"Are you wearing a hat?"

"In our forecast just ahead," the CNN guy said, "great weather for all you people trying to get your Christmas shopping d—"

Mom turned the TV down.

"Mom, turn it back up," I said, motioning wildly

"No, I'm not wearing a hat," Sueann said. "What does that have to do with whether I broke up with David or not?"

The weather map behind the CNN guy was covered with 62, 65, 70, 68. *"Mom,"* I said.

She fumbled with the remote.

"You won't believe what he did the other day," Sueann said, outraged. "Gave me an engagement ring! Can you imag—"

"—unseasonably warm temperatures and *lots* of sunshine," the weather guy blared out. "Continuing right through Christmas."

"I mean, what was I thinking?" Sueann said.

"Shh," I said. "I'm trying to listen to the weather."

"It's supposed to be nice all next week," Mom said.

⊣•••⊢

It was nice all the next week. Allison called to tell me Dakota was back home. "The doctors don't know what it was, some kind of bug or something, but whatever it was, it's completely gone. She's back taking ice skating and tap-dancing lessons, and next week I'm signing both girls up for junior Band."

"You did the right thing," Gary said grudgingly. "Marcie told me her knee was really hurting. When she was still talking to me, that is."

"The reconciliation's off, huh?"

"Yeah," he said, "but I haven't given up. The way she acted proves to me that her love for me is still there, if I can only reach it."

All it proved to me was that it took an invasion from outer space to make her seem even marginally human, but I didn't say so.

"I've talked her into going into marriage counseling with me," he said. "You were right not to trust me either. That's the mistake they always make in those body-snatcher movies, trusting people."

Well, yes and no. If I'd trusted Jim Bridgeman, I wouldn't have had to do all those thermostats alone.

"You were the one who turned the heat up at the pizza place where Sueann and her fiancé were having dinner," I said after Jim told me he'd figured out what the aliens' weakness was after seeing me turn up the thermostat on fifth. "You were the one who'd checked out *Attack of the Soul Killers.*"

"I tried to talk to you," he said. "I don't blame you for not trusting me. I should have taken my hat off, but I didn't want you to see my bald spot."

"You can't go by appearances," I said.

—|•••|—

By December fifteenth, hat sales were down, the mall was jammed with ill-tempered shoppers, at City Hall an animal-rights group was protesting Santa Claus's wearing fur, and Gary's wife had skipped their first marriage-counseling session and then blamed it on him.

It's now four days till Christmas, and things are completely back to normal. Nobody at work's wearing a hat except Jim, Solveig's naming her baby Durango, Hunziger's suing management for firing him, antidepressant sales are up, and my mother called just now to tell me Sueann has a new boyfriend who's a terrorist, and to ask me if I'd sent out my Christmas newsletters yet. And had I met anyone lately at work.

"Yes," I said. "I'm bringing him to Christmas dinner."

Yesterday Betty Holland filed a sexual harassment suit against Nathan Steinberg for kissing her under the mistletoe, and I was nearly run over on my way home from work. But the world has been made safe from cankers, leaf wilt, and galls.

And it makes an interesting Christmas Newsletter.

Whether it's true or not.

Wishing you and yours a very Merry Christmas and a Happy New Year,

*Nan Johnson*

———|*Travel Quides*

# Fire Watch

History hath triumphed over time, which besides it nothing
but eternity hath triumphed over.
—Sir Walter Raleigh

September 20—Of course the first thing I looked for was the fire
watch stone. And of course it wasn't there yet. It wasn't dedicated
until 1951, accompanying speech by the Very Reverend Dean Walter
Matthews, and this is only 1940. I knew that. I went to see the fire watch
stone only yesterday, with some kind of misplaced notion that seeing the
scene of the crime would somehow help. It didn't.

The only things that would have helped were a crash course in London during the Blitz and a little more time. I had not gotten either.

"Traveling in time is not like taking the tube, Mr. Bartholomew," the
esteemed Dunworthy had said, blinking at me through those antique
spectacles of his. "Either you report on the twentieth or you don't go
at all."

"But I'm not ready," I'd said. "Look, it took me four years to get
ready to travel with St. Paul. *St. Paul.* Not St. Paul's. You can't expect me
to get ready for London in the Blitz in two days."

"Yes," Dunworthy had said. "We can." End of conversation.

"Two days!" I had shouted at my roommate Kivrin. "All because
some computer adds an *'s.* And the esteemed Dunworthy doesn't even
bat an eye when I tell him. 'Time travel is not like taking the tube, young
man,' he says. 'I'd suggest you get ready. You're leaving day after tomorrow.' The man's a total incompetent."

"No," she said. "He isn't. He's the best there is. He wrote the book
on St. Paul's. Perhaps you should listen to what he says."

I had expected Kivrin to be at least a little sympathetic. She had been practically hysterical when she got her practicum changed from fifteenth- to fourteenth-century England, and how did either century qualify as a practicum? Even counting infectious diseases they couldn't have been more than a five. The Blitz is an eight, and St. Paul's itself is, with my luck, a ten.

"You think I should go see Dunworthy again?" I said.

"Yes."

"And then what? I've got two days. I don't know the money, the language, the history. Nothing."

"He's a good man," Kivrin said. "I think you'd better listen to him while you can." Good old Kivrin. Always the sympathetic ear.

The good man was responsible for my standing just inside the propped-open west doors, gawking like the country boy I was supposed to be, looking for a stone that wasn't there. Thanks to the good man, I was about as unprepared for my practicum as it was possible for him to make me.

I couldn't see more than a few feet into the church. I could see a candle gleaming feebly a long way off and a closer blur of white moving toward me. A verger, or possibly the Very Reverend Dean himself. I pulled out the letter from my clergyman uncle in Wales that was supposed to gain me access to the dean, and patted my back pocket to make sure I hadn't lost the microfiche *Oxford English Dictionary, Revised, with Historical Supplements,* I'd smuggled out of the Bodleian. I couldn't pull it out in the middle of the conversation, but with luck I could muddle through the first encounter by context and look up the words I didn't know later.

"Are you from the ayarpee?" he said. He was no older than I am, a head shorter and much thinner. Almost ascetic looking. He reminded me of Kivrin. He was not wearing white, but clutching it to his chest. In other circumstances I would have thought it was a pillow. In other circumstances I would know what was being said to me, but there had been no time to unlearn sub-Mediterranean Latin and Jewish law and learn Cockney and air raid procedures. Two days, and the esteemed Dunworthy, who wanted to talk about the sacred burdens of the historian instead of telling me what the ayarpee was.

"Are you?" he demanded again

I considered whipping out the OED after all on the grounds that Wales was a foreign country, but I didn't think they had microfilm in 1940.

Ayarpee. It could be anything, including a nickname for the fire watch, in which case the impulse to say no was not safe at all. "No," I said.

He lunged suddenly toward and past me and peered out the open doors. "Damn," he said, coming back to me. "Where are they then? Bunch of lazy bourgeois tarts!" And so much for getting by on context.

He looked at me closely, suspiciously, as if he thought I was only pretending not to be with the ayarpee. "The church is closed," he said finally.

I held up the envelope and said, "My name's Bartholomew. Is Dean Matthews in?"

He looked out the door a moment longer as if he expected the lazy bourgeois tarts at any moment and intended to attack them with the white bundle; then he turned and said, as if he were guiding a tour, "This way, please," and took off into the gloom.

He led me to the right and down the south aisle of the nave. Thank God I had memorized the floor plan or at that moment, heading into total darkness, led by a raving verger, the whole bizarre metaphor of my situation would have been enough to send me out the west doors and back to St. John's Wood. It helped a little to know where I was. We should have been passing number twenty-six: Hunt's painting of "The Light of the World"—Jesus with his lantern—but it was too dark to see it. We could have used the lantern ourselves.

He stopped abruptly ahead of me, still raving. "We weren't asking for the bloody savoy, just a few cots. Nelson's better off than we are—at least he's got a pillow provided." He brandished the white bundle like a torch in the darkness. It was a pillow after all. "We asked for them over a fortnight ago, and here we still are, sleeping on the bleeding generals from Trafalgar because those bitches want to play tea and crumpets with the tommies at victoria and the hell with us!"

He didn't seem to expect me to answer his outburst, which was good, because I had understood perhaps one key word in three. He stomped on ahead, moving out of sight of the one pathetic altar candle and stopping again at a black hole. Number twenty-five: stairs to the Whispering Gallery, the Dome, the library (not open to the public). Up the stairs, down a hall, stop again at a medieval door and knock.

"I've got to go wait for them," he said. "If I'm not there they'll likely take them over to the Abbey. Tell the Dean to ring them up again, will you?" and he took off down the stone steps, still holding his pillow like a shield against him.

He had knocked, but the door was at least a foot of solid oak, and it was obvious the Very Reverend Dean had not heard. I was going to have to knock again. Yes, well, and the man holding the pinpoint had to let go of it, too, but even knowing it will all be over in a moment and you won't feel a thing doesn't make it any easier to say, "Now!" So I stood in front of the door, cursing the history department and the esteemed Dunworthy and the computer that had made the mistake and brought me here to this dark door with only a letter from a fictitious uncle that I trusted no more than I trusted the rest of them.

Even the old reliable Bodleian had let me down. The batch of research stuff I cross-ordered through Balliol and the main terminal is probably sitting in my room right now, a century out of reach. And Kivrin, who had already done her practicum and should have been bursting with advice, walked around as silent as a saint until I begged her to help me.

"Did you go to see Dunworthy?" she said.

"Yes. You want to know what priceless bit of information he had for me? 'Silence and humility are the sacred burdens of the historian.' He also told me I would love St. Paul's. Golden gems from the Master. Unfortunately, what I need to know are the times and places of the bombs so one doesn't fall on me." I flopped down on the bed. "Any suggestions?"

"How good are you at memory retrieval?" she said.

I sat up. "I'm pretty good. You think I should assimilate?"

"There isn't time for that," she said. "I think you should put everything you can directly into long-term."

"You mean endorphins?" I said.

The biggest problem with using memory-assistance drugs to put information into your long-term memory is that it never sits, even for a microsecond, in your short-term memory, and that makes retrieval complicated, not to mention unnerving. It gives you the most unsettling sense of déjà vu to suddenly know something you're positive you've never seen or heard before.

The main problem, though, is not eerie sensations but retrieval. Nobody knows exactly how the brain gets what it wants out of storage, but short-term is definitely involved. That brief, sometimes microscopic, time information spends in short-term is apparently used for something besides tip-of-the-tongue availability. The whole complex sort-and-file process of retrieval is apparently centered in short-term, and without it, and without the help of the drugs that put it there or artificial substitutes, information can be impossible to retrieve. I'd used endorphins for examinations and never had any difficulty with retrieval, and it looked like it was the only way to store all the information I needed in anything approaching the time I had left, but it also meant that I would never have known any of the things I needed to know, even for long enough to have forgotten them. If and when I could retrieve the information, I would know it. Till then I was as ignorant of it as if it were not stored in some cobwebbed corner of my mind at all.

"You can retrieve without artificials, can't you?" Kivrin said, looking skeptical.

"I guess I'll have to."

"Under stress? Without sleep? Low body endorphin levels?" What exactly had her practicum been? She had never said a word about it, and undergraduates are not supposed to ask. Stress factors in the Middle Ages? I thought everybody slept through them.

"I hope so," I said. "Anyway I'm willing to try this idea if you think it will help."

She looked at me with that martyred expression and said, "Nothing will help." Thank you, St. Kivrin of Balliol.

But I tried it anyway. It was better than sitting in Dunworthy's rooms having him blink at me through his historically accurate eyeglasses and tell me I was going to love St. Paul's. When my Bodleian requests didn't come, I overloaded my credit and bought out Blackwell's. Tapes on World War II, Celtic literature, history of mass transit, tourist guidebooks, everything I could think of. Then I rented a high-speed recorder and shot up. When I came out of it, I was so panicked by the feeling of not knowing any more than I had when I started that I took the tube to London and raced up Ludgate Hill to see if the fire watch stone would trigger any memories. It didn't.

"Your endorphin levels aren't back to normal yet," I told myself and tried to relax, but that was impossible with the prospect of the practicum looming up before me. And those are real bullets, kid. Just because you're a history major doing his practicum doesn't mean you can't get killed. I read history books all the way home on the tube and right up until Dunworthy's flunkies came to take me to St. John's Wood this morning.

Then I jammed the microfiche OED in my back pocket and went off feeling as if I would have to survive by my native wit and hoping I could get hold of artificials in 1940. Surely I could get through the first day without mishap, I thought, and now here I was, stopped cold by almost the first word that was spoken to me.

Well, not quite. In spite of Kivrin's advice that I not put anything in short-term, I'd memorized the British money, a map of the tube system, a map of my own Oxford. It had gotten me this far. Surely I would be able to deal with the Dean.

Just as I had almost gotten up the courage to knock, he opened the door, and as with the pinpoint, it really was over quickly and without pain. I handed him my letter and he shook my hand and said something understandable like, "Glad to have another man, Bartholomew." He looked strained and tired and as if he might collapse if I told him the Blitz had just started. I know, I know: Keep your mouth shut. The sacred silence, etc.

He said, "We'll get Langby to show you round, shall we?" I assumed that was my Verger of the Pillow, and I was right. He met us at the foot of the stairs, puffing a little but jubilant.

"The cots came," he said to Dean Matthews. "You'd have thought they were doing us a favor. All high heels and hoity-toity. 'You made us miss our tea, luv,' one of them said to me. 'Yes, well, and a good thing, too,' I said. 'You look as if you could stand to lose a stone or two.'"

Even Dean Matthews looked as though he did not completely understand him. He said, "Did you set them up in the crypt?" and then introduced us. "Mr. Bartholomew's just got in from Wales," he said. "He's come to join our volunteers." Volunteers, not fire watch.

Langby showed me round, pointing out various dimnesses in the general gloom and then dragged me down to see the ten folding canvas cots set up among the tombs in the crypt, also in passing, Lord Nelson's black marble sarcophagus. He told me I don't have to stand a watch the first night and suggested I go to bed, since sleep is the most precious commodity in the raids. I could well believe it. He was clutching that silly pillow to his breast like his beloved.

"Do you hear the sirens down here?" I asked, wondering if he buried his head in it.

He looked round at the low stone ceilings. "Some do, some don't. Brinton has to have his Horlich's. Bence-Jones would sleep if the roof fell in on him. I have to have a pillow. The important thing is to get your eight in no matter what. If you don't, you turn into one of the walking dead. And then you get killed."

On that cheering note he went off to post the watches for tonight, leaving his pillow on one of the cots with orders for me to let nobody touch it. So here I sit, waiting for my first air raid siren and trying to get all this down before I turn into one of the walking or non-walking dead.

I've used the stolen OED to decipher a little Langby. Middling success. A tart is either a pastry or a prostitute (I assume the latter, although I was wrong about the pillow). Bourgeois is a catchall term for all the faults of the middle class. A Tommy's a soldier. Ayarpee I could not find under any spelling and I had nearly given up when something in long-term about the use of acronyms and abbreviations in wartime popped forward (bless you, St. Kivrin) and I realized it must be an abbreviation. ARP. Air Raid Precautions. Of course. Where else would you get the bleeding cots from?

*September 21*—Now that I'm past the first shock of being here, I realize that the history department neglected to tell me what I'm supposed to do in the three-odd months of this practicum. They handed me this journal, the letter from my uncle, and ten pounds in pre-war money and sent me packing into the past. The ten pounds (already depleted by train and tube fares) is supposed to last me until the end of December and get me back to St. John's Wood for pickup when the second letter calling me back to Wales to sick uncle's bedside comes. Till then I live here in the crypt with Nelson, who, Langby tells me, is pickled in alcohol inside his coffin. If we take a direct hit, will he burn like a torch or simply trickle out in a decaying stream onto the crypt floor, I wonder. Board is provided by a gas ring, over which are cooked wretched tea and indescribable kippers. To pay for all this luxury I am to stand on the roofs of St. Paul's and put out incendiaries.

I must also accomplish the purpose of this practicum, whatever it may be. Right now the only purpose I care about is staying alive until the second letter from uncle arrives and I can go home.

I am doing make-work until Langby has time to "show me the ropes." I've cleaned the skillet they cook the foul little fishes in, stacked wooden folding chairs at the altar end of the crypt (flat instead of standing because they tend to collapse like bombs in the middle of the night), and tried to sleep.

I am apparently not one of the lucky ones who can sleep through the raids. I spent most of the night wondering what St. Paul's risk rating is.

Practica have to be at least a six. Last night I was convinced this was a ten, with the crypt as ground zero, and that I might as well have applied for Denver.

The most interesting thing that's happened so far is that I've seen a cat. I am fascinated, but trying not to appear so, since they seem commonplace here.

*September 22*—Still in the crypt. Langby comes dashing through periodically cursing various government agencies (all abbreviated) and promising to take me up on the roofs. In the meantime I've run out of make-work and taught myself to work a stirrup pump. Kivrin was overly concerned about my memory retrieval abilities. I have not had any trouble so far. Quite the opposite. I called up firefighting information and got the whole manual with pictures, including instructions on the use of the stirrup pump. If the kippers set Lord Nelson on fire, I shall be a hero.

Excitement last night. The sirens went early and some of the chars who clean offices in the City sheltered in the crypt with us. One of them woke me out of a sound sleep, going like an air raid siren. Seems she'd seen a mouse. We had to go whacking at tombs and under the cots with a rubber boot to persuade her it was gone. Obviously what the history department had in mind: murdering mice.

*September 24*—Langby took me on rounds. Into the choir, where I had to learn the stirrup pump all over again, assigned rubber boots and a tin helmet. Langby says Commander Allen is getting us asbestos firemen's coats, but hasn't yet, so it's my own wool coat and muffler and very cold on the roofs even in September. It feels like November and looks it, too, bleak and cheerless with no sun. Up to the dome and onto the roofs, which should be flat but in fact are littered with towers, pinnacles, gutters, statues, all designed expressly to catch and hold incendiaries out of reach. Shown how to smother an incendiary with sand before it burns through the roof and sets the church on fire. Shown the ropes (literally) lying in a heap at the base of the dome in case somebody has to go up one of the west towers or over the top of the dome. Back inside and down to the Whispering Gallery.

Langby kept up a running commentary through the whole tour, part practical instruction, part church history. Before we went up into the Gallery he dragged me over to the south door to tell me how Christopher

Wren stood in the smoking rubble of Old St. Paul's and asked a workman to bring him a stone from the graveyard to mark the cornerstone. On the stone was written in Latin, "I shall rise again," and Wren was so impressed by the irony that he had the word inscribed above the door. Langby looked as smug as if he had not told me a story every first-year history student knows, but I suppose without the impact of the fire watch stone, the other is just a nice story.

Langby raced me up the steps and onto the narrow balcony circling the Whispering Gallery. He was already halfway round to the other side, shouting dimensions and acoustics at me. He stopped facing the wall opposite and said softly, "You can hear me whispering because of the shape of the dome. The sound waves are reinforced around the perimeter of the dome. It sounds like the very crack of doom up here during a raid. The dome is one hundred and seven feet across. It is eighty feet above the nave."

I looked down. The railing went out from under me and the black-and-white marble floor came up with dizzying speed. I hung onto something in front of me and dropped to my knees, staggered and sick at heart. The sun had come out, and all of St. Paul's seemed drenched in gold. Even the carved wood of the choir, the white stone pillars, the leaden pipes of the organ, all of it golden, golden.

Langby was beside me, trying to pull me free. "Bartholomew," he shouted, "what's wrong? For God's sake, man. "

I knew I must tell him that if I let go, St. Paul's and all the past would fall in on me, and that I must not let that happen because I was an historian. I said something, but it was not what I intended because Langby merely tightened his grip. He hauled me violently free of the railing and back onto the stairway, then let me collapse limply on the steps and stood back from me, not speaking.

"I don't know what happened in there," I said. "I've never been afraid of heights before."

"You're shaking," he said sharply. "You'd better lie down." He led me back to the crypt.

*September 25*—Memory retrieval: ARP manual. Symptoms of bombing victims. Stage one—shock; stupefaction; unawareness of injuries; words may not make sense except to victim. Stage two—shivering; nausea; injuries, losses felt; return to reality. Stage three—talkativeness that cannot be controlled; desire to explain shock behavior to rescuers.

Langby must surely recognize the symptoms, but how does he account for the fact there was no bomb? I can hardly explain my shock behavior to him, and it isn't just the sacred silence of the historian that stops me.

He has not said anything, in fact assigned me my first watches for tomorrow night as if nothing had happened, and he seems no more preoccupied than anyone else. Everyone I've met so far is jittery (one thing I had in short-term was how calm everyone was during the raids) and the raids have not come near us since I got here. They've been mostly over the East End and the docks.

There was a reference tonight to a UXB, and I have been thinking about the Dean's manner and the church being closed when I'm almost sure I remember reading it was open through the entire Blitz. As soon as I get a chance, I'll try to retrieve the events of September. As to retrieving anything else, I don't see how I can hope to remember the right information until I know what it is I am supposed to do here, if anything.

There are no guidelines for historians, and no restrictions either. I could tell everyone I'm from the future if I thought they would believe me. I could murder Hitler if I could get to Germany. Or could I? Time paradox talk abounds in the history department, and the graduate students back from their practica don't say a word one way or the other. Is there a tough, immutable past? Or is there a new past every day and do we, the historians, make it? And what are the consequences of what we do, if there are consequences? And how do we dare do anything without knowing them? Must we interfere boldly, hoping we do not bring about all our downfalls? Or must we do nothing at all, not interfere, stand by and watch St. Paul's burn to the ground if need be so that we don't change the future?

All those are fine questions for a late-night study session. They do not matter here. I could no more let St. Paul's burn down than I could kill Hitler. No, that is not true. I found that out yesterday in the Whispering Gallery. I could kill Hitler if I caught him setting fire to St. Paul's.

*September 26*—I met a young woman today. Dean Matthews has opened the church, so the watch have been doing duties as chars and people have started coming in again. The young woman reminded me of Kivrin, though Kivrin is a good deal taller and would never frizz her hair like that. She looked as if she had been crying. Kivrin has looked like that since she got back from her practicum. The Middle Ages were too much for her. I wonder how she would have coped with this. By pouring out her fears to the local priest, no doubt, as I sincerely hoped her look-alike was not going to do.

"May I help you?" I said, not wanting in the least to help. "I'm a volunteer."

She looked distressed. "You're not paid?" she said, and wiped at her reddened nose with a handkerchief. "I read about St. Paul's and the fire watch and all, and I thought perhaps there's a position there for me. In the canteen, like, or something. A paying position." There were tears in her red-rimmed eyes.

"I'm afraid we don't have a canteen," I said as kindly as I could, considering how impatient Kivrin always makes me, "and it's not actually a real shelter. Some of the watch sleep in the crypt. I'm afraid we're all volunteers, though."

"That won't do, then," she said. She dabbed at her eyes with the handkerchief. "I love St. Paul's, but I can't take on volunteer work, not with my little brother Tom back from the country." I was not reading this situation properly. For all the outward signs of distress she sounded quite cheerful and no closer to tears than when she had come in. "I've got to get us a proper place to stay. With Tom back, we can't go on sleeping in the tubes."

A sudden feeling of dread, the kind of sharp pain you get sometimes from involuntary retrieval, went over me. "The tubes?" I said, trying to get at the memory.

"Marble Arch, usually" she went on. "My brother Tom saves us a place early and I go…" She stopped, held the handkerchief close to her nose, and exploded into it. "I'm sorry," she said, "this awful cold!"

Red nose, watering eyes, sneezing. Respiratory infection. It was a wonder I hadn't told her not to cry. It's only by luck that I haven't made some unforgivable mistake so far, and this is not because I can't get at the long-term memory. I don't have half the information I need even stored: cats and colds and the way St. Paul's looks in full sun. It's only a matter of time before I am stopped cold by something I do not know. Nevertheless, I am going to try for retrieval tonight after I come off watch. At least I can find out whether and when something is going to fall on me.

I have seen the cat once or twice. He is coal-black with a white patch on his throat that looks as if it were painted on for the blackout.

*September 27*—I have just come down from the roofs. I am still shaking.

Early in the raid the bombing was mostly over the East End. The view was incredible. Searchlights everywhere, the sky pink from the fires and reflecting in the Thames, the exploding shells sparkling like fireworks. There was a constant, deafening thunder broken by the occasional droning of the planes high overhead, then the repeating stutter of the ack-ack guns.

About midnight the bombs began falling quite near with a horrible sound like a train running over me. It took every bit of will I had to keep from flinging myself flat on the roof, but Langby was watching. I didn't want to give him the satisfaction of watching a repeat performance of my behavior in the dome. I kept my head up and my sand bucket firmly in hand and felt quite proud of myself.

The bombs stopped roaring past about three, and there was a lull of about half an hour, and then a clatter like hail on the roofs. Everybody except Langby dived for shovels and stirrup pumps. He was watching me. And I was watching the incendiary.

It had fallen only a few meters from me, behind the clock tower. It was much smaller than I had imagined, only about thirty centimeters long. It was sputtering violently, throwing greenish-white fire almost to where I was standing. In a minute it would simmer down into a molten mass and begin to burn through the roof. Flames and the frantic shouts of firemen, and then the white rubble stretching for miles, and nothing, nothing left, not even the fire watch stone.

It was the Whispering Gallery all over again. I felt that I had said something, and when I looked at Langby's face he was smiling crookedly.

"St. Paul's will burn down," I said. "There won't be anything left."

"Yes," Langby said. "That's the idea, isn't it? Burn St. Paul's to the ground? Isn't that the plan?"

"Whose plan?" I said stupidly

"Hitler's, of course," Langby said. "Who did you think I meant?" and, almost casually, picked up his stirrup pump.

The page of the ARP manual flashed suddenly before me. I poured the bucket of sand around the still sputtering bomb, snatched up another bucket and dumped that on top of it. Black smoke billowed up in such a cloud that I could hardly find my shovel. I felt for the smothered bomb with the tip of it and scooped it into the empty bucket, then shoveled the sand in on top of it. Tears were streaming down my face from the acrid smoke. I turned to wipe them on my sleeve and saw Langby

He had not made a move to help me. He smiled. "It's not a bad plan, actually. But of course we won't let it happen. That's what the fire watch is here for. To see that it doesn't happen. Right, Bartholomew?"

I know now what the purpose of my practicum is. I must stop Langby from burning down St. Paul's.

*September 28*—I try to tell myself I was mistaken about Langby last night, that I misunderstood what he said. Why would he want to burn down St. Paul's unless he is a Nazi spy? How can a Nazi spy have gotten on the fire watch? I think about my faked letter of introduction and shudder.

How can I find out? If I set him some test, some fatal thing that only a loyal Englishman in 1940 would know, I fear I am the one who would be caught out. I *must* get my retrieval working properly.

Until then, I shall watch Langby. For the time being at least that should be easy. Langby has just posted the watches for the next two weeks. We stand every one together.

*September 30*—I know what happened in September. Langby told me.

Last night in the choir, putting on our coats and boots, he said, "They've already tried once, you know."

I had no idea what he meant. I felt as helpless as that first day when he asked me if I was from the ayarpee.

"The plan to destroy St. Paul's. They've already tried once. The tenth of September. A high explosive bomb. But of course you didn't know about that. You were in Wales."

I was not even listening. The minute he had said "high explosive bomb," I had remembered it all. It had burrowed in under the road and lodged on the foundations. The bomb squad had tried to defuse it, but there was a leaking gas main. They decided to evacuate St. Paul's, but Dean Matthews refused to leave, and they got it out after all and exploded it in Barking Marshes. Instant and complete retrieval.

"The bomb squad saved her that time," Langby was saying. "It seems there's always somebody about."

"Yes," I said, "there is," and walked away from him.

*October 1*—I thought last night's retrieval of the events of September tenth meant some sort of breakthrough, but I have been lying here on my cot most of the night trying for Nazi spies in St. Paul's and getting nothing. Do I have to know exactly what I'm looking for before I can remember it? What good does that do me?

Maybe Langby is not a Nazi spy. Then what is he? An arsonist? A madman? The crypt is hardly conducive to thought, being not at all as silent as a tomb. The chars talk most of the night and the sound of the bombs is muffled, which somehow makes it worse. I find myself straining to hear them. When I did get to sleep this morning, I dreamed about one of the tube shelters being hit, broken mains, drowning people.

*October 4*—I tried to catch the cat today. I had some idea of persuading it to dispatch the mouse that has been terrifying the chars. I also wanted to see one up close. I took the water bucket I had used with the stirrup pump last night to put out some burning shrapnel from one of the antiaircraft guns. It still had a bit of water in it, but not enough to drown the cat, and my plan was to clamp the bucket over him, reach under, and pick him up, then carry him down to the crypt and point him at the mouse. I did not even come close to him.

I swung the bucket, and as I did so, perhaps an inch of water splashed out. I thought I remembered that the cat was a domesticated animal, but I must have been wrong about that. The cat's wide complacent face pulled back into a skull-like mask that was absolutely terrifying, vicious claws extended from what I had thought were harmless paws, and the cat let out a sound to top the chars.

In my surprise I dropped the bucket and it rolled against one of the pillars. The cat disappeared. Behind me, Langby said, "That's no way to catch a cat."

"Obviously," I said, and bent to retrieve the bucket.

"Cats hate water," he said, still in that expressionless voice.

"Oh," I said, and started in front of him to take the bucket back to the choir. "I didn't know that."

"Everybody knows it. Even the stupid Welsh."

*October 8*—We have been standing double watches for a week—bomber's moon. Langby didn't show up on the roofs, so I went looking for him in the church. I found him standing by the west doors talking to an old man. The man had a newspaper tucked under his arm and he handed it to Langby, but Langby gave it back to him. When the man saw me, he ducked out. Langby said, "Tourist. Wanted to know where the Windmill Theater is. Read in the paper the girls are starkers."

I know I looked as if I didn't believe him because he said, "You look rotten, old man. Not getting enough sleep, are you? I'll get somebody to take the first watch for you tonight."

"No," I said coldly. "I'll stand my own watch. I like being on the roofs," and added silently, *where I can watch you.*

He shrugged and said, "I suppose it's better than being down in the crypt. At least on the roofs you can hear the one that gets you."

*October 10*—I thought the double watches might be good for me, take my mind off my inability to retrieve. The watched-pot idea. Actually, it sometimes works. A few hours of thinking about something else, or a good night's sleep, and the fact pops forward without any prompting, without any artificials.

The good night's sleep is out of the question. Not only do the chars talk constantly, but the cat has moved into the crypt and sidles up to everyone, making siren noises and begging for kippers. I am moving my cot out of the transept and over by Nelson before I go on watch. He may be pickled, but he keeps his mouth shut.

*October 11*—I dreamed Trafalgar, ships' guns and smoke and falling plaster and Langby shouting my name. My first waking thought was that the folding chairs had gone off. I could not see for all the smoke.

"I'm coming," I said, limping toward Langby and pulling on my boots. There was a heap of plaster and tangled folding chairs in the transept. Langby was digging in it. "Bartholomew!" he shouted, flinging a chunk of plaster aside. "Bartholomew!"

I still had the idea it was smoke. I ran back for the stirrup pump and then knelt beside him and began pulling on a splintered chair back. It resisted, and it came to me suddenly, *There is a body under here. I will reach for a piece of the ceiling and find it is a hand.* I leaned back on my heels, determined not to be sick, then went at the pile again.

Langby was going far too fast, jabbing with a chair leg. I grabbed his hand to stop him, and he struggled against me as if I were a piece of rubble to be thrown aside. He picked up a large flat square of plaster, and under it was the floor. I turned and looked behind me. Both chars huddled in the recess by the altar. "Who are you looking for?" I said, keeping hold of Langby's arm.

"Bartholomew," he said, and swept the rubble aside, his hands bleeding through the coating of smoky dust.

"I'm here," I said. "I'm all right." I choked on the white dust. "I moved my cot out of the transept."

He turned sharply to the chars and then said quite calmly, "What's under here?"

"Only the gas ring," one of them said timidly from the shadowed recess, "and Mrs. Galbraith's pocketbook." He dug through the mess until he had found them both. The gas ring was leaking at a merry rate, though the flame had gone out.

"You've saved St. Paul's and me after all," I said, standing there in my underwear and boots, holding the useless stirrup pump. "We might all have been asphyxiated."

He stood up. "I shouldn't have saved you," he said.

Stage one: shock, stupefaction, unawareness of injuries, words may not make sense except to victim. He would not know his hand was bleeding yet. He would not remember what he had said. He had said he shouldn't have saved my life.

"I shouldn't have saved you," he repeated. "I have my duty to think of."

"You're bleeding," I said sharply. "You'd better lie down." I sounded just like Langby in the gallery.

*October 13*—It was a high explosive bomb. It blew a hole in the Choir, and some of the marble statuary is broken, but the ceiling of the crypt did not collapse, which is what I thought at first. It only jarred some plaster loose.

I do not think Langby has any idea what he said. That should give me some sort of advantage, now that I am sure where the danger lies, now that I am sure it will not come crashing down from some other direction. But what good is all this knowing, when I do not know what he will do? Or when?

Surely I have the facts of yesterday's bomb in long-term, but even falling plaster did not jar them loose this time. I am not even trying for retrieval, now. I lie in the darkness waiting for the roof to fall in on me. And remembering how Langby saved my life.

*October 15*—The girl came in again today. She still has the cold, but she has gotten her paying position. It was a joy to see her. She was wearing a smart uniform and open-toed shoes, and her hair was in an elaborate frizz around her face. We are still cleaning up the mess from the bomb, and Langby was out with Allen getting wood to board up the Choir, so I let the girl chatter at me while I swept. The dust made her sneeze, but at least this time I knew what she was doing.

She told me her name is Enola and that she's working for the WVS, running one of the mobile canteens that are sent to the fires. She came, of all things, to thank me for the job. She said that after she told the WVS that there was no proper shelter with a canteen for St. Paul's, they gave her a run in the City. "So I'll just pop in when I'm close and let you know how I'm making out, won't I just?"

She and her brother Tom are still sleeping in the tubes. I asked her if that was safe and she said probably not, but at least down there you couldn't hear the one that got you and that was a blessing.

*October 18*—I am so tired I can hardly write this. Nine incendiaries tonight and a land mine that looked as though it was going to catch on the dome till the wind drifted its parachute away from the church. I put out two of the incendiaries. I have done that at least twenty times since I got here and helped with dozens of others, and still it is not enough. One incendiary, one moment of not watching Langby, could undo it all.

I know that is partly why I feel so tired. I wear myself out every night trying to do my job and watch Langby, making sure none of the incendiaries falls without my seeing it. Then I go back to the crypt and wear myself out trying to retrieve something, anything, about spies, fires, St. Paul's in the fall of 1940, anything. It haunts me that I am not doing enough, but I do not know what else to do. Without the retrieval, I am as helpless as these poor people here, with no idea what will happen tomorrow.

If I have to, I will go on doing this till I am called home. He cannot burn down St. Paul's so long as I am here to put out the incendiaries. "I have my duty," Langby said in the crypt.

And I have mine.

*October 21*—It's been nearly two weeks since the blast and I just now realized we haven't seen the cat since. He wasn't in the mess in the crypt. Even after Langby and I were sure there was no one in there, we sifted through the stuff twice more. He could have been in the Choir, though.

Old Bence-Jones says not to worry. "He's all right," he said. "The jerries could bomb London right down to the ground and the cats would waltz out to greet them. You know why? They don't love anybody. That's what gets half of us killed. Old lady out in Stepney got killed the other night trying to save her cat. Bloody cat was in the Anderson."

"Then where is he?"

"Someplace safe, you can bet on that. If he's not around St. Paul's, it means we're for it. That old saw about the rats deserting a sinking ship, that's a mistake, that is. It's cats, not rats."

*October 25*—Langby's tourist showed up again. He cannot still be looking for the Windmill Theatre. He had a newspaper under his arm again today, and he asked for Langby, but Langby was across town with Allen, trying to get the asbestos firemen's coats. I saw the name of the paper. It was *The Worker*. A Nazi newspaper?

*November 2*—I've been up on the roofs for a week straight, helping some incompetent workmen patch the hole the bomb made. They're doing a terrible job. There's still a great gap on one side a man could fall into, but they insist it'll be all right because, after all, you wouldn't fall clear through but only as far as the ceiling, and "the fall can't kill you." They don't seem to understand it's a perfect hiding place for an incendiary.

And that is all Langby needs. He does not even have to set a fire to destroy St. Paul's. All he needs to do is let one burn uncaught until it is too late.

I could not get anywhere with the workmen. I went down into the church to complain to Matthews, and saw Langby and his tourist behind a pillar, close to one of the windows. Langby was holding a newspaper and talking to the man. When I came down from the library an hour later, they were still there. So is the gap. Matthews says we'll put planks across it and hope for the best.

*November 5*—I have given up trying to retrieve. I am so far behind on my sleep I can't even retrieve information on a newspaper whose name I already know. Double watches the permanent thing now. Our chars have abandoned us altogether (like the cat), so the crypt is quiet, but I cannot sleep.

If I do manage to doze off, I dream. Yesterday I dreamed Kivrin was on the roofs, dressed like a saint. "What was the secret of your practicum?" I said. "What were you supposed to find out?"

She wiped her nose with a handkerchief and said, "Two things. One, that silence and humility are the sacred burdens of the historian. Two"—she stopped and sneezed into the handkerchief—"don't sleep in the tubes."

My only hope is to get hold of an artificial and induce a trance. That's a problem. I'm positive it's too early for chemical endorphins and probably hallucinogens. Alcohol is definitely available, but I need something more concentrated than ale, the only alcohol I know by name. I do not dare ask the watch. Langby is suspicious enough of me already. It's back to the OED, to look up a word I don't know.

*November 11*—The cat's back. Langby was out with Allen again, still trying for the asbestos coats, so I thought it was safe to leave St. Paul's. I went to the grocers for supplies, and hopefully an artificial. It was late, and the sirens sounded before I had even gotten to Cheapside, but the raids do not usually start until after dark. It took awhile to get all the groceries and to get up my courage to ask whether he had any alcohol— he told me to go to a pub—and when I came out of the shop, it was as if I had pitched suddenly into a hole.

I had no idea where St. Paul's lay, or the street, or the shop I had just come from. I stood on what was no longer the sidewalk, clutching my brown-paper parcel of kippers and bread with a hand I could not have seen if I held it up before my face. I reached up to wrap my muffler closer about my neck and prayed for my eyes to adjust, but there was no reduced light to adjust to. I would have been glad of the moon, for all St. Paul's watch cursed it and called it a fifth columnist. Or a bus, with its shuttered headlights giving just enough light to orient myself by. Or a searchlight. Or the kickback flare of an ack-ack gun. Anything.

Just then I did see a bus, two narrow yellow slits a long way off. I started toward it and nearly pitched off the curb. Which meant the bus was sideways in the street, which meant it was not a bus. A cat meowed, quite near, and rubbed against my leg. I looked down into the yellow lights I had thought belonged to the bus. His eyes were picking up light from somewhere, though I would have sworn there was not a light for miles, and reflecting it flatly up at me.

"A warden'll get you for those lights, old tom," I said, and then as a plane droned overhead, "Or a jerry."

The world exploded suddenly into light, the searchlights and a glow along the Thames seeming to happen almost simultaneously, lighting my way home.

"Come to fetch me, did you, old tom?" I said gaily. "Where've you been? Knew we were out of kippers, didn't you? I call that loyalty." I talked to him all the way home and gave him half a tin of the kippers for saving my life. Bence-Jones said he smelled the milk at the grocer's.

*November 13*—I dreamed I was lost in the blackout. I could not see my hands in front of my face, and Dunworthy came and shone a pocket torch at me, but I could only see where I had come from and not where I was going.

"What good is that to them?" I said. "They need a light to show them where they're going."

"Even the light from the Thames? Even the light from the fires and the ack-ack guns?" Dunworthy said.

"Yes. Anything is better than this awful darkness." So he came closer to give me the pocket torch. It was not a pocket torch, after all, but Christ's lantern from the Hunt picture in the south nave. I shone it on the curb before me so I could find my way home, but it shone instead on the fire watch stone and I hastily put the light out.

*November 20*—I tried to talk to Langby today. "I've seen you talking to the old gentleman," I said. It sounded like an accusation. I meant it to. I wanted him to think it was and stop whatever he was planning.

"Reading," he said. "Not talking." He was putting things in order in the choir, piling up sandbags.

"I've seen you reading then," I said belligerently, and he dropped a sandbag and straightened.

"What of it?" he said. "It's a free country. I can read to an old man if I want, same as you can talk to that little WVS tart."

"What do you read?" I said.

"Whatever he wants. He's an old man. He used to come home from his job, have a bit of brandy and listen to his wife read the papers to him. She got killed in one of the raids. Now I read to him. I don't see what business it is of yours."

It sounded true. It didn't have the careful casualness of a lie, and I almost believed him, except that I had heard the tone of truth from him before. In the crypt. After the bomb.

"I thought he was a tourist looking for the Windmill," I said.

He looked blank only a second, and then he said, "Oh, yes, that. He came in with the paper and asked me to tell him where it was. I looked it up to find the address. Clever, that. I didn't guess he couldn't read it for himself." But it was enough. I knew that he was lying.

He heaved a sandbag almost at my feet. "Of course you wouldn't understand a thing like that, would you? A simple act of human kindness?"

"No," I said coldly. "I wouldn't."

None of this proves anything. He gave away nothing, except perhaps the name of an artificial, and I can hardly go to Dean Matthews and accuse Langby of reading aloud.

I waited till he had finished in the choir and gone down to the crypt. Then I lugged one of the sandbags up to the roof and over to the chasm. The planking has held so far, but everyone walks gingerly around it, as if it were a grave. I cut the sandbag open and spilled the loose sand into the bottom. If it has occurred to Langby that this is the perfect spot for an incendiary, perhaps the sand will smother it.

*November 21*—I gave Enola some of "uncle's" money today and asked her to get me the brandy. She was more reluctant than I thought she'd be, so there must be societal complications I am not aware of, but she agreed.

I don't know what she came for. She started to tell me about her brother and some prank he'd pulled in the tubes that got him in trouble with the guard, but after I asked her about the brandy, she left without finishing the story.

*November 25*—Enola came today, but without bringing the brandy. She is going to Bath for the holidays to see her aunt. At least she will be away from the raids for a while. I will not have to worry about her. She finished the story of her brother and told me she hopes to persuade this aunt to take Tom for the duration of the Blitz but is not at all sure the aunt will be willing.

Young Tom is apparently not so much an engaging scapegrace as a near criminal. He has been caught twice picking pockets in the Bank tube shelter, and they have had to go back to Marble Arch. I comforted her as best I could, told her all boys were bad at one time or another. What I really wanted to say was that she needn't worry at all, that young Tom strikes me as a true survivor type, like my own tom, like Langby, totally unconcerned with anybody but himself, well-equipped to survive the Blitz and rise to prominence in the future.

Then I asked her whether she had gotten the brandy.

She looked down at her open-toed shoes and muttered unhappily, "I thought you'd forgotten all about that."

I made up some story about the watch taking turns buying a bottle, and she seemed less unhappy, but I am not convinced she will not use this trip to Bath as an excuse to do nothing. I will have to leave St. Paul's and buy it myself, and I don't dare leave Langby alone in the church. I made her promise to bring the brandy today before she leaves. But she is still not back, and the sirens have already gone.

*November 26*—No Enola, and she said their train left at noon. I suppose I should be grateful that at least she is safely out of London. Perhaps in Bath she will be able to get over her cold.

Tonight one of the ARP girls breezed in to borrow half our cots and tell us about a mess over in the East End where a surface shelter was hit. Four dead, twelve wounded. "At least it wasn't one of the tube shelters!" she said. "Then you'd see a real mess, wouldn't you?"

*November 30*—I dreamed I took the cat to St. John's Wood.

"Is this a rescue mission?" Dunworthy said.

"No, sir," I said proudly. "I know what I was supposed to find in my practicum. The perfect survivor. Tough and resourceful and selfish. This is the only one I could find. I had to kill Langby, you know, to keep him from burning down St. Paul's. Enola's brother has gone to Bath, and the others will never make it. Enola wears open-toed shoes in the winter and sleeps in the tubes and puts her hair up on metal pins so it will curl. She cannot possibly survive the Blitz."

Dunworthy said, "Perhaps you should have rescued her instead. What did you say her name was?"

"Kivrin," I said, and woke up cold and shivering.

*December 5*—I dreamed Langby had the pinpoint bomb. He carried it under his arm like a brown paper parcel, coming out of St. Paul's Station and around Ludgate Hill to the west doors.

"This is not fair," I said, barring his way with my arm. "There is no fire watch on duty."

He clutched the bomb to his chest like a pillow. "That is your fault," he said, and before I could get to my stirrup pump and bucket, he tossed it in the door.

The pinpoint was not even invented until the end of the twentieth century, and it was another ten years before the dispossessed communists got hold of it and turned it into something that could be carried under your arm. A parcel that could blow a quarter mile of the City into oblivion. Thank God that is one dream that cannot come true.

It was a sunlit morning in the dream, and this morning when I came off watch the sun was shining for the first time in weeks. I went down to the crypt and then came up again, making the rounds of the roofs twice more, then the steps and the grounds and all the treacherous alleyways between, where an incendiary could be missed. I felt better after that, but when I got to sleep I dreamed again, this time of fire and Langby watching it, smiling.

*December 15*—I found the cat this morning. Heavy raids last night, but most of them over toward Canning Town and nothing on the roofs to speak of. Nevertheless the cat was quite dead. I found him lying on the steps this morning when I made my own, private rounds. Concussion. There was not a mark on him anywhere except the white blackout patch on his throat, but when I picked him up, he was all jelly under the skin.

I could not think what to do with him. I thought for one mad moment of asking Matthews if I could bury him in the crypt. Honorable death in war or something. Trafalgar, Waterloo, London, died in battle. I ended by wrapping him in my muffler and taking him down Ludgate Hill to a building that had been bombed out and burying him in the rubble. It will do no good. The rubble will be no protection from dogs or rats, and I shall never get another muffler. I have gone through nearly all of uncle's money.

I should not be sitting here. I haven't checked the alleyways or the rest of the steps, and there might be a dud or a delayed incendiary or something that I missed.

When I came here, I thought of myself as the noble rescuer, the savior of the past. I am not doing very well at the job. At least Enola is out of it. I wish there were some way I could send St. Paul's to Bath for safekeeping. There were hardly any raids last night. Bence-Jones said cats can survive anything. What if he was coming to get me, to show me the way home? All the bombs were over Canning Town.

*December 16*—Enola has been back a week. Seeing her, standing on the west steps where I found the cat, sleeping in Marble Arch and not safe at all, was more than I could absorb. "I thought you were in Bath," I said stupidly.

"My aunt said she'd take Tom but not me as well. She's got a houseful of evacuation children, and what a noisy lot. Where is your muffler?" she said. "It's dreadful cold up here on the hill."

"I..." I said, unable to answer, "I lost it."

"You'll never get another one," she said. "They're going to start rationing clothes. And wool, too. You'll never get another one like that."

"I know," I said, blinking at her.

"Good things just thrown away" she said. "It's absolutely criminal, that's what it is."

I don't think I said anything to that, just turned and walked away with my head down, looking for bombs and dead animals.

*December 20*—Langby isn't a Nazi. He's a communist. I can hardly write this. A communist.

One of the chars found *The Worker* wedged behind a pillar and brought it down to the crypt as we were coming off the first watch.

"Bloody communists," Bence-Jones said. "Helping Hitler, they are. Talking against the king, stirring up trouble in the shelters. Traitors, that's what they are."

"They love England same as you," the char said.

"They don't love nobody but themselves, bloody selfish lot. I wouldn't be surprised to hear they were ringing Hitler up on the telephone," Bence-Jones said. "'Ello, Adolf, here's where to drop the bombs.'"

The kettle on the gas ring whistled. The char stood up and poured the hot water into a chipped teapot, then sat back down. "Just because they speak their minds don't mean they'd burn down old St. Paul's, does it now?"

"Of course not," Langby said, coming down the stairs. He sat down and pulled off his boots, stretching his feet in their wool socks. "Who wouldn't burn down St. Paul's?"

"The communists," Bence-Jones said, looking straight at him, and I wondered if he suspected Langby too.

Langby never batted an eye. "I wouldn't worry about them if I were you," he said. "It's the jerries that are doing their bloody best to burn her down tonight. Six incendiaries so far, and one almost went into that great hole over the choir." He held out his cup to the char, and she poured him a cup of tea.

I wanted to kill him, smashing him to dust and rubble on the floor of the crypt while Bence-Jones and the char looked on in helpless surprise, shouting warnings to them and the rest of the watch. "Do you know what the communists did?" I wanted to shout. "Do you? We have to stop him." I even stood up and started toward him as he sat with his feet stretched out before him and his asbestos coat still over his shoulders.

And then the thought of the Gallery drenched in gold, the communist coming out of the tube station with the package so casually under his arm, made me sick with the same staggering vertigo of guilt and helplessness, and I sat back down on the edge of my cot and tried to think what to do.

They do not realize the danger. Even Bence-Jones, for all his talk of traitors, thinks they are capable only of talking against the king. They do not know, cannot know, what the communists will become. Stalin is an ally. Communists mean Russia. They have never heard of Karinsky or the New Russia or any of the things that will make "communist" into a synonym for "monster." They will never know it. By the time the communists become what they became, there will be no fire watch. Only I know what it means to hear the name "communist" uttered here, so carelessly, in St. Paul's.

A communist. I should have known. I should have known.

*December 22*—Double watches again. I have not had any sleep and I am getting very unsteady on my feet. I nearly pitched into the chasm this morning, only saved myself by dropping to my knees. My endorphin levels are fluctuating wildly, and I know I must get some sleep soon or I will become one of Langby's walking dead, but I am afraid to leave him alone on the roofs, alone in the church with his communist party leader, alone anywhere. I have taken to watching him when he sleeps.

If I could just get hold of an artificial, I think I could induce a trance, in spite of my poor condition. But I cannot even go out to a pub. Langby is on the roofs constantly, waiting for his chance. When Enola comes again I must convince her to get the brandy for me. There are only a few days left.

*December 28*—Enola came this morning while I was on the west porch, picking up the Christmas tree. It has been knocked over three nights running by concussion. I righted the tree and was bending down to pick up the scattered tinsel when Enola appeared suddenly out of the fog like some cheerful saint. She stooped quickly and kissed me on the cheek. Then she straightened up, her nose red from her perennial cold, and handed me a box wrapped in colored paper.

"Merry Christmas," she said. "Go on then, open it. It's a gift."

My reflexes are almost totally gone. I knew the box was far too shallow for a bottle of brandy. Nevertheless, I believed she had remembered, had brought me my salvation. "You darling," I said, and tore it open.

It was a muffler. Gray wool. I stared at it for fully half a minute without realizing what it was. "Where's the brandy?" I said.

She looked shocked. Her nose got redder and her eyes started to blur. "You need this more. You haven't any clothing coupons and you have to be outside all the time. It's been so dreadful cold."

"I *needed* the brandy," I said angrily.

"I was only trying to be kind," she started, and I cut her off.

"Kind?" I said. "I asked you for brandy. I don't recall ever saying I needed a muffler. "I shoved it back at her and began untangling a string of colored lights that had shattered when the tree fell.

She got that same holy martyr look Kivrin is so wonderful at. "I worry about you all the time up here," she said in a rush. "They're *trying* for St. Paul's, you know. And it's so close to the river. I didn't think you should be drinking. I—it's a crime when they're trying so hard to kill us all that you won't take care of yourself. It's like you're in it with them. I worry someday I'll come up to St. Paul's and you won't be here."

"Well, and what exactly am I supposed to do with a muffler? Hold it over my head when they drop the bombs?"

She turned and ran, disappearing into the gray fog before she had gone down two steps. I started after her, still holding the string of broken lights, tripped over it, and fell almost all the way to the bottom of the steps.

Langby picked me up. "You're off watches," he said grimly.

"You can't do that," I said.

"Oh, yes, I can. I don't want any walking dead on the roofs with me."

I let him lead me down here to the crypt, make me a cup of tea, put me to bed, all very solicitous. No indication that this is what he has been waiting for. I will lie here till the sirens go. Once I am on the roofs he will not be able to send me back without seeming suspicious. Do you know what he said before he left, asbestos coat and rubber boots, the dedicated fire watcher? "I want you to get some sleep." As if I could sleep with Langby on the roofs. I would be burned alive.

*December 30*—The sirens woke me, and old Bence-Jones said, "That should have done you some good. You've slept the clock round."

"What day is it?" I said, going for my boots.

"The twenty-ninth," he said, and as I dived for the door, "No need to hurry. They're late tonight. Perhaps they won't come at all. That'd be a blessing, that would. The tide's out."

I stopped by the door to the stairs, holding on to the cool stone. "Is St. Paul's all right?"

"She's still standing," he said. "Have a bad dream?"

"Yes," I said, remembering the bad dreams of all the past weeks—the dead cat in my arms in St. John's Wood, Langby with his parcel and his *Worker* under his arm, the fire watch stone garishly lit by Christ's lantern. Then I remembered I had not dreamed at all. I had slept the kind of sleep I had prayed for, the kind of sleep that would help me remember.

Then I remembered. Not St. Paul's, burned to the ground by the communists. A headline from the dailies. "Marble Arch hit. Eighteen killed by blast." The date was not clear except for the year. 1940. There were exactly two more days left in 1940. I grabbed my coat and muffler and ran up the stairs and across the marble floor.

"Where the hell do you think you're going?" Langby shouted to me. I couldn't see him.

"I have to save Enola," I said, and my voice echoed in the dark sanctuary. "They're going to bomb Marble Arch."

"You can't leave now," he shouted after me, standing where the fire watch stone would be. "The tide's out. You dirty—"

I didn't hear the rest of it. I had already flung myself down the steps and into a taxi. It took almost all the money I had, the money I had so carefully hoarded for the trip back to St. John's Wood. Shelling started while we were still in Oxford Street, and the driver refused to go any farther. He let me out into pitch blackness, and I saw I would never make it in time.

Blast. Enola crumpled on the stairway down to the tube, her opentoed shoes still on her feet, not a mark on her. And when I try to lift her, jelly under the skin. I would have to wrap her in the muffler she gave me, because I was too late. I had gone back a hundred years to be too late to save her.

I ran the last blocks, guided by the gun emplacement that had to be in Hyde Park, and skidded down the steps into Marble Arch. The woman in the ticket booth took my last shilling for a ticket to St. Paul's Station. I stuck it in my pocket and raced toward the stairs.

"No running," she said placidly. "To your left, please." The door to the right was blocked off by wooden barricades, the metal gates beyond pulled to and chained. The board with names on it for the stations was x-ed with tape, and a new sign that read ALL TRAINS was nailed to the barricade, pointing left.

Enola was not on the stopped escalators or sitting against the wall in the hallway. I came to the first stairway and could not get through. A family had set out, just where I wanted to step, a communal tea of bread and butter, a little pot of jam sealed with waxed paper, and a kettle on a ring like the one Langby and I had rescued out of the rubble, all of it spread on a cloth embroidered at the corners with flowers. I stood staring down at the layered tea, spread like a waterfall down the steps.

"I—Marble Arch—" I said. Another twenty killed by flying tiles. "You shouldn't be here."

"We've as much right as anyone," the man said belligerently, "and who are you to tell us to move on?"

A woman lifting saucers out of a cardboard box looked up at me, frightened. The kettle began to whistle.

"It's you that should move on," the man said. "Go on then." He stood off to one side so I could pass. I edged past the embroidered cloth apologetically.

"I'm sorry," I said. "I'm looking for someone. On the platform."

"You'll never find her in there, mate," the man said, thumbing in that direction. I hurried past him, nearly stepping on the tea cloth, and rounded the corner into hell.

It was not hell. Shopgirls folded coats and leaned back against them, cheerful or sullen or disagreeable, but certainly not damned. Two boys scuffled for a shilling and lost it on the tracks. They bent over the edge, debating whether to go after it, and the station guard yelled to them to back away. A train rumbled through, full of people. A mosquito landed on the guard's hand and he reached out to slap it and missed. The boys laughed.

And behind and before them, stretching in all directions down the deadly tile curves of the tunnel like casualties, backed into the entranceways and onto the stairs, were people. Hundreds and hundreds of people.

I stumbled back onto the stairs, knocking over a teacup. It spilled like a flood across the cloth.

"I told you, mate," the man said cheerfully. "It's hell in there, ain't it? And worse below."

"Hell," I said. "Yes." I would never find her. I would never save her. I looked at the woman mopping up the tea, and it came to me that I could not save her either. Enola or the cat or any of them, lost here in the endless stairways and cul-de-sacs of time. They were already dead a hundred years, past saving. The past is beyond saving. Surely that was the lesson the history department sent me all this way to learn. Well, fine, I've learned it. Can I go home now?

Of course not, dear boy. You have foolishly spent all your money on taxicabs and brandy, and tonight is the night the Germans burn the City. (Now it is too late, I remember it all. Twenty-eight incendiaries on the roofs.) Langby must have his chance, and you must learn the hardest lesson of all and the one you should have known from the beginning. You cannot save St. Paul's.

I went back out onto the platform and stood behind the yellow line until a train pulled up. I took my ticket out and held it in my hand all the way to St. Paul's Station. When I got there, smoke billowed toward me like an easy spray of water. I could not see St. Paul's.

"The tide's out," a woman said in a voice devoid of hope, and I went down in a snake pit of limp cloth hoses. My hands came up covered with rank-smelling mud, and I understood finally (and too late) the significance of the tide. There was no water to fight the fires.

A policeman barred my way and I stood helplessly before him with no idea what to say. "No civilians allowed here," he said. "St. Paul's is for it." The smoke billowed like a thundercloud, alive with sparks, and the dome rose golden above it.

"I'm fire watch," I said, and his arm fell away, and then I was on the roofs.

My endorphin levels must have been going up and down like an air raid siren. I do not have any short-term from then on, just moments that do not fit together: the people in the church when we brought Langby down, huddled in a corner playing cards, the whirlwind of burning scraps of wood in the dome, the ambulance driver who wore open-toed shoes like Enola and smeared salve on my burned hands. And in the center, the one clear moment when I went after Langby on a rope and saved his life.

I stood by the dome, blinking against the smoke. The City was on fire and it seemed as if St. Paul's would ignite from the heat, would crumble from the noise alone. Bence-Jones was by the northwest tower, hitting at an incendiary with a spade. Langby was too close to the patched place where the bomb had gone through, looking toward me. An incendiary clattered behind him. I turned to grab a shovel, and when I turned back, he was gone.

"Langby!" I shouted, and could not hear my own voice. He had fallen into the chasm and nobody saw him or the incendiary. Except me. I do not remember how I got across the roof. I think I called for a rope. I got a rope. I tied it around my waist, gave the ends of it into the hands of the fire watch, and went over the side. The fires lit the walls of the hole almost all the way to the bottom. Below me I could see a pile of whitish rubble. He's under there, I thought, and jumped free of the wall. The space was so narrow there was nowhere to throw the rubble. I was afraid I would inadvertently stone him, and I tried to toss the pieces of planking and plaster over my shoulder, but there was barely room to turn. For one awful moment I thought he might not be there at all, that the pieces of splintered wood would brush away to reveal empty pavement, as they had in the crypt.

I was numbed by the indignity of crawling over him. If he was dead I did not think I could bear the shame of stepping on his helpless body Then his hand came up like a ghost's and grabbed my ankle, and within seconds I had whirled and had his head free.

He was the ghastly white that no longer frightens me. "I put the bomb out," he said. I stared at him, so overwhelmed with relief I could not speak. For one hysterical moment I thought I would even laugh, I was so glad to see him. I finally realized what it was I was supposed to say.

"Are you all right?" I said.

"Yes," he said, and tried to raise himself on one elbow. "So much the worse for you."

He could not get up. He grunted with pain when he tried to shift his weight to his right side and lay back, the uneven rubble crunching sickeningly under him. I tried to lift him gently so I could see where he was hurt. He must have fallen on something.

"It's no use," he said, breathing hard. "I put it out."

I spared him a startled glance, afraid that he was delirious and went back to rolling him onto his side.

"I know you were counting on this one," he went on, not resisting me at all. "It was bound to happen sooner or later with all these roofs. Only I went after it. What'll you tell your friends?"

His asbestos coat was torn down the back in a long gash. Under it his back was charred and smoking. He had fallen on the incendiary. "Oh, my God," I said, trying frantically to see how badly he was burned without touching him. I had no way of knowing how deep the burns went, but they seemed to extend only in the narrow space where the coat had torn. I tried to pull the bomb out from under him, but the casing was as hot as a stove. It was not melting, though. My sand and Langby's body had smothered it. I had no idea if it would start up again when it was exposed to the air. I looked around, a little wildly, for the bucket and stirrup pump Langby must have dropped when he fell.

"Looking for a weapon?" Langby said, so clearly it was hard to believe he was hurt at all. "Why not just leave me here? A bit of overexposure and I'd be done for by morning. Or would you rather do your dirty work in private?"

I stood up and yelled to the men on the roof above us. One of them shone a pocket torch down at us, but its light didn't reach.

"Is he dead?" somebody shouted down to me.

"Send for an ambulance," I said. "He's been burned."

I helped Langby up, trying to support his back without touching the burn. He staggered a little and then leaned against the wall, watching me as I tried to bury the incendiary, using a piece of the planking as a scoop. The rope came down and I tied Langby to it. He had not spoken since I helped him up. He let me tie the rope around his waist, still looking steadily at me. "I should have let you smother in the crypt," he said.

He stood leaning easily, almost relaxed against the wooden supports, his hands holding him up. I put his hands on the slack rope and wrapped it once around them for the grip I knew he didn't have. "I've been onto you since that day in the Gallery. I knew you weren't afraid of heights. You came down here without any fear of heights when you thought I'd ruined your precious plans. What was it? An attack of conscience? Kneeling there like a baby, whining, 'What have we done? What have we done?' You made me sick. But you know what gave you away first? The cat. Everybody knows cats hate water. Everybody but a dirty Nazi spy."

There was a tug on the rope. "Come ahead," I said, and the rope tautened.

"That WVS tart? Was she a spy, too? Supposed to meet you in Marble Arch? Telling me it was going to be bombed. You're a rotten spy, Bartholomew. Your friends already blew it up in September. It's open again."

The rope jerked suddenly and began to lift Langby He twisted his hands to get a better grip. His right shoulder scraped the wall. I put up my hands and pushed him gently so that his left side was to the wall. "You're making a big mistake, you know," he said. "You should have killed me. I'll tell."

I stood in the darkness, waiting for the rope. Langby was unconscious when he reached the roof. I walked past the fire watch to the dome and down to the crypt.

This morning the letter from my uncle came and with it a five-pound note.

*December 31*—Two of Dunworthy's flunkies met me in St. John's Wood to tell me I was late for my exams. I did not even protest. I shuffled obediently after them without even considering how unfair it was to give an exam to one of the walking dead. I had not slept in—how long? Since yesterday when I went to find Enola. I had not slept in a hundred years.

Dunworthy was in the Examination Buildings, blinking at me. One of the flunkies handed me a test paper and the other one called time. I turned the paper over and left an oily smudge from the ointment on my burns. I stared uncomprehendingly at them. I had grabbed at the incendiary when I turned Langby over, but these burns were on the backs of my hands. The answer came to me suddenly in Langby's unyielding voice. "They're rope burns, you fool. Don't they teach you Nazi spies the proper way to come up a rope?"

I looked down at the test. It read, "Number of incendiaries that fell on St. Paul's_____Number of land mines_____Number of high explosive bombs_____Method most commonly used for extinguishing incendiaries_____land mines_____high explosive bombs_____Number of volunteers on first watch_____second watch_____ Casualties_____Fatalities_____" The questions made no sense. There was only a short space, long enough for the writing of a number, after any of the questions. Method most commonly used for extinguishing incendiaries. How would I ever fit what I knew into that narrow space? Where were the questions about Enola and Langby and the cat?

I went up to Dunworthy's desk. "St. Paul's almost burned down last night," I said. "What kind of questions are these?"

"You should be answering questions, Mr. Bartholomew, not asking them."

"There aren't any questions about the people," I said. The outer casing of my anger began to melt.

"Of course there are," Dunworthy said, flipping to the second page of the test. "Number of casualties, 1940. Blast, shrapnel, other."

"Other?" I said. At any moment the roof would collapse on me in a shower of plaster dust and fury. "Other? Langby put out a fire with his own body. Enola has a cold that keeps getting worse. The cat…" I snatched the paper back from him and scrawled "one cat" in the narrow space next to "blast." "Don't you care about them at all?"

"They're important from a statistical point of view," he said, "but as individuals they are hardly relevant to the course of history."

My reflexes were shot. It was amazing to me that Dunworthy's were almost as slow. I grazed the side of his jaw and knocked his glasses off. "Of course they're relevant!" I shouted. "They *are* the history, not all these bloody numbers!"

The reflexes of the flunkies were very fast. They did not let me start another swing at him before they had me by both arms and were hauling me out of the room.

"They're back there in the past with nobody to save them. They can't see their hands in front of their faces and there are bombs falling down on them and you tell me they aren't important? You call that being an historian?"

The flunkies dragged me out the door and down the hall. "Langby saved St. Paul's. How much more important can a person get? You're no historian! You're nothing but a—" I wanted to call him a terrible name, but the only curses I could summon up were Langby's. "You're nothing but a dirty Nazi spy!" I bellowed. "You're nothing but a lazy bourgeois tart!"

They dumped me on my hands and knees outside the door and slammed it in my face. "I wouldn't be an historian if you paid me!" I shouted, and went to see the fire watch stone.

*December 31*—I am having to write this in bits and pieces. My hands are in pretty bad shape, and Dunworthy's boys didn't help matters much. Kivrin comes in periodically, wearing her St. Joan look, and smears so much salve on my hands that I can't hold a pencil.

St. Paul's Station is not there, of course, so I got out at Holborn and walked, thinking about my last meeting with Dean Matthews on the morning after the burning of the city. This morning.

"I understand you saved Langby's life," he said. "I also understand that between you, you saved St. Paul's last night."

I showed him the letter from my uncle and he stared at it as if he could not think what it was. "Nothing stays saved forever," he said, and for a terrible moment I thought he was going to tell me Langby had died. "We shall have to keep on saving St. Paul's until Hitler decides to bomb something else."

The raids on London are almost over, I wanted to tell him. He'll start bombing the countryside in a matter of weeks. Canterbury, Bath, aiming always at the cathedrals. You and St. Paul's will both outlast the war and live to dedicate the fire watch stone.

"I am hopeful, though," he said. "I think the worst is over."

"Yes, sir." I thought of the stone, its letters still readable after all this time. No, sir, the worst is not over.

I managed to keep my bearings almost to the top of Ludgate Hill. Then I lost my way completely, wandering about like a man in a grave-yard. I had not remembered that the rubble looked so much like the white plaster dust Langby had tried to dig me out of. I could not find the stone anywhere. In the end I nearly fell over it, jumping back as if I had stepped on a body.

It is all that's left. Hiroshima is supposed to have had a handful of un-touched trees at ground zero. Denver the capitol steps. Neither of them says, "Remember men and women of St. Paul's Watch who by the grace of God saved this cathedral." The grace of God.

Part of the stone is sheared off. Historians argue there was another line that said, "for all time," but I do not believe that, not if Dean Matthews had anything to do with it. And none of the watch it was dedicated to would have believed it for a minute. We saved St. Paul's every time we put out an incendiary, and only until the next one fell. Keeping watch on the danger spots, putting out the little fires with sand and stirrup pumps, the big ones with our bodies, in order to keep the whole vast complex structure from burning down. Which sounds to me like a course description for History Practicum 401. What a fine time to discover what historians are for when I have tossed my chance for being one out the windows as easily as they tossed the pinpoint bomb in! No, sir, the worst is not over.

There are flash burns on the stone, where legend says the Dean of St. Paul's was kneeling when the bomb went off. Totally apocryphal, of course, since the front door is hardly an appropriate place for prayers. It is more likely the shadow of a tourist who wandered in to ask the whereabouts of the Windmill Theatre, or the imprint of a girl bringing a volunteer his muffler. Or a cat.

Nothing is saved forever, Dean Matthews, and I knew that when I walked in the west doors that first day, blinking into the gloom, but it is pretty bad nevertheless. Standing here knee-deep in rubble out of which I will not be able to dig any folding chairs or friends, knowing that Langby died thinking I was a Nazi spy, knowing that Enola came one day and I wasn't there. It's pretty bad.

But it is not as bad as it could be. They are both dead, and Dean Matthews too, but they died without knowing what I knew all along, what sent me to my knees in the Whispering Gallery, sick with grief and guilt: that in the end none of us saved St. Paul's. And Langby cannot turn to me, stunned and sick at heart, and say, "Who did this? Your friends the Nazis?" And I would have to say, "No, the communists." That would be the worst.

I have come back to the room and let Kivrin smear more salve on my hands. She wants me to get some sleep. I know I should pack and get gone. It will be humiliating to have them come and throw me out, but I do not have the strength to fight her. She looks so much like Enola.

*January 1*—I have apparently slept not only through the night, but through the morning mail drop as well. When I woke up just now, I found Kivrin sitting on the end of the bed holding an envelope. "Your grades came," she said.

I put my arm over my eyes. "They can be marvelously efficient when they want to, can't they?"

"Yes," Kivrin said.

"Well, let's see it," I said, sitting up. "How long do I have before they come and throw me out?"

She handed the flimsy computer envelope to me. I tore it along the perforation. "Wait," she said. "Before you open it, I want to say something." She put her hand gently on my burns. "You're wrong about the history department. They're very good."

It was not exactly what I expected her to say. "Good is not the word I'd use to describe Dunworthy," I said and yanked the inside slip free.

Kivrin's look did not change, not even when I sat there with the print-out on my knees where she could surely see it.

"Well," I said.

The slip was hand-signed by the esteemed Dunworthy. I have taken a first. With honors.

*January 2*—Two things came in the mail today. One was Kivrin's assignment. The history department thinks of everything—even to keeping her here long enough to nursemaid me, even to coming up with a prefabricated trial by fire to send their history majors through.

I think I wanted to believe that was what they had done, Enola and Langby only hired actors, the cat a clever android with its clockwork innards taken out for the final effect, not so much because I wanted to believe Dunworthy was not good at all, but because then I would not have this nagging pain at not knowing what had happened to them.

"You said your practicum was England in 1400?" I said, watching her as suspiciously as I had watched Langby.

"1348," she said, and her face went slack with memory. "The plague year."

"My God," I said. "How could they do that? The plague's a ten."

"I have a natural immunity," she said, and looked at her hands.

Because I could not think of anything to say I opened the other piece of mail. It was a report on Enola. Computer-printed, facts and dates and statistics, all the numbers the history department so dearly loves, but it told me what I thought I would have to go without knowing: that she had gotten over her cold and survived the Blitz. Young Tom had been killed in the Baedaker raids on Bath, but Enola had lived until 2006, ten years before they blew up St. Paul's.

I don't know whether I believe the report or not, but it does not matter. It is, like Langby's reading aloud to the old man, a simple act of human kindness. They think of everything.

Not quite. They did not tell me what happened to Langby. But I find as I write this that I already know: I saved his life. It does not seem to matter that he might have died in hospital next day, and I find, in spite of all the hard lessons the history department has tried to teach me, I do not quite believe this one: that nothing is saved forever. It seems to me that perhaps Langby is.

*January 3*—I went to see Dunworthy today. I don't know what I intended to say—some pompous drivel about my willingness to serve in the fire watch of history, standing guard against the falling incendiaries of the human heart, silent and saintly.

But he blinked at me nearsightedly across his desk, and it seemed to me that he was blinking at that last bright image of St. Paul's in sunlight before it was gone forever and that he knew better than anyone that the past cannot be saved, and I said instead, "I'm sorry that I broke your glasses, sir."

"How did you like St. Paul's?" he said, and like my first meeting with Enola, I felt I must be somehow reading the signals all wrong, that he was not feeling loss, but something quite different.

"I loved it, sir," I said.

"Yes," he said. "So do I."

Dean Matthews is wrong. I have fought with memory my whole practicum only to find that it is not the enemy at all, and being an historian is not some saintly burden after all. Because Dunworthy is not blinking against the fatal sunlight of the last morning, but into the gloom of that first afternoon, looking in the great west doors of St. Paul's at what is, like Langby, like all of it, every moment, in us, saved forever.

# Nonstop to Portales

Every town's got a claim to fame. No town is too little and dried out to have some kind of tourist attraction. John Garfield's grave, Willa Cather's house, the dahlia capital of America. And if they don't have a house or a grave or a Pony Express station, they make something up. Sasquatch footprints in Oregon. The Martha lights in Texas. Elvis sightings. Something.

Except, apparently, Portales, New Mexico.

"Sights?" the cute Hispanic girl at the desk of the Portales Inn said when I asked what there was to see. "There's Billy the Kid's grave over in Fort Sumner. It's about seventy miles."

I'd just driven all the way from Bisbee, Arizona. The last thing I wanted to do was get back in a car and drive a hundred and sixty miles round trip to see a crooked wooden tombstone with the name worn off.

"Isn't there anything famous to see in town?"

"In Portales?" she said, and it was obvious from her tone there wasn't.

"There's Blackwater Draw Museum on the way up to Clovis," she said finally. "You take Highway 70 north about eight miles and it's on your right. It's an archaeological dig. Or you could drive out west of town and see the peanut fields."

Great. Bones and dirt.

"Thanks," I said and went back up to my room.

It was my own fault. Cross wasn't going to be back till tomorrow, but I'd decided to come to Portales a day early to "take a look around" before I talked to him, but that was no excuse. I'd been in little towns all over the west for the last five years. I knew how long it took to look around. About fifteen minutes. And five to see it had dead end written all over it. So here I was in Sightless Portales on a Sunday with nothing to do for a whole day but think about Cross's offer and try to come up with a reason not to take it.

"It's a good, steady job," my friend Denny'd said when he called to tell me Cross needed somebody. "Portales is a nice town. And it's got to be better than spending your life in a car. Driving all over kingdom come trying to sell inventions to people who don't want them. What kind of future is there in that?"

No future at all. The farmers weren't interested in solar powered irrigation equipment or water conservation devices. And lately Hammond, the guy I worked for, hadn't seemed very interested in them either.

My room didn't have air-conditioning. I cranked the window open and turned the TV on. It didn't have cable either. I watched five minutes of a sermon and then called Hammond.

"It's Carter Stewart," I said as if I were in the habit of calling him on Sundays. "I'm in Portales. I got here earlier than I thought, and the guy I'm supposed to see isn't here till tomorrow. You got any other customers you want me to look up?"

"In Portales?" he said, sounding barely interested. "Who were you supposed to see there?"

"Hudd at Southwest Agricultural Supply. I've got an appointment with him at eleven." And an appointment with Cross at ten, I thought. "I got in last night. Bisbee didn't take as long as I thought it would."

"Hudd's our only contact in Portales," he said.

"Anybody in Clovis? Or Tucumcari?"

"No," he said, too fast to have looked them up. "There's nobody much in that part of the state."

"They're big into peanuts here. You want me to try and talk to some peanut farmers?"

"Why don't you just take the day off?" he said.

"Yeah, thanks," I said, and hung up and went back downstairs.

There was a dried-up old guy at the desk now, but the word must have spread. "You wanna see something really interesting?" he said. "Down in Roswell's where the Air Force has got that space alien they won't let anybody see. You take Highway 70 south—"

"Didn't anybody famous ever live here in Portales?" I asked. "A vice-president? Billy the Kid's cousin?"

He shook his head.

"What about buildings? A railroad station? A courthouse?"

"There's a courthouse, but it's closed on Sundays. The Air Force claims it wasn't a spaceship, that it was some kind of spy plane, but I know a guy who saw it coming down. He said it was shaped like a big long cigar and had lights all over it."

"Highway 70?" I said, to get away from him. "Thanks," and went out into the parking lot.

I could see the top of the courthouse over the dry-looking treetops, only a couple of blocks away. It was closed on Sundays, but it was better than sitting in my room watching Falwell and thinking about the job I was going to have to take unless something happened between now and to-morrow morning. And better than getting back in the car to go see something Roswell had made up so it'd have a tourist attraction. And maybe I'd get lucky, and the courthouse would turn out to be the site of the last hanging in New Mexico. Or the first peace march. I walked downtown.

The streets around the courthouse looked like your typical small-town post-Wal-Mart business district. No drugstore, no grocery store, no dimestore. There was an Anthony's standing empty, and a restaurant that would be in another six months, a Western clothing store with a dusty denim shirt and two concho belts in the window, a bank with a sign in the window saying "New Location."

The courthouse was red brick and looked like every other courthouse from Nelson, Nebraska, to Tyler, Texas. It stood in a square of grass and trees. I walked around it twice, looking at the war memorial and the flag-pole and trying not to think about Hammond and Bisbee. It hadn't taken as long as I'd thought because I hadn't even been able to get in to see the buyer, and Hammond hadn't cared enough to even ask how it had gone. Or to bother to look up his contacts in Tucumcari. And it wasn't just that it was Sunday. He'd sounded that way the last two times I'd called him. Like a man getting ready to give up, to pull out.

Which meant I should take Cross's job offer and be grateful.

"It's a forty-hour week," he'd said. "You'll have time to work on your inventions."

Right. Or else settle into a routine and forget about them. Five years ago when I'd taken the job with Hammond, Denny'd said, "You'll be able to see the sights. The Grand Canyon, Mount Rushmore, Yellow-stone." Yeah, well, I'd seen them. Cave of the Winds, Amazing Mystery House, Indian curios, Genuine Live Jackalope.

I walked around the courthouse square again and then went down to the railroad tracks to look at the grain elevator and walked back to the courthouse again. The whole thing took ten minutes. I thought about walking over to the university, but it was getting hot. In another half hour the grass would start browning and the streets would start getting soft, and it would be even hotter out here than in my room. I started back to the Portales Inn.

The street I was on was shady, with white wooden houses, the kind I'd probably live in if I took Cross's job, the kind I'd work on my inventions in. If I could get the parts for them at Southwest Agricultural Supply. Or Wal-Mart. If I really did work on them. If I didn't just give up after awhile.

I turned down a side street. And ran into a dead end. Which was pretty appropriate, under the circumstances. "At least this would be a real job, not a dead end like the one you're in now," Cross'd said. "You've got to think about the future."

Yeah, well, I was the only one. Nobody else was doing it. They kept on using oil like it was water, kept on using water like the Ogalala Aquifer was going to last forever, kept planting and polluting and populating. I'd already thought about the future, and I knew what it was going to be. Another dead end. Another Dust Bowl. The land used up, the oil wells and the water table pumped dry, Bisbee and Clovis and Tucumcari turned into ghost towns. The Great American Desert all over again, with nobody but a few Indians left on it, waiting in their casinos for customers who weren't going to come. And me, sitting in Portales, working a forty-hour-a-week job.

I backtracked and went the other way. I didn't run into any other dead ends, or any sights either, and by 10:15 I was back at the Portales Inn, with only twenty-four hours to kill and Billy the Kid's grave looking better by the minute.

There was a tour bus in the Inn's parking lot. NONSTOP TOURS, it said in red and gray letters, and a long line of people was getting on it. A young woman was standing by the door of the bus, ticking off names on a clipboard. She was cute, with short yellow hair and a nice figure. She was wearing a light blue T-shirt and a short denim skirt.

An older couple in Bermuda shorts and Disney World T-shirts were climbing the stairs onto the bus, slowing up the line.

"Hi," I said to the tour guide. "What's going on?"

She looked up from her list at me, startled, and the old couple froze halfway up the steps. The tour guide looked down at her clipboard and then back up at me, and the startled look was gone, but her cheeks were as red as the letters on the side of the bus.

"We're taking a tour of the local sights," she said. She motioned to the next person in line, a fat guy in a Hawaiian shirt, and the old couple went on up the steps and into the bus.

"I didn't think there were any," I said. "Local sights."

The fat guy was gaping at me.

"Name?" the tour guide said.

"Giles H. Paul," he said, still staring at me. She motioned him onto the bus.

"Name?" I said, and she looked startled all over again. "What's your name? It's probably on that clipboard in case you've forgotten it."

She smiled. "Tonia Randall."

"So, Tonia, where's this tour headed?"

"We're going out to the ranch."

"The ranch?"

"Where he grew up," she said, her cheeks flaming again. She motioned to the next person in line. "Where he got his start."

Where who started to what? I wanted to ask, but she was busy with a tall man who moved almost as stiffly as the old couple, and anyway, it was obvious everybody in line knew who she was talking about. They couldn't wait to get on the bus, and the young couple who were last in line kept pointing things out to their little kid—the courthouse, the Portales Inn sign, a big tree on the other side of the street.

"Is it private? Your tour?" I said. "Can anybody pay to go on it?" And what was I doing? I'd taken a tour in the Black Hills one time, when I'd had my job about a month and still wanted to see the sights, and it was even more depressing than thinking about the future. Looking out blue-tinted windows while the tour guide tells memorized facts and unfunny jokes. Trooping off the bus to look at Wild Bill Hickok's grave for five minutes, trooping back on. Listening to bawling kids and complaining wives. I didn't want to go on this tour.

But when Tonia blushed and said, "No, I'm sorry," I felt a rush of disappointment at not seeing her again.

"Sure," I said, because I didn't want her to see it. "Just wondering. Well, have a nice time," and started for the front door of the Inn.

"Wait," she said, leaving the couple and their kid standing there and coming over to me. "Do you live here in Portales?"

"No," I said, and realized I'd decided not to take the job. "Just passing through. I came to town to see a guy. I got here early, and there's nothing to do. That ever happen to you?"

She smiled, as if I'd said something funny. "So you don't know anyone here?"

"No," I said.

"Do you know the person you've got the appointment with?"

I shook my head, wondering what that had to do with anything.

She consulted her clipboard again. "It seems a pity for you to miss seeing it," she said, "and if you're just passing through...just a minute." She walked back to the bus, stepped up inside, and said something to the driver. They consulted a few minutes, and then she came back down the steps. The couple and their kid came up to her, and she stopped a minute and checked their names off and waved them onto the bus, and then came back over to me. "The bus is full. Do you mind standing?"

Bawling kids, videocams, *and* no place to sit to go see the ranch where somebody I'd probably never heard of got his start. At least I'd heard of Billy the Kid, and if I drove over to Fort Sumner I could take as long as I wanted to look at his grave. "No," I said. "I wouldn't mind." I pulled out my wallet. "Maybe I better ask before we go any farther, how much is the tour?"

She looked startled again. "No charge. Because the tour's already full."

"Great," I said. "I'd like to go."

She smiled and motioned me on board with her clipboard. Inside, it looked more like a city bus than a tour bus—the front and back seats were sideways along the walls, and there were straps for hanging onto. There was even a cord for signaling your stop, which might come in handy if the tour turned out to be as bad as the Wild Bill Hickok tour. I grabbed hold of a strap near the front.

The bus was packed with people of all ages. A white-haired man older than the Disney World couple, middle-aged people, teenagers, kids. I counted at least four under age five. I wondered if I should yank the cord right now.

Tonia counted heads and nodded to the driver. The door whooshed shut, and the bus lumbered out of the parking lot and slowly through a neighborhood of trees and tract houses. The Disney World couple were sitting in the front seat. They scooted over to make room for me, and I gestured to Tonia, but she motioned me to sit down.

She put down her clipboard and held on to the pole just behind the driver's seat. "The first stop on today's tour," she said, "will be the house. He did the greater part of his work here," and I began to wonder if I was going to go the whole tour without ever finding out who the tour was about. When she'd said "the ranch," I'd assumed it was some Old West figure, but these houses had all been built in the thirties and forties.

"He moved into this house with his wife, Blanche, shortly after they were married."

The bus ground down its gears and stopped next to a white house with a porch on a corner lot.

"He lived here from 1947 to…" She paused and looked sideways at me. "…he present. It was while he was living here that he wrote *Seetee Ship* and *The Black Sun* and came up with the idea of genetic engineering."

He was a writer, which narrowed it down some, but none of the titles she'd mentioned rang a bell. But he was famous enough to fill a tour bus, so his books must have been turned into movies. Tom Clancy? Stephen King? I'd have expected both of them to have a lot fancier houses.

"The windows in front are the living room," Tonia said. "You can't see his study from here. It's on the south side of the house. That's where he keeps his Grand Master Nebula Award, right above where he works."

That didn't ring a bell either, but everybody looked impressed, and the couple with the kid got out of their seats to peer out the tinted windows. "The two rear windows are the kitchen, where he read the paper and watched TV at breakfast before going to work. He used a typewriter and then in later years a personal computer. He's not at home this weekend. He's out of town at a science fiction convention."

Which was probably a good thing. I wondered how he felt about tour buses parking out front, whoever he was. A science fiction writer. Isaac Asimov, maybe.

The driver put the bus in gear and pulled away from the curb. "As we drive past the front of the house," Tonia said, "you'll be able to see his easy chair, where he did most of his reading."

The bus ground up through the gears and started winding through more neighborhood streets. "Jack Williamson worked on the *Portales News-Tribune* from 1947 to 1948 and then, with the publication of *Darker Than You Think,* quit journalism to write full-time," she said, pausing and glancing at me again, but if she was expecting me to be looking as impressed as everybody else, I wasn't. I'd read a lot of paperbacks in a lot of un-air-conditioned motel rooms the last five years, but the name Jack Williamson didn't ring a bell at all.

"From 1960 to 1977, Jack Williamson was a professor at Eastern New Mexico University, which we're coming up on now," Tonia said.

The bus pulled into the college's parking lot and everybody looked eagerly out the windows, even though the campus looked just like every other western college's, brick and glass and not enough trees, sprinklers watering the brownish grass.

"This is the Campus Union," she said, pointing. The bus made a slow circuit of the parking lot. "And this is Becky Sharp Auditorium, where the annual lecture in his honor is held every spring. It's the week of April twelfth this year."

It struck me that they hadn't planned very well. They'd managed to miss not only their hero but the annual week in his honor, too.

"Over there is the building where he teaches a science fiction class with Patrice Caldwell," she said, pointing, "and that, of course, is Golden Library, where the Williamson Collection of his works and awards is housed." Everyone nodded in recognition.

I expected the driver to open the doors and everybody to pile out to look at the library, but the bus picked up speed and headed out of town.

"We aren't going to the library?" I said.

She shook her head. "Not this tour. At this time the collection's still very small."

The bus geared up and headed west and south out of town on a two-lane road. "New Mexico State Highway 18," a sign read. "Out your windows you can see the *Llano Estacado,* or Staked Plains," Tonia said. "They were named, as Jack Williamson says in his auto-biography, *Wonder's Child,* for the stakes Coronado used to mark his way across the plain. Jack Williamson's family moved here in a covered wagon in 1915 to a homestead claim in the sandhills. Here Jack did farm chores, hauled water, collected firewood, and read *Treasure Island* and *David Copperfield.*"

At least I'd heard of those books. And Jack had to be at least seventy-nine years old.

"The farm was very poor, with poor soil and almost no water, and after three years the family was forced to move off it and onto a series of sharecrop farms to make ends meet. During this time Jack went to school at Richland and at Center, where he met Blanche Slaten, his future wife. Any questions?"

This had the Deadwood tour all beat for boring, but a bunch of hands went up, and she went down the aisle to answer them, leaning over their seats and pointing out the tinted windows. The old couple got up and went back to talk to the fat guy, holding on to the straps above his seat and gesturing excitedly.

I looked out the window. The Spanish should have named it the *Llano Flatto*. There wasn't a bump or a dip in it all the way to the horizon.

Everybody, including the kids, was looking out the windows, even though there wasn't anything much to look at. A plowed field of red dirt, a few bored-looking cows, green rows of sprouting green that must be the peanuts, another plowed field. I was getting to see the dirt after all.

Tonia came back to the front and sat down beside me. "Enjoying the tour so far?" she said.

I couldn't think of a good answer to that. "How far is the ranch?" I said.

"Twenty miles. There used to be a town named Pep, but now there's just the ranch…" She paused and then said, "What's your name? You didn't tell me."

"Carter Stewart," I said.

"Really?" She smiled at the funniest things. "Are you named after Carter Leigh in 'Nonstop to Mars'?"

I didn't know what that was. One of Jack Williamson's books, apparently. "I don't know. Maybe."

"I'm named after Tonia Andros in 'Dead Star Station.' And the driver's named after Giles Habibula."

The tall guy had his hand up again. "I'll be right back," she said, and hurried down the aisle.

The fat guy's name had been Giles, too, which wasn't exactly a common name, and I'd seen the name "Lethonee" on Tonia's clipboard, which had to be out of a book. But how could somebody I'd never even heard of be so famous people were named after his characters?

They must be a fan club, the kind that makes pilgrimages to Graceland and names their kids Paul and Ringo. They didn't look the part, though. They should be wearing Jack Williamson T-shirts and Spock ears, not Disney World T-shirts. The elderly couple came back and sat down next to me. They smiled and started looking out the window.

They didn't act the part either. The fans I'd met had always had a certain defensiveness, an attitude of "I know you think I'm crazy to like this stuff, and maybe I am," and they always insisted on explaining how they got to be fans and why you should be one, too. These people had none of that. They acted like coming out here was the most normal thing in the world, even Tonia. And if they were science fiction fans, why weren't they touring Isaac Asimov's ranch? Or William Shatner's?

Tonia came back again and stood over me, holding on to a hanging strap. "You said you were in Portales to see somebody?" she said.

"Yeah. He's supposed to offer me a job."

"In Portales?" she said, making that sound exciting. "Are you going to take it?"

I'd made up my mind back there in that dead end, but I said, "I don't know. I don't think so. It's a desk job, a steady paycheck, and I wouldn't have to do all the driving I'm doing now." I found myself telling her about Hammond and the things I wanted to invent and how I was afraid the job would be a dead end.

"'I had no future,'" she said. "Jack Williamson said that at this year's Williamson Lecture. 'I had no future. I was a poor kid in the middle of the Depression, without education, without money, without prospects.'"

"It's not the Depression, but otherwise I know how he felt. If I don't take Cross's job, I may not have one. And if I do take it—" I shrugged. "Either way I'm not going anywhere."

"Oh, but to have a chance to live in the same town with Jack Williamson," Tonia said. "To run into him at the supermarket, and maybe even get to take one of his classes."

"Maybe you should take Cross's job offer," I said.

"I can't." Her cheeks went bright red again. "I've already got a job." She straightened up and addressed the tour group. "We'll be coming to the turnoff to the ranch soon," she said. "Jack Williamson lived here with his family from 1915 till World War II, when he joined the army, and again after the war until he married Blanche."

The bus slowed almost to a stop and turned onto a dirt road hardly as wide as the bus was that led off between two fields of fenced pastureland.

"The farm was originally a homestead," Tonia said, and everyone murmured appreciatively and looked out the windows at more dirt and a couple of clumps of yucca.

"He was living here when he read his first issue of *Amazing Stories Quarterly*," she said, "and when he submitted his first story to *Amazing*. That was 'The Metal Man,' which, as you remember from yesterday, he saw in the window of the drugstore."

"I see it!" the tall man shouted, leaning forward over the back of the driver's seat. "I see it!" Everyone craned forward, trying to see, and we pulled up in front of some outbuildings and stopped.

The driver whooshed the doors open, and everyone filed off the bus and stood in the rutted dirt road, looking excitedly at the unpainted sheds and the water trough. A black heifer looked up incuriously and then went back to chewing on the side of one of the sheds.

Tonia assembled everyone in the road with her clipboard.

"That's the ranch house over there," she said, pointing at a low green house with a fenced yard and a willow tree. "Jack Williamson lived here with his parents, his brother Jim, and his sisters Jo and Katie. It was here that Jack Williamson wrote 'The Girl from Mars' and *The Legion of Space*, working at the kitchen table. His uncle had given him a basket-model Remington typewriter with a dim purple ribbon, and he typed his stories on it after everyone had gone to bed. Jack Williamson's brother Jim…" she paused and glanced at me, "owns the ranch at this time. He and his wife are in Arizona this weekend."

Amazing. They'd managed to miss them all, but nobody seemed to mind, and it struck me suddenly what was unusual about this tour. Nobody complained. That's all they'd done on the Wild Bill Hickok tour. Half of them hadn't known who he was, and the other half had complained that it was too expensive, too hot, too far, the windows on the bus didn't open, the gift shop didn't sell Coke. If their tour guide had announced the wax museum was closed, he'd have had a riot on his hands.

"It was difficult for him to write in the midst of the family," she said, leading off away from the house toward a pasture. "There were frequent interruptions and too much noise, so in 1934 he built a separate cabin. Be careful," she said, skirting around a clump of sagebrush. "There are sometimes rattlesnakes."

That apparently didn't bother anybody either. They trooped after her across a field of dry, spiny grass and gathered around a weathered gray shack.

"This is the actual cabin he wrote in," Tonia said.

I wouldn't have called it a cabin. It hardly even qualified as a shack. When I'd first seen it as we pulled up, I'd thought it was an abandoned outhouse. Four gray wood-slat walls, half falling down, a sagging gray shelf, some rusted cans. When Tonia started talking, a farm cat leaped down from where it had been sleeping under what was left of the roof and took off like a shot across the field.

"It had a desk, files, bookshelves, and later a separate bedroom," Tonia said.

It didn't look big enough for a typewriter, let alone a bed, but this was obviously what all these people had come to see. They stood reverently before it in the spiky grass, like it was the Washington Monument or something, and gazed at the weathered boards and rusted cans, not saying anything.

"He installed electric lights," Tonia said, "which were run by a small windmill, and a bath. He still had occasional interruptions—from snakes and once from a skunk who took up residence under the cabin. He wrote 'Dead Star Station' here, and 'The Meteor Girl,' his first story to include time travel. 'If the field were strong enough,'" he said in the story, "'we could bring physical objects through space-time instead of mere visual images.'"

They all found that amusing for no reason I could see and then stood there some more, looking reverent. Tonia came over to me. "Well, what do you think?" she said, smiling.

"Tell me about him seeing 'The Metal Man' in the drugstore," I said.

"Oh, I forgot you weren't with us at the drugstore," she said. "Jack Williamson sent his first story to *Amazing Stories* in 1928 and then never heard anything back. In the fall of that year he was shopping for groceries, and he looked in the window of a drugstore and saw a magazine with a picture on the cover that looked like it could be his story, and when he went in, he was so excited to see his story in print, he bought all three copies of the magazine and went off without the groceries he'd been carrying."

"So then he had prospects?"

She said seriously, "He said, 'I had no future. And then I looked in the drugstore window and saw Hugo Gernsback's *Amazing Stories,* and it gave me a future.'"

"I wish somebody would give me a future," I said.

"'No one can predict the future, he can only point the way.' He said that, too."

She went over to the shack and addressed the group. "He also wrote 'Nonstop to Mars,' my favorite story, in this cabin," she said to the group, "and it was right here that he proposed the idea of colonizing Mars and…" She paused, but this time it was the stiff tall man she glanced at. "…invented the idea of androids."

They continued to look. All of them walked around the shack two or three times, pointing at loose boards and tin cans, stepping back to get a better look, walking around it again. None of them seemed to be in any hurry to go. The Deadwood tour had lasted all of ten minutes at Mount Moriali Cemetery, with one of the kids whining, "Can't we *go* now?" the whole time, but this group acted like they could stay here all day. One of them got out a notebook and started writing things down. The couple with the kid took her over to the heifer, and all three of them patted her gingerly.

After a while Tonia and the driver passed out paper bags and everybody sat down in the pasture, rattlesnakes and all, and had lunch. Stale sandwiches, cardboard cookies, cans of lukewarm Coke, but nobody complained. Or left any litter.

They neatly packed everything back in the bags and then walked around the shack some more, looking in the empty windows and scaring a couple more farm cats, or just sat and looked at it. A couple of them went over to the fence and gazed longingly over it at the ranch house.

"It's too bad there's nobody around to show them the house," I said. "People don't usually go off and leave a ranch with nobody to look after the animals. I wonder if there's somebody around. Whoever it is would probably give you a tour of the ranch house."

"It's Jack's niece Betty," Tonia said promptly. "She had to go up to Clovis today to get a part for the water pump. She won't be back till four." She stood up, brushing dead grass and dirt off her skirt. "All right, everybody. It's time to go."

There was a discontented murmuring, and one of the kids said, "Do we have to go already?", but everybody picked up their lunch bags and Coke cans and started for the bus. Tonia ticked off their names on her clipboard as they got on like she was afraid one of them might jump ship and take up residence among the rattlesnakes.

"Carter Stewart," I told her. "Where to next? The drugstore?"

She shook her head. "We went there yesterday. Where's Underhill?" She started across the road again, with me following her.

The tall man was standing silently in front of the shack, looking in at the empty room. He stood absolutely motionless, his eyes fixed on the gray weathered boards, and when Tonia said, "Underhill? I'm afraid we need to go," he continued to stand there for a long minute, like he was trying to store up the memory. Then he turned and walked stiffly past us and back to the bus.

Tonia counted heads again, and the bus made a slow circle past the ranchhouse, turning around, and started back along the dirt road. Nobody said anything, and when we got to the highway, everyone turned around in their seats for a last look. The old couple dabbed at their eyes, and one of the kids stood up on the rear seat and waved goodbye. The tall man was sitting with his head buried in his hands.

"The cabin you've just seen was where it all started," Tonia said, "with a copy of a pulp magazine and a lot of imagination." She told how Jack Williamson had become a meteorologist and a college professor, as well as a science fiction writer, traveled to Italy, Mexico, the Great Wall of China, all of which must have been impossible for him to imagine, sitting all alone in that poor excuse for a shack, typing on an old typewriter with a faded ribbon.

I was only half listening. I was thinking about the tall guy, Underhill, and trying to figure out what was wrong about him. It wasn't his stiffness—I'd been at least that stiff after a day in the car. It was something else. I thought about him standing there, looking at the shack, so fixed, like he was trying to carry the image away with him.

He probably just forgot his camera, I thought, and realized what had been nagging at me. Nobody had a camera. Tourists always have cameras. The Wild Bill Hickok gang had all had cameras, even the kids. And videocams. One guy had kept a videocam glued to his face the whole time and never seen a thing. They'd spent the whole tour snapping Wild Bill's tombstone, snapping the figures in the wax museum even though there were signs that said, NO PICTURES, snapping each other in front of the saloon, in front of the cemetery, in front of the bus. And then buying up slides and postcards in the gift shop in case the pictures didn't turn out.

No cameras. No gift shop. No littering or trespassing or whining. What kind of tour is this? I thought.

"He predicted 'a new Golden Age of fair cities, of new laws and new machines,'" Tonia was saying, "'of human capabilities undreamed of, of a civilization that has conquered matter and Nature, distance and time, disease and death.'"

He'd imagined the same kind of future I'd imagined. I wondered if he'd ever tried selling his ideas to farmers. Which brought me back to the job, which I'd managed to avoid thinking about almost all day.

Tonia came and stood across from me, holding on to the center pole. "'A poor country kid, poorly educated, unhappy with his whole environment, longing for something else,'" she said. "That's how Jack Williamson described himself in 1928." She looked at me. "You're not going to take the job, are you?"

"I don't think so," I said. "I don't know."

She looked out the window at the fields and cows, looking disappointed. "When he first moved here, this was all sagebrush and drought and dust. He couldn't imagine what was going to happen any more than you can right now."

"And the answer's in a drugstore window?"

"The answer was inside him," she said. She stood up and addressed the group. "We'll be coming into Portales in a minute," she said. "In 1928, Jack Williamson wrote, 'Science is the doorway to the future, scientifiction, the golden key. It goes ahead and lights the way. And when science sees the things made real in the author's mind, it makes them real indeed.'"

The tour group applauded, and the bus pulled into the parking lot of the Portales Inn. I waited for the rush, but nobody moved. "We're not staying here," Tonia explained.

"Oh," I said, getting up. "You didn't have to give me door-to-door service. You could have let me out at wherever you're staying, and I could have walked over."

"That's all right," Tonia said, smiling.

"Well," I said, unwilling to say goodbye. "Thanks for a really interesting tour. Can I take you to dinner or something? To thank you for letting me come?"

"I can't," she said. "I have to check everybody in and everything."

"Yeah," I said. "Well…"

Giles the driver opened the door with a whoosh of air.

"Thanks," I said. I nodded to the old couple. "Thanks for sharing your seat," and stepped down off the bus.

"Why don't you come with us tomorrow?" she said. "We're going to go see Number 5516."

Number 5516 sounded like a county highway and probably was, the road Jack Williamson walked to school along or something, complete with peanuts and dirt, at which the group would gaze reverently and not take pictures. "I've got an appointment tomorrow," I said, and realized I didn't want to say goodbye to her. "Next time. When's your next tour?"

"I thought you were just passing through."

"Like you said, a lot of nice people live around here. Do you bring a lot of tours through here?"

"Now and then," she said, her cheeks bright red.

I watched the bus pull out of the parking lot and down the street. I looked at my watch. 4:45. At least an hour till I could justify dinner. At least five hours till I could justify bed. I went in the Inn and then changed my mind and went back out to the car and drove out to see where Cross's office was so I wouldn't have trouble in the morning, in case it was hard to find.

It wasn't. It was on the south edge of town on Highway 70, a little past the Motel Super 8. The tour bus wasn't in the parking lot of the Super 8, or at the Hillcrest, or the Sands Motel. They must have gone to Roswell or Tucumcari for the night. I looked at my watch again. It was 5:05.

I drove back through town, looking for someplace to eat. McDonald's, Taco Bell, Burger King. There's nothing wrong with fast food, except that it's fast. I needed a place where it took half an hour to get a menu and another twenty minutes before they took your order.

I ended up eating at Pizza Hut (personal pan pizza in under five minutes or your money back). "Do you get a lot of tour bus business?" I asked the waitress.

"In Portales? You have to be kidding," she said. "In case you haven't noticed, Portales is right on the road to nowhere. Do you want a box for the rest of that pizza?"

The box was a good idea. It took her ten minutes to bring it, which meant it was nearly six by the time I left. Only four hours left to kill. I filled up the car at Allsup's and bought a sixpack of Coke. Next to the magazines was a rack of paperbacks.

"Any Jack Williamson books?" I asked the kid at the counter.

"Who?" he said.

I spun the rack around slowly. John Grisham. Danielle Steel. Stephen King's latest thousand-page effort. No Jack Williamson. "Is there a bookstore in town?" I asked the kid.

"Huh?"

He'd never heard of that either. "A place where I can buy a book?"

"Alco has books, I think," he said. "But they closed at five."

"How about a drugstore?" I said, thinking of that copy of *Amazing Stories*.

Still blank. I gave up, paid him for the gas and the sixpack, and started out to the car.

"You mean a drugstore like aspirin and stuff?" the kid said. "There's Van Winkle's."

"When do they close?" I asked, and got directions.

Van Winkle's was a grocery store. It had two aisles of "aspirin and stuff" and half an aisle of paperbacks. More Grisham. *Jurassic Park*. Tom Clancy. And *The Legion of Time* by Jack Williamson. It looked like it had been there a while. It had a faded fifties-style cover and dog-eared edges.

I took it up to the check-out. "What's it like having a famous writer living here?" I asked the middle-aged clerk.

She picked up the book. "The guy who wrote this lives in Portales?" she said. "Really?"

Which brought us up to 6:22. But at least now I had something to read. I went back to the Portales Inn and up to my room, opened a can of Coke and all the windows, and sat down to read *The Legion of Time,* which was about a girl who'd traveled back in time to tell the hero about the future.

"The future has been held to be as real as the past," the book said, and the girl in the book was able to travel between one and the other as easily as the tour had traveled down New Mexico Highway 18.

I closed the book and thought about the tour. They didn't have a single camera, and they weren't afraid of rattlesnakes. And they'd looked out at the Llano Flatto like they'd never seen a field or a cow before. And they all knew who Jack Williamson was, unlike the kid at Allsup's or the clerk at Van Winkle's. They were all willing to spend two days looking at abandoned shacks and dirt roads—no, wait, *three* days. Tonia'd said they'd gone to the drugstore yesterday.

I had an idea. I opened the drawer of the nightstand, looking for a phone book. There wasn't one. I went downstairs to the lobby and asked for one. The blue-haired lady at the desk handed me one about the size of *The Legion of Time,* and I flipped to the Yellow Pages.

There was a Thrifty Drug, which was a chain, and a couple that sounded locally owned but weren't downtown. "Where's B. and J. Drugs?" I asked. "Is it close to downtown?"

"A couple of blocks," the old lady said.

"How long has it been in business?"

"Let's see," she said. "it was there when Nora was little because I remember buying medicine that time she had the croup. She would have been six, or was that when she had the measles? No, the measles were the summer she..."

I'd have to ask B. and J. "I've got another question," I said, and hoped I wouldn't get an answer like the last one. "What time does the university library open tomorrow?"

She gave me a brochure. The library opened at 8:00 and the Williamson Collection at 9:30. I went back up to the room and tried B. and J. Drugs. They weren't open.

It was getting dark. I closed the curtains over the open windows and opened the book again. "The world is a long corridor, and time is a lantern carried steadily along the hall," it said, and, a few pages later, "If time were simply an extension of the universe, was tomorrow as real as yesterday? If one could leap forward—"

Or back, I thought. "Jack Williamson lived in this house from 1947 to…" Tonia'd said, and paused and then said, "…the present," and I'd thought the sideways glance was to see my reaction to his name, but what if she'd intended to say, "from 1947 to 1998"? Or "2015"?

What if that was why she kept pausing when she talked, because she had to remember to say "Jack Williamson *is*" instead of "Jack Williamson *was*", "*does* most of his writing" instead of "*did* most of his writing," had to remember what year it was and what hadn't happened yet?

"'If the field were strong enough,'" I remembered Tonia saying out at the ranch, "'we could bring physical objects through space-time instead of mere visual images.'" And the tour group had all smiled.

What if they were the physical objects? What if the tour had traveled through time instead of space? But that didn't make any sense. If they could travel through time they could have come on a weekend Jack Williamson was home, or during the week of the Williamson Lectureship.

I read on, looking for explanations. The book talked about quantum mechanics and probability, about how changing one thing in the past could affect the whole future. Maybe that was why they had to come when Jack Williamson was out of town, to avoid doing something to him that might change the future.

Or maybe Nonstop Tours was just incompetent and they'd come on the wrong weekend. And the reason they didn't have cameras was because they all forgot them. And they were all really tourists, and *The Legion of Time* was just a science fiction book and I was making up crackpot theories to avoid thinking about Cross and the job.

But if they were ordinary tourists, what were they doing spending a day staring at a tumbledown shack in the middle of nowhere? Even if they were tourists from the future, there was no reason to travel back in time to see a science fiction writer when they could see presidents or rock stars.

Unless they lived in a future where all the things he'd predicted in his stories had come true. What if they had genetic engineering and androids and spaceships? What if in their world they'd terraformed planets and gone to Mars and explored the galaxy? That would make Jack Williamson their forefather, their founder. And they'd want to come back and see where it all started.

The next morning, I left my stuff at the Portales Inn and went over to the library. Checkout wasn't till noon, and I wanted to wait till I'd found out a few things before I made up my mind whether to take the job or not. On the way there I drove past B. and J. Drugs and then College Drug. Neither of them were open, and I couldn't tell from their outsides how old they were.

The library opened at eight and the room with the Williamson collection in it at 9:30, which was cutting it close. I was there at 9:15, looking in through the glass at the books. There was a bronze plaque on the wall and a big mobile of the planets.

Tonia had said the collection "isn't very big at this point," but from what I could see, it looked pretty big to me. Rows and rows of books, filing cabinets, boxes, photographs.

A young guy in chinos and wire-rimmed glasses unlocked the door to let me in. "Wow! Lined up and waiting to get in! This is a first," he said, which answered my first question.

I asked it anyway. "Do you get many visitors?"

"A few," he said. "Not as many as I think there should be for a man who practically invented the future. Androids, terraforming, antimatter, he imagined them all. We'll have more visitors in two weeks. That's when the Williamson Lectureship week is. We get quite a few visitors then. The writers who are speaking usually drop in."

He switched on the lights. "Let me show you around," he said. "We're adding to the collection all the time." He took down a long flat box. "This is the comic strip Jack did, *Beyond Mars*. And here is where we keep his original manuscripts." He opened one of the filing cabinets and pulled out a sheaf of typed yellow sheets. "Have you ever met Jack?"

"No," I said, looking at an oil painting of a white-haired man with a long, pleasant-looking face. "What's he like?"

"Oh, the nicest man you've ever met. It's hard to believe he's one of the founders of science fiction. He's in here all the time. Wonderful guy. He's working on a new book, *The Black Sun*. He's out of town this weekend, or I'd take you over and introduce you. He's always delighted to meet his fans. Is there anything specific you wanted to know about him?"

"Yes," I said. "Somebody told me about him seeing the magazine with his first story in it in a drugstore. Which drugstore was that?"

"It was one in Canyon, Texas. He and his sister were going to school down there."

"Do you know the name of the drugstore?" I said. "I'd like to go see it."

"Oh, it went out of business years ago," he said. "I think it was torn down."

"We went there yesterday," Tonia had said, and what day exactly was that? The day Jack saw it and bought all three copies and forgot his groceries? And what were they wearing that day? Print dresses and double-breasted suits and hats?

"I've got the issue here," he said, taking a crumbling magazine out of a plastic slipcover. It had a garish picture of a man being pulled up out of a crater by a brilliant crystal. "December, 1928. Too bad the drugstore's not there anymore. You can see the cabin where he wrote his first stories, though. It's still out on the ranch his brother owns. You go out west of town and turn south on State Highway 18. Just ask Betty to show you around."

"Have you ever had a tour group in here?" I interrupted.

"A *tour* group?" he said, and then must have decided I was kidding. "He's not quite that famous."

Yet, I thought, and wondered when Nonstop Tours visited the library. Ten years from now? A hundred? And what were they wearing that day?

I looked at my watch. It was 9:45. "I've got to go," I said. "I've got an appointment." I started out and then turned back. "This person who told me about the drugstore, they mentioned something about Number 5516. Is that one of his books?"

"5516? No, that's the asteroid they're naming after him. How'd you know about that? It's supposed to be a surprise. They're giving him the plaque Lectureship week."

"An asteroid," I said. I started out again.

"Thanks for coming in," the librarian said. "Are you just visiting or do you live here?"

"I live here," I said.

"Well, then, come again."

I went down the stairs and out to the car. It was 9:50. Just enough time to get to Cross's and tell him I'd take the job.

I went out to the parking lot. There weren't any tour buses driving through it, which must mean Jack Williamson was back from his convention.

After my meeting with Cross I was going to go over to his house and introduce myself. "I know how you felt when you saw that *Amazing Stories* in the drugstore," I'd tell him. "I'm interested in the future, too. I liked what you said about it, about science fiction lighting the way and science making the future real."

I got in the car and drove through town to Highway 70. An asteroid. I should have gone with them. "It'll be fun," Tonia said. It certainly would be.

Next time, I thought. Only I want to see some of this terraforming. I want to go to Mars.

I turned south on Highway 70 towards Cross's office. Roswell 92 miles, the sign said.

"Come again," I said, leaning out the window and looking up. "Come again!"


## AFTERWORD

Two years ago I had the privilege of speaking at the Jack Williamson Lectureship Weekend in Portales, New Mexico. It gave me the opportunity not only to spend time with Jack, but also to do the "onsite research" for this story, which consisted of a delightful day at the ranch with Jack's family, highlighted by wonderful conversation and the best asparagus (and the most) I have ever eaten in my life. When I was asked to do a story for this collection, I knew exactly what I wanted to write about.

Writing the story also gave me the chance to reread all of Jack's early stories. A lot of the science fiction written in the thirties and forties dates badly (and not just because of the heat rays and vacuum tubes) and has only historical interest. But Jack's stuff is as fresh as it was the day it was written. "Deadstar Station," "Jamboree," and, of course, "Nonstop to Mars," would sell in a flash to *Analog* or *The Magazine of Fantasy and Science Fiction* today.

Mostly though, "Nonstop to Portales" let me write about Jack, who is my flat-out favorite person in the field. He is a man of extraordinary talent and consummate humility, of penetrating intelligence and great kindness, a scholar and a gentleman. We are unbelievably lucky to have him as one of the forefathers of the field.

—Connie Willis, 1996

# Parking Fines and Other Violations

# Ado

The Monday before spring break I told my English lit class we were going to do Shakespeare. The weather in Colorado is usually wretched this time of year. We get all the snow the ski resorts needed in December, use up our scheduled snow days, and end up going an extra week in June. The forecast on the *Today* show hadn't predicted any snow till Saturday, but with luck it would arrive sooner.

My announcement generated a lot of excitement. Paula dived for her corder and rewound it to make sure she'd gotten my every word, Edwin Summer looked smug, and Delilah snatched up her books and stomped out, slamming the door so hard it woke Rick up. I passed out the release/refusal slips and told them they had to have them back in by Wednesday. I gave one to Sharon to give Delilah.

"Shakespeare is considered one of our greatest writers, possibly *the* greatest," I said for the benefit of Paula's corder. "On Wednesday I will be talking about Shakespeare's life, and on Thursday and Friday we will be reading his work."

Wendy raised her hand. "Are we going to read all the plays?"

I sometimes wonder where Wendy has been the last few years—certainly not in this school, possibly not in this universe. "What we're studying hasn't been decided yet," I said. "The principal and I are meeting tomorrow."

"It had better be one of the tragedies," Edwin said darkly.

By lunch the news was all over the school. "Good luck," Greg Jefferson, the biology teacher, said in the teachers' lounge. "I just got done doing evolution."

"Is it really that time of year again?" Karen Miller said. She teaches American lit across the hall. "I'm not even up to the Civil War yet."

"It's that time of year again," I said. "Can you take my class during your free period tomorrow? I've got to meet with Harrows."

"I can take them all morning. Just have your kids come into my room tomorrow. We're doing 'Thanatopsis.' Another thirty kids won't matter."

"'Thanatopsis'?" I said, impressed. "The whole thing?"

"All but lines ten and sixty-eight. It's a terrible poem, you know. I don't think anybody understands it well enough to protest. And I'm not telling anybody what the title means."

"Cheer up," Greg said. "Maybe we'll have a blizzard."

⊣ • • • ⊢

Tuesday was clear, with a forecast of temps in the sixties. Delilah was outside the school when I got there, wearing a red "Seniors Against Devil Worship in the Schools" T-shirt and shorts. She was carrying a picket sign that said, "Shakespeare is Satan's Spokesman." "Shakespeare" and "Satan" were both misspelled.

"We're not starting Shakespeare till tomorrow," I told her. "There's no reason for you not to be in class. Ms. Miller is teaching 'Thanatopsis.'"

"Not lines ten and sixty-eight, she's not. Besides, Bryant was a Theist, which is the same thing as a Satanist." She handed me her refusal slip and a fat manila envelope. "Our protests are in there." She lowered her voice. "What does the word 'thanatopsis' really mean?"

"It's an Indian word. It means, 'One who uses her religion to ditch class and get a tan.'"

I went inside, got Shakespeare out of the vault in the library, and went into the office. Ms. Harrows already had the Shakespeare file and her box of Kleenex out. "Do you have to do this?" she said, blowing her nose.

"As long as Edwin Summer's in my class, I do. His mother's head of the President's Task Force on Lack of Familiarity with the Classics." I added Delilah's list of protests to the stack and sat down at the computer.

"Well, it may be easier than we think," she said. "There have been a lot of suits since last year, which takes care of *Macbeth, The Tempest, Midsummer Night's Dream, The Winter's Tale,* and *Richard III.*"

"Delilah's been a busy girl," I said. I fed in the unexpurgated disk and the excise and reformat programs. "I don't remember there being any witchcraft in *Richard III.*"

She sneezed and grabbed for another Kleenex. "There's not. That was a slander suit. Filed by his great-great-grand-something. He claims there's no conclusive proof that Richard III killed the little princes. It doesn't matter anyway. The Royal Society for the Restoration of Divine Right of Kings has an injunction against all the history plays. What's the weather supposed to be like?"

"Terrible," I said. "Warm and sunny." I called up the catalog and deleted *Henry IV, Parts I and II,* and the rest of her list. *"The Taming of the Shrew?"*

"Angry Women's Alliance. Also *Merry Wives of Windsor, Romeo and Juliet,* and *Love's Labour's Lost.*"

"*Othello?* Never mind. I know that one. *The Merchant of Venice?* The Anti-Defamation League?"

"No. American Bar Association. And Morticians International. They object to the use of the word 'casket' in Act III." She blew her nose.

⊣ ••• ⊢

It took us first and second period to deal with the plays and most of the third to finish the sonnets. "I've got a class fourth period and then lunch duty," I said. "We'll have to finish up the rest of them this afternoon."

"Is there anything left for this afternoon?" Ms. Harrows asked.

"*As You Like It* and *Hamlet,*" I said. "Good heavens, how did they miss *Hamlet?*"

"Are you sure about *As You Like It?*" Ms. Harrows said, leafing through her stack. "I thought somebody'd filed a restraining order against it."

"Probably the Mothers Against Transvestites," I said. "Rosalind dresses up like a man in Act II."

"No, here it is. The Sierra Club. 'Destructive attitudes toward the environment.'" She looked up. "What destructive attitudes?"

"Orlando carves Rosalind's name on a tree." I leaned back in my chair so I could see out the window. The sun was still shining maliciously down. "I guess we go with *Hamlet.* This should make Edwin and his mother happy."

"We've still got the line-by-lines to go," Ms. Harrows said. "I think my throat is getting sore."

⊣ ••• ⊢

I got Karen to take my afternoon classes. It was sophomore lit and we'd been doing Beatrix Potter—all she had to do was pass out a worksheet on *Squirrel Nutkin*. I had outside lunch duty. It was so hot I had to take my jacket off. The College Students for Christ were marching around the school carrying picket signs that said, "Shakespeare was a Secular Humanist."

Delilah was lying on the front steps, reeking of suntan oil. She waved her "Shakespeare is Satan's Spokesman" sign languidly at me. "'Ye have sinned a great sin,'" she quoted. "'Blot me, I pray thee, out of thy book which thou has written.' Exodus Chapter 32, Verse 30."

"First Corinthians 13:3," I said. "'Though I give my body to be burned and have not charity, it profiteth me nothing.'"

—| • • • |—

"I called the doctor," Ms, Harrows said. She was standing by the window looking out at the blazing sun. "He thinks I might have pneumonia."

I sat down at the computer and fed in *Hamlet*. "Look on the bright side. At least we've got the E and R programs. We don't have to do it by hand the way we used to."

She sat down behind the stack. "How shall we do this? By group or by line?"

"We might as well take it from the top."

"Line one. 'Who's there?' The National Coalition Against Contractions."

"Let's do it by group," I said.

"All right. We'll get the big ones out of the way first. The Commission on Poison Prevention feels the 'graphic depiction of poisoning in the murder of Hamlet's father may lead to copycat crimes.' They cite a case in New Jersey where a sixteen-year-old poured Drano in his father's ear after reading the play. Just a minute. Let me get a Kleenex. The Literature Liberation Front objects to the phrases, 'Frailty, thy name is woman,' and 'O, most pernicious woman,' the 'What a piece of work is man' speech, and the queen."

"The whole queen?"

She checked her notes. "Yes. All lines, references, and allusions." She felt under her jaw, first one side, then the other. "I think my glands are swollen. Would that go along with pneumonia?"

Greg Jefferson came in, carrying a grocery sack. "I thought you could use some combat rations. How's it going?"

"We lost the queen," I said. "Next?"

"The National Cutlery Council objects to the depiction of swords as deadly weapons. 'Swords don't kill people. People kill people.' The Copenhagen Chamber of Commerce objects to the line, 'Something is rotten in the state of Denmark.' Students Against Suicide, the International Federation of Florists, and the Red Cross object to Ophelia's drowning."

Greg was setting out the bottles of cough syrup and cold tablets on the desk. He handed me a bottle of Valium. "The International Federation of Florists?" he said.

"She fell in picking flowers," I said. "What was the weather like out there?"

"Just like summer," he said. "Delilah's using an aluminum sun reflector."

"Ass," Ms. Harrows said.

"Beg pardon?" Greg said.

"ASS, the Association of Summer Sunbathers, objects to the line, 'I am too much I' the sun,'" Ms. Harrows said, and took a swig from the bottle of cough syrup.

We were only half-finished by the time school let out. The Nuns' Network objected to the line "Get thee to a nunnery," Fat and Proud of It wanted the passage beginning "Oh, that this too too solid flesh should melt" removed, and we didn't even get to Delilah's list, which was eight pages long.

"What play are we going to do?" Wendy asked me on my way out.

"*Hamlet,*" I said.

"*Hamlet?*" she said. "Is that the one about the guy whose uncle murders the king and then the queen marries the uncle?"

"Not anymore," I said.

Delilah was waiting for me outside. "'Many of them brought their books together and burned them,'" she quoted. "Acts 19:19."

"'Look not upon me, because I am black, because the sun hath looked upon me,'" I said.

It was overcast Wednesday but still warm. The Veterans for a Clean America and the Subliminal Seduction Sentinels were picnicking on the lawn. Delilah had on a halter top. "That thing you said yesterday about the sun turning people black, what was that from?"

"The Bible," I said. "Song of Solomon. Chapter 1, Verse 6."

"Oh," she said, relieved. "That's not in the Bible anymore. We threw it out."

Ms. Harrows had left a note for me. She was at the doctor's. I was supposed to meet with her third period.

"Do we get to start today?" Wendy asked.

"If everybody remembered to bring in their slips. I'm going to lecture on Shakespeare's life," I said. "You don't know what the forecast for today is, do you?"

"Yeah, it's supposed to be great."

I had her collect the refusal slips while I went over my notes. Last year Delilah's sister Jezebel had filed a grievance halfway through the lecture for "trying to preach promiscuity, birth control, and abortion by saying Anne Hathaway got pregnant before she got married." "Promiscuity," "abortion," "pregnant," and "before" had all been misspelled.

Everybody had remembered their slips. I sent the refusals to the library and started to lecture.

"Shakespeare—" I said. Paula's corder clicked on. "William Shakespeare was born on April twenty-third, 1564, in Stratford-on-Avon."

Rick, who hadn't raised his hand all year or even given an indication that he was sentient, raised his hand. "Do you intend to give equal time to the Baconian theory?" he said. "Bacon was not born on April twenty-third, 1564. He was born on January twenty-second, 1561."

⊢•••⊢

Ms. Harrows wasn't back from the doctor's by third period, so I started on Delilah's list. She objected to forty-three references to spirits, ghosts, and related matters, twenty-one obscene words, ("obscene" misspelled), and seventy-eight others that she thought might be obscene, such as pajock and cockles.

Ms. Harrows came in as I was finishing the list and threw her briefcase down. "Stress induced!" she said. "I have pneumonia, and he says my symptoms are stress induced!"

"Is it still cloudy out?"

"It is seventy-two degrees out. Where are we?"

"Morticians International," I said. "Again. 'Death presented as universal and inevitable.'" I peered at the paper. "That doesn't sound right."

Ms. Harrows took the paper away from me. "That's their 'Thanatopsis' protest. They had their national convention last week. They filed a whole set at once, and I haven't had a chance to sort through them." She rummaged around in her stack. "Here's the one on *Hamlet*. 'Negative portrayal of interment-preparation personnel—'"

"The gravedigger."

"'—And inaccurate representation of burial regulations. Neither a hermetically sealed coffin nor a vault appear in the scene.'"

We worked until five o'clock. The Society for the Advancement of Philosophy considered the line "There are more things in heaven and earth, Horatio, than are dreamt of in your philosophy" a slur on their profession. The Actors' Guild challenged Hamlet's hiring of nonunion employees, and the Drapery Defense League objected to Polonius being stabbed while hiding behind a curtain. "The clear implication of the scene is that the arras is dangerous," they had written in their brief. "Draperies don't kill people. People kill people."

Ms. Harrows put the paper down on top of the stack and took a swig of cough syrup. "And that's it. Anything left?"

"I think so," I said, punching reformat and scanning the screen. "Yes, a couple of things. How about, 'There is a willow grows aslant a brook / That shows his hoar leaves in the glassy stream.'"

"You'll never get away with 'hoar,'" Ms. Harrows said.

Thursday I got to school at seven-thirty to print out thirty copies of *Hamlet* for my class. It had turned colder and even cloudier in the night. Delilah was wearing a parka and mittens. Her face was a deep scarlet, and her nose had begun to peel.

"'Hath the Lord as great delight in burnt offerings as in obeying the voice of the Lord?'" I asked. "First Samuel 15:22." I patted her on the shoulder.

"Yeow," she said.

I passed out *Hamlet* and assigned Wendy and Rick to read the parts of Hamlet and Horatio.

"'The air bites shrewdly; it is very cold,'" Wendy read.

"Where are we?" Rick said. I pointed out the place to him. "Oh. 'It is a nipping and an eager air.'"

"'What hour now?'" Wendy read.

"'I think it lacks of twelve.'"

Wendy turned her paper over and looked at the back. "That's it?" she said. "That's all there is to *Hamlet?* I thought his uncle killed his father and then the ghost told him his mother was in on it and he said 'To be or not to be' and Ophelia killed herself and stuff." She turned the paper back over. "This can't be the whole play."

"It better not be the whole play," Delilah said. She came in, carrying her picket sign. "There'd better not be any ghosts in it. Or cockles."

"Did you need some Solarcaine, Delilah?" I asked her.

"I need a Magic Marker," she said with dignity.

I got her one out of the desk. She left, walking a little stiffly, as if it hurt to move.

"You can't just take parts of the play out because somebody doesn't like them," Wendy said. "If you do, the play doesn't make any sense. I bet if Shakespeare were here, he wouldn't let you just take things out—"

"Assuming Shakespeare wrote it," Rick said. "If you take every other letter in line two except the first three and the last six, they spell 'pig,' which is obviously a code word for Bacon."

"Snow day!" Ms. Harrow said over the intercom. Everybody raced to the windows. "We will have early dismissal today at nine-thirty."

I looked at the clock. It was 9:28.

"The Overprotective Parents Organization has filed the following protest: 'It is now snowing, and as the forecast predicts more snow, and as snow can result in slippery streets, poor visibility, bus accidents, frostbite, and avalanches, we demand that school be closed today and tomorrow so as not to endanger our children.' Buses will leave at nine thirty-five. Have a nice spring break!"

"The snow isn't even sticking on the ground," Wendy said. "Now we'll never get to do Shakespeare."

⊣•••⊢

Delilah was out in the hall, on her knees next to her picket sign, crossing out the word "man" in "Spokesman."

"The Feminists for a Fair Language are here," she said disgustedly. "They've got a court order," She wrote "person" above the crossed-out "man." "A court order! Can you believe that? I mean, what's happening to our right to freedom of speech?"

"You misspelled 'person,'" I said.

# All My Darling Daughters

BARRETT: I'll have her dog...Octavius.
OCTAVIUS: Sir?
BARRETT: Her dog must be destroyed. At once.
OCTAVIUS: I really d-don't see what the p-poor little beast
has d-done to...
—The Barretts of Wimpole Street

The first thing my new roommate did was tell me her life story. Then she tossed up all over my bunk. Welcome to Hell. I know, I know. It was my own fucked fault that I was stuck with the stupid little scut in the first place. Daddy's darling had let her grades slip till she was back in the freshman dorm and she would stay there until the admin reported she was being a good little girl again. But he didn't have to put me in the charity ward, with all the little scholarship freshmen from the front colonies—frightened virgies one and all. The richies had usually had their share of jig-jig in boarding school, even if they were mostly edge. And they were willing to learn.

Not this one. She wouldn't know a bone from a vaj, and wouldn't know what went into which either. Ugly, too. Her hair was chopped off in an old-fashioned bob I thought nobody, not even front kids, wore anymore. Her name was Zibet and she was from some godspit colony called Marylebone Weep and her mother was dead and she had three sisters and her father hadn't wanted her to come. She told me all this in a rush of what she probably thought was friendliness before she tossed her supper all over me and my nice new slickspin sheets.

The sheets were the sum total of good things about the vacation Daddy Dear had sent me on over summer break. Being stranded in a forest of slimy slicksa trees and noble natives was supposed to build my character and teach me the hazards of bad grades. But the noble natives were good at more than weaving their precious product with its near frictionless surface. Jig-jig on slickspin is something entirely different, and I was close to being an expert on the subject. I'd bet even Brown didn't know about this one. I'd be more than glad to teach him.

"I'm so sorry," she kept saying in a kind of hiccup while her face turned red and then white and then red again like a fucked alert bell, and big tears seeped down her face and dripped on the mess. "I guess I got a little sick on the shuttle."

"I guess. Don't bawl, for jig's sake, it's no big deal. Don't they have laundries in Mary Boning It?"

"Marylebone Weep. It's a natural spring."

"So are you, kid. So are you." I scooped up the wad, with the muck inside. "No big deal. The dorm mother will take care of it."

She was in no shape to take the sheets down herself, and I figured Mumsy would take one look at those big fat tears and assign me a new roommate. This one was not exactly perfect. I could see right now I couldn't expect her to do her homework and not bawl giant tears while Brown and I jig-jigged on the new sheets. But she didn't have leprosy, she didn't weigh eight hundred pounds, and she hadn't gone for my vaj when I bent over to pick up the sheets. I could do a lot worse.

I could also be doing some better. Seeing Mumsy on my first day back was not my idea of a good start. But I trotted downstairs with the scutty wad and knocked on the dorm mother's door.

She is no dumb lady. You have to stand in a little box of an entryway waiting for her to answer your knock. The box works on the same principle as a rat cage, except that she's added her own little touch. Three big mirrors that probably cost her a year's salary to cart up from earth. Never mind—as a weapon, they were a real bargain. Because, Jesus Jiggin' Mary, you stand there and sweat and the mirrors tell you your skirt isn't straight and your hair looks scutty and that bead of sweat on your upper lip is going to give it away immediately that you are scared scutless. By the time she answers the door—five minutes if she's feeling kindly—you're either edge or you're not there. No dumb lady.

I was not on the defensive, and my skirts are never straight, so the mirrors didn't have any effect on me, but the five minutes took their toll.

That box didn't have any ventilation and I was way too close to those sheets. But I had my speech all ready. No need to remind her who I was. The admin had probably filled her in but good. And I'd get nowhere telling her they were my sheets. Let her think they were the virgie's.

When she opened the door I gave her a brilliant smile and said, "My roommate's had a little problem. She's a new freshman, and I think she got a little excited coming up on the shuttle and—"

I expected her to launch into the "supplies are precious, everything must be recycled, cleanliness is next to godliness" speech you get for everything you do on this godspit campus. Instead she said, "What did you do to her?"

"What did I—look, she's the one who tossed up. What do you think I did, stuck my fingers down her throat?"

"Did you give her something? Samurai? Float? Alcohol?"

"Jiggin' Jesus, she just got here. She walked in, she said she was from Mary's Prick or something, she tossed up."

"And?"

"And what? I may look depraved, but I don't think freshmen vomit at the sight of me."

From her expression, I figured Mumsy might. I stuck the smelly wad of sheets at her. "Look," I said, "I don't care what you do. It's not my problem. The kid needs clean sheets."

Her expression for the mucky mess was kinder than the one she had for me. "Recycling is not until Wednesday. She will have to sleep on her mattress until then."

Mary Masting, she could knit a sheet by Wednesday, especially with all the cotton flying around this fucked campus. I grabbed the sheets back.

"Jig you, scut," I said.

I got two months' dorm restricks and a date with the admin.

I went down to third level and did the sheets myself. It cost a fortune. They want you to have an awareness of the harm you are doing the delicate environment by failing to abide, etc. Total scut. The environment's about as delicate as a senior's vaj. When Old Man Moulton bought this thirdhand Hell-Five, he had some edge dream of turning it into the college he went to as a boy. Whatever possessed him to even buy the old castoff is something nobody's ever figured out. There must have been a Lagrangian point on the top of his head.

The realtor must have talked hard and fast to make him think Hell could ever look like Ames, Iowa. At least there'd been some technical advances since it was first built or we'd all be floating around the godspit place. But he couldn't stop at simply gravitizing the place, fixing the plumbing, and hiring a few good teachers. Oh, no, he had to build a sandstone campus, put in a football field, and plant trees! This all cost a fortune, of course, which put it out of the reach of everybody but richies and trust kids, except for Moulton's charity scholarship cases. But you couldn't jig jig in a plastic bag to fulfill your fatherly instincts back then, so Moulton had to build himself a college. And here we sit, stuck out in space with a bunch of fucked cottonwood trees that are trying to take over.

Jesus Bonin' Mary, cottonwoods! I mean, so what if we're a hundred years out of date. I can take the freshman beanies and the pep rallies. Dorm curfews didn't stop anybody a hundred years ago either. And face it, pleated skirts and cardigans make for easy access. But those godspit trees!

At first they tried the nature-dupe stuff. Freeze your vaj in winter, suffocate in summer, just like good old Iowa. The trees were at least bearable then. Everybody choked in cotton for a month, they baled the stuff up like Mississippi slaves and shipped it down to earth and that was it. But finally something was too expensive even for Daddy Moulton and we went on even-clime like all the other Hell-Fives. Nobody bothered to tell the trees, of course, so now they just spit and drop leaves whenever they feel like it, which is all the time. You can hardly make it to class without choking to death.

The trees do their dirty work down under, too, rooting happily away through the plumbing and the buried cables so that nothing works. Ever. I think the whole outer shell could blow away and nobody would ever know. The fucked root system would hold us together. And the admin wonders why we call it Hell. I'd like to upset this delicate balance once and for all.

I ran the sheets through on disinfect and put them in the spin. While I was sitting there, thinking evil thoughts about freshmen and figuring how to get off restricks, Arabel came wandering in.

"Tavvy, hi! When did you get back?" She is always too sweet for words. We played lezzies as freshmen, and sometimes I think she's sorry it's over. "There's a great party," she said.

"I'm on restricks," I said. Arabel's not the world's greatest authority on parties. I mean, herself and a plastic bone would be a great party. "Where is it?"

"My room. Brown's there," she said languidly. This was calculated to make me rush out of my pants and up the stairs, no doubt. I watched my sheets spin.

"So what are you doing down here?" I said.

"I came down for some float. Our machine's out. Why don't you come on over? Restricks never stopped you before."

"I've been to your parties, Arabel. Washing my sheets might be more exciting."

"You're right," she said, "it might." She fiddled with the machine. This was not like her at all.

"What's up?"

"Nothing's up." She sounded puzzled. "It's samurai-party time without the samurai. Not a bone in sight and no hope of any. That's why I came down here."

"Brown, too?" I asked. He was into a lot of edge stuff, but I couldn't quite imagine celibacy.

"Brown, too. They all just sit there."

"They're on something, then. Something new they brought back from vacation." I couldn't see what she was so upset about.

"No," she said. "They're not on anything. This is different. Come see. Please."

Well, maybe this was all a trick to get me to one of Arabel's scutty parties and maybe not. But I didn't want Mumsy to think she'd hurt my feelings by putting me on restricks. I threw the lock on the spin so no-body'd steal the sheets and went with her.

⊣•••⊢

For once Arabel hadn't exaggerated. It was a godspit party, even by her low standards. You could tell that the minute you walked in. The girls looked unhappy, the boys looked uninterested. It couldn't be all bad, though. At least Brown was back. I walked over to where he was standing.

"Tavvy," he said, smiling, "how was your summer? Learn anything new from the natives?"

"More than my fucked father intended." I smiled back at him.

"I'm sure he had your best interests at heart," he said. I started to say something clever to that, then realized he wasn't kidding. Brown was trust just like I was. He had to be kidding. Only he wasn't. He wasn't smiling anymore either.

"He just wanted to protect you, for your own good."

Jiggin' Jesus, he had to be on something. "I don't need any protecting," I said. "As you well know."

"Yeah," he said, sounding disappointed. "Yeah." He moved away.

What in the scut was going on? Brown leaned against the wall, watching Sept and Arabel. She had her sweater off and was shimmying out of her skirt, which I have seen before, sometimes even helped with. What I had never seen before was the look of absolute desperation on her face. Something was very wrong. Sept stripped, and his bone was as big as Arabel could have wanted, but the look on her face didn't change. Sept shook his head almost disapprovingly at Brown and went down on Arabel.

"I haven't had any straight-up all summer," Brown said from behind me, his hand on my vaj. "Let's get out of here."

Gladly. "We can't go to my room," I said. "I've got a virgie for a roommate. How about yours?"

"No!" he said, and then more quietly, "I've got the same problem. New guy just off the shuttle. I want to break him in gently."

You're lying, Brown, I thought. And you're about to back out of this, too. "I know a place," I said, and practically raced him to the laundry room so he wouldn't have time to change his mind.

I spread one of the dried slickspin sheets on the floor and went down as fast as I could get out of my clothes. Brown was in no hurry, and the frictionless sheet seemed to relax him. He smoothed his hands the full length of my body. "Tavvy," he said, brushing his lips along the line from my hips to my neck, "your skin's so soft. I'd almost forgotten." He was talking to himself.

Forgotten what, for fucked's sake, he couldn't have been without any jig-jig all summer or he'd be showing it now, and he acted like he had all the time in the world.

"Almost forgotten..nothing like.."

Like what? I thought furiously. Just what have you got in that room? And what has it got that I haven't? I spread my legs and forced him down between them. He raised his head a little, frowning, then he started that

304

long, slow, torturing passage down my skin again. Jiggin' Jesus, how long did he think I could wait?

"Come on," I whispered, trying to maneuver him with my hips. "Put it in, Brown. I want to jig jig. Please."

He stood up in a motion so abrupt that my head smacked against the laundry-room floor. He pulled on his clothes, looking…what? Guilty? Angry?

I sat up. "What in the holy scut do you think you're doing?"

"You wouldn't understand. I just keep thinking about your father."

"My *father*? What in the scut are you talking about?"

"Look, I can't explain it. I just can't…" And left. Like that. With me ready to go off any minute and what do I get? A cracked head.

"I don't have a father, you scutty godfucker!" I shouted after him.

I yanked my clothes on and started pulling the other sheet out of the spin with a viciousness I would have liked to have spent on Brown. Arabel was back, watching from the laundry-room door. Her face still had that strained look.

"Did you see that last charming scene?" I asked her, snagging the sheet on the spin handle and ripping a hole in one corner.

"I didn't have to. I can imagine it went pretty much the way mine did." She leaned unhappily against the door. "I think they've all gone bent over the summer."

"Maybe." I wadded the sheets together into a ball. I didn't think that was it, though. Brown wouldn't have lied about a new boy in his room in that case. And he wouldn't have kept talking about my father in that edge way. I walked past Arabel. "Don't worry, Arabel, if we have to go lezzy again, you know you're my first choice."

She didn't even look particularly happy about that.

My idiot roommate was awake, sitting bolt upright on the bunk where I'd left her. The poor brainless thing had probably been sitting there the whole time I'd been gone. I made up the bunk, stripped off my clothes for the second time tonight, and crawled in. "You can turn out the light any time," I said.

She hopped over to the wall plate, swathed in a nightgown that dated as far back as Old Man Moulton's college days, or farther. "Did you get in trouble?" she asked, her eyes wide.

"Of course not. I wasn't the one who tossed up. If anybody's in trouble, it's you," I added maliciously.

She seemed to sag against the flat wallplate as if she were clinging to it for support. "My father—will they tell my father?" Her face was flashing red and white again. And where would the vomit land this time? That would teach me to take out my frustrations on my roommate.

"Your father? Of course not. Nobody's in trouble. It was a couple of fucked sheets, that's all."

She didn't seem to hear me, "He said he'd come and get me if I got in trouble. He said he'd make me go home."

I sat up in the bunk. I'd never seen a freshman yet that wasn't dying to go home, at least not one like Zibet, with a whole loving family waiting for her instead of a trust and a couple of snotty lawyers. But Zibet here was scared scutless at the idea. Maybe the whole campus was going edge. "You didn't get in trouble," I repeated. "There's nothing to worry about."

She was still hanging onto that wallplate for dear life.

"Come on"—Mary Masting, she was probably having an attack of some kind and I'd get blamed for that, too. "You're safe here. Your father doesn't even know about it."

She seemed to relax a little. "Thank you for not getting me in trouble," she said and crawled back into her own bunk. She didn't turn the light off.

Jiggin' Jesus, it wasn't worth it. I got out of bed and turned the fucked light off myself.

"You're a good person, you know that," she said softly into the darkness. Definitely edge. I settled down under the covers, planning to masty myself to sleep, since I couldn't get anything any other way, but very quietly. I didn't want any more hysterics.

A hearty voice suddenly exploded into the room. "To the young men of Moulton College, to all my strong sons, I say—"

"What's that?" Zibet whispered.

"First night in Hell," I said, and got out of bed for the thirtieth time.

"May all your noble endeavors be crowned with success," Old Man Moulton said.

I slapped my palm against the wallplate and then fumbled through my still-unpacked shuttle bag for a nail file. I stepped up on Zibet's bunk with it and started to unscrew the intercom.

"To the young women of Moulton College," he boomed again, "to all my darling daughters." He stopped. I tossed the screws and file back in the bag, smacked the plate, and flung myself back in bed.

"Who was that?" Zibet whispered.

"Our founding father," I said, and then remembering the effect the word "father" seemed to be having on everyone in this edge place I added hastily, "That's the last time you'll have to hear him. I'll put some plast in the works tomorrow and put the screws back in so the dorm mother won't figure it out. We will live in blessed silence for the rest of the semester."

She didn't answer. She was already asleep, gently snoring. Which meant so far I had misguessed every single thing today. Great start to the semester.

⊣•••⊢

The admin knew all about the party. "You *do* know the meaning of the word restricks, I presume?" he said.

He was an old scut, probably forty-five. Dear Daddy's age. He was fairly good-looking, probably exercising like edge to keep the old belly in for the freshman girls. He was liable to get a hernia. He probably jig jigged into a plastic bag, too, just like Daddy, to carry on the family name. Jiggin' Jesus, there oughta be a law.

"You're a trust student, Octavia?"

"That's right." You think I'd be stuck with a fucked name like Octavia if I wasn't?

"Neither parent?"

"No. Paid mother-surr. Trust name till twenty-one." I watched his face to see what effect that had on him. I'd seen a lot of scared faces that way.

"There's no one to write to, then, except your lawyers. No way to expel you. And restricks don't seem to have any appreciable effect on you. I don't quite know what would."

I'll bet you don't. I kept watching him, and he kept watching me, maybe wondering if I was his darling daughter, if that expensive jism in the plastic bag had turned out to be what he was boning after right now.

"What exactly was it you called your dorm mother?"

"Scut," I said.

"I've longed to call her that myself a time or two."

The sympathetic buildup. I waited, pretty sure of what was coming.

"About this party—I've heard the boys have something new going. What is it?"

The question wasn't what I'd expected. "I don't know," I said and then realized I'd let my guard down. "Do you think I'd tell you if I knew?"

"No, of course not. I admire that. You're quite a young woman, you know. Outspoken, loyal, very pretty, too, if I may say so."

Um-hmm. And you just happen to have a job for me, don't you?

"My secretary's quit. She likes younger men, she says, although if what I hear is true, maybe she's better off with me. It's a good job. Lots of extras. Unless, of course, you're like my secretary and prefer boys to men."

Well, and here was the way out. No more virgie freshmen, no more restricks. Very tempting. Only he was at least forty-five, and somehow I couldn't quite stomach the idea of jig jig with my own father. Sorry, sir.

"If it's the trust problem that's bothering you, I assure you there are ways to check."

Liar. Nobody knows who their kids are. That's why we've got these storybook trust names, so we can't show up on Daddy's doorstep: Hi, I'm your darling daughter. The trust protects them against scenes like that. Only sometimes with a scut like the admin here, you wonder just who's being protected from whom.

"Do you remember what I told my dorm mother?" I said.

"Yes."

"Double to you."

Restricks for the rest of the year and a godspit alert band welded onto my wrist.

"I know what they've got," Arabel whispered to me in class. It was the only time I ever saw her. The godspit alert band went off if I even mastied without permission.

"What?" I asked, pretty much without caring.

"Tell you after."

I met her outside, in a blizzard of flying leaves and cotton. The circulation system had gone edge again. "Animals," she said.

"Animals?"

"Little repulsive things about as long as your arm. Tessels, they're called. Repulsive little brown animals."

"I don't believe it," I said. "It's got to be more than beasties. That's elementary school stuff. Are they bioenhanced?"

"You mean pheromones or something?" She frowned. "I don't know. I sure didn't see anything attractive about them, but the boys—Brown brought his to a party, carrying it around on his arm, calling it Daughter Ann. They all swarmed around it, petting it, saying things like 'Come to Daddy.' It was really edge."

I shrugged. "Well, if you're right, we don't have anything to worry about. Even if they're bio-enhanced, how long can beasties hold their attention? It'll all be over by midterms."

"Can't you come over? I never see you." She sounded like she was ready to go lezzy.

I held up the banded wrist. "Can't. Listen, Arabel, I'll be late to my next class," I said, and hurried off through the flailing yellow and white. I didn't have a next class. I went back to the dorm and took some float.

When I came out of it, Zibet was there, sitting on her bunk with her knees hunched up, writing busily in a notebook. She looked much better than the first time I saw her. Her hair had grown out some and showed enough curl at the ends to pick up on her features. She didn't look strained. In fact she looked almost happy.

"What are you doing?" I hoped I said. The first couple of sentences out of float it's anybody's guess what's going to come out.

"Recopying my notes," she said. Jiggin', the things that make some people happy. I wondered if she'd found a boyfriend and that was what had given her that pretty pink color. If she had, she was doing better than Arabel. Or me.

"For who?"

"What?" she looked blank.

"What boy are you copying your notes for?"

"Boy?" Now there was an edge to her voice. She looked frightened.

I said carefully, "I figure you've got to have a boyfriend." And watched her go edge again. Mary doing Jesus, that must not have come out right at all. I wondered what I'd really said to send her off like that.

She backed up against the bunk wall like I was after her with something and held her notebook flat against her chest. "Why do you think that?"

Think what? Holy scut, I should have told her about float before I went off on it. I'd have to answer her now like it was still a real conversation instead of a caged rat being poked with a stick, and hope I could explain later. "I don't know why I think that. You just looked—"

"It's true, then," she said, and the strain was right back, blinking red and white.

"What is?" I said, still wondering what it was the float had garbled my innocent comment into.

"I had braids like you before I came here. You probably wondered about that." Holy scut, I'd said something mean about her choppy hair.

"My father..."—she clutched the notebook like she had clutched the wallplate that night, hanging on for dear life. "My father cut them off." She was admitting some awful thing to me and I had no idea what.

"Why did he do that?"

"He said I tempted...men with it. He said I was a—that I made men think wicked thoughts about me. He said it was my fault that it happened. He cut off all my hair."

It was coming to me finally that I had asked her just what I thought I had: whether she had a boyfriend.

"Do you think I—do that?" she asked me pleadingly.

Are you kidding? She couldn't have tempted Brown in one of his bone-a-virgin moods. I couldn't say that to her, though, and on the other hand, I knew if I said yes it was going to be toss-up time in dormland again. I felt sorry for her, poor kid, her braids chopped off and her scut of a father scaring the hell out of her with a bunch of lies. No wonder she'd been so edge when she first got here.

"Do you?" she persisted.

"You want to know what I think," I said, standing up a little unsteadily. "I think fathers are a pile of scut." I thought of Arabel's story. Little brown animals as long as your arm and Brown saying, "Your father only wants to protect you." "Worse than a pile of scut," I said. "All of them."

She looked at me, backed up against the wall, as if she would like to believe me.

"You want to know what my father did to me?" I said. "He didn't cut my braids off. Oh, no, this is lots better. You know about trust kids?"

She shook her head.

"Okay. My father wants to carry on his precious name and his precious jig juice, but he doesn't want any of the trouble. So he sets up a trust. He pays a lot of money, he goes jig jig in a plastic bag, and presto he's a father, and the lawyers are left with all the dirty work. Like taking care of me and sending me someplace for summer break and paying my tuition at this godspit school. Like putting one of these on me." I held up my wrist with the ugly alert band on it. "He never even saw me. He doesn't even know who I am. Trust me. I know about scutty fathers."

"I wish…" Zibet said. She opened her book and started copying her notes again. I eased down onto my bunk, starting to feel the post-float headache. When I looked at her again, she was dripping tears all over her precious notes. Jiggin' Jesus, everything I said was wrong. The most I could hope for in this edge place was that the boys would be done playing beasties by midterms and I could get my grades up.

By midterms the circulation system had broken down completely. The campus was knee-deep in leaves and cotton. You could hardly walk. I trudged through the leaves to class, head down. I didn't even see Brown until it was too late.

He had the animal on his arm. "This is Daughter Ann," Brown said. "Daughter Ann, meet Tavvy."

"Go jig yourself," I said, brushing by him.

He grabbed my wrist, holding on hard and pressing his fingers against the alert band until it hurt. "That's not polite, Tavvy. Daughter Ann wants to meet you. Don't you, sweetheart?" He held the animal out to me. Arabel had been right. Hideous little things. I had never gotten a close look at one before. It had a sharp little brown face, with dull eyes and a tiny pink mouth. Its fur was coarse and brown, and its body hung limply off Brown's arm. He had put a ribbon around its neck.

"Just your type," I said. "Ugly as mud and a hole big enough for even you to find."

His grip tightened. "You can't talk that way to my…"

"Hi," Zibet said behind me. I whirled around. This was all I needed.

"Hi," I said, and yanked my wrist free. "Brown, this is my roommate. My freshman roommate. Zibet, Brown."

"And this is Daughter Ann," he said, holding the animal up so that its tender pink mouth gaped stupidly at us. Its tail was up. I could see tender pink at the other end, too. And Arabel wonders what the attraction is?

"Nice to meet you, freshman roommate," Brown muttered and pulled the animal back close to him. "Come to Papa," he said, and stalked off through the leaves.

I rubbed my poor wrist. Please, please let her not ask me what a tessel's for? I have had about all I can take for one day. I'm not about to explain Brown's nasty habits to a virgie.

I had underestimated her. She shuddered a little and pulled her notebooks against her chest. "Poor little beast," she said.

⊣•••⊢

"What do you know about sin?" she asked me suddenly that night. At least she had turned off the light. That was some improvement.

"A lot," I said. "How do you think I got this charming bracelet?"

"I mean really doing something wrong. To somebody else. To save yourself." She stopped. I didn't answer her, and she didn't say anything more for a long time. "I know about the admin," she said finally.

I couldn't have been more surprised if Old Scut Moulton had suddenly shouted, "Bless you, my daughter," over the intercom.

"You're a good person, I can tell that." There was a dreamy quality to her voice. If it had been anybody but her I'd have thought she was masting. "There are things you wouldn't do, not even to save yourself."

"And you're a hardened criminal, I suppose?"

"There are things you wouldn't do," she repeated sleepily, and then said quite clearly and irrelevantly, "My sister's coming for Christmas."

Jiggin', she was full of surprises tonight. "I thought you were going home for Christmas," I said.

"I'm never going home," she said.

⊣•••⊢

"Tavvy!" Arabel shouted halfway across campus. "Hello!"

The boys are over it, I thought, and how in the scut am I going to get rid of this alert band? I felt so relieved I could have cried.

"Tavvy," she said again. "I haven't seen you in weeks!"

"What's going on?" I asked her, wondering why she didn't just blurt it out about the boys in her usual breakneck fashion.

"What do you mean?" she said, wide-eyed, and I knew it wasn't the boys. They still had the tessels, Brown and Sept and all the rest of them. They still had the tessels. It's only beasties, I told myself fiercely, it's only beasties and why are you so edge about it? Your father has your best interests at heart. Come to Daddy

"The admin's secretary quit," Arabel said. "I got put on restricks for a samurai party in my room." She shrugged. "It was the best offer I'd had all fall."

Oh, but you're trust, Arabel. You're trust. He could be your father. Come to Papa.

"You look terrible," Arabel said. "Are you doing too much float?"

I shook my head. "Do you know what it is the boys do with them?"

"Tavvy, sweetheart, if you can't figure out what that big pink hole is for—"

"My roommate's father cut her hair off," I said. "She's a virgie. She's never done anything. He cut off all her hair."

"Hey," Arabel said, "you are really edging it. Listen, how long have you been without jig jig? I can set you up, younger guys than the admin, nothing to worry about. Guaranteed no trusters. I could set you up."

I shook my head. "I don't want any."

"Listen, I'm worried about you. I don't want you to go edge on me. Let me ask the admin about your alert band at least. "

"No," I said clearly "I'm all right, Arabel. I've got to get to class."

"Don't let this tessel thing get to you, Tavvy. It's only beasties."

"Yeah." I walked steadily away from her across the spitting, leaf-littered campus. As soon as I was out of her line of sight, I slumped against one of the giant cottonwoods and hung on to it like Zibet had clung to that wallplate. For dear life.

Zibet didn't say another thing about her sister until right before Christmas break. Her hair, which I had thought was growing out, looked choppier than ever. The old look of strain was back and getting worse every day. She looked like a radiation victim.

I wasn't looking that good myself. I couldn't sleep, and float gave me headaches that lasted a week. The alert band started a rash that had worked its way halfway up my arm. And Arabel was right. I was going edge. I couldn't get the tessels off my mind. If you'd asked me last summer what I thought of beasties, I'd have said it was great fun for everyone, especially the animals. Now the thought of Brown with that hideous little brown and pink thing on his arm was enough to make me toss up. I keep thinking about your father. If it's the trust thing you're worried about, I can find out for you. He has your best interests at heart. Come to Papa.

My lawyers hadn't succeeded in convincing the admin to let me go to Aspen for Christmas, or anywhere else. They'd managed to wangle full privileges as soon as everybody was gone, but not to get the alert band off. I figured if my dorm mother got a good look at what it was doing to my arm, though, she'd let me have it off for a few days and give it a chance to heal. The circulation system was working again, blowing winds of hurricane force all across Hell. Merry Christmas, everybody

On the last day of class I walked into our dark room, hit the wallplate, and froze. There sat Zibet in the dark. On my bed. With a tessel in her lap.

"Where did you get that?" I whispered.

"I stole it," she said.

I locked the door behind me and pushed one of the desk chairs against it. "How?"

"They were all at a party in somebody else's room."

"You went in the boys' dorm?"

She didn't answer.

"You're a freshman. They could send you home for that," I said, disbelieving. This was the girl who had gone quite literally up the wall over the sheets, who had said, "I'm never going home again."

"Nobody saw me," she said calmly "They were all at a party."

"You're edge," I said. "Whose is it, do you know?"

"It's Daughter Ann."

I grabbed the top sheet off my bunk and started lining my shuttle bag with it. Holy scut, this would be the first place Brown would look. I rifled through my desk drawer for a pair of scissors to cut some air slits with. Zibet still sat petting the horrid thing.

"We've got to hide it," I said. "This time I'm not kidding. You really are in trouble."

She didn't hear me. "My sister Henra's pretty. She has long braids like you. She's good like you, too," and then in an almost pleading voice, "she's only fifteen."

⊣•••⊢

Brown demanded and got a room check that started, you guessed it, with our room. The tessel wasn't there. I'd put it in the shuttle bag and hidden it in one of the spins down in the laundry room. I'd wadded the other slickspin sheet in front of it, which I felt was a fitting irony for Brown, only he was too enraged to see it.

"I want another check," he said after the dorm mother had given him the grand tour. "I know it's here." He turned to me. "I know you've got it."

"The last shuttle's in ten minutes," the dorm mother said. "There isn't time for another check."

"She's got it. I can tell by the look on her face. She's hidden it somewhere. Somewhere in this dorm."

The dorm mother looked like she'd like to have him in her Skinner box for about an hour. She shook her head.

"You lose, Brown," I said. "You stay and you'll miss your shuttle and be stuck in Hell over Christmas. You leave and you lose your darling Daughter Ann. You lose either way, Brown."

He grabbed my wrist. The rash was almost unbearable under the band. My wrist had started to swell, puffing out purplish-red over the metal. I tried to free myself with my other hand, but his grip was as hard and vengeful as his face. "Octavia here was at a samurai party in the boys' dorm last week," he said to the dorm mother.

"That's not true," I said. I could hardly talk. The pain from his grip was making me so nauseated I felt faint.

"I find that difficult to believe," the dorm mother said, "since she is confined by an alert band."

"This?" Brown said, and yanked my arm up. I cried out. "This thing?" He twisted it around my wrist. "She can take it off any time she wants. Didn't you know that?" He dropped my wrist and looked at me contemptuously "Tavvy's too smart to let a little thing like an alert band stop her, aren't you, Tavvy?"

I cradled my throbbing wrist against my body and tried not to black out. It isn't beasties, I thought frantically. He would never do this to me just for beasties. It's something worse. Worse. He must never, never get it back.

"There's the call for the shuttle," the dorm mother said. "Octavia, your break privileges are canceled."

Brown shot a triumphant glance at me and followed her out. It took every bit of strength I had to wait till the last shuttle was gone before I went to get the tessel. I carried it back to the room with my good hand. The restricks hardly mattered. There was no place to go anyway. And the tessel was safe. "Everything will be all right," I said to the tessel.

Only everything wasn't all right. Henra, the pretty sister, wasn't pretty. Her hair had been cut off, as short as scissors could make it. She was flushed bright red and crying. Zibet's face had gone stony white and stayed that way. I didn't think from the looks of her that she'd ever cry again. Isn't it wonderful what a semester of college can do for you?

Restricks or no, I had to get out of there. I took my books and camped down in the laundry room. I wrote two term papers, read three textbooks, and like Zibet, recopied all my notes. He cut off my hair. He said I tempted men and that was why it happened. Your father was only trying to protect you. Come to Papa. I turned on all the spins at once so I couldn't hear myself think and typed the term papers.

I made it to the last day of break, gritting my teeth to keep from thinking about Brown, about tessels, about everything. Zibet and her sister came down to the laundry room to tell me Henra was going back on the first shuttle. I said goodbye. "I hope you can come back," I said, knowing I sounded stupid, knowing there was nothing in the world that could make me go back to Marylebone Weep if I were Henra.

"I am coming back. As soon as I graduate."

"It's only two years," Zibet said. Two years ago Zibet had the same sweet face as her sister. Two years from now, Henra too would look like death warmed over. What fun to grow up in Marylebone Weep, where you're a wreck at seventeen.

"Come back with me, Zibet," Henra said.

"I can't. "

Toss-up time. I went back to the room, propped myself on my bunk with a stack of books, and started reading. The tessel had been asleep on the foot of the bunk, its gaping pink vaj sticking up. It crawled onto my lap and lay there. I picked it up. It didn't resist. Even with it living in the room, I'd never really looked at it closely. I saw now that it couldn't resist if it tried. It had tiny little paws with soft pink underpads and no claws. It had no teeth, either, just the soft little rosebud mouth, only a quarter of the size of the opening at the other end. If it had been enhanced with pheromones, I sure couldn't tell it. Maybe its attraction was simply that it had no defenses, that it couldn't fight even if it wanted to.

I laid it over my lap and stuck an exploratory finger a little way into the vaj. I'd done enough lezzing when I was a freshman to know what a good vaj should feel like. I eased the finger farther in.

It screamed.

I yanked the hand free, balled it into a fist, and crammed it against my mouth hard to keep from screaming myself. Horrible, awful, pitiful sound. Helpless. Hopeless. The sound a woman must make when she's being raped. No. Worse. The sound a child must make. I thought, I have never heard a sound like that in my whole life, and at the same instant, this is the sound I have been hearing all semester. Pheromones. Oh, no, a far greater attraction than some chemical. Or is fear a chemical, too?

I put the poor little beast onto the bed, went into the bathroom, and washed my hands for about an hour. I thought Zibet hadn't known what the tessels were for, that she hadn't had more than the vaguest idea what the boys were doing to them. But she had known. Known and tried to keep it from me. Known and gone into the boys' dorm all by herself to steal one. We should have stolen them all, all of them, gotten them away from those scutting god-fucking…I had thought of a lot of names for my father over the years. None of them was bad enough for this. Scutting Jesus jiggers. Fucking piles of scut.

Zibet was standing in the door of the bathroom.

"Oh, Zibet," I said, and stopped.

"My sister's going home this afternoon," she said.

"No," I said, "Oh, no," and ran past her out of the room.

I guess I had kind of a little breakdown. Anyway, I can't account very well for the time. Which is edge, because the thing I remember most vividly is the feeling that I needed to hurry, that something awful would happen if I didn't hurry.

I know I broke restricks because I remember sitting out under the cottonwoods and thinking what a wonderful sense of humor Old Man Moulton had. He sent up Christmas lights for the bare cottonwoods, and the cotton and the brittle yellow leaves blew against them and caught fire. The smell of burning was everywhere. I remember thinking clearly, smokes and fires, how appropriate for Christmas in Hell.

But when I tried to think about the tessels, about what to do, the thoughts got all muddy and confused, like I'd taken too much float. Sometimes it was Zibet Brown wanted and not Daughter Ann at all, and I would say, "You cut off her hair. I'll never give her back to you. Never." And she would struggle and struggle against him. But she had no claws, no teeth. Sometimes it was the admin, and he would say, "If it's the trust thing you're worried about, I can find out for you," and I would say, "You only want the tessels for yourself." And sometimes Zibet's father said, "I am only trying to protect you. Come to Papa." And I would climb up on the bunk to unscrew the intercom but I couldn't shut him up. "I don't need protecting," I would say to him. Zibet would struggle and struggle.

A dangling bit of cotton had stuck to one of the Christmas lights. It caught fire and dropped into the brown broken leaves. The smell of smoke was everywhere. Somebody should report that. Hell could burn down, or was it burn up, with nobody here over Christmas break. I should tell somebody. That was it, I had to tell somebody. But there was nobody to tell. I wanted my father. And he wasn't there. He had never been there. He had paid his money, spilled his juice, and thrown me to the wolves. But at least he wasn't one of them. He wasn't one of them.

There was nobody to tell. "What did you do to it?" Arabel said. "Did you give it something? Samurai? Float? Alcohol?"

"I didn't…"

"Consider yourself on restricks."

"It isn't beasties," I said. "They call them Baby Dear and Daughter Ann. And they're the fathers. They're the fathers. But the tessels don't have any claws. They don't have any teeth. They don't even know what jig-jig is."

"He has her best interests at heart," Arabel said.

"What are you talking about? He cut off all her hair. You should have seen her, hanging onto the wallplate for dear life! She struggled and struggled, but it didn't do any good. She doesn't have any claws. She doesn't have any teeth. She's only fifteen. We have to hurry."

"It'll all be over by midterms," Arabel said. "I can fix you up. Guaranteed no trusters."

I was standing in the dorm mother's Skinner box, pounding on her door. I did not know how I had gotten there. My face looked back at me from the dorm mother's mirrors. Arabel's face: strained and desperate. Flashing red and white and red again like an alert band: my roommate's face. She would not believe me. She would put me on restricks. She would have me expelled. It didn't matter. When she answered the door, I could not run. I had to tell somebody before the whole place caught on fire.

"Oh, my dear," she said, and put her arms around me.

I knew before I opened the door that Zibet was sitting on my bunk in the dark. I pressed the wallplate and kept my bandaged hand on it, as if I might need it for support. "Zibet," I said. "Everything's going to be all right. The dorm mother's going to confiscate the tessels. They're going to outlaw animals on campus. Everything will be all right."

She looked up at me. "I sent it home with her," she said.

"What?" I said blankly.

"He won't...leave us alone. He—I sent Daughter Ann home with her." No. Oh, no.

"Henra's good like you. She won't save herself. She'll never last the two years." She looked steadily at me. "I have two other sisters. The youngest is only ten."

"You sent the tessel home?" I said. "To your *father?*"

"Yes."

"It can't protect itself," I said. "It doesn't have any claws. It can't protect itself."

"I told you you didn't know anything about sin," she said, and turned away.

I never asked the dorm mother what they did with the tessels they took away from the boys. I hope, for their own sakes, that somebody put them out of their misery.

# In the Late Cretaceous

"It was in the late Cretaceous that predators reached their full flowering," Dr. Othniel said. "Of course, carnivorous dinosaurs were present from the Middle Triassic on, but it was in the Late Cretaceous, with the arrival of the albertosaurus, the velociraptor, the deinonychus, and of course, the tyrannosaurus rex, that the predatory dinosaur reached its full strength, speed, and sophistication."

Dr. Othniel wrote "LATE CRETACEOUS—PREDATORS" on the board. He suffered from arthritis and a tendency to stoop, and the combination made him write only on the lower third of the chalkboard. He wrote "ALBERTOSAURUS, COELOPHYSIS, VELOCIRAPTOR, DEINONYCHUS, TYRANNOSAURUS REX," in a column under "LATE CRETACEOUS—PREDATORS," which put "TYRANNOSAURUS REX" just above the chalk tray.

"Of all these," Dr. Othniel said, "tyrannosaurus rex is the most famous, and deservedly so."

Dr. Othniel's students wrote in their notebooks "#1 LC. predator TRX" or "No predators in the Late Cretaceous" or "I have a new roommate. Her name is Traci. Signed, Deanna." One of them composed a lengthy letter protesting the unfairness of his parking tickets.

"This flowering of the predators was partly due to the unprecedented abundance of prey. Herbivores such as the triceratops, the chasmosaurus, and the duck-billed hadrosaur roamed the continents in enormous herds."

He had to move an eraser so he could write "PREY—HADROSAURS" under "TYRANNOSAURUS REX." His students wrote "Pray—duck-billed platypus," and "My new roommate Traci has an absolutely wow boyfriend named Todd," and "If you think I'm going to pay this ticket, you're crazy!"

"The hadrosaurs were easy prey. They had no horns or bony frills like the triceratops," he said. "They did, however, have large bony crests, which may have been used to trumpet warnings to each other or to hear or smell the presence of predators." He squeezed "HOLLOW BONY CREST" in under "HADROSAURS" and raised his head, as if he had heard something.

One of his sophomores, who was writing "I don't even have a car," glanced toward the door, but there wasn't anyone there.

Dr. Othniel straightened, vertebra by vertebra, until the top of his bald head was nearly even with the top of the blackboard. He lifted his chin, as if he were sniffing the air, and then bent over again, frowning. "Warnings, however, were not enough against the fifty-foot-tall tyrannosaurus rex, with his five-foot-long jaws and seven-inch-long teeth," he said. He wrote "JAWS—5 FT., TEETH—7 IN." down among the erasers.

His students wrote "The Parking Authority is run by a bunch of Nazis," and "Deanna + Todd," and "TRX had five feet."

⊣•••⊢

After her Advanced Antecedents class, Dr. Sarah Wright collected her mail and took it to her office. There was a manila envelope from the State Department of Education, a letter from the Campus Parking Authority marked "Third Notice: Pay Your Outstanding Tickets Immediately," and a formal-looking square envelope from the dean's office, none of which she wanted to open.

She had no outstanding parking tickets, the legislature was going to cut state funding of universities by another eighteen percent, and the letter from the dean was probably notifying her that the entire amount was going to come out of Paleontology's hide.

There was also a stapled brochure from a flight school she had written to during spring break after she had graded 143 papers, none of which had gotten off the ground. The brochure had an eagle, some clouds, and the header "Do you ever just want to get away from it all?"

She pried the staple free and opened it. "Do you ever get, like, fed up with your job and want to blow it off?" it read. "Do you ever feel like you just want to bag everything and do something really neat instead?"

It went on in this vein, which reminded her of her students' papers, for several illustrated paragraphs before it got down to hard facts, which were that the Lindbergh Flight Academy charged three thousand dollars for their course, "including private, commercial, instrument, CFI, CFII, written tests, and flight tests. Lodging extra. Not responsible for injuries, fatalities, or other accidents."

She wondered if the "other accidents" covered budget cuts from the legislature.

Her TA, Chuck, came in, eating a Twinkie and waving a formal-looking square envelope. "Did you get one of these?" he asked.

"Yes," Sarah said, picking up hers. "I was just going to open it. What is it, an invitation to a slaughter?"

"No, a reception for some guy. The dean's having it this afternoon. In the Faculty Library."

Sarah looked at the invitation suspiciously. "I thought the dean was at an educational conference."

"She's back."

Sarah tore open the envelope and pulled out the invitation. "'The dean cordially invites you to a reception for Dr. Jerry King,'" she muttered. "Dr. Jerry King?" She opened the manila envelope and scanned through the legislature report, looking for his name. "Who is he, do you know?"

"Nope."

At least he wasn't one of the budget-cut supporters. His name wasn't on the list. "Did the rest of the department get these?"

"I don't know. Othniel got one. I saw it in his box," Chuck said. "I don't think he can reach it. His box is on the top row."

Dr. Robert Walker came in, waving a piece of paper. "Look at this! Another ticket for not having a parking sticker! I have a parking sticker! I have two parking stickers! One on the bumper and one on the windshield. Why can't they see them?"

"Did you get one of these, Robert?" Sarah asked, showing him the invitation. "The dean's having a reception this afternoon. Is it about the funding cuts?"

"I don't know," Robert said. "They're right there in plain sight. I even drew an arrow in Magic Marker to the one on the bumper."

"The legislature's cut our funding again," Sarah said. "I'll bet you anything the dean's going to eliminate a position. She was over here last week looking at our enrollment figures."

"The whole university's enrollment is down," Robert said, going over to the window and looking out. "Nobody can afford to go to college anymore, especially when it costs eighty dollars a semester for a parking sticker. Not that the stickers do any good. You still get parking tickets."

"We've got to fight this," Sarah said. "If she eliminates one of our positions, we'll be the smallest department on campus, and the next thing you know, we'll have been merged with Geology. We've got to organize the department and put up a fight. Do you have any ideas, Robert?"

"You know," Robert said, still looking out the window, "maybe if I posted someone out by my car—"

"Your car?"

"Yeah. I could hire a student to sit on the back bumper, and when the Parking Authority comes by, he could point to the sticker. It would cost a lot, but—Stop that!" he shouted suddenly. He wrenched the window open and leaned out. "You can't give me a parking ticket!" he shouted down at the parking lot. "I have two stickers! What are you, blind?" He pulled his head in and bolted out of the office and down the stairs, yelling, "They just gave me another ticket! Can you believe that?"

"No," Sarah said. She picked up the flight-school brochure and looked longingly at the picture of the eagle.

"Do you think they'll have food?" Chuck said. He was looking at the dean's invitation.

"I hope not," Sarah said.

"Why not?"

"Grazing," she said. "The big predators always attack when the hadrosaurs are grazing."

"If they do have food, what kind do you think they'll have?" Chuck asked wistfully.

"It depends," Sarah said, turning the brochure over. "Tea and cookies, usually."

"Homemade?"

"Not unless there's bad news. Cheese and crackers means somebody's getting the ax. Liver pâté means a budget cut. Of course, if the budget cut's big enough, there won't be any money for refreshments."

On the back of the brochure it said in italics "Become Upwardly Mobile," and underneath, in boldface:

FAA-APPROVED
TUITION WAIVERS AVAILABLE
FREE PARKING

"There have been radical changes in our knowledge of the dinosaurs over the past few years," Dr. Albertson said, holding the micropaleontology textbook up, "so radical that what came before is obsolete." He opened the book to the front. "Turn to the introduction."

His students opened their books, which had cost $64.95.

"Have you all turned to the introduction?" Dr. Albertson asked, taking hold of the top corner of the first page. "Good. Now tear it out." He ripped out the page. "It's useless, completely archaic."

Actually, although there had been some recent revisions in theories regarding dinosaur behavior and physiology, particularly in the larger predators, there hadn't been any at all at the microscopic level. But Dr. Albertson had seen Robin Williams do this in a movie and been very impressed.

His students, who had been hoping to sell them back to the university bookstore for $32.47, were less so. One of them asked hopefully, "Can't we just promise not to read it?"

"Absolutely not," Dr. Albertson said, yanking out a handful of pages. "Come on. Tear them out."

He threw the pages in a metal wastebasket and held the wastebasket out to a marketing minor who was quietly tucking the torn-out pages into the back of the book with an eye to selling it as a pre-edited version. "That's right, all of them," Dr. Albertson said. "Every outdated, old-fashioned page."

Someone knocked on the door. He handed the wastebasket to the marketing minor and left the slaughter to open it. It was Sarah Wright with a squarish envelope.

"There's a reception for the dean this afternoon," she said. "We need the whole department there."

"Do we have to tear out the title page, too?" a psychology minor asked.

"The legislature's just cut funding another eighteen percent, and I'm afraid they're going to try to eliminate one of our positions."

"You can count on my support one hundred percent," he said.

"Good," Sarah said, sighing with relief. "As long as we stick together, we've got a chance."

Dr. Albertson shut the door behind her, glancing at his watch. He had planned to stand on his desk before the end of class, but now there wouldn't be time. He had to settle for the inspirational coda.

"Ostracods, diatoms, fusilinids, these are what we stay alive for," he said. "Carpe diem! Seize the day!"

The psych minor raised his hand. "Can I borrow your Scotch tape?" he asked. "I accidentally tore out Chapters One and Two."

There was brie at the reception. And sherry and spinach puffs and a tray of strawberries with cellophane-flagged toothpicks stuck like daggers into them. Sarah took a strawberry and a rapid head count of the department. Everyone else seemed to be there except Robert, who was probably parking his car, and Dr. Othniel.

"Did you make sure Dr. Othniel saw his invitation?" she asked her TA, who was eating strawberries two at a time.

"Yeah," Chuck said with his mouth full. "He's here." He gestured with his plate toward a high-backed wing chair by the fire.

Sarah went over and checked. Dr. Othniel was asleep. She went back over to the table and had another strawberry. She wondered which one was Dr. King. There were only three men she didn't recognize. Two of them were obviously Physics Department—they were making a fusion reactor out of a Styrofoam cup and several of the fancy toothpicks. The third looked likely. He was tall and distinguished and was wearing a tweed jacket with patches on the elbows, but after a few minutes he disappeared into the kitchen and came back with a tray of liver pâté and crackers.

Robert came in, carrying his suit jacket and looking out of breath. "You will *not* believe what happened to me," he said.

"You got a parking ticket," Sarah said. "Were you able to find out anything about this Dr. King?"

"He's an educational consultant," Robert said. "What *is* the point of spending eighty dollars a semester for a parking sticker when there are never any places to park in the permit lots? You know where I had to park? Behind the football stadium! That's five blocks farther away than my house!"

"An educational consultant?" Sarah said. "What's the dean up to?" She stared thoughtfully at her strawberry. "An educational consultant..."

"Author of *What's Wrong with Our Entire Educational System*," Dr. Albertson said. He took a plate and put a spinach puff on it. "He's an expert on restructionary implementation."

"What's that?" Chuck said, making a sandwich out of the liver pâté and two bacon balls.

Dr. Albertson looked superior. "Surely they teach you graduate assistants about restructionary implementation," he said, which meant he didn't know either. He took a bite of spinach puff. "You should try these," he said. "I was just talking to the dean. She told me she made them herself."

"We're dead," Sarah said.

"There's Dr. King now," Dr. Albertson said, pointing to a lumbering man wearing a polo shirt and Sansabelt slacks.

The dean went over to greet him, clasping his hands in hers. "Sorry I'm late," he boomed out. "I couldn't find a parking place so I parked out in front."

Dr. Othniel suddenly emerged from the wing chair, looking wildly around. Sarah beckoned to him with her toothpick, and he stooped his way over to them, sat down next to the brie, and went back to sleep.

The dean moved to the center of the room and clapped her hands for attention. Dr. Othniel jerked at the sound. "I don't want to interrupt the fun," the dean said, "And *please,* do go on eating and drinking, but I just wanted you all to meet Dr. Jerry King. Dr. King will be working with the Paleontology Department on something I'm sure you'll all find terribly exciting. Dr. King, would you like to say a few words?"

Dr. King smiled, a large friendly grin that reminded Sarah of the practice jaw in Field Techniques. "We all know the tremendous impactization technology has had on our modern society," he said.

"Impactization?" Chuck said, eating a lemon tart the distinguished-looking gentleman had just brought out from the kitchen. "I thought 'impact' was a verb."

"It is," Sarah said. "And once, back in the Late Cretaceous, it was a noun."

"Shh," Dr. Albertson said, looking disapproving.

"As we move into the twenty-first century, our society is transformizing radically, but is education? No. We are still teaching the same old subjects in the same old ways." He smiled at the dean. "Until today. Today marks the beginning of a wonderful innovationary experiment in education, a whole new instructionary dynamic in teaching paleontology. I'll be thinktanking with you dinosaur guys and gals next week, but until then I want you to think about one word."

"Extinction," Sarah murmured.

"That word is 'relevantness.' Does paleontology have relevantness to our modern society? How can we make it have relevantness? Think about it. Relevantness."

There was a spattering of applause from the departments Dr. King would not be thinktanking with. Robert poured a large glass of sherry and drank it down. "It's not fair," he said. "First the Parking Authority and now this."

"Pilots make a lot of money," Sarah said. "And the only word they have to think about is 'crash.'"

Dr. Albertson raised his hand.

"Yes?" the dean asked.

"I just wanted Dr. King to know," he said, "that he can count on my support one hundred percent."

"Are you supposed to eat this white crust thing on the cheese?" Chuck asked.

Dr. King put a memo in the Paleontology Department's boxes the next day. It read "Group ideating session next Mon. Dr. Wright's office. 2 P.M. J. King. P .S. I will be doing observational datatizing this Tues. and Thurs."

"We'll all do some observational datatizing," Sarah said, even more alarmed by Dr. King's preempting her office without asking her than by the brie.

She went to find her TA, who was in her office eating a Snickers. "I want you to go find out about Dr. King's background," she told him.

"Why?"

"Because he used to be a junior-high girl's basketball coach. Maybe we can get some dirt on him and one of his seventh grade forwards."

"How do you know he used to be a junior-high coach?"

"All educational consultants used to be junior-high coaches. Or social-studies teachers." She looked at the memo disgustedly. "What do you suppose observational datatizing consists of?"

⊣•••⊢

Observational datatizing consisted of wandering around the halls of the Earth Sciences building with a clipboard listening to Dr. Albertson.

"Okay, how much you got?" Dr. Albertson was saying to his class. He was wearing a butcher's apron and a paper fast-food hat and was cutting apples into halves, quarters, and thirds with a cleaver, which had noth-ing to do with depauperate fauna, but which he had seen Edward James Olmos do in *Stand and Deliver*. He had been very impressed.

"Yip, that'll do it," he was saying in an Hispanic accent when Dr. King appeared suddenly at the back of the room with his clipboard.

"But the key question here is *relevantness*," Dr. Albertson said hastily. "How do the depauperate fauna affectate on our lives today?"

His students looked wary. One of them crossed his arms protectively over his textbook as though he thought he was going to be asked to tear out more pages.

"Depauperate fauna have a great deal of relevantness to our modern society," Dr. Albertson said, but Dr. King had wandered back into the hall and into Dr. Othniel's class.

"The usual mode of the tyrannosaurus rex was to approach a herd of hadrosaurs from cover," Dr. Othniel, who did not see Dr. King because he was writing on the board, said. "He would then attack suddenly and retreat." He wrote "1. OBSERVE, 2. ATTACK, 3. RETREAT," in a col-umn on the board, the letters of each getting smaller and squinchier as he approached the chalk tray.

His students wrote "1. Sneak up, 2. Bite ass, 3. Beat it," and "Todd called last night. I told him Traci wasn't there. We talked forever."

Dr. King wrote "RELEVANTNESS?" in large block letters on his clip-board and wandered out again.

"The jaws and teeth of the tyrannosaurus were capable of inflicting a fatal wound with a single bite. It would then follow at a distance, wait-ing for its victim to bleed to death," Dr. Othniel said.

⊣•••⊢

Robert was late to the meeting on Monday. "You will not believe what happened to me!" he said. "I had to park in the daily permit lot, and while I was getting the permit out of the machine, they gave me a ticket!"

Dr. King, who was sitting at Sarah's desk wearing a pair of gray sweats, a whistle, and a baseball cap with "Dan Quayle Junior High" on it, said, "I know you're all as excited about this educationing experiment we're about to embarkate on as I am."

"More," Dr. Albertson said.

Sarah glared at him. "Will this experiment involve eliminating positions?"

Dr. King smiled at her. His teeth reminded her of some she'd seen at the Denver Museum of Natural History. "'Positions,' 'classes,' 'departments,' all those terms are irrelevantatious. We need to reassessmentize our entire concept of education, its relevantatiousness to modern society. How many of you are using paradigmic bonding in your classes?"

Dr. Albertson raised his hand.

"Paradigmic bonding, experiential role-playing, modular cognition. I assessmentized some of your classes last week. I saw no computer-learner linkages, no multimedial instruction, no cognitive tracking. In one class"—Dr. King smiled largely at Dr. Othniel—"I saw a blackboard being used. Methodologies like that are extinct."

"So are dinosaurs," Sarah muttered. "Why don't you say something, Robert?"

"Dr. King," Robert said, "do you plan to extend this reorganization to other departments?"

Good, Sarah thought, send him over to pester English Lit.

"Yes," Dr. King said, beaming. "Paleontology is only an initiatory pretest. Eventually we intend to expand it to encompassate the entire university. Why?"

"There's one department that drastically needs reorganization," Robert said. "I don't know if you're aware of this, but the Parking Authority is completely out of control. The sign distinctly says you're supposed to park your car first and *then* go get the daily permit out of the machine."

┤•••├

"What did you find out about Dr. King?" Sarah asked Chuck Tuesday morning.

"He didn't coach junior-high girl's basketball," he said, drinking a lime Slurpee. "It was junior-high wrestling."

"Oh," Sarah said. "Then find out where he got his doctorate. Maybe we can get the college to rescind it for using words like 'assessmentize.'"

"I don't think I'd better," Chuck said. "I mean, I've only got one semester till I graduate. And besides," he said, sucking on the Slurpee, "some of his ideas made sense. I mean, a lot of that stuff we learn in class does seem kind of pointless. I mean, what does the Late Cretaceous have to do with us, really? It might be fun to role-play and stuff."

"Fine," Sarah said. "Role-play this. You are a coryhosaurus. You're smart and fast, but not fast enough because a tyrannosaurus rex has just taken a bite out of your flank. What do you do?"

"Gosh, that's a tough one," Chuck said, slurping meditatively. "What would you do?"

"Grow a wishbone."

Tuesday afternoon, as soon as her one o'clock class was over, Sarah went to Robert's office. He wasn't there. She waited outside for half an hour, reading the announcement for a semester at sea, and then went over to the Parking Authority office.

He was standing near the front of a line that wound down the stairs and out the door. It was composed mostly of students, though the person at the head of the line was a frail-looking old man. He was flapping a green slip at the young man behind the counter. The young man had a blond crew cut and looked like an adolescent Himmler.

"...a heart attack," the old man at the head of the line was saying. Sarah wondered if he had had one when he got his parking ticket or if he intended to have one now.

Sarah tried to get to Robert, but two students were blocking the door. She recognized one of the freshmen from Dr. Othniel's class. "Oh, Todd," the freshman was saying to a boy in a tank undershirt and jeans, "I knew you'd help me. I tried to get Traci to come with me—I mean, after all, it was her car—but I think she had a date."

"A date?" Todd said.

"Well, I don't know for sure. It's hard to keep track of all her guys. I couldn't do that. I mean"—she lowered her eyes demurely—"if you were *my* boyfriend, I'd never even think about other guys."

"Excuse me," Sarah said, "but I need to talk to Dr. Walker."

Todd stepped to one side, and instead of stepping to the other, the freshman from Dr. Othniel's class squeezed over next to him. Sarah slid past and worked her way up to Robert, ignoring the nasty looks of the other people in line.

"Don't tell me you got a ticket, too," Robert said.

"No," she said. "We have to do something about Dr. King."

"We certainly do," Robert said indignantly.

"Oh, I'm so glad you feel that way. Dr. Othniel's useless. He doesn't even realize what's going on, and Dr. Albertson's giving a lecture on 'The Impactization of Microscopic Fossils on Twentieth-Century Society.'"

"Which is what?"

"I have no idea. When I was in there, he was showing a videotape of *The Land Before Time*."

"I had a coronary thrombosis!" the old man shouted.

"Unauthorized vehicles are not allowed in permit lots," the Hitler Youth said. "However, we have initiated a preliminary study of the incident."

"A preliminary study!" the old man said, clutching his left arm. "The last one you did took five years!"

"We need another meeting with Dr. King," Sarah said. "We need to tell him relevance is not the issue, that paleontology is important in and of itself, and not because brontosaurus earrings are trendy. Surely he'll see reason. We have science and logic on our side."

Robert looked at the old man at the counter.

"What is there to study?" he was saying. "You ticketed the ambulance while the paramedics were giving me CPR!"

"I'm not sure reason will work," Robert said doubtfully.

"Well, then, how about a petition? We've got to do something, or we'll all be showing episodes of *The Flintstones*. He's a dangerous man!"

"He certainly is," Robert said. "Do you know what I just got? A citation for parking in front of the Faculty Library."

"Will you forget about your stupid parking tickets for a minute?" Sarah said. "You won't have any reason to park unless we get rid of King. I know Albertson's students would all sign a petition. Yesterday he made them cut the illustrations out of their textbooks and make a collage."

"The Parking Authority doesn't acknowledge petitions," Robert said. "You heard what Dr. King told the dean at the reception. He said, 'I'm parked right outside.' He left a note on his windshield that said the Paleontology Department had given him permission to park there." He waved the green paper at her. "Do you know where I parked? Fifteen blocks away. And I'm the one who gets a citation for improperly authorizing parking permission!"

"Good-bye, Robert," Sarah said.

"Wait a minute! Where are you going? We haven't figured out a plan of action yet."

Sarah worked her way back through the line. The two students were still blocking the door. "I'm sure Traci will understand," the freshman from Dr. Othniel's class was saying, "I mean, it isn't like you two were *serious* or anything."

"Wait a minute!" Robert shouted from his place in line. "What are you going to do?"

"Evolve," Sarah said.

—|•••|—

On Wednesday there was another memo in Paleontology's boxes. It was on green paper, and Robert snatched it up and took off for the Parking Authority office, muttering dark threats. He was already there and standing in line behind a young woman in a wheelchair and two firemen when he finally unfolded it and read it.

"I *know* I was parking in a handicapped spot," the young woman was saying when Robert let out a whoop and ran back to the Earth Sciences building.

Sarah had a one o'clock class, but she wasn't there. Her students, who were spending their time waiting erasing marks in their textbooks so they could resell them at the bookstore, didn't know where she was. Neither did Dr. Albertson, who was making a papier-mâché foraminifer.

Robert went into Dr. Othniel's class. "The prevalence of predators in the Late Cretaceous," Dr. Othniel was saying, "led to severe evolutionary pressures, resulting in aquatic and aeronautical adaptations."

Robert tried to get his attention, but he was writing "BIRDS" in the chalk tray.

He went out in the hall. Sarah's TA was standing outside her office, eating a bag of Doritos.

"Have you seen Dr. Wright?" Robert asked.

"She's gone," Chuck said, munching.

"Gone? You mean, resigned?" he said, horrified. "But she doesn't have to." He waved the green paper at Chuck. "Dr. King's going to do a preliminary study, a—what does he call it?—a preinitiatory survey of prevailing paleontological pedagogy. We won't have to worry about him for another five years at least."

"She saw it," Chuck said, pulling a jar of salsa out of his back pocket. "She said it was too late. She'd already paid her tuition." He unscrewed the lid.

"Her tuition?" Robert said. "What are you talking about? Where did she go?"

333

"She flew the coop." He dug in the bag and pulled out a chip. He dipped it in the sauce. "Oh, and she left something for you." He handed Robert the jar of salsa and the chips and dug in his other back pocket. He handed Robert the flight brochure and a green plastic square.

"It's her parking sticker," Robert said

"Yeah," Chuck said. "She said she won't be needing it where she's going."

"That's all? She didn't say anything else?"

"Oh, yeah," he said, dipping a chip into the salsa Robert still held. "She said to watch out for falling rocks."

⊣•••⊢

"The predatory dinosaurs flourished for the entire Late Cretaceous," Dr. Othniel said, "and then, along with their prey, disappeared. Various theories have been advanced for their extinction, none of which has been authoritatively proved."

"I'll bet they couldn't find a parking place," a student who had written one of the letters to the Parking Authority and who had finally given up and traded his Volkswagen in on a skateboard, whispered.

"What?" Dr. Othniel said, looking vaguely around. He turned back to the board. "The diminishing food supply, the rise of mammals, the depradations of smaller predators, all undoubtedly contributed."

He wrote:

"1. FOOD SUPPLY

2. MAMMALS

3. COMPETITION," on the bottom one fifth of the board.

His students wrote "I thought it was an asteroid," and "My new roommate Terri is trying to steal Todd away from me! Can you believe that? Signed, Deanna."

"The demise of the dinosaurs—" Dr. Othniel said, and stopped. He straightened slowly, vertebra by vertebra, until he was nearly erect. He lifted his chin, as if he were sniffing the air, and then walked over to the open window, leaned out, and stood there for several minutes, scanning the clear and empty sky.

———| Royalty

# The Curse of Kings

There was a curse. It lay on all of us, though we didn't know it. Anyway Lacau didn't. Standing there, reading the tomb seal out loud to me in my cage, he didn't have a clue who the warning was meant for. And the Sandalman, standing on the black ridge watching the bodies burn, had no idea he had already fallen victim to it.

The princess knew, leaning her head in hopelessness against the wall of her tomb ten thousand years ago. And Evelyn, eaten alive by it, she knew. She tried to tell me that last night on Colchis while we waited for the ship.

The electricity was off again, and Lacau had lit a photosene lamp and put it close to the translator so I could see the dials. Evelyn's voice had gotten so bad that the fix needed constant adjusting. The lamp's flame lit only the space around me. Lacau, bending over the hammock, was in total darkness.

Evelyn's bey sat by the lamp, watching the reddish flame, her mouth open and her black teeth shining in the light. I expected her to stick her hand in the flame any minute, but she didn't. The air was still and full of dust. The lamp flame didn't even flicker.

"Evie," Lacau said. "We don't have any time left. The Sandalman's soldiers will be here before morning. They'll never let us leave."

Evelyn said something, but the translator didn't pick it up.

"Move the mike closer," I said. "I didn't get that."

"Evie," he said again. "We need you to tell us when happened. Can you do that for us, Evie? Tell us what happened?"

She tried again. I had the volume dial kicked as high as it would go, and the translator picked it up this time, but only as static. Evelyn started to cough, a sharp, terrible sound that the translator turned into a scream.

"For God's sake, put her on the respirator," I said.

"I can't," he said. "The power pack is dead." And the other respirator has to be plugged in, I thought, and you've used up all the extension cords. But I didn't say it. Because if he put her on the respirator he would have to unplug the refrigerator.

"Then get her a drink of water," I said.

He took the Coke* bottle off the crate by the hammock, put the straw in it, and leaned into the darkness to tilt Evelyn's head forward so she could drink. I turned the translator off. It was bad enough listening to her try to talk. I didn't think I could stand listening to her try to drink.

After what seemed like an hour, he set the Coke bottle down on the crate again. "Evelyn," he said. "Try to tell us what happened. Did you go in the tomb?"

I switched the translator back on and kept my finger ready on the record button. There was no point in recording the tortured sounds she was making.

"Curse," Evelyn said clearly, and I pushed the button down. "Don't open it. Don't open it." She stopped and tried to swallow. "Wuhdayuh?"

"What day is it?" the translator said.

She tried to swallow again, and Lacau reached for the Coke bottle, pulled the straw out, and handed it to the bey. "Go get some more water." The little bey stood up, her black eyes still fixed on the flame, and took the bottle. "Hurry," Lacau said.

"Hurry," Evelyn said. "Before bey."

"Did you open the tomb when the bey went to get the Sandalman?"

"Oh, don't open it. Don't open it. Sorry. Didn't know."

"Didn't know what, Evelyn?" Lacau said.

The bey was still staring, fascinated, at the flame, her mouth open so that I could see her shiny black teeth. I looked at the thick green bottle she was holding in her dirty-looking hands. The straw in it was glass, too, thick and uneven and full of bubbles, probably made out at the bottling plant. Its sides were scored with long scratches. Evelyn had made those scratches when she sucked the water up through the straw. One more day and she'll have it cut to ribbons, I thought, and then remembered we didn't have one more day. Not unless Evelyn's bey suddenly pitched forward into the red flame, honeycombs sharpening on her dirty brown skin, inside her throat, inside her lungs.

"Hurry," Evelyn said into the hypnotic silence, and the little bey looked over at the hammock as if she had just woken up and hurried out

---

* Coke® and Coca-Cola® are registered trademarks of the Coca-Cola Company.

of the room with the Coke bottle. "Hurry. What day is it? Have to save the treasure. He'll murder her."

"Who, Evelyn? Who'll murder her? Who will he murder?"

"We shouldn't have gone in," she said, and let her breath out in a sigh that sounded like sand scratching on glass. "Beware. Curse of kings."

"She's quoting what was on the door seal," Lacau said. He straightened up. "They did go in the tomb," he said. "I suppose you got that on your recorder."

"No," I said, and pushed "erase." "She still isn't down from the dilaudid. I'll start recording when she starts making sense."

"The Commission would have found for the Sandalman," Lacau said. "Howard swore they didn't go in, that they waited for the Sandalman."

"What difference does it make?" I said. "Evelyn won't be alive to testify at any Commission hearing and neither will we if the Sandalman and his soldiers get here before the ship, so what the hell difference does it make? There won't be any treasure left either after the commission gets through, so why are we making this damned recording? By the time the Commission hears it, it'll be too late to save her."

"What if it *was* something in the tomb, after all? What if it *was* a virus?"

"It wasn't," I said. "The Sandalman poisoned them. If it was a virus, then why doesn't the bey have it? She was in the tomb with them, wasn't she?"

"Hurry," somebody said, and I thought for a minute it was Evelyn, but it was the bey. She came running into the room, the Coke bottle splashing water everywhere.

"What is it?" Lacau said. "Is the ship here?"

She yanked at his hand. "Hurry," she said, and dragged him down the long hall of packing crates.

"Hurry," Evelyn said softly, like an echo, and I got up and went over to the hammock. I could hardly see her, which made it a little easier. I unclenched my fists and said, "It's me, Evelyn. It's Jack."

"Jack," she said. I could hardly hear her. Lacau had clipped the mike to the plastic mesh that was pulled up to her neck, but she was fading fast and starting to wheeze again. She needed a shot of the morphate. It would ease her breathing, but this soon after the dilaudid it would put her out like a light.

"I delivered the message to the Sandalman," I said, leaning over to catch what she would say. "What was in the message, Evelyn?"

"Jack," she said. "What day is it?"

I had to think. It felt like I had been here years. "Wednesday," I said.

"Tomorrow," she said. She closed her eyes and seemed to relax almost into sleep.

I was not going to get anything out of her. I sprayed on plasticgloves, picked up the injection kit, and broke it open. The morphate would put her out in minutes, but until then she would be free from the pain and maybe coherent.

Her arm had fallen over the side of the hammock. I moved the lamp a little closer and tried to find a place to give the injection. Her whole arm was covered with a network of honeycombed white ridges, some of them nearly two centimeters high now. They had softened and thickened since the first time I'd seen her. Then they had been thin and razor-sharp. There was no way I was going to be able to find a vein among them, but as I watched, the heat from the photosene flame softened a circle of skin on her forearm, and the five-sided ridges collapsed around it so I could get the hypo in.

I jabbed twice before blood pooled up in the soft depression where the needle had gone in. It dripped onto the floor. I looked around, but there was nothing to wipe it up with. Lacau had used the last of the cotton this morning. I took a piece of paper off my notebook and blotted the blood with it.

The bey had come back in. She ducked under my elbow with a piece of plastic mesh held out flat. I folded the paper up and dropped it in the center of the plastic. The bey folded the plastic mesh over it and folded up the ends, making it into a kind of packet, careful not to touch the blood. I stood and looked at it.

"Jack," Evelyn said. "She was murdered."

"Murdered?" I said and reached over to adjust the fix again. All I got was feedback. "Who was murdered, Evelyn?"

"The princess. They killed her. For the treasure." The morphate was taking effect. I could make her words out easily, though they didn't make sense. Nobody had murdered the princess. She had been dead ten thousand years. I leaned farther over her.

"Tell me what was in the message you gave me to take to the Sandalman, Evelyn," I said.

The lights came on. She put her hand over her face as if to hide it. "Murdered the Sandalman's bey. Had to. To save the treasure."

I looked over at the little bey. She was still holding the packet of plastic, turning it over and over in her dirty-looking hands.

"Nobody murdered the bey," I said. "She's right here."

She didn't hear me. The shot was taking effect. Her hand relaxed and then slid down to her breast. Where it had pressed against her forehead and cheek, the fingers had left deep imprints in the wax-soft skin. The pressure of her fingers had flattened the honeycombed ridges at the ends of her fingers and pushed them back so that the ends of her bones were sticking out.

She opened her eyes. "Jack," she said clearly, and her voice was so hopeless I reached over and turned the translator off. "Too late."

Lacau pushed past me and lifted up the mesh drape. "What did she say?" he demanded.

"Nothing," I said, peeling off the plastic gloves and throwing them in the open packing crate we were using for the things Evelyn had touched. The bey was still playing with the plastic packet she had wrapped around the blood-soaked paper. I grabbed it away from her and put it in the box. "She's delirious," I said. "I gave her her shot. Is the ship here?"

"No," he said, "but the Sandalman is."

"Curse," Evelyn said. But I didn't believe her.

I had been burning eight columns about a curse when I intercepted the message from Lacau. I was halfway across Colchis's endless desert continent with the Lisii team. I had run out of stories on the team's incredible find, which consisted of two clay pots and some black bones. Two pots was more than Howard's team out at the Spine had come up with in five years, and my hotline had been making noises about pulling me off on the next circuit ship.

I didn't think they would as long as AP kept Bradstreet on the planet. When and if anybody found the treasure they were all looking for, the hotline that had somebody on Colchis would be the one that got the scoop. And in the meantime good stories would see to it that I was in the right place at the right time when the story of the century finally broke, so I'd hotfooted it up north to cover a two-bit suhundulim massacre and then out here to Lisii. When the pots gave out I made up a curse.

It wasn't much of a curse—no murders, no avalanches, no mysterious fires—but every time somebody sprained an ankle or got bitten by a kheper, I got at least four columns out of it.

After my first one, headered, "Curse of Kings Strikes Again," went out, Howard, over at the Spine, sent me a ground-to-ground that read, "The curse has to be in the same place as the treasure, Jackie-boy!"

I burned back, "If the treasure's over there, what am I doing stuck out here? Find something so I can come back."

I didn't get an answer to that, and the Lisii team didn't find any more bones, and the curse grew and grew. Six rocks the size of my thumbnail rattled down a lava slope the Lisii team had just walked down, and I headered my story, "Mysterious Rockfall Nearly Buries Archaeologists: Is King's Curse Responsible?" and was feeding it into the burner when I heard the sizzle I'd set up to alert me to the consul's transmissions. Hotline reporters weren't supposed to trespass on official transmissions, and Lacau, the consul over at the Spine, had double-cooked his to make sure we didn't, but burners have only so many firelines, and I'd had enough time on Lisii to try them all.

It was a ship-in-area request. He'd put, "Hurry," at the end of it. The circuit ship was only a month away, and he couldn't wait for it. They'd found something.

I burned the rest of my story. Then I hit ground-to-ground and sent Howard a copy of the header with the tag, "Found anything yet?" I didn't get an answer.

I went out and found the team and asked them if there was anything anybody needed from the base camp, one of my shock boards had gone bad and I was going to run in. I made a list of what they wanted, loaded my equipment in the jeep, and took off for the Spine.

I burned stories all the way, sending them ground-to-ground to the relay I kept in my tent back at Lisii, so it would look to Bradstreet like my stories were still coming from there. I had to stop the jeep every time and set up the burn equipment, but I didn't want him heading for the Spine. He was still up north, waiting for another massacre, but he had a Swallow that could get him to the Spine in a day and a half.

So I sent out a story headered, "Khepers Threaten Team's Life— Curse's Agents?" about the tick-like khepers, who sucked the blood out of anybody dumb enough to stick his hand down a hole. Since the Lisii team made their living doing just that, their arms were spotted with white circles of dead skin where the poison had entered their blood. The bites didn't heal, and your blood was toxic for a week or so, which prompted somebody to put up a sign on the barracks that read, "No Nibbling Allowed," with a skull-and-crossbones under it. I didn't say that in my story, of course. I made them out to be agents of the dead curse, wreaking vengeance on whoever dared disturb the sleep of Colchis's ancient kings.

The second day out I intercepted an answer from a ship. It was an Amenti freighter, and it was a long way away, but it was coming. It could make it in a week. Lacau's answer was only one word. "Hurry."

If I was going to beat the ship in, I couldn't waste any more time burning stories. I pulled out some back-up tapes I'd made, deliberately dateless, and sent those: a flattering piece on Lacau, the long-suffering consul who has to keep the peace and divide the treasure, interviews with Howard and Borchardt, a not-so-flattering piece on the local dictator-type, the Sandalman, a recap of the accidental discovery of the ransacked tombs in the Spine that had brought Howard and his gang here in the first place. I was taking a risk doing all these stories on the Spine, but I hoped Bradstreet would check the transmission-point and decide I was trying to throw him off. With luck he'd tear off to Lisii in his damned Swallow, convinced the team had struck pay dirt and I was trying to keep it a secret till I got my scoop.

I skidded into the Sandalman's village six days after I left Lisii. I was still a day and a half from the Spine, but with the ship due in two days they had to be here, where it would land, and not out at the Spine.

There was a deathly silence over the white clay settlement that reminded me of someplace else. It was a little after five. Afternoon nap time. Nobody would be up till at least six, but I knocked on the consul's door anyway. Nobody was home, and the place was locked up tight. I peeked in through the cloth blinds, but I couldn't see much. What I could see was that Lacau's burn equipment wasn't on the desk, and that worried me. There was nobody home in the low building the Spine team used as a barracks either, and where the hell was everybody? They wouldn't still be out at the Spine, not with a ship coming in tomorrow. Maybe the ship had come and gone two days ahead of schedule.

I hadn't burned a story since the day before yesterday. I'd run out of tapes and I hadn't dared risk taking the time to stop and set up the equipment when it might mean getting there too late. Over at Lisii I had been careful every once in awhile to let my stories pile up for two or three days and then send them all at once so that Bradstreet wouldn't immediately jump to conclusions when I missed a deadline. He was going to catch on pretty soon, though, and I didn't have anything else to do. I wasn't going to go tearing off to the Spine until I'd talked to somebody and made sure that was where they were, and I couldn't go at night anyway, so I sat down on the low clay step of the barracks porch, set up my burn equipment, and ran a check on the ship. Still on its way. It would be here day after tomorrow. So where was the team? Curse Strikes Again? Team Disappears?

I couldn't do that story, so I whipped off a couple of columns on the one member of the Howard team I hadn't met—Evelyn Herbert. She'd joined the team right after I went north to cover the massacre, and I didn't know much about her. Bradstreet had said she was beautiful. Actually that wasn't what he'd said. He said she was the most beautiful woman he'd ever seen, but that was because we were stuck in Khamsin and had drunk a fifth of gin in endless bottles of Coke. "She has this face," he said, "like Helen of Troy's. A face that could launch..." The comparison had petered out since if there was anything on Colchis to launch neither of us was sober enough to think of it. "Even the Sandalman's crazy about her."

I had refused to believe that. "No, really," Bradstreet had protested sloppily, "he's given her presents, he even gave her her own bey, he wanted her to move into his private compound but she wouldn't. I tell you, you've got to see her. She's beautiful."

I still hadn't believed it, but it made a good story. I burned it as the romance of the century, and that took care of yesterday's story. But what about today's?

I went around and knocked on all the doors again. It was still awfully quiet, and I'd remembered what it reminded me of—Khamsin right after the massacre. What if Lacau's hysterical, "hurry!" had had something to do with the Sandalman? What if the Sandalman had taken one look at the treasure and decided he wanted it all for himself? I sat back down, and burned a story on the Commission. Whenever there was a controversy over archaeological finds, the Commission on Antiquities came and sat on it until everybody was bored and ready to give up. Everyone took them far more seriously than they deserved to be taken. Once they'd even been called in to settle who owned a planet when a dig turned up proof that the so-called natives had really landed in a spaceship several thousand years before. The Commission took this on with a straight face, even if it was like the Neanderthals demanding Earth back, listened to evidence for something over four years, as if they were actually going to do something, and finally recessed to review the accumulated heaps of testimony and let the opposing sides fight it out for themselves. They were still in recess ten years later, but I didn't say that in the story. I wrote up the Commission as the arm of archeological justice—fair but stern and woe to anybody who gets greedy. Maybe it would make the Sandalman think twice about massacreing Howard's team and taking all the treasure for himself, if he hadn't done that already.

There still weren't any signs of life, and what if that meant there weren't any signs of life? I went the round of the doors again, afraid one of them would swing open on a heap of bodies. But unlike Khamsin, there were no signs of destruction either. There hadn't been a massacre. They were probably all over at the Sandalman's divvying up the treasure.

There was no way to see into the high-walled compound. I rattled the fancy iron gate, and a bey I didn't recognize came out. She was carrying a photosene lantern, bringing it out to be lit before the sun went down, and I was not sure she'd heard me banging on the gate. She looked old.

It's hard to tell with beys, who never get bigger than twelve-year-olds. Their black hair doesn't turn gray and they don't usually lose their black teeth, but this one was wearing a black robe instead of a shift, which meant she had a high station in the Sandalman's household even though I didn't remember her, and her forearms were covered with kheper bites. Either she was exceptionally curious, even for a bey, or she'd been around awhile.

"Is the Sandalman here?" I said.

She didn't answer. She hung the lantern on a hook off to the inside of the gate and watched as the pool of photo-chemical liquid in its base caught fire.

"I need to see the Sandalman," I said more loudly: She must be hard of hearing.

"No one in," she said, her dished face impassive. Did that mean the Sandalman wasn't there or that she wasn't supposed to let anybody in?

"Is the Sandalman here?" I said. "I want to see him."

"No one in," she repeated. The Sandalman's other bey had been a lot easier to get information out of. I had given her a pocket mirror and made a friend for life. The fact that she wasn't here probably meant the Sandalman wasn't either. But where had they gone?

"I'm a reporter," I said, and stuck my press card at her. "Show him this. I think he'll want to talk to me."

She looked at the card, rubbed her dirty-looking finger along the smooth plastic, and turned it over.

"Where is he? Out at the Spine?"

The bey turned the card back over to the front. She poked at the hot-line's holo-banner with the same finger, as if she could stick it between the three-dimensional letters.

"Where's Lacau? Where's Howard? Where's the Sandalman?"

She held the card up sideways and peered along its edge. She flipped it over, looking at the letters, and turned it sideways again, slowly, watching the three-dimensional effect go flat.

"Look," I said. "You can keep the press card. It's a present. Just tell your boss I'm here."

She was trying to pry the 3-D letters up with the tip of her black fingernail. I should never have given her the press card.

I opened up my knapsack, got out a bottle of Coke, and held it out to her, just this side of the gate. She actually looked up from the press card long enough to grab for it. I took a step backward. "Where are the dig men?" I said, and then remembered it's the bey women who run things, if you could call running errands for the suhundulim and drinking Cokes running things, but at least they were up most of the day. The male beys slept, and the females ignored them and any other male who wasn't giving them a direct order, but they might notice a female. "Where's Evelyn Herbert?"

"Big cloud," she said.

Big cloud? What did that mean? This wasn't the season for the big desert-drenching thunderstorms. A fire? A ship?

"Where?" I said.

She reached for the Coke bottle. I let her almost get it. "Big cloud where?"

She pointed east to where the lava spills formed a low ridge. The flat basin beyond was where they landed the ships. What if some other ship had responded to Lacau's message? Some ship that had already been and gone, team and treasure with it?

"Ship?" I said.

"No," she said, and made a lunge through the bars for the Coke. "Big cloud."

I gave it to her. She retreated to the front steps of the main house and sat down. She took a swig of the Coke and turned the press card over and over in her other hand, making it flash in the sunlight.

"How long has it been there?" I said.

She didn't even act like she'd heard me.

On the way out to the ridge I convinced myself the bey had seen a dust devil. I didn't want to believe a ship had been and gone with the treasure and the team. Maybe if it was a ship, it was still there.

It wasn't. I could see the half-mile circle of scorched dirt where they always landed the ships even before I got to the top of the ridge, and it was empty, but I went on up. And there was the big cloud. A plasticmesh geodome in the middle of the basin. The consul's landrover was parked on the far side of it and several crawlers that they must have used to bring the treasure down from the Spine.

I hid the jeep behind a hump of lava and then crept around behind the rocks until I could see in the front door. There were a couple of suhundulim guarding the tent, which was the best proof yet that there was a treasure. The Commission's only ruling said that the archaeologist's government got half of everything and the "natives" got the other half. The Sandalman would be making sure he got his half. I was surprised Howard hadn't posted a guard, too, since the ruling said any tampering with the treasure meant forfeiture of the whole thing by the offending party. At Lisii the guards had practically sat on those poor skeletons and clay shards to make sure nobody sneaked a shinbone in his pocket and hoping somebody would so they could claim the whole treasure by default.

I'd never get past the Sandalman's guards. If I wanted a story I'd have to go in the back door. I crept as far back as the jeep and then down the ridge, keeping as much rock between me and the guards as I could. I didn't take my burn equipment. I wasn't sure I could even get in, and I didn't want somebody confiscating it on the grounds that burning a story was tampering. Besides, the black lava was honeycombed with sharp-edged holes. I didn't want to risk dropping my equipment and breaking it.

I kept out of sight as long as I could and then ran across the open sand to the side of the dome away from the consul's landrover and ducked under the outer layer of mesh. The tent didn't have a back door. I hadn't expected it to. The Lisii team had a tent just like this for storing their clay pots, and the only way in was under the mesh at the bottom.

But the sides of this "big cloud" were packed with boxes and equipment right up to the walls.

I edged along the side of the tent until I came to a place where the plastic gave a little, and slit it with my knife. I looked through the slit, saw nothing but more plastic mesh a few feet away, and squeezed through.

I scared the little bey who was standing there half to death. She flattened herself against one of the packing cases, clutching a Coke bottle with a straw in it.

She'd scared me, too. "Shh," I said, and put my finger to my lips, but she didn't scream. She hung onto the Coke bottle for dear life and started edging away from me.

"Hey," I said softly. "'Don't be scared. You know me." Now I knew where the Sandalman had to be because here was his bey. The old one at the gate must have been left to guard the compound while they were out here. "Remember, I gave you the mirror?" I whispered. "Where's your boss? Where's the Sandalman?"

She stopped and looked at me, her big eyes wide. "Mirror," she said, and nodded, but she didn't come any closer and she let go of the Coke bottle.

"Where's the Sandalman?" I asked her again. No answer. "Where are dig men?" I said. Still no answer. "Where is Evelyn Herbert?"

"Evelyn," she said, and stretched out one dirty-looking arm to point in the direction of a plastic curtain. I ducked through it.

This area of the tent was draped on all sides with plastic mesh, making a kind of low-ceilinged room. The packing cases that were stacked against the side of the tent shut out most of the evening light, and I could hardly see. There was some kind of hammock affair near the wall, hung with more plastic. I could hear someone breathing heavily, unevenly.

"Evelyn?" I said.

The bey had followed me into the room. "Is there a light?" I said to her. She ducked past me and pulled on a string to light a single light bulb hanging from a tangle of cords. Then she backed over against the far wall. The breathing was coming from the hammock.

"Evelyn?" I said, and lifted up the plastic drape.

"Oh," I said, and it came out like a groan. I put my hand over my mouth as if I were trying to get out of a fire, choking on the smoke, smothering, and backed way from the hammock. I practically backed into the little bey, who was pressed so flat against the flimsy wall I thought she was going to go right through it.

"What's wrong with her?" I grabbed her by her bony little shoulders. "What happened?"

I was scaring her to death. There was no way she could answer me. I let go of her shoulders and she pressed herself into the plastic folds of the wall till she nearly disappeared.

"What's wrong with her?" I whispered, and knew my voice still sounded terrifying. "Is it some kind of virus?"

"Curse," the little bey said, and the lights went out.

I stood there in the dark, and I could hear Evelyn's ragged, tortured breathing and the rapid, frightened sound of my own, and for one minute I believed the bey. Then the light came on again, and I looked over at the plastic-draped hammock, and knew I was standing only a few feet away from the biggest story I was ever going to get.

"Curse," the little bey repeated, and I thought, "No, it's not a curse. It's my scoop."

I went over to the hammock again and lifted the plastic drape with two fingers and looked at what had been Evelyn Herbert. A padded mesh blanket was pulled up to her neck, and her hands were crossed over her chest. They were covered with a network of white ridges, even on the fingernails. In the depressions between the ridges the skin was so thin it was transparent. I could see the veins and the raw flesh tissue under them.

Whatever it was covered her face, too, even her eyelids and the inside of her open mouth. Over her cheekbones the white honeycombs were thicker and farther apart; and they looked so soft I thought her bones would poke through at any moment. My skin crawled at the thought that the plastic might be covered with the virus, that I might already have been infected when I came into the room.

She opened her eyes, and I gripped the plastic so hard I almost yanked it down. Tiny honeycombs, so fine they looked like spiderwebs, filmed her eyes. I don't know if she could see me or not.

"Evelyn," I said. "My name is Jack Merton. I'm a reporter. Can you talk?"

She made a strangled sound. I couldn't make it out. She shut her eyes and tried again, and this time I understood her.

"Help me," she said.

"What do you want me to do?" I said.

She made a series of sounds that had to be words but I had no idea what they were. I wished to God the translator was here instead of in the jeep.

She tried to raise herself up by the muscles in her shoulders and back, not even attempting to use her hands. She coughed, a hard, scraping sound, as if she were trying to clear her throat, and made a sound.

"I've got a machine that will make it easier for you to talk," I said. "A translator. Out in my jeep. I'll go get it."

She said clearly, "No," and then the same string of unintelligible sounds.

"I can't understand you," I said, and she reached out suddenly and took hold of my shirt. I backed away so fast I knocked into the lightbulb and sent it swinging. The little bey edged out from the wall to watch it.

"Treasure," Evelyn said, and took a long dragging breath. "Sandalman. Poy. Son."

"Poison?" I said. The light swung wildly over her. I looked at my shirt front. It was cut to pieces where she had grabbed it, slashed into long ribbons by those ridges on her hands. "Who poisoned you? The Sandalman?"

"Help me," she said.

"Was the treasure poisoned, Evelyn?"

She tried to shake her head.

"Take...message."

"Message? To who?"

"San...man," she said, and her muscles gave way and she sank back against the hammock, coughing and taking little rasping breaths in between.

I stepped back so her coughing couldn't reach me. "Why? Are you trying to warn the Sandalman that somebody poisoned you? Why do you want me to take a message to the Sandalman?"

She had stopped coughing. She lay looking up at me. "Help me," she said.

"If I take your message to the Sandalman, will you tell me what happened?" I said. "Will you tell me who poisoned you?"

She tried to nod and started coughing again. The little bey sprang forward with a Coke bottle, stuck a glass straw in it, and tipped it forward so Evelyn could drink. Some of the water spilled onto her chin and into her mouth, and the bey wiped it away with the tail of her dirty-looking shift. Evelyn tried to raise herself up again, and the bey helped her, putting her arm around Evelyn's ridge-covered shoulders. The ridges there were as thick as those on her face, and they didn't seem to cut the bey. If anything, they seemed to flatten a little under the weight of the bey's arm. She stuck the straw in Evelyn's mouth. Evelyn choked and started coughing again. The bey waited, and then tried again, and this time Evelyn got a drink. She lay back.

"Yes," she said, more clearly than she had said anything so far. "Lamp."

I thought I had misunderstood her. "What's the message, Evelyn?" I said. "What do you want to tell him?"

"Lamp," she said again, and tried to gesture with her hand. I turned around and looked. A photosene lamp stood on an upturned plastic cargo carton. Next to it were two disposable injection kits, the kind you find in portable first aid kits, and a plastic packet. The bey handed it to me. I took it from her gingerly, hoping Evelyn hadn't touched the packet, that the bey had put the message inside for her: Then I looked at her hands again and my slashed shirt and knew the bey had not only had to put the message in the plastic envelope, she had probably had to write it out for her, too. I hoped it was readable.

I stuck it in the foil-lined pouch I used for my spare burn-charges and tried to fight the feeling that I needed to wash my hands. I went back over to the hammock. "Where is he? Is he here, in the dome?"

She tried to shake her head again. I was beginning to be able to understand her motions, but I wished again for the translator so I could be sure of what she was saying. "No," she said, and coughed. "Not here. Compound. Village."

"He's in the compound? Are you sure? I was there this afternoon. I didn't see anybody but one of his beys."

She sighed, a terrible sound like a candle guttering out in the wind. "Compound. Hurry."

"All right," I said. "I'll try to get back before dark."

"Hurry," she said, and started to cough again.

⊣ • • • ⊢

I ducked out the way I had come. On the way out I asked the bey if the Sandalman was really back at the compound.

"North," she said. "Soldiers." Which could mean any number of things.

"He's gone north?" I said. "He isn't at the compound?"

"Compound," she said. "Treasure."

"But he's not here, in the tent? Are you sure?"

"Compound," she said. "Soldiers."

I gave up. I glanced around the plastic-hung hall I was in, wondering if I should try to find Howard or Lacau or somebody before I went traipsing back to the compound to look for the Sandalman. There was hardly any light left. If I waited much longer, it would be dark, and I couldn't run the risk of being kept here by an indignant Lacau, with the message burning a hole in my pocket. At least if I went back to the jeep I could read the message, and that might give me a clue as to what in the hell was going on around here. I thought there was a good chance the Sandalman actually was in the compound. If he had gone north he wouldn't have left his bey behind.

I went back out through the slit I'd made and hotfooted it across the space of open plain to the safety of the ridge. Once there, I took my stick-light out and kept it trained on my feet so I wouldn't fall in a hole. I stopped halfway up in the shadow of a long black crevice, to catch my breath and read the message. There wouldn't be enough light if I waited till I got up to the jeep. It was already dark enough that I was going to have to use the sticklight. I pulled the burn pouch out of my shirt and started to open it.

"Come back!" a voice shouted directly beneath me. I flattened myself into the crevice like Evelyn's bey. The sticklight skittered away and down a hole.

"Come back! You don't have to touch him! I'll do that!" I raised my head a little and looked down. It had been some freak of acoustics produced by the face of the lava ridge. Lacau was nowhere near me. He, and two stocky figures in white robes who had to be suhundulim, were on the other side of the tent, so far away I could hardly make them out in the deepening twilight, though Lacau's voice was coming through as clearly as if he were standing directly beneath me.

"I'll do the burying, for God's sake. All you have to do is dig the grave." Lacau turned and gestured toward the tent, and his voice cut off. Whose grave? I looked where he was gesturing and could make out a bluish-gray shape on the sand. A body wrapped in plastic. "The Sandalman sent you here to guard the treasure, and that includes doing what I tell you," Lacau said. "When he gets back, I'll..."

I didn't hear the rest of it, but whatever he had said had not convinced them. They continued to back away from him, and after a minute they turned and ran. I was glad it was nearly dark so I couldn't see them. The suhundulim have always given me the creeps. Bands of herniated muscle ripple under their skin, especially on their faces and their hands and feet. When Bradstreet burns stories about them, he describes them as looking like welts or rope burns, but he's crazy. They look like snakes. The Sandalman isn't too bad—he's got a lot on his feet, which Bradstreet said looked like sandals when he burned the story that gave the Sandalman his name, but hardly any on his face.

The Sandalman. He must be at the compound because Lacau had said, "When he gets back." None of them were looking my way, so I went up and over the ridge as quietly as I could in case the echo thing worked both ways.

There was still enough light in the west to drive by. I thought about stopping midway, switching on the headlights, and reading Evelyn's message in their beam, but I didn't want Lacau to see my lights and figure out where I'd been. I could read the message by one of the lights in the village before I got to the Sandalman's.

I didn't turn on my lights until I couldn't see my hand in front of my face, and when I did I saw I'd practically crashed into the village wall. There weren't any lights along the wall. I left my jeep lights on, wishing I could drive the jeep into the village.

As soon as I was inside the wall, I could see the lantern I'd watched the bey hand out. It was the only light in the whole place, and there was still that massacre-quiet. Maybe they'd found out what was lying in that hammock in the plastic-dome and had taken off like the suhundulim guards.

I went over to the Sandalman's gate and looked up at the lantern. It was just out of my reach or I would have lifted it off its hook and gone off to the shelter of an alley where I could read the message without anybody seeing me. Including the Sandalman. I didn't think he'd take kindly to somebody opening his mail. I huddled against the wall and pulled out the burn pouch.

"No one in," the bey said. She still had the press card in her hand. It looked gnawed around the edges. She must have been sitting on the steps ever since this afternoon, trying to get the holo-letters out.

"I have to see the Sandalman," I said. "Let me in. I have a message for him."

She was looking at the burn pouch curiously. I stuck it back in my pocket.

"Let me in," I said. "Go tell the Sandalman I'm here and I want to see him. Tell him I have a message for him."

"Message," the bey said, watching the pocket whore the burn pouch had gone.

I gave up and pulled the pouch out of my shirt. I took the plastic packet out and showed it to her. "Message. For Sandalman. Let me in."

"No one in," she said. "I take." Her hand lunged through the iron gate.

I yanked the packet away from her. "Message not for you. For Sandalman. Take me to Sandalman. Now."

I had frightened her. She backed away from the gate toward the steps. "No one in," she said, and sat down. She began turning the press card over and over in her dirty-looking hands.

"I'll give you something," I said. "If you take the message to the Sandalman, I'll give you something. Better than the press card."

She came back to the gate, still looking suspicious. I had no idea what I had on me that she might like. I rummaged in my torn shirt pocket and came up with a pen that had holo-letters down its side. "I'll give you this," I said, holding it out in one hand. "You tell Sandalman I have message for him." I held the packet out, too, so she would understand. "Let me in," I said.

She was faster than a striking snake. One minute, she was edging forward, looking at the pen. The next she had the packet. She grabbed the lantern off its hook and ran up the steps.

"Don't," I said. "Wait." The door shut behind her. I couldn't see a thing.

Great. The bey would make a nice meal of the message, I was no closer to a story than I had been, and Evelyn would probably be dead by the time I got back to the dome. I felt my way along the wall till I could see the jeep's lights. They were starting to dim. Great. Now the battery was going. I would not have been surprised to find Bradstreet sitting in the driver's seat, burning a story on my equipment.

⊣•••⊢

I didn't have a prayer of finding my way back to the dome in the pitch black that was Colchis's night, so I left the lights on and hoped Lacau wouldn't see me coming. Even with them on, I high-centered the jeep twice and crashed into a chunk of lava that cast no shadow at all.

I took my shredded shirt off and left it in the jeep. It took me forever to get down the ridge in the dark, carrying the translator and my burn equipment, and the slit I had made in the tent wasn't big enough for me and the bulky boxes. I set them down, slipped through the slit backwards, and pulled the burn box through after me. I hefted the translator onto my shoulder.

"What took you so long, Jack?" Lacau said. "The Sandalman's guards have been gone a couple of hours. I knew I shouldn't have tried to get them to help me. Now they've run away and you've gotten in. Is Bradstreet here, too?"

I turned around. Lacau was standing there, looking like he hadn't slept in a week.

"Why don't you go right back out the way you came in and I'll pretend I never saw you?" he said.

"I'm here to get a story," I said. "You don't really think I'll leave till I get it, do you? I want to see Howard."

"No," Lacau said.

"Right to know," I said, and reached automatically for the press card the bey was probably chewing on right now. If she hadn't already started on Evelyn's message. "You can't deny a hotline reporter access to the principals in a story."

"He's dead," Lacau said. "I buried him this afternoon."

I tried to look like I had come to get a story about a treasure, like I'd never seen the horror that lay in the hammock down the hall, and I guess I did okay because Lacau didn't look suspicious. Maybe he had stopped looking and feeling shock and didn't expect it from me. Or maybe I looked just like I was supposed to.

"Dead?" I said, and tried to remember what he looked like, but all I could see was what was left of Evelyn's face, and her hands clutching my shirt, sharp as a razor and not even looking like a hand.

"What about Callender?"

"He's dead, too. They're all dead except Borchardt and Herbert, and they can't talk. You got here too late."

The strap of the translator was digging into my bare shoulder. I shifted to adjust it.

"What's that?" he said. "A translator? Can it do anything with distorted language? With somebody who can't talk because of...can it do that?"

"Yes," I said. "What's going on? What happened to Howard and the others?"

"I'm confiscating your burn equipment," he said. "And your translator."

"You can't do that," I said, and started to back away from him. "Hotline reporters have free access."

"Not in here they don't. Give me the translator."

"What do you need it for? I thought you said Borchardt and Herbert couldn't talk."

Lacau reached behind him. "Pick up the burn equipment and come this way," he said, and pulled out a photosene flamethrower made out of what looked like a Coke bottle and a mirror, one of the homemade jobs the suhundulim had massacred everybody with. Lacau tilted it so the mirror was under the light bulb hanging above us. I picked up the burn equipment.

He led me away from Evelyn, through a maze of cargo cartons and boxes to the center of the tent. Plastic mesh was draped over where I thought Borchardt might be lying in a hammock like Evelyn's. If he'd hoped to get me lost, it hadn't worked. I could find Evelyn easily. All I had to do was follow the web-like tangle of electrical cords.

The center area looked like a warehouse, piles of open crates everywhere, shovels and picks and sifters, all the archaeologists' equipment, stacked against them. Their packs and sleeping bags were over at one side in a tangled heap next to a pile of flattened cargo cartons. In the middle was a wire cage and facing it, directly under another mess of electrical cords and plugged into it, was a refrigerator. It was big, an ancient double-door commercial job, and I would have bet it came from the Coca-Cola bottling plant. No sign of the treasure, unless it was all already packed. Or in cold storage. I wondered what the cage was for.

"Put down the equipment," Lacau said, and started fiddling with the mirror again. "Get in the cage."

"Where's your burn equipment?" I said.

"None of your business."

"Look," I said. "You've got your job to do, and I've got mine. All I want is a story."

"A story?" Lacau said. He shoved me into the cage. "How about this for a story? You've just been exposed to a deadly virus. You're under quarantine," he said, and reached up and turned out the light.

—|•••|—

Boy, I really knew how to get a story. First the Sandalman's bey and now Lacau, and I was no closer to knowing what was going on than when I was back at Lisii, and maybe only hours away from coming down with what was eating Evelyn. I rattled the wire mesh and yelled for Lacau awhile. Then I played with the lock and yelled some more, but I couldn't see anything or hear anything except the wheezing hum of the refrigerator. Its silence was the only way I could tell when the electricity went off, which it did at least four times during the night. After awhile I hunched against the corner of the cage and tried to sleep.

As soon as it was light, I took off my clothes and checked myself all over for honeycombs. I couldn't see any. I pulled my pants and shoes back on, scribbled a message on a page of my notebook and started banging on the cage again. The bey came in. She had a tray. It had a hard chunk of local bread, a harder one of cheese, and a bottle of Coke with a glass straw in it. It better not be the same one Evelyn had been drinking out of.

"Who else is here?" I asked the bey, but she looked skittish. I had really scared her last night.

I smiled at her. "You remember me, don't you? I gave you a mirror." She didn't smile back. "Are there other beys here?"

She set the tray down on a carton and poked the bread through at me a chunk at a time. "What other beys are here besides you?" I said.

She couldn't get the Coke bottle through the wire without its spilling all over. After a minute or two of her trying, I said, "Here, look, let's cooperate;" and I leaned forward and sucked on the straw while she held the bottle.

When I straightened up, she said, "Only me. No beys. Only me."

"Look," I said. "I want you to take a message to Lacau."

She didn't answer, but at least she didn't back away. I pulled out my trusty holo-lettered pen and held it close to my body. I wasn't going to make the same mistake as last night. "I'll give you pen if you take message to Lacau."

She backed away and stood pressed against the refrigerator, her large black eyes fastened on the pen. I scribbled Lacau's name on the message with it, and put it back in my pocket, and her eyes followed it, fascinated. "I gave you mirror," I said. "I give you this." She darted forward to take the message I was holding out to her, and I finished my breakfast and took a nap and wondered what had happened to the message I had given the Sandalman's bey.

When I woke up again, it was fully light, and I could see a lot of things I'd missed last night. My burn equipment was still here, on the other side of the sleeping bags, but I couldn't see the translator anywhere.

One of the packing crates, a little one, was right outside the cage. I wriggled my hand through a square of wire and pulled the box in close enough to pull the masking tape off. I wondered who had packed the treasure. Howard's team? Or had they started dropping like flies as soon as they found it? The crate looked like too good a job for the suhundulim to have done it. It looked almost like Lacau's style, but why would he pack it? His job was just to keep it from being stolen.

Masking tape and padded mesh and bubbles, all very neat. I pushed my hand through the wire till it stuck, tipped the box a little forward with my other hand, and was able to get a grip on something. I pulled it out.

It was a vase of some kind. I was holding it by the long, narrow neck. In it was a silver tube that was supposed to look like a flower, a lily maybe; widening out and then narrowing toward the open top. The sides of the tube were etched with fine lines. The vase itself was made of some kind of blue ceramic, as thin as eggshell. I wrapped it up in plastic mesh and laid it back in the box. I rummaged in the bubbles some more and came up with something that looked like a cross between one of Lisii's clay pots and something a bey had chewed on for awhile and then spit out.

"That's the door seal," Lacau said. "According to Borchardt, it says, 'Beware the curse of kings and keepers that turn men's dreams to blood.'" He took the clay tablet out of my hands.

"Did you get my message?" I said, trying to pull my hands back through the cage wire. I scraped my wrist. It started to bleed. "Well," I said, "did you get the message?"

He threw a chewed wad of paper at me. "More or less," he said. "Beys tend to be curious about anything you give them. What was in the message?"

"I want to make a deal with you."

Lacau started to put the door seal back in the carton. "I already know how to work the translator," he said. "And the burn equipment."

"Nobody knows I'm here. I've been relaying stories back to Lisii ground-to-ground for burning."

"What kind of stories?" he said. He had straightened up, still holding the door seal.

"Fillers. The local wildlife, old interviews, the Commission. Human interest stuff."

"The Commission?" he said. He had made a sudden, lurching movement as if he had almost dropped the door seal and then caught it at the last instant. I wondered if he was okay. He looked terrible.

"I've got a relay set up back in Lisii. My transmissions go out through it, and Bradstreet thinks I'm still in Lisii. If I stop burning stories, he'll know something's up. He's got a Swallow. He could be here as soon as tomorrow."

Lacau put the vase carefully in the carton and piled bubbles around it. He taped it shut and put down the masking tape. "What's your deal?"

"I start filing stories again that will convince Bradstreet I'm still in Lisii."

"And in return?"

"You tell me what's going on. You let me interview the team. You give me a scoop."

"Can you keep him away till day after tomorrow?"

"What happens tomorrow?"

"Can you?"

"Yes."

He thought about it. "The ship will be here tomorrow morning," he said slowly. "I'm going to need help loading the treasure."

"I'll help you," I said.

"No private interviews, no private access to the burn equipment. I get censorship of the stories you file."

"Okay," I said.

"You don't file the story on this till we're off Colchis."

I would have agreed to anything. This was not just a local bit of nastiness, minor potentate poisons a few strangers. There was a story here like no story I had ever had, and I would have agreed to kiss the Sandalman's snaky feet to get it.

"Deal," I said.

Lacau took a deep breath. "We found a treasure in the Spine," he said. "Three weeks ago. A princess's tomb. It's worth...I don't know. Most of the artifacts are made of silver, and their archaeological value alone is beyond price.

"A week ago, two days after we'd finished clearing the tomb and bringing it down here where we could work on it, the team came down with...something. A virus of some kind. Just the team. Not the Sandalman's representative, not the bearers who brought the stuff down from the Spine. Nobody but the team. The Sandalman claims they opened the tomb themselves without waiting for local authorization." He stopped.

"And if they did, that would mean they forfeit and the Sandalman gets the whole thing. Convenient. Where was the Sandalman's rep while they were supposedly doing all this?"

"It was his bey. She went back to get the Sandalman. The team stayed behind to guard the treasure. Howard swears, swore they didn't go in, that they waited until the Sandalman and his bearers got there. He says, said the team was poisoned."

"Poy son," Evelyn had said. "Sandalman."

"The Sandalman claims it was some kind of guard poison put in the tomb by the ancients, that the team touched it when they opened the tomb illegally."

"Who did Howard say poisoned them?" I said.

"He didn't. The...this thing they caught went into their throats. Howard couldn't talk at all after the first day. Evelyn Herbert is still able to talk, but she's very hard to understand. That's why I need the translator. I need to talk to Evelyn and find out how they were poisoned."

I thought about what he had said. Some kind of guard poison in the tomb. I knew about that. I had burned stories about the poisons the ancient of all cultures put in their tombs to keep defilers from ransacking them, the contact poisons they put on the artifacts themselves. I had handled the door seal.

Lacau was watching me. He said, "I helped bring the treasure down from the Spine. So did the bearers. And I've been handling the bodies. I've been wearing plasticgloves, but that wouldn't protect me from airborne or droplet infection. Whatever it is, I don't think it's contagious."

"Do you think it's a poison, like Howard said?" I asked..

"My official position is that it's a virus that was present in the tomb and that the entire party, including the Sandalman's representative, was exposed to it when the tomb was opened."

"And the Sandalman."

"The Sandalman's bey entered the tomb before he did. Then the team. Then the Sandalman. My official position is that the virus was anerobic and that after the tomb had been open to the air a few minutes, it was no longer virulent."

"But you don't believe that?"

"No."

"Then why take that position? Why not accuse the Sandalman? If the treasure's what you want, that'll make sure you get it. The Commission..."

"The Commission will close the planet and investigate the charges."

"And you don't want that?"

I wanted to ask why not, but I figured I'd better be out of the cage before I asked that. "But if it's a virus, what's your excuse for why the bey hasn't come down with it?" I said.

"Difference in body chemistry and size. I declared the quarantine, and the Sandalman went along with it, more or less. He agreed to give us an extension of a week to allow for the variation in incubation time of the virus in the bey before he files his complaint with the Commission. The week's up day after tomorrow. If the bey comes down with it in the next two days…"

Which explained why the Sandalman's bey was here, in quarantine with the archaeologists, when no one else, not even the Sandalman's guards, would set foot inside the tent. She was not Evelyn's nurse. She was the sole hope of the expedition.

And she was not going to catch anything. The Sandalman had agreed to the extension. He had been willing to leave her with the team. He would never have done that if he had thought there was even the slightest chance of her coming down with it. So there was not any chance. Unless Evelyn knew what the poison was. Unless she had threatened to poison the Sandalman's bey. Unless that was what was in the message.

"Why didn't he just kill the team right there in the tomb?" I said. "If all he wants is the treasure, why didn't he see to it they were buried by a rockfall or something and call it an accident?"

"There'd still have been an investigation. He couldn't risk that."

I was about to ask why he couldn't, but I'd thought of something more important. "Where is he anyway?"

"He's gone north to Khamsin to get an army," he said.

Khamsin. So the Sandalman wasn't at the compound after all, and the bey was probably making a nice meal of Evelyn's message by now. And when he arrived in Khamsin nothing I could say would convince Bradstreet something wasn't going on. I wondered if Lacau had figured that out yet.

He unlocked the cage. "I'm taking you to see Evelyn Herbert," he said. "But I want you to file a story first."

"Okay," I said. I had already decided what I was going to send. I wasn't going to be able to fool Bradstreet, but maybe I could throw him off just long enough for me to get my scoop.

"I want a printout first," Lacau said.

"This burner doesn't use one," I said, "but you can put the message on hold and then delete whatever you want from the monitor before we burn it." I pointed to the hold button.

"All right," he said.

"I put it in lock," I said, but he kept his hand on the hold key through the whole message.

I typed in a private priority that read, "Big Doings at the Spine. Hold 12-column."

"You're trying to get him out to the Spine?" Lacau said. "That won't work. He'll see the dome. Anyway, he can't uncook an official message, can he?"

"Of course he can. How do you think I knew you had a ship coming in? But he also knows that I know he can and he won't trust this message. This is the one he'll believe." I tapped the code for ground transmission, fed in the message; and waited for the burner to tell me it wouldn't go through. It couldn't do that until Lacau let go of the hold key, and I didn't even have to ask him. He raised his hand and put it over his chin and watched the screen.

I waited the length of time it would have taken me to weigh odds that Bradstreet would ignore a local message if it weren't flagged with a priority and then decide to send it straight. "Coming back as fast as I can. Stall," I typed. I signed it, "Jackie."

"Who's this message going to?"' Lacau said.

"Nobody. I've got a relay set up in my tent. It'll put the message in store and hold it. I'll file a story in the morning about the Spine. It'll be transmitted from here, which is a day's trip from the Spine."

"So he'll think you're doing just what you said. Heading for Lisii."

"Yes," I said. "Now do I get to see Evelyn Herbert?"

"Yes," he said, and started back along the maze of boxes and electrical cords with me following. Halfway there he stopped and said, as if he had just remembered, "This...thing they've come down with is pretty bad. They look...I want you to be prepared," he said.

"I'm a reporter," I said, so that if I didn't look horrified enough Lacau would think it was because I was used to seeing horrors, but I made the speech for nothing. I didn't have any trouble registering shock. Evelyn looked just as bad the second time.

⊣ ••• ⊢

Lacau had put some kind of contraption across her chest. It was plugged into the spiderweb of cords overhead. I set up the translator. There wasn't much I could really do until Evelyn did a fix for us, but I fiddled with it anyway, and the bey watched me, all eyes. Lacau sprayed on plasticgloves and went over to the hammock to look at her.

"I gave her her shot half an hour ago," he said. "It'll be a few more minutes."

"What are you giving her?" I said.

"Dilaudid and sulfadine morphates. It was all there was in the first aid kit. There were IV packs, but they kept leaking."

He said that without emotion, as if he had not had the horror of trying to put an IV in an arm that could cut an IV pack to ribbons. He did not seem at all afraid of her.

"The dilaudid puts her out cold for about an hour, and then after that she's pretty lucid, but in a lot of pain. The morphates are better for pain, but they put her under after only a couple of minutes."

"If it's going to be awhile, I'm going to show the bey the translator, okay?" I said. "If I take it apart and explain everything, we decrease our chances of finding it taken apart tomorrow morning. Is that all right?"

He nodded and went over to look at Evelyn again.

I pulled the face off the box, motioned the bey over, and started my spiel. Every burn chip, every hold strip, every circuit. I pulled them all out and let her handle them, hold them up to the light, stick them in her mouth, and finally put them back in the way they belonged with her own dirty little hands. Halfway through the electricity went off again, and we sat for five full minutes in twilight, but Lacau made no move to get up or to light the photosene lamp.

"It's the respirator," he said. "I've got one on Borchardt, too. It keeps overloading the generator." I wished the lights would come back on so I could see his face more clearly. I was more than ready to believe the generator could overload. The one out at Lisii was off half the time without benefit of respirators, but I was still sure he was lying. It was that double-door refrigerator next to my cage that was overloading the generator and making the lights go out. And what was in that refrigerator? Coca-Cola?

The lights came on. Lacau leaned over Evelyn, and the little bey and I snapped the last burn chip in place and put the face back on the translator. I gave the bey a burned-out hold strip to keep, and she went off in a corner to examine it.

Lacau said, "Evelyn?" and she murmured something.

"I think we're about ready," he said. "What do you want her to say?"

I handed him a clip mike to fasten on the plastic drape above her head. "Refrigerator," I said, and knew I'd gone too far. I was liable to find myself back in the cage. "Have her say anything you want so I can get a fix. Her name. Anything."

"Evie," he said, and his voice was surprisingly gentle. "We have a machine here that can help you talk. I want you to say your name."

She said something, but the box didn't pick it up. "The mike's not close enough," I said.

Lacau pulled the plastic drape down a little, and she made a sound again, and this time it came out of the box as static. I twiddled dials to get an initial sound, but couldn't get it to match.

"Have her try it again. I'm not getting anything," I said, and punched hold so I could hang onto the sound and work with it, but it was still noise, no matter what I did. I began to wonder if the bey had put one of the tubes in backwards.

"Can you try it again?" Lacau said gently. "Evelyn?" and this time he bent so far over her he was practically touching her. Noise.

"There's something the matter with the box," I said.

"She's not saying, 'Evelyn,'" Lacau said.

"What's she saying then?"

Lacau straightened up and looked at me. "Message," he said.

The lights went out again, just for a few seconds, and while they were out I said, trying to sound a little impatient and not at all nervous, "Okay, then, I'll get a fix on 'message.' Have her say it again."

The lights came back on, and then the centering lights on the translator blinked on, and her voice, sounding like a woman's voice now, said, "Message," and then, "Something to tell you."

There was a deadly silence. I was surprised the box wasn't picking up my heartbeat and making it into the word "caught." The lights went out again and stayed out. Evelyn started wheezing. The wheezing got rapidly worse.

"Can't you switch the respirator onto batteries?" I said.

"No," Lacau said. "I'll have to get the other one." He pulled out a sticklight and used it to light the photosene lamp. He picked the lamp up by its base and went out.

As soon as I couldn't see the wavering shadows along the hall of boxes anymore, I felt my way over to the bed. I nearly tripped over the bey, who was sitting cross-legged by the bed, sucking on the hold strip. "Get water," I said.

"Evelyn," I said, using the sound she was making to tell me where she was. "Evelyn, it's me. Jack, I was here before."

The wheezing stopped, just like that, as if she were holding her breath. "I gave the message to the Sandalman," I said. "I handed it to him myself."

She said something, but I was too far away from the translator to pick it up. It sounded like "light."

"I went right away. As soon as I left you last night."

This time I made out the word. "Good," she said, and the lights went on.

"What was in the message, Evelyn?"

"What message?" Lacau said.

He set the respirator down beside the bed. I could see why he hadn't wanted to use it. It was the kind that fastened over the trachea and cut off all speech.

"What were you trying to say, Evie?" he said.

"Message," she said. "Sandalman. Good."

"She's not making any sense," I said. "Is she still under the morphates? Ask her something you know the answer to."

"Evelyn," he said. "Who was with you out on the Spine?"

"Howard. Callender. Borchardt." She stopped a minute as if she were trying to remember. "Bey."

"That's fine. You don't have to tell me the others. When you found the treasure, what did you do?"

"Waited. Sent bey. Waited Sandalman."

"Did you go in the tomb?" He had been over these questions before. I could tell by the way he asked them, but on the last question his tone changed, and I waited to hear her answer, too.

"No," she said, and the word came through absolutely clearly. "Waited Sandalman."

"What were you trying to tell me, Evelyn? Yesterday. You kept trying to tell me something, and I couldn't understand you. But now I've got a translator. What were you trying to tell me?"

What would she say to him? Never mind? I got somebody else to deliver it? It crossed my mind, then and later, that she could not tell us apart, that her ears were filled with honeycombs, too, and our voices bending over her sounded the same to her. That wasn't true, of course. She knew exactly who she was talking to until the very last. But right then I held my breath, my hand hovering over the switch, thinking that if I waited she might tell Lacau I'd been in here before. Thinking, too, that if I waited she would tell me what was in the message.

"Were you trying to tell me about the poison, Evelyn?"

"Too late," she said.

Lacau turned around. "I didn't catch that," he said. "What did she say?"

"I think she said, 'treasure.'"

"Treasure," she said. "Curse." Her breathing steadied. The translator stopped picking it up. Lacau stood up and let the drape down over her.

"She's asleep," he said. "She never lasts long on the morphates." He turned around and looked at me. The bey had been waiting for her chance. She grabbed the Coke bottle off the cargo carton and ducked past him. He turned and looked at her.

"Maybe she's right," he said tonelessly. "Maybe it is a curse."

I was watching the bey too, as she stood there waiting for Evelyn to wake up so she could give her a drink, no taller than a ten-year-old, clutching the Coke bottle in one hand and the hold strip I had given her in the other. I tried to think what she would look like when the poison started working on her.

"I think sometimes I could almost do it," Lacau said.

"Do what?" I said.

"I think I could poison the Sandalman's bey to save the treasure if I knew what the poison was. That's a kind of curse, isn't it, wanting something so badly you'd kill somebody for it?"

"Yes," I said. The bey stuck the hold strip in her mouth.

"Ever since I saw the treasure, I..."

I stood up. "You'd kill a harmless bey for a goddamned blue vase?" I said angrily. "When you'll get the treasure anyway? You can take blood samples. You can prove the team was poisoned. The Commission will award you the treasure."

"The Commission will close the planet."

"What difference will that make?"

"They will destroy the treasure," Lacau said, as if he'd forgotten I was there.

"What are you talking about? They won't let the Sandalman or his cronies anywhere near the treasure. They'll see to it nobody damages the merchandise. They'll take their own sweet time about it, but you'll get your treasure."

"You haven't seen the treasure;" he said. "You..." He put up his hands in a gesture of despair. "You don't understand."

"Then maybe you'd better show me this wonderful treasure," I said.

His shoulders slumped. "All right," he said, and everything in me said: Story.

He locked me in the cage again while he hooked the respirator back up to Borchardt. I didn't ask to go with him. I had known Borchardt almost as long as I had Howard, although I hadn't liked him as well. But I wouldn't have wished this on him. It was nearly noon. The sun was practically overhead and hot enough to burn a hole right through the plastic. Lacau came back in half an hour, looking worse than ever.

He sat down on a packing crate and put his hands up to his head. "Borchardt's dead," he said: "He died while we were in with Evelyn."

"Let me out of the cage," I said.

"Borchardt had a theory about the beys," Lacau said. "About their curiosity. He looked on it as a curse."

"Curse," Evelyn's bey had said, huddled against the wall.

"Let me out of the cage," I said.

"He thought that when the suhundulim came the beys were curious about them and the 'snakes underneath,' so curious they let them stay. And the suhundulim enslaved them. Borchardt maintained the beys were a great people with a highly developed civilization until the suhundulim came and took Colchis away from them."

"Let me out of the cage, Lacau."

He bent over and dug down into the packing case beside him. "This could never have been made by a suhundulim," he said, and pulled it out, spilling plastic bubbles everywhere. "It's spun silver strung with ceramic beads so tiny you can't see them except under a microscope. No suhundulim could make that."

"No," I said. It did not look like beads strung on a silver wire. It looked like a cloud, a majestic desert thunderhead. When Lacau turned it in the light coming through the plastic roof, it shaded into rose and lavender. It was beautiful.

"A suhundulim could make this, however," he said, and turned it around so I could see the other side. It was mashed flat, a dull gray mass. "One of the Sandalman's bearers dropped it bringing it out of the tomb."

He laid it carefully back in its nest of plastic bubbles and taped the box shut. He walked over and stood in front of the cage. "They will close the planet," he said. "Even if we could keep it out of the Sandalman's hands, the Commission will take a year, two years, to make a decision, maybe longer."

"Let me out," I said.

He turned and opened the double doors of the refrigerator and stepped back so I could see what was inside. "The electricity goes off all the time. Sometimes it stays off for days," he said.

From the moment I had intercepted Lacau's message, I had known it was the story of the century. I had felt it in my bones. And here it was.

It was a statue of a girl. A child, twelve maybe. No older than that. She sat on a block of solid beaten silver. She was wearing a white and blue dress with trailing fringes, and she was leaning against the side wall of the refrigerator, her hand and forearm flat against it and her head leaning on her hand, as if she were overcome by some great grief. I couldn't see her face.

Her black hair was bound in the same silver stuff the cloud had been made of, and around her neck was a collar of the blue faience etched in silver. One knee was slightly forward, and I could see her foot in a silver shoe. She was made of wax, soft and white as skin, and I knew that if she could somehow turn her sorrowing face and look at me, it would be the face I had waited all my life to see. I clutched the wire of the cage and could not get my breath.

"The beys' civilization was very advanced," Lacau said. "Arts, science, embalming." He smiled at my uncomprehending frown. "She's not a statue. She's a bey princess.

"The embalming process turned the tissues to wax." He leaned over her. "The tomb was in a cave that was naturally refrigerated, but we had to bring her down from the Spine. Howard sent me back to try to find temp control equipment and coolants. This was all I could find. It was out at the bottling plant," Lacau said, and lifted the blue-and-white fringe of her trailing skirt. "We didn't try to move her till the last day. The Sandalman's bearers bumped her against the door of the tomb getting her out," he said.

The wax of her leg was flattened and pushed up. Nearly half of the black femur was exposed.

No wonder Evelyn's first word to me had been, "Hurry." No wonder Lacau had laughed when I told him the Commission would keep the treasure safe. The investigation would take a year or more, and she would sit here with the electricity flickering on and off.

"We have to get her off the planet," I said, and my hands clutched the mesh so hard the wire cut nearly through to the bone.

"Yes," Lacau said, in a tone that told me what I should have known.

"The Sandalman won't let her off Colchis," I said. "He's afraid the Commission will try to take the planet away from him." And I had burned a story about the Commission to scare him. "They won't do anything. They're not going to give Colchis to a bunch of ten-year-olds who keep sticking things in their mouths, no matter who was here first."

"I know," Lacau said.

"He poisoned the team," I said, and turned to look at the princess, her beautiful face that I could not see turned to the wall in some ancient grief. He had killed the team, and when he got back from the north with his army he would kill us. And destroy the princess. "Where's your burn equipment?" I said.

"The Sandalman has it."

"Then he knows when the ship will be here. We've got to get her out of here."

"Yes," Lacau said. He let go of the blue-and-white fringe, and it fell across her foot. He shut the door of the refrigerator.

"Let me out of the cage," I said. "I'll help you. Whatever you're going to do, I'll help you."

He looked at me a long minute, as if he were trying to decide whether he could trust me. "I'll let you out," he said finally. "But not yet."

It was dark again before he came to get me. He had come through the center area twice. The first time he got a shovel from the jumble of equipment stacked against the cargo cartons. The second time he opened the refrigerator again to get out an injection kit for Evelyn's shot, and I stood in the cage and stared at the princess, waiting for her to turn her head. Sitting there afterwards, waiting for Lacau to finish doing whatever it was he did not trust me to help him with, I was surprised to see that the wire of the cage had not mashed and flattened my hands like tallow.

It had been dark over an hour when Lacau came and let me out. He had a coil of yellow extension cords with him, and the shovel. He leaned it against the pile of flattened cartons, dumped the cords on the floor beside it, and unlocked the cage.

"We have to move the refrigerator," he said. "We'll put it against the back wall of the tent so we can load it into the ship as soon as it lands."

I went over to the heap of cords and began to untangle them. I didn't ask him where he'd gotten them. One of them looked like the cord to Evelyn's respirator. We plugged the cords together, and then Lacau unplugged the refrigerator. My grip on the cord tightened as he did it, even though I knew he was going to plug it into the extension cord and hook it up again and the whole process wasn't going to take more than thirty seconds. He plugged it in carefully, as if he were afraid the lights would go off when he did it, but they didn't even flicker.

They dimmed a little when we picked the refrigerator up between us, but it weighed less than I thought it would. As soon as we shuffled past the first row of packing crates, I saw what Lacau had been doing at least part of the day. He'd moved as many boxes as he could to the east side of the tent and up against the wall, leaving a passage wide enough for us to get through with the refrigerator and a space for it against the wall of the tent. He'd hooked a light up, too. The extension cord didn't quite reach, and we had to set the refrigerator down a few meters from the wall of the tent. It was still close enough. If the ship got here in time.

"Is the Sandalman here yet?" I said. Lacau was walking rapidly back to the center area, and I wasn't at all sure I should follow him. I wasn't going to let myself be locked in that cage for the Sandalman's soldiers to find. I stayed where I was.

"Do you have a recorder?" Lacau said. He stopped and looked at me. "Do you have a recorder?"

"No," I said.

"I want you to record Evelyn's testimony," he said. "We'll need it if the Commission is called in."

"I don't have a recorder," I said.

"I won't lock you in again," he said. He reached in his pocket and tossed me something. It was the handlock to the cage. "If you don't trust me, you can give it to Evelyn's bey."

"There's a record button on the translator," I said.

And we went in and interviewed Evelyn and she told me there was a curse and I didn't believe her. And the Sandalman came.

—|•••|—

Lacau seemed unconcerned that the Sandalman was camped on the ridge above us. "I've unscrewed all the light bulbs," he said, "and they can't see into this room. I put a tarp on the roof this afternoon." He sat back down next to Evelyn. "They have lanterns, but they won't try coming down that ridge at night."

"What happens when the sun comes up?" I said.

"I think she's coming around," he said. "Turn the recorder on. Evelyn, we've got a recorder here. We need you to tell us what happened. Can you talk?"

"Last day," Evelyn said.

"Yes," Lacau said. "This is the last day. The ship will be here in the morning to take us home. We'll get you to a doctor."

"Last day," she said again. "In tomb. Loading princess. Cold."

"What was that last word?" Lacau said.

"It sounded like, 'cold,'" I said.

"It was cold in the tomb, wasn't it, Evie? Is that what you mean?"

She tried to shake her head. "Coke," she said. "Sandalman. Here. Must be thirsty. Coke."

"The Sandalman gave you a Coke? Was the poison in the Coke? Is that how he poisoned the team?"

"Yes," she said, and it came out like a sigh, as if that was what she had been trying to tell us all along.

"What kind of poison was it, Evelyn?"

"Blue."

Lacau jerked around to look at me. "Did she say, 'blood'?"

I shook my head. "Ask her again," I said.

"Blood," Evelyn said clearly. "Keep her."

"What's she talking about?" I said. "A kheper bite can't kill you. It doesn't even make you sick."

"No," Lacau said, "but enough kheper poison could. I should have seen the similarities, the replacement of the cell structure, the waxiness. The ancient beys used a concentrated distillation of kheper-infected blood for embalming. 'Beware the curse of kings and khepers.' How do you suppose the Sandalman figured it out?"

Maybe he hadn't had to, I thought. Maybe he'd had the poison all along. Maybe his ancestors, landing on Colchis, had been as curious as the beys they were going to steal a planet from. "Show us how your embalming process works," they might have said, and then, when they'd seen the obvious benefits, they'd said to the smartest of the beys, just like the Sandalman had said to Howard and Evelyn and the rest of the team, "Here. Have a Coke. You must be thirsty."

I thought of the beautiful princess, leaning against her hand. And Evelyn. And Evelyn's bey, sitting in front of the photosene flame, all unaware.

"Is it contagious?" I said for the last time. "Would Evelyn's blood be poisonous, too?"

Lacau blinked at me as if he could not make out what I was saying. "Only if you drank it, I think," he said after a minute. He looked down at Evelyn. "She was asking me to poison the bey," he said. "But I couldn't understand her. It was before you got here with the translator."

"You'd have done it, wouldn't you?" I said. "If you'd known what the poison was, that her blood was poisonous, you'd have killed the bey to save the treasure?"

He wasn't listening to me. He was looking up at the roof of the tent where the tarp didn't quite cover. "Is it getting light?" he said.

"Not for another hour," I said.

"No," he said, "I would have done almost anything for her." His voice was so full of longing it embarrassed me to listen to him. "But not that."

He gave Evelyn a second shot and blew out the lamp. After a few minutes he said, "There are three injection kits left. In the morning I'm going to give Evelyn all of them." I wondered if he was looking at me the way he had when I was in the cage, wondering if he could trust me to do what had to be done.

"Will it kill her?" I said.

"I hope so," he said. "There's no way we can move her."

"I know," I said, and we sat in the darkness for a long time.

"Two days," he said, and his voice was full of that same longing. "The incubation period was only two days."

And then we sat there not saying anything, waiting for the sun to come up.

When it did, Lacau took me into what had been Howard's room, where he had cut a flap-like window in the plastic wall that faced the ridge, and I saw what he had done. The Sandalman's soldiers lined the top of the ridge. They were too far away to be able to see the snakes rippling across their faces, but I knew they were looking down at the dome, and on the sand in front of us, laid end to end, were the bodies.

"How long have they been there?" I said.

"I put them out there yesterday afternoon. After Borchardt died."

"You dug Howard up,?" I said. Howard was lying nearest us. He did not look as bad as I had imagined he would. He had almost no honeycombs, and although his skin looked waxy and soft like the skin over Evelyn's cheekbones, he looked almost like I remembered him. The sun had done that. He was melting out there in the sun.

"Yes," he said. "The Sandalman knows it's a poison, but the rest of the suhundulim don't. They'll never cross that line of bodies. They're afraid of catching the virus."

"He'll tell them," I said.

"Would you believe him?" he said. "Would you cross that line because he told you it wasn't a virus?"

"It's a good thing you left me in the cage," I said. "I wouldn't have helped you do this."

Light flashed from the ridge. "Are they firing at us?" I said.

"No," he said. "The Sandalman's head bey has something shiny in her hand that's reflecting the sunlight."

It was the bey from the compound. She had my press card and was moving it back and forth so it flashed sunlight.

"She wasn't there before," Lacau said. "The Sandalman must have brought her out to show his soldiers she hasn't caught the virus and they won't either."

"What?" I said. "Why would she catch it? I thought Evelyn's bey was the one who was with the team."

He was frowning at me. "Evelyn's bey never went anywhere near the Spine. She's a maidservant the Sandalman gave Evelyn. How did you get the idea she was the Sandalman's representative?" He looked at me in disbelief. "You don't think the Sandalman would let us anywhere near his bey after we'd negotiated for the extra days, do you? He wouldn't have trusted us not to poison her like he poisoned the team. He locked her up tight in his compound before he went north," he said bitterly.

"And Evelyn knew that," I said. "She knew the Sandalman had gone north. She knew he'd left his bey behind. Didn't she?"

Lacau didn't answer. He was watching the bey. The Sandalman offered her something, and she took it. It looked like a bucket. She had to stick the press card in her mouth to free both hands so she could lift it. The Sandalman said something to her, and she started down the ridge, spilling liquid from the bucket as she went. The Sandalman had left his bey behind at the compound, locked up, but the guards had run off like the guards at the dome, and a curious bey could open any lock.

"She doesn't seem to be sick, does she?" Lacau said bitterly. "And our week is up. The team caught it in two days."

"Two," I said. "Did Evelyn know the Sandalman left his bey behind?"

"Yes," Lacau said, watching the ridge. "I told her."

The little bey was down the ridge and onto the plain. The Sandalman yelled something at her, and she began to run. The bucket banged against her legs, and more liquid spilled out. As soon as she reached the line of bodies, she stopped and looked back at the ridge. The Sandalman yelled again. He was a long way away, but the ridge amplified his voice. I could hear him quite clearly.

"Pour," he said. "Pour fire," and the little bey tipped the bucket and started down the row.

"Photosene," Lacau said tonelessly. "The sunlight will ignite it."

A lot had spilled out of the bucket on the way down, none of it on the bey, for which I was thankful. There were only a few drops left to shake over Howard. The bey dropped the bucket and danced back. At the other end of the row, Callender's shirt took fire. I shut my eyes.

"Two lousy days," Lacau said. Callender's mustache was on fire. Borchardt smouldered and then flared up yellowly like a candle. Lacau didn't even see me leave.

I followed the electrical cords back to Evelyn's room, half-running. The bey wasn't there. I flipped on the translator and yanked the drape up and looked down at her. "What was in the message, Evelyn?" I said.

The sound of her breathing was so loud nothing was going to get through on the translator. Her eyes were closed.

"You knew the Sandalman had already gone north when you sent me back to the compound, didn't you?" The translator was picking up my own voice and echoing it back to me. "You knew I was lying when I told you I'd delivered the message to the Sandalman. But you didn't care. Because the message wasn't for him. It was for his bey."

She said something. The translator couldn't do anything with it, but it didn't matter. I knew what it was. "Yes," she said, and I felt a sudden desire to hit her; to watch the honeycombed cheeks cave in under the force of my hand and mash against bone.

"You knew she'd put it in her mouth, didn't you?"

"Yes," she said; and opened her eyes. There was a dull roaring outside.

"You murdered her," I said.

"Had to. To save the treasure," she said. "Sorry. Curse."

"There isn't any curse," I said, clenching my hands at my sides so I wouldn't hit her. "That was just a story you made up to stall me till the poison could take effect, wasn't it?"

She started to cough. The bey darted in front of me with the Coke bottle. She put the straw in Evelyn's mouth, propped Evelyn's head up with her hand, and tilted her gently forward so she could drink.

"You'd have killed your own bey, too, if you had to, wouldn't you?" I said. "For the treasure. For the goddamned treasure!"

"Curse," Evelyn, said.

"The ship's here," Lacau said behind me, "but we'll never make it. Howard's the only one left. They're sending the bey down with more photosene."

"We'll make it," I said, and switched the translator off. I took out my knife and slit the wall of the tent behind Evelyn's hammock. Evelyn's bey scampered to her feet and came over to where we were standing. The Sandalman's bey was halfway across the plain with the bucket. She was moving more slowly this time, and none of the photosene was splashing out. Above, on the ridge, the Sandalman's soldiers edged forward.

"We can load the treasure," I said. "Evelyn's seen to that."

The bey made it to the bodies. She started to tip the bucket onto Howard, then seemed to change her mind, and set the bucket down. The Sandalman yelled something at her. She took hold of the bucket, let go of it again, and fell over.

"You see," I said. "It was a virus after all."

There was a sound from above her like a stuttering sigh, and the Sandalman's soldiers began to back away from the edge of the ridge.

⊣ • • • ⊢

375

A loading crew was there before we even had the back of the tent sliced open. Lacau pointed them at the nearest boxes, and they didn't even ask any questions. They just started carrying them out to the ship. Lacau and I picked up the refrigerator, gently, gently, so as not to bang the princess's shins, and carried her across the sand to the ship's loading bay.

The captain took one look at her and yelled for the rest of his crew to come and help load. "Hurry," he said after us. "They're bringing up some kind of weapon on the ridge there."

We hurried. We handed stuff out the back door, and the crew ran the boxes across the sand faster than Evelyn's bey getting a drink of water in a Coke bottle; and we still weren't fast enough. There was a soft whoosh and splat on the roof overhead, and liquid trickled down the plastic mesh over our heads.

"He's got a photosene cannon," Lacau said. "Is the blue vase out?"

"Where's Evelyn's bey?" I said, and took off for Evelyn's room. The mesh drape above the hammock was already melting, the fire slicing through it like a knife. The little bey was flattened against the inner wall where I had seen her that first night, watching the fire. I grabbed her up under my arm and dived for the center area.

I couldn't get through. The packing cases that lined the tent were a wall of roaring flame. I ducked back into Evelyn's room. I saw immediately that we could not get out that way either, and just as immediately I remembered the slit I'd made in the wall.

I clamped my hand over the bey's mouth so she wouldn't breathe in the fumes from the melting plastic, held my breath, and started past the hammock.

Evelyn was still alive.

I could not hear her wheezing above the fire, but I could see her chest rise and fall before it began to melt. She was lying with her face pressed against the side of the melting hammock, and she turned her face toward me as I stopped as if she had heard me. The honeycombs on her face widened and flattened, and then smoothed out with the heat, and for a minute I saw her as she must have looked when Bradstreet saw her and said that she was beautiful, as she must have looked when the Sandalman gave her his own bey. The face she turned to me was the face that I had waited all my life to see. And only saw too late.

She guttered out like a candle, and I stood there and watched her, and by the time she was dead the roof had caved in on Lacau and two of the crew. And the blue vase had already been broken in a mad dash to the ship with the last of the treasure.

But we saved the princess. And I got my story.

It is the story of the century, At least that's what Bradstreet's boss called it when he fired him. My boss is asking for forty columns a day. I give them to him.

They are great stories. In them Evelyn is a beautiful victim and Lacau is a hero. I am a hero, too. After all, I helped save the treasure. The stories I burn don't tell how Lacau dug up Howard and built a fort with him or how I got the Lisii team killed. In the stories I burn there is only one villain.

I send forty columns a day out over the burner and try to put the blue vase back together and in what time is left I write this story, which I will not send anywhere. The bey fiddles with the lights.

Our cabin has a system of air-current-sensitive highlights that dim and brighten automatically as you move. The bey cannot get enough of them. She does not even mess with the blue vase or try to put the pieces in her mouth.

I have figured out what the vase is, by the way. The etched lines on the silver straw that looks like a lily are scratches. I am piecing together a ten-thousand-year-old Coke bottle. Here. You must be thirsty. The beys may have had a wonderful civilization, but years before the Sandalman's grandparents even showed up, they were busy poisoning princesses. They murdered her; and she must have known it, and that's why she leans her head against her hand so hopelessly. They murdered her for what? For a treasure? For a planet? For a story? And didn't anybody try to save her?

The first thing Evelyn said to me was, "Help me." What if I had? What if I had said the hell with the story and called Bradstreet, sent him over to get the Lisii team's doctor and evacuate the rest of the team? What if, while he was still on the way, I had burned a message to the Sandalman that said, "You can have the princess if you'll let us off the planet?" and then plugged in that trachea respirator that wouldn't let her talk but might have kept her alive till we could get her onto a ship?

I like to think that I would have done that if I had known her, if it had not been, as she said, "Too late." But I don't know. The Sandalman, who was so enamoured of her that he gave her his own bey, stood in the tomb and offered her poison in a Coke bottle. And Lacau knew her, but what he went back for, what he died for, was not her but a blue vase.

"There was a curse," I say.

Evelyn's bey drifts slowly across the room, and the lights brighten and then dim again as she passes. "All," she says, and sits down on the bunk. The reading light at the end of the bed goes on.

"What?" I say, and wish I still had the translator.

"Curse everybody," she says. "You. Me. All." She crosses her dirty-looking hands over her breast and lies down on the bed. The lights go out. It is just like old times.

In a minute she'll get tired of it being dark and get up, and I'll go back to labeling the jigsawed pieces of the blue vase so a team of archaeologists who have not yet been killed by the curse can put it back together. But for now I have to sit in the dark.

"Curse everybody." Even the Lisii team. Because of the relay in my tent, the Sandalman thought they were helping me get the treasure off Colchis. He buried them alive in the cave they were excavating. He couldn't kill Bradstreet because he was halfway to the Spine with a broken-down Swallow, and by the time he got it fixed the Commission had landed, and he'd been fired, and my boss had hired him to file stories on the hearings. They have the Sandalman in custody in a geodome like the one he burned down. The rest of the suhundulim sit in on the Commission's hearings, but the beys, according to Bradstreet, don't pay any attention to them. They are more interested in the Commission's judicial wigs. They have stolen four of them so far.

Evelyn's bey gets up and then flops back down on the bunk, trying to make the highlights flicker. She is not at all curious about this story I am writing, this tale of murder and poison and other curses men fall victim to. Maybe her people got enough of that in the good old days. Maybe Borchardt was wrong and the suhundulim didn't take Colchis away from them at all. Maybe the minute they landed, the beys said, "Here. Take it. Hurry."

She has fallen asleep. I can hear her quiet, even breathing. She is not under the curse, at least.

I saved her, and I saved the princess, even though I was a thousand years too late. So maybe I am not entirely in its clutches either. But in a few minutes I will go turn on a light and finish this story, and when I'm done with it I'll put it in a nice, safe place. Like a tomb. Or a refrigerator.

Why? Because having gotten this story at such great cost I am determined to tell it? Or because the curse of kings stands all around me like a cage, hangs overhead like a tangle of electrical cords?

"The curse of kings and keepers," I say, and my bey scrambles off the bunk and tears out of the cabin to fetch me a drink of water in a Coke bottle she must have been carrying when I dragged her on board, as if I were her new patient and lay under a drape of plasticmesh, already dying.

# Even the Queen

The phone sang as I was looking over the defense's motion to dismiss. "It's the universal ring," my law clerk Bysshe said, reaching for it. "It's probably the defendant. They don't let you use signatures from jail."

"No, it's not," I said. "It's my mother."

"Oh." Bysshe reached for the receiver. "Why isn't she using her signature?"

"Because she knows I don't want to talk to her. She must have found out what Perdita's done."

"Your daughter Perdita?" he asked, holding the receiver against his chest. "The one with the little girl?"

"No, that's Viola. Perdita's my younger daughter. The one with no sense."

"What's she done?"

"She's joined the Cyclists."

Bysshe looked inquiringly blank, but I was not in the mood to enlighten him. Or in the mood to talk to Mother. "I know exactly what Mother will say. She'll ask me why I didn't tell her, and then she'll demand to know what I'm going to do about it, and there is nothing I can do about it, or I obviously would have done it already."

Bysshe looked bewildered. "Do you want me to tell her you're in court?"

"No." I reached for the receiver. "I'll have to talk to her sooner or later." I took it from him. "Hello, Mother," I said.

"Traci," Mother said dramatically, "Perdita has become a Cyclist."

"I know."

"Why didn't you tell me?"

"I thought Perdita should tell you herself."

"Perdita!" She snorted. "She wouldn't tell me. She knows what I'd have to say about it. I suppose you told Karen."

"Karen's not here. She's in Iraq." The only good thing about this whole debacle was that thanks to Iraq's eagerness to show it was a responsible world-community member and its previous penchant for self-destruction, my mother-in-law was in the one place on the planet where the phone service was bad enough that I could claim I'd tried to call her but couldn't get through, and she'd have to believe me.

The Liberation has freed us from all sorts of indignities and scourges, including Iraq's Saddams, but mothers-in-law aren't one of them, and I was almost happy with Perdita for her excellent timing. When I didn't want to kill her.

"What's Karen doing in Iraq?" Mother asked.

"Negotiating a Palestinian homeland."

"And meanwhile her granddaughter is ruining her life," she said irrelevantly. "Did you tell Viola?"

"I *told* you, Mother. I thought Perdita should tell all of you herself."

"Well, she didn't. And this morning one of my patients, Carol Chen, called me and demanded to know what I was keeping from her. I had no idea what she was talking about."

"How did Carol Chen find out?"

"From her daughter, who almost joined the Cyclists last year. *Her* family talked her out of it," she said accusingly. "Carol was convinced the medical community had discovered some terrible side effect of ammenerol and were covering it up. I cannot believe you didn't tell me, Traci."

And I cannot believe I didn't have Bysshe tell her I was in court, I thought. "I told you, Mother. I thought it was Perdita's place to tell you. After all, it's her decision."

"Oh, *Trac*i!" Mother said. "You cannot mean that!"

In the first fine flush of freedom after the Liberation, I had entertained hopes that it would change everything—that it would somehow do away with inequality and matriarchal dominance and those humorless women determined to eliminate the word "manhole" and third-person singular pronouns from the language.

Of course it didn't. Men still make more money, "herstory" is still a blight on the semantic landscape, and my mother can still say, "Oh, *Trac*i!" in a tone that reduces me to preadolescence.

"Her decision!" Mother said. "Do you mean to tell me you plan to stand idly by and allow your daughter to make the mistake of her life?"

"What can I do? She's twenty-two years old and of sound mind."

"If she were of sound mind, she wouldn't be doing this. Didn't you try to talk her out of it?"

"Of course I did, Mother."

"And?"

"And I didn't succeed. She's determined to become a Cyclist."

"Well, there must be something we can do. Get an injunction or hire a deprogrammer or sue the Cyclists for brainwashing. You're a judge, there must be some law you can invoke—"

"The law is called personal sovereignty, Mother, and since it was what made the Liberation possible in the first place, it can hardly be used against Perdita. Her decision meets all the criteria for a case of personal sovereignty: It's a personal decision, it was made by a sovereign adult, it affects no one else—"

"What about my practice? Carol Chen is convinced shunts cause cancer."

"Any effect on your practice is considered an indirect effect. Like secondary smoke. It doesn't apply. Mother, whether we like it or not, Perdita has a perfect right to do this, and we don't have any right to interfere. A free society has to be based on respecting others' opinions and leaving each other alone. We have to respect Perdita's right to make her own decisions."

All of which was true. It was too bad I hadn't said any of it to Perdita when she called. What I had said, in a tone that sounded exactly like my mother's, was "Oh, Perdita!"

"This is all your fault, you know," Mother said. "I *told* you you shouldn't have let her get that tattoo over her shunt. And don't tell me it's a free society. What good is a free society when it allows my granddaughter to ruin her life?" She hung up.

I handed the receiver back to Bysshe.

"I really liked what you said about respecting your daughter's right to make her own decisions," he said. He held out my robe. "And about not interfering in her life."

"I want you to research the precedents on deprogramming for me," I said, sliding my arms into the sleeves. "And find out if the Cyclists have been charged with any free-choice violations—brainwashing, intimidation, coercion."

The phone sang, another universal. "Hello, who's calling?" Bysshe said cautiously. His voice became suddenly friendlier. "Just a minute." He put his hand over the receiver. "It's your daughter Viola."

I took the receiver. "Hello, Viola."

"I just talked to Grandma," she said. "You will not believe what Perdita's done now. She's joined the Cyclists."

"I know," I said.

"You *know*? And you didn't tell me? I can't believe this. You never tell me anything."

"I thought Perdita should tell you herself," I said tiredly.

"Are you kidding? She never tells me anything either. That time she had eyebrow implants, she didn't tell me for three weeks, and when she got the laser tattoo, she didn't tell me at all. *Twidge* told me. You should have called me. Did you tell Grandma Karen?"

"She's in Baghdad," I said.

"I know," Viola said. "I called her."

"Oh, Viola, you didn't!"

"Unlike you, Mom, I believe in telling members of our family about matters that concern them."

"What did she say?" I asked, a kind of numbness settling over me now that the shock had worn off.

"I couldn't get through to her. The phone service over there is terrible. I got somebody who didn't speak English, and then I got cut off, and when I tried again, they said the whole city was down."

Thank you, I breathed silently. Thank you, thank you, thank you.

"Grandma Karen has a right to know, Mother. Think of the effect this could have on Twidge. She thinks Perdita's wonderful. When Perdita got the eyebrow implants, Twidge glued LEDs to hers, and I almost never got them off. What if Twidge decides to join the Cyclists, too?"

"Twidge is only nine. By the time she's supposed to get her shunt, Perdita will have long since quit." I hope, I added silently. Perdita had had the tattoo for a year and a half now and showed no signs of tiring of it. "Besides, Twidge has more sense."

"It's true. Oh, Mother, how *could* Perdita do this? Didn't you tell her about how awful it was?"

"Yes," I said. "And inconvenient. And unpleasant and unbalancing and painful. None of it made the slightest impact on her. She told me she thought it would be fun."

Bysshe was pointing to his watch and mouthing, "Time for court."

"Fun!" Viola said. "When she saw what I went through that time? Honestly, Mother, sometimes I think she's completely brain dead. Can't you have her declared incompetent and locked up or something?"

"No," I said, trying to zip up my robe with one hand. "Viola, I have to go. I'm late for court. I'm afraid there's nothing we can do to stop her. She's a rational adult."

"Rational!" Viola said. "Her eyebrows light up, Mother. She has Custer's Last Stand lased on her arm."

I handed the phone to Bysshe. "Tell Viola I'll talk to her tomorrow." I zipped up my robe. "And then call Baghdad and see how long they expect the phones to be out." I started into the courtroom. "And if there are any more universal calls, make sure they're local before you answer."

⊣•••⊢

Bysshe couldn't get through to Baghdad, which I took as a good sign, and my mother-in-law didn't call. Mother did, in the afternoon, to ask if lobotomies were legal.

She called again the next day. I was in the middle of my Personal Sovereignty class, explaining the inherent right of citizens in a free society to make complete jackasses of themselves. They weren't buying it.

"I think it's your mother," Bysshe whispered to me as he handed me the phone. "She's still using the universal. But it's local. I checked."

"Hello, Mother," I said.

"It's all arranged," Mother said. "We're having lunch with Perdita at McGregor's. It's on the corner of Twelfth Street and Larimer."

"I'm in the middle of class," I said.

"I know. I won't keep you. I just wanted to tell you not to worry. I've taken care of everything."

I didn't like the sound of that. "What have you done?"

"Invited Perdita to lunch with us. I told you. At McGregor's."

"Who is 'us,' Mother?"

"Just the family," she said innocently. "You and Viola."

Well, at least she hadn't brought in the deprogrammer. Yet. "What are you up to, Mother?"

"Perdita said the same thing. Can't a grandmother ask her granddaughters to lunch? Be there at twelve-thirty."

"Bysshe and I have a court-calendar meeting at three."

"Oh, we'll be done by then. And bring Bysshe with you. He can provide a man's point of view."

She hung up.

"You'll have to go to lunch with me, Bysshe," I said. "Sorry."

"Why? What's going to happen at lunch?"

"I have no idea."

⊣•••⊢

On the way over to McGregor's, Bysshe told me what he'd found out about the Cyclists. "They're not a cult. There's no religious connection. They seem to have grown out of a pre-Liberation women's group," he said, looking at his notes, "although there are also links to the pro-choice movement, the University of Wisconsin, and the Museum of Modern Art."

"What?"

"They call their group leaders 'docents.' Their philosophy seems to be a mix of pre-Liberation radical feminism and the environmental primitivism of the eighties. They're floratarians and they don't wear shoes."

"Or shunts," I said. We pulled up in front of McGregor's and got out of the car. "Any mind-control convictions?" I asked hopefully.

"No. A bunch of suits against individual members, all of which they won."

"On grounds of personal sovereignty."

"Yeah. And a criminal one by a member whose family tried to deprogram her. The deprogrammer was sentenced to twenty years, and the family got twelve."

"Be sure to tell Mother about that one," I said, and opened the door to McGregor's.

It was one of those restaurants with a morning-glory vine twining around the maitre d's desk and garden plots between the tables.

"Perdita suggested it," Mother said, guiding Bysshe and me past the onions to our table. "She told me a lot of the Cyclists are floratarians."

"Is she here?" I asked, sidestepping a cucumber frame.

"Not yet." She pointed past a rose arbor. "There's our table."

Our table was a wicker affair under a mulberry tree. Viola and Twidge were seated on the far side next to a trellis of runner beans, looking at menus.

"What are you doing here, Twidge?" I asked. "Why aren't you in school?"

"I am," she said, holding up her LCD slate. "I'm remoting today."

"I thought she should be part of this discussion," Viola said. "After all, she'll be getting her shunt soon."

"My friend Kensy says she isn't going to get one. Like Perdita," Twidge said.

"I'm sure Kensy will change her mind when the time comes," Mother said. "Perdita will change hers, too. Bysshe, why don't you sit next to Viola?"

Bysshe slid obediently past the trellis and sat down in the wicker chair at the far end of the table. Twidge reached across Viola and handed him a menu. "This is a great restaurant," she said. "You don't have to wear shoes." She held up a bare foot to illustrate. "And if you get hungry while you're waiting, you can just pick something." She twisted around in her chair, picked two of the green beans, gave one to Bysshe, and bit into the other one. "I bet Kensy doesn't. Kensy says a shunt hurts worse than braces."

"It doesn't hurt as much as not having one," Viola said, shooting me a Now-Do-You-See-What-My-Sister's-Caused? look.

"Traci, why don't you sit across from Viola?" Mother said to me. "And we'll put Perdita next to you when she comes."

"If she comes," Viola said.

"I told her one o'clock," Mother said, sitting dawn at the near end. "So we'd have a chance to plan our strategy before she gets here. I talked to Carol Chen—"

"Her daughter nearly joined the Cyclists last year," I explained to Bysshe and Viola.

"*She* said they had a family gathering, like this, and simply talked to her daughter, and she decided she didn't want to be a Cyclist after all." She looked around the table. "So I thought we'd do the same thing with Perdita. I think we should start by explaining the significance of the Liberation and the days of dark oppression that preceded it—"

"*I* think," Viola interrupted, "we should try to talk her into just going off the ammenerol for a few months instead of having the shunt removed. If she comes. Which she won't."

"Why not?"

"Would you? I mean, it's like the Inquisition. Her sitting here while all of us 'explain' at her. Perdita may be crazy, but she's not stupid."

"It's hardly the Inquisition," Mother said. She looked anxiously past me toward the door. "I'm sure Perdita—" She stopped, stood up, and plunged off suddenly through the asparagus.

I turned around, half expecting Perdita with light-up lips or a full-body tattoo, but I couldn't see through the leaves. I pushed at the branches.

"Is it Perdita?" Viola said, leaning forward.

I peered around the mulberry bush. "Oh, my God," I said.

It was my mother-in-law, wearing a black abayah and a silk yarmulke. She swept toward us through a pumpkin patch, robes billowing and eyes flashing. Mother hurried in her wake of trampled radishes, looking daggers at me.

I turned them on Viola. "It's your Grandmother Karen," I said accusingly. "You told me you didn't get through to her."

"I didn't," she said. "Twidge, sit up straight. And put your slate down."

There was an ominous rustling in the rose arbor, as of leaves shrinking back in terror, and my mother-in-law arrived.

"Karen!" I said, trying to sound pleased. "What on earth are you doing here? I thought you were in Baghdad."

"I came back as soon as I got Viola's message," she said, glaring at everyone in turn. "Who's this?" she demanded, pointing at Bysshe. "Viola's new live-in?"

"No!" Bysshe said, looking horrified.

"This is my law clerk, Mother," I said. "Bysshe Adams-Hardy."

"Twidge, why aren't you in school?"

"I *am*," Twidge said. "I'm remoting." She held up her slate. "See? Math."

"I see," she said, turning to glower at me. "It's a serious enough matter to require my great-grandchild's being pulled out of school *and* the hiring of legal assistance, and yet you didn't deem it important enough to notify *me*. Of course, you *never* tell me anything, Traci."

She swirled herself into the end chair, sending leaves and sweet-pea blossoms flying and decapitating the broccoli centerpiece. "I didn't get Viola's cry for help until yesterday. Viola, you should never leave messages with Hassim. His English is virtually nonexistent. I had to get him to hum me your ring. I recognized your signature, but the phones were out, so I flew home. In the middle of negotiations, I might add."

"How *are* negotiations going, Grandma Karen?" Viola asked.

"They *were* going extremely well. The Israelis have given the Palestinians half of Jerusalem, and they've agreed to time-share the Golan Heights." She turned to glare momentarily at me. "*They* know the importance of communication." She turned back to Viola. "So why are they picking on you, Viola? Don't they like your new live-in?"

"I am *not* her live-in," Bysshe protested.

I have often wondered how on earth my mother-in-law became a mediator and what she does in all those negotiation sessions with Serbs and

Catholics and North and South Koreans and Protestants and Croats. She takes sides, jumps to conclusions, misinterprets everything you say, refuses to listen. And yet she talked South Africa into a Mandelan government and would probably get the Palestinians to observe Yom Kippur. Maybe she just bullies everyone into submission. Or maybe they have to band together to protect themselves against her.

Bysshe was still protesting. "I never even met Viola till today. I've only talked to her on the phone a couple of times."

"You must have done *something*," Karen said to Viola. "They're obviously out for your blood."

"Not mine," Viola said.-"Perdita's. She's joined the Cyclists."

"The Cyclists? I left the West Bank negotiations because you don't approve of Perdita joining a biking club? How am I supposed to explain this to the president of Iraq? She will *not* understand, and neither do I. A biking club!"

"The Cyclists do not ride bicycles," Mother said.

"They menstruate," Twidge said.

There was a dead silence of at least a minute, and I thought, it's finally happened. My mother-in-law and I are actually going to be on the same side of a family argument.

"All this fuss is over Perdita's having her shunt removed?" Karen said finally. "She's of age, isn't she? And this is obviously a case where personal sovereignty applies. You should know that, Traci. After all, you're a judge."

I should have known it was too good to be true.

"You mean you approve of her setting back the Liberation twenty years?" Mother said.

"I hardly think it's that serious," Karen said. "There are antishunt groups in the Middle East, too, you know, but no one takes them seriously. Not even the Iraqis, and they still wear the veil."

"Perdita is taking them seriously."

Karen dismissed Perdita with a wave of her black sleeve. "They're a trend, a fad. Like microskirts. Or those dreadful electronic eyebrows. A few women wear silly fashions like that for a little while, but you don't see women as a whole giving up pants or going back to wearing hats."

"But Perdita..." Viola said.

"If Perdita wants to have her period, I say let her. Women functioned perfectly well without shunts for thousands of years."

Mother brought her fist down on the table. "Women also functioned *perfectly well* with concubinage, cholera, and corsets," she said, emphasizing each word with her fist. "But that is no reason to take them on voluntarily, and I have no intention of allowing Perdita—"

"Speaking of Perdita, where is the poor child?" Karen said.

"She'll be here any minute," Mother said. "I invited her to lunch so we could discuss this with her."

"Ha!" Karen said. "So you could browbeat her into changing her mind, you mean. Well, I have no intention of collaborating with you. *I* intend to listen to the poor thing's point of view with interest and an open mind. 'Respect,' that's the key word, and one you all seem to have forgotten. Respect and common courtesy."

A barefoot young woman wearing a flowered smock and a red scarf tied around her left arm carne up to the table with a sheaf of pink folders.

"It's about time," Karen said, snatching one of the folders away from her. "Your service here is dreadful. I've been sitting here for ten minutes. She snapped the folder open. "I don't suppose you have Scotch."

"My name is Evangeline," the young woman said. "I'm Perdita's docent." She took the folder away from Karen. "She wasn't able to join you for lunch, but she asked me to come in her place and explain the Cyclist philosophy to you."

She sat down in the wicker chair next to me.

"The Cyclists are dedicated to freedom," she said. "Freedom from artificiality, freedom from body-controlling drugs and hormones, freedom from the male patriarchy that attempts to impose them on us. As you probably already know, we do not wear shunts."

She pointed to the red scarf around her arm. "Instead, we wear this as a badge of our freedom and our femaleness. I'm wearing it today to announce that my time of fertility has come."

"We had that, too," Mother said, "only we wore it on the back of our skirts."

I laughed.

The docent glared at me. "Male domination of women's bodies began long before the so-called 'Liberation,' with government regulation of abortion and fetal rights, scientific control of fertility, and finally the development of ammenerol, which eliminated the reproductive cycle altogether. This was all part of a carefully planned takeover of women's bodies, and by extension, their identities, by the male patriarchal regime."

"What an interesting point of view!" Karen said enthusiastically.

It certainly was. In point of fact, ammenerol hadn't been invented to eliminate menstruation at all. It had been developed for shrinking malignant tumors, and its uterine lining-absorbing properties had only been discovered by accident.

"Are you trying to tell us," Mother said, "that men *forced* shunts on women? We had to *fight* everyone to get ammenerol approved by the FDA!"

It was true. What surrogate mothers and antiabortionists and the fetal-rights issue had failed to do in uniting women, the prospect of not having to menstruate did. Women had organized rallies, petitioned, elected senators, passed amendments, been excommunicated, and gone to jail, all in the name of Liberation.

"Men were *against* it," Mother said, getting rather red in the face. "And the religious right, and the maxipad manufacturers, and the Catholic Church—

"They knew they'd have to allow women priests," Viola said.

"Which they did," I said.

"The Liberation hasn't freed you," the docent said loudly. "Except from the natural rhythms of your life, the very wellspring of your femaleness."

She leaned over and picked a daisy that was growing under the table. "We in the Cyclists celebrate the onset of our menses and rejoice in our bodies," she said, holding the daisy up. "Whenever a Cyclist comes into blossom, as we call it, she is honored with flowers and poems and songs. Then we join hands and tell what we like best about our menses."

"Water retention," I said.

"Or lying in bed with a heating pad for three days a month," Mother said.

"*I* think I like the anxiety attacks best," Viola said. "When I went off the ammenerol, so I could have Twidge, I'd have these days where I was convinced the space station was going to fall on me."

A middle-aged woman in overalls and a straw hat had come over while Viola was talking and was standing next to Mother's chair. "I had these mood swings," she said. "One minute I'd feel cheerful and the next like Lizzie Borden."

"Who's Lizzie Borden?" Twidge asked.

"She killed her parents," Bysshe said. "With an ax."

Karen and the docent glared at both of them. "Aren't you supposed to be working on your math, Twidge?" Karen said.

"I've always wondered if Lizzie Borden had PMS," Viola said, "and that was why—"

"No," Mother said. "It was having to live before tampons and ibuprofen. An obvious case of justifiable homicide."

"I hardly think this sort of levity is helpful," Karen said, glowering at everyone.

"Are you our waitress?" I asked the straw-hatted woman hastily.

"Yes," she said, producing a slate from her overalls pocket

"Do you serve wine?" I asked.

"Yes. Dandelion, cowslip, and primrose."

"We'll take them all."

"A bottle of each?"

"For now," I said. "Unless you have them in kegs."

"Our specials for today are watermelon salad and *choufleur gratinée*," she said, smiling at everyone. Karen and the docent did not smile back. "You handpick your own cauliflower from the patch up front. The floratarian special is sautéed lily buds with marigold butter."

There was a temporary truce while everyone ordered. "I'll have the sweet peas," the docent said, "and a glass of rose water."

Bysshe leaned over to Viola. "I'm sorry I sounded so horrified when your grandmother asked if I was your live-in," he said.

"That's okay," Viola said. "Grandma Karen can be pretty scary."

"I just didn't want you to think I didn't like you. I do. Like you, I mean."

"Don't they have soyburgers?" Twidge asked.

As soon as the waitress left, the docent began passing out the pink folders she'd brought with her. "These will explain the working philosophy of the Cyclists," she said, handing me one, "along with practical information on the menstrual cycle." She handed Twidge one.

"It looks just like those books we used to get in junior high," Mother said, looking at hers. "'A Special Gift,' they were called, and they had all these pictures of girls with pink ribbons in their hair, playing tennis and smiling. Blatant misrepresentation."

She was right. There was even the same drawing of the fallopian tubes I remembered from my middle-school movie, a drawing that had always reminded me of *Alien* in the early stages.

"Oh, yuck," Twidge said. "This is disgusting."

"Do your math," Karen said.

Bysshe looked sick. "Did women really *do* this stuff?"

The wine arrived, and I poured everyone a large glass. The docent pursed her lips disapprovingly and shook her head. "The Cyclists do not use the artificial stimulants or hormones that the male patriarchy has forced on women to render them docile and subservient."

"How long do you menstruate?" Twidge asked.

"Forever," Mother said.

"Four to six days," the docent said. "It's there in the booklet."

"No, I mean, your whole life or what?"

"A woman has her menarche at twelve years old on the average and ceases menstruating at age fifty-five."

"I had my first period at eleven," the waitress said, setting a bouquet down in front of me. "At school."

"I had my last one on the day the FDA approved ammenerol," Mother said.

"Three hundred and sixty-five divided by twenty-eight," Twidge said, writing on her slate. "Times forty-three years." She looked up. "That's five hundred and fifty-nine periods."

"That can't be right," Mother said, taking the slate away from her. "It's at least five thousand."

"And they all start on the day you leave on a trip," Viola said.

"Or get married," the waitress said. Mother began writing on the slate.

I took advantage of the cease-fire to pour everyone some more dandelion wine.

Mother looked up from the slate. "Do you realize with a period of five days, you'd be menstruating for nearly three thousand days? That's over eight solid years."

"And in between there's PMS," the waitress said, delivering flowers.

"What's PMS?" Twidge asked.

"Premenstrual syndrome was the name the male medical establishment fabricated for the natural variation in hormonal levels that signal the onset of menstruation," the docent said. "This mild and entirely normal fluctuation was exaggerated by men into a debility." She looked at Karen for confirmation.

"I used to cut my hair," Karen said.

The docent looked uneasy.

"Once I chopped off one whole side," Karen went on. "Bob had to hide the scissors every month. And the car keys. I'd start to cry every time I hit a red light."

"Did you swell up?" Mother asked, pouring Karen another glass of dandelion wine.

"I looked just like Orson Welles."

"Who's Orson Welles?" Twidge asked.

"Your comments reflect the self-loathing thrust on you by the patriarchy," the docent said. "Men have brainwashed women into thinking menstruation is evil and unclean. Women even called their menses 'the curse' because they accepted men's judgment."

"I called it the curse because I thought a witch must have laid a curse on me," Viola said. "Like in 'Sleeping Beauty.'"

Everyone looked at her.

"Well, I did," she said. "It was the only reason I could think of for such an awful thing happening to me." She handed the folder back to the docent. "It still is."

"I think you were awfully brave," Bysshe said to Viola, "going off the ammenerol to have Twidge."

"It was awful," Viola said. "You can't imagine."

Mother sighed. "When I got my period, I asked my mother if Annette had it, too."

"Who's Annette?" Twidge said.

"A Mouseketeer," Mother said, and added, at Twidge's uncomprehending look, "On TV."

"High-rez," Viola said.

"The Mickey Mouse Club," Mother said.

"There was a high-rezzer called the Mickey Mouse Club?" Twidge said incredulously.

"They were days of dark oppression in many ways," I said.

Mother glared at me. "Annette was every young girl's ideal," she said to Twidge. "Her hair was curly, she had actual breasts, her pleated skirt was always pressed, and I could not imagine that she could have anything so *messy* and undignified. Mr. Disney would never have allowed it. And if Annette didn't have one, I wasn't going to have one either. So I asked my mother—"

"What did she say?" Twidge cut in.

"She said every woman had periods," Mother said. "So I asked her, 'Even the Queen of England?' And she said, 'Even the Queen.'"

"Really?" Twidge said. "But she's so *old!*"

"She isn't having it now," the docent said irritatedly. "I told you, menopause occurs at age fifty-five."

"And then you have hot flashes," Karen said, "and osteoporosis and so much hair on your upper lip, you look like Mark Twain."

"Who's—" Twidge said.

"You are simply reiterating negative male propaganda," the docent interrupted, looking very red in the face.

"You know what I've always wondered?" Karen said, leaning conspiratorially close to Mother. "If Maggie Thatcher's menopause was responsible for the Falklands War."

"Who's Maggie Thatcher?" Twidge said.

The docent, who was now as red in the face as her scarf, stood up. "It is clear there is no point in trying to talk to you. You've all been completely brainwashed by the male patriarchy." She began grabbing up her folders. "You're blind, all of you! You don't even see that you're victims of a male conspiracy to deprive you of your biological identity, of your very womanhood. The Liberation wasn't a liberation at all. It was only another kind of slavery."

"Even if that were true," I said, "even if it had been a conspiracy to bring us under male domination, it would have been worth it."

"She's right, you know," Karen said to Mother. "Traci's absolutely right. There are some things worth giving up anything for, even your freedom, and getting rid of your period is definitely one of them."

"Victims!" the docent shouted. "You've been stripped of your femininity, and you don't even care!" She stomped out, destroying several squash and a row of gladiolas in the process.

"You know what I hated most before the Liberation?" Karen said, pouring the last of the dandelion wine into her glass. "Sanitary belts."

"And those cardboard tampon applicators," Mother said.

"I'm never going to join the Cyclists," Twidge said.

"Good," I said.

"Can I have dessert?"

I called the waitress over, and Twidge ordered sugared violets. "Anyone else want dessert?" I asked. "Or more primrose wine?"

"I think it's wonderful the way you're trying to help your sister," Bysshe said, leaning closer to Viola.

"And those Modess ads," Mother said. "You remember, with those glamorous women in satin-brocade evening dresses and long white gloves, and below the picture was written, 'Modess, because...' I thought Modess was a perfume."

Karen giggled. "I thought it was a brand of *champagne!*"

"I don't think we'd better have any more wine," I said.

⊣•••⊢

The phone started singing the minute I got to my chambers the next morning, the universal ring.

"Karen went back to Iraq, didn't she?" I asked Bysshe.

"Yeah," he said. "Viola said there was some snag over whether to put Disneyland on the West Bank or not."

"When did Viola call?"

Bysshe looked sheepish. "I had breakfast with her and Twidge this morning."

"Oh." I picked up the phone. "It's probably Mother with a plan to kidnap Perdita. Hello?"

"This is Evangeline, Perdita's docent," the voice on the phone said. "I hope you're happy. You've bullied Perdita into surrendering to the enslaving male patriarchy."

"I have?" I said.

"You obviously employed mind control, and I want you to know we intend to file charges." She hung up. The phone rang again immediately, another universal.

"What is the good of signatures when no one ever uses them?" I said, and picked up the phone.

"Hi, Mom," Perdita said. "I thought you'd want to know I've changed my mind about joining the Cyclists."

"Really?" I said, trying not to sound jubilant.

"I found out they wear this red scarf thing on their arm. It covers up Sitting Bull's horse."

"That is a problem," I said.

"Well, that's not all. My docent told me about your lunch. Did Grandma Karen really tell you you were right?"

"Yes."

"Gosh! I didn't believe that part. Well, anyway, my docent said you wouldn't listen to her about how great menstruating is, that you all kept talking about the negative aspects of it, like bloating and cramps and crabbiness, and I said, 'What are cramps?' and she said, 'Menstrual bleeding frequently causes headaches and discomfort,' and I said, 'Bleeding?

Nobody ever said anything about bleeding!' Why didn't you tell me there was blood involved, Mother?"

I had, but I felt it wiser to keep silent.

"And you didn't say a word about its being painful. And all the hormone fluctuations! Anybody'd have to be crazy to want to go through that when they didn't have to! How did you stand it before the Liberation?"

"They were days of dark oppression," I said.

"I *guess!* Well, anyway, I quit, and so my docent is really mad. But I told her it was a case of personal sovereignty, and she has to respect my decision. I'm still going to become a floratarian, though, and I *don't* want you to try to talk me out of it."

"I wouldn't dream of it," I said.

"You know, this whole thing is really your fault, Mom! If you'd told me about the pain part in the first place, none of this would have happened. Viola's right! You never tell us *anything!*"

# Inn

Christmas Eve. The organ played the last notes of "O Come, O Come Emmanuel," and the choir sat down. Reverend Will hobbled slowly to the pulpit, clutching his sheaf of yellowed typewritten sheets.

In the choir, Dee leaned over to Sharon and whispered, "Here we go. Twenty-four minutes and counting."

On Sharon's other side, Virginia murmured, "'And all went to be taxed, every one into his own city.'"

Reverend Wall set the papers on the pulpit, looked rheumily out over the congregation, and said, "'And all went to be taxed, every one into his own city. And Joseph also went up from Galilee, out of the city of Nazareth, into Judea, unto the city of David, which is called Bethlehem, because he was of the house and lineage of David. To be taxed with Mary, his espoused wife, being great with child.'" He paused.

"We know nothing of that journey up from Nazareth," Virginia whispered.

"We know nothing of that journey up from Nazareth," Reverend Wall said, in a wavering voice, "what adventures befell the young couple, what inns they stopped at along the way. All we know is that on a Christmas Eve like this one they arrived in Bethlehem, and there was no room for then at the inn."

Virginia was scribbling something on the margin of her bulletin. Dee started to cough. "Do you have any cough drops?" she whispered to Sharon.

"What happened to the ones I gave you last night?" Sharon whispered back.

"Though we know nothing of their journey," Reverend Wall said, his voice growing stronger, "we know much of the world they lived in. It was a world of censuses and soldiers, of bureaucrats and politicians, a world busy with property and rules and its own affairs."

*Dee started to cough again. She rummaged in the pocket of her music folder and came up with a paper-wrapped cough drop. She unwrapped it and popped it into her mouth.*

*"...a world too busy with its own business to even notice an insignificant couple from far away," Reverend Wall intoned.*

*Virginia passed her bulletin to Sharon. Dee leaned over to read it, too. It read, "What happened here last night after the rehearsal? When I came home from the mall, there were police cars outside."*

*Dee grabbed the bulletin and rummaged in her folder again. She found a pencil, scribbled "Somebody broke into the church," and passed it across Sharon to Virginia.*

*"You're kidding," Virginia whispered. "Were they caught?"*

*"No," Sharon said.*

The rehearsal on the twenty-third was supposed to start at seven. By a quarter to eight the choir was still standing at the back of the sanctuary, waiting to sing the processional, the shepherds and angels were bouncing off the walls, and Reverend Wall, in his chair behind the pulpit, had nodded off. The assistant minister, Reverend Lisa Farrison, was moving poinsettias onto the chancel steps to make room for the manger, and the choir director, Rose Henderson, was on her knees, hammering wooden bases onto the cardboard palm trees. They had fallen down twice already.

"What do you think are the chances we'll still be here when it's time for the Christmas Eve service to start tomorrow night?" Sharon said, leaning against the sanctuary door.

"I can't be," Virginia said, looking at her watch. "I've got to be out at the mall before nine. Megan suddenly announced she wants Senior Prom Barbie."

"My throat feels terrible," Dee said, feeling her glands. "Is it hot in here, or am I getting a fever?"

"It's hot in these robes," Sharon said. "Why are we wearing them? This is a rehearsal."

"Rose wanted everything to be exactly like it's going to be tomorrow night."

"If I'm exactly like this tomorrow night, I'll be dead," Dee said, trying to clear her throat. "I can't get sick. I don't have any of the presents wrapped, and I haven't even thought about what we're having for Christmas dinner."

"At least you *have* presents," Virginia said. "I have eight people left to buy for. Not counting Senior Prom Barbie."

"I don't have anything done. Christmas cards, shopping, wrapping, baking, nothing, and Bill's parents are coming," Sharon said. "Come on, let's get this show on the road."

Rose and one of the junior choir angels hoisted the palm trees to standing. They listed badly to the right, as if Bethlehem were experiencing a hurricane. "Is that straight?" Rose called to the back of the church.

"Yes," Sharon said.

"Lying in church," Dee said. "Tsk, tsk."

"All right," Rose said, picking up a bulletin. "Listen up, everybody. Here's the order of worship. Introit by the brass quartet, processional, opening prayer, announcements—Reverend Farrison, is that where you want to talk about the 'Least of These' Project?"

"Yes," Reverend Farrison said. She walked to the front of the sanctuary. "And can I make a quick announcement right now?" She turned and faced the choir. "If anybody has anything else to donate, you need to bring it to the church by tomorrow morning at nine," she said briskly. "That's when we're going to deliver them to the homeless. We still need blankets and canned goods. Bring them to the Fellowship Hall."

She walked back down the aisle, and Rose started in on her list again. "Announcements, 'O Come, O Come, Emmanuel,' Reverend Wall's sermon—"

Reverend Wall nodded awake at his name. "Ah," he said, and hobbled toward the pulpit, clutching a sheaf of yellowed typewritten papers.

"Oh, no," Sharon said. "Not a Christmas pageant *and* a sermon. We'll be here forever."

"Not *a* sermon," Virginia said. "*The* sermon. All twenty-four minutes of it. I've got it memorized. He's given it every year since he came."

"Longer than that," Dee said. "I swear last year I heard him say something in it about World War I."

"'And all went to be taxed, every one into his own city,'" Reverend Wall said. "'And Joseph also went up from Galilee, out of the city of Nazareth.'"

"Oh, *no*," Sharon said. "He's going to give the whole sermon right now."

"We know nothing of that journey up from Bethlehem," he said.

"Thank you, Reverend Wall," Rose said. "After the sermon, the choir sings 'O Little Town of Bethlehem', and Mary and Joseph—"

"What message does the story of their journey hold for us?" Reverend Wall said, picking up steam.

Rose was hurrying up the aisle and up the chancel steps. "Reverend Wall, you don't need to run through your sermon right now."

"What does it say to us," he asked, "struggling to recover from a world war?"

Dee nudged Sharon.

"Reverend *Wall*," Rose said, reaching the pulpit. "I'm afraid we don't have time to go through your whole sermon right now. We need to run through the pageant now."

"Ah," he said, and gathered up his papers.

"All right," Rose said. "The choir sings 'O Little Town of Bethlehem', and Mary and Joseph, you come down the aisle."

Mary and Joseph, wearing bathrobes and Birkenstocks, assembled themselves at the back of the sanctuary, and started down the center aisle.

"No, no, Mary and Joseph, not that way," Rose said. "The wise men from the East have to come down the center aisle, and you're coming up from Nazareth. You two come down the side aisle."

Mary and Joseph obliged, taking the aisle at a trot.

"No, no, slow *down*," Rose said. "You're tired. You've walked all the way from Nazareth. Try it again."

They raced each other to the back of the church and started again, slower at first and then picking up speed.

"The congregation won't be able to see them," Rose said, shaking her head. "What about lighting the side aisle? Can we do that, Reverend Farrison?"

"She's not here," Dee said. "She went to get something."

"I'll go get her," Sharon said, and went down the hall.

Miriam Hoskins was just going into the adult Sunday school room with a paper plate of frosted cookies. "Do you know where Reverend Farrison is?" Sharon asked her.

"She was in the office a minute ago," Miriam said, pointing with the plate.

Sharon went down to the office. Reverend Farrison was standing at the desk, talking on the phone. "How soon can the van be here?" She motioned to Sharon she'd be a minute. "Well, can you find out?"

Sharon waited, looking at the desk. There was a glass dish of paper-wrapped cough drops next to the phone, and beside it a can of smoked oysters and three cans of water chestnuts. Probably for the 'Least of These' Project, she thought ruefully.

"Fifteen minutes? All right. Thank you," Reverend Farrison said, and hung up. "Just a minute," she told Sharon, and went to the outside door. She opened it and leaned out. Sharon could feel the icy air as she stood there. She wondered if it had started snowing.

"The van will be here in a few minutes," Reverend Farrison said to someone outside.

Sharon looked out the stained-glass panels on either side of the door, trying to see who was out there.

"It'll take you to the shelter," Reverend Farrison said. "No, you'll have to wait outside." She shut the door. "Now," she said, turning to Sharon, "what did you want, Mrs. Englert?"

Sharon said, still looking out the window, "They need you in the sanctuary." It was starting to snow. The flakes looked blue through the glass.

"I'll be right there," Reverend Farrison said. "I was just taking care of some homeless. That's the second couple we've had tonight. We always get them at Christmas. What's the problem? The palm trees?"

"What?" Sharon said, still looking at the snow.

Reverend Farrison followed her gaze. "The shelter van's coming for them in a few minutes," she said. "We can't let them stay in here unsupervised. First Methodist's had their collection stolen twice in the last month, and we've got all the donations for the 'Least of These' Project in there." She gestured toward the Fellowship Hall.

I thought they were *for* the homeless, Sharon thought. "Couldn't they just wait in the sanctuary or something?" she said.

Reverend Farrison sighed. "Letting them in isn't doing them a kindness. They come here instead of the shelter because the shelter confiscates their liquor." She started down the hall. "What did they need me for?"

"Oh," Sharon said, "the lights. They wanted to know if they could get lights over the side aisle for Mary and Joseph."

"I don't know," she said. "The lights in this church are such a mess." She stopped at the bank of switches next to the stairs that led down to the choir room and the Sunday school rooms. "Tell me what this turns on."

She flicked a switch. The hall light went off. She switched it back on and tried another one.

"That's the light in the office," Sharon said, "and the downstairs hall, and that one's the adult Sunday school room."

"What's this one?" Reverend Farrison said.

There was a yelp from the choir members. Kids screamed.

"The sanctuary," Sharon said. "Okay, that's the side aisle lights." She called down to the sanctuary. "How's that?"

"Fine," Rose called. "No, wait, the organ's off."

Reverend Farrison flicked another switch, and the organ came on with a groan.

"Now the side lights are off," Sharon said, "and so's the pulpit light."

"I told you they were a mess," Reverend Farrison said. She flicked another switch. "What did that do?"

"It turned the porch light off."

"Good. We'll leave it off. Maybe it will discourage any more homeless from coming," she said. "Reverend Wall let a homeless man wait inside last week, and he relieved himself on the carpet in the adult Sunday school room. We had to have it cleaned." She looked reprovingly at Sharon. "With these people, you can't let your compassion get the better of you."

No, Sharon thought. Jesus did, and look what happened to him.

⊣•••⊢

*"The innkeeper could have turned them away," Reverend Wall intoned. "He was a busy man, and his inn was full of travelers. He could have shut the door on Mary and Joseph."*

*Virginia leaned across Sharon to Dee. "Did whoever broke in take anything?"*

*"No," Sharon said.*

*"Whoever it was urinated on the floor in the nursery," Dee whispered, and Reverend Wall trailed off confusedly and looked over at the choir.*

*Dee began coughing loudly, trying to smother it with her hand. He smiled vaguely at her and started again. "The innkeeper could have turned them away."*

*Dee waited a minute, and then opened her hymnal to her bulletin and began writing on it. She passed it to Virginia, who read it and then passed it back to Sharon.*

*"Reverend Farrison thinks some of the homeless got in," it read. "They tore up the palm trees, too. Ripped the bases right off. Can you imagine anybody doing something like that?"*

*"As the innkeeper found room for Mary and Joseph that Christmas Eve long ago," Reverend Wall said, building to a finish "let us find room in our hearts for Christ. Amen."*

*The organ began the intro to "O Little Town of Bethlehem," and Mary and Joseph appeared at the back with Miriam Hoskins. She adjusted Mary's white veil and whispered something to them. Joseph pulled at his glued-on beard.*

*"What route did they finally decide on?" Virginia whispered. "In from the side or straight down the middle?"*

*"Side aisle," Sharon whispered.*

*The choir stood up. "'O little town of Bethlehem, how still we see thee lie,'" they sang. "Above thy deep and dreamless sleep, the silent stars go by.'"*

*Mary and Joseph started up the side aisle, taking the slow, measured steps Rose had coached them in, side by side. No, Sharon thought. That's not right. They didn't look like that. Joseph should be a little ahead of Mary, protecting her, and her hand should be on her stomach, protecting the baby.*

⊣••⊢

They eventually decided to wait on the decision of how Mary and Joseph would come, and started through the pageant. Mary and Joseph knocked on the door of the inn, and the innkeeper, grinning broadly, told them there wasn't any room.

"Patrick, don't look so happy," Rose said. "You're supposed to be in a bad mood. You're busy and tired, and you don't have any rooms left."

Patrick attempted a scowl. "I have no rooms left," he said, "but you can stay in the stable." He led them over to the manger, and Mary knelt down behind it.

"Where's the baby Jesus?" Rose said.

"He's not due till tomorrow night," Virginia whispered.

"Does anybody have a baby doll they can bring?" Rose asked.

One of the angels raised her hand, and Rose said, "Fine. Mary, use the blanket for now, and choir, you sing the first verse of 'Away in a Manger.'

Shepherds," she called to the back of the sanctuary, "as soon as 'Away in a Manger' is over, come up and stand on this side." She pointed.

The shepherds picked up an assortment of hockey sticks, broom handles, and canes taped to one-by-twos and adjusted their headcloths.

"All right, let's run through it," Rose said. "Organ?"

The organ played the opening chord, and the choir stood up.

"A-way," Dee sang and started to cough, choking into her hand. "Do—cough—drop?" she managed to gasp out between spasms.

"I saw some in the office," Sharon said, and ran down the chancel steps, down the aisle, and out into the hall.

It was dark, but she didn't want to take the time to try to find the right switch. She could more or less see her way by the lights from the sanctuary, and she thought she knew right where the cough drops were.

The office lights were off, too, and the porch light Reverend Farrison had turned off to discourage the homeless. She opened the office door, felt her way over to the desk and patted around till she found the glass dish. She grabbed a handful of cough drops and felt her way back out into the hall.

The choir was singing "It Came Upon a Midnight Clear," but after two measures they stopped, and in the sudden silence Sharon heard knocking.

She started for the door and then hesitated, wondering if this was the same couple Reverend Farrison had turned away earlier, coming back to make trouble, but the knocking was soft, almost diffident, and through the stained-glass panels she could see it was snowing hard.

She switched the cough drops to her left hand, opened the door a little, and looked out. There were two people standing on the porch, one in front of the other. It was too dark to do more than make out their outlines, and at first glance it looked like two women, but then the one in front said in a young man's voice, *"Erkas."*

"I'm sorry," Sharon said. "I don't speak Spanish. Are you looking for a place to stay?" The snow was turning to sleet, and the wind was picking up.

*"Kumrah,"* the young man said, making a sound like he was clearing his throat, and then a whole string of words she didn't recognize.

"Just a minute," she said, and shut the door. She went back into the office, felt for the phone, and, squinting at the buttons in the near-darkness, punched in the shelter number.

It was busy. She held down the receiver, waited a minute, and tried again. Still busy. She went back to the door, hoping they'd given up and gone away.

"*Erkas,*" the man said as soon as she opened it.

"I'm sorry," she said. "I'm trying to call the homeless shelter," and he began talking rapidly, excitedly.

He stepped forward and put his hand on the door. He had a blanket draped over him, which was why she'd mistaken him for a woman. "*Erkas,*" he said, and he sounded upset, desperate, and yet somehow still diffident, timid.

"*Bott lom,*" he said, gesturing toward the woman who was standing back almost to the edge of the porch, but Sharon wasn't looking at her. She was looking at their feet.

They were wearing sandals. At first she thought they were barefoot and she squinted through the darkness, horrified. Barefoot in the snow! Then she glimpsed the dark line of a strap, but they still might as well be. And it was snowing hard.

She couldn't leave them outside, but she didn't dare bring them into the hall to wait for the van either, not with Reverend Farrison around.

The office was out—the phone might ring—and she couldn't put them in the Fellowship Hall with all the stuff for the homeless in there.

"Just a minute," she said, shutting the door, and went to see if Miriam was still in the adult Sunday school room. It was dark, so she obviously wasn't, but there was a lamp on the table by the door. She switched it on. No, this wouldn't work either, not with the communion silver in a display case against the wall, and anyway, there was a stack of paper cups on the table, and the plates of Christmas cookies Miriam had been carrying, which meant there'd be refreshments in here after the pageant. She switched off the light, and went out into the hall.

Not Reverend Wall's office—it was locked anyway—and certainly not Reverend Farrison's, and if she took them downstairs to one of the Sunday school rooms, she'd just have to sneak them back up again.

The furnace room? It was between the adult Sunday school room and the Fellowship Hall. She tried the doorknob. It opened, and she looked in. The furnace filled practically the whole room, and what it didn't was taken up by a stack of folding chairs. There wasn't a light switch she could find, but the pilot light gave off enough light to maneuver by. And it was warmer than the porch.

She went back to the door, looked down the hall to make sure nobody was coming, and let them in. "You can wait in here," she said, even though it was obvious they couldn't understand her.

They followed her through the dark hall to the furnace room, and she opened out two of the folding chairs so they could sit down, and motioned them in.

"It Came Upon a Midnight Clear" ground to a halt, and Rose's voice came drifting out of the sanctuary. "Shepherd's crooks are not weapons. All right. Angel?"

"I'll call the shelter," Sharon said hastily and shut the door on them.

She crossed to the office and tried the shelter again. "Please, please answer," she said, and when they did, she was so surprised, she forgot to tell them the couple would be inside.

"It'll be at least half an hour," the man said. "Or forty-five minutes."

"Forty-five minutes?"

"It's like this whenever it gets below zero," the man said. "We'll try to make it sooner."

At least she'd done the right thing—they couldn't possibly stand out in that snow for forty-five minutes. The right thing, she thought ruefully, sticking them in the furnace room. But at least it was warm in there and out of the snow. And they were safe, as long as nobody came out to see what had happened to her.

"Dee," she said suddenly. Sharon was supposed to have come out to get her some cough drops.

They were lying on the desk where she'd laid them while she phoned. She snatched them up and took off down the hall and into the sanctuary.

The angel was on the chancel steps, exhorting the shepherds not to be afraid. Sharon threaded her way through them up to the chancel and sat down between Dee and Virginia.

She handed the cough drops to Dee, who said, "What took you so long?"

"I had to make a phone call. What did I miss?"

"Not a thing. We're still on the shepherds. One of the palm trees fell over and had to be fixed, and then Reverend Farrison stopped the rehearsal to tell everybody not to let homeless people into the church, that Holy Trinity had had its sanctuary vandalized."

"Oh," she said. She gazed out over the sanctuary, looking for Reverend Farrison.

"All right, now, after the angel makes her speech," Rose said, "she's joined by a multitude of angels. That's *you*, junior choir. No. Line up on the steps. Organ?"

The organ struck up "Hark, the Herald Angels Sing," and the junior choir began singing in piping, nearly inaudible voices.

Sharon couldn't see Reverend Farrison anywhere. "Do you know where Reverend Farrison went?" she whispered to Dee.

"She went out just as you came in. She had to get something from the office."

The office. What if she heard them in the furnace room and opened the door and found them in there? She half stood.

"Choir," Rose said, glaring directly at Sharon. "Will you help the junior choir by humming along with them?"

Sharon sat back down, and after a minute Reverend Farrison came in from the back, carrying a pair of scissors.

"'Late in time, behold Him come,'" the junior choir sang, and Miriam stood up and went out.

"Where's Miriam going?" Sharon whispered.

"How would I know?" Dee said, looking curiously at her. "To get the refreshments ready, probably. Is something the matter?"

"No," she said.

Rose was glaring at Sharon again. Sharon hummed, "'Light and life to all He brings,'" willing the song to be over so she could go out, but as soon as it was over, Rose said, "All right, wise men," and a sixth-grader carrying a jewelry box started down the center aisle. "Choir, 'We Three Kings.' Organ?"

There were four long verses to "We Three Kings of Orient Are." Sharon couldn't wait.

"I have to go to the bathroom," she said. She set her folder on her chair and ducked down the stairs behind the chancel and through the narrow room that led to the side aisle. The choir called it the flower room because that was where they stored the out-of-season altar arrangements. They used it for sneaking out when they needed to leave church early, but right now there was barely room to squeeze through. The floor was covered with music stands and pots of silk Easter lilies, and a huge spray of red roses stood in front of the door to the sanctuary.

Sharon shoved it into the corner, stepping gingerly among the lilies, and opened the door.

"Balthazar, lay the gold in front of the manger, don't drop it. Mary, you're the Mother of God. Try not to look so scared," Rose said.

Sharon hurried down the side aisle and out into the hall, where the other two kings were waiting, holding perfume bottles.

"'Westward leading, still proceeding, guide us to thy perfect light,'" the choir sang.

The hall and office lights were still off, but light was spilling out of the adult Sunday school room all the way to the end of the hall. She could see that the furnace-room door was still shut.

I'll call the shelter again, she thought, and see if I can hurry them up, and if I can't, I'll take them downstairs till everybody's gone, and then take them to the shelter myself.

She tiptoed past the open door of the adult Sunday school room so Miriam wouldn't see her, and then half-sprinted down to the office and opened the door.

"Hi," Miriam said, looking up from the desk. She had an aluminum pitcher in one hand and was rummaging in the top drawer with the other. "Do you know where the secretary keeps the key to the kitchen? It's locked, and I can't get in."

"No," Sharon said, her heart still pounding.

"I need a spoon to stir the Kool-Aid," Miriam said, opening and shutting the side drawers of the desk. "She must have taken them home with her. I don't blame her. First Baptist had theirs stolen last month. They had to change all the locks."

Sharon glanced uneasily at the furnace-room door.

"Oh, well," Miriam said, opening the top drawer again. "I'll have to make do with this." She pulled out a plastic ruler. "The kids won't care."

She started out and then stopped. "They're not done in there yet, are they?"

"No," Sharon said. "They're still on the wise men. I needed to call my husband to tell him to take the turkey out of the freezer."

"I've got to do that when I get home," Miriam said. She went across the hall and into the library, leaving the door open. Sharon waited a minute and then called the shelter. It was busy. She held her watch to the light from the hall. They'd said half an hour to forty-five minutes. By that time the rehearsal would be over and the hall would be full of people.

Less than half an hour. They were already singing "Myrrh is mine, its bitter perfume." All that was left was "Silent Night" and then "Joy to the World," and the angels would come streaming out for cookies and Kool-Aid.

She went over to the front door and peered out. Below zero, the woman at the shelter had said, and now there was sleet, slanting sharply across the parking lot.

She couldn't send them out in that without any shoes. And she couldn't keep them up here, not with the kids right next door. She was going to have to move them downstairs.

But where? Not the choir room. The choir would be taking their folders and robes back down there, and the pageant kids would be getting their coats out of the Sunday school rooms. And the kitchen was locked.

The nursery? That might work. It was at the other end of the hall from the choir room, but she would have to take them past the adult Sunday school room to the stairs, and the door was open.

"'Si-i-lent night, ho-oh-ly night,'" came drifting out of the sanctuary, and then was cut off, and she could hear Reverend Farrison's voice lecturing, probably about the dangers of letting the homeless into the church.

She glanced again at the furnace-room door and then went into the adult Sunday school room. Miriam was setting out the paper cups on the table. She looked up. "Did you get through to your husband?"

"Yes," Sharon said. Miriam looked expectant.

"Can I have a cookie?" Sharon said at random.

"Take one of the stars. The kids like the Santas and the Christmas trees the best."

She grabbed up a bright yellow-frosted star. "Thanks," she said, and went out pulling the door shut behind her.

"Leave it open," Miriam said. "I want to be able to hear when they're done."

Sharon opened the door back up half as far as she'd shut it, afraid any less would bring Miriam to the door to open it herself, and walked quietly to the furnace room.

The choir was on the last verse of "Silent Night." After that there was only "Joy to the World" and then the benediction. Open door or no open door, she was going to have to move them now. She opened the furnace-room door.

They were standing where she had left them between the folding chairs, and she knew, without any proof, that they had stood there like that the whole time she had been gone.

The young man was standing slightly in front of the woman, the way he had at the door, only he wasn't a man, he was a boy, his beard as thin and wispy as an adolescent's, and the woman was even younger, a child of ten maybe, only she had to be older, because now that there was light from the half-open door of the adult Sunday school room Sharon could see that she was pregnant.

She regarded all this—the girl's awkward bulkiness and the boy's beard, the fact that they had not sat down, the fact that it was the light from the adult Sunday school room that was making her see now what she hadn't before—with some part of her mind that was still functioning, that was still thinking how long the van from the shelter would take, how to get them past Reverend Farrison, some part of her mind that was taking in the details that proved what she had already known the moment she opened the door.

"What are you *doing* here?" she whispered, and the boy opened his hands in a gesture of helplessness. "*Erkas,*" he said.

And that still-functioning part of her mind put her fingers to her lips in a gesture he obviously understood because they both looked instantly frightened. "You have to come with me," she whispered.

But then it stopped functioning altogether, and she was half-running them past the open door and onto the stairs, not even hearing the organ blaring out "Joy to the world, the Lord is come,'" whispering, "Hurry! Hurry!" and they didn't know how to get down the steps, the girl turned around and came down backwards, her hands flat on the steps above, and the boy helped her down, step by step as if they were clambering down rocks, and she tried to pull the girl along faster and nearly made her stumble, and even that didn't bring her to her senses.

She hissed, "Like this," and showed them how to walk down the steps, facing forward, one hand on the rail, and they paid no attention, they came down backwards like toddlers, and it took forever, the hymn she wasn't hearing was already at the end of the third verse and they were only halfway down, all of them panting hard, and Sharon scurrying back up above them as if that would hurry them, past wondering how she would ever get them up the stairs again, past thinking she would have to call the van and tell them not to come, thinking only; Hurry, hurry, and How did they *get* here?

She did not come to herself until she had herded them somehow down the hall and into the nursery, thinking, It can't be locked, please don't let it be locked, and it wasn't, and gotten them inside and pulled the door shut and tried to lock it, and it didn't have a lock, and she thought, That must be why it wasn't locked, an actual coherent thought, her first one since that moment when she opened the furnace-room door, and seemed to come to herself.

She stared at them, breathing hard, and it was them, their never having seen stairs before was proof of that, if she needed any proof, but she didn't, she had known it the instant she saw them, there was no question.

She wondered if this was some sort of vision, the kind people were always getting where they saw Jesus' face on a refrigerator, or the Virgin Mary dressed in blue and white, surrounded by roses. But their rough brown cloaks were dripping melted snow on the nursery carpet, their feet in the useless sandals were bright red with cold, and they looked too frightened.

And they didn't look at all like they did in religious pictures. They were too short, his hair was greasy and his face was tough-looking, like a young punk's, and her veil looked like a grubby dishtowel and it didn't hang loose, it was tied around her neck and knotted in the back, and they were too young, almost as young as the children upstairs dressed like them.

They were looking around the room frightenedly, at the white crib and the rocking chair and the light fixture overhead. The boy fumbled in his sash and brought out a leather sack. He held it out to Sharon.

"How did you *get* here?" she said wonderingly. "You're supposed to be on your way to Bethlehem."

He thrust the bag at her, and when she didn't take it, untied the leather string and took out a crude-looking coin and held it out.

"You don't have to pay me," she said, which was ridiculous. He couldn't understand her. She held a flat hand up, pushing the coin away and shaking her head. That was a universal sign, wasn't it? And what was the sign for welcome? She spread her arms out, smiling at the youngsters. "You are welcome to stay here," she said, trying to put the meaning of the words into her voice. "Sit down. Rest."

They remained standing. Sharon pulled the rocking chair. "Sit, please."

Mary looked frightened, and Sharon put her hands on the arms of the chair and sat down to show her how. Joseph immediately knelt, and Mary tried awkwardly to.

"No, no!" Sharon said, and stood up so fast she set the rocking chair swinging. "Don't kneel. I'm nobody." She looked hopelessly at them. "How did you get here? You're not supposed to be here."

Joseph stood up. *"Erkas,"* he said, and went over to the bulletin board.

It was covered with colored pictures from Jesus' life: Jesus healing the lame boy, Jesus in the temple, Jesus in the Garden of Gethsemane.

He pointed to the picture of the Nativity scene. *"Kumrah,"* he said.

Does he recognize himself? she wondered, but he was pointing at the donkey standing by the manger. *"Erkas,"* he said. *"Erkas."*

Did that mean "donkey," or something else? Was he demanding to know what she had done with theirs, or trying to ask her if she had one? In all the pictures, all the versions of the story Mary was riding a donkey, but she had thought they'd gotten that part of the story wrong, as they had gotten everything else wrong, their faces, their clothes, and above all their youth, their helplessness.

*"Kumrah erkas,"* he said. *"Kumrah erkas. Bott lom?"*

"I don't know," she said. "I don't know where Bethlehem is."

Or what to do with you, she thought. Her first instinct was to hide them here until the rehearsal was over and everybody had gone home. She couldn't let Reverend Farrison find them.

But surely as soon as she saw who they were, she would—what? Fall to her knees? Or call for the shelter's van? "That's the second couple tonight," she'd said when she shut the door. Sharon wondered suddenly if it was them she'd turned away, if they'd wandered around the parking lot, lost and frightened, and then knocked on the door again.

She couldn't let Reverend Farrison find them, but there was no reason for her to come into the nursery. All the children were upstairs, and the refreshments were in the adult Sunday school room. But what if she checked the rooms before she locked up?

I'll take them home with me, Sharon thought. They'll be safe there. If she could get them up the stairs and out of the parking lot before the rehearsal ended.

I got them down here without anybody seeing them, she thought. But even if she could manage it, which she doubted, if they didn't die of fright when she started the car and the seat belts closed down over them, home was no better than the shelter.

They had gotten lost through some accident of time and space, and ended up at the church. The way back—if there was a way back, there

had to be a way back, they had to be at Bethlehem by tomorrow night—
was here.

It occurred to her suddenly that maybe she shouldn't have let them
in, that the way back was outside the north door. But I couldn't *not* let
them in, she protested, it was snowing, and they didn't have any shoes.

But maybe if she'd turned them away, they would have walked off the
porch and back into their own time. Maybe they still could.

She said, "Stay here," putting her hand up to show them what she
meant, and went out of the nursery into the hall, shutting the door tightly
behind her.

The choir was still singing "Joy to the World." They must have had
to stop again. Sharon ran silently up the stairs and past the adult Sunday
school room. Its door was still half-open, and she could see the plates of
cookies on the table. She opened the north door, hesitating a moment as
if she expected to see sand and camels, and leaned out. It was still sleeting, and the cars had an inch of snow on them.

She looked around for something to wedge the door open with,
pushed one of the potted palms over, and went out on the porch. It was
slick, and she had to take hold of the wall to keep her footing. She
stepped carefully to the edge of the porch and peered into the sleet, already shivering, looking for what? A lessening of the sleet, a spot where
the darkness was darker, or not so dark? A light?

Nothing. After a minute she stepped off the porch, moving as cautiously as Mary and Joseph had going down the stairs, and made a circuit of the parking lot.

Nothing. If the way back had been out here, it wasn't now, and she
was going to freeze if she stayed out here. She went back inside, and then
stood there, staring at the door, trying to think what to do. I've got to get
help, she thought, hugging her arms to herself for warmth. I've got to tell
somebody. She started down the hall to the sanctuary.

The organ had stopped. "Mary and Joseph, I need to talk to you for
a minute," Rose's voice said. "Shepherds, leave your crooks on the front
pew. The rest of you, there are refreshments in the adult Sunday school
room. Choir, don't leave. I need to go over some things with you."

There was a clatter of sticks and then a stampede, and Sharon was overwhelmed by shepherds elbowing their way to the refreshments. One of the
wise men caught his Air Jordan in his robe and nearly fell down, and two
of the angels lost their tinsel halos in their eagerness to reach the cookies.

Sharon fought through them and into the back of the sanctuary. Rose was in the side aisle, showing Mary and Joseph how to walk, and the choir was gathering up their music. Sharon couldn't see Dee.

Virginia came down the center aisle, stripping off her robe as she walked. Sharon went to meet her. "Do you know where Dee is?" she asked her.

"She went home," Virginia said, handing Sharon a folder. "You left this on your chair." Dee's voice was giving out completely, and I said, "This is silly. Go home and go to bed."

"Virginia…" Sharon said.

"Can you put my robe away for me?" Virginia said, pulling her stole off her head. "I've got exactly ten minutes to get to the mall."

Sharon nodded absently, and Virginia draped it over her arm and hurried out. Sharon scanned the choir, wondering who else she could confide in.

Rose dismissed Mary and Joseph, who went off at a run, and crossed to the center aisle. "Rehearsal tomorrow night at 6:15," she said. "I need you in your robes and up here right on time, because I've got to practice with the brass quartet at 6:40. Any questions?"

Yes, Sharon thought, looking around the sanctuary. Who can I get to help me?

"What are we singing for the processional?" one of the tenors asked.

"'*Adeste Fideles*,'" Rose said. "Before you leave, let's line up so you can see who your partner is."

Reverend Wall was sitting in one of the back pews, looking at the notes to his sermon. Sharon sidled along the pew and sat down next to him.

"Reverend Wall," she said, and then had no idea how to start. "Do you know what *erkas* means? I think it's Hebrew."

He raised his head from his notes and peered at her. "It's Aramaic. It means 'lost.'"

"Lost." He'd been trying to tell her at the door, in the furnace room, downstairs. "We're lost."

"Forgotten," Reverend Wall said. "Misplaced."

Misplaced, all right. By two thousand years, an ocean, and how many miles?

"When Mary and Joseph journeyed up to Bethlehem from Nazareth, how did they go?" she asked, hoping he would say, "Why are you asking all these questions?" so she could tell him, but he said, "Ah. You weren't listening to my sermon. We know nothing of that journey, only that they arrived in Bethlehem."

Not at this rate, she thought.

"Pass in the anthem," Rose said from the chancel. "I've only got thirty copies, and I don't want to come up short tomorrow night."

Sharon looked up. The choir was leaving. "On this journey, was there anyplace where they might have gotten lost?" she said hurriedly.

"'*Erkas*' can also mean 'hidden, passed out of sight,'" he said. "Aramaic is very similar to Hebrew. In Hebrew, the word—"

"Reverend Wall," Reverend Farrison said from the center aisle. "I need to talk to you about the benediction."

"Ah. Do you want me to give it now?" he said, and stood up, clutching his papers.

Sharon took the opportunity to grab her folder and duck out. She ran downstairs after the choir.

There was no reason for any of the choir to go into the nursery, but she stationed herself in the hall, sorting through the music in her folder as if she were putting it in order, and trying to think what to do.

Maybe, if everyone went into the choir room, she could duck into the nursery or one of the Sunday school rooms and hide until everybody was gone. But she didn't know whether Reverend Farrison checked each of the rooms before leaving. Or worse, locked them.

She could tell her she needed to stay late, to practice the anthem, but she didn't think Reverend Farrison would trust her to lock up, and she didn't want to call attention to herself, to make Reverend Farrison think, "Where's Sharon Englert? I didn't see her leave." Maybe she could hide in the chancel, or the flower room, but that meant leaving the nursery unguarded.

She had to decide. The crowd was thinning out, the choir handing Rose their music and putting on their coats and boots. She had to do something. Reverend Farrison could come down the stairs any minute to search the nursery. But she continued to stand there, sorting blindly through her music, and Reverend Farrison came down the steps, carrying a ring of keys.

Sharon stepped back protectively, the way Joseph had, but Reverend Farrison didn't even see her. She went up to Rose and said, "Can you lock up for me? I've got to be at Emmanuel Lutheran at 9:30 to collect their Least of These contributions."

"I was supposed to go meet with the brass quartet—" Rose said reluctantly.

Don't let Rose talk you out of it, Sharon thought.

"Be sure to lock *all* the doors, including the Fellowship Hall," Reverend Farrison said, handing her the keys.

"No, I've got mine," Rose said. "But—"

"And check the parking lot. There were some homeless hanging around earlier. Thanks."

She ran upstairs, and Sharon immediately went over to Rose. "Rose," she said.

Rose held out her hand for Sharon's anthem.

Sharon shuffled through her music and handed it to her. "I was wondering," she said, trying to keep her voice casual, "I need to stay and practice the music for tomorrow. I'd be glad to lock up for you. I could drop the keys by your house tomorrow morning."

"Oh, you're a godsend," Rose said. She handed Sharon the stack of music and got her keys out of her purse. "These are the keys to the outside doors, north door, east door, Fellowship Hall," she said, ticking them off so fast, Sharon couldn't see which was which, but it didn't matter. She could figure them out after everybody left.

"This is the choir-room door," Rose said. She handed them to Sharon. "I *really* appreciate this. The brass quartet couldn't come to the rehearsal, they had a concert tonight, and I really need to go over the introit with them. They're having a terrible time with the middle part."

So am I, Sharon thought.

Rose yanked on her coat. "And after I meet with them, I've got to go over to Miriam Berg's and pick up the baby Jesus." She stopped, her arm half in her coat sleeve. "Did you need me to stay and go over the music with you?"

"No!" Sharon said, alarmed. "No, I'll be fine. I just need to run through it a couple of times."

"Okay. Great. Thanks again," she said, patting her pockets for her keys. She took the keyring away from Sharon and unhooked her car keys. "You're a godsend, I mean it," she said, and took off up the stairs at a trot.

Two of the altos came out, pulling on their gloves. "Do you know what I've got to face when I get home?" Julia said. "Putting up the tree."

They handed their music to Sharon.

"I hate Christmas," Karen said. "By the time it's over, I'm worn to a frazzle."

They hurried up the stairs, still talking, and Sharon leaned into the choir room to make sure it was empty, dumped the music and Rose's robe on a chair, took off her robe, and went upstairs.

Miriam was coming out of the adult Sunday school room, carrying a pitcher of Kool-Aid. "Come on, Elizabeth," she called into the room. "We've got to get to Buymore before it closes. She managed to completely destroy her halo," she said to Sharon, "so now I've got to go buy some more tinsel. Elizabeth, we're the last ones here."

Elizabeth strolled out, holding a Christmas-tree cookie in her mittened hand. She stopped halfway to the door to lick the cookie's frosting.

"Elizabeth," Miriam said. "Come on."

Sharon held the door for them, and Miriam went out, ducking her head against the driving sleet. Elizabeth dawdled after her, looking up at the sky.

Miriam waved. "See you tomorrow night."

"I'll be here," Sharon said, and shut the door. I'll *still* be here, she thought. And what if they are? What happens then? Does the Christmas pageant disappear, and all the rest of it? The cookies and the shopping and the Senior Prom Barbies? And the church?

She watched Miriam and Elizabeth through the stained-glass panel till she saw the car's taillights, purple through the blue glass, pull out of the parking lot, and then tried the keys one after the other, till she found the right one, and locked the door.

She checked quickly in the sanctuary and the bathrooms, in case somebody was still there, and then ran down the stairs to the nursery to make sure *they* were still there, that they hadn't disappeared.

They were there, sitting on the floor next to the rocking chair and sharing what looked like dried dates from an unfolded cloth. Joseph started to stand up as soon as he saw her poke her head in the door, but she motioned him back down. "Stay here," she said softly, and realized she didn't need to whisper. "I'll be back in a few minutes. I'm just going to lock the doors."

She pulled the door shut, and went back upstairs. It hadn't occurred to her they'd be hungry, and she had no idea what they were used to eating—unleavened bread? Lamb? Whatever it was, there probably wasn't any in the kitchen, but the deacons had had an Advent supper last week.

419

With luck, there might be some chili in the refrigerator. Or, better yet, some crackers.

The kitchen was locked. She'd forgotten Miriam had said that, and anyway, one of the keys must open it. None of them did, and after she'd tried all of them twice she remembered they were Rose's keys, not Reverend Farrison's, and turned the lights on in the Fellowship Hall. There was tons of food in there, stacked on tables alongside the blankets and used clothes and toys. And all of it was in cans, just the way Reverend Farrison had specified in the bulletin.

Miriam had taken the Kool-Aid home, but Sharon hadn't seen her carrying any cookies. The kids probably ate them all, she thought, but she went into the adult Sunday school room and looked. There was half a paper-plateful left, and Miriam had been right—the kids liked the Christmas trees and Santas the best—the only ones left were yellow stars. There was a stack of paper cups, too. She picked them both up and took them downstairs.

"I brought you some food," she said, and set the plate on the floor between them.

They were staring in alarm at her, and Joseph was scrambling to his feet.

"It's food," she said, bringing her hand to her mouth and pretending to chew. "Cakes."

Joseph was pulling on Mary's arm, trying to yank her up, and they were both staring, horrified, at her jeans and sweatshirt. She realized suddenly they must not have recognized her without her choir robe. Worse, the robe looked at least a little like their clothes, but this getup must have looked totally alien.

"I'll bring you something to drink," she said hastily, showing them the paper cups, and went out. She ran down to the choir room. Her robe was still draped over the chair where she'd dumped it, along with Rose's and the music. She put the robe on and then filled the paper cups at the water fountain and carried them back to the nursery.

They were standing, but when they saw her in the robe, they sat back down. She handed Mary one of the paper cups, but she only looked at her fearfully. Sharon held it out to Joseph. He took it, too firmly, and it crumpled, water spurting onto the carpet.

"That's okay; it doesn't matter," Sharon said, cursing herself for being an idiot. "I'll get you a real cup."

She ran upstairs, trying to think where there would be one. The coffee cups were in the kitchen, and so were the glasses, and she hadn't seen anything in the Fellowship Hall or the adult Sunday school room.

She smiled suddenly. "I'll get you a real cup," she repeated, and went into the adult Sunday school room and took the silver Communion chalice out of the display case. There were silver plates, too. She wished she'd thought of it sooner.

She went into the Fellowship Hall and got a blanket and took the things downstairs. She filled the chalice with water and took it in to them, and handed Mary the chalice, and this time Marv took it without hesitation and drank deeply from it.

Sharon gave Joseph the blanket. "I'll leave you alone so you can eat and rest," she said, and went out into the hall, pulling the door nearly shut again.

She went down to the choir room and hung up Rose's robe and stacked the music neatly on the table. Then she went up to the furnace room and folded up the folding chairs and stacked them against the wall. She checked the east door and the one in the Fellowship Hall. They were both locked.

She turned off the lights in the Fellowship Hall and the office, and then thought, "I should call the shelter," and turned them back on. It had been an hour since she'd called. They had probably already come and not found anyone, but in case they were running really late, she'd better call.

The line was busy. She tried it twice and then called home. Bill's parents were there. "I'm going to be late," she told him. "The rehearsal's running long," and hung up, wondering how many lies she'd told so far tonight.

Well, it went with the territory, didn't it? Joseph lying about the baby being his, and the wise men sneaking out the back way, the Holy Family hightailing it to Egypt and the innkeeper lying to Herod's soldiers about where they'd gone.

And in the meantime, more hiding. She went back downstairs and opened the door gently, trying not to startle them, and then just stood there, watching.

They had eaten the cookies. The empty paper plate stood on the floor next to the chalice, not a crumb on it. Mary lay curled up like the child she was under the blanket, and Joseph sat with his back to the rocking chair, guarding her.

421

Poor things, she thought, leaning her cheek against the door. Poor things. So young, and so far away from home. She wondered what they made of it all. Did they think they had wandered into a palace in some strange kingdom? There's stranger yet to come, she thought, shepherds and angels and old men from the east, bearing jewelry boxes and perfume bottles. And then Cana. And Jerusalem. And Golgotha.

But for the moment, a place to sleep, out of the weather, and something to eat, and a few minutes of peace. How still we see thee lie. She stood there a long time, her cheek resting against the door, watching Mary sleep and Joseph trying to stay awake.

His head nodded forward, and he jerked it back, waking himself up and saw Sharon. He stood up immediately careful not to wake Mary, and came over to her, looking worried. *"Erkas kumrah,"* he said. *"Bott lom?"*

"I'll go find it," she said.

She went upstairs and turned the lights on again and went into the Fellowship Hall. The way back wasn't out the north door, but maybe they had knocked at one of the other doors first and then come around to it when no one answered. The Fellowship Hall door was on the northwest corner. She unlocked it, trying key after key, and opened it. The sleet was slashing down harder than ever. It had already covered up the tire tracks in the parking lot.

She shut the door and tried the east door, which nobody used except for the Sunday service, and then the north door again. Nothing. Sleet and wind and icy air.

Now what? They had been on their way to Bethlehem from Nazareth, and somewhere along the way they had taken a wrong turn. But how? And where? She didn't even know what direction they'd been heading in. Up. Joseph had gone *up* from Nazareth, which meant north, and in "The First Nowell" it said the star was in the northwest.

She needed a map. The ministers' offices were locked, but there were books on the bottom shelf of the display case in the adult Sunday school room. Maybe one was an atlas.

It wasn't. They were all self-help books, about coping with grief and codependency and teenage pregnancy, except for an ancient-looking concordance and a Bible dictionary.

The Bible dictionary had a set of maps at the back. Early Israelite Settlements in Canaan, The Assyrian Empire, The Wanderings of the Israelites in the Wilderness. She flipped forward. The Journeys of Paul. She turned back a page. Palestine in New Testament Times.

She found Jerusalem easily and Bethlehem should be northwest of it. There was Nazareth, where Mary and Joseph had started from, so Bethlehem had to be farther north.

It wasn't there. She traced her finger over the towns, reading the tiny print. Cana, Kedesh, Jericho, but no Bethlehem. Which was ridiculous. It had to be there. She started down from the north, marking each of the towns with her finger.

When she finally found it, it wasn't at all where it was supposed to be. Like them, she thought. It was south and a little west of Jerusalem, so close it couldn't be more than a few miles from the city.

She looked down at the bottom of the page for the map scale, and there was an inset labeled "Mary and Joseph's Journey to Bethlehem," with their route marked in broken red.

Nazareth was almost due north of Bethlehem, but they had gone east to the Jordan River, and then south along its banks. At Jericho they'd turned back west toward Jerusalem through an empty brown space marked "Judean Desert."

She wondered if that was where they had gotten lost, the donkey wandering off to find water and them going after it and losing the path. If it was, then the way back lay southwest, but the church didn't have any doors that opened in that direction, and even if it did, they would open on a twentieth-century parking lot and snow, not on first-century Palestine.

How had they gotten here? There was nothing in the map to tell her what might have happened on their journey to cause this.

She put the dictionary back and pulled out the concordance.

There was a sound. A key, and somebody opening the door. She slapped the book shut, shoved it back into the bookcase, and went out into the hall. Reverend Farrison was standing at the door, looking scared. "Oh, Sharon," she said, putting her hand to her chest. "What are you still doing here? You scared me half to death."

That makes two of us, Sharon thought, her heart thumping. "I had to stay and practice," she said. "I told Rose I'd lock up. What are you doing here?"

"I got a call from the shelter," she said, opening the office door. "They got a call from us to pick up a homeless couple, but when they got here there was nobody outside."

She went in the office and looked behind the desk, in the corner next to the filing cabinets. "I was worried they got into the church," she said, coming out. "The last thing we need is someone vandalizing the church two days before Christmas." She shut the office door behind her. "Did you check all the doors?"

Yes, she thought, and none of them led anywhere. "Yes," she said. "They were all locked. And anyway, I would have heard anybody trying to get in. I heard you."

Reverend Farrison opened the door to the furnace room. "They could have sneaked in and hidden when everyone was leaving." She looked in at the stacked folding chairs and then shut the door. She started down the hall toward the stairs.

"I checked the whole church," Sharon said, following her.

She stopped at the stairs, looking speculatively down the steps.

"I was nervous about being alone," Sharon said desperately, "so I turned on all the lights and checked all the Sunday school rooms and the choir room and the bathrooms. There isn't anybody here."

She looked up from the stairs and toward the end of the hall. "What about the sanctuary?"

"The sanctuary?" Sharon said blankly

She had already started down the hall toward it, and Sharon followed her, relieved, and then, suddenly, hopeful. Maybe there was a door she'd missed. A sanctuary door that faced southwest. "Is there a door in the sanctuary?"

Reverend Farrison looked irritated. "If someone went out the east door, they could have gotten in and hidden in the sanctuary. Did you check the pews?" She went into the sanctuary. "We've had a lot of trouble lately with homeless people sleeping in the pews. You take that side, and I'll take this one," she said, going over to the side aisle. She started along the rows of padded pews, bending down to look under each one. "Our Lady of Sorrows had their Communion silver stolen right off the altar."

The Communion silver, Sharon thought, working her way along the rows. She'd forgotten about the chalice.

Reverend Farrison had reached the front. She opened the flower-room door, glanced in, closed it, and went up into the chancel. "Did you check the adult Sunday school room?" she said, bending down to look under the chairs.

"Nobody could have hidden in there. The junior choir was in there, having refreshments," Sharon said, and knew it wouldn't do any good. Reverend Farrison was going to insist on checking it anyway, and once she'd found the display case open, the chalice missing, she would go through all the other rooms, one after the other. Till she came to the nursery.

"Do you think it's a good idea us doing this?" Sharon said. "I mean, if there is somebody in the church, they might be dangerous. I think we should wait. I'll call my husband, and when he gets here, the three of us can check—"

"I called the police," Reverend Farrison said, coming down the steps from the chancel and down the center aisle. "They'll be here any minute."

The police. And there they were, hiding in the nursery, a bearded punk and a pregnant teenager, caught redhanded with the Communion silver.

Reverend Farrison started out into the hall.

"I didn't check the Fellowship Hall," Sharon said rapidly. "I mean, I checked the door, but I didn't turn on the lights, and with all those presents for the homeless in there…"

She led Reverend Farrison down the hall, past the stairs. "They could have gotten in the north door during the rehearsal and hidden under one of the tables."

Reverend Farrison stopped at the bank of lights and began flicking them. The sanctuary lights went off, and the light over the stairs came on.

Third from the top, Sharon thought, watching Reverend Farrison hit the switch. Please. Don't let the adult Sunday school room come on.

The office lights came on, and the hall light went out. "This church's top priority after Christmas is labeling these lights," Reverend Farrison said, and the Fellowship Hall light came on.

Sharon followed her right to the door and then, as Reverend Farrison went in, Sharon said, "You check in here. I'll check the adult Sunday school room," and shut the door on her.

She went to the adult Sunday school room door, opened it, waited a full minute, and then shut it silently. She crept down the hall to the light bank, switched the stairs light off and shot down the darkened stairs, along the hall, and into the nursery.

They were already scrambling to their feet. Mary had put her hand on the seat of the rocking chair to pull herself up and had set it rocking, but she didn't let go of it.

"Come with me," Sharon whispered, grabbing up the chalice. It was half-full of water, and Sharon looked around hurriedly, and then poured it out on the carpet and tucked it under her arm.

"Hurry!" Sharon whispered, opening the door, and there was no need to motion them forward to put her fingers to her lips. They followed her swiftly, silently, down the hall, Mary's head ducked, and Joseph's arms held at his sides, ready to come up defensively, ready to protect her.

Sharon walked to the stairs, dreading the thought of trying to get them up them. She thought for a moment of putting them in the choir room and locking them in. She had the key, and she could tell Reverend Farrison she'd checked it and then locked it to make sure no one got in. But if it didn't work, they'd be trapped, with no way out. She had to get them upstairs.

She halted at the foot of the stairs, looking up around the landing and listening. "We have to hurry;" she said, taking hold of the railing to show them how to climb, and started up the stairs.

This time they did much better, still putting their hands on the steps in front of them instead of the rail, but climbing up quickly. Three-fourths of the way up, Joseph even took hold of the rail.

Sharon did better, too, her mind steadily now on how to escape Reverend Farrison, what to say to the police, where to take them.

Not the furnace room, even though Reverend Farrison had already looked in there. It was too close to the door, and the police would start with the hall. And not the sanctuary. It was too open.

She stopped just below the top of the stairs, motioning them to keep down, and they instantly pressed themselves back into the shadows. Why was it those signals were universal—danger, silence, run? Because it's a dangerous world, she thought, then and now, and there's worse to come. Herod, and the flight into Egypt. And Judas. And the police.

She crept to the top of the stairs and looked toward the sanctuary and then the door. Reverend Farrison must still be in the Fellowship Hall. She wasn't in the hall, and if she'd gone in the adult Sunday school room, she'd have seen the missing chalice and sent up a hue and cry.

Sharon bit her lip, wondering if there was time to put it back, if she dared leave them here on the stairs while she sneaked in and put it in the display case, but it was too late. The police were here. She could see their red and blue lights flashing purely through the stained-glass door panels. In another minute they'd be at the door, knocking, and Reverend Farrison would come out of the Fellowship Hall, and there'd be no time for anything.

She'd have to hide them in the sanctuary until Reverend Farrison took the police downstairs. and then move them—where? The furnace room? It was still too close to the door. The Fellowship Hall?

She waved them upward, like John Wayne in one of his war movies, along the hall and into the sanctuary. Reverend Farrison had turned off the lights, but there was still enough light from the chancel cross to see by. She laid the chalice in the back pew and led them along the back row to the shadowed side aisle, and then pushed them ahead of her to the front, listening intently for the sound of knocking.

Joseph went ahead with his eyes on the ground, as if he expected more sudden stairs, but Mary had her head up, looking toward the chancel, toward the cross.

Don't look at it, Sharon thought. Don't look at it. She hurried ahead to the flower room.

There was a muffled sound like thunder, and the bang of a door shutting.

"In here," she whispered, and opened the flower-room door.

She'd been on the other side of the sanctuary when Reverend Farrison checked the flower room. Sharon understood now why she had given it only the most cursory of glances. It had been full before. Now it was crammed with the palm trees and the manger. They'd heaped the rest of the props in it—the innkeeper's lantern and the baby blanket. She pushed the manger back, and one of its crossed legs caught on a music stand and tipped it over. She lunged for it, steadied it, and then stopped, listening.

Knocking out in the hall. And the sound of a door shutting. Voices. She let go of the music stand and pushed them into the flower room, shoving Mary into the corner against the spray of roses and nearly knocking over another music stand.

She motioned to Joseph to stand on the other side and flattened herself against a palm tree, shut the door, and realized the moment she did that it was a mistake.

They couldn't stand here in the dark like this—the slightest movement by any of them would bring everything clattering down, and Mary couldn't stay squashed uncomfortably into the corner like that for long.

She should have left the door slightly open, so there was enough light from the cross to see by so she could hear where the police were. She couldn't hear anything with the door shut except the sound of their own light breathing and the clank of the lantern when she tried to shift her weight, and she couldn't risk opening the door again, not when they might already be in the sanctuary, looking for her. She should have shut Mary and Joseph in here and gone back into the hall to head the police off. Reverend Farrison would be looking for her, and if she didn't find her, she'd take it as one more proof that there was a dangerous homeless person in the church and insist on the police searching every nook and cranny.

Maybe she could go out through the choir loft, Sharon thought, if she could move the music stands out of the way, or at least shift things around so they could hide behind them, but she couldn't do either in the dark.

She knelt carefully, slowly, keeping her back perfectly straight, and put her hand out behind her, feeling for the top of the manger. She patted spiky straw till she found the baby blanket and pulled it out. They must have put the wise men's perfume bottles in the manger, too. They clinked wildly as she pulled the blanket out.

She knelt farther, feeling for the narrow space under the door, and jammed the blanket into it. It didn't quite reach the whole length of the door, but it was the best she could do. She straightened, still slowly, and patted the wall for the light switch.

Her hand brushed it. Please, she prayed, don't let this turn on some other light, and flicked it on.

Neither of them had moved, not even to shift their hands. Mary, pressed against the roses, took a caught breath, and then released it slowly, as if she had been holding it the whole time.

They watched Sharon as she knelt again to tuck in a corner of the blanket and then turned slowly around so she was facing into the room. She reached across the manger for one of the music stands and stacked it against the one behind it, working as gingerly, as slowly, as if she were defusing a bomb. She reached across the manger again, lifted one of the music stands and set it on the straw so she could push the manger back far enough to give her space to move. The stand tipped and Joseph steadied it.

Sharon picked up one of the cardboard palm trees. She worked the plywood base free, set it in the manger, and slid the palm tree flat along the wall next to Mary, and then did the other one.

That gave them some space. There was nothing Sharon could do about the rest of the music stands. Their metal frames were tangled together, and against the outside wall was a tall metal cabinet, with pots of Easter lilies in front of it. She could move the lilies to the top of the cabinet at least.

She listened carefully with her ear to the door for a minute, and then stepped carefully over the manger between two lilies. She bent and picked up one of them and set it on top of the cabinet and then stopped, frowning at the wall. She bent down again, moving her hand along the floor in a slow semicircle.

Cold air, and it was coming from behind the cabinet . She stood on tiptoe and looked behind it. "There's a door," she whispered. "To the outside."

"Sharon!" a muffled voice called from the sanctuary.

Mary froze, and Joseph moved so he was between her and the door. Sharon put her hand on the light switch and waited, listening.

"Mrs. Englert?" a man's voice called. Another one, farther off, "Her car's still here," and then Reverend Farrison's voice again, "Maybe she went downstairs."

Silence. Sharon put her ear against the door and listened, and then edged past Joseph to the side of the cabinet and peered behind it. The door opened outward. They wouldn't have to move the cabinet out very far, just enough for her to squeeze through and open the door, and then there'd be enough space for all of them to get through, even Mary. There were bushes on this side of the church. They could hide underneath them until after the police left.

She motioned Joseph to help her, and together they pushed the cabinet a few inches out from the wall. It knocked one of the Easter lilies over, and Mary stooped awkwardly and picked it up, cradling it in her arms.

They pushed again. This time it made a jangling noise, as if there were coat hangers inside, and Sharon thought she heard voices again, but there was no help for it. She squeezed into the narrow space, thinking, What if it's locked? and opened the door.

Onto warmth. Onto a clear sky, black and pebbled with stars.

"How—" she said stupidly, looking down at the ground in front of the door. It was rocky, with bare dirt in between. There was a faint breeze, and she could smell dust and something sweet. Oranges?

She turned to say, "I found it. I found the door," but Joseph was already leading Mary through it, pushing at the cabinet to make the space wider. Mary was still carrying the Easter lily, and Sharon took it from her and set it against the base of the door to prop it open and went out into the darkness.

The light from the open door lit the ground in front of them and at its edge was a stretch of pale dirt. The path, she thought, but when she got closer, she saw it was the dried bed of a narrow stream. Beyond it the rocky ground rose up steeply. They must be at the bottom of a draw, and she wondered if this was where they had gotten lost.

"*Bott lom?*" Joseph said behind her.

She turned around. "*Bott lom?*" he said again, gesturing in front and to the sides, the way he'd done in the nursery. Which way?

She had no idea. The door faced west, and if the direction held true, and if this was the Judean Desert it should lie to the southwest. "That direction," she said, and pointed up the steepest part of the slope. "You go that way, I think."

They didn't move. They stood watching her, Joseph standing slightly in front of Mary, waiting for her to lead them.

"I'm not—" she said, and stopped. Leaving them here was no better than leaving them in the furnace room. Or out in the snow. She looked back at the door, almost wishing for Reverend Farrison and the police, and then set off toward what she hoped was the southwest, clambering awkwardly up the slope, her shoes slipping on the rocks.

How did they do this, she thought, grabbing at a dry clump of weed for a handhold, even with a donkey? There was no way Mary could make it up this slope. She looked back, worried.

They were following easily, sturdily, as certain of themselves as she had been on the stairs.

But what if at the top of this draw there was another one, or a drop-off? And no path. She dug in her toes and scrambled up.

There was a sudden sound, and Sharon whirled around and looked back at the door, but it still stood half-open, with the lily at its foot and the manger behind.

The sound scraped again, closer, and she caught the crunch of footsteps and then a sharp wheeze.

"It's the donkey," she said, and it plodded up to her as if it were glad to see her.

She reached under it for its reins, which were nothing but a ragged rope, and it took a step toward her and blared in her ear, "Haw!" and then a wheeze that was practically a laugh.

She laughed, too, and patted his neck. "Don't wander off again," she said, leading him over to Joseph, who was waiting where she'd left them. "Stay on the path." She scrambled on up to the top of the slope, suddenly certain the path would be there, too.

It wasn't, but it didn't matter. Because there to the southwest was Jerusalem, distant and white in the starlight, lit by a hundred hearthfires, a thousand oil lamps, and beyond it, slightly to the west, three stars low in the sky, so close they were almost touching.

They came up beside her, leading the donkey. *"Bott lom,"* she said, pointing. "There, where the star is."

Joseph was fumbling in his sash again, holding out the little leather bag.

"No," she said, pushing it back to him. "You'll need it for the inn in Bethlehem."

He put the bag back reluctantly, and she wished suddenly she had something to give them. Frankincense. Or myrrh.

"Hunh-*haw*," the donkey brayed, and started down the hill. Joseph lunged after him, grabbing for the rope, and Mary followed them, her head ducked.

"Be careful," Sharon said. "Watch out for King Herod." She raised her hand in a wave, the sleeve of her choir robe billowing out in the warm breeze like a wing, but they didn't see her. They went on down the hill, Mary with her hand on the donkey for steadiness, Joseph a little ahead. When they were nearly at the bottom, Joseph stopped and pointed at the ground and led the donkey off at an angle out of her sight, and Sharon knew they'd found the path.

She stood there for a minute, enjoying the scented breeze, looking at the almost-star, and then went back down the slope, skidding on the rocks and loose dirt, and took the Easter lily out of the door and shut it. She pushed the cabinet back into position, took the blanket out from under the door, switched off the light, and went out into the darkened sanctuary.

There was no one there. She went and got the chalice, stuck it into the wide sleeve of her robe, and looked out into the hall. There was no one there either. She went into the adult Sunday school room and put the chalice back into the display case and then went downstairs.

"*Where* have you been?" Reverend Farrison said. Two uniformed policemen came out of the nursery, carrying flashlights.

Sharon unzipped her choir robe and took it off. "I checked the Communion silver," she said. "None of it's missing." She went into the choir room and hung up her robe.

"We looked in there," Reverend Farrison said, following her in. "You weren't there."

"I thought I heard somebody at the door," she said.

*By the end of the second verse of "O Little Town of Bethlehem," Mary and Joseph were only three fourths of the way to the front of the sanctuary.*

*"At this rate, they won't make it to Bethlehem by Easter," Dee whispered. "Can't they get a move on?"*

*"They'll get there," Sharon whispered, watching them. They paced slowly, unperturbedly, up the aisle, their eyes on the chancel. "'How silently, how silently,'" Sharon sang, "'the wondrous gift is given.'"*

*They, went past the second pew from the front and out of the choir's sight. The innkeeper came to the top of the chancel steps with his lantern, determinedly solemn.*

*"'So God imparts to human hearts,
The blessings of his heaven.'"*

*"Where did they go?" Virginia whispered, craning her neck to try and see them. "Did they sneak out the back way or something?"*

*Mary and Joseph reappeared, walking slowly, sedately, toward the palm trees and the manger. The innkeeper came down the steps, trying hard to look like he wasn't waiting for then, like he wasn't overjoyed to see them.*

*"'No ear may hear his coming,
But in this world of sin...'"*

*At the back of the sanctuary; the shepherds assembled, clanking their staffs, and Miriam handed the wise men their jewelry box and perfume bottles. Elizabeth adjusted her tinsel halo.*

*"'Where meek souls will receive him still,
The dear Christ enters in.'"*

*Joseph and Mary came to the center and stopped. Joseph stepped in front of Mary and knocked on an imaginary door, and the innkeeper came forward, grinning from ear to ear, to open it.*

# Matters of Life and Death

# Samaritan

*The people of the Countrie, when they travaile in the
Woods, make fires where they sleepe in the night; and in the
morning, when they are gone, the Pongoes [orangutans] will
come and sit about the fire, till it goeth out: for they have no
understanding to lay the wood together.*
                                    —Andrew Battell, 1625

Reverend Hoyt knew immediately what Natalie wanted. His assistant
pastor knocked on the half-open door of his study and then sailed
in, dragging Esau by one hand behind her. The triumphant smile on her
face was proof enough of what she was going to say.

"Reverend Hoyt, Esau has something he wants to tell you." She
turned to the orangutan. He was standing up straight, something Reverend
Hoyt knew was hard for him to do. He came almost to Natalie's
shoulder. His thick, squat body was covered almost entirely with long,
neatly brushed auburn hair. He had only a little hair on top of his head.
He had slicked it down with water. His wide face, inset and shadowed by
his cheek flaps, was as impassive as ever.

Natalie signed something to him. He stood silent, his long arms hanging
limply at his sides. She turned back to Reverend Hoyt. "He wants to
be baptized! Isn't that wonderful? Tell him, Esau."

He had seen it coming. The Reverend Natalie Abreu, twenty-two and
only one year out of Princeton, was one enthusiasm after another. She
had revamped the Sunday school, taken over the grief counseling department,
and initiated a standard of priestly attire that outraged Reverend

Hoyt's Presbyterian soul. Today she had on a trailing cassock with a red-and-gold-embroidered stole edged with fringe. It must be Pentecost. She was short and had close-cropped brown hair. She flew about her official duties like a misplaced choirboy in her ridiculous robes and surplices and chasubles. She had taken over Esau, too.

She had not known how to use American Sign Language when she came. Reverend Hoyt knew only the bare minimum of signs himself, "yes" and "no" and "come here." The jobs he wanted Esau to do he had acted out mostly in pantomime. He had asked Natalie to learn a basic vocabulary so they could communicate better with the orang. She had memorized the entire Ameslan handbook. She rattled on to Esau for hours at a time, her fingers flying, telling him Bible stories and helping him with his reading.

"How do you know he wants to be baptized?"

"He told me. You know how we had the confirmation class last Sunday and he asked me all about confirmation and I said, 'Now they are God's children, members of God's family' And Esau said, 'I would like very much to be God's beloved child, too.'"

It was always disconcerting to hear Natalie translate what Esau said. She changed what was obviously labored and fragmented language into rhapsodies of adjectives, clauses, and modifiers. It was like watching one of those foreign films in which the actor rattled on for a paragraph and the subtitle only printed a cryptic, "That is so." This was reversed, of course. Esau had signed something like, "Me like be child God," if that, and Natalie had transformed it into something a seminary professor would say. It was impossible to have any real communication with Esau this way, but it was better than pantomime.

"Esau," he began resignedly, "do you love God?"

"Of course he loves God," Natalie said. "He'd hardly want to be baptized if he didn't, would he?"

"Natalie," he said patiently, "I need to talk to Esau. Please ask him, 'Do you love God?"'

She looked disgusted but signed out the question. Reverend Hoyt winced. The sign for God was dreadful. It looked like a sideways salute. How could you ask someone if they loved a salute?

Esau nodded. He looked terribly uncomfortable standing there. It infuriated Reverend Hoyt that Natalie insisted on his standing up. His backbone simply wasn't made for it. She had tried to get him to wear clothes, too. She had bought him a workman's uniform of coveralls and a cap and shoes. Reverend Hoyt had not even been patient with her that time. "Why on earth would we put shoes on him?" he had said. "He was hired because he has feet he can use like hands. He needs them both if he's going to get up among the beams. Besides which, he is already clothed. His hair covers him far more appropriately than those ridiculous robes you wear cover you!" After that Natalie had worn some dreadful Benedictine thing made of horsehair and rope until Reverend Hoyt apologized. He had not given in on the matter of clothes for Esau, however.

"Tell Esau to sit down in the chair," he said. He smiled at the orangutan as he said it. He sat down also. Natalie remained standing. The orangutan climbed into the chair frontwards, then turned around. His short legs stuck out straight in front of him. His body hunched forward. He wrapped his long arms around himself, then glanced up at Natalie, and hastily let them hang at his sides. Natalie looked profoundly embarrassed.

"Esau," he began again, motioning to Natalie to translate "baptism is a serious matter. It means that you love God and want to serve him. Do you know what serve means?"

Esau nodded slowly, then made a peculiar sign, tapping the side of his head with the flat of his hand.

"What did he say, Natalie? And no embellishments, please. Just translate."

"It's a sign I taught him," she said stiffly. "In Sunday school. The word wasn't in the book. It means talents. He means—"

"Do you know the story of the ten talents, Esau?"

She translated. Again he nodded.

"And would you serve God with your talents?"

This whole conversation was insane. He could not discuss Christian service with an orangutan. It made no sense. They were not free agents. They belonged to the Cheyenne Mountain Primate Research facility at what had been the old zoo. It was there that the first orangs had signed to each other. A young one raised until the age of three with humans, had lost both human parents in an accident and had been returned to the Center. He had a vocabulary of over twenty words in American Sign Language and could make simple commands. Before the end of the year, the entire colony of orangs had the same vocabulary and could form declarative sentences. Cheyenne Mountain did its best to educate their orangs and find them useful jobs out in society, but they still owned them. They came to get Esau once a month to breed him with females at the Center. He didn't blame them. Orangs were now extinct in the wild. Cheyenne Mountain was doing the best they could to keep the species alive and they were not unkind to them, but he felt sorry for Esau, who would always serve.

He tried something else. "Do you love God, Esau?" he asked again. He made the sign for "love" himself.

Esau nodded. He made the sign for "love."

"And do you know that God loves you?"

He hesitated. He looked at Reverend Hoyt solemnly with his round brown eyes and blinked. His eyelids were lighter than the rest of his face, a sandy color. He made his right hand into a fist and faced it out toward Reverend Hoyt. He put the short thumb outside and across the fingers, then moved it straight up, then tucked it inside, all very methodically.

"S-A-M-" Natalie spelled. "Oh, he means the good Samaritan, that was our Bible story last week. He has forgotten the sign we made for it." She turned to Esau and dropped her flat hand to her open palm. "Good, Esau. Good Samaritan." She made the S fist and tapped her waist with it twice. "Good Samaritan. Remember?"

Esau looked at her. He put his fist up again and out toward Reverend Hoyt. "S-" he repeated, "A-M-A-R-" He spelled it all the way through.

Natalie was upset. She signed rapidly at Esau. "Don't you remember, Esau? Good Samaritan. He remembers the story. You can see that. He's just forgotten the sign for it, that's all." She took his hands and tried to force them into the flattened positions for "good." He resisted.

"No," Reverend Hoyt said, "I don't think that's what he's talking about."

Natalie was nearly in tears. "He knows all his Bible stories. And he can read. He's read almost all of the New Testament by himself."

"I know, Natalie," Reverend Hoyt said patiently.

"Well, are you going to baptize him?"

He looked at the orang sitting hunched in the chair before him. "I'll have to give the matter some thought."

She looked stubborn. "Why? He only wants to be baptized. The Ecumenical Church baptizes people, doesn't it? We baptized fourteen people last Sunday. All he wants is to be baptized."

"I will have to give the matter some thought."

She looked as if she wanted to say something. "Come on, Esau," she said, signing to the ape to follow her.

He got out of the chair clumsily, trying to face forward while he did. Trying to please Natalie, Reverend Hoyt thought. Is that why he wants to be baptized, too, to please Natalie?

Reverend Hoyt sat at his desk for some time. Then he walked down the endless hall from his office to the sanctuary. He stood at the side door and looked into the vast sunlit chamber. The church was one of the first great Ecumenical cathedrals, built before the Rapture. It was nearly four stories high, vaulted with great open pine beams from the Colorado mountains. The famous Lazetti window reached the full four stories and was made of stained glass set in strips of steel.

The first floor, behind the pulpit and the choir loft, was in shadow, dark browns and greens rising to a few slender palm trees. Above that was the sunset. Powerful orange, rich rose, deep mauve dimmed to delicate peach and cream and lavender far over the heads of the congregation. At about the third-floor level the windows changed imperceptibly from pastel-tinted to clear window glass. In the evenings the Denver sunset, rising above the smog, blended with the clouds of the window. Real stars came out behind the single inset star of beveled glass near the peak of the window.

Esau was up among the beams. He swung arm over arm, one hand trailing a white dusting cloth. His long hairy arms moved surely among the crosspieces as he worked. They had tried ladders before Esau came, but they scratched the wood of the beams and were not safe. One had come crashing down within inches of the Lazetti window.

Reverend Hoyt decided to say nothing until he had made up his mind on the matter. To Natalie's insistent questions, he gave the same patient answer. "I have not decided." On Sunday he preached the sermon on humility he had already planned.

Reading the final scripture, however, he suddenly caught sight of Esau huddled on one of the pine crosspieces, his arms wrapped around a buttress for support, watching him as he read. "'But as for me, my feet had almost stumbled, my steps had well-nigh slipped. I was stupid and ignorant. I was like a beast toward thee.'"

441

He looked out over his congregation. They looked satisfied with themselves, smug. He looked at Esau.

"'Nevertheless I am continually with thee; thou dost hold my hand. Afterward thou wilt receive me to glory. My flesh and my heart may fail, but God is the strength of my heart and my portion forever.'" He banged the Bible shut. "I have not said everything I intend to say on the subject of humility, a subject very few of you know anything about." The congregation looked surprised. Natalie, in a bright red robe with a yellow silk chasuble over it, beamed.

He made Natalie shout the benediction over the uproar afterwards and went out the organist's door and back to the parsonage. He turned down the bell on the telephone to almost nothing. An hour later Natalie arrived with Esau in tow. She was excited. Her cheeks were as red as her robe. "Oh, I'm so glad you decided to say something after all. I was hoping you would. You'll see, they'll all think it's a wonderful idea! I wish you'd baptized him, though. Just think how surprised everyone would have been! The first baptism ever, and in our church! Oh, Esau, aren't you excited! You're going to be baptized!"

"I haven't decided yet, Natalie. I told the congregation the matter had come up, that's all."

"But you'll see, they'll think it's a wonderful idea."

He sent her home, telling her not to accept any calls or talk to any reporters, an edict he knew she would ignore completely. He kept Esau with him, fixing a nice supper for them both and turning the television on to a baseball game. Esau picked up Reverend Hoyt's cat, an old tom that allowed people in the parsonage only on sufferance, and carried him over to his chair in front of the TV. Reverend Hoyt expected an explosion of claws and hurt feelings, but tom settled down quite happily in Esau's lap.

When bedtime came, Esau set him down gently on the end of the guest bed and stroked him twice. Then he crawled into the bed forwards, which always embarrassed Natalie so. Reverend Hoyt tucked him in. It was a foolish thing to do. Esau was fully grown. He lived alone and took care of himself. Still, it seemed the thing to do.

Esau lay there looking up at him. He raised up on one arm to see if the cat was still there, and turned over on his side, wrapping his arms around his neck. Reverend Hoyt turned off the light. He didn't know the sign for "good night," so he just waved, a tentative little wave, from the door. Esau waved back.

Esau ate breakfast with the cat in his lap. Reverend Hoyt had turned the phone back up, and it rang insistently. He motioned to Esau that it was time to go over to the church. Esau signed something, pointing to the cat. He clearly wanted to take it with him. Reverend Hoyt signed one rather gentle "no" at him, pinching his first two fingers and thumb together, but smiling so Esau would not think he was angry.

Esau put the cat down on the chair. Together they walked to the church. Reverend Hoyt wished there were some way he could tell him it was not necessary for him to walk upright all the time. At the door of Reverend Hoyt's study Esau signed, "Work?" Reverend Hoyt nodded and tried to push his door open. Letters shoved under the door had wedged it shut. He knelt and pulled a handful free. The door swung open, and he picked up another handful from the floor and put them on his desk. Esau peeked in the door and waved at him. Reverend Hoyt waved back, and Esau shambled off to the sanctuary. Reverend Hoyt shut the door.

Behind his desk was a little clutter of sharp-edged glass and a large rock. There was a star-shaped hole above them in the glass doors. He took the message off the rock. It read, "'And I saw a beast coming up out of the earth, and upon his head the names of blasphemy.'"

Reverend Hoyt cleaned up the broken glass and called the bishop. He read through his mail, keeping an eye out for her through the glass doors. She always came in the back way through the parking lot. His office was at the very end of the business wing of the church, the hardest thing to get to. It had been intended that way to give him as much privacy as possible. There had been a little courtyard with a crab apple tree in it outside the glass doors. Five years ago the courtyard and the crab apple tree had both been sacrificed to parking space, and now he had no privacy at all, but an excellent view of all comings and goings. It was the only way he knew what was going on in the church. From his office he couldn't hear a thing.

The bishop arrived on her bicycle. Her short curly gray hair had been swept back from her face by the wind. She was very tanned. She was wearing a light green pantsuit, but she had a black robe over her arm. He let her in through the glass doors.

"I wasn't sure if it was an official occasion or not. I decided I'd better bring something along in case you were going to drop another bombshell."

"I know," he sighed, sitting down behind his littered desk. "It was a stupid thing to do. Thank you for coming, Moira."

"You could at least have warned me. The first call I got was some reporter raving that the End was coming, I thought the Charies had taken over again. Then some idiot called to ask what the church's position on pigs' souls was. It was another twenty minutes before I was able to find out exactly what you'd done. In the meantime, Will, I'm afraid I called you a number of highly uncharitable names." She reached out and patted his hand. "All of which I take back. How are you doing, dear?"

"I didn't intend to say anything until I'd decided what to do," he said thoughtfully. "I was going to call you this week about it. I told Natalie that when she brought Esau in."

"I knew it. This is Natalie Abreu's brainchild, isn't it? I thought I detected the hand of an assistant pastor in all this. Honestly, Will, they are all alike. Isn't there some way to keep them in seminary another ten years until they calm down a little? Causes and ideas and reforms and more causes. It wears me out.

"Mine is into choirs: youth choirs, boy choirs, madrigals, antiphonals, glees. We barely have time for the sermon there are so many choirs. My church doesn't look like a church. It looks like a military parade. Battalions of colored robes trooping in and out, chanting responses." She paused. "There are times when I'd like to throttle him. Right now I'd like to throttle Natalie. Whatever put it into her head?"

Reverend Hoyt shook his head. "She's very fond of him."

"So she's been filling him with a lot of Bible stories and scripture. Has she been taking him to Sunday school?"

"Yes. First grade, I think."

"Well, then, you can claim indoctrination, can't you? Say it wasn't his own idea but was forced on him?"

"I can say that about three-fourths of the Sunday school class. Moira, that's the problem. There isn't any argument that I can use against him that wouldn't apply to half the congregation. He's lonely. He needs a strong father figure. He likes the pretty robes and candles. Instinct. Conditioning. Sexual sublimation. Maybe those things are true of Esau, but they're true of a lot of people I've baptized, too. And I never said to them, 'Why do you really want to be baptized?'"

"He's doing it to please Natalie."

"Of course. And how many assistant pastors go to seminary to please their parents?" He paced the narrow space behind his desk. "I don't suppose there's anything in church law?"

"I looked. The Ecumenical Church is just a baby, Will. We barely have the organizational bylaws written down, let alone all the odds and ends. And twenty years is not enough time to build a base of precedent. I'm sorry, Will. I even went back to pre-unification law, thinking we might be able to borrow something obscure. But no luck."

The liberal churches had flirted with the idea of unification for more than twenty-five years without getting more accomplished than a few statements of good will. Then the Charismatics had declared the Rapture, and the churches had dived for cover right into the arms of ecumenism.

The fundamentalist Charismatic movement had gained strength all through the eighties. They had been committed to the imminent coming of the End, with its persecutions and Antichrist. On a sultry Tuesday in 1989 they had suddenly announced that the End was not only in sight but here, and that all true Christians must unite to do battle against the Beast. The Beast was never specifically named, but most true Christians concluded he resided somewhere among the liberal churches. There was fervent prayer on Methodist front lawns. Young men ranted up the aisles of Episcopal churches during mass. A great many stained glass windows, including all but one of the Lazettis, were broken. A few churches burned.

The Rapture lost considerable momentum when two years later the skies still had not rolled back like a scroll and swallowed up the faithful, but the Charies were a force the newly born United Ecumenical Church refused to take lightly. She was a rather hodgepodge church, it was true, but she stood like a bulwark against the Charies.

"There wasn't anything?" Reverend Hoyt asked. "But the bishops can at least make a ruling, can't they?"

"The bishops have no authority over you in this matter. The United Church of Christ insisted on self-determination in matters within an individual church, including election of officers, distribution of communion, and baptism. It was the only way we could get them in," she finished apologetically.

"I've never understood that. There they were all by themselves with the Charismatics moving in like wolves. They didn't have any choice. They had to come in. So how did they get a plum like self-determination?"

"It worked both ways, remember. We could hardly stand by and let the Charies get them. Besides, everyone else had fiddled away their compromise points on trespassers versus debtors and translations of the Bible. You Presbyterians, as I recall, were determined to stick in the magic word 'predestination' everywhere you could."

Reverend Hoyt had a feeling the purpose of this was to get him to smile. He smiled. "And what was it you Catholics nearly walked out over? Oh, yes, grape juice."

"Will, the point is I cannot give you bishop's counsel on this. It's your problem. You're the one who'll have to come to a fair and rational decision."

"Fair and rational?" He picked up a handful of mail. "With advice like this?"

"You asked for it, remember? Ranting from the pulpit about humility?"

"Listen to this: 'You can't baptize an ape. They don't have souls. One time I was in San Diego in the zoo there. We went to the ape house and right there, in front of the visitors and everything, were these two orangitangs...'" He looked up from the letter. "Here she apparently had some trouble deciding what words were most appropriate. Her pen has blotted." He continued to read "'...two orangitangs doing it.' That's underlined. 'The worst of it is that they were laying there just enjoying it. So you see, even if you think they are nice sometimes...' etc. This, from a woman who's had three husbands and who knows how many 'little lapses,' as she calls them. She says I can't baptize him on the grounds that he likes sex."

He flipped through more papers. "The deacons think it would have what they call a negative effect on the total amount of pledges. The ushers don't want tourists in here with cameras. Three men and nine women think baptizing him would somehow let loose his animal lusts and no one would be safe in the church alone."

He held up another letter triumphantly, this one written on pale pink rosebudded stationery. "'You asked us Sunday what we thought about apes having souls. I think so. I like to sit in back because of my arthritis which is very bad. During the invocation there were three tots in front of me with their little hands folded in prayer and just inside the vestry door was your ape, with his head bowed and his hands folded too.'" He held up the paper. "My only ally. And she thinks it's cute to watch a full-grown orangutan fold his little hannies. How am I supposed to come to any kind of decision with advice like this? Even Natalie's determined to make him into something he isn't. Clothes and good manners and standing up straight. And I'm supposed to decide!"

Moira had listened to his rantings with a patient expression. Now she stood up. "That's right, Will. It is your decision, not Natalie's, not your congregation's, not the Charies'. You're supposed to decide."

He watched her to her bicycle through the star of broken glass. "Damn the Congregationalists!" he said under his breath.

He sorted all the mail into three piles of "for" and "against" and "wildly insane," then threw all of them into the wastebasket. He called in Natalie and Esau so he could give Esau the order to put up the protective plastic webbing over the big stained glass window. Natalie was alarmed. "What is it?" she asked when Esau had left with the storeroom key in his hand. "Have there been threats?"

He showed her the message from the rock, but didn't mention the letters. "I'll take him home again with me tonight," he said. "When does he have to go to Colorado Springs?"

"Tomorrow." She had fished a letter out of the wastebasket and was reading it. "We could cancel. They already know the situation," she said and then blushed.

"No. He's probably safer there than here." He let some of the tiredness creep into his voice.

"You aren't going to do it, are you?" Natalie said suddenly. "Because of a lot of creeps!" She slammed the letter down on his desk. "You're going to listen to them, aren't you? A lot of creeps who don't even know what a soul is and you're going to let them tell you Esau doesn't have one!" She went to the door, the tails of the yellow stole flying. "Maybe I should just tell them to keep him tomorrow, since you don't want him."

The door's slamming dislodged another splinter of glass.

Reverend Hoyt went to the South Denver Library and checked out books on apes and St. Augustine and sign language. He read them in his office until it was nearly dark outside. Then he went to get Esau. The protective webbing was up on the outside of the window. There was a ladder standing in the sanctuary. The window let in the dark blue evening light and the beginning stars.

Esau was sitting in one of the back pews, his short legs straight out in front of him on the velvet cushions. His arms hung down, palms out. He was resting. The dustcloth lay beside him. His wide face held no expression except the limpness of fatigue. His eyes were sad beyond anything Reverend Hoyt had ever seen.

When he saw Reverend Hoyt he climbed down off the pew quite readily. They walked to the parish house. Esau immediately went to find the cat.

The people from Cheyenne Mountain came quite early the next morning. Reverend Hoyt noticed their van in the parking lot. He saw Natalie walk Esau to the van. The young man from the center opened the door and said something to Natalie. She nodded and smiled rather shyly at him. Esau got in the back seat of the van. Natalie leaned in and hugged him goodbye. When the van drove off he was sitting looking out the window, his face impassive. Natalie did not look in Reverend Hoyt's direction.

They brought him back about noon the next day. Reverend Hoyt saw the van again, and shortly afterward Natalie brought the young man to his office. She was dressed all in white, a childishly full surplice over a white robe. She looked like an angel in a Sunday school program. Pentecost must be over and Trinity begun. She was still subdued, more than the situation of having her friends argue for her would seem to merit. Reverend Hoyt wondered how often this same young man came for Esau.

"I thought you would like to know how things are going down at the Center, sir," the young man said briskly. "Esau passed his physical, though there is some question of whether he might need glasses. He has a slight case of astigmatism. Otherwise he is in excellent physical condition for a male of his age. His attitude toward the breeding program has also improved markedly in the past few months. Male orangs become rather solitary, neurotic beings as they mature, sometimes becoming very depressed. Esau was not, up until a few months ago, willing to breed at all. Now he participates regularly and has impregnated one female.

"What I came to say, sir, is that we feel Esau's job and the friends he has made here have made him a much happier and better adjusted ape than he was before. You are to be congratulated. We would hate to see anything interfere with the emotional well-being he has achieved so far."

This is the best argument of all, Reverend Hoyt thought. A happy ape is a breeding ape. A baptized ape is a happy ape. Therefore…

"I understand," he said, looking at the young man. "I have been reading about orangutans, but I have questions. If you could give me some time this afternoon, I would appreciate it."

The young man glanced at his watch. Natalie looked uncomfortable. "Perhaps after the news conference. That lasts until…" He turned to Natalie. "Is it four o'clock, Reverend Abreu?"

She tried to smile. "Yes, four. We should be going. Reverend Hoyt, if you'd like to come—"

"I believe the bishop is coming later this afternoon, thank you." The young man took Natalie's arm. "After the press conference," Reverend Hoyt continued, "please have Esau put the ladder away. Tell him he does not need to use it."

"But—"

"Thank you, Reverend Abreu."

Natalie and her young man went to their press conference. He closed all the books he had checked out from the library and stacked them on the end of his desk. Then he put his head in his hands and tried to think.

"Where's Esau?" the bishop said when she came in.

"In the sanctuary, I suppose. He's supposed to he putting the webbing on the inside of the window."

"I didn't see him."

"Maybe Natalie took him with her to her press conference."

She sat down. "What have you decided?"

I don't know. Yesterday I managed to convince myself he was one of the lower animals. This morning at three I woke from a dream in which he was made a saint. I am no closer to knowing what to do than I have ever been."

"Have you thought, as my archbishop would say, who cannot forget his Baptist upbringing, about what our dear Lord would do?"

"You mean, 'Who is my neighbor? And Jesus answering said, A certain man went down from Jerusalem to Jericho and fell among thieves.' Esau said that, you know. When I asked him if he knew that God loved him he spelled out the word Samaritan."

"I wonder," Moira said thoughtfully. "Did he mean the good Samaritan or—"

"The odd thing about it was that Natalie'd apparently taught him some kind of shorthand sign for good Samaritan, but he wouldn't use it. He kept spelling the word out, letter by letter."

"'How is it that thou, being a Jew, askest drink of me, which am a woman of Samaria?'"

"What?"

"John 4. That's what the Samaritan woman said to Jesus at the well."

"You know, one of the first apes they raised with human parents used to have to do this test where she sorted through a pile of pictures and separated the humans from the apes. She could do it perfectly, except for one mistake. She always put her own picture in the human pile." He stood up and went and stood at the doors. "I have thought all along that the reason he wanted to be baptized was because he didn't know he wasn't human. But he knows. He knows."

"Yes," said the bishop. "I think he does."

They walked together as far as the sanctuary "I didn't want to ride my bicycle today," she said. "The reporters recognize it. What is that noise?"

It was a peculiar sound, a sort of heavy wheezing. Esau was sitting on the floor by one of the pews, his chest and head leaning on the seat. He was making the noise.

"Will," Moira said. "The ladder's down. I think he fell."

He whirled. The ladder lay full-length along the middle aisle. The plastic webbing was draped like fish net over the front pews. He knelt by Esau, forgetting to sign. 'Are you all right?"

Esau looked up at him. His eyes were clouded. There was blood and saliva under his nose and on his chin. "Go get Natalie," Reverend Hoyt said.

Natalie was in the door, looking like a childish angel. The young man from Cheyenne Mountain was with her. Her face went as white as her surplice. "Go call the doctor," she whispered to him, and was instantly on her knees by Esau. "Esau, are you all right? Is he sick?"

Reverend Hoyt did not know how to tell her. "I'm afraid he fell, Natalie."

"Off the ladder," she said immediately. "He fell off the ladder."

"Do you think we should lay him down, get his feet up?" Moira asked. "He must be in shock."

Reverend Hoyt lifted Esau's lip a little. The gums were grayish blue. Esau gave a little cough and spewed out a stream of frothy blood onto his chest.

"Oh," Natalie sobbed and put her hand over her mouth.

"I think he can breathe better in this position," Reverend Hoyt said. Moira got a blanket from somewhere. Reverend Hoyt put it over him, tucking it in at his shoulders. Natalie wiped his mouth and nose with the tail of her surplice. They waited for the doctor.

The doctor was a tall man with owlish glasses. Reverend Hoyt didn't know him. He eased Esau onto his back on the floor and jammed the velvet pew cushion under his feet to prop them up. He looked at Esau's gums, as Reverend Hoyt had done, and took his pulse. He worked slowly and methodically to set up the intravenous equipment and shave a space on Esau's arm. It had a calming effect on Natalie, She leaned back on her heels, and some of the color came back to her cheeks. Reverend Hoyt could see that there was almost no blood pressure. When the doctor inserted the needle and attached it to the plastic tube of sugar water, no blood backed up into the tube.

The doctor examined Esau gently, having Natalie sign questions to him. He did not answer. His breathing eased a little, but blood bubbled out of his nose. "We've got a peritoneal hernia here," the doctor said. "The organs have been pushed up into the rib cage and aren't giving the lungs enough space. He must have struck something when he fell." The corner of the pew. "He's very shocky. How long ago did this happen?"

"Before I came," Moira said, standing to the side. "I didn't see the ladder when I came." She collected herself. "Before three."

"We'll take him in as soon as we get a little bit more fluid in him." He turned to the young man. "Did you call the ambulance?"

The young man nodded. Esau coughed again. The blood was bright red and full of bubbles. The doctor said, "He's bleeding into the lungs." He adjusted the intravenous equipment slowly "If you will all leave for just a few moments, I'll try to see if I can get him some additional air space in the lungs."

Natalie put both hands over her mouth and hiccuped a sob.

"No," Reverend Hoyt said.

The doctor's look was unmistakable. You know what's coming. I am counting on you to be sensible and get people out of here so they don't have to see it.

"No," he said again, more softly. "We would like to do something first. Natalie, go and get the baptismal bowl and my prayer book."

She stood up, wiping a bloody hand across her tears. She did not say anything as she went.

"Esau," Reverend Hoyt said. Please God, let me remember what few signs I know. "Esau God's child." He signed the foolish little salute for God. He held his hand out waist-high for child. He had no idea how to show a possessive.

Esau's breathing was shallower. He raised his right hand a little and made a fist. "S-A-M-"

"No!" Reverend Hoyt jammed his two fingers against his thumb viciously. He shook his head vigorously. "No! Esau God's childl" The signs would not say what he wanted them to. He crossed his fists on his chest, the sign for love, Esau tried to make the same sign. He could not move his left arm at all. He looked at Reverend Hoyt and raised his right hand. He waved.

Natalie was standing over them, holding the bowl. She was shivering. He motioned her to kneel beside him and sign. He handed the bowl to Moira. "I baptize thee, Esau," he said steadily, and dipped his hand in the water, "in the name of the Father"—he put his damp hand gently on the scraggly red head—"and of the Son, and of the Holy Ghost. Amen."

He stood up and looked at the bishop. He put his arm around Natalie and led her into the nave. After a few minutes the doctor called them back.

Esau was on his back, his arms flung out on either side, his little brown eyes open and unseeing. "He was just too shocky," the doctor said. "There was nothing but blood left in his lungs." He handed his card to Reverend Hoyt. "My number's on there. If there's anything I can do."

"Thank you," Reverend Hoyt said. "You've been very kind."

The young man from Cheyenne Mountain said, "The Center will arrange for disposal of the body."

Natalie was looking at the card. "No," she said. Her robe was covered with blood, and damp. "No, thank you."

There was something in her tone the young man was afraid to question. He went out with the doctor.

Natalie sat down on the floor next to Esau's body. "He called a vet," she said. "He told me he'd help me get Esau baptized, and then he called a vet, like he was an animal!" She started to cry, reaching out and patting the limp palm of Esau's hand. "Oh, my dear friend," she said. "My dear friend."

Moira spent the night with Natalie. In the morning she brought her to Reverend Hoyt's once. "I'll talk to the reporters for you today," she said. She hugged them both goodbye.

Natalie sat down in the chair opposite Reverend Hoyt's desk. She was wearing a simple blue skirt and blouse. She held a wadded Kleenex in her hands. "There isn't anything you can say to me, is there?" she asked quite steadily. "I ought to know, after a whole year of counseling everybody else." She sounded sad. "He *was* in pain, he *did* suffer a long time, it *was* my fault."

"I wasn't going to say any of those things to you, Natalie," he said gently.

She was twisting the Kleenex, trying to get to the point where she could speak without crying. "Esau told me that you tucked him in when he stayed with you. He told me all about your cat, too." She was not going to make it. "I want to thank you...for being so kind to him. And for baptizing him, even though you didn't think he was a person." The tears came, little choking sobs. "I know that you did it for me." She stopped, her lips trembling.

He didn't know how to help her. "God chooses to believe that we have souls because He loves us," he said. "I think He loves Esau, too. I know we did."

"I'm glad it was me that killed him," Natalie said tearfully. "And not somebody that hated him, like the Charies or something. At least nobody hurt him on purpose."

"No," Reverend Hoyt said. "Not on purpose."

"He *was* a person, you know, not just an animal."

"I know," he said. He felt very sorry for her.

She stood up and wiped at her eyes with the sodden Kleenex. "I'd better go see what can be done about the sanctuary." She looked totally and finally humiliated, standing there in the blue dress. Natalie the unquenchable quenched at last. He could not bear it.

"Natalie," he said, "I know you'll be busy, but if you have the time, would you mind finding a white robe for Sunday for me to wear? I have been meaning to ask you. So many of the congregation have told me how much they thought your robes added to the service. And a stole perhaps. What is the color for Trinity Sunday?"

"White," she said promptly, and then looked ashamed. "White and gold."

# Cash Crop

"Oh, Haze," Sombra said. "Aren't you excited about tomorrow? Our new dresses and the school all decorated with flowers?"

"Yes," I said, trying to see down the hill to the peach tree. Francie always waited by the peach tree after school, triumphant that she had made it home before the downer. But this morning Mother had come to take her home, and I could not see any figure standing beside the stunted tree.

"I can hardly wait to see the flowers!" Sombra said. "Mamita says they always bring yellow roses. And red carnations. Do you know what carnations look like, Haze?"

I shook my head. The only flowers I had ever seen were my mother's greentent geraniums.

Earlier today the district nurse had talked to Mother for a long time. I had heard the words "scarlet fever" and "northern," and the nurse's face had become flushed and angry as she spoke. "Flowers!" she had said angrily. "They buy us off with flowers and antibiotics when they should be sending us a centrifuge so we can make our own antibiotics. They take our grain and give us flowers!" And Mother had hurried Francie home.

"Just think," Sombra said, looking up at the dusty haze, "right now the *Magassar*'s orbiting. Floating up there in space with its hold full of flowers." She was shivering, hugging her arms across her chest. We had ridden the dustdowner home, clinging to the narrow seat under the sprinklers, and both of us were wet from the spray.

Dirty downers, my father called them. "They buy us off with the downers when they could be doing climate control, when they could be eliminating the strep altogether." All I seemed to be able to think of today were angry words against the government. There shouldn't be, with graduation coming. The government had sent a special ship just for the occasion of our first graduating class. They had already sent fabric for graduation clothes with the last grain ship, and although Sombra's romantic notions about the ship floating overhead with its hold full of flowers were not quite right and the *Magassar* was instead already filling its massive hold with compressed grain and alcohol from the orbiting silos, when it did land tomorrow there would be gifts and special foods from earth, fresh fruits and chocolate, and Sombra's flowers. Yet all I heard were angry words.

Father had threatened to dismantle the dustdowner that circled our stead daily and build a cannon out of it. "Then when the government men tell me they're doing all they can about the strep, I can tell them what I think." The government's argument was that the strep outbreaks were being caused by the dust, so they sent the automated sprinklers crawling up and down the adobe-hard roads between the steads, wasting Haven's already scarce water, and stirring up dust with their heavy wheels that their sprinklers didn't even touch. The quarantine and sterilization regulations the first steaders set up did more to keep the strep under control than the downers ever would.

The steaders made their own use of them, hitching supplies and messages on the back to send them between the steads. During quarantines the district nurse sent antibiotics that way and sometimes a coffin, And all the kids caught them on the way to and from school, if they could time it, arriving damp and disheveled at their angry mothers', who told them they would get a chill and catch the strep, who forced the government-supplied Schultz-Charlton strips into their mouths and wrapped them in blankets. I had seen Mamita Turillo do it to Sombra and Mother to Francie. Not to me. I was never chilled. The breeze on my wet shirt and jeans today was cool, but not cold.

"Oh, you're never cold," Sombra said now, her teeth chattering. "It isn't fair."

Even in winter I slept under a thin blanket and forgot my coat at school. Even in Haven's sudden intense summer that was nearly here, my dust-colored cheeks didn't flush like Sombra's red ones. Sweat didn't curl my dust-colored hair as it did her black hair. Sombra looked like a greentent flower, her body tall and narrow, her cheeks and hair bright splashes of color. I only came to Sombra's shoulder, and I looked more like the flowers Mother tried to plant outside the greentent, dusty and pinched and they never bloomed.

I was not the only one. A few of the first-generation steaders, like Old Man Phelps, were short and hardy, and more and more of the new hands Mamita boarded fresh off the emigration ships looked like me. I looked out across our stead and Sombra's with the bare hard road and low mud fence dividing the pale sweeps of winter wheat, and the pinkish-brown haze in the sky above them. Maybe the emigration people had decided to send people as colorless and dusty as Haven itself in the hope the strep would overlook them.

I could see Father's peach tree at the corner of our stead, where Sombra would turn to go another quarter-mile to her house, but no Francie. Only one thing would have made Mother come and get her, somebody sick here in western.

"Sombra," I said, "do you know of anybody sick in this district?"

"Yes," she said, unconcerned. "Old Man Phelps. I heard the district nurse tell your mother."

"Scarlet fever?" I said blankly, but it could not be anything else. It was always scarlet fever. Stray streptococci brought by the first steaders had taken to Haven's dry, dusty climate like cherrybrights to a tree. It was always there, waiting for a shortage of antibiotics. There had been a heart-stopping outbreak in northern three weeks ago, seventeen reported, mostly children, and a local had been slapped on the district by the district nurse. It shouldn't have spread to western. What was worse, Mr. Phelps brought us within two of a planetwide quarantine. Mr. Phelps, one of the oldtimers who never got the strep, down with scarlet fever.

"The district nurse told your mother there was nothing to worry about. Mr. Phelps lives alone, and she said she could stop an outbreak with the antibiotics the *Magassar*'s bringing."

"If the *Magassar* lands," I said. A faint scratchiness of fear was beginning behind my throat. Two more reported cases and the *Magassar* would go back to earth without even landing. There would be no graduation.

Sombra said, "Mamita says there's no reason for them to quarantine us without antibiotics. She says they could drop the antibiotics from orbit. Do you think that's true?"

The scratchiness became almost an ache. "No, of course not. If they could, they would. They wouldn't leave us without any antibiotics if there was any way to get them to us." But I was remembering something from a long time ago, when little Willie died. Mother telling me to get out of the house, out of her sight, and Father saying, "Don't take it out on Haze. It's the government that's left us to the wolves. Blame them. Blame me— I brought you here, knowing what they were doing. But not Haze. She can't help being what she is." The ache was worse. I swallowed hard, and when it didn't go away, I pressed the flat of my hand against the hollow space between my collarbones and swallowed again. This time it went away.

"Of course not," I said again, feeling much better. "Don't worry about Mr. Phelps. He won't stop our graduation. There's got to be an incubation period, and by the time it's up, the *Magassar* will already be on the ground. The local's probably already got it stopped."

We were nearly down the long hill to the corner, and I didn't want to leave her thinking about a possible quarantine. I said, "Mother finished our dresses last night. Are you going to come over to try yours on?" Sombra's flushed cheeks darkened. "To make sure about the hem," I said hesitantly. "To see how we're going to look tomorrow."

Sombra shook her dark head. "I'm sure it'll be all right," she said uncomfortably. "Mamita has a lot of chores for me today. With the *Magassar* coming in tomorrow. She's taking the new hands to board again, and so she said she wanted me to bring in everything ripe from the greentent for the supper tomorrow night. I wish Mamita had made our dresses," she finished unhappily.

"It's all right," I said. "I'll bring it over tomorrow morning. We'll get dressed together."

It had been a mistake to mention the dresses, and a worse one to have had Mother make them for us. I had been to Sombra's house countless times, with Mamita bright and cheerful as a cherrybright, feeding us vegetables from the greentent and asking us about school, reaching up on tiptoe to pull Sombra's curls away from her face and, no taller than me, hugging me goodbye when I left. Mother was rigid and erect as one of the tallgrasses that shaded our porch when Sombra came home with me. She had not spoken a dozen words to her during all the fittings. We should have had Mamita make the dresses.

Yesterday Sombra had tried on her dress timidly. I had not seen it so nearly finished before, with the red ribbons pinned where they would be threaded through the bodice. "Oh, Sombra, you look so beautiful!" I had blurted out, "Oh, Mama, it's the loveliest dress I've ever seen."

Mother had turned on me with a look that made Sombra gasp. "I will not allow you to call me that," she had said, and slammed the door behind her. Sombra had shimmied out of the dress and into her jeans so fast she nearly tore the thin white cotton.

"It's because of the babies," I had said helplessly. "She had seven babies that died between Francie and me. Little Willie lived to be three. I remember when he died. It was a planetwide and there wasn't anything to give him and he laid upstairs in the big bed crying, 'Mama! Mama!' for five days."

Sombra had her shirt buttoned and her books scooped up. "She lets Francie call her Mama," she said, her cheeks flaming with anger.

"That's different," I had said.

"How is it different? Mamita lost nine babies to the strep. Nine."

"But she has you and the twins left. And all Mother has is Francie."

"And you. She has you." I had not known how to explain to her that Francie, with her blue eyes and yellow hair, made her think of San Francisco, of earth. Francie and the geraniums she tended so carefully in the hot damp air of the greentent. And when she looked at me, what did she think? She had found me that day after Willie died, hiding in the greentent, and had switched me. What was she thinking then? And what did she think this morning when the district nurse told her Mr. Phelps had scarlet fever and we were within two of a planetwide? The scratchiness had returned, this time as a dull ache. I knotted my hand into a fist and pushed against it, but it did no good. I wondered if I'd better take a strip when I got home.

"You're worried about them imposing a quarantine, aren't you?" Sombra said. We were nearly down the hill, and I had not said anything the whole way.

"I was wondering if they'll have pink carnations tomorrow," I said. "I was wondering if they'll give us some to wear in our hair?"

"Of course. Mamita said so. You'll have red roses. You'll be so pretty." The long walk down the dusty hill had dried us off. She looked hot now, the sweat on her forehead curling her dark hair. "Let's sit down a minute, all right?" She sank down on the low mudbrick fence and fanned herself with her books. "It's so hot today."

I looked over her head at the peach tree. It was no taller than me and folded-in on itself so that it barely gave any shade at all. Its leaves were narrow and so pale a green the dust made them look the same color as the wheat. There were little pinkish-white specks between the leaves. I squinted at them.

"Don't you think it's hot?" Sombra said.

This was the only one of Father's trees that had lived past the ponics tanks. It had lasted five years now, though it had never borne fruit. And now there were the pale specks all over it, which could be moths or sorrel ants. The ache pressed dully against the hard bone of my sternum, bending me forward under it. I put the edge of my fist against the pain, pressing hard into the bone, willing myself to straighten. Mother was always telling me to stand up straight, to try to look at least as tall as I could, not like some hunched dwarf, and I would straighten automatically, my whole body responding. I willed myself to hear her voice now. My shoulder blades pulled back, stretching the ache with it till it had pulled out to nothing. I stood still, breathing hard.

"I can't sit down," I said breathlessly. "I have to go right home."

"But it's so hot! Do I feel hot to you?" She pulled me onto the wall with her and pressed her cheek against mine. It was burning against my chilled face.

"A little," I said. I must take a strip when I get home. And tell Father about the tree.

"You're not getting sick, are you?" she said. "You can't get sick, Haze, not for graduation. You go right home and go to bed, all right? I don't want you sending us under a planetwide."

"I will," I promised her, climbing over the fence and into the field for a closer look at the tree. The specks were larger than I had thought, almost the size of...

"Oh, Sombra," I shouted after her delightedly, "we won't go under a planetwide, and I'm not getting sick either. I've had a good omen. There'll be flowers for graduation."

"How do you know?" she shouted back.

"I thought the tree had something wrong with it," I said. "But it doesn't. It's in bloom!"

She grinned in happy surprise. "You mean blossoms?" She was over the low fence in an easy step and peering eagerly at the tiny tight blossoms. "Oh, they're just starting to come out, aren't they? Oh, Haze, think how pretty they'll be!"

A red cherrybright whizzed through the air over our heads and lighted unafraid on the top of the tree, shaking the branch in our faces. The folded blossoms bowed and dipped.

"The pink blossoms are for my ribbons," Sombra said happily, "and the cherrybright's for your red ribbons!" She put her arm around my waist. It felt warm through my thin shirt. "And you know what they mean?"

"That we'll be beautiful tomorrow! That nothing can possibly go wrong because we're going to graduate!"

"Oh, Haze," she said, hugging me, "I can hardly wait." She ran back to the road. "Bring my dress over first thing in the morning and we'll get ready together. Everything's going to be perfect," she shouted to me. "The day is full of omens."

⊣ • • • ⊢

No one was in the house but Francie, sitting at the kitchen table, dawdling over her lessons with a strip in her mouth.

"Papa's in the greentent. With Mama," she said, taking the strip out of her mouth so she could talk. It was the bright red of a negative reading. Active strep blanched the strips like a person going white from fear. "Are you scared?" she said.

"Of what?"

"Mama says two more and they'll call a planetwide. There won't be any graduation."

"There will so, Francie. There hasn't been a planetwide in ages."

"How do you know?"

"I just know," I said, thinking of the peach tree and what Father would say when he saw it was in bloom. He would think it was a good omen, too. I smiled at Francie and went out to find Father.

He stood in the door of the greentent, blocking it with his bulk. Mother stood across the ponics tanks from him, holding onto one of the metal supports. Through the thick plastic, she looked as if she were drowning. Her hand clutched the strut so hard I thought she would pull the whole tent down.

"It's what they want," Father said. "It ties us to them. We'll be doing just what they want."

"I don't care," she said.

"It will take away every chance of a cash crop. You know that, don't you?"

"Mr. Phelps died this morning. There have been seventeen cases in northern."

"The *Magassar* will be landing tomorrow. We don't have to…"

"No," she said, and looked steadily at him. "You owe it to me."

His hand on the doorframe tightened until I could see the veins stand out on his hands.

"The peach tree's in bloom," I blurted, and they both turned to look at me, Father with blank drowned eyes, Mother with a look like triumph. "It's a good sign, don't you think?" I said into the silence. "An omen. It means the *Magassar* will land tomorrow and everything will be all right…anyway, it has to have some kind of incubation period, doesn't it? People can't just catch it in one day."

"It's a new strain," Mother said. She had let go of the strut and was pushing dirt around the base of a geranium. "The district nurse said it appears to have a very short incubation period."

"She doesn't know that," I said earnestly. "How could she know that for sure?"

She looked up, but at my father, not at me. "Mr. Phelps had taken a strip that morning. It was negative. You would not have expected Mr. Phelps to get it at all, let alone so quickly. Maybe others you wouldn't expect will get it, too."

The call box, attached to the plastic feederlines above the ponics tanks, barked suddenly. The sharp, short signal that called the district nurse. The signal that meant our district. Mother looked at me. "What did I tell you?" she said.

My father let go of the doorframe, and took a step toward her. "Move your geraniums to ponics," he said, "I need the plaindirt to plant more corn in." He turned and walked away.

I helped Mother move the geraniums into the tanks, my body tensed for the alerting bark of the box, but it did not ring again. After supper we stayed in the kitchen, and when we went up to bed, Father carried the little box with him, trailing its wires like ribbons, but the box did not sound again. Oh, yes, the day was full of omens.

⊣ • • ⊢

The pale pink haze was gone in the morning, replaced with the clear chill to the sky that meant night frost. I took Father down to the tree before breakfast to look at the peach blossoms. They dropped like scraps of paper at his feet when he put out his hand to a branch. "The frost got them," he said, as if he didn't even mind.

"Not all of them," I said. Some of them, crumpled and tight, like little knots against the cold, still clung to the branches. "The frost didn't get all of them," I said. "It's supposed to be warm today. I knew it would be warm for graduation." He was looking past me, past the tree. I turned to look. A cherrybright fluttered on Sombra's fence. Our good omen.

"No!" Father said sharply, and then more gently as I turned back to him in surprise, "the frost didn't get them all. Some of them are still alive." He took my arm, and steered me back to the house, keeping himself between the tree and me, as if the frozen blossoms were my disappointment and I could not bear to see them.

At the greentent I stopped. "I have to take Sombra her dress," I said, barely able to keep the excitement of the day out of my voice. "We have to get ready for graduation." He did not let go of my arm, but his hand seemed to go suddenly lifeless. I patted his cold hand and ran into the house to get Sombra's dress and down the steps past him with it over my arm, fluttering pink ribbons as I ran. He still stood there, as if he had finally seen the frozen blossoms and could not hide his grief.

It was not a cherrybright. It was a quarantine sticker, tied to one of the distance markers. I stood for a moment by the peach tree looking at it as my father had done, the dress as heavy on my arm as my hand had been on his. "No!" I said, as sharply as he had and took off running.

I could not even let myself think what breaking quarantine meant. "I don't care," I told myself, catching my breath at the last corner of the fence. "It's graduation," I would tell Mamita. "The *Magassar* will be landing with all those flowers. We have to be there."

Mamita would look reluctant, thinking of the consequences.

"One of the hands has it, doesn't he? The new ones always get it. But this is our *graduation!* You can't let him spoil it. Think of all the flowers," I would say. "Sombra has to see them. She'll die if she doesn't see them. Give her a strip. Give us both one. We won't get it."

I climbed over the fence, careful of the dress. Even folded double, it almost dragged on the ground. The gate would be locked. I cut through the field at a dead run and came up to the house the back way, past the greentent. The door stood open, but I could not see anyone through the plastic. Sombra must have hurried through her chores to get ready and left the door open. Mamita would kill her. I could not stop to shut it now, because someone might see me and turn me in. I had to get to Mamita and convince her first.

I knocked at the back door, leaning against the scratchy stalk of a tallgrass, too breathless for a moment to say any of the things I had planned to say. Then Mamita opened the door, and I knew I would never say any of them.

I could hear a baby crying in the house. Mamita passed her hand over her chest, pressing as if there were a pain there. Then she put her hand up to her forehead. There were brilliant scarlet creases on the inside of her elbows. "Why, Haze, what are you doing here?" she said.

"I brought Sombra's dress," I said.

A sudden, hitting anger flared out of her black eyes, and I stumbled back, raking my arm against the tallgrass. It came to me much later that she must have thought I brought the dress for Sornbra's laying out, that she had felt the same anger as Mother did when she saw me standing and still healthy while the babies died, one after the other. I did not think of that then. All I could think was that it was not one of the hands, that it was Sombra who was sick.

"For graduation," I said, holding the dress out insistently. If I could make her take it, then it would not be true.

"Thank you, Haze," she said, but she didn't take it. "Her father's already gone," she said. "Sombra's..." and in that breath of a second, I thought she was going to say that she was dead already, too, and I could not, would not let her say that.

"The *Magassar* will be landing this morning. I could go over there for you. I could catch a downer. I'd be back in no time. The *Magassar*'s bringing a whole load of antibiotics. I heard the district nurse say so."

"He died before the district nurse could get here. He wouldn't let me call until we found Sombra in the greentent. He didn't want to spoil her graduation."

"But the *Magassar*..."

She put her hand on my shoulder. "Sombra was the twentieth," she said.

I still could not take in what she was saying. "There was only one call. That makes nineteen." One call. Sombra and her father. One call.

"You should go home and take a strip, dear," she said. "You'll have been exposed." She put her hand to my cheek, and it burned like a brand. "Tell your mother thank you for the dress," she said, and shut the door in my face.

⊣•••⊢

When Francie found me, I was sitting under the peach tree with Sombra's dress across my lap like a blanket. The last of the blossoms fell on the dress, already dead and dying like the flowers aboard the *Magassar*.

"Papa says for you to come up to the house," Francie said. Mama had curled her hair with sugar water for graduation. The curls were stiff against her pink cheeks.

"There isn't any graduation," I said.

"I know *that*," she said disdainfully. "Mamma's been making me take strips all morning long. She thinks I'm going to get it."

"No," I said, my cheeks burning from the brand of Sombra's cheek, Mamita's hand. The pain pressed against my sternum and would not go away. "I'm going to get it."

"I *told* Mama I didn't even sit near her. And how you never let me walk home with you two, how you always ride the downer. She sent for me as soon as she found out about Mr. Phelps, and Sombra wasn't even sick then. But she wouldn't listen. Anyway, you never get sick. She probably won't even make you take a strip. And Sombra wasn't sick yesterday, was she? So you probably weren't exposed either. Mama says the incubation period is really short." She remembered why she had been sent. "Papa says you're supposed to come *now*." She flounced off.

I stood up, still careful of the white dress, and followed Francie through the field of scratchy wheat. They don't know about my breaking quarantine, I thought in amazement. I wondered why Father had sent for me. Perhaps he knew and wanted to talk to me before he turned me in. "What does he want?" I said.

"I don't know. He said I was supposed to come and get you before the downer came. There's been one already, with a coffin. For Mr. Utrillo."

I stopped and looked back toward the road. The downer rattled past the peach tree, spraying water over the scattered blossoms, wetting the coffin it pulled behind it. Sombra's coffin. He had at least tried to spare me that. And now I would have to try to spare him my dying, as much as I could.

I imposed my own quarantine, sneaking a strip as soon as I got back to the house. I had been afraid that Mother would make me take one, but she didn't, although Francie was already sitting at the kitchen table when

I came in, protesting the bright red strip Mother held in her hand. I held the strip I had stolen behind my back until I could get out to the green-tent. I took it there, huddled under the ponics tank in case it took a long time. It blanched white as soon as the paper was in my mouth. I did not need the strip to tell me I was getting sick. Sombra's cheek, her mother's hand, burned on my face like a brand.

No one reported me. I did not doubt that Mamita, much as she loved me, would have turned me in. This was more than a planetwide. It was a local, too. The *Magassar* had already broken its orbit and was heading for home. We were on our own, and the only way to stop it was to keep the quarantine from being broken. Which meant Mamita had the fever, too, that maybe all the people on the Turillo stead were dead or sick with it and no one to help them.

I tried to stay out of everyone's way, especially Francie's. I talked with my head averted and asked to do the wash and the dishes so I could sterilize my own things. I picked a fight with Francie and called her a tagalong, so that she avoided me as carefully as I did her. Mother paid no attention to me. She had eyes only for Francie.

⊣ • • • ⊢

Three weeks after Sombra died, Father said at supper, "The local's off at Turillos'. Mamita's over it. The district nurse cleared her this afternoon."

"The twins?" Mother said.

He shook his head. "Both of them died. But none of the hands came down with it. Six months here and not one of them has had so much as a white strip."

"It was an unusual strain," Mother said. "It doesn't prove anything. They could all die tomorrow."

"I doubt it," he said. "The incubation period was very short, as you said. But none of the hands got it." He put a subtle emphasis on the word 'none.'

"Yet," Mother said. "I'm sure Haven isn't through coming up with new strains. We're still without antibiotics." The fear I had expected was not in her voice.

"They intercepted the *Magassar* halfway home and told them we'd had no new cases in a week. They're holding where they are for a week, and then if there are no other reporteds, they'll come back." He smiled at me. "I'm full of good news today, Haze. The peaches didn't freeze after all. We're getting some fruit starting."

He turned and looked at Mother, and said in the same cheerful tone, "You'll have to move the geraniums out of the ponics."

Mother put her hand up to her cheek as if he had hit her. "I talked to Mamita," he said. "She said she'll buy all the corn we can give her. Cash crop."

"Can I move the flowers back to plaindirt?" she asked.

"No," Father said. "I'll need to put the corn wherever I can."

She looked at him across the table as if he were her enemy, and he looked just as steadily back. It was as if a bargain had been struck between them, and the price she was paying was her precious flowers. I wondered what price Father had paid.

"If the peaches aren't frozen, they could be our cash crop, Father," I said urgently. "They'll ripen almost as fast as the corn and you know how hungry everyone will be for real fruit."

"No," Father said. His eyes never left her face. "We need the cash from the corn. To pay for something. Don't we?"

"Yes," she said, and pushed her chair back from the table. "You have your cash crop and I have mine."

"I want to put the corn in tomorrow," he shouted after her. "Pull your geraniums out this afternoon." Francie was staring at him wide-eyed. "Come on, Haze," he said more quietly, "I'll show you the peaches."

They did not even look like fruit. But they were there, hard little swellings like pebbles where the tight blossoms had been. "You see," he said, "we'll have our cash crop yet."

The quarantine sticker was gone from Sombra's fence. My strip had been white again this morning, and the ache that never quite left me was deeper, into my lungs now.

"First-generation colonies don't have cash crops," Father said. "They're too busy hanging on, too busy trying to stay alive. They're abjectly grateful for what the government gives them—greentents, antibiotics, anything. Second-generation aren't so grateful. The wheat's doing well and they start noticing that the government's help isn't all that helpful. Third-generation colonies aren't grateful at all. They have cash crops and they can buy what they need from earth, not beg for it. Fourth-generation stop growing wheat altogether and start manufacturing what they need and to hell with earth."

"We're fourth-generation," I said, not understanding.

Father had carried down a bucket of lime-sulphur and water and a wad of cloth rags to paint the peaches with. He dipped a rag in the bucket and pulled it out dripping. "No, Haze," he said. "We're first-generation, and if the government has its way, we'll be first-generation forever. The strep keeps us down, keeps us fighting for our lives. We can't develop light industry. We can't even keep our children alive long enough to graduate them from high school. We've been here nearly seventy years, Haze, and this is our first graduation."

"They could drop the antibiotics without landing, couldn't they?" I said. Little Willie upstairs in the big bed, crying for Mama. "They could wipe it out altogether if they wanted to." Father was bending over the sulphur-smelling bucket, dipping the rag in the liquid. "Why aren't you doing something about it?"

I expected him to say there was nothing they could do, that it was impossible to manufacture antibiotics without filters and centrifuges and reagents, which the government would never ship us. I expected him to say that the only manufactured goods they shipped were those guaranteed not to be vandalized for parts and that the main virtue of the dust-downers as far as the government saw it was that they could not be turned into equipment for making antibiotics. But he wiped industriously at a peach and said, "We will be second-generation yet, Haze," he said. "We'll have our cash crops, and the government won't be able to stop us. They're shipping us the one thing we need right now, and they don't even know it."

I knelt by the bucket, dipping the worn cloth in the sulphur-smelling liquid.

"When I first tried to grow peaches, Haze, I used ordinary peach seeds from back home. I started them in the ponics tanks and some of them lived long enough to bloom and I crossed them with others that had survived. Do you remember that, Haze? When the greentent was full of peach trees?"

I shook my head, still kneeling by the bucket. I could not even imagine it. Now there was no room for anything, not even Mother's geraniums.

"I bred for what I thought they needed—a thick skin to stand the sorrel ants and a short trunk to stand the wind, but I couldn't do any genetic engineering. There isn't any equipment. I could only cross the ones that did well, the ones that lived long enough to bloom. I knew what I was breeding for, but not what I would get. I never thought it would be so...stunted and turned in upon itself..."

He was not looking at the tree. He was looking at me. The rag he held was dripping whitish water on the toe of his shoe. "We have people working in emigration, some of them colonists, some of them not, looking at the gene prints and deciding on the emigration permits. We all thought your mother...her genetic prints were almost exactly like Mr. Phelps', and he'd never had the strep. I've only had it twice in all these years. If it was a few points off, still it would be close enough, we thought. You cannot do the same things to people that you do to peach trees. Because it matters when they die.

"All I have left is this one pale and stunted tree," he said, and squeezed out the rag on the ground and began painting the fruit again. "And you."

⊣•••⊢

The next day we trenched the tree, filling the narrow moat with dried mud and straw to keep the sorrel ants away. Father did not say anything more, and I could not tell anything from his face.

The day after that I had a negative strip, and I looked at it a long time, thinking about how I was never hot, never cold, how I had never had strep as a child. But Mr. Phelps had died of scarlet fever. Mr. Phelps, who looked like me and never felt the cold. And Mother's gene prints were almost like Mr. Phelps'.

I ran down to the tree, almost tripping in the tangle of ripening wheat. Father was standing by the tree, examining one of the peaches. It was no larger that I could see, but it had lost a little of its greenish cast.

"Do you think we should put a moth net on?" he said. "It's a little early for moths."

"Father," I said, "I don't think anything we do will help or hurt it. I think it's all in the seed."

He smiled, and his smile told me what I had been afraid to see before. "So I've been told," he said.

"I'm immune to the strep, aren't I?"

"Her prints were almost exactly those of Mr. Phelps. I had only had the strep twice. We thought it would be close enough, and after you were born, we were sure it would." He looked through me, as he had done on that day when he saw the sticker on Sombra's fence. "I have done the best I can for her. I have tried to remember that it was not her fault, that I brought her here to this, that it is my fault for thinking of her as I thought of my peach trees. I have let her turn Francie into a greentent flower that cannot possibly survive. I have let her treat you like a stepchild because I knew you could survive no matter what she did to you. I have let her…" He stopped and passed his hand over his chest. "There is a cache of blackmarket penicillin in the greentent for Francie. It took the cash crop to do it. It will save her once." He looked away from me toward Turillos'. "I think it's time to send you to Mamita's. She's got all the hands to do for. She'll need you."

He sent me back to the house to pack my things. The day was very hot. Halfway across the field I put my hand up to my forehead, and I could feel the damp sweat curling my hair. It will be cooler under the peach tree, I thought, and started back toward the tree. But halfway there the haze seemed to thicken almost to clouds with a fine pink tint, and the temperature to drop. It will be warmer in the greentent, I thought, shivering. I turned back the way I had come.

I hit one of the supports in the greentent when I fell. Francie will see that it's down, I thought, Francie will find me. I tried to pull myself up by the edge of the ponics tanks, but I had cut my hand when I fell and it bled into the tanks.

Mother found me. Francie had seen the greentent sagging heavily on one side and run to the house to tell her. Mother stood over me for a long time, as if she could not think what to do.

"What's wrong with her?" Francie asked from the doorway.

"Did you touch her?" Mother said.

"No, Mama."

"Are you sure?"

"Yes, Mama," she said, her bright blue eyes full of tears. "Shouldn't I go get Papa?"

And at last she knelt beside me and put her cool hand on my hot cheek. "She has the scarlet fever," she said to Francie. "Go into the house."

⊣•••⊢

They put me in the big bed in the front bedroom because of Francie. I tried to keep the covers on, but it was so hot that I kicked them off without meaning to, and then I shivered so that they had to bring more blankets off Francie's bed.

"How is she?" Father said.

"No better," Mother said. "Her fever still hasn't broken." Her voice was less afraid than it had been in the greentent. I wondered if the planetwide had been lifted.

"I called the district nurse."

"Why?" Mother said, still in that quiet voice. "She doesn't have anything to give her. The *Magassar* won't come back again."

"There's the penicillin." I wondered if they looked as they had looked that day in the greentent, each clutching the frame of the bed as they had held onto the supports of the greentent.

Mother put her hand to my cheek. It felt cool. "No," she said quietly.

"She'll die without it," he said. I could hardly hear his voice.

"There isn't any penicillin," Mother said, and her voice was as still as her hand on my cheek. "I gave it to Francie."

Something worried at the edge of my mind. I tried to get a hold on it, but my teeth were chattering so badly I could not. The pain in my chest burned like a flame. I thought if I could press with my hand against it, the pain would lessen, but my hand felt muffled, and when I tried to look at it, it was as white as a positive strip.

Mamita had told me to take a strip when I got home. I did and it was white. But that could not be right, because the incubation period was very short, and I had not gotten sick for nearly a month. But I already had it, I thought. That day Sombra had asked if I was getting sick and there had been that pain behind my sternum that nearly doubled me over by the tree, I had already been getting sick.

I was edging closer to the worrisome thing, but it was so cold. I never felt the cold. Or the heat. Sombra had leaned forward to me on the wall and said, "Don't I feel hot?" and the pain had almost doubled me over. She was already getting sick, but so was I. I had been getting sick that day, and I had gotten over it.

I pulled my hand free of the blankets, and that started me shivering again. The hand was still white and clumsily heavy. I put it over the hollow space between my collarbones and pressed and pressed, my whole body straightening, tautening with the pain until it stretched to nothing.

Then I got up and put on my graduation dress, fumbling over the buttons with my bandaged hand, a little weak from the fever, but better, better.

⊣•••⊢

Father was standing by the peach tree, throwing the peaches at the road. They bounced when they hit the hard mud and rolled against Turillos' fence.

"Oh, Papa," I said, "don't do that."

He did not seem to hear me. The dustdowner was kicking up its little trail of dust far down the road. He picked a hard peach off the tree, covered it with his big fist in a grip that should have smashed it, and pitched it at the distant downer.

"Papa," I said again. He whirled violently as if he would throw the peach at me. I stepped back in surprise.

"She killed you," he said, "to save her precious Francie. She let you die up there crying out her name. Putting her hand on your cheek and tucking you in. She murdered you!" He flung the peach down violently. It rolled to my feet. "Murderer!" He turned to wrench another peach off the tree.

I put up my hand in protest. "Papa, don't! Not your cash crop!"

He dropped his hands and stared limply at the dustdowner rattling down the road toward us. It was pulling a coffin behind it. My coffin. "You were my cash crop," he said quietly.

I remembered Mamita's face when she thought I'd brought the dress for Sombra's laying out. I looked down at my white shroudlike dress and my hand wrapped in the white bandage. "Oh, Papa," I said, finally understanding. "I didn't die. I got better."

"She gave the penicillin to Francie," he said. "While you were still in the greentent. Before she even let Francie come to get me. Your hand was bleeding. She gave her the penicillin before she even bandaged your hand."

"It doesn't matter," I said. "I didn't need the medicine. I got over the scarlet fever by myself."

It was finally coming to him, bit by bit, like it had come to me in the big bed. "You were supposed to be immune," he said. "But you got it anyway. You were supposed to be immune."

"I'm not immune, Papa, but I can get over the strep myself. I've been doing it all along, all my life." I picked up the peach at my feet and handed it to him. He looked at it numbly.

"We were breeding for immunity," he said.

"I know, Papa. You knew what you were breeding for, but you didn't know what you'd get." I wanted to put my arms around him. "Haven will always be coming up with new strains. It would be impossible to be immune to all of them."

He took a knife out of his pocket, slowly, as if he were still asleep. He cut into the peach in his hand, sawing through the thick, dusty skin to the sudden softness underneath. He bit into it, and I watched his face anxiously.

"Is it all right, Papa?" I said. "Is it sweet?"

"Sweet beyond hope," he said, and put his arms around me, holding me close. "Oh, my sweet Haze, we bred to fight the strep, and look, look what we got!"

He held me by the shoulders and looked down at me. "I want you to go to Mamita's. You can't help here. But the hands all have gene prints like yours." His eyes were full of tears. "You are my cash crop after all."

"Now run," he said and walked away from me, back through the field toward the house. I stood for a minute, watching him, unable to call to him, to shout after him how much I loved them all. I climbed over the fence and stood in the road, looking at the litter of unhurt peaches. The downer was finishing its determined circuit at the top of the hill. If I hurried I could ride my own coffin to Mamita's and not even get my graduation dress wet. It seemed to me suddenly the most joyous chance in the world—to ride my own coffin, triumphant in my white dress with its fluttering red ribbons.

I stopped to catch my breath at the top of the hill and looked back at the peach tree. Francie was standing by it, with her hand raised almost in a question. Mama had done her hair in sugar curls for some occasion, and they did not move in the dusty wind that fluttered the red ribbons on my dress. She seemed as still as the brown haze that surrounded her, hugging her thin arms against her chest. I was too far away to see her shivering. Perhaps I would not have known what it meant if I had: I was not bred to read omens.

"I'll bring you some penicillin," I shouted, though she would have no idea of what I was saying. I shouted past her to Papa, who was too far away already to hear me. "I'll bring you some if I have to walk all the way to the *Magassar*."

"Don't worry!" I shouted. "They'll lift the planetwide. I know it." The dustdowner rattled past me, drowning out my words, and I ran to pull myself up onto the splintery edge of the coffin. "Don't worry, Francie!" I shouted again, putting my bandaged hand up to my mouth and holding on tight with the other. "We're all going to live forever!"

# Jack

The night Jack joined our post, Vi was late. So was the Luftwaffe. The sirens still hadn't gone by eight o'clock.

"Perhaps our Violet's tired of the RAF and begun on the aircraft spotters," Morris said, "and they're so taken by her charms, they've forgotten to wind the sirens."

"You'd best watch out, then," Swales said, taking off his tin warden's hat. He'd just come back from patrol. We made room for him at the linoleum-covered table, moving our teacups and the litter of gas masks and pocket torches. Twickenham shuffled his papers into one pile next to his typewriter and went on typing.

Swales sat down and poured himself a cup of tea. "She'll set her cap for the ARP next," he said, reaching for the milk. Morris pushed it toward him. "And none of us will be safe." He grinned at me. "Especially the young ones, Jack."

"I'm safe," I said. "I'm being called up soon. Twickenham's the one who should be worrying."

Twickenham looked up from his typing at the sound of his name. "Worrying about what?" he asked, his hands poised over the keyboard.

"Our Violet setting her cap for you," Swales said. "Girls always go for poets."

"I'm a journalist, not a poet. What about Renfrew?" He nodded his head toward the cots in the other room.

"Renfrew!" Swales boomed, pushing his chair back and starting into the room.

"Shh," I said. "Don't wake him. He hasn't slept all week."

"You're right. It wouldn't be fair in his weakened condition." He sat back down. "And Morris is married. What about your son, Morris? He's a pilot, isn't he? Stationed in London?"

Morris shook his head. "Quincy's up at North Weald."

"Lucky, that," Swales said. "Looks as if that leaves you, Twickenham."

"Sorry," Twickenham said, typing. "She's not my type."

"She's not anyone's type, is she?" Swales said.

"The RAF's," Morris said, and we all fell silent, thinking of Vi and her bewildering popularity with the RAF pilots in and around London. She had pale eyelashes and colorless brown hair she put up in flat little pin curls while she was on duty, which was against regulations, though Mrs. Lucy didn't say anything to her about them. Vi was dumpy and rather stupid, and yet she was out constantly with one pilot after another, going to dances and parties.

"I still say she makes it all up," Swales said. "She buys all those things she says they give her herself, all those oranges and chocolate. She buys them on the black market."

"On a full-time's salary?" I said. We only made two pounds a week, and the things she brought home to the post—sweets and sherry and cigarettes—couldn't be bought on that. Vi shared them round freely, though liquor and cigarettes were against regulations as well. Mrs. Lucy didn't say anything about them, either.

She never reprimanded her wardens about anything, except being malicious about Vi, and we never gossiped in her presence. I wondered where she was. I hadn't seen her since I came in.

"Where's Mrs. Lucy?" I asked. "She's not late as well, is she?"

Morris nodded toward the pantry door. "She's in her office. Olmwood's replacement is here. She's filling him in."

Olmwood had been our best part-time, a huge out-of-work collier who could lift a house beam by himself, which was why Nelson, using his authority as district warden, had had him transferred to his own post.

"I hope the new man's not any good," Swales said. "Or Nelson will steal him."

"I saw Olmwood yesterday," Morris said. "He looked like Renfrew, only worse. He told me Nelson keeps them out the whole night patrolling and looking for incendiaries."

There was no point in that. You couldn't see where the incendiaries were falling from the street, and if there was an incident, nobody was anywhere to be found. Mrs. Lucy had assigned patrols at the beginning of the Blitz, but within a week she'd stopped them at midnight so we could get some sleep. Mrs. Lucy said she saw no point in our getting killed when everyone was already in bed anyway.

476

"Olmwood says Nelson makes them wear their gas masks the entire time they're on duty and holds stirrup-pump drills twice a shift," Morris said.

"Stirrup-pump drills!" Swales exploded. "How difficult does he think it is to learn to use one? Nelson's not getting me on his post, I don't care if Churchill himself signs the transfer papers."

The pantry door opened. Mrs. Lucy poked her head out. "It's half past eight. The spotter'd better go upstairs even if the sirens haven't gone," she said. "Who's on duty tonight?"

"Vi," I said, "but she hasn't come in yet."

"Oh, dear," she said. "Perhaps someone had better go look for her."

"I'll go," I said, and started pulling on my boots.

"Thank you, Jack," she said. She shut the door.

I stood up and tucked my pocket torch into my belt. I picked up my gas mask and slung it over my arm in case I ran into Nelson. The regulations said they were to be worn while patrolling, but Mrs. Lucy had realized early on that you couldn't see anything with them on. Which is why, I thought, she has the best post in the district, including Admiral Nelson's.

Mrs. Lucy opened the door again and leaned out for a moment. "She usually comes by underground. Sloane Square," she said. "Take care."

"Right," Swales said. "Vi might be lurking outside in the dark, waiting to pounce!" He grabbed Twickenham round the neck and hugged him to his chest.

"I'll be careful," I said, and went up the basement stairs and out onto the street.

I went the way Vi usually came from Sloane Square Station, but there was no one in the blacked-out streets except a girl hurrying to the underground station, carrying a blanket, a pillow, and a dress on a hanger.

I walked the rest of the way to the tube station with her to make sure she found her way, though it wasn't that dark. The nearly full moon was up, and there was a fire still burning down by the docks from the raid of the night before.

"Thanks awfully," the girl said, switching the hanger to her other hand so she could shake hands with me. She was much nicer looking than Vi, with blond, very curly hair. "I work for this old stewpot at John Lewis's, and she won't let me leave even a minute before closing, will she, even if the sirens have gone."

I waited outside the station for a few minutes and then walked up to the Brompton Road, thinking Vi might have come in at South Kensington instead, but I didn't see her, and she still wasn't at the post when I got back.

"We've a new theory for why the sirens haven't gone," Swales said. "We've decided our Vi's set her cap for the Luftwaffe, and they've surrendered."

"Where's Mrs. Lucy?" I asked.

"Still in with the new man," Twickenham said.

"I'd better tell Mrs. Lucy I couldn't find her," I said, and started for the pantry.

Halfway there the door opened, and Mrs. Lucy and the new man came out. He was scarcely a replacement for the burly Olmwood. He was not much older than I was, slightly built, hardly the sort to lift housebeams. His face was thin and rather pale, and I wondered if he was a student.

"This is our new part-time, Mr. Settle," Mrs. Lucy said. She pointed to each of us in turn. "Mr. Morris, Mr. Twickenham, Mr. Swales, Mr. Harker." She smiled at the part-time and then at me. "Mr. Harker's name is Jack, too," she said. "I shall have to work at keeping you straight."

"A pair of jacks," Swales said. "Not a bad hand."

The part-time smiled.

"Cots are in there if you'd like to have a lie-down," Mrs. Lucy said, "and if the raids are close, the coal cellar's reinforced. I'm afraid the rest of the basement isn't, but I'm attempting to rectify that." She waved the papers in her hand. "I've applied to the district warden for reinforcing beams. Gas masks are in there," she said, pointing at a wooden chest, "batteries for the torches are in here"—she pulled a drawer open—"and the duty roster's posted on this wall." She pointed at the neat columns. "Patrols here and watches here. As you can see, Miss Westen has the first watch for tonight."

"She's still not here," Twickenham said, not even pausing in his typing.

"I couldn't find her," I said.

"Oh, dear," she said. "I do hope she's all right. Mr. Twickenham, would you mind terribly taking Vi's watch?"

"I'll take it," Jack said. "Where do I go?"

"I'll show him," I said, starting for the stairs.

"No, wait," Mrs. Lucy said. "Mr. Settle, I hate to put you to work before you've even had a chance to become acquainted with everyone, and there really isn't any need to go up till after the sirens have gone. Come and sit down, both of you." She took the flowered cozy off the teapot. "Would you like a cup of tea, Mr. Settle?"

"No, thank you," he said.

She put the cozy back on and smiled at him. "You're from Yorkshire, Mr. Settle," she said as if we were all at a tea party. "Whereabouts?"

"Newcastle," he said politely.

"What brings you to London?" Morris said.

"The war," he said, still politely.

"Wanted to do your bit, eh?"

"Yes."

"That's what my son Quincy said. 'Dad,' he says, 'I want to do my bit for England. I'm going to be a pilot.' Downed twenty-one planes, he has, my Quincy," Morris told Jack, "and been shot down twice himself. Oh, he's had some scrapes, I could tell you, but it's all top secret."

Jack nodded.

There were times I wondered whether Morris, like Violet with her RAF pilots, had invented his son's exploits. Sometimes I even wondered if he had invented the son, though if that were the case, he might surely have made up a better name than Quincy.

"'Dad,' he says to me out of the blue, 'I've got to do my bit,' and he shows me his enlistment papers. You could've knocked me over with a feather. Not that he's not patriotic, you understand, but he'd had his little difficulties at school, sowed his wild oats, so to speak, and here he was, saying, 'Dad, I want to do my bit.'"

The sirens went, taking up one after the other. Mrs. Lucy said, "Ah, well, here they are now," as if the last guest had finally arrived at her tea party, and Jack stood up.

"If you'll just show me where the spotter's post is, Mr. Harker," he said.

"Jack," I said. "It's a name that should be easy for you to remember."

I took him upstairs to what had been Mrs. Lucy's cook's garret bedroom—unlike the street, a perfect place to watch for incendiaries. It was on the fourth floor, higher than most of the buildings on the street so one could see anything that fell on the roofs around. One could see the Thames, too, between the chimney pots, and in the other direction the searchlights in Hyde Park.

Mrs. Lucy had set a wing-backed chair by the window, from which the glass had been removed, and the narrow landing at the head of the stairs had been reinforced with heavy oak beams that even Olmwood couldn't have lifted.

"One ducks out here when the bombs get close," I said, shining the torch on the beams. "It'll be a swish and then a sort of rising whine." I led him into the bedroom. "If you see incendiaries, call out and try to mark exactly where they fall on the roofs." I showed him how to use the gunsight mounted on a wooden base that we used for a sextant and handed him the binoculars. "Anything else you need?" I asked.

"No," he said soberly. "Thank you."

I left him and went back downstairs. They were still discussing Violet.

"I'm really becoming worried about her," Mrs. Lucy said. One of the ack-ack guns started up, and there was the dull crump of bombs far away, and we all stopped to listen.

"ME 109's," Morris said. "They're coming in from the south again."

"I do hope she has the sense to get to a shelter," Mrs. Lucy said, and Vi burst in the door.

"Sorry I'm late," she said, setting a box tied with string on the table next to Twickenham's typewriter. She was out of breath and her face was suffused with color. "I know I'm supposed to be on watch, but Harry took me out to see his plane this afternoon, and I had a horrid time getting back." She heaved herself out of her coat and hung it over the back of Jack's chair. "You'll never believe what he's named it! The *Sweet Violet!*" She untied the string on the box. "We were so late we hadn't time for tea, and he said, 'You take this to your post and have a good tea, and I'll keep the jerries busy till you've finished,'" She reached in the box and lifted out a torte with sugar icing. "He's painted the name on the nose and put little violets in purple all round it," she said, setting it on the table. "One for every jerry he's shot down."

We stared at the cake. Eggs and sugar had been rationed since the beginning of the year, and they'd been in short supply even before that. I hadn't seen a fancy torte like this in over a year.

"It's raspberry filling," she said, slicing through the cake with a knife. "They hadn't any chocolate." She held the knife up, dripping jam. "Now, who wants some, then?"

"I do," I said. I had been hungry since the beginning of the war and ravenous since I'd joined the ARP, especially for sweets, and I had my piece eaten before she'd finished setting slices on Mrs. Lucy's Wedgwood plates and passing them round.

There was still a quarter left. "Who's upstairs taking my watch?" she said, sucking a bit of raspberry jam off her finger.

"The new part-time," I said. "I'll take it up to him."

She cut a slice and eased it off the knife and onto the plate. "What's he like?" she asked.

"He's from Yorkshire," Twickenham said, looking at Mrs. Lucy. "What did he do up there before the war?"

Mrs. Lucy looked at her cake, as if surprised that it was nearly eaten. "He didn't say," she said.

"I meant, is he handsome?" Vi said, putting a fork on the plate with the slice of cake. "Perhaps I should take it up to him myself."

"He's puny. Pale," Swales said, his mouth full of cake. "Looks as if he's got consumption."

"Nelson won't steal him anytime soon, that's certain," Morris said.

"Oh, well, then," Vi said, and handed the plate to me.

I took it and went upstairs, stopping on the second-floor landing to shift it to my left hand and switch on my pocket torch.

Jack was standing by the window, the binoculars dangling from his neck, looking out past the rooftops toward the river. The moon was up, reflecting whitely off the water like one of the German flares, lighting the bombers' way.

"Anything in our sector yet?" I said.

"No," he said, without turning round. "They're still to the east."

"I've brought you some raspberry cake," I said.

He turned and looked at me.

I held the cake out. "Violet's young man in the RAF sent it."

"No, thank you," he said. "I'm not fond of cake."

I looked at him with the same disbelief I had felt for Violet's name emblazoned on a Spitfire. "There's plenty," I said. "She brought a whole torte."

"I'm not hungry, thanks. You eat it."

"Are you sure? One can't get this sort of thing these days."

"I'm certain," he said, and turned back to the window.

I looked hesitantly at the slice of cake, guilty about my greed but hating to see it go to waste and still hungry. At the least I should stay up and keep him company.

"Violet's the warden whose watch you took, the one who was late," I said. I sat down on the floor, my back to the painted baseboard, and started to eat. "She's full-time. We've got five full-timers. Violet and I and

Renfrew—you haven't met him yet, he was asleep. He's had rather a bad time. Can't sleep in the day—and Morris and Twickenham. And then there's Petersby. He's part-time like you."

He didn't turn around while I was talking or say anything, only continued looking out the window. A scattering of flares drifted down, lighting the room.

"They're a nice lot," I said, cutting a bite of cake with my fork. In the odd light from the flares the jam filling looked black. "Swales can be rather a nuisance with his teasing sometimes, and Twickenham will ask you all sorts of questions, but they're good men on an incident."

He turned around. "Questions?"

"For the post newspaper. Notice sheet, really, information on new sorts of bombs, ARP regulations, that sort of thing. All Twickenham's supposed to do is type it and send it round to the other posts, but I think he's always fancied himself an author, and now he's got his chance. He's named the notice sheet *Twickenham's Twitterings,* and he adds all sorts of things—drawings, news, gossip, interviews."

While I had been talking, the drone of engines overhead had been growing steadily louder. It passed, there was a sighing whoosh and then a whistle that turned into a whine.

"Stairs," I said, dropping my plate. I grabbed his arm and yanked him into the shelter of the landing. We crouched against the blast, my hands over my head, but nothing happened. The whine became a scream and then sounded suddenly farther off. I peeked round the reinforcing beam at the open window. Light flashed and then the crump came, at least three sectors away. "Lees," I said, going over to the window to see if I could tell exactly where it was. "High explosive bomb." Jack focused the binoculars where I was pointing.

I went out to the landing, cupped my hands, and shouted down the stairs, "HE. Lees." The planes were still too close to bother sitting down again. "Twickenham's done interviews with all the wardens," I said, leaning against the wall. "He'll want to know what you did before the war, why you became a warden, that sort of thing. He wrote up a piece on Vi last week."

Jack had lowered the binoculars and was watching where I had pointed. The fires didn't start right away with a high explosive bomb. It took a bit for the ruptured gas mains and scattered coal fires to catch. "What was she before the war?" he asked.

"Vi? A stenographer," I said. "And something of a wallflower, I should think. The war's been rather a blessing for our Vi."

"A blessing," Jack said, looking out at the high explosive in Lees. From where I was sitting, I couldn't see his face except in silhouette, and I couldn't tell whether he disapproved of the word or was merely bemused by it.

"I didn't mean a blessing exactly. One can scarcely call something as dreadful as this a blessing. But the war's given Vi a chance she wouldn't have had otherwise. Morris says without it she'd have died an old maid, and now she's got all sorts of beaus." A flare drifted down, white and then red. "Morris says the war's the best thing that ever happened to her."

"Morris," he said, as if he didn't know which one that was.

"Sandy hair, toothbrush mustache," I said. "His son's a pilot."

"Doing his bit," he said, and I could see his face clearly in the reddish light, but I still couldn't read his expression.

A stick of incendiaries came down over the river, glittering like sparklers, and fires sprang up everywhere.

The next night there was a bad incident off Old Church Street, two HEs. Mrs. Lucy sent Jack and me over to see if we could help. It was completely overcast, which was supposed to stop the Luftwaffe but obviously hadn't, and very dark. By the time we reached the King's Road, I had completely lost my bearings.

I knew the incident had to be close, though, because I could smell it. It wasn't truly a smell; it was a painful sharpness in the nose from the plaster dust and smoke and whatever explosive the Germans put in their bombs. It always made Vi sneeze.

I tried to make out landmarks, but all I could see was the slightly darker outline of a hill on my left. I thought blankly, We must be lost. There aren't any hills in Chelsea, and then realized it must be the incident.

"The first thing we do is find the incident officer," I told Jack. I looked round for the officer's blue light, but I couldn't see it. It must be behind the hill.

I scrabbled up it with Jack behind me, trying not to slip on the uncertain slope. The light was on the far side of another, lower hill, a ghostly bluish blur off to the left. "It's over there," I said. "We must report in. Nelson's likely to be the incident officer, and he's a stickler for procedure."

I started down, skidding on the broken bricks and plaster. "Be careful," I called back to Jack. "There are all sorts of jagged pieces of wood and glass."

"Jack," he said.

I turned around. He had stopped halfway down the hill and was looking up, as if he had heard something. I glanced up, afraid the bombers were coming back, but couldn't hear anything over the antiaircraft guns. Jack stood motionless, his head down now, looking at the rubble.

"What is it?" I said.

He didn't answer. He snatched his torch out of his pocket and swung it wildly round.

"You can't do that!" I shouted. "There's a blackout on!"

He snapped it off. "Go and find something to dig with," he said, and dropped to his knees. "There's someone alive under here."

He wrenched the bannister free and began stabbing into the rubble with its broken end.

I looked stupidly at him. "How do you know?"

He jabbed viciously at the mess. "Get a pickax. This stuff's hard as rock." He looked up at me impatiently. "Hurry!"

The incident officer was someone I didn't know. I was glad. Nelson would have refused to give me a pickax without the necessary authorization of duties. This officer, who was younger than me and broken out in spots under his powdering of brick dust, didn't have a pickax, but he gave me two shovels without any argument.

The dust and smoke were clearing a bit by the time I started back across the mounds, and a shower of flares drifted down over by the river, lighting everything in a fuzzy, overbright light like headlights in a fog. I could see Jack on his hands and knees halfway down the mound, stabbing with the bannister. He looked like he was murdering someone with a knife, plunging it in again and again.

Another shower of flares came down, much closer. I ducked and hurried across to Jack, offering him one of the shovels.

"That's no good," he said, waving it away.

"What's wrong? Can't you hear the voice anymore?" He went on jabbing with the bannister. "What?" he said, and looked in the flare's dazzling light like he had no idea what I was talking about.

"The voice you heard," I said. "Has it stopped calling?"

"It's this stuff," he said. "There's no way to get a shovel into it. Did you bring any baskets?"

I hadn't, but farther down the mound I had seen a large tin saucepan. I fetched it for him and began digging. He was right, of course. I got one good shovelful and then struck an end of a floor joist and bent the blade of the shovel. I tried to get it under the joist so I could pry it upward, but it was wedged under a large section of beam farther on. I gave it up, broke off another of the bannisters, and got down beside Jack.

The beam was not the only thing holding the joist down. The rubble looked loose—bricks and chunks of plaster and pieces of wood—but it was as solid as cement. Swales, who showed up out of nowhere when we were three feet down, said, "It's the clay. All London's built on it. Hard as statues." He had brought two buckets with him and the news that Nelson had shown up and had had a fight with the spotty officer over whose incident it was.

"'It's *my* incident,' Nelson says, and gets out the map to show him how this side of King's Road is in his district," Swales said gleefully, "and the incident officer says, 'Your incident? Who wants the bloody thing, I say,' he says."

Even with Swales helping, the going was so slow, whoever was under there would probably have suffocated or bled to death before we could get to him. Jack didn't stop at all, even when the bombs were directly overhead. He seemed to know exactly where he was going, though none of us heard anything in those brief intervals of silence, and Jack seemed scarcely to listen.

The bannister he was using broke off in the iron-hard clay, and he took mine and kept digging. A broken clock came up, and an egg cup. Morris arrived. He had been evacuating people from two streets over where a bomb had buried itself in the middle of the street without exploding. Swales told him the story of Nelson and the spotty young officer and then went off to see what he could find out about the inhabitants of the house.

Jack came up out of the hole. "I need braces," he said. "The sides are collapsing."

I found some unbroken bed slats at the base of the mound. One of the slats was too long for the shaft. Jack sawed it halfway through and then broke it off.

Swales came back. "Nobody in the house," he shouted down the hole. "The colonel and Mrs. Godalming went to Surrey this morning." The all clear sounded, drowning out his words.

"Jack," Jack said from the hole.

"Jack," he said again, more urgently.

I leaned over the tunnel.

"What time is it?" he said.

"About five," I said. "The all clear just went."

"Is it getting light?"

"Not yet," I said. "Have you found anything?"

"Yes," he said. "Give us a hand."

I eased myself into the hole. I could understand his question; it was pitch-dark down here. I switched my torch on. It lit up our faces from beneath like spectres.

"In there," he said, and reached for a bannister just like the one he'd been digging with.

"Is he under a stairway?" I said, and the bannister clutched at his hand.

It only took a minute or two to get him out. Jack pulled on the arm I had mistaken for a bannister, and I scrabbled through the last few inches of plaster and clay to the little cave he was in, formed by an icebox and a door leaning against each other.

"Colonel Godalming?" I said, reaching for him.

He shook off my hand. "Where the bleeding hell have you people been?" he said. "Taking a tea break?"

He was in full evening dress, and his big mustache was covered with plaster dust. "What sort of country is this, leaving a man to dig himself out?" he shouted, brandishing a serving spoon full of plaster in Jack's face. "I could have dug all the way to China in the time it took you blighters to get me out!"

Hands came down into the hole and hoisted him up. "Blasted incompetents!" he yelled. We pushed on the seat of his elegant trousers. "Slackers, the lot of you! Couldn't find the nose in front of your own face!"

⊣•••⊢

Colonel Godalming had in fact left for Surrey the day before but had decided to come back for his hunting rifle, in case of invasion. "Can't rely on the blasted Civil Defence to stop the jerries," he had said as I led him down to the ambulance.

It was starting to get light. The incident was smaller than I'd thought, not much more than two blocks square. What I had taken for a mound to the south was actually a squat office block, and beyond it the row houses hadn't even had their windows blown out.

The ambulance had pulled up as near as possible to the mound. I helped him over to it. "What's your name?" he said, ignoring the doors I'd opened. "I intend to report you to your superiors. And the other one. Practically pulled my arm out of its socket. Where's he got to?"

"He had to go to his day job," I said. As soon as we had Godalming out, Jack had switched on his pocket torch again to glance at his watch and said, "I've got to leave."

I told him I'd check him out with the incident officer and started to help Godalming down the mound. Now I was sorry I hadn't gone with him.

"Day job!" Godalming snorted. "Gone off to take a nap is more like it. Lazy slacker. Nearly breaks my arm and then goes off and leaves me to die. I'll have his job!"

"Without him we'd never even have found you," I said angrily. "He's the one who heard your cries for help."

"Cries for help!" the colonel said, going red in the face. "Cries for help! Why would I cry out to a lot of damned slackers?"

The ambulance driver got out of the car and came round to see what the delay was.

"Accused me of crying out like a damned coward!" he blustered to her. "I didn't make a sound. Knew it wouldn't do any good. Knew if I didn't dig myself out, I'd be there till Kingdom Come! Nearly had myself out, too, and then he comes along and accuses me of blubbering like a baby! It's monstrous, that's what it is! Monstrous!"

She took hold of his arm.

"What do you think you're doing, young woman? You should be at home instead of out running about in short skirts! It's indecent, that's what it is!"

She shoved him, still protesting, onto a bunk and covered him up with a blanket. I slammed the doors to, watched her off, and then made a circuit of the incident, looking for Swales and Morris. The rising sun appeared between two bands of cloud, reddening the mounds and glinting off a broken mirror.

I couldn't find either of them, so I reported in to Nelson, who was talking angrily on a field telephone and who nodded and waved me off when I tried to tell him about Jack, and then went back to the post.

Swales was already regaling Morris and Vi, who were eating breakfast, with an imitation of Colonel Godalming. Mrs. Lucy was still filling out papers, apparently the same form as when we'd left.

"Huge mustaches," Swales was saying, his hands two feet apart to illustrate their size, "like a walrus's, and tails, if you please. 'Oi siy, this is disgriceful!'" he sputtered, his right eye squinted shut with an imaginary monocle. "'Wot's the Impire coming to when a man cahn't even be rescued!'" He dropped into his natural voice. "I thought he was going to have our two Jacks court-martialed on the spot." He peered round me. "Where's Settle?"

"He had to go to his day job," I said.

"Just as well," he said, screwing the monocle back in. "The colonel looked like he was coming back with the Royal Lancers." He raised his arm, gripping an imaginary sword. "Charge!"

Vi tittered. Mrs. Lucy looked up and said, "Violet, make Jack some toast. Sit down, Jack. You look done in."

I took my helmet off and started to set it on the table. It was caked with plaster dust, so thick it was impossible to see the red W through it. I hung it on my chair and sat down.

Morris shoved a plate of kippers at me. "You never know what they're going to do when you get them out," he said. "Some of them fall all over you, sobbing, and some act like they're doing you a favor. I had one old woman acted all offended, claimed I made an improper advance when I was working her leg free."

Renfrew came in from the other room, wrapped in a blanket. He looked as bad as I thought I must, his face slack and gray with fatigue. "Where was the incident?" he asked anxiously.

"Just off Old Church Street. In Nelson's sector," I added to reassure him.

But he said nervously, "They're coming closer every night. Have you noticed that?"

"No, they aren't," Vi said. "We haven't had anything in our sector all week."

Renfrew ignored her. "First Gloucester Road and then Ixworth Place and now Old Church Street. It's as if they're circling, searching for something."

"London," Mrs. Lucy said briskly. "And if we don't enforce the black-out, they're likely to find it." She handed Morris a typed list. "Reported infractions from last night. Go round and reprimand them." She put her hand on Renfrew's shoulder. "Why don't you go have a nice liedown, Mr. Renfrew, while I cook you breakfast?"

"I'm not hungry," he said, but he let her lead him, clutching his blanket, back to the cot.

We watched Mrs. Lucy spread the blanket over him and then lean down and tuck it in around his shoulders, and then Swales said, "You know who this Godalming fellow reminds me of? A lady we rescued over in Gower Street," he said, yawning. "Hauled her out and asked her if her husband was in there with her. 'No,' she says, 'the bleedin' coward's at the front.'"

We all laughed.

"People like this colonel person don't deserve to be rescued," Vi said, spreading oleo on a slice of toast. "You should have left him there awhile and seen how he liked that."

"He was lucky they didn't leave him there altogether," Morris said. "The register had him in Surrey with his wife."

"Lucky he had such a loud voice," Swales said. He twirled the end of an enormous mustache. "Oi siy," he boomed. "Get me out of here im-meejutly, you slackers!"

But he said he didn't call out, I thought, and could hear Jack shouting over the din of the antiaircraft guns, the drone of the planes, "There's someone under here."

Mrs. Lucy came back to the table. "I've applied for reinforcements for the post," she said, standing her papers on end and tamping them into an even stack. "Someone from the Town Hall will be coming to inspect in the next few days." She picked up two bottles of ale and an ashtray and carried them over to the dustbin.

"Applied for reinforcements?" Swales asked. "Why? Afraid Colonel Godalming'll be back with the heavy artillery?"

There was a loud banging on the door.

"Oi siy," Swales said. "Here he is now, and he's brought his hounds."

Mrs. Lucy opened the door. "Worse," Vi whispered, diving for the last bottle of ale. "It's Nelson." She passed the bottle to me under the table, and I passed it to Renfrew, who tucked it under his blanket.

"Mr. Nelson," Mrs. Lucy said as if she were delighted to see him, "do come in. And how are things over your way?"

"We took a beating last night," he said, glaring at us as though we were responsible.

"He's had a complaint from the colonel," Swales whispered to me. "You're done for, mate."

"Oh, I'm so sorry to hear that," Mrs. Lucy said. "Now, how may I help you?"

He pulled a folded paper from the pocket of his uniform and carefully opened it out. "This was forwarded to me from the City Engineer," he said. "All requests for material improvements are to be sent to the district warden, not over his head to the Town Hall."

"Oh, I'm so *glad*," Mrs. Lucy said, leading him into the pantry. "It is such a comfort to deal with someone one knows, rather than a faceless bureaucracy. If I had realized you were the proper person to appeal to, I should have contacted you *immediately*." She shut the door.

Renfrew took the ale bottle out from under his blanket and buried it in the dustbin. Violet began taking out her bobby pins.

"We'll never get our reinforcements now," Swales said. "Not with Adolf von Nelson in charge."

"Shh," Vi said, yanking at her snaillike curls. "You don't want him to hear you."

"Olmwood told me he makes them keep working at an incident, even when the bombs are right overhead. Thinks all the posts should do it."

"Shh!" Vi said.

"He's a bleeding Nazi!" Swales said, but he lowered his voice. "Got two of his wardens killed that way. You better not let him find out you and Jack are good at finding bodies, or you'll be out there dodging shrapnel, too."

Good at finding bodies. I thought of Jack, standing motionless, looking at the rubble and saying, "There's someone alive under here. Hurry."

"That's why Nelson steals from the other posts," Vi said, scooping her bobby pins off the table and into her haversack. "Because he does his own in." She pulled out a comb and began yanking it through her snarled curls.

The pantry door opened and Nelson and Mrs. Lucy came out, Nelson still holding the unfolded paper. She was still wearing her tea-party smile, but it was a bit thin. "I'm sure you can see it's unrealistic to expect nine people to huddle in a coal cellar for hours at a time," she said.

"There are people all over London 'huddling in coal cellars for hours at a time,' as you put it," Nelson said coldly, "who do not wish their Civil Defence funds spent on frivolities."

"I do not consider the safety of my wardens a frivolity," she said, "though it is clear to me that you do, as witnessed by your very poor record."

Nelson stared for a full minute at Mrs. Lucy, trying to think of a retort, and then turned on me. "Your uniform is a disgrace, warden," he said, and stomped out.

─┤ • • • ├─

Whatever it was Jack had used to find Colonel Godalming, it didn't work on incendiaries. He searched as haphazardly for them as the rest of us, Vi, who had been on spotter duty, shouting directions: "No, farther down Fulham Road. In the grocer's."

She had apparently been daydreaming about her pilots, instead of spotting. The incendiary was not in the grocer's but in the butcher's three doors down, and by the time Jack and I got to it, the meat locker was on fire. It wasn't hard to put out, there were no furniture or curtains to catch, and the cold kept the wooden shelves from catching, but the butcher was extravagantly grateful. He insisted on wrapping up five pounds of lamb chops in white paper and thrusting them into Jack's arms.

"Did you really have to be at your day job so early, or were you only trying to escape the colonel?" I asked Jack on the way back to the post.

"Was he that bad?" he said, handing me the parcel of lamb chops.

"He nearly took my head off when I said you'd heard him shouting. Said he didn't call for help. Said he was digging himself out." The white butcher's paper was so bright, the Luftwaffe would think it was a searchlight. I tucked the parcel inside my overalls so it wouldn't show. "What sort of work is it, your day job?" I asked.

"War work," he said.

"Did they transfer you? Is that why you came to London?"

"No," he said. "I wanted to come." We turned into Mrs. Lucy's street. "Why did you join the ARP?"

"I'm waiting to be called up," I said, "so no one would hire me."

"And you wanted to do your bit."

"Yes," I said, wishing I could see his face.

"What about Mrs. Lucy? Why did she become a warden?"

"Mrs. Lucy?" I said blankly. The question had never even occurred to me. She was the best warden in London. It was her natural calling, and I'd thought of her as always having been one. "I've no idea," I said.

"It's her house, she's a widow. Perhaps the Civil Defence commandeered it, and she had to become one. It's the tallest in the street." I tried to remember what Twickenham had written about her in his interview. "Before the war she had something to do with a church."

"A church," he said, and I wished again I could see his face. I couldn't tell in the dark whether he spoke in contempt or longing.

"She was a deaconess or something," I said. "What sort of war work is it? Munitions?"

"No," he said, and walked on ahead.

Mrs. Lucy met us at the door of the post. I gave her the package of lamb chops, and Jack went upstairs to replace Vi as spotter. Mrs. Lucy cooked the chops up immediately, running upstairs to the kitchen during a lull in the raids for salt and a jar of mint sauce, standing over the gas ring at the end of the table and turning them for what seemed an eternity. They smelled wonderful.

Twickenham passed round newly run-off copies of *Twickenham's Twitterings*. "Something for you to read while you wait for your dinner," he said proudly.

The lead article was about the change in address of Sub-Post D, which had taken a partial hit that broke the water mains.

"Had Nelson refused them reinforcements, too?" Swales asked.

"Listen to this," Petersby said. He read aloud from the news sheet. "'The crime rate in London has risen twenty-eight percent since the beginning of the blackout.'"

"And no wonder," Vi said, coming down from upstairs. "You can't see your nose in front of your face at night, let alone someone lurking in an alley. I'm always afraid someone's going to jump out at me while I'm on patrol."

"All those houses standing empty, and half of London sleeping in the shelters," Swales said. "It's easy pickings. If I was a bad'un, I'd come straight to London."

"It's disgusting," Morris said indignantly. "The idea of someone taking advantage of there being a war to commit crimes."

"Oh, Mr. Morris, that reminds me. Your son telephoned," Mrs. Lucy said, cutting into a chop to see if it was done. Blood welled up. "He said he'd a surprise for you, and you were to come out to"—she switched the fork to her left hand and rummaged in her overall pocket till she found a slip of paper—"North Weald on Monday, I think. His commanding officer's made the necessary travel arrangements for you. I wrote it all down." She handed it to him and went back to turning the chops.

"A surprise?" Morris said, sounding worried. "He's not in trouble, is he? His commanding officer wants to see me?"

"I don't know. He didn't say what it was about. Only that he wanted you to come."

Vi went over to Mrs. Lucy and peered into the skillet. "I'm glad it was the butcher's and not the grocer's," she said. "Rutabagas wouldn't have cooked up half so nice."

Mrs. Lucy speared a chop, put it on a plate, and handed it to Vi. "Take this up to Jack," she said.

"He doesn't want any," Vi said. She took the plate and sat down at the table.

"Did he say why he didn't?" I asked.

She looked curiously at me. "I suppose he's not hungry," she said. "Or perhaps he doesn't like lamb chops."

"I do hope he's not in any trouble," Morris said, and it took me a minute to realize he was talking about his son. "He's not a bad boy, but he does things without thinking. Youthful high spirits, that's all it is."

"He didn't eat the cake either," I said. "Did he say why he didn't want the lamb chop?"

"If Mr. Settle doesn't want it, then take it to Mr. Renfrew," Mrs. Lucy said sharply. She snatched the plate away from Vi. "And don't let him tell you he's not hungry. He must eat. He's getting very run-down."

Vi sighed and stood up. Mrs. Lucy handed her back the plate, and she went into the other room.

"We all need to eat plenty of good food and get lots of sleep," Mrs. Lucy said reprovingly. "To keep our strength up."

"I've written an article about it in the *Twitterings*," Twickenham said, beaming. "It's known as 'walking death.' It's brought about by lack of sleep and poor nutrition, with the anxiety of the raids. The walking dead exhibit slowed reaction time and impaired judgment, which result in increased accidents on the job."

"Well, I won't have any walking dead among my wardens," Mrs. Lucy said, dishing up the rest of the chops. "As soon as you've had these, I want you all to go to bed."

The chops tasted even better than they had smelled. I ate mine, reading Twickenham's article on the walking dead. It said that loss of appetite was a common reaction to the raids. It also said that lack of sleep could cause compulsive behavior and odd fixations. "The walking dead may become convinced that they are being poisoned or that a friend or relative is a German agent. They may hallucinate, hearing voices, seeing visions, or believing fantastical things."

"He was in trouble at school, before the war, but he's steadied down since he joined up," Morris said. "I wonder what he's done."

At three the next morning a land mine exploded in almost the same spot off Old Church Street as the HEs. Nelson sent Olmwood to ask for help, and Mrs. Lucy ordered Swales, Jack, and me to go with him.

"The mine didn't land more'n two houses away from the first crater," Olmwood said while we were getting on our gear. "The jerries couldn't have come closer if they'd been aiming at it."

"I know what they're aiming at," Renfrew said from the doorway. He looked terrible, pale and drawn as a ghost. "And I know why you've applied for reinforcements for the post. It's me, isn't it? They're after me."

"They're not after any of us," Mrs. Lucy said firmly. "They're two miles up. They're not aiming at anything."

"Why would Hitler want to bomb you more than the rest of us?" Swales said.

"I don't know." He sank down on one of the chairs and put his head in his hands. "I don't know. But they're after me. I can feel it."

Mrs. Lucy had sent Swales, Jack, and me to the incident because "you've been there before. You'll know the terrain." But that was a fond hope. Since they explode above ground, land mines do considerably more damage then HEs. There was now a hill where the incident officer's tent had been, and three more beyond it, a mountain range in the middle of London. Swales started up the nearest peak to look for the incident officer's light.

"Jack, over here!" somebody called from the hill behind us, and both of us scrambled up a slope toward the voice.

A group of five men were halfway up the hill looking down into a hole.

"Jack!" the man yelled again. He was wearing a blue foreman's arm band, and he was looking straight past us at someone toiling up the slope

494

with what looked like a stirrup pump. I thought, surely they're not trying to fight a fire down that shaft, and then saw it wasn't a pump. It was, in fact, an automobile jack, and the man with the blue arm band reached between us for it, lowered it down the hole, and scrambled in after it.

The rest of the rescue squad stood looking down into the blackness as if they could actually see something. After a while they began handing empty buckets down into the hole and pulling them out heaped full of broken bricks and pieces of splintered wood. None of them took any notice of us, even when Jack held out his hands to take one of the buckets.

"We're from Chelsea," I shouted to the foreman over the din of the planes and bombs. "What can we do to help?"

They went on bucket-brigading. A china teapot came up on the top of one load, covered with dust but not even chipped.

I tried again. "Who is it down there?"

"Two of 'em," the man nearest me said. He plucked the teapot off the heap and handed it to the man wearing a balaclava under his helmet. "Man and a woman."

"We're from Chelsea," I shouted over a burst of antiaircraft fire. "What do you want us to do?"

He took the teapot away from the man with the balaclava and handed it to me. "Take this down to the pavement with the other valuables."

It took me a long while to get down the slope, holding the teapot in one hand and the lid on with the other and trying to keep my footing among the broken bricks, and even longer to find any pavement. The land mine had heaved most of it up, and the street with it.

I finally found it, a square of unbroken pavement in front of a blown-out bakery, with the "valuables" neatly lined up against it: a radio, a boot, two serving spoons like the one Colonel Godalming had threatened me with, a lady's beaded evening bag. A rescue worker was standing guard next to them.

"Halt!" he said, stepping in front of them as I came up, holding a pocket torch or a gun. "No one's allowed inside the incident perimeter."

"I'm ARP," I said hastily. "Jack Harker. Chelsea." I held up the teapot. "They sent me down with this."

It was a torch. He flicked it on and off, an eye blink. "Sorry," he said. "We've had a good deal of looting recently." He took the teapot and placed it at the end of the line next to the evening bag. "Caught a man last week going through the pockets of the bodies laid out in the street waiting for the mortuary van. Terrible how some people will take advantage of a thing like this."

I went back up to where the rescue workers were digging. Jack was at the mouth of the shaft, hauling buckets up and handing them back. I got in line behind him.

"Have they found them yet?" I asked him as soon as there was a lull in the bombing.

"Quiet!" a voice shouted from the hole, and the man in the balaclava repeated, "Quiet, everyone! We must have absolute quiet!"

Everyone stopped working and listened. Jack had handed me a bucket full of bricks, and the handle cut into my hands. For a second there was absolute silence, and then the drone of a plane and the distant swish and crump of an HE.

"Don't worry," the voice from the hole shouted, "we're nearly there." The buckets began coming up out of the hole again.

I hadn't heard anything, but apparently down in the shaft they had, a voice or the sound of tapping, and I felt relieved, both that one of them at least was still alive, and that the diggers were on course. I'd been on an incident in October where we'd had to stop halfway down and sink a new shaft because the rubble kept distorting and displacing the sound. Even if the shaft was directly above the victim, it tended to go crooked in working past obstacles, and the only way to keep it straight was with frequent soundings. I thought of Jack digging for Colonel Godalming with the bannister. He hadn't taken any soundings at all. He had seemed to know exactly where he was going.

The men in the shaft called for the jack again, and Jack and I lowered it down to them. As the man below it reached up to take it, Jack stopped. He raised his head, as if he were listening.

"What is it?" I said. I couldn't hear anything but the ack-ack guns in Hyde Park. "Did you hear someone calling?"

"Where's the bloody jack?" the foreman shouted.

"It's too late," Jack said to me. "They're dead."

"Come along, get it down here," the foreman shouted. "We haven't got all day."

He handed the jack down.

"Quiet," the foreman shouted, and above us, like a ghostly echo, we could hear the balaclava call, "Quiet, please, everyone."

A church clock began to chime, and I could hear the balaclava say irritatedly, "We must have absolute quiet."

The clock chimed four and stopped, and there was a skittering sound of dirt falling on metal. Then silence, and a faint sound.

"Quiet!" the foreman called again, and there was another silence, and the sound again. A whimper. Or a moan. "We hear you," he shouted. "Don't be afraid."

"One of them's still alive," I said.

Jack didn't say anything.

"We just *heard* them," I said angrily.

Jack shook his head.

"We'll need lumber for bracing," the man in the balaclava said to Jack, and I expected him to tell him it was no use, but he went off immediately and came back dragging a white-painted bookcase.

It still had three books in it. I helped Jack and the balaclava knock the shelves out of the case and then took the books down to the store of "valuables." The guard was sitting on the pavement going through the beaded evening bag.

"Taking inventory," he said, scrambling up hastily. He jammed a lipstick and a handkerchief into the bag. "So's to make certain nothing gets stolen."

"I've brought you something to read," I said, and laid the books next to the teapot. "*Crime and Punishment.*"

I toiled back up the hill and helped Jack lower the bookshelves down the shaft, and after a few minutes buckets began coming up again. We reformed our scraggly bucket brigade, the balaclava at the head of it and me and then Jack at its end.

The all clear went. As soon as it wound down, the foreman took another sounding. This time we didn't hear anything, and when the buckets started again, I handed them to Jack without looking at him.

It began to get light in the east, a slow graying of the hills above us. Two of them, several stories high, stood where the row houses that had escaped the night before had been, and we were still in their shadow, though I could see the shaft now, with the end of one of the white bookshelves sticking up from it like a gravestone.

The buckets began to come more slowly.

"Put out your cigarettes!" the foreman called up, and we all stopped, trying to catch the smell of gas. If they were dead, as Jack had said, it was most likely gas leaking in from the broken mains that had killed them, and not internal injuries. The week before we had brought up a boy and his dog, not a scratch on them. The dog had barked and whimpered almost up to when we found them, and the ambulance driver said she thought they'd only been dead a few minutes.

I couldn't smell any gas, and after a minute the foreman said, excited, "I see them!"

The balaclava leaned over the shaft, his hands on his knees. "Are they alive?"

"Yes! Fetch an ambulance!"

The balaclava went leaping down the hill, skidding on broken bricks that skittered down in a minor avalanche.

I knelt over the shaft. "Will they need a stretcher?" I called down.

"No," the foreman said, and I knew by the sound of his voice they were dead.

"Both of them?" I said.

"Yes."

I stood up. "How did you know they were dead?" I said, turning to look at Jack. "How did—"

He wasn't there. I looked down the hill. The balaclava was nearly to the bottom—grabbing at a broken window sash to stop his headlong descent, his wake a smoky cloud of brick dust—but Jack was nowhere to be seen.

It was nearly dawn. I could see the gray hills and at the far end of them the warden and his "valuables." There was another rescue party on the third hill over, still digging. I could see Swales handing down a bucket.

"Give a hand here," the foreman said impatiently, and hoisted the jack up to me. I hauled it over to the side and then came back and helped the foreman out of the shaft. His hands were filthy, covered in reddish-brown mud.

"Was it the gas that killed them?" I asked, even though he was already pulling out a packet of cigarettes.

"No," he said, shaking a cigarette out and taking it between his teeth. He patted the front of his coverall, leaving red stains.

"How long have they been dead?" I asked.

He found his matches, struck one, and lit the cigarette. "Shortly after we last heard them, I should say," he said, and I thought, but they were already dead by then. And Jack knew it. "They've been dead at least two hours."

I looked at my watch. I read a little past six. "But the mine didn't kill them?"

He took the cigarette between his fingers and blew a long puff of smoke. When he put the cigarette back in his mouth, there was a red smear on it. "Loss of blood."

The next night the Luftwaffe was early. I hadn't gotten much sleep after the incident. Morris had fretted about his son the whole day, and Swales had teased Renfrew mercilessly. "Goring's found out about your spying," he said, "and now he's sent his Stukas after you."

I finally went up to the fourth floor and tried to sleep in the spotter's chair, but it was too light. The afternoon was cloudy, and the fires burning in the East End gave the sky a nasty reddish cast.

Someone had left a copy of *Twickenham's Twitterings* on the floor. I read the article on the walking dead again, and then, still unable to sleep, the rest of the news sheet. There was an account of Hitler's invasion of Transylvania, and a recipe for butterless strawberry tart, and the account of the crime rate. "London is currently the perfect place for the criminal element," Nelson was quoted as saying. "We must constantly be on the lookout for wrongdoing."

Below the recipe was a story about a Scottish terrier named Bonny Charlie who had barked and scrabbled wildly at the ruins of a collapsed house till wardens heeded his cries, dug down, and discovered two unharmed children.

I must have fallen asleep reading that, because the next thing I knew Morris was shaking me and telling me the sirens had gone. It was only five o'clock.

At half past we had an HE in our sector. It was just three blocks from the post, and the walls shook, and plaster rained down on Twickenham's typewriter and on Renfrew, lying awake in his cot.

"Frivolities, my foot," Mrs. Lucy muttered as we dived for our tin hats. "We need those reinforcing beams."

The part-times hadn't come on duty yet. Mrs. Lucy left Renfrew to send them on. We knew exactly where the incident was—Morris had been looking in that direction when it went—but we still had difficulty finding it. It was still evening, but by the time we had gone half a block, it was pitch-black.

The first time that had happened, I thought it was some sort of after-blindness from the blast, but it's only the brick and plaster dust from the collapsed buildings. It rises up in a haze that's darker than any blackout curtain, obscuring everything. When Mrs. Lucy set up shop on a stretch of sidewalk and switched on the blue incident light, it glowed spectrally in the man-made fog.

"Only two families still in the street," she said, holding the register up to the light. "The Kirkcuddy family and the Hodgsons."

"Are they an old couple?" Morris asked, appearing suddenly out of the fog.

She peered at the register. "Yes. Pensioners."

"I found them," he said in that flat voice that meant they were dead. "Blast."

"Oh, dear," she said. "The Kirkcuddys are a mother and two children. They've an Anderson shelter." She held the register closer to the blue light. "Everyone else has been using the tube shelter." She unfolded a map and showed us where the Kirckcuddys' backyard had been, but it was no help. We spent the next hour wandering blindly over the mounds, listening for sounds that were impossible to hear over the Luftwaffe's comments and the ack-ack's replies.

Petersby showed up a little past eight and Jack a few minutes later, and Mrs. Lucy set them to wandering in the fog, too.

"Over here," Jack shouted almost immediately, and my heart gave an odd jerk.

"Oh, good, he's heard them," Mrs. Lucy said. "Jack, go and find him."

"Over here," he called again, and I started off in the direction of his voice, almost afraid of what I would find, but I hadn't gone ten steps before I could hear it, too. A baby crying, and a hollow, echoing sound like someone banging a fist against tin.

"Don't stop," Vi shouted. She was kneeling next to Jack in a shallow crater. "Keep making noise. We're coming." She looked up at me. "Tell Mrs. Lucy to ring the rescue squad."

I blundered my way back to Mrs. Lucy through the darkness. She had already rung up the rescue squad. She sent me to Sloane Square to make sure the rest of the inhabitants of the block were safely there.

The dust had lifted a little but not enough for me to see where I was going. I pitched off a curb into the street and tripped over a pile of debris and then a body. When I shone my torch on it, I saw it was the girl I had walked to the shelter two nights before.

She was sitting against the tiled entrance to the station, still holding a dress on a hanger in her limp hand. The old stewpot at John Lewis's never let her off even a minute before closing, and the Luftwaffe had been early. She had been killed by blast, or by flying glass. Her face and neck and hands were covered with tiny cuts, and glass crunched underfoot when I moved her legs together.

I went back to the incident and waited for the mortuary van and went with them to the shelter. It took me three hours to find the families on my list. By the time I got back to the incident, the rescue squad was five feet down.

"They're nearly there," Vi said, dumping a basket on the far side of the crater. "All that's coming up now is dirt and the occasional rosebush."

"Where's Jack?" I said.

"He went for a saw." She took the basket back and handed it to one of the rescue squad, who had to put his cigarette into his mouth to free his hands before he could take it. "There was a board, but they dug past it."

I leaned over the hole. I could hear the sound of banging but not the baby. "Are they still alive?"

She shook her head. "We haven't heard the baby for an hour or so. We keep calling, but there's no answer. We're afraid the banging may be something mechanical."

I wondered if they were dead, and Jack, knowing it, had not gone for a saw at all but off to that day job of his.

Swales came up. "Guess who's in hospital?" he said.

"Who?" Vi said.

"Olmwood. Nelson had his wardens out walking patrols during a raid, and he caught a piece of shrapnel from one of the ack-acks in the leg. Nearly took it off."

The rescue worker with the cigarette handed a heaping basket to Vi. She took it, staggering a little under the weight, and carried it off.

"You'd better not let Nelson see you working like that," Swales called after her, "or he'll have you transferred to his sector. Where's Morris?" he said, and went off, presumably to tell him and whoever else he could find about Olmwood.

Jack came up, carrying the saw.

"They don't need it," the rescue worker said, the cigarette dangling from the side of his mouth. "Mobile's here," he said, and went off for a cup of tea. Jack knelt and handed the saw down the hole.

"Are they still alive?" I asked.

Jack leaned over the hole, his hands clutching the edges. The banging was incredibly loud. It must have been deafening inside the Anderson. Jack stared into the hole as if he heard neither the banging nor any voice.

He stood up, still looking into the hole. "They're farther to the left," he said.

How can they be farther to the left? I thought. We can hear them. They're directly under us. "Are they alive?" I said.

"Yes."

Swales came back. "He's a spy, that's what he is," he said. "Hitler sent him here to kill off our best men one by one. I told you his name was Adolf von Nelson."

The Kirkcuddys were farther to the left. The rescue squad had to widen the tunnel, cut the top of the Anderson open, and pry it back, like opening a can of tomatoes. It took till nine o'clock in the morning, but they were all alive.

Jack left sometime before it got light. I didn't see him go. Swales was telling me about Olmwood's injury, and when I turned around, Jack was gone.

"Has Jack told you where this job of his is that he has to leave so early for?" I asked Vi when I got back to the post.

She had propped a mirror against one of the gas masks and was putting her hair up in pin curls. "No," she said, dipping a comb in a glass of water and wetting a lock of her hair. "Jack, could you reach me my bobby pins? I've a date this afternoon, and I want to look my best."

I pushed the pins across to her. "What sort of job is it? Did Jack say?"

"No. Some sort of war work, I should think." She wound a lock of hair around her finger. "He's had ten kills. Four Stukas and six 109's."

I sat down next to Twickenham, who was typing up the incident report. "Have you interviewed Jack yet?"

"When would I have had time?" Twickenham asked. "We haven't had a quiet night since he came."

Renfrew shuffled in from the other room. He had a blanket wrapped round him Indian style and a bedspread over his shoulders. He looked terrible, pale and drawn as a ghost.

"Would you like some breakfast?" Vi asked, prying a pin open with her teeth.

He shook his head. "Did Nelson approve the reinforcements?"

"No," Twickenham said in spite of Vi's signaling him not to.

"You must tell Nelson it's an emergency," he said, hugging the blanket to him as if he were cold. "I know why they're after me. It was before the war. When Hitler invaded Czechoslovakia. I wrote a letter to the *Times*."

I was grateful Swales wasn't there. A letter to the *Times*.

"Come, now, why don't you go and lie down for a bit?" Vi said, securing a curl with a bobby pin as she stood up. "You're tired, that's all, and that's what's getting you so worried. They don't even get the *Times* over there."

She took his arm, and he went docilely with her into the other room. I heard him say, "I called him a lowland bully. In the letter." The person suffering from severe sleep loss may hallucinate, hearing voices, seeing visions, or believing fantastical things.

"Has he mentioned what sort of day job he has?" I asked Twickenham.

"Who?" he asked, still typing.

"Jack."

"No, but whatever it is, let's hope he's as good at it as he is at finding bodies." He stopped and peered at what he'd just typed. "This makes five, doesn't it?"

Vi came back. "And we'd best not let von Nelson find out about it," she said. She sat down and dipped the comb into the glass of water. "He'd take him like he took Olmwood, and we're already shorthanded, with Renfrew the way he is."

Mrs. Lucy came in carrying the incident light, disappeared into the pantry with it, and came out again carrying an application form. "Might I use the typewriter, Mr. Twickenham?" she asked.

He pulled his sheet of paper out of the typewriter and stood up. Mrs. Lucy sat down, rolled in the form, and began typing. "I've decided to apply directly to Civil Defence for reinforcements," she said.

"What sort of day job does Jack have?" I asked ha

"War work," she said. She pulled the application out, turned it over, rolled it back in. "Jack, would you mind taking this over to headquarters?"

"Works days," Vi said, making a pin curl on the back of her head. "Raids every night. When does he sleep?"

"I don't know," I said.

"He'd best be careful," she said. "Or he'll turn into one of the walking dead, like Renfrew."

Mrs. Lucy signed the application form, folded it in half, and gave it to me. I took it to Civil Defence headquarters and spent half a day trying to find the right office to give it to.

"It's not the correct form," the sixth girl said. "She needs to file an A-114, Exterior Improvements."

"It's not exterior," I said. "The post is applying for reinforcing beams for the cellar."

"Reinforcements are classified as exterior improvements," she said. She handed me the form, which looked identical to the one Mrs. Lucy had already filled out, and I left.

On the way out Nelson stopped me. I thought he was going to tell me my uniform was a disgrace again, but instead he pointed to my tin hat and demanded, "Why aren't you wearing a regulation helmet, warden? 'All ARP wardens shall wear a helmet with the letter W in red on the front,'" he quoted.

I took my hat off and looked at it. The red W had partly chipped away so that it looked like a V.

"What post are you?" he barked.

"Forty-eight. Chelsea," I said, and wondered if he expected me to salute.

"Mrs. Lucy is your warden," he said disgustedly, and I expected his next question to be what was I doing at Civil Defence, but instead he said, "I heard about Colonel Godalming. Your post has been having good luck locating casualties these last few raids."

"Yes, sir," was obviously the wrong answer, and "No, sir," would make him suspicious. "We found three people in an Anderson last night," I said. "One of the children had the wits to bang on the roof with a pair of pliers."

"I've heard that the person finding them is a new man, Settle." He sounded friendly, almost jovial. Like Hitler at Munich.

"Settle?" I said blankly. "Mrs. Lucy was the one who found the Anderson."

⊣ • • • ⊢

Morris's son Quincy's surprise was the Victoria Cross. "A medal," he said over and over. "Who'd have thought it, my Quincy with a medal? Fifteen planes he shot down."

It had been presented at a special ceremony at Quincy's commanding officer's headquarters, and the Duchess of York herself had been there. Morris had pinned the medal on Quincy himself.

"I wore my suit," he told us for the hundredth time. "In case he was in trouble I wanted to make a good impression, and a good thing, too. What would the Duchess of York have thought if I'd gone looking like this?"

He looked pretty bad. We all did. We'd had two breadbaskets of incendiaries, one right after the other, and Vi had been on watch. We had had to save the butcher's again, and a baker's two blocks farther down, and a thirteenth-century crucifix.

"I *told* him it went through the altar roof," Vi had said disgustedly when she and I finally got it out. "Your friend Jack couldn't find an incendiary if it fell on him."

"You told Jack the incendiary came down on the church?" I said, looking up at the carved wooden figure. The bottom of the cross was blackened, and Christ's nailed feet, as if he had been burnt at the stake instead of crucified.

"Yes," she said. "I even told him it was the altar." She looked back up the nave. "And he could have seen it as soon as he came into the church."

"What did he say? That it wasn't there?"

Vi was looking speculatively up at the roof. "It could have been caught in the rafters and come down after. It hardly matters, does it? We put it out. Come on, let's get back to the post," she said, shivering. "I'm freezing."

I was freezing, too. We were both sopping wet. The AFS had stormed up after we had the fire under control and sprayed everything in sight with icy water.

"Pinned it on myself, I did," Morris said. "The Duchess of York kissed him on both cheeks and said he was the pride of England." He had brought a bottle of wine to celebrate the Cross. He got Renfrew up and brought him to the table, draped in his blankets, and ordered Twickenham to put his typewriter away. Petersby brought in extra chairs, and Mrs. Lucy went upstairs to get her crystal.

"Only eight, I'm afraid," she said, coming back with the stemmed goblets in her blackened hands. "The Germans have broken the rest. Who's willing to make do with the tooth glass?"

"I don't care for any, thank you," Jack said. "I don't drink."

"What's that?" Morris said jovially. He had taken off his tin helmet, and below the white line it left, he looked like he was wearing blackface in a music-hall show. "You've got to toast my boy at least. Just imagine. My Quincy with a medal."

Mrs. Lucy rinsed out the porcelain tooth glass and handed it to Vi, who was pouring out the wine. They passed the goblets round. Jack took the tooth glass.

"To my son Quincy, the best pilot in the RAF!" Morris said, raising his goblet.

"May he shoot down the entire Luftwaffe!" Swales shouted. "And put an end to this bloody war!"

"So a man can get a decent night's sleep!" Renfrew said, and everyone laughed.

We drank. Jack raised his glass with the others, but when Vi took the bottle round again, he put his hand over the mouth of it.

"Just think of it," Morris said. "My son Quincy with a medal. He had his troubles in school, in with a bad lot, problems with the police. I worried about him, I did, wondered what he'd come to, and then this war comes along and here he is a hero."

"To heroes!" Petersby said.

We drank again, and Vi dribbled out the last of the wine into Morris's glass. "That's the lot, I'm afraid." She brightened. "I've a bottle of cherry cordial Charlie gave me."

Mrs. Lucy made a face. "Just a minute," she said, disappeared into the pantry, and came back with two cobwebbed bottles of port, which she poured out generously and a little sloppily.

"The presence of intoxicating beverages on post is strictly forbidden," she said. "A fine of five shillings will be imposed for a first offence, one pound for subsequent offences." She took out a pound note and laid it on the table. "I wonder what Nelson was before the war?"

"A monster," Vi said.

I looked across at Jack. He still had his hand over his glass.

"A headmaster," Swales said. "No, I've got it. An Inland Revenue collector!"

Everyone laughed.

"I was a horrid person before the war," Mrs. Lucy said.

Vi giggled.

"I was a deaconess, one of those dreadful women who arranges the flowers in the sanctuary and gets up jumble sales and bullies the rector. 'The Terror of the Churchwardens,' that's what I used to be. I was determined that they should put the hymnals front side out on the backs of the pews. Morris knows. He sang in the choir."

"It's true," Morris said. "She used to instruct the choir on the proper way to queue up."

I tried to imagine her as a stickler, as a petty tyrant like Nelson, and failed.

"Sometimes it takes something dreadful like a war for one to find one's proper job," she said, staring at her glass.

"To the war!" Swales said gaily.

"I'm not sure we should toast something so terrible as that," Twickenham said doubtfully.

"It isn't all that terrible," Vi said. "I mean, without it, we wouldn't all be here together, would we?"

"And you'd never have met all those pilots of yours, would you, Vi?" Swales said.

"There's nothing wrong with making the best of a bad job," Vi said, miffed.

"Some people do more than that," Swales said. "Some people take positive advantage of the war. Like Colonel Godalming. I had a word with one of the AFS volunteers. Seems the colonel didn't come back for his hunting rifle, after all." He leaned forward confidingly. "Seems he was having a bit on with a blond dancer from the Windmill. *Seems* his wife thought he was out shooting grouse in Surrey, and now she's asking all sorts of unpleasant questions."

"He's not the only one taking advantage," Morris said. "That night you got the Kirkcuddys out, Jack, I found an old couple killed by blast. I put them by the road for the mortuary van, and later I saw somebody over there, bending over the bodies, doing something to them. I thought, he must be straightening them out before the rigor sets in, but then it comes to me. He's robbing them. Dead bodies."

"And who's to say they were killed by blast?" Swales said. "Who's to say they weren't murdered? There's lot of bodies, aren't there, and nobody looks close at them. Who's to say they were all killed by the Germans?"

"How did we get onto this?" Petersby said. "We're supposed to be celebrating Quincy Morris's medal, not talking about murderers." He raised his glass. "To Quincy Morris!"

"And the RAF!" Vi said.

"To making the best of a bad job," Mrs. Lucy said.

"Hear, hear," Jack said softly, and raised his glass, but he still didn't drink.

Jack found four people in the next three days. I did not hear any of them until well after we had started digging, and the last one, a fat woman in striped pyjamas and a pink hair net, I never did hear, though she said when we brought her up that she had "called and called between prayers."

Twickenham wrote it all up for the *Twitterings,* tossing out the article on Quincy Morris's medal and typing up a new master's. When Mrs. Lucy borrowed the typewriter to fill out the A-114, she said, "What's this?"

"My lead story," he said. "'Settle Finds Four in Rubble.'" He handed her the master's.

"'Jack Settle, the newest addition to Post Forty-eight,'" she read, "'located four air-raid victims last night. "I wanted to be useful," says the modest Mr. Settle when asked why he came to London from Yorkshire. And he's been useful since his very first night on the job when he—'" She handed it back to him. "Sorry. You can't print that. Nelson's been nosing about, asking questions. He's already taken one of my wardens and nearly got him killed. I won't let him have another."

"That's censorship!" Twickenham said, outraged.

"There's a war on," Mrs. Lucy said, "and we're shorthanded. I've relieved Mr. Renfrew of duty. He's going to stay with his sister in Birmingham. And I wouldn't let Nelson have another one of my wardens if we were overstaffed. He's already got Olmwood nearly killed."

She handed me the A-114 and asked me to take it to Civil Defence. I did. The girl I had spoken to wasn't there, and the girl who was said, "This is for interior improvements. You need to fill out a D-268."

"I did," I said, "and I was told that reinforcements qualified as exterior improvements."

"Only if they're on the outside." She handed me a D-268. "Sorry," she said apologetically. "I'd help you if I could, but my boss is a stickler for the correct forms."

"There's something else you can do for me," I said. "I was supposed to take one of our part-times a message at his day job, but I've lost the address. If you could look it up for me. Jack Settle? If not, I've got to go all the way back to Chelsea to get it."

She looked back over her shoulder and then said, "Wait a mo," and darted down the hall. She came back with a sheet of paper.

"Settle?" she said. "Post Forty-eight, Chelsea?"

"That's the one," I said. "I need his work address."

"He hasn't got one."

He had left the incident while we were still getting the fat woman out. It was starting to get light. We had a rope under her, and a makeshift winch, and he had abruptly handed his end to Swales and said, "I've got to leave for my day job."

"You're certain?" I said.

"I'm certain." She handed me the sheet of paper. It was Jack's approval for employment as a part-time warden, signed by Mrs. Lucy. The spaces for work and home addresses had been left blank. "This is all there was in the file," she said. "No work permit, no identity card, not even a ration card. We keep copies of all that, so he must not have a job."

I took the D-268 back to the post, but Mrs. Lucy wasn't there. "One of Nelson's wardens came round with a new regulation," Twickenham said, running off copies on the duplicating machine. "All wardens will be out on patrol unless on telephone or spotter duty. *All* wardens. She went off to give him what-for," he said, sounding pleased. He was apparently over his anger at her for censoring his story on Jack.

I picked up one of the still-wet copies of the news sheet. The lead story was about Hitler's invasion of Greece. He had put the article about Quincy Morris's medal down in the right-hand corner under a list of "What the War Has Done for Us." Number one was, "It's made us discover capabilities we didn't know we had."

"Mrs. Lucy called him a murderer," Twickenham said.

A murderer.

"What did you want to tell her?" Twickenham said.

That Jack doesn't have a job, I thought. Or a ration card. That he didn't put out the incendiary in the church even though Vi told him it had gone through the altar roof. That he knew the Anderson was farther to the left.

"It's still the wrong form," I said, taking out the D-268.

"That's easily remedied," he said. He rolled the application into the typewriter, typed for a few minutes, handed it back to me.

"Mrs. Lucy has to sign it," I said, and he snatched it back, whipped out a fountain pen, and signed her name.

"What were you before the war?" I asked. "A forger?"

"You'd be surprised." He handed the form back to me. "You look dreadful, Jack. Have you had any sleep this last week?"

"When would I have had the chance?"

"Why don't you lie down now while no one's here?" he said, reaching for my arm the way Vi had reached for Renfrew's. "I'll take the form back to Civil Defence for you."

I shook off his arm. "I'm all right."

I walked back to Civil Defence. The girl who had tried to find Jack's file wasn't there, and the first girl was. I was sorry I hadn't brought the A-114 along as well, but she scrutinized the form without comment and stamped the back. "It will take approximately six weeks to process," she said.

"Six weeks!" I said. "Hitler could have invaded the entire Empire by then."

"In that case, you'll very likely have to file a different form."

I didn't go back to the post. Mrs. Lucy would doubtless be back by the time I returned, but what could I say to her? I suspect Jack. Of what? Of not liking lamb chops and cake? Of having to leave early for work? Of rescuing children from the rubble?

He had said he had a job, and the girl couldn't find his work permit, but it took the Civil Defence six weeks to process a request for a few beams. It would probably take them till the end of the war to file the work permits. Or perhaps his had been in the file, and the girl had missed it. Loss of sleep can result in mistakes on the job. And odd fixations.

I walked to Sloane Square Station. There was no sign of where the young woman had been. They had even swept the glass up. Her stewpot of a boss at John Lewis's never let her go till closing time, even if the sirens had gone, even if it was dark. She had had to hurry through the blacked-out streets all alone, carrying her dress for the next day on a hanger, listening to the guns and trying to make out how far off the planes were. If someone had been stalking her, she would never have heard him, never have seen him in the darkness. Whoever found her would think she had been killed by flying glass.

He doesn't eat, I would say to Mrs. Lucy. He didn't put out an incendiary in a church. He always leaves the incidents before dawn, even when we don't have the casualties up. The Luftwaffe is trying to kill me. It was a letter I wrote to the *Times*. The walking dead may hallucinate, hearing voices, seeing visions, or believing fantastical things.

The sirens went. I must have been standing there for hours, staring at the sidewalk. I went back to the post. Mrs. Lucy was there. "You look dreadful, Jack. How long's it been since you've slept?"

"I don't know," I said. "Where's Jack?"

"On watch," Mrs. Lucy said.

"You'd best be careful," Vi said, setting chocolates on a plate. "Or you'll turn into one of the walking dead. Would you like a sweet? Eddie gave them to me."

The telephone pipped. Mrs. Lucy answered it, spoke a minute, hung up. "Slaney needs help on an incident," she said. "They've asked for Jack."

⊣ • • • ⊢

She sent both of us. We found the incident without any trouble. There was no dust cloud, no smell except from a fire burning off to one side. "This didn't just happen," I said. "It's a day old, at least."

I was wrong. It was two days old. The rescue squads had been working straight through, and there were still at least thirty people unaccounted for. Some of the rescue squad were digging halfheartedly halfway up a mound, but most of them were standing about, smoking and looking like they were casualties themselves. Jack went up to where the men were digging, shook his head, and set off across the mound.

"Heard you had a bodysniffer," one of the smokers said to me. "They've got one in Whitechapel, too. Crawls round the incident on his hands and knees, sniffing like a bloodhound. Yours do that?"

"No," I said.

"Over here," Jack said.

"Says he can read their minds, the one in Whitechapel does," he said, putting out his cigarette and taking up a pickax. He clambered up the slope to where Jack was already digging.

It was easy to see because of the fire, and fairly easy to dig, but halfway down we struck the massive headboard of a bed.

"We'll have to go in from the side," Jack said.

"The hell with that," the man who'd told me about the bodysniffer said. "How do you know somebody's down there? I don't hear anything."

Jack didn't answer him. He moved down the slope and began digging into its side.

"They've been in there two days," the man said. "They're dead and I'm not getting overtime." He flung down the pickax and stalked off to the mobile canteen. Jack didn't even notice he was gone. He handed me baskets, and I emptied them, and occasionally Jack said, "Saw," or "Tin-snips," and I handed them to him. I was off getting the stretcher when he brought her out.

She was perhaps thirteen. She was wearing a white nightgown, or perhaps it only looked white because of the plaster dust. Jack's face was ghastly with it. He had picked her up in his arms, and she had fastened her arms about his neck and buried her face against his shoulder. They were both outlined by the fire.

I brought the stretcher up, and Jack knelt down and tried to lay her on it, but she would not let go of his neck. "It's all right," he said gently. "You're safe now."

He unclasped her hands and folded them on her chest. Her nightgown was streaked with dried blood, but it didn't seem to be hers. I wondered who else had been in there with her. "What's your name?" Jack said.

"Mina," she said. It was no more than a whisper.

"My name's Jack," he said. He nodded at me. "So's his. We're going to carry you down to the ambulance now. Don't be afraid. You're safe now."

The ambulance wasn't there yet. We laid the stretcher on the side-walk, and I went over to the incident officer to see if it was on its way. Before I could get back, somebody shouted, "Here's another," and I went and helped dig out a hand that the foreman had found, and then the body all the blood had come from. When I looked down the hill, the girl was still lying there on the stretcher, and Jack was bending over it.

I went out to Whitechapel to see the bodysniffer the next day. He wasn't there. "He's a part-time," the post warden told me, clearing off a chair so I could sit down. The post was a mess, dirty clothes and dishes everywhere.

An old woman in a print wrapper was frying up kidneys in a skillet. "Works days in munitions out to Dorking," she said.

"How exactly is he able to locate the bodies?" I asked. "I heard—"

"That he reads their minds?" the woman said. She scraped the kidneys onto a plate and handed it to the post warden. "He's heard it, too, more's the pity, and it's gone straight to his head. 'I can feel them under here,' he says to the rescue squads, like he was Houdini or something, and points to where they're supposed to start digging."

"Then how does he find them?"

"Luck," the warden said.

"I think he smells 'em," the woman said. "That's why they call 'em bodysniffers."

The warden snorted. "Over the stink the jerries put in the bombs and the gas and all the rest of it?"

"If he were a—" I said, and didn't finish it. "If he had an acute sense of smell, perhaps he could smell the blood."

"You can't even smell the bodies when they've been dead a week," the warden said, his mouth full of kidneys. "He hears them screaming, same as us."

"He's got better hearing than us," the woman said, switching happily to his theory. "Most of us are half-deaf from the guns, and he isn't."

I hadn't been able to hear the fat woman in the pink hair net, although she'd said she had called for help. But Jack, just down from Yorkshire, where they hadn't been deafened by antiaircraft guns for weeks, could. There was nothing sinister about it. Some people had better hearing than others.

"We pulled an army colonel out last week who claimed he didn't cry out," I said.

"He's lying," the warden said, sawing at a kidney. "We had a nanny, two days ago, prim and proper as you please, swore the whole time we was getting her out, words to make a sailor blush, and then claimed she didn't. 'Unclean words have never crossed my lips and never will,' she says to me." He brandished his fork at me. "Your colonel cried out, all right. He just won't admit it."

"I didn't make a sound," Colonel Godalming had said, brandishing his serving spoon. "Knew it wouldn't do any good," and perhaps the warden was right, and it was only bluster. But he hadn't wanted his wife to know he was in London, to find out about the dancer at the Windmill. He had had good reason to keep silent, to try to dig himself out.

I went home and rang up a girl I knew in the ambulance service and asked her to find out where they had taken Mina. She rang me back in a few minutes with the answer, and I took the tube over to St. George's Hospital. The others had all cried out, or banged on the roof of the Anderson, except Mina. She had been so frightened when Jack got her out, she couldn't speak above a whisper, but that didn't mean she hadn't cried or whimpered.

"When you were buried last night, did you call for help?" I would ask her, and she would answer me in her mouse voice, "I called and called between prayers. Why?" And I would say, "It's nothing, an odd fixation brought on by lack of sleep. Jack spends his days in Dorking, at a munitions plant, and has exceptionally acute hearing." And there is no more truth to my theory than to Renfrew's belief that the raids were brought on by his letter to the *Times*.

St. George's had an entrance marked "Casualty Clearing Station." I asked the nursing sister behind the desk if I could see Mina.

"She was brought in last night. The James Street incident."

She looked at a penciled and crossed-over roster. "I don't show an admission by that name."

"I'm certain she was brought here," I said, twisting my head round to read the list. "There isn't another St. George's, is there?"

She shook her head and lifted up the roster to look at a second sheet.

"Here she is," she said, and I had heard the rescue squads use that tone of voice often enough to know what it meant, but that was impossible. She had been under that headboard. The blood on her nightgown hadn't even been hers.

"I'm so sorry," the sister said.

"When did she die?" I said.

"This morning," she said, checking the second list, which was much longer than the first.

"Did anyone else come to see her?"

"I don't know. I've just been on since eleven."

"What did she die of?"

She looked at me as if I were insane.

"What was the listed cause of death?" I said.

She had to find Mina's name on the roster again. "Shock due to loss of blood," she said, and I thanked her and went to find Jack.

┤•••├

514

He found me. I had gone back to the post and waited till everyone was asleep and Mrs. Lucy had gone upstairs and then sneaked into the pantry to look up Jack's address in Mrs. Lucy's files. It had not been there, as I had known it wouldn't. And if there had been an address, what would it have turned out to be when I went to find it? A gutted house? A mound of rubble?

I had gone to Sloane Square Station, knowing he wouldn't be there, but having no other place to look. He could have been anywhere. London was full of empty houses, bombed-out cellars, secret places to hide until it got dark. That was why he had come here.

"If I was a bad'un, I'd head straight for London," Swales had said. But the criminal element weren't the only ones who had come, drawn by the blackout and the easy pickings and the bodies. Drawn by the blood.

I stood there until it started to get dark, watching two boys scrabble in the gutter for sweets that had been blown out of a confectioner's front window, and then walked back to a doorway down the street from the post, where I could see the door, and waited. The sirens went. Swales left on patrol. Petersby went in. Morris came out, stopping to peer at the sky as if he were looking for his son Quincy's plane. Mrs. Lucy must not have managed to talk Nelson out of the patrols.

It got dark. The searchlights began to crisscross the sky, catching the silver of the barrage balloons. The planes started coming in from the east, a low hum. Vi hurried in, wearing high heels and carrying a box tied with string. Petersby and Twickenham left on patrol. Vi came out, fastening her helmet strap under her chin and eating something.

"I've been looking for you everywhere," Jack said.

I turned around. He had driven up in a lorry marked ATS. He had left the door open and the motor running. "I've got the beams," he said. "For reinforcing the post. The incident we were on last night, all these beams were lying on top, and I asked the owner of the house if I could buy them from him."

He gestured to the back of the lorry, where jagged ends of wood were sticking out. "Come along, then, we can get them up tonight if we hurry." He started toward the truck. "Where were you? I've looked everywhere for you."

"I went to St. George's Hospital," I said.

He stopped, his hand on the open door of the truck. "Mina's dead," I said, "but you knew that, didn't you?"

He didn't say anything.

"The nurse said she died of loss of blood," I said. A flare drifted down, lighting his face with a deadly whiteness. "I know what you are."

"If we hurry, we can get the reinforcements up before the raid starts," he said. He started to pull the door to.

I put my hand on it to keep him from closing it. "War work," I said bitterly. "What do you do, make sure you're alone in the tunnel with them or go to see them in hospital afterward?"

He let go of the door.

"Brilliant stroke, volunteering for the ARP," I said. "Nobody's going to suspect the noble air-raid warden, especially when he's so good at locating casualties. And if some of those casualties die later, if somebody's found dead on the street after a raid, well, it's only to be expected. There's a war on."

The drone overhead got suddenly louder, and a whole shower of flares came down. The searchlights wheeled, trying to find the planes. Jack took hold of my arm.

"Get down," he said, and tried to drag me into the doorway.

I shook his arm off. "I'd kill you if I could," I said. "But I can't, can I?" I waved my hand at the sky. "And neither can they. Your sort don't die, do they?"

There was a long swish, and the rising scream. "I *will* kill you, though," I shouted over it. "If you touch Vi or Mrs. Lucy."

"Mrs. Lucy," he said, and I couldn't tell if he said it with astonishment or contempt.

"Or Vi or any of the rest of them. I'll drive a stake through your heart or whatever it takes," I said, and the air fell apart.

There was a long sound like an enormous monster growling. It seemed to go on and on. I tried to put my hands over my ears, but I had to hang on to the road to keep from falling. The roar became a scream, and the sidewalk shook itself sharply, and I fell off.

"Are you all right?" Jack said.

I was sitting next to the lorry, which was on its side. The beams had spilled out the back. "Were we hit?" I said.

"No," he said, but I already knew that, and before he had finished pulling me to my feet, I was running toward the post that we couldn't see for the dust.

⊣ • • • ⊢

Mrs. Lucy had told Nelson having everyone out on patrol would mean no one could be found in an emergency, but that was not true. They were all there within minutes, Swales and Morris and Violet, clattering up in her high heels, and Petersby. They ran up, one after the other, and then stopped and looked stupidly at the space that had been Mrs. Lucy's house, as if they couldn't make out what it was.

"Where's Renfrew?" Jack said.

"In Birmingham," Vi said.

"He wasn't here," I explained. "He's on sick leave." I peered through the smoke and dust, trying to see their faces. "Where's Twickenham?"

"Here," he said.

"Where's Mrs. Lucy?" I said.

"Over here," Jack said, and pointed down into the rubble.

We dug all night. Two different rescue squads came to help. They called down every half hour, but there was no answer. Vi borrowed a light from somewhere, draped a blue head scarf over it, and set up as incident officer. An ambulance came, sat awhile, left to go to another incident, came back. Nelson took over as incident officer, and Vi came back up to help. "Is she alive?" she asked.

"She'd better be," I said, looking at Jack.

It began to mist. The planes came over again, dropping flares and incendiaries, but no one stopped work. Twickenham's typewriter came up in the baskets, and one of Mrs. Lucy's wineglasses.

At around three Morris thought he heard something, and we stopped and called down, but there was no answer. The mist turned into a drizzle. At half past four I shouted to Mrs. Lucy, and she called back, from far underground, "I'm here."

"Are you all right?" I shouted.

"My leg's hurt. I think it's broken," she shouted, her voice calm. "I seem to be under the table."

"Don't worry," I shouted. "We're nearly there."

The drizzle turned the plaster dust into a slippery, disgusting mess. We had to brace the tunnel repeatedly and cover it with a tarpaulin, and then it was too dark to see to dig. Swales lay above us, holding a pocket torch over our heads so we could see. The all clear went.

"Jack!" Mrs. Lucy called up.

"Yes!" I shouted.

"Was that the all clear?"

"Yes," I shouted. "Don't worry. We'll have you out soon now."

"What time is it?"

It was too dark in the tunnel to see my watch. I made a guess. "A little after five.

"Is Jack there?"

"Yes."

"He mustn't stay," she said. "Tell him to go home."

The rain stopped, and it began to get light. Jack glanced vaguely up at the sky.

"Don't even think about it," I said. "You're not going anywhere." We ran into one and then another of the oak beams that had reinforced the landing on the fourth floor and had to saw through them. Swales reported that Morris had called Nelson "a bloody murderer." Vi brought us paper cups of tea.

We called down to Mrs. Lucy, but there wasn't any answer. "She's probably dozed off," Twickenham said, and the others nodded as if they believed him.

We could smell the gas long before we got to her, but Jack kept on digging, and like the others, I told myself that she was all right, that we would get to her in time.

She was not under the table after all, but under part of the pantry door. We had to call for a jack to get it off her. It took Morris a long time to come back with it, but it didn't matter. She was lying perfectly straight, her arms folded across her chest and her eyes closed as if she were asleep. Her left leg had been taken off at the knee. Jack knelt beside her and cradled her head.

"Keep your hands off her," I said.

I made Swales come down and help get her out. Vi and Twickenham put her on the stretcher. Petersby went for the ambulance. "She was never a horrid person, you know," Morris said. "Never."

It began to rain again, the sky so dark, it was impossible to tell whether the sun had come up yet or not. Swales brought a tarp to cover Mrs. Lucy.

Petersby came back. "The ambulance has gone off again," he said. "I've sent for the mortuary van, but they said they doubt they can be here before half past eight."

I looked at Jack. He was standing over the tarp, his hands slackly at his sides. He looked worse then Renfrew ever had, impossibly tired, his face gray with wet plaster dust. "We'll wait," I said.

"There's no point in all of us standing here in the rain for two hours," Morris said. "I'll wait here with the…I'll wait here. Jack"—he turned to him—"go and report to Nelson."

"I'll do it," Vi said. "Jack needs to get to his day job."

"Is she up?" Nelson said. He clambered over the fourth-floor beams to where we were standing. "Is she dead?" He glared at Morris and then at my hat, and I wondered if he were going to reprimand me for the condition of my uniform.

"Which of you found her?" he demanded.

I looked at Jack. "Settle did," I said. "He's a regular wonder. He's found six this week alone."

Two days after Mrs. Lucy's funeral, a memo came through from Civil Defence transferring Jack to Nelson's post, and I got my official notice to report for duty. I was sent to basic training and then on to Portsmouth. Vi sent me food packets, and Twickenham posted me copies of his *Twitterings*.

The post had relocated across the street from the butcher's in a house belonging to a Miss Arthur, who had subsequently joined the post. "Miss Arthur loves knitting and flower arranging and will make a valuable addition to our brave little band," Twickenham had written. Vi had got engaged to a pilot in the RAF. Hitler had bombed Birmingham. Jack, in Nelson's post now, had saved sixteen people in one week, a record for the ARP.

After two weeks I was shipped to North Africa, out of the reach of the mails. When I finally got Morris's letter, it was three months old. Jack had been killed while rescuing a child at an incident. A delayed-action bomb had fallen nearby, but "that bloody murderer Nelson" had refused to allow the rescue squad to evacuate. The DA had gone off, the tunnel Jack was working in had collapsed, and he'd been killed. They had gotten the child out, though, and she was unhurt except for a few cuts.

But he isn't dead, I thought. It's impossible to kill him. I had tried, but even betraying him to von Nelson hadn't worked, and he was still somewhere in London, hidden by the blackout and the noise of the bombs and the number of dead bodies, and who would notice a few more?

In January I helped take out a tank battalion at Tobruk. I killed nine Germans before I caught a piece of shrapnel. I was shipped to Gibraltar to hospital, where the rest of my mail caught up with me. Vi had gotten married, the raids had let up considerably, Jack had been awarded the George Cross posthumously.

In March I was sent back to hospital in England for surgery. It was near North Weald, where Morris's son Quincy was stationed. He came to see me after the surgery. He looked the very picture of an RAF pilot, firm-jawed, steely-eyed, rakish grin, not at all like a delinquent minor. He was flying nightly bombing missions over Germany, he told me, "giving Hitler a bit of our own back."

"I heard you're to get a medal," he said, looking at the wall above my head as if he expected to see violets painted there, nine of them, one for each kill.

I asked him about his father. He was fine, he told me. He'd been appointed Senior Warden. "I admire you ARP people," he said, "saving lives and all that."

He meant it. He was flying nightly bombing missions over Germany, reducing their cities to rubble, creating incidents for their air-raid wardens to scrabble through looking for dead children. I wondered if they had bodysniffers there, too, and if they were monsters like Jack.

"Dad wrote to me about your friend Jack," Quincy said. "It must have been rough, hearing so far away from home and all."

He looked genuinely sympathetic, and I supposed he was. He had shot down twenty-eight planes and killed who knows how many fat women in hair nets and thirteen-year-old girls, but no one had ever thought to call him a monster. The Duchess of York had called him the pride of England and kissed him on both cheeks.

"I went with Dad to Vi Westen's wedding," he said. "Pretty as a picture she was."

I thought of Vi, with her pin curls and her plain face. It was as though the war had transformed her into someone completely different, someone pretty and sought after.

"There were strawberries and two kinds of cake," he said. "One of the wardens—Tottenham?—read a poem in honor of the happy couple. Wrote it himself."

It was as if the war had transformed Twickenham as well, and Mrs. Lucy, who had been the terror of the churchwardens. What the War Has Done for Us. But it hadn't transformed them. All that was wanted was for someone to give Vi a bit of attention for all her latent sweetness to blossom. Every girl is pretty when she knows she's sought after.

Twickenham had always longed to be a writer. Nelson had always been a bully and a stickler, and Mrs. Lucy, in spite of what she said, had never been either. "Sometimes it takes something dreadful like a war for one to find one's proper job," she'd said.

Like Quincy, who had been, in spite of what Morris said, a bad boy, headed for a life of petty crime or worse, when the war came along. And suddenly his wildness and daring and "high spirits" were virtues, were just what was needed.

What the War Has Done for Us, Number Two. It has made jobs that didn't exist before. Like RAF pilot. Like post warden. Like bodysniffer.

"Did they find Jack's body?" I asked, though I knew the answer. No, Quincy would say, we couldn't find it, or there was nothing left.

"Didn't Dad tell you?" Quincy said with an anxious look at the transfusion bag hanging above the bed. "They had to dig past him to get to the little girl. It was pretty bad, Dad said. The blast from the DA had driven the leg of a chair straight through his chest."

So I had killed him after all. Nelson and Hitler and I.

"I shouldn't have told you that," Quincy said, watching the blood drip from the bag into my veins as if it were a bad sign. "I know he was a friend of yours. I wouldn't have told you only Dad said to tell you yours was the last name he said before he died. Just before the DA went up. 'Jack,' he said, like he knew what was going to happen, Dad said, and called out your name."

He didn't though, I thought. And "that bloody murderer Nelson" hadn't refused to evacuate him. Jack had just gone on working, oblivious to Nelson and the DA, stabbing at the rubble as though he were trying to murder it, calling out "saw" and "wire cutters" and "braces." Calling out "jack." Oblivious to everything except getting them out before the gas killed them, before they bled to death. Oblivious to everything but his job.

I had been wrong about why he had joined the ARP, about why he had come to London. He must have lived a terrible life up there in York-shire, full of darkness and self-hatred and killing. When the war came, when he began reading of people buried in the rubble, of rescue wardens searching blindly for them, it must have seemed a godsend. A blessing.

It wasn't, I think, that he was trying to atone for what he'd done, for what he was. It's impossible, at any rate. I had killed only ten people, counting Jack, and had helped rescue nearly twenty, but it doesn't cancel out. And I don't think that was what he wanted. What he had wanted was to be useful.

"Here's to making the best of a bad job," Mrs. Lucy had said, and that was all any of them had been doing: Swales with his jokes and gossip, and Twickenham, and Jack, and if they found friendship or love or atonement as well, it was no less than they deserved. And it was still a bad job.

"I should be going," Quincy said, looking worriedly at me. "You need your rest, and I need to be getting back to work. The German army's halfway to Cairo, and Yugoslavia's joined the Axis." He looked excited, happy. "You must rest and get well. We need you back in this war."

"I'm glad you came," I said.

"Yes, well, Dad wanted me to tell you that about Jack calling for you." He stood up. "Tough luck, your getting it in the neck like this." He slapped his flight cap against his leg. "I hate this war," he said, but he was lying.

"So do I," I said.

"They'll have you back killing jerries in no time," he said.

"Yes."

He put his cap on at a rakish angle and went off to bomb lecherous retired colonels and children and widows who had not yet managed to get reinforcing beams out of the Hamburg Civil Defence and paint violets on his plane. Doing his bit.

A sister brought in a tray. She had a large red cross sewn to the bib of her apron.

"No, thanks, I'm not hungry," I said.

"You must keep your strength up," she said. She set the tray beside the bed and went out.

"The war's been rather a blessing for our Vi," I had told Jack, and perhaps it was. But not for most people. Not for girls who worked at John Lewis's for old stewpots who never let them leave early even when the sirens had gone. Not for those people who discovered hidden capabilities for insanity or betrayal or bleeding to death. Or murder.

The sirens went. The nurse came in to check my transfusion and take the tray away. I lay there for a long time, watching the blood come down into my arm.

"Jack," I said, and didn't know who I called out to, or if I had made a sound.

# The Last of the Winnebagos

O n the way out to Tempe I saw a dead jackal in the road. I was in the
far left lane of Van Buren, ten lanes away from it, and its long legs
were facing away from me, the squarish muzzle flat against the pavement so
it looked narrower than it really was, and for a minute I thought it was a dog.

I had not seen an animal in the road like that for fifteen years. They
can't get onto the dividers, of course, and most of the multiways are
fenced. And people are more careful of their animals.

The jackal was probably somebody's pet. This part of Phoenix was
mostly residential, and after all this time, people still think they can turn
the nasty, carrion-loving creatures into pets. Which was no reason to have
hit it and, worse, left it there. It's a felony to strike an animal and another one to not report it, but whoever had hit it was long gone.

I pulled the Hitori over onto the center shoulder and sat there awhile,
staring at the empty multiway. I wondered who had hit it and whether
they had stopped to see if it was dead.

Katie had stopped. She had hit the brakes so hard, she sent the car
into a skid that brought it up against the ditch, and jumped out of the
Jeep. I was still running toward him, floundering in the snow. We made
it to him almost at the same time. I knelt beside him, the camera dangling from my neck, its broken case hanging half-open.

"I hit him," Katie had said. "I hit him with the Jeep."

I looked in the rearview mirror. I couldn't even see over the pile of
camera equipment in the backseat with the eisenstadt balanced on top. I
got out. I had come nearly a mile, and looking back, I couldn't see the
jackal, though I knew now that's what it was.

"McCombe! David! Are you there yet?" Ramirez's voice said from
inside the car.

I leaned in. "No," I shouted in the general direction of the phone's
mike. "I'm still on the multiway."

"Mother of God, what's taking you so long? The governor's conference is at twelve, and I want you to go out to Scottsdale and do a layout on the closing of Taliessin West. The appointment's for ten. Listen, McCombe, I got the poop on the Amblers for you. They bill themselves as 'One Hundred Percent Authentic,' but they're not. Their RV isn't really a Winnebago, it's an Open Road. It *is* the last RV on the road, though, according to Highway Patrol. A man named Eldridge was touring with one, also *not* a Winnebago, a Shasta, until March, but he lost his license in Oklahoma for using a tanker lane, so this is it. Recreation vehicles are banned in all but four states. Texas has legislation in committee, and Utah has a full-divided bill coming up next month. Arizona will be next, so take lots of pictures, Davey boy. This may be your last chance. And get some of the zoo."

"What about the Amblers?" I said.

"Their name *is* Ambler, believe it or not. I ran a lifeline on them. He was a welder. She was a bank teller. No kids. They've been doing this since eighty-nine when he retired. Nineteen years. David, are you using the eisenstadt?"

We had been through this the last three times I'd been on a shoot. "I'm not *there* yet," I said.

"Well, I want you to use it at the governor's conference. Set it on his desk if you can."

I intended to set it on a desk, all right. One of the desks at the back, and let it get some nice shots of the rear ends of reporters as they reached wildly for a little clear airspace to shoot their pictures in, some of them holding their vidcams in their upstretched arms and aiming them in what they hope is the right direction because they can't see the governor at all, let it get a nice shot of one of the reporter's arms as he knocked it facedown on the desk.

"This one's a new model. It's got a trigger. It's set for faces, full-lengths, and vehicles."

So great. I come home with a hundred-frame cartridge full of passersby and tricycles. How the hell did it know when to click the shutter or which one the governor was in a press conference of eight hundred people, full-length or face? It was supposed to have all kinds of fancy light-metrics and computer-composition features, but all it could really do was mindlessly snap whatever passed in front of its idiot lens, just like the highway speed cameras.

It had probably been designed by the same government types who'd put the highway cameras along the road instead of overhead so that all it takes is a little speed to reduce the new side-license plates to a blur, and people go faster than ever. A great camera, the eisenstadt. I could hardly wait to use it.

"Sun-Co's very interested in the eisenstadt," Ramirez said. She didn't say good-bye. She never does. She just stops talking and then starts up again later. I looked back in the direction of the jackal.

The multiway was completely deserted. New cars and singles don't use the undivided multiways much, even during rush hours. Too many of the little cars have been squashed by tankers. Usually there are at least a few obsoletes and renegade semis taking advantage of the Patrol's being on the dividers, but there wasn't anybody at all.

I got back in the car and backed up even with the jackal. I turned off the ignition but didn't get out. I could see the trickle of blood from its mouth from here. A tanker went roaring past out of nowhere, trying to beat the cameras, straddling the three middle lanes and crushing the jackal's rear half to a bloody mush. It was a good thing I hadn't been trying to cross the road. He never would have even seen me.

I started the car and drove to the nearest off-ramp to find a phone. There was one at an old 7-Eleven on McDowell.

"I'm calling to report a dead animal on the road," I told the woman who answered the Society's phone.

"Name and number?"

"It's a jackal," I said. "It's between Thirtieth and Thirty-second on Van Buren. It's in the far right lane."

"Did you render emergency assistance?"

"There was no assistance to be rendered. It was dead."

"Did you move the animal to the side of the road?"

"No."

"Why not?" she said, her tone suddenly sharper, more alert.

Because I thought it was a dog. "I didn't have a shovel," I said, and hung up.

I got out to Tempe by eight-thirty, in spite of the fact that every tanker in the state suddenly decided to take Van Buren. I got pushed out onto the shoulder and drove on that most of the way.

The Winnebago was set up in the fairgrounds between Phoenix and Tempe, next to the old zoo. The flyer had said they would be open from nine to nine, and I had wanted to get most of my pictures before they opened, but it was already a quarter to nine, and even if there were no cars in the dusty parking lot, I was probably too late.

It's a tough job being a photographer. The minute most people see a camera, their real faces close like a shutter in too much light, and all that's left is their camera face, their public face. It's a smiling face, except in the case of Saudi terrorists or senators, but, smiling or not, it shows no real emotion. Actors, politicians, people who have their pictures taken all the time are the worst. The longer the person's been in the public eye, the easier it is for me to get great vidcam footage and the harder it is to get anything approaching a real photograph, and the Amblers had been at this for nearly twenty years. By a quarter to nine they would already have their camera faces on.

I parked down at the foot of the hill next to the clump of ocotillos and yucca where the zoo sign had been, pulled my Nikon longshot out of the mess in the backseat, and took some shots of the sign they'd set up by the multiway: "See a Genuine Winnebago. One Hundred Percent Authentic."

The Genuine Winnebago was parked longways against the stone banks of cacti and palms at the front of the zoo. Ramirez had said it wasn't a real Winnebago, but it had the identifying W with its extending stripes running the length of the RV, and it seemed to me to be the right shape, though I hadn't seen one in at least ten years.

I was probably the wrong person for this story. I had never had any great love for RVs, and my first thought when Ramirez called with the assignment was that there are some things that should be extinct, like mosquitoes and lane dividers, and RVs are right at the top of the list. They had been everywhere in the mountains when I'd lived in Colorado, crawling along in the left-hand lane, taking up two lanes even in the days when a lane was fifteen feet wide, with a train of cursing cars behind them.

I'd been behind one on Independence Pass that had stopped cold while a ten-year-old got out to snap pictures of the scenery with an Instamatic, and one of them had tried to take the curve in front of my house and ended up in my ditch, looking like a beached whale. But that was always a bad curve.

An old man in an ironed short-sleeved shirt came out the side door and around to the front end and began washing the Winnebago with a sponge and a bucket. I wondered where he had gotten the water. According to Ramirez's advance work, which she'd sent me over the modem about the Winnebago, it had maybe a fifty-gallon water tank, tops, which is barely enough for drinking water, a shower, and maybe washing a dish or two, and there certainly weren't any hookups here at the zoo, but he was swilling water onto the front bumper and even over the tires as if he had more than enough.

I took a few shots of the RV standing in the huge expanse of parking lot and then hit the longshot to full for a picture of the old man working on the bumper. He had large reddish-brown freckles on his arms and the top of his bald head, and he scrubbed away at the bumper with a vengeance. After a minute he stopped and stepped back, and then called to his wife. He looked worried, or maybe just crabby. I was too far away to tell if he had snapped out her name impatiently or simply called her to come and look, and I couldn't see his face. She opened the metal side door, with its narrow louvered window, and stepped down onto the metal step.

The old man asked her something, and she, still standing on the step, looked out toward the multiway and shook her head, and then came around to the front, wiping her hands on a dishtowel, and they both stood there looking at his handiwork.

They were One Hundred Percent Authentic, even if the Winnebago wasn't, down to her flowered blouse and polyester slacks, probably also one hundred percent, and the cross-stitched rooster on the dishtowel. She had on brown leather slip-ons like I remembered my grandmother wearing, and I was willing to bet she had set her thinning white hair on bobby pins. Their bio said they were in their eighties, but I would have put them in their nineties, although I wondered if they were too perfect and therefore fake, like the Winnebago. But she went on wiping her hands on the dishtowel the way my grandmother had when she was upset, even though I couldn't see if her face was showing any emotion, and that action at least was authentic.

She apparently told him the bumper looked fine because he dropped the dripping sponge into the bucket and went around behind the Winnebago. She went back inside, shutting the metal door behind her even though it had to be already at least 110 out, and they hadn't even bothered to park under what scanty shade the palms provided.

I put the longshot back in the car. The old man came around the front with a big plywood sign. He propped it against the vehicle's side. "The

Last of the Winnebagos," the sign read in somebody's idea of what Indian writing should look like. "See a vanishing breed. Admission—Adults—$8.00, Children under twelve—$5.00. Open 9 A.M. to Sunset." He strung up a row of red and yellow flags and then picked up the bucket and started toward the door, but halfway there he stopped and took a few steps down the parking lot to where I thought he probably had a good view of the road, and then went back, walking like an old man, and took another swipe at the bumper with the sponge.

"Are you done with the RV yet, McCombe?" Ramirez said on the car phone.

I slung the camera into the back. "I just got here. Every tanker in Arizona was on Van Buren this morning. Why the hell don't you have me do a piece on abuses of the multiway system by water-haulers?"

"Because I want you to get to Tempe alive. The governor's press conference has been moved to one, so you're okay. Have you used the eisenstadt yet?"

"I told you, I just got here. I haven't even turned the damned thing on."

"You don't turn it on. It self-activates when you set it bottom down on a level surface."

Great. It had probably already shot its hundred-frame cartridge on the way here.

"Well, if you don't use it on the Winnebago, make sure you use it at the governor's conference," she said. "By the way, have you thought any more about moving to investigative?"

That was why Sun-Co was really so interested in the eisenstadt. It had been easier to send a photographer who could write stories than it had to send a photographer and a reporter, especially in the little one-seater Hitoris they were ordering now, which was how I got to be a photojournalist. And since that had worked out so well, why send either? Send an eisenstadt and a DAT deck and you won't need an Hitori and way-mile credits to get them there. You can send them through the mail. They can sit unnoticed on the old governor's desk, and after a while somebody in a one-seater who wouldn't have to be either a photographer or a reporter can sneak in to retrieve them and a dozen others.

"No," I said, glancing back up the hill. The old man gave one last swipe to the front bumper and then walked over to one of the zoo's old stone-edged planters and dumped the bucket in on a tangle of prickly pear, which would probably think it was a spring shower and bloom before I made it up the hill. "Look, if I'm going to get any pictures before the touristas arrive, I'd better go."

"I wish you'd think about it. And use the eisenstadt this time. You'll like it once you try it. Even *you'll* forget it's a camera."

"I'll bet," I said. I looked back down the multiway. Nobody at all was coming now. Maybe that was what all the Amblers' anxiety was about—I should have asked Ramirez what their average daily attendance was and what sort of people used up credits to come this far out and see an old beat-up RV. The curve into Tempe alone was 3.2 miles. Maybe nobody came at all. If that was the case, I might have a chance of getting some decent pictures. I got in the Hitori and drove up the steep drive.

"Howdy," the old man said, all smiles, holding out his reddish-brown freckled hand to shake mine. "Name's Jake Ambler. And this here's Winnie," he said, patting the metal side of the RV, "Last of the Winnebagos. Is there just the one of you?"

"David McCombe," I said, holding out my press pass. "I'm a photographer. Sun-Co. Phoenix *Sun,* Tempe-Mesa *Tribune,* Glendale *Star,* and affiliated stations. I was wondering if I could take some pictures of your vehicle?" I touched my pocket and turned the taper on.

"You bet. We've always cooperated with the media, Mrs. Ambler and me. I was just cleaning old Winnie up," he said. "She got pretty dusty on the way down from Globe." He didn't make any attempt to tell his wife I was there, even though she could hardly avoid hearing us, and she didn't open the metal door again. "We been on the road now with Winnie for almost twenty years. Bought her in 1992 in Forest City, Iowa, where they were made. The wife didn't want to buy her, didn't know if she'd like traveling, but now she's the one wouldn't part with it."

He was well into his spiel now, an open, friendly, I-have-nothing-to-hide expression on his face that hid everything. There was no point in taking any stills, so I got out the vidcam and shot the TV footage while he led me around the RV.

"This up here," he said, standing with one foot on the flimsy metal ladder and patting the metal bar around the top, "is the luggage rack, and this is the holding tank. It'll hold thirty gallons and has an automatic electric pump that hooks up to any waste hookup. Empties in five minutes, and you don't even get your hands dirty." He held up his fat pink hands palms forward as if to show me. "Water tank," he said, slapping a silver metal tank next to it. "Holds forty gallons, which is plenty for just the two of us. Interior space is a hundred fifty cubic feet with six feet four of headroom. That's plenty even for a tall guy like yourself."

He gave me the whole tour. His manner was easy, just short of slap-on-the-back hearty, but he looked relieved when an ancient VW bug came chugging cattycornered up through the parking lot. He must have thought they wouldn't have any customers either.

A family piled out, Japanese tourists, a woman with short black hair, a man in shorts, two kids. One of the kids had a ferret on a leash.

"I'll just look around while you tend to the paying customers," I told him.

I locked the vidcam in the car, took the longshot, and went up toward the zoo. I took a wide-angle of the zoo sign for Ramirez. I could see it now—she'd run a caption like, "The old zoo stands empty today. No sound of lion's roar, of elephant's trumpeting, of children's laughter, can be heard here. The old Phoenix Zoo, last of its kind—while just outside its gates stands yet another last of its kind. Story on page 10." Maybe it would be a good idea to let the eisenstadts and the computers take over.

I went inside. I hadn't been out here in years. In the late eighties there had been a big flap over zoo policy. I had taken the pictures, but I hadn't covered the story since there were still such things as reporters back then. I had photographed the cages in question and the new zoo director, who had caused all the flap by stopping the zoo's renovation project cold and giving the money to a wildlife protection group.

"I refuse to spend money on cages when in a few years we'll have nothing to put in them. The timber wolf, the California condor, the grizzly bear, are in imminent danger of becoming extinct, and it's our responsibility to save them, not make a comfortable prison for the last survivors."

The Society had called him an alarmist, which just goes to show you how much things can change. Well, he was an alarmist, wasn't he? The grizzly bear isn't extinct in the wild—it's Colorado's biggest tourist draw, and there are so many whooping cranes Texas is talking about limited hunting.

In all the uproar, the zoo had ceased to exist, and the animals all went to an even more comfortable prison in Sun City—sixteen acres of savanna land for the zebras and lions, and snow manufactured daily for the polar bears.

They hadn't really been cages, in spite of what the zoo director said. The old capybara enclosure, which was the first thing inside the gate, was a nice little meadow with a low stone wall around it. A family of prairie dogs had taken up residence in the middle of it.

I went back to the gate and looked down at the Winnebago. The family circled the Winnebago, the man bending down to look underneath the body. One of the kids was hanging off the ladder at the back of the RV. The ferret was nosing around the front wheel Jake Ambler had so carefully scrubbed down, looking like it was about ready to lift its leg, if ferrets do that. The kid yanked on its leash and then picked it up in his arms. The mother said something to him. Her nose was sunburned.

Katie's nose had been sunburned. She had had that white cream on it that skiers used to use. She was wearing a parka and jeans and bulky pink-and-white moonboots that she couldn't run in, but she still made it to Aberfan before I did. I pushed past her and knelt over him.

"I hit him," she said bewilderedly. "I hit a dog."

"Get back in the jeep, damn it!" I shouted at her. I stripped off my sweater and tried to wrap him in it. "We've got to get him to the vet."

"Is he dead?" Katie said, her face as pale as the cream on her nose.

"No!" I had shouted. "No, he isn't dead."

The mother turned and looked up toward the zoo, her hand shading her face. She caught sight of the camera, dropped her hand, and smiled, a toothy, impossible smile. People in the public eye are the worst, but even people having a snapshot taken close down somehow, and it isn't just the phony smile. It's as if that old superstition is true, and cameras do really steal the soul.

I pretended to take her picture and then lowered the camera. The zoo director had put up a row of tombstone-shaped signs in front of the gate, one for each endangered species. They were covered with plastic, which hadn't helped much. I wiped the streaky dust off the one in front of me. "Canis latrans," it said, with two green stars after it. "Coyote. North American wild dog. Due to large-scale poisoning by ranchers, who saw it as a threat to cattle and sheep, the coyote is nearly extinct in the wild." Underneath there was a photograph of a ragged coyote sitting on its haunches and an explanation of the stars. Blue—endangered species. Yellow—endangered habitat. Red—extinct in the wild.

After Misha died, I had come out here to photograph the dingo and the coyotes and the wolves, but they were already in the process of moving the zoo, so I couldn't get any pictures, and it probably wouldn't have done any good. The coyote in the picture had faded to a greenish-yellow,

and its yellow eyes were almost white, but it stared out of the picture looking as hearty and unconcerned as Jake Ambler, wearing its camera face.

The mother had gone back to the bug and was herding the kids inside. Mr. Ambler walked the father back to the car, shaking his shining
bald head, and the man talked some more, leaning on the open door, and
then got in and drove off. I walked back down.

If he was bothered by the fact that they had only stayed ten minutes
and that, as far as I had been able to see, no money had changed hands,
it didn't show in his face. He led me around to the side of the RV and
pointed to a chipped and faded collection of decals along the painted bar
of the W. "These here are the states we've been in." He pointed to the one
nearest the front. "Every state in the Union, plus Canada and Mexico.
Last state we were in was Nevada."

Up this close it was easy to see where he had painted out the name
of the original RV and covered it with the bar of red. The paint had the
dull look of unauthenticity. He had covered up the "Open Road" with a
burnt-wood plaque that read "The Amblin' Amblers."

He pointed at a bumper sticker next to the door that said, "I got lucky in
Vegas at Caesar's Palace," and had a picture of a naked showgirl. "We could-
n't find a decal for Nevada. I don't think they make them anymore. And you
know something else you can't find? Steering-wheel covers. You know the
kind. That keep the wheel from burning your hands when it gets hot?"

"Do you do all the driving? I asked.

He hesitated before answering, and I wondered if one of them didn't
have a license. I'd have to look it up in the lifeline. "Mrs. Ambler spells
me sometimes, but I do most of it. Mrs. Ambler reads the map. Damn
maps nowadays are so hard to read. Half the time you can't tell what
kind of road it is. They don't make them like they used to."

We talked for a while more about all the things you couldn't find a
decent one of anymore and the sad state things had gotten in generally,
and then I announced I wanted to talk to Mrs. Ambler, got the vidcam
and the eisenstadt out of the car, and went inside the Winnebago.

She still had the dishtowel in her hand, even though there couldn't
possibly be space for that many dishes in the tiny RV. The inside was even
smaller than I had thought it would be, low enough that I had to duck
and so narrow I had to hold the Nikon close to my body to keep from
hitting the lens on the passenger seat. It felt like an oven inside, and it was
only nine o'clock in the morning.

I set the eisenstadt down on the kitchen counter, making sure its concealed lens was facing out. If it would work anywhere, it would be here. There was basically nowhere for Mrs. Ambler to go that she could get out of range. There was nowhere I could go either, and sorry, Ramirez, there are just some things a live photographer can do better than a preprogrammed one, like stay out of the picture.

"This is the galley," Mrs. Ambler said, folding her dishtowel and hanging it from a plastic ring on the cupboard below the sink with the cross-stitch design showing. It wasn't a rooster after all. It was a poodle wearing a sunbonnet and carrying a basket. "Shop on Wednesday," the motto underneath said.

"As you can see, we have a double sink with a handpump faucet. The refrigerator is LP-electric and holds four cubic feet. Back here is the dinette area. The table folds up into the rear wall, and we have our bed. And this is our bathroom."

She was as bad as her husband. "How long have you had the Winnebago?" I said to stop the spiel. Sometimes, if you can get people talking about something besides what they intended to talk about, you can disarm them into something like a natural expression.

"Nineteen years," she said, lifting up the lid of the chemical toilet. "We bought it in 1992. I didn't want to buy it—I didn't like the idea of selling our house and going gallivanting off like a couple of hippies, but Jake went ahead and bought it, and now I wouldn't trade it for anything. The shower operates on a forty-gallon pressurized water system." She stood back so I could get a picture of the shower stall, so narrow you wouldn't have to worry about dropping the soap. I dutifully took some vidcam footage.

"You live here full-time then?" I said, trying not to let my voice convey how impossible that prospect sounded. Ramirez had said they were from Minnesota. I had assumed they had a house there and only went on the road for part of the year.

"Jake says the great outdoors is our home," she said. I gave up trying to get a picture of her and snapped a few high-quality detail stills for the papers: the "Pilot" sign taped on the dashboard in front of the driver's seat, the crocheted granny-square afghan on the uncomfortable-looking couch, a row of salt and pepper shakers in the back windows—Indian children, black Scottie dogs, ears of corn.

"Sometimes we live on the open prairies and sometimes on the seashore," she said. She went over to the sink and hand-pumped a scant two cups of water into a little pan and set it on the two-burner stove. She took down two turquoise Melmac cups and flowered saucers and a jar of freeze-dried and spooned a little into the cups. "Last year we were in the Colorado Rockies. We can have a house on a lake or in the desert, and when we get tired of it, we just move on. Oh, my, the things we've seen."

I didn't believe her. Colorado had been one of the first states to ban recreational vehicles, even before the gas crunch and the multiways. It had banned them on the passes first and then shut them out of the national forests, and by the time I left, they weren't even allowed on the interstates.

Ramirez had said RVs were banned outright in forty-seven states. New Mexico was one, Utah had heavy restricks, and daytime travel was forbidden in all the western states. Whatever they'd seen, and it sure wasn't Colorado, they had seen it in the dark or on some unpatrolled multiway, going like sixty to outrun the cameras. Not exactly the footloose and fancy-free life they tried to paint.

The water boiled. Mrs. Ambler poured it into the cups, spilling a little on the turquoise saucers. She blotted it up with the dishtowel. "We came down here because of the snow. They get winter so early in Colorado."

"I know," I said. It had snowed two feet, and it was only the middle of September. Nobody even had their snow tires on. The aspens hadn't turned yet, and some of the branches broke under the weight of the snow. Katie's nose was still sunburned from the summer.

"Where did you come from just now?" I asked her.

"Globe," she said, and opened the door to yell to her husband. "Jake! Coffee!" She carried the cups to the table-that-converts-into-a-bed. "It has leaves that you can put in it so it seats six," she said.

I sat down at the table so she was on the side where the eisenstadt could catch her. The sun was coming in through the cranked-open back windows, already hot. Mrs. Ambler got onto her knees on the plaid cushions and let down a woven cloth shade, carefully, so it wouldn't knock the salt and pepper shakers off.

There were some snapshots stuck up between the ceramic ears of corn. I picked one up. It was a square Polaroid from the days when you had to peel off the print and glue it to a stiff card: The two of them, looking exactly the way they did now, with that friendly, impenetrable camera smile, were standing in front of a blur of orange rock—the Grand Canyon? Zion? Monument Valley? Polaroid had always chosen color over definition. Mrs. Ambler was holding a little blur in her arms that could have been a cat but wasn't. It was a dog.

"That's Jake and me at Devil's Tower," she said, taking the picture away from me. "And Taco. You can't tell from this picture, but she was the cutest little thing: a chihuahua." She handed it back to me and rummaged behind the salt and pepper shakers. "Sweetest little dog you ever saw. This will give you a better idea."

The picture she handed me was considerably better, a matte print done with a decent camera. Mrs. Ambler was holding the chihuahua in this one, too, standing in front of the Winnebago.

"She used to sit on the arm of Jake's chair while he drove, and when we came to a red light she'd look at it, and when it turned green she'd bark to tell him to go. She was the smartest little thing."

I looked at the dog's flaring, pointed ears, its bulging eyes and rat's snout. The dogs never come through. I took dozens of pictures, there at the end, and they might as well have been calendar shots. Nothing of the real dog at all. I decided it was the lack of muscles in their faces—they could not smile, in spite of what their owners claimed. It is the muscles in the face that make people leap across the years in pictures. The expressions on dogs' faces were what breeding had fastened on them—the gloomy bloodhound, the alert collie, the rakish mutt—and anything else was wishful thinking on the part of the doting master, who would also swear that a color-blind chihuahua with a brain pan the size of a Mexican jumping bean could tell when the light changed.

My theory of the facial muscles doesn't really hold water, of course. Cats can't smile either, and they come through. Smugness, slyness, disdain—all of those expressions come through beautifully, and they don't have any muscles in their faces either, so maybe it's love that you can't capture in a picture because love was the only expression dogs were capable of.

I was still looking at the picture. "She is a cute little thing," I said, and handed it back to her. "She wasn't very big, was she?"

"I could carry Taco in my jacket pocket. We didn't name her Taco. We got her from a man in California that named her that," she said, as if she could see herself that the dog didn't come through in the picture. As if, had she named the dog herself, it would have been different. Then the name would have been a more real name, and Taco would have, by default, become more real as well. As if a name could convey what the picture didn't—all the things the little dog did and was and meant to her.

Names don't do it either, of course. I had named Aberfan myself. The vet's assistant, when he heard it, typed it in as Abraham.

"Age?" he had said calmly, even though he had no business typing all this into a computer—he should have been in the operating room with the vet.

"You've got that in there, damn it," I shouted.

He looked calmly puzzled. "I don't know any Abraham...."

"Aberfan, damn it. Aberfan!"

"Here it is," the assistant said imperturbably.

Katie, standing across the desk, looked up from the screen. "He had the newparvo and lived through it?" she said bleakly.

"He had the newparvo and lived through it," I said, "until you came along."

"I had an Australian shepherd," I told Mrs. Ambler.

Jake came into the Winnebago, carrying the plastic bucket. "Well, it's about time," Mrs. Ambler said. "Your coffee's getting cold."

"I was just going to finish washing off Winnie," he said. He wedged the bucket into the tiny sink and began pumping vigorously with the heel of his hand. "She got mighty dusty coming down through all that sand."

"I was telling Mr. McCombe here about Taco," she said, getting up and taking him the cup and saucer. "Here, drink your coffee before it gets cold."

"I'll be in in a minute," he said. He stopped pumping and tugged the bucket out of the sink.

"Mr. McCombe had a dog," she said, still holding the cup out to him. "He had an Australian shepherd. I was telling him about Taco."

"He's not interested in that," Jake said. They exchanged one of those warning looks that married couples are so good at. "Tell him about the Winnebago. That's what he's here for."

Jake went back outside. I screwed the longshot's lens cap on and put the vidcam back in its case. She took the little pan off the miniature stove and poured the coffee back into it. "I think I've got all the pictures I need," I said to her back.

She didn't turn around. "He never liked Taco. He wouldn't even let her sleep on the bed with us. Said it made his legs cramp. A little dog like that that didn't weigh anything."

I took the longshot's lens cap back off.

"You know what we were doing the day she died? We were out shopping. I didn't want to leave her alone, but Jake said she'd be fine. It was ninety degrees that day, and he just kept on going from store to store, and when we got back she was dead." She set the pan on the stove and turned on the burner. "The vet said it was the newparvo, but it wasn't. She died from the heat, poor little thing."

I set the Nikon down gently on the Formica table and estimated the settings.

"When did Taco die?" I asked her, to make her turn around.

"Ninety-six," she said. She turned back to me, and I let my hand come down on the button in an almost soundless click, but her public face was still in place: apologetic now, smiling, a little sheepish. "My, that was a long time ago."

I stood up and collected my cameras. "I think I've got all the pictures I need," I said again. "If I don't, I'll come back out."

"Don't forget your briefcase," she said, handing me the eisenstadt. "Did your dog die of the newparvo, too?"

"He died fifteen years ago," I said. "In ninety-eight."

She nodded understandingly. "The third wave," she said.

I went outside. Jake was standing behind the Winnebago, under the back window, holding the bucket. He shifted it to his left hand and held out his right hand to me. "You get all the pictures you needed?" he asked.

"Yeah," I said. "I think your wife showed me about everything." I shook his hand.

"You come on back out if you need any more pictures," he said, and sounded, if possible, even more jovial, openhanded, friendly than he had before. "Mrs. Ambler and me, we always cooperate with the media."

"Your wife was telling me about your chihuahua," I said, more to see the effect on him than anything else.

"Yeah, the wife still misses that little dog after all these years," he said, and he looked the way she had, mildly apologetic, still smiling. "It died of the newparvo. I told her she ought to get it vaccinated, but she kept putting it off." He shook his head. "Of course, it wasn't really her fault. You know whose fault the newparvo really was, don't you?"

Yeah, I knew. It was the communists' fault, and it didn't matter that all their dogs had died, too, because he would say their chemical warfare had gotten out of hand or that everybody knows commies hate dogs. Or maybe it was the fault of the Japanese, though I doubted that. He was, after all, in a tourist business. Or the Democrats or the atheists or all of them put together, and even that was One Hundred Percent Authentic—

portrait of the kind of man who drives a Winnebago—but I didn't want to hear it. I walked over to the Hitori and slung the eisenstadt in the back.

"You know who really killed your dog, don't you?" he called after me.

"Yes," I said, and got in the car.

⊣ • • • ⊢

I went home, fighting my way through a fleet of red-painted water tankers who weren't even bothering to try to outrun the cameras and thinking about Taco. My grandmother had had a chihuahua. Perdita. Meanest dog that ever lived. Used to lurk behind the door waiting to take Labrador-sized chunks out of my leg. And my grandmother's. It developed some lingering chihauhua ailment that made it incontinent and even more ill-tempered, if that was possible.

Toward the end, it wouldn't even let my grandmother near it, but she refused to have it put to sleep and was unfailingly kind to it, even though I never saw any indication that the dog felt anything but unrelieved spite toward her. If the newparvo hadn't come along, it probably would still have been around making her life miserable.

I wondered what Taco, the wonder dog, able to distinguish red and green at a single intersection, had really been like, and if it had died of heat prostration. And what it had been like for the Amblers, living all that time in 150 cubic feet together and blaming each other for their own guilt.

I called Ramirez as soon as I got home, breaking in without announcing myself, the way she always did. "I need a lifeline," I said.

"I'm glad you called," she said. "You got a call from the Society. And how's this as a slant for your story? 'The Winnebago and the Winnebagos.' They're an Indian tribe. In Minnesota, I think—why the hell aren't you at the governor's conference?"

"I came home," I said. "What did the Society want?"

"They didn't say. They asked for your schedule. I told them you were with the governor in Tempe. Is this about a story?"

"Yeah."

"Well, you run a proposal past me before you write it. The last thing the paper needs is to get in trouble with the Society."

"The lifeline's for Katherine Powell." I spelled it.

She spelled it back to me. "Is she connected with the Society story?"

"No."

"Then what is she connected with? I've got to put something on the request-for-info."

"Put down background."

"For the Winnebago story?"

"Yes," I said. "For the Winnebago story. How long will it take?"

"That depends. When do you plan to tell me why you ditched the governor's conference? *And* Taliessin West. Jesus Maria, I'll have to call the *Republic* and see if they'll trade footage. I'm sure they'll be thrilled to have shots of an extinct RV. That is, assuming you got any shots. You did make it out to the zoo, didn't you?"

"Yes. I got vidcam footage, stills, the works. I even used the eisenstadt."

"Mind sending your pictures in while I look up your old flame, or is that too much to ask? I don't know how long this will take. It took me two days to get clearance on the Amblers. Do you want the whole thing—pictures, documentation?"

"No. Just a résumé. And a phone number."

She cut out, still not saying good-bye. If phones still had receivers, Ramirez would be a great one for hanging up on people. I highwired the vidcam footage and the eisenstadts in to the paper and then fed the eisenstadt cartridge into the developer. I was more than a little curious about what kind of pictures it would take, in spite of the fact that it was trying to do me out of a job. At least it used high-res film and not some damn two-hundred-thousand-pixel TV substitute. I didn't believe it could compose, and I doubted if the eisenstadt would be able to do foreground-background either, but it might, under certain circumstances, get a picture I couldn't.

The doorbell rang. I answered the door. A lanky young man in a Hawaiian shirt and baggies was standing on the front step, and there was another man in a Society uniform out in the driveway.

"Mr. McCombe?" he said, extending a hand. "Jim Hunter. Humane Society."

I don't know what I'd expected—that they wouldn't bother to trace the call? That they'd let somebody get away with leaving a dead animal on the road?

"I just wanted to stop by and thank you on behalf of the Society for phoning in that report on the jackal. Can I come in?"

He smiled, an open, friendly, smug smile, as if he expected me to be stupid enough to say, "I don't know what you're talking about," and slam the screen door on his hand.

"Just doing my duty," I said, smiling back at him.

"Well, we really appreciate responsible citizens like you. It makes our job a whole lot easier." He pulled a folded readout from his shirt pocket. "I just need to double-check a couple of things. You're a reporter for Sun-Co, is that right?"

"Photojournalist," I said.

"And the Hitori you were driving belongs to the paper?"

I nodded.

"It has a phone. Why didn't you use it to make the call?"

The uniform was bending over the Hitori.

"I didn't realize it had a phone. The paper just bought the Hitoris. This is only the second time I've had one out."

Since they knew the paper had had phones put in, they also knew what I'd just told them. I wondered where they'd gotten the info. Public phones were supposed to be tap free, and if they'd read the license number off one of the cameras, they wouldn't know who'd had the car unless they'd talked to Ramirez, and if they'd talked to her, she wouldn't have been talking blithely about the last thing she needed being trouble with the Society.

"You didn't know the car had a phone," he said, "so you drove to—" He consulted the readout, somehow giving the impression he was taking notes. I'd have bet there was a taper in the pocket of that shirt. "—the 7-Eleven at McDowell and Fortieth Street, and made the call from there. Why didn't you give the Society rep your name and address?"

"I was in a hurry," I said. "I had two assignments to cover before noon, the second out in Scottsdale."

"Which is why you didn't render assistance to the animal either. Because you were in a hurry."

You bastard, I thought. "No," I said. "I didn't render assistance because there wasn't any assistance to be rendered. The—it was dead."

"And how did you know that, Mr. McCombe?"

"There was blood coming out of its mouth," I said.

I had thought that that was a good sign, that he wasn't bleeding anywhere else. The blood had come out of Aberfan's mouth when he tried to lift his head, just a little trickle, sinking into the hard-packed snow. It had stopped before we even got him into the car. "It's all right, boy," I told him. "We'll be there in a minute."

Katie started the Jeep, killed it, started it again, backed it up to where she could turn around.

Aberfan lay limply across my lap, his tail against the gear shift. "Just lie still, boy," I said. I patted his neck. It was wet, and I raised my hand and looked at the palm, afraid it was blood. It was only water from the melted snow. I dried his neck and the top of his head with the sleeve of my sweater.

"How far is it?" Katie said. She was clutching the steering wheel with both hands and sitting stiffly forward in the seat. The windshield wipers flipped back and forth, trying to keep up with the snow.

"About five miles," I said, and she stepped on the gas pedal and then let up on it again as we began to skid.

"On the right side of the highway."

Aberfan raised his head off my lap and looked at me. His gums were gray, and he was panting, but I couldn't see any more blood. He tried to lick my hand. "You'll make it, Aberfan," I said. "You made it before, remember?"

"But you didn't get out of the car and go check, to make sure it was dead?" Hunter said.

"No."

"And you don't have any idea who hit the jackal?" he said, and made it sound like the accusation it was.

"No."

He glanced back at the uniform, who had moved around the car to the other side. "Whew," Hunter said, shaking his Hawaiian collar, "it's like an oven out here. Mind if I come in?" which meant the uniform needed more privacy. Well, then, by all means, give him more privacy. The sooner he sprayed print-fix on the bumper and tires and peeled off the incriminating traces of jackal blood that weren't there and stuck them in the evidence bags he was carrying in the pockets of that uniform, the sooner they'd leave. I opened the screen door wider.

"Oh, this is great," Hunter said, still trying to generate a breeze with his collar. "These old adobe houses stay so cool." He glanced around the room at the developer and the enlarger, the couch, the dry-mounted photographs on the wall. "You don't have any idea who might have hit the jackal?"

"I figure it was a tanker," I said. "What else would be on Van Buren that time of morning?"

I was almost sure it had been a car or a small truck. A tanker would have left the jackal a spot on the pavement. But a tanker would get a license suspension and two weeks of having to run water into Santa Fe instead of Phoenix, and probably not that. Rumor at the paper had it the Society was in the water board's pocket. If it was a car, on the other hand, the Society would take away the car and stick its driver with a prison sentence.

"They're all trying to beat the cameras," I said. "The tanker probably didn't even know it'd hit it."

"What?" he said.

"I said, it had to be a tanker. There isn't anything else on Van Buren during rush hour."

I expected him to say, "Except for you," but he didn't. He wasn't even listening. "Is this your dog?" he said.

He was looking at the photograph of Perdita. "No," I said. "That was my grandmother's dog."

"What is it?"

A nasty little beast. And when it died of the newparvo, my grandmother had cried like a baby. "A chihuahua."

He looked around at the other walls. "Did you take all these pictures of dogs?" His whole manner had changed, taking on a politeness that made me realize just how insolent he had intended to be before. The one on the road wasn't the only jackal around.

"Some of them," I said. He was looking at the photograph next to it. "I didn't take that one."

"I know what this one is," he said, pointing at it. "It's a boxer, right?"

"An English bulldog," I said.

"Oh, right. Weren't those the ones that were exterminated? For being vicious?"

"No," I said.

He moved on to the picture over the developer, like a tourist in a museum. "I bet you didn't take this one either," he said, pointing at the high shoes, the old-fashioned hat on the stout old woman holding the dogs in her arms.

"That's a photograph of Beatrix Potter, the English children's author," I said. "She wrote *Peter Rabbit.*"

He wasn't interested. "What kind of dogs are those?"

"Pekingese."

"It's a great picture of them."

It is, in fact, a terrible picture of them. One of them has wrenched his face away from the camera, and the other sits grimly in her owner's hand, waiting for its chance. Obviously neither of them liked having its picture taken, though you can't tell that from their expressions. They reveal nothing in their little flat-nosed faces, in their black little eyes.

Beatrix Potter, on the other hand, comes through beautifully, in spite of the attempt to smile for the camera and the fact that she must have had to hold on to the Pekes for dear life, or maybe because of that. The fierce, humorous love she felt for her fierce, humorous little dogs is all there in her face. She must never, in spite of *Peter Rabbit* and its attendant fame, have developed a public face. Everything she felt was right there, unprotected, unshuttered. Like Katie.

"Are any of these your dog?" Hunter asked. He was standing looking at the picture of Misha that hung above the couch.

"No." I said.

"How come you don't have any pictures of your dog?" he asked, and I wondered how he knew I had had a dog and what else he knew.

"He didn't like having his picture taken."

He folded up the readout, stuck it in his pocket, and turned around to look at the photo of Perdita again. "He looks like he was a real nice little dog," he said.

The uniform was waiting on the front step, obviously finished with whatever he had done to the car.

"We'll let you know if we find out who's responsible," Hunter said, and they left. On the way out to the street the uniform tried to tell him what he'd found, but Hunter cut him off. The suspect has a house full of photographs of dogs, therefore he didn't run over a poor facsimile of one on Van Buren this morning. Case closed.

I went back over to the developer and fed the eisenstadt film in. "Positives, one two three order, five seconds," I said, and watched as the pictures came up on the developer's screen. Ramirez had said the eisenstadt automatically turned on whenever it was set upright on a level surface. She was right. It had taken a half-dozen shots on the way out to Tempe. Two shots of the Hitori it must have taken when I set it down to load the car, open door of same with prickly pear in the foreground, a blurred shot of palm trees and buildings with a minuscule, sharp-focused glimpse of the traffic on the expressway. Vehicles and people. There was a great shot of the red tanker that had clipped the jackal and ten or so of the yucca I had parked next to at the foot of the hill.

It had gotten two nice shots of my forearm as I set it down on the kitchen counter of the Winnebago and some beautifully composed still lifes of Melmac with Spoons. Vehicles and people. The rest of the pictures were dead losses: my back, the open bathroom door, Jake's back, and Mrs. Ambler's public face.

Except the last one. She had been standing right in front of the eisenstadt, looking almost directly into the lens. "When I think of that poor thing, all alone," she had said, and by the time she turned around, she had her public face back on, but for a minute there, looking at what she thought was a briefcase and remembering, there she was, the person I had tried all morning to get a picture of.

I took it into the living room and sat down and looked at it awhile.

"So you knew this Katherine Powell in Colorado," Ramirez said, breaking in without preamble, and the highwire slid silently forward and began to print out the lifeline. "I always suspected you of having some deep dark secret in your past. Is she the reason you moved to Phoenix?"

I was watching the highwire advance the paper. Katherine Powell, 4628 Dutchman Drive, Apache Junction. Forty miles away.

"Holy Mother, you were really cradle-robbing. According to my calculations, she was seventeen when you lived there."

Sixteen.

"Are you the owner of the dog?" the vet had asked her, his face slackening into pity when he saw how young she was.

"No." she said. "I'm the one who hit him."

"My God," he said. "How old are you?"

"Sixteen," she said, and her face was wide open. "I just got my license."

"Aren't you even going to tell me what she has to do with this Winnebago thing?" Ramirez said.

"I moved down here to get away from the snow," I said, and cut out without saying good-bye.

The lifeline was still rolling silently forward. Hacker at Hewlett-Packard. Fired in 2008, probably during the unionization. Divorced. Two kids. She had moved to Arizona five years after I did. Management programmer for Toshiba. Arizona driver's license.

I went back to the developer and looked at the picture of Mrs. Ambler. I had said dogs never came through. That wasn't true. Taco wasn't in the blurry snapshots Mrs. Ambler had been so anxious to show me, in the stories she had been so anxious to tell. But she was in this picture, reflected in the pain and love and loss on Mrs. Ambler's face. I could see her plain as day, perched on the arm of the driver's seat, barking impatiently when the light turned green.

I put a new cartridge in the eisenstadt and went out to see Katie.

I had to take Van Buren—it was almost four o'clock, and the rush hour would have started on the dividers—but the jackal was gone anyway. The Society is efficient. Like Hitler and his Nazis.

"Why don't you have any pictures of your dog?" Hunter had asked. The question could have been based on the assumption that anyone who would fill his living room with photographs of dogs must have had one of his own, but it wasn't. He had known about Aberfan, which meant he'd had access to my lifeline, which meant all kinds of things. My lifeline was privacy coded, so I had to be notified before anybody could get access, except, it appeared, the Society. A reporter I knew at the paper, Dolores Chiwere, had tried to do a story awhile back claiming that the Society had an illegal link to the lifeline banks, but she hadn't been able to come up with enough evidence to convince her editor. I wondered if this counted.

The lifeline would have told them about Aberfan but not about how he died. Killing a dog wasn't a crime in those days, and I hadn't pressed charges against Katie for reckless driving or even called the police.

"I think you should," the vet's assistant had said. "There are less than a hundred dogs left. People can't just go around killing them."

"My God, man, it was snowing and slick," the vet had said angrily, "and she's just a kid."

"She's old enough to have a license," I said, looking at Katie. She was fumbling in her purse for her driver's license. "She's old enough to have been on the roads."

Katie found her license and gave it to me. It was so new it was still shiny. Katherine Powell. She had turned sixteen two weeks ago.

"This won't bring him back," the vet had said, and taken the license out of my hand and given it back to her. "You go on home now."

"I need her name for the records," the vet's assistant had said.

She had stepped forward. "Katie Powell," she had said.

"We'll do the paperwork later," the vet had said firmly.

They never did do the paperwork, though. The next week the third wave hit, and I suppose there hadn't seemed any point.

I slowed down at the zoo entrance and looked up into the parking lot as I went past. The Amblers were doing a booming business. There were at least five cars and twice as many kids clustered around the Winnebago.

"Where the hell are you?" Ramirez said. "And where the hell are your pictures? I talked the *Republic* into a trade, but they insisted on scoop rights. I need your stills now!"

"I'll send them in as soon as I get home," I said. "I'm on a story."

"The hell you are! You're on your way out to see your old girlfriend. Well, not on the paper's credits, you're not."

"Did you get the stuff on the Winnebago Indians?" I asked her.

"Yes. They were in Wisconsin, but they're not anymore. In the mid-seventies there were sixteen hundred of them on the reservation and about forty-five hundred altogether, but by 2000 the number was down to five hundred, and now they don't think there are any left, and nobody knows what happened to them."

I'll tell you what happened to them, I thought. Almost all of them were killed in the first wave, and people blamed the government and the Japanese and the ozone layer, and after the second wave hit, the Society passed all kinds of laws to protect the survivors, but it was too late, they were already below the minimum-survival population limit, and then the third wave polished off the rest of them, and the last of the Winnebagos sat in a cage somewhere, and if I had been there, I would probably have taken his picture.

"I called the Bureau of Indian Affairs," Ramirez said, "and they're supposed to call me back, and you don't give a damn about the Winnebagos. You just wanted to get me off the subject. What's this story you're on?"

I looked around the dashboard for an exclusion button.

"What the hell is going on, David? First you ditch two big stories, now you can't even get your pictures in. Jesus, if something's wrong, you can tell me. I want to help. It has something to do with Colorado, doesn't it?"

I found the exclusion button and cut her off.

Van Buren got crowded as the afternoon rush spilled over off the divideds. Out past the curve, where Van Buren turns into Apache Boulevard, they were putting in new lanes. The cement forms were already up on the eastbound side, and they were building the wooden forms up in two of the six lanes on my side.

The Amblers must have just beaten the workmen, though at the rate the men were working right now, leaning on their shovels in the hot afternoon sun and smoking stew, it had probably taken them six weeks to do this stretch.

Mesa was still open multiway, but as soon as I was through downtown, the construction started again, and this stretch was nearly done—forms up on both sides and most of the cement poured. The Amblers couldn't have come in from Globe on this road. The lanes were barely wide enough for the Hitori, and the tanker lanes were gated. Superstition Mountain is full-divided, and the old highway down from Roosevelt is, too, which meant they hadn't come in from Globe at all. I wondered how they had come in—probably in some tanker lane on a multiway.

"Oh, my, the things we've seen," Mrs. Ambler had said. I wondered how much they'd been able to see skittering across the dark desert like a couple of kangaroo mice, trying to beat the cameras.

The roadworkers didn't have the new exit signs up yet, and I missed the exit for Apache Junction and had to go halfway to Superior, trapped in my narrow, cement-sided lane, till I hit a change-lanes and could get turned around.

Katie's address was in Superstition Estates, a development pushed up as close to the base of Superstition Mountain as it could get. I thought about what I would say to Katie when I got there. I had said maybe ten sentences altogether to her, most of them shouted directions, in the two hours we had been together. In the Jeep on the way to the vet's I had talked to Aberfan, and after we got there, sitting in the waiting room, we hadn't talked at all.

It occurred to me that I might not recognize her. I didn't really remember what she looked like—only the sunburned nose and that terrible openness, and now, fifteen years later, it seemed unlikely that she would have either of them. The Arizona sun would have taken care of the first, and she had gotten married and divorced, been fired, had who knows what else happen to her in fifteen years to close her face. In which case, there had been no point in my driving all the way out here. But Mrs. Ambler had had an almost impenetrable public face, and you could still catch her off guard. If you got her talking about the dogs. If she didn't know she was being photographed.

Katie's house was an old-style passive solar, with flat black panels on the roof. It looked presentable, but not compulsively neat. There wasn't any grass—tankers won't waste their credits coming this far out, and Apache Junction isn't big enough to match the bribes and incentives of Phoenix or Tempe—but the front yard was laid out with alternating patches of black lava chips and prickly pear. The side yard had a parched-looking palo verde tree, and there was a cat tied to it. A little girl was playing under the tree with toy cars.

I took the eisenstadt out of the back and went up to the front door and rang the bell. At the last moment, when it was too late to change my mind, walk away, because she was already opening the screen door, it occurred to me that she might not recognize me, that I might have to tell her who I was.

Her nose wasn't sunburned, and she had put on the weight a sixteen-year-old puts on to get to be thirty, but otherwise she looked the same as she had that day in front of my house. And her face hadn't completely closed. I could tell, looking at her, that she recognized me and that she had known I was coming. She must have put a notify on her lifeline to have them warn her if I asked her whereabouts. I thought about what that meant.

She opened the screen door a little, the way I had to the Humane Society. "What do you want?" she said.

I had never seen her angry, not even when I turned on her at the vet's. "I wanted to see you," I said.

I had thought I might tell her I had run across her name while I was working on a story and wondered if it was the same person or that I was doing a piece on the last of the passive solars. "I saw a dead jackal on the road this morning," I said.

"And you thought I killed it?" she said. She tried to shut the screen door.

I put out my hand without thinking, to stop her. "No," I said. I took my hand off the door. "No, of course I don't think that. Can I come in? I just want to talk to you."

The little girl had come over, clutching her toy cars to her pink T-shirt, and was standing off to the side, watching curiously.

"Come on inside, Jana," Katie said, and opened the screen door a fraction wider. The little girl scooted through. "Go on in the kitchen," she said. "I'll fix you some Kool-Aid." She looked up at me. "I used to have nightmares about your coming. I'd dream that I'd go to the door and there you'd be."

"It's really hot out here," I said, and knew I sounded like Hunter. "Can I come in?"

She opened the screen door all the way. "I've got to make my daughter something to drink," she said, and led the way into the kitchen, the little girl dancing in front of her.

"What kind of Kool-Aid do you want?" Katie asked her, and she shouted, "Red!"

The kitchen counter faced the stove, refrigerator, and water cooler across a narrow aisle that opened out into an alcove with a table and chairs. I put the eisenstadt down on the table and then sat down myself so she wouldn't suggest moving into another room.

Katie reached a plastic pitcher down from one of the shelves and stuck it under the water tank to fill it. Jana dumped her cars on the counter, clambered up beside them, and began opening the cupboard doors.

"How old's your little girl?" I asked.

Katie got a wooden spoon out of the drawer next to the stove and brought it and the pitcher over to the table. "She's four," she said. "Did you find the Kool-Aid?" she asked the little girl.

"Yes," the little girl said, but it wasn't Kool-Aid. It was a pinkish cube she peeled a plastic wrapping off of. It fizzed and turned a thinnish red when she dropped it into the pitcher. Kool-Aid must have become extinct, too, along with Winnebagos and passive solar. Or else changed beyond recognition. Like the Humane Society.

Katie poured the red stuff into a glass with a cartoon whale on it.

"Is she your only one?" I asked.

"No, I have a little boy," she said, but warily, as if she wasn't sure she wanted to tell me, even though if I'd requested the lifeline, I already had access to all this information. Jana asked if she could have a cookie and then took it and her Kool-Aid back down the hall and outside. I could hear the screen door slam.

Katie put the pitcher in the refrigerator and leaned against the kitchen counter, her arms folded across her chest. "What do you want?"

She was just out of range of the eisenstadt, her face in the shadow of the narrow aisle.

"There was a dead jackal on the road this morning," I said. I kept my voice low so she would lean forward into the light to try and hear me. "It'd been hit by a car, and it was lying funny, at an angle. It looked like a dog. I wanted to talk to somebody who remembered Aberfan, somebody who knew him."

"I didn't know him," she said. "I only killed him, remember? That's why you did this, isn't it, because I killed Aberfan?"

She didn't look at the eisenstadt, hadn't even glanced at it when I set it on the table, but I wondered suddenly if she knew what I was up to. She was still carefully out of range. And what if I said to her, "That's right. That's why I did this, because you killed him, and I didn't have any pictures of him. You owe me. If I can't have a picture of Aberfan, you at least owe me a picture of you remembering him."

Only she didn't remember him, didn't know anything about him except what she had seen on the way to the vet's, Aberfan lying on my lap and looking up at me, already dying. I had had no business coming here, dredging all this up again. No business.

"At first I thought you were going to have me arrested," Katie said, "and then after all the dogs died, I thought you were going to kill me."

The screen door banged. "Forgot my cars," the little girl said, and scooped them into the tail of her T-shirt. Katie tousled her hair as she went past and then folded her arms again.

"'It wasn't my fault,' I was going to tell you when you came to kill me," she said. "'It was snowy. He ran right in front of me. I didn't even see him.' I looked up everything I could find about newparvo. Preparing for the defense. How it mutated from parvovirus and from cat distemper before that and then kept on mutating, so they couldn't come up with a vaccine. How even before the third wave they were below the minimum survival population. How it was the fault of the people who owned the last survivors because they wouldn't risk their dogs to breed them. How the scientists didn't come up with a vaccine until only the jackals were left. 'You're wrong,' I was going to tell you. 'It was the puppy-mill owners' fault that all the dogs died. If they hadn't kept their dogs in such unsanitary conditions, it never would have gotten out of control in the first place.' I had my defense all ready. But you'd moved away."

Jana banged in again, carrying the empty whale glass. She had a red smear across the whole lower half of her face. "I need some more," she said, making "some more" into one word. She held the glass in both hands while Katie opened the refrigerator and poured her another glassful.

"Wait a minute, honey," she said. "You've got Kool-Aid all over you," and bent to wipe Jana's face with a paper towel.

Katie hadn't said a word in her defense while we waited at the vet's, not, "It was snowy," or, "He ran right out in front of me," or, "I didn't even see him." She had sat silently beside me, twisting her mittens in her lap, until the vet came out and told me Aberfan was dead, and then she had said, "I didn't know there were any left in Colorado. I thought they were all dead."

And I had turned to her, to a sixteen-year-old not even old enough to know how to shut her face, and said, "Now they all are. Thanks to you."

"That kind of talk isn't necessary," the vet had said warningly.

I had wrenched away from the hand he tried to put on my shoulder. "How does it feel to have killed one of the last dogs in the world?" I shouted at her. "How does it feel to be responsible for the extinction of an entire species?"

The screen door banged again. Katie was looking at me, still holding the reddened paper towel.

"You moved away," she said, "and I thought maybe that meant you'd forgiven me, but it didn't, did it?" She came over to the table and wiped at the red circle the glass had left. "Why did you do it? To punish me? Or did you think that's what I'd been doing the last fifteen years, roaring around the roads murdering animals?"

"What?" I said.

"The Society's already been here."

"The Society?" I said, not understanding.

"Yes," she said, still looking at the red-stained towel. "They said you had reported a dead animal on Van Buren. They wanted to know where I was this morning between eight and nine A.M."

I nearly ran down a roadworker on the way back into Phoenix. He leaped for the still-wet cement barrier, dropping the shovel he'd been leaning on all day, and I ran right over it.

The Society had already been there. They had left my house and gone straight to hers. Only that wasn't possible, because I hadn't even called Katie then. I hadn't even seen the picture of Mrs. Ambler yet. Which meant they had gone to see Ramirez after they left me, and the last thing Ramirez and the paper needed was trouble with the Society.

"I thought it was suspicious when he didn't go to the governor's conference," she had told them, "and just now he called and asked for a lifeline on this person here. Katherine Powell, 4628 Dutchman Drive. He knew her in Colorado."

"Ramirez!" I shouted at the car phone. "I want to talk to you!" There wasn't any answer.

I swore at her for a good ten miles before I remembered I had the exclusion button on. I punched it off. "Ramirez, where the hell are you?"

"I could ask you the same question," she said. She sounded even angrier than Katie, but not as angry as I was. "You cut me off, you won't tell me what's going on."

"So you decided you had it figured out for yourself, and you told your little theory to the Society."

"What?" she said, and I recognized that tone, too. I had heard it in my own voice when Katie told me the Society had been there. Ramirez hadn't told anybody anything, she didn't even know what I was talking about, but I was going too fast to stop.

"You told the Society I'd asked for Katie's lifeline, didn't you?" I shouted.

"No," she said. "I didn't. Don't you think it's time you told me what's going on?"

"Did the Society come see you this afternoon?"

"No. I told you. They called this morning and wanted to talk to you. I told them you were at the governor's conference."

"And they didn't call back later?"

"No. Are you in trouble?"

I hit the exclusion button. "Yes," I said. "Yes, I'm in trouble."

Ramirez hadn't told them. Maybe somebody else at the paper had, but I didn't think so. There had after all been Dolores Chiwere's story about their having illegal access to the lifelines. "How come you don't have any pictures of your dog?" Hunter had asked me, which meant they'd read my lifeline, too. So they knew we had both lived in Colorado, in the same town, when Aberfan died.

"What did you tell them?" I had demanded of Katie. She had been standing there in the kitchen still messing with the Kool-Aid-stained towel, and I had wanted to yank it out of her hands and make her look at me. "What did you tell the Society?"

She looked up at me. "I told them I was on Indian School Road, picking up the month's programming assignments from my company. Unfortunately, I could just as easily have driven in on Van Buren."

"About Aberfan!" I shouted. "What did you tell them about Aberfan?"

She looked steadily at me. "I didn't tell them anything. I assumed you'd already told them."

I had taken hold of her shoulders. "If they come back, don't tell them anything. Not even if they arrest you. I'll take care of this. I'll…"

But I hadn't told her what I'd do because I didn't know. I had run out of her house, colliding with Jana in the hall on her way in for another refill, and roared off for home, even though I didn't have any idea what I would do when I got there.

Call the Society and tell them to leave Katie alone, that she had nothing to do with this? That would be even more suspicious than everything else I'd done so far, and you couldn't get much more suspicious than that.

I had seen a dead jackal on the road (or so I said), and instead of reporting it immediately on the phone right there in my car, I'd driven to a convenience store two miles away. I'd called the Society, but I'd refused to give them my name and number. And then I'd canceled two shoots without telling my boss and asked for the lifeline of one Katherine Powell, whom I had known fifteen years ago and who could have been on Van Buren at the time of the accident.

The connection was obvious, and how long would it take them to make the connection that fifteen years ago was when Aberfan had died?

Apache was beginning to fill up with rush-hour overflow and a whole fleet of tankers. The overflow obviously spent all their time driving divideds—nobody bothered to signal that they were changing lanes. Nobody even gave an indication that they knew what a lane was. Going around the curve from Tempe and onto Van Buren, they were all over the road. I moved over into the tanker lane.

My lifeline didn't have the vet's name on it. They were just getting started in those days, and there was a lot of nervousness about invasion of privacy. Nothing went on-line without the person's permission, especially not medical and bank records, and the lifelines were little more than puff bios: family, occupation, hobbies, pets. The only things on the lifeline besides Aberfan's name was the date of his death and my address at the time, but that was probably enough. There were only two vets in town.

The vet hadn't written Katie's name down on Aberfan's record. He had handed her driver's license back to her without even looking at it, but Katie had told her name to the vet's assistant. He might have written it down. There was no way I could find out. I couldn't ask for the vet's lifeline because the Society had access to the lifelines. They'd get to him before I could. I could maybe have the paper get the vet's records for me, but I'd have to tell Ramirez what was going on, and the phone was probably tapped, too. And if I showed up at the paper, Ramirez would confiscate the car. I couldn't go there.

Wherever the hell I was going, I was driving too fast to get there. When the tanker ahead of me slowed down to ninety, I practically climbed up his back bumper. I had gone past the place where the jackal had been hit without ever seeing it. Even without the traffic, there probably hadn't been anything to see. What the Society hadn't taken care of, the overflow probably had, and anyway, there hadn't been any evidence to begin with. If there had been, if the cameras had seen the car that hit it, they wouldn't have come after me. And Katie.

The Society couldn't charge her with Aberfan's death—killing an animal hadn't been a crime back then—but if they found out about Aberfan they would charge her with the jackal's death, and it wouldn't matter if a hundred witnesses, a hundred highway cameras had seen her on Indian School Road. It wouldn't matter if the print-fix on her car was clean. She had killed one of the last dogs, hadn't she? They would crucify her.

I should never have left Katie. "Don't tell them anything," I had told her, but she had never been afraid of admitting guilt. When the receptionist had asked her what had happened, she had said, "I hit him," just like that, no attempt to make excuses, to run off, to lay the blame on someone else.

I had run off to try to stop the Society from finding out that Katie had hit Aberfan, and meanwhile the Society was probably back at Katie's, asking her how she'd happened to know me in Colorado, asking her how Aberfan died.

I was wrong about the Society. They weren't at Katie's house. They were at mine, standing on the porch, waiting for me to let them in.

"You're a hard man to track down," Hunter said.

The uniform grinned. "Where you been?"

"Sorry," I said, fishing my keys out of my pocket. "I thought you were all done with me. I've already told you everything I know about the incident."

Hunter stepped back just far enough for me to get the screen door open and the key in the lock. "Officer Segura and I just need to ask you a couple more questions."

"Where'd you go this afternoon?" Segura asked.

"I went to see an old friend of mine."

"Who?"

"Come on, come on," Hunter said. "Let the guy get in his own front door before you start badgering him with a lot of questions."

I opened the door. "Did the cameras get a picture of the tanker that hit the jackal?" I asked.

"Tanker?" Segura said.

"I told you," I said, "I figure it had to be a tanker. The jackal was lying in the tanker lane." I led the way into the living room, depositing my keys on the computer and switching the phone to exclusion while I talked. The last thing I needed was Ramirez bursting in with, "What's going on? Are you in trouble?"

"It was probably a renegade that hit it, which would explain why he didn't stop." I gestured at them to sit down.

Hunter did. Segura started for the couch and then stopped, staring at the photos on the wall above it. "Jesus, will you look at all the dogs!" he said. "Did you take all these pictures?"

"I took some of them. That one in the middle is Misha."

"The last dog, right?"

"Yes," I said.

"No kidding. The very last one."

No kidding. She was being kept in isolation at the Society's research facility in St. Louis when I saw her. I had talked them into letting me shoot her, but it had to be from outside the quarantine area. The picture had an unfocused look that came from shooting it through a wiremesh-reinforced window in the door, but I wouldn't have done any better if they'd let me inside. Misha was past having any expression to photograph. She hadn't eaten in a week at that point. She lay with her head on her paws, staring at the door, the whole time I was there.

"You wouldn't consider selling this picture to the Society, would you?"

"No, I wouldn't."

He nodded understandingly. "I guess people were pretty upset when she died."

Pretty upset. They had turned on anyone who had anything to do with it—the puppy-mill owners, the scientists who hadn't come up with a vaccine, Misha's vet—and a lot of others who hadn't. And they had handed over their civil rights to a bunch of jackals who were able to grab them because everybody felt so guilty. Pretty upset.

"What's this one?" Segura asked. He had already moved on to the picture next to it.

"It's General Patton's bull terrier Willie."

They fed and cleaned up after Misha with those robot arms they used to use in the nuclear plants. Her owner, a tired-looking woman, was allowed to watch her through the wire-mesh window but had to stay off to the side because Misha flung herself barking against the door whenever she saw her.

"You should make them let you in," I had told her. "It's cruel to keep her locked up like that. You should make them let you take her back home."

"And let her get the newparvo?" she said.

There was nobody left for Misha to get the newparvo from, but I didn't say that. I set the light readings on the camera, trying not to lean into Misha's line of vision.

"You know what killed them, don't you?" she said. "The ozone layer. All those holes. The radiation got in and caused it."

It was the communists, it was the Mexicans, it was the government. And the only people who acknowledged their guilt weren't guilty at all.

"This one here looks kind of like a jackal," Segura said. He was looking at a picture I had taken of a German shepherd after Aberfan died. "Dogs were a lot like jackals, weren't they?"

"No," I said, and sat down on the shelf in front of the developer's screen, across from Hunter. "I already told you everything I know about the jackal. I saw it lying in the road, and I called you."

"You said when you saw the jackal it was in the far right lane," Hunter said.

"That's right."

"And you were in the far left lane?"

"I was in the far left lane."

They were going to take me over my story, point by point, and when I couldn't remember what I'd said before, they were going to say, "Are you sure that's what you saw, Mr. McCombe? Are you sure you didn't see the jackal get hit? Katherine Powell hit it, didn't she?"

"You told us this morning you stopped, but the jackal was already dead. Is that right?" Hunter asked.

"No," I said.

Segura looked up. Hunter touched his hand casually to his pocket and then brought it back to his knee, turning on the taper.

"I didn't stop for about a mile. Then I backed up and looked at it, but it was dead. There was blood coming out of its mouth."

Hunter didn't say anything. He kept his hands on his knees and waited—an old journalist's trick: If you wait long enough, they'll say something they didn't intend to, just to fill the silence.

"The jackal's body was at a peculiar angle," I said, right on cue. "The way it was lying, it didn't look like a jackal. I thought it was a dog." I waited till the silence got uncomfortable again. "It brought back a lot of terrible memories," I said. "I wasn't even thinking. I just wanted to get away from it. After a few minutes I realized I should have called the Society, and I stopped at the 7-Eleven."

I waited again, till Segura began to shoot uncomfortable glances at Hunter, and then started in again. "I thought I'd be okay, that I could go ahead and work, but after I got to my first shoot, I knew I wasn't going to make it, so I came home." Candor. Openness. If the Amblers can do it, so can you. "I guess I was still in shock or something. I didn't even call my boss and have her get somebody to cover the governor's conference. All I could think about was—" I stopped and rubbed my hand across my face. "I needed to talk to somebody. I had the paper look up an old friend of mine, Katherine Powell."

I stopped, I hoped this time for good. I had admitted lying to them and confessed to two crimes: leaving the scene of the accident and using press access to get a lifeline for personal use, and maybe that would be enough to satisfy them. I didn't want to say anything about going to see Katie. They would know she would have told me about their visit and decide this confession was an attempt to get her off, and maybe they'd been watching the house and knew it anyway, and this was all wasted effort.

The silence dragged on. Hunter's hands tapped his knees twice and then subsided. The story didn't explain why I'd picked Katie, who I hadn't seen in fifteen years, who I knew in Colorado, to go see, but maybe, maybe they wouldn't make the connection.

"This Katherine Powell," Hunter said, "you knew her in Colorado, is that right?"

"We lived in the same little town."

We waited.

"Isn't that when your dog died?" Segura said suddenly. Hunter shot him a glance of pure rage, and I thought, it isn't a taper he's got in that shirt pocket. It's the vet's records, and Katie's name is on them.

"Yes," I said. "He died in September of ninety-eight."

Segura opened his mouth.

"In the third wave?" Hunter asked before he could say anything.

"No," I said. "He was hit by a car."

They both looked genuinely shocked. The Amblers could have taken lessons from them. "Who hit it?" Segura asked, and Hunter leaned forward, his hand moving reflexively toward his pocket.

"I don't know," I said. "It was a hit and run. Whoever it was just left him lying there in the road. That's why when I saw the jackal, it...that was how I met Katherine Powell. She stopped and helped me. She helped me get him into her car, and we took him to the vet's, but it was too late."

Hunter's public face was pretty indestructible, but Segura's wasn't. He looked surprised and enlightened and disappointed all at once.

"That's why I wanted to see her," I said unnecessarily.

"Your dog was hit on what day?" Hunter asked.

"September thirtieth."

"What was the vet's name?"

He hadn't changed his way of asking the questions, but he no longer cared what the answers were. He had thought he'd found a connection, a cover-up, but here we were, a couple of dog lovers, a couple of Good Samaritans, and his theory had collapsed. He was done with the interview, he was just finishing up, and all I had to do was be careful not to relax too soon.

I frowned. "I don't remember his name. Cooper, I think."

"What kind of car did you say hit your dog?"

"I don't know," I said, thinking, not a Jeep. Make it something besides a Jeep. "I didn't see him get hit. The vet said it was something big, a pickup maybe. Or a Winnebago."

And I knew who had hit the jackal. It had all been right there in front of me—the old man using up their forty-gallon water supply to wash the bumper, the lies about their coming in from Globe—only I had been too intent on keeping them from finding out about Katie, on getting the picture of Aberfan, to see it. It was like the damned parvo. When you had it licked in one place, it broke out somewhere else.

"Were there any identifying tire tracks?" Hunter said.

"What?" I said. "No. It was snowing that day." It had to show in my face, and he hadn't missed anything yet. I passed my hand over my eyes. "I'm sorry. These questions are bringing it all back."

"Sorry," Hunter said.

"Can't we get this stuff from the police report?" Segura asked.

"There wasn't a police report," I said. "It wasn't a crime to kill a dog when Aberfan died."

It was the right thing to say. The look of shock on their faces was the real thing this time, and they looked at each other in disbelief instead of at me. They asked a few more questions and then stood up to leave. I walked them to the door.

"Thank you for your cooperation, Mr. McCombe," Hunter said. "We appreciate what a difficult experience this has been for you."

I shut the screen door between us. The Amblers would have been going too fast, trying to beat the cameras because they weren't even supposed to be on Van Buren. It was almost rush hour, and they were in the tanker lane, and they hadn't even seen the jackal till they hit it, and then it was too late. They had to know the penalty for hitting an animal was jail and confiscation of the vehicle, and there wasn't anybody else on the road.

"Oh, one more question," Hunter said from halfway down the walk. "You said you went to your first assignment this morning. What was it?"

Candid. Open. "It was out at the old zoo. A sideshow kind of thing."

—| ••• |—

I watched them all the way out to their car and down the street. Then I latched the screen, pulled the inside door shut, and locked it, too. It had been right there in front of me—the ferret sniffing the wheel, the bumper, Jake anxiously watching the road. I had thought he was looking for customers, but he wasn't. He was expecting to see the Society drive up. "He's not interested in that," he had said when Mrs. Ambler said she had been telling me about Taco. He had listened to our whole conversation, standing under the back window with his guilty bucket, ready to come back in and cut her off if she said too much, and I hadn't tumbled to any of it. I had been so intent on Aberfan I hadn't even seen it when I looked right through the lens at it. And what kind of an excuse was that? Katie hadn't even tried to use it, and she was learning to drive.

I went and got the Nikon and pulled the film out of it. It was too late to do anything about the eisenstadt pictures or the vidcam footage, but I didn't think there was anything in them. Jake had already washed the bumper by the time I'd taken those pictures.

I fed the longshot film into the developer. "Positives, one two three order, fifteen seconds," I said, and waited for the image to come on the screen.

I wondered who had been driving. Jake, probably. "He never liked Taco," she had said, and there was no mistaking the bitterness in her voice. "I didn't want to buy the Winnebago."

They would both lose their licenses, no matter who was driving, and the Society would confiscate the Winnebago. They would probably not send two octogenarian specimens of Americana like the Amblers to prison. They wouldn't have to. The trial would take six months, and Texas already had legislation in committee.

The first picture came up. A light-setting shot of an ocotillo.

Even if they got off, even if they didn't end up taking away the Winnebago for unauthorized use of a tanker lane or failure to purchase a sales-tax permit, the Amblers had six months left at the outside. Utah was all ready to pass a full-divided bill, and Arizona would be next. In spite of the road crews' stew-slowed pace, Phoenix would be all-divided by the time the investigation was over, and they'd be completely boxed in. Permanent residents of the zoo. Like the coyote.

A shot of the zoo sign, half-hidden in the cactus. A close-up of the Amblers' balloon-trailing sign. The Winnebago in the parking lot.

"Hold," I said. "Crop." I indicated the areas with my finger. "Enlarge to full screen."

The longshot takes great pictures, sharp contrast, excellent detail. The developer only had a five-hundred-thousand-pixel screen, but the dark smear on the bumper was easy to see, and the developed picture would be much clearer. You'd be able to see every splatter, every grayish-yellow hair. The Society's computers would probably be able to type the blood from it.

"Continue," I said, and the next picture came on the screen. Artsy shot of the Winnebago and the zoo entrance. Jake washing the bumper. Red-handed.

Maybe Hunter had bought my story, but he didn't have any other suspects, and how long would it be before he decided to ask Katie a few more questions? If he thought it was the Amblers, he'd leave her alone.

The Japanese family clustered around the waste-disposal tank. Close-up of the decals on the side. Interiors—Mrs. Ambler in the galley, the up-right-coffin shower stall, Mrs. Ambler making coffee.

No wonder she had looked that way in the eisenstadt shot, her face full of memory and grief and loss. Maybe in the instant before they hit it, it had looked like a dog to her, too.

All I had to do was tell Hunter about the Amblers, and Katie was off the hook. It should be easy. I had done it before.

"Stop," I said to a shot of the salt-and-pepper collection. The black-and-white Scottie dogs had painted red-plaid bows and red tongues. "Expose," I said. "One through twenty-four."

The screen went to question marks and started beeping. I should have known better. The developer could handle a lot of orders, but asking it to expose perfectly good film went against its whole memory, and I didn't have time to give it the step-by-steps that would convince it I meant what I said.

"Eject," I said. The Scotties blinked out. The developer spat out the film, rerolled into its protective case.

The doorbell rang. I switched on the overhead and pulled the film out to full length and held it directly under the light. I had told Hunter an RV hit Aberfan, and he had said on the way out, almost an afterthought, "That first shoot you went to, what was it?" And after he left, what had he done, gone out to check on the sideshow kind of thing, gotten Mrs. Ambler to spill her guts? There hadn't been time to do that and get back. He must have called Ramirez. I was glad I had locked the door.

I turned off the overhead. I rerolled the film, fed it back into the developer, and gave it a direction it could handle. "Permanganate bath, full strength, one through twenty-four. Remove one hundred percent emulsion. No notify."

The screen went dark. It would take the developer at least fifteen minutes to run the film through the bleach bath, and the Society's computers could probably enhance a picture out of two crystals of silver and thin air, but at least the detail wouldn't be there. I unlocked the door.

It was Katie.

She held up the eisenstadt. "You forgot your briefcase," she said.

I stared blankly at it. I hadn't even realized I didn't have it. I must have left it on the kitchen table when I went tearing out, running down little girls and stewed roadworkers in my rush to keep Katie from getting involved. And here she was, and Hunter would be back any minute, saying, "That shoot you went on this morning, did you take any pictures?"

"It isn't a briefcase," I said.

"I wanted to tell you," she said, and stopped. "I shouldn't have accused you of telling the Society I'd killed the jackal. I don't know why you came to see me today, but I know you're not capable of—"

"You have no idea what I'm capable of," I said. I opened the door enough to reach for the eisenstadt. "Thanks for bringing it back. I'll get the paper to reimburse your way-mile credits."

Go home. Go home. If you're here when the Society comes back, they'll ask you how you met me, and I just destroyed the evidence that could shift the blame to the Amblers. I took hold of the eisenstadt's handle and started to shut the door.

She put her hand on the door. The screen door and the fading light made her look unfocused, like Misha. "Are you in trouble?"

"No," I said. "Look, I'm very busy."

"Why did you come to see me?" she asked. "Did you kill the jackal?"

"No," I said, but I opened the door and let her in.

I went over to the developer and asked for a visual status. It was only on the sixth frame. "I'm destroying evidence," I said to Katie. "I took a picture this morning of the vehicle that hit it, only I didn't know it was the guilty party until a half an hour ago." I motioned for her to sit down on the couch. "They're in their eighties. They were driving on a road they weren't supposed to be on, in an obsolete recreation vehicle, worrying about the cameras and the tankers. There's no way they could have seen it in time to stop. The Society won't see it that way, though. They're determined to blame somebody, anybody, even though it won't bring them back."

She set her canvas carryit and the eisenstadt down on the table next to the couch.

"The Society was here when I got home," I said. "They'd figured out we were both in Colorado when Aberfan died. I told them it was a hit and run, and you'd stopped to help me. They had the vet's records, and your name was on them."

I couldn't read her face. "If they come back, you tell them that you gave me a ride to the vet's." I went back to the developer. The longshot film was done. "Eject," I said, and the developer spit it into my hand. I fed it into the recycler.

"McCombe! Where the hell are you?" Ramirez's voice exploded into the room, and I jumped and started for the door, but she wasn't there. The phone was flashing. "McCombe! This is important!"

Ramirez was on the phone and using some override I didn't even know existed. I went over and pushed it back to access. The lights went out. "I'm here," I said.

"You won't believe what just happened!" She sounded outraged. "A couple of terrorist types from the Society just stormed in here and confiscated the stuff you sent me!"

All I'd sent her was the vidcam footage and the shots from the eisenstadt, and there shouldn't have been anything on those. Jake had already washed the bumper. "What stuff?" I said.

"The prints from the eisenstadt!" she said, still shouting. "Which I didn't have a chance to look at when they came in because I was too busy trying to work a trade on your governor's conference, not to mention trying to track you down! I had hardcopies made and sent the originals straight down to composing with your vidcam footage. I finally got to them half an hour ago, and while I'm sorting through them, this Society creep just grabs them away from me. No warrants, no 'would you mind?'—nothing. Right out of my hand. Like a bunch of—"

"Jackals," I said. "You're sure it wasn't the vidcam footage?" There wasn't anything in the eisenstadt shots except Mrs. Ambler and Taco, and even Hunter couldn't have put that together, could he?

"Of course I'm sure," Ramirez said, her voice bouncing off the walls. "It was one of the prints from the eisenstadt. I never even saw the vidcam stuff. I sent it straight to composing. I told you."

I went over to the developer and fed the cartridge in. The first dozen shots were nothing, stuff the eisenstadt had taken from the backseat of the car. "Start with frame ten," I said. "Positives. One two three order. Five seconds."

"What did you say?" Ramirez demanded.

"I said, did they say what they were looking for?"

"Are you kidding? I wasn't even there as far as they were concerned. They split up the pile and started through them on my desk."

The yucca at the foot of the hill. More yucca. My forearm as I set the eisenstadt down on the counter. My back.

"Whatever it was they were looking for, they found it," Ramirez said.

I glanced at Katie. She met my gaze steadily, unafraid. She had never been afraid, not even when I told her she had killed all the dogs, not even when I showed up on her doorstep after fifteen years.

"The one in the uniform showed it to the other one," Ramirez was saying, "and said, 'You were wrong about the woman doing it. Look at this.'"

"Did you get a look at the picture?"

Still life of cups and spoons. Mrs. Ambler's arm. Mrs. Ambler's back.

"I tried. It was a truck of some kind."

"A truck? Are you sure? Not a Winnebago?"

"A truck. What the hell is going on over there?"

I didn't answer. Jake's back. Open shower door. Still life with Sanka. Mrs. Ambler remembering Taco.

"What woman are they talking about?" Ramirez said. "The one you wanted the lifeline on?"

"No," I said. The picture of Mrs. Ambler was the last one on the cartridge. The developer went back to the beginning. Bottom half of the Hitori. Open car door. Prickly pear. "Did they say anything else?"

"The one in uniform pointed to something on the hardcopy and said, 'See. There's his number on the side. Can you make it out?'"

Blurred palm trees and the expressway. The tanker hitting the jackal.

"Stop," I said. The image froze.

"What?" Ramirez said.

It was a great action shot, the back wheels passing right over the mess that been the jackal's hind legs. The jackal was already dead, of course, but you couldn't see that or the already drying blood coming out of its mouth because of the angle. You couldn't see the truck's license number either because of the speed the tanker was going, but the number was there, waiting for the Society's computers. It looked like the tanker had just hit it.

"What did they do with the picture?" I asked.

"They took it into the chief's office. I tried to call up the originals from composing, but the chief had already sent for them *and* your vidcam footage. Then I tried to get you, but I couldn't get past your damned exclusion."

"Are they still in there with the chief?"

"They just left. They're on their way over to your house. The chief told me to tell you he wants 'full cooperation,' which means hand over the negatives and any other film you just took this morning. He told *me* to keep my hands off. No story. Case closed."

"How long ago did they leave?"

"Five minutes. You've got plenty of time to make me a print. Don't highwire it. I'll come pick it up."

"What happened to, 'The last thing I need is trouble with the Society'?"

"It'll take them at least twenty minutes to get to your place. Hide it somewhere the Society won't find it."

"I can't," I said, and listened to her furious silence. "My developer's broken. It just ate my longshot film," I said, and hit the exclusion button again.

"You want to see who hit the jackal?" I said to Katie, and motioned her over to the developer. "One of Phoenix's finest."

She came and stood in front of the screen, looking at the picture. If the Society's computers were really good, they could probably prove the jackal was already dead, but the Society wouldn't keep the film long enough for that. Hunter and Segura had probably already destroyed the highwire copies. Maybe I should offer to run the cartridge sheet through the permanganate bath for them when they got here, just to save time.

I looked at Katie. "It looks guilty as hell, doesn't it?" I said. "Only it isn't." She didn't say anything, didn't move. "It would have killed the jackal if it had hit it. It was going at least ninety. But the jackal was already dead."

She looked across at me.

"The Society would have sent the Amblers to jail. It would have confiscated the house they've lived in for fifteen years for an accident that was nobody's fault. They didn't even see it coming. It just ran right out in front of them."

Katie put her hand up to the screen and touched the jackal's image.

"They've suffered enough," I said, looking at her. It was getting dark. I hadn't turned on any lights, and the red image of the tanker made her nose look sunburned.

"All these years she's blamed him for her dog's death, and he didn't do it," I said. "A Winnebago's a hundred square feet on the inside. That's about as big as this developer, and they've lived inside it for fifteen years, while the lanes got narrower and the highways shut down, hardly enough room to breathe, let alone live, and her blaming him for something he didn't do."

In the ruddy light from the screen she looked sixteen.

"They won't do anything to the driver, not with the tankers hauling thousands of gallons of water into Phoenix every day. Even the Society won't run the risk of a boycott. They'll destroy the negatives and call the case closed. And the Society won't go after the Amblers," I said. "Or you."

I turned back to the developer. "Go," I said, and the image changed. Yucca. Yucca. My forearm. My back. Cups and spoons.

"Besides," I said. "I'm an old hand at shifting the blame." Mrs. Ambler's arm. Mrs. Ambler's back. Open shower door. "Did I ever tell you about Aberfan?"

Katie was still watching the screen, her face pale now from the light-blue 200 percent Formica shower stall.

"The Society already thinks the tanker did it. The only one I've got to convince is my editor." I reached across to the phone and took the exclusion off. "Ramirez," I said, "wanta go after the Society?"

Jake's back. Cups, spoons, and Sanka.

"I did," Ramirez said in a voice that could have frozen the Salt River, "but your developer was broken, and you couldn't get me a picture."

Mrs. Ambler and Taco.

I hit the exclusion button again and left my hand on it. "Stop," I said. "Print." The screen went dark, and the print slid out into the tray. "Reduce frame. Permanganate bath by one percent. Follow on screen." I took my hand off. "What's Dolores Chiwere doing these days, Ramirez?"

"She's working investigative. Why?"

I didn't answer. The picture of Mrs. Ambler faded a little, a little more.

"The Society *does* have a link to the lifelines!" Ramirez said, not quite as fast as Hunter, but almost. "That's why you requested your old girlfriend's line, isn't it? You're running a sting."

I had been wondering how to get Ramirez off Katie's trail, and she had done it herself, jumping to conclusions just like the Society. With a little effort, I could convince Katie, too: Do you know why I really came to see you today? To catch the Society. I had to pick somebody the Society couldn't possibly know about from my lifeline, somebody I didn't have any known connection with.

Katie watched the screen, looking like she already half believed it. The picture of Mrs. Ambler faded some more. Any known connection.

"Stop," I said.

"What about the truck?" Ramirez demanded. "What does it have to do with this sting of yours?"

"Nothing," I said. "And neither does the water board, which is an even bigger bully than the Society. So do what the chief says. Full cooperation. Case closed. We'll get them on lifeline tapping."

She digested that, or maybe she'd already hung up and was calling Dolores Chiwere. I looked at the image of Mrs. Ambler on the screen. It had faded enough to look slightly overexposed but not enough to look tampered with. And Taco was gone.

I looked at Katie. "The Society will be here in another fifteen minutes," I said, "which gives me just enough time to tell you about Aberfan." I gestured at the couch. "Sit down."

She came and sat down. "He was a great dog," I said. "He loved the snow. He'd dig through it and toss it up with his muzzle and snap at the snowflakes, trying to catch them."

Ramirez had obviously hung up, but she would call back if she couldn't track down Chiwere. I put the exclusion back on and went over to the developer. The image of Mrs. Ambler was still on the screen. The bath hadn't affected the detail that much. You could still see the wrinkles, the thin white hair, but the guilt, or blame, the look of loss and love, was gone. She looked serene, almost happy.

"There are hardly any good pictures of dogs," I said. "They lack the necessary muscles to take good pictures, and Aberfan lunged at you as soon as he saw the camera."

I turned the developer off. Without the light from the screen, it was almost dark in the room. I turned on the overhead.

"There were less than a hundred dogs left in the United States, and he'd already had the newparvo once and nearly died. The only pictures I had of him had been taken when he was asleep. I wanted a picture of Aberfan playing in the snow."

I leaned against the narrow shelf in front of the developer's screen. Katie looked the way she had at the vet's, sitting there with her hands clenched, waiting for me to tell her something terrible.

"I wanted a picture of him playing in the snow, but he always lunged at the camera," I said, "so I let him out in the front yard, and then I sneaked out the side door and went across the road to some pine trees where he wouldn't be able to see me. But he did."

"And he ran across the road," Katie said. "And I hit him."

She was looking down at her hands. I waited for her to look up, dreading what I would see in her face. Or not see.

"It took me a long time to find out where you'd gone," she said to her hands. "I was afraid you'd refuse me access to your lifeline. I finally saw one of your pictures in a newspaper, and I moved to Phoenix, but after I got here, I was afraid to call you for fear you'd hang up on me."

She twisted her hands the way she had twisted her mittens at the vet's. "My husband said I was obsessed with it, that I should have gotten over it by now, everybody else had, that they were only dogs anyway." She looked up, and I braced my hands against the developer. "He said forgiveness wasn't something somebody else could give you, but I didn't want you to forgive me exactly. I just wanted to tell you I was sorry."

There hadn't been any reproach, any accusation in her face when I told her she was responsible for the extinction of a species that day at the vet's, and there wasn't now. Maybe she didn't have the facial muscles for it, I thought bitterly.

"Do you know why I came to see you today?" I said angrily. "My camera broke when I tried to catch Aberfan. I didn't get any pictures." I grabbed the picture of Mrs. Ambler out of the developer's tray and flung it at her. "Her dog died of newparvo. They left it in the Winnebago, and when they came back, it was dead."

"Poor thing," she said, but she wasn't looking at the picture. She was looking at me.

"She didn't know she was having her picture taken. I thought if I got you talking about Aberfan, I could get a picture like that of you."

And surely now I would see it, the look I had really wanted when I set the eisenstadt down on Katie's kitchen table, the look I still wanted, even though the eisenstadt was facing the wrong way, the look of betrayal the dogs had never given us. Not even Misha. Not even Aberfan. How does it feel to be responsible for the extinction of an entire species?

I pointed at the eisenstadt. "It's not a briefcase. It's a camera. I was going to take your picture without your even knowing it."

She had never known Aberfan. She had never known Mrs. Ambler either, but in that instant before she started to cry, she looked like both of them. She put her hand up to her mouth. "Oh," she said, and the love, the loss was there in her voice, too. "If you'd had it then, it wouldn't have happened."

I looked at the eisenstadt. If I had had it, I could have set it on the porch and Aberfan would never have even noticed it. He would have burrowed through the snow and tossed it up with his nose, and I could have thrown snow up in big glittering sprays that he would have leapt at, and it never would have happened. Katie Powell would have driven past, and I would have stopped to wave at her, and she, sixteen years old and just learning to drive, would maybe even have risked taking a mittened hand off the steering wheel to wave back, and Aberfan would have wagged his tail into a blizzard and then barked at the snow he'd churned up.

He wouldn't have caught the third wave. He would have lived to be an old dog, fourteen or fifteen, too old to play in the snow anymore, and even if he had been the last dog in the world, I would not have let them lock him up in a cage, I would not have let them take him away. If I had had the eisenstadt.

No wonder I hated it.

It had been at least fifteen minutes since Ramirez called. The Society would be here any minute. "You shouldn't be here when the Society comes," I said, and Katie nodded and smudged the tears off her cheeks and stood up, reaching for her carryit.

"Do you ever take pictures?" she said, shouldering the carryit. "I mean, besides for the papers?"

"I don't know if I'll be taking pictures for them much longer. Photo-journalists are becoming an extinct breed."

"Maybe you could come take some pictures of Jana and Kevin. Kids grow up so fast, they're gone before you know it."

"I'd like that," I said. I opened the screen door for her and looked both ways down the street at the darkness. "All clear," I said, and she went out. I shut the screen door between us.

She turned and looked at me one last time with her dear, open face that even I hadn't been able to close. "I miss them," she said.

I put my hand up to the screen. "I miss them, too."

I watched her to make sure she turned the corner and then went back in the living room and took down the picture of Misha. I propped it against the developer so Segura would be able to see it from the door. In a month or so, when the Amblers were safely in Texas and the Society had forgotten about Katie, I'd call Segura and tell him I might be willing to sell it to the Society, and then in a day or so I'd tell him I'd changed my mind. When he came out to try to talk me into it, I'd tell him about Perdita and Beatrix Potter, and he would tell me about the Society.

Chiwere and Ramirez would have to take the credit for the story—I didn't want Hunter putting anything else together—and it would take more than one story to break them, but it was a start.

569

Katie had left the print of Mrs. Ambler on the couch. I picked it up and looked at it a minute and then fed it into the developer. "Recycle," I said.

I picked up the eisenstadt from the table by the couch and took the film cartridge out. I started to pull the film out to expose it, and then shoved it into the developer instead and turned it on. "Positives, one two three order, five seconds."

I had apparently set the camera on its activator again—there were ten shots or so of the back seat of the Hitori. Vehicles and people. The pictures of Katie were all in shadow. There was a Still Life of Kool-Aid Pitcher with Whale Glass and another one of Jana's toy cars, and some near-black frames that meant Katie had laid the eisenstadt facedown when she brought it to me.

"Two seconds," I said, and waited for the developer to flash the last shots so I could make sure there wasn't anything else on the cartridge and then expose it before the Society got here. All but the last frame was of the darkness that was all the eisenstadt could see lying on its face. The last one was of me.

The trick in getting good pictures is to make people forget they're being photographed. Distract them. Get them talking about something they care about.

"Stop," I said, and the image froze.

Aberfan was a great dog. He loved to play in the snow, and after I had murdered him, he lifted his head off my lap and tried to lick my hand.

The Society would be here any minute to take the longshot film and destroy it, and this one would have to go, too, along with the rest of the cartridge. I couldn't risk Hunter's being reminded of Katie. Or Segura taking a notion to do a print-fix and peel on Jana's toy cars.

It was too bad. The eisenstadt takes great pictures. "Even you'll forget it's a camera," Ramirez had said in her spiel, and that was certainly true. I was looking straight into the lens.

And it was all there, Misha and Taco and Perdita and the look he gave me on the way to the vet's while I stroked his poor head and told him it would be all right, that look of love and pity I had been trying to capture all these years. The picture of Aberfan.

The Society would be here any minute. "Eject," I said, and cracked the cartridge open, and exposed it to the light.

# And Afterwards

# Service for the Burial of the Dead

I should not have come, Anne thought, clenching her gloved hands in her lap. She had come early so that she could sit well to the back, but not so early that people would talk. She had hesitated at the back of the church for only a moment, to take a deep breath and put her head up proudly, and in that moment old Mr. Finn had swooped down on her, taken her arm, and led her to the empty pew behind the one tied off with black ribbon for the mourning family.

I should not have come alone, she thought. I should have made my father come. Even as she thought it she saw her father's red and angry face as she tied on her black bonnet.

"You are going to the funeral, then?" he had said.

"Yes, Father." She had buttoned her gray pelisse over her gray silk, tied her chip bonnet under her chin.

"And not even wear black?"

She had calmly put on her gloves. "My black cloak is ruined," she had said, thinking of his face that night when she came in, the black wool cloak soaked with frozen rain, the hem of her black merino heavy with mud. He had thought she'd killed Elliott even then, before the news that he was missing, before they had started dragging the river. He still believed it and would have shown it in his red, guilty face when he walked her down the aisle at the funeral. But he would at least have walked her to a safe corner, protecting her from the talk of the townspeople, if not from their thoughts. Perhaps they thought she had murdered Elliott, too, or perhaps they only thought she had no pride, and that at least was true.

She had lost what little pride she had that night, waiting on the island for Elliott. She had not even thought what it would mean when she agreed to meet him. She had thought only of wearing her warmest clothes against the November rain, the black merino, the black wool cloak, her sturdy boots. Only after she had stood in the rain for hours under the oak tree, its bare branches no protection from the wind or the approaching dark, had she thought what a terrible thing she was doing. When he comes, I must say no, she thought, the winter rain dripping off her ruined bonnet.

He had no intention of throwing Victoria over as he had thrown her over. Victoria was small and fair and had a wealthy father. The marriage was set for Christmas. Victoria's brother, now at sea, had been sent for to be best man at the wedding. Elliott had not even been kind enough to tell her of his engagement. Her father had told her. "No," she had said, and thought as she said it that it must be true because she had never, in all the time she had loved Elliott, been able to say no to him.

Was that why she had agreed to meet him on the island? Because she still could not say "no," even when it meant her downfall? It did not matter. He had not come. She had waited nearly all night, and when she crept home, chilled to the bone, she knew she would not have been able to say no if he had. She could summon no anger at him, and when they found his boat, no grief. She did not feel anything and that had helped her to walk with old Mr. Finn to the front of the church, her eyes dry, no guilty color in her cheeks.

But I cannot, cannot sit here and face Victoria, she thought. I cannot do that to her. She has never done anything to me.

It was already too late for her to walk back down the aisle. There was a side door quite close to her that the minister entered by. It led down a hall to the choir's robing room and the vestry. There was a door just outside the vestry that led to the sideyard of the church. If she hurried, she could escape that way before Reverend Sprague brought the family in.

Escape. Was that how it would look? The murderess overcome by guilt? The discarded sweetheart overcome by remorse or grief or shame? It doesn't matter what they think, Anne thought. I cannot do this to Victoria.

She put her gloved hand on the back of the pew in front of her. Behind her a man coughed, trying to muffle the sound with his hand. Anne pulled her handkerchief from her muff and put it to her mouth. She coughed twice, paused, coughed again, and stood up and walked quickly to the side door.

She shut the door behind her and hurried along the drafty hall, shivering in the thin silk and the light pelisse.

"Let us pray," Reverend Sprague said, and she found herself almost upon the family. They stood in a dejected little knot, their heads bowed, Victoria and her father and Elliott's father. The face of Elliott's father was gray, and he leaned heavily on his cane, his eyes open and staring blindly at the wall.

Ann backed hastily down the hall to the robing room. The door was locked, but there was a large key in the keyhole. She turned it, rattling it loudly in her haste. "Amen," she could hear Reverend Sprague say, and she pulled the key free, opened the door and slipped inside, pulling the door to behind her. It was very dark. Anne felt along the wall for a lamp sconce. Her foot brushed against something, and she bent down. It was a candle in a metal holder. Two phosphorus matches lay in the candle-holder, and she struck one, lit the candle, and still kneeling, looked at the room.

It looked as if it had not been used in years. Reverend Sprague did not approve of robes and other "papist trappings" except at Christmas. The black robes hanging on their pegs were heavy with dust. Two black-varnished pews stood against one wall, and several wooden chairs. Anne stood up, holding the candle. She shook the dust from the hem of her dress and went to the door. The organ had begun.

She blew out the candle and set it on one of the dusty pews, still listening. The organ stopped, and then started again, and she could hear the low rumble of the congregation singing. She felt her way to the door and opened it a little to make certain no one was in the hall. Then she let herself out and replaced the key in the lock. The organ ground into the amen. She nearly ran down the hall.

Anne was almost at the door before she saw the man. He had just come in and had turned to close the door gently behind him. Anne did not recognize him. He had reddish-brown hair under a soft, dark cap and was wearing a short dark coat and heavy boots. Victoria's brother, Anne thought, and waited for him to turn.

He seemed to be having some trouble with the door. He could not seem to shut it, and when he straightened, Anne could see a thin line of light where the door was still open. The man turned around.

"Elliott," Anne said.

He smiled disarmingly. "You look as though you'd seen a ghost," he said. "Did I frighten you?" he said, as though he were amused at the idea. The organ began again.

"Elliott," she said. He didn't seem to hear her. He was looking toward the sanctuary. Under the dark open coat he was wearing a white silk shirt and a black damask vest. Anne thought of her own ruined cloak. He had not come to meet her after all. He had left her standing on the island in the rain all night long. He had left them all thinking he was dead. "Where have you been?" she whispered.

"Away," he said lightly. "When you didn't come to meet me I decided to go up to Hartford. What's going on in there? A funeral?"

"Your funeral," she said. She could not get her voice above a whisper. "We thought you were drowned. They dragged the river."

"I have always liked funerals," Elliott said as if he had not heard her. "The weeping fiancée, the distraught father, the minister extolling the deceased's virtues. Are there flowers?"

"Flowers?" Anne said blankly. "They found the boat, Elliott. It was all broken apart."

"Of course there are flowers. Hothouse lilies. Victoria's father will have sent all the way to New York for them. Well, he can afford it. Tell me, are little Vicky's pretty gray eyes red from weeping?"

Anne did not answer him. He turned suddenly away from her. "As you won't tell me anything, I shall have to go see for myself." He started down the hall, his boots making a terrible noise on the wooden floor.

"You mustn't go in there, Elliott," Anne said. She started to put her hand on Elliott's arm, but she drew it back.

Elliott wheeled to face her. "First you won't meet me on the island, and now you keep me from my own funeral. Yet you never said no to me when we met on the island, our island, last summer, did you, sweet Anne?"

"I did meet you…" she stammered. "I waited all night—I—Elliott, your father collapsed when he heard the news. His heart—"

"—might stop at the sight of me. I should like to see that. You see, sweet Anne, you give me even more reason to attend my funeral. Unless you are trying to keep me to yourself. Is that it, Anne? Are you sorry now you didn't meet me on the island?"

She stood there, thinking miserably, I cannot stop him. I have not ever been able to stop him from doing anything he wanted.

He had turned again and was nearly to the door of the sanctuary. "Wait," Anne said. She hurried to him, brushing past the door of the robing room as she did. The key clattered out of the lock, and the door swung open.

Elliott stopped and looked at the key on the floor between them. "You would lock me in a hideaway and keep me all to yourself, is that it?"

"You mustn't go in there, Elliott," she repeated stolidly, thinking of his father leaning on his cane, of Victoria's bent head, of Elliott's easy smile when he went into the sanctuary to greet them. "You look as if you'd seen a ghost," he would say lightly, and watch the color leave his father's face.

"I won't let you," she said.

"How are you going to stop me?" he said. "Did you plan to lock me in the robing room and come to me at night, as you came to the island last summer? If you long for me so much, how can I resist you? Very well, sweet Anne, lock me in." He stepped inside the door and stood there smiling easily. "It is sad that I must miss my own funeral, but I do it to please you, Anne."

The organ had stopped again, and in the sudden silence Anne knelt and picked up the key.

"Elliott," she said uncertainly.

He folded his arms across his chest. "You want me all to yourself. Then you shall have me. No one, not even Vicky, will know that I am here. It will be our secret, sweet Anne. I will be your prisoner, and you will come to me." He gestured toward the door. "Lock me in, Anne. The funeral is nearly over."

Anne looked at the heavy key in her hand. There was a sudden burst of music and singing from the sanctuary. Anne looked uneasily toward the sanctuary door. In a moment Reverend Sprague would open that door.

"You will come, won't you, Anne?" Elliott said. He was leaning against the wall. "You won't forget?"

"There's a candle on the pew," Anne said, and shut the door in his face. She turned the key in the lock, and then, not knowing what else to do, thrust the key into her muff, and ran for the sideyard door.

⊣•••⊢

She was too late. People were already spilling out the double doors onto the dead brown grass of the sideyard. The biting wind caught the door and slammed it shut. Everyone stopped and looked up at Anne.

Anne walked through them as if they were not even there, unmindful of how she held her head, of how she looked in the gray pelisse and the guilty chip bonnet. She did not even hear the light footsteps behind her until a soft voice called to her.

"Anne? Miss Lawrence? Please wait."

She turned. It was Victoria Thatcher, her pretty gray eyes red with weeping. She was clutching a little black prayer book. "I wanted to tell you how grateful I am you came," she said.

Anne was suddenly furious with her tearstained face, her gentle words. He doesn't love you, she almost said. He wanted to meet me at night on the island, and I went. He's in the robing room now, waiting for me. He isn't dead, but I wish he were and so should you.

"Your kindness means a great deal to me," Victoria said haltingly. "I—my father has just now gone to Hartford to attend to some business of Elliott's, and I have no friends here. Elliott's father has been kindness itself, but he is not well, and I—you were very kind to come. Please say you will be kind again and come to tea someday."

"I..."

Victoria bit her lip and ducked her head, then looked straight up at Anne. "I know what they are saying about Elliott's death. I want you to know that I don't believe them. I know you didn't..." She stopped and ducked her head again. "I know you pray for his soul, as I do."

He doesn't have a soul, Anne thought. You should pray for his father and for yourself. And what is it that you don't believe? That I murdered him? Or that I met him on the island?

Victoria looked up at Anne again, her gray eyes filled with tears. "Please, if you loved Elliott, too, then that is all the more reason to be friends now that he is gone."

But he isn't gone, Anne thought desperately. He is sitting in the robing room laughing to think of us standing here. He is not dead, but I wish that he were. For your sake. For all our sakes.

"Thank you for inviting me to tea," Anne said, and walked rapidly away.

—| • • • |—

Anne went to the church after supper, taking ham and cake wrapped in brown paper. Elliott was sitting in the dark. "I had to wait until my father had his supper," Anne said, lighting the candle. "I had to sneak out of the house."

Elliott grinned. "It's not the first time, is it?"

She put the parcel down on the pew next to the candle. "You cannot stay here," she said.

He opened up the package. "I rather like it here. It is dry at least, too cold, but otherwise very comfortable. I have good food and you to do my bidding. There will be few enough tears of joy at my resurrection. Why shouldn't I stay here?"

"Your father has taken to his bed."

"From joy? Has the bereaved fiancée taken to her bed, too? She never would take to mine."

"Victoria is caring for your father. Her own father has gone to Hartford to settle your affairs. You can't let them persist in thinking you are dead."

"Ah, but I can. And must. At least until Victoria's father pays my debts. And until you pay for not meeting me at the island."

"It is wrong to do this, Elliott," she said. "I shall tell."

"I do not think so," he said. "For I should have to say then that I had never gone on the river at all, but only hidden away with you. And then what will happen to my poor stayabed father and my rich Victoria? You will not tell."

"I will not come again," she said. "I will not bring you your supper."

"And leave the minister to find my bones? Oh, you will come again, sweet Anne."

"No," Anne said. "I won't." She did not lock the door, in the hope that he would change his mind, but she took the key. In case, she thought, without even knowing the meaning of her own words. In case I need it.

Anne's father answered the door before she could get halfway down the stairs. She saw the sudden stiffening of his back, the sudden grayness of his ears and neck, and she thought, It is Elliott.

She had gone to the church every night for three days, taking him food and candles and once a comforter because he complained of the cold, taking the same useless arguments. Victoria's father came home, spent a morning at the bank, and left again. Victoria went past every morning on her way to visit Elliott's father, looking smaller and more pale every day. There was still no word from her brother. On the third day she wrote asking Anne to tea.

Anne had shown the note to Elliott. "How can you do this to her?" she said.

"To you, you mean. You accepted, of course. It should be rather a lark."

"I refused. You must think about what you are putting her through, Elliott."

"And what about what I've been through? In an open boat in the middle of the night in the middle of a storm. I don't even remember getting ashore. I had to walk halfway to Haddam before I was able to borrow a horse at an inn. Think what you've put me through, Anne, all because you didn't choose to meet me. Now I don't choose to meet them." He fumbled with the comforter, trying to cover his knees.

Anne had felt too tired to fight him anymore. She had put the packet of food down on the pew and turned away.

"Leave the door open," Elliott had said. "I don't like being shut in this coffin of a room. And tell me when Victoria's father comes home again with all my debts honored."

He will never come out, Anne had thought despairingly, but now, standing on the landing watching her father, she thought, He has come out after all, and hurried down the steps. When she reached the foot of the stairs, her father turned to her and said accusingly, "It is Miss Thatcher. She has come to call." He walked past her up the stairs without another word.

"It was improper of me to come," Victoria said. "Now your father is angry with me."

"He is angry with me. You have done nothing improper, unless showing kindness is improper." They were still standing in the wind at the door. "Won't you come in?" Anne said. "I'll make some tea."

Victoria put her hand on Anne's arm. "I did not come to call. I—now I must ask a kindness of you." She had not worn gloves, and her hand was icy even through the wool of Anne's sleeve.

"Come in and tell me," she said, and once more she thought, It's Elliott. Victoria stepped into the hall, but she would not let Anne take her black cloak or bonnet, and when Anne went to shut the door, she said, "I cannot stay. I must go to Dr. Sawyers. He—a body has been found in the river. Near Haddam. I must go to see if it is Elliott."

A tremendous wave of anger swept over Anne at Elliott. She almost said, "He is not dead. He's in the robing room," but Victoria, once she had started, could not seem to stop. "My father has gone to Hartford," she said. "There was some trouble about gambling debts of Elliott's. My brother is still at sea. We have had no news of his ship. Elliott's father is too ill to go. My father went in his place to Hartford, and now there is no one to see to this. I cannot ask Elliott's father. It would kill him to see—I came to ask your father, but now I fear I have angered him and there is no one else to—"

"I will go with you," Anne said, throwing on her gray pelisse. It was far too light for the cold day, but she was afraid to take the time to go back upstairs for something heavier for fear Victoria would be too distraught to wait. I cannot let Elliott do this, she thought. I will tell her what he has done.

But there was no chance. Victoria walked so fast that Anne nearly ran to keep up with her, and the words flowed out of her in great painful spurts, as if an artery had been cut somewhere. "My brother should be here by now. There's been no word from New London, where they are to dock. He cannot have been delayed in port. But the storms have been so fierce I fear for his ship. I wrote him on the day that Elliott was first missed. I knew that he was dead, that first day. My father said not to worry, that he was only delayed, that we must not give up hope, and now my brother Roger is delayed, and there is no one to tell me not to worry."

They were on Dr. Sawyer's doorstep. Victoria knocked, her bare hands red from the cold, and the doctor let them in immediately. He did not take their wraps. "It will be cold," he said, and led them swiftly down the hall past his office to the back of his house. "I am so sorry your father is not here. It is no work for young ladies." If they would only stop, she would tell them, but they did not stop, even for a moment. Anne hurried after them.

The doctor opened the door into a large square room. It made Anne think of a kitchen because of the long table. There was a sheet over the table, dragging almost to the floor. Victoria was very pale. "I do not like this at all, Victoria," Dr. Sawyer said, speaking more and more rapidly. "If your father were here—It is a nasty business."

Anne thought, As soon as she sees it isn't Elliott, I will tell them. Dr. Sawyer pulled the sheet back from the body.

It was as if the time, so hurried along by them, had stopped stock-still. The man had been dead several days. Since the storm, Anne thought. He was drowned in the storm. His black coat was still damp and stained like her cloak had been when she had tried to wash away the mud. He was wearing a white silk shirt and a black damask vest. There was a gray silk handkerchief in the vest pocket, wrinkled and water-spotted. He looked cold.

Victoria put her hand out toward the body and then drew it back and groped for Anne's hand. "I'm sorry," Dr. Sawyer said, and looked down at the body lying on the table.

It was Elliott.

—|•••|—

"It's about time you got here," Elliott said, getting up. He had been lying on the pew, his coat folded up under his head. He had unbuttoned his shirt and opened his black vest. "I've been wasting away."

Anne handed him the parcel silently, looking at him. There was a gray silk handkerchief in the pocket of his vest.

"Did you go to tea at Vicky's?" he said, unwrapping the brown paper from the slices of bread, the baked ham, the russets. He was having some difficulty with the string. "Comforting the bereaved and all that? What fun!"

"No," Anne said. She watched him, waiting. He could not untie the string. He laid the packet on the seat beside him. "We went to Dr. Sawyer's."

"Why? Is my revered father sinking or does pretty Vicky have the vapors?"

"We went to see a body, to see if we could identify it."

"Ugh. A grisly business, I should imagine. Pretty Vicky fainting with relief at the sight of some bloated stranger, Dr. Sawyer ready with the smelling salts—"

"It was your body, Elliott."

She had expected him to look shocked or furtive or frightened. Instead, he put his hands behind his head and leaned back against them, smiling at her. "How is that possible, sweet Anne? Or have you been having the vapors, too?"

"How did you get from the river to Haddam, Elliott? You never told me."

He did not change his position. "A horse was grazing by the riverside. I leaped upon his back, the true horseman, and galloped home to you."

"You said you got the horse at an inn."

582

"I didn't want to offend your sensibilities by telling you I stole the horse. Perhaps I overjudged your sense of delicacy. You seem to have no qualms about accusing me of—what is it exactly you're accusing me of? Murdering some harmless passerby and dressing him in my clothes? Impossible. As you can see, I am still wearing them."

"My cloak is ruined beyond repair," she said slowly. "My boots were caked with mud. The hem of my dress was stained and torn. How did you manage to ride a horse all the way from Haddam in a storm and arrive with your boots polished and your coat brushed?"

He sat up suddenly and grabbed for her hands. She stepped back. "You did all that for me, Anne?" he said. "Waiting on the island, drenched and dirty? No wonder you are angry. But this is no way to punish me. Locking me in this dusty room, telling me ghost stories. I'll buy you a new cloak, darling."

"Why haven't you eaten anything I've brought you? You said you were famished. You said you hadn't eaten for days."

He let go of her hands. "When should I have eaten it? You've been here all this time, badgering me with silly questions. I'll eat it now." He picked up the paper packet and set it on his lap.

Anne watched him. His hands were windburned to a dark red. The body's hands had had no color. It was as if the river had washed it away.

Elliott fumbled with the brown paper on the bread. "Bread and cake and my own sweet Anne. What man could ask for more?" But he still didn't open the packet, and after a few minutes he replaced it on the seat. "I'll eat it after you've gone," he said petulantly "You've made me lose my appetite with all this talk of dead men."

When she went back the next day, he was fully dressed, his gray handkerchief neatly folded in his vest pocket, his coat on. "What time's the funeral?" he said gaily. "The second funeral, of course. How many funerals shall I have, I wonder? And will I have to pay for all the flowers when I return?"

"It is this afternoon," Anne said, wondering as soon as she said it if she should not have lied to him. She had dressed for the funeral, thinking all the while she would not go see him, that it was too dangerous, concentrating on dressing warmly in her brushed and cleaned wool merino, on taking her muff. But the key was in her muff, and as soon as she saw it, she knew that she had meant to go see him all along. It was just like the night she had gone to meet him on the island. She had not cared about warmth then, only about not being seen, and she had dressed in her black cloak and her black dress, her black bonnet, as if she were going someplace else altogether. As if, she realized now, she were dressing for a funeral.

"This afternoon," he repeated. "Then Victoria's father is back from Hartford?"

"Yes."

"And my father, is he well enough to attend? Leaning on his cane and murmuring, 'A bad end. I knew he would come to a bad end.' Is it to be a graveside service?" Elliott said, picking up his hat.

"Yes," she said in alarm. "Where are you going?"

"With you, of course. To the funeral. I missed my first one."

"You can't," she said, and backed slightly toward the door, clutching the key inside her muff.

"I think," he said coldly, "that this little game has gone on long enough. I never should have let you dissuade me from walking in on the first funeral. I certainly shall not let you keep me from this one."

Anne was so horrified she could not move. "You'll kill your father," she said.

"Well, and good riddance. You shall have someone to bury then besides this poor stranger who is masquerading as me."

"We are burying you, Elliott," she said, and there was something in his face when she said that that gave him away. "You know you're dead, don't you, Elliott?" she said quietly.

He put his hat on. "We shall see if my fiancée thinks I am dead. Or her father. How glad he will be to see me alive and free of debt! He shall welcome me with open arms, his son-in-law to be. And pretty Vicky, she shall be a bride instead of a widow."

Anne thought of Victoria's kind gray eyes, her little hand holding Anne's hand in the doctor's kitchen, of Victoria's father, grim-faced and protective, his hand on his daughter's shoulder. "Why are you doing this terrible thing, Elliott?" Anne said.

"I do not like coffins. They are small and dark and dusty. And cold. Like this room. I will not let them lock me in the grave as you have locked me in."

Anne sucked in her breath sharply.

"They will be so overjoyed they will quite forget what they have gone to the cemetery to do." He smiled disarmingly at her. "They will quite forget to bury me."

Anne backed against the door. "I won't let you," she said.

"Dear Anne, how will you stop me?"

She had not locked him in, not since the funeral. She had left the door unlocked each night in the hope that he would come out. "Leave the door open," he had shouted after her, but he had not opened it himself. When she went back the door was still shut, as if she had locked him in. "I will lock you in," she said aloud, and clutched the key inside her muff.

Elliott laughed. "What good will that do? If I am a ghost, I should be able to pass through the walls and come floating across the cemetery to you, shouldn't I, Anne?"

"No," she said steadily. "I won't let you."

"No?" he said, and laughed again. "When have you ever said no to me and meant it? You do not mean it now." He took a step toward her. "Come. We will go together."

"No!" she said, and whirled, opening and shutting the door behind her in one motion, pulling on the knob with all her strength till she could get the key into the lock and turn it. Elliott's hand was on the knob on the other side, turning it.

"Stop this foolishness and let me out, Anne," he said, half laughing, half stern.

"No," she said.

She put the key in the muff, and then, as if that had taken all her strength, she walked a few steps into the sanctuary and sank down on a pew. It was the one she had sat in that day of the funeral, and she put her arms down on the pew in front of her and buried her head in them. Inside the muff, her hand still clutched the key.

"Can I be of help, Miss Lawrence?" Reverend Sprague said kindly. He was wearing his heavy black coat and carrying the Service for the Burial of the Dead.

"Yes," Anne said, and stood up to go to the cemetery with him.

⊣ • • • ⊢

The coffin was already in the grave. The dirt was heaped around the edges, as dry and pale as the grass. The sky was heavy and gray. It was very cold. Victoria came forward to greet Reverend Sprague and speak to Anne. "I am so glad you came," she said, taking Anne's gloved hand. "We have only just heard," she said, her gray eyes filling with tears, and Anne thought suddenly, He has already been here.

Victoria's father came and put his arm around his daughter. "We have had word from New London," he said. "My son's ship was lost in a storm. With all hands."

"No," Anne said. "Your brother."

"We still hope and pray he may not be lost," Victoria's father said. "They were very near the coast."

"He is not lost," Anne said, almost to herself, "he will come today," and she did not know of whom she spoke.

"Let us pray," Reverend Sprague said, and Anne thought, Yes, yes, hurry. They all moved closer to the grave as if that could somehow shelter them from the iron-gray sky. "'In the midst of life we are in death,'" Reverend Sprague read. "'Of whom may we seek for succor, but of thee, O Lord?'"

Anne closed her eyes.

"'For we must all appear before the judgment seat of Christ.'" It was beginning to snow. Reverend Sprague stopped to look at the flakes falling on the book and lost the page altogether. When he found it, he said, "Pardon me," and began again. "'In the midst of life...'"

Hurry Anne thought. Oh, hurry.

Far away, at the other side of the cemetery, across the endless stretch of grayish-brown grass and gray-black stones, someone was coming. The minister hesitated. Go on, Anne thought. Go on.

"'That every one may receive the things done in his body, according to that he hath done, whether it be good or bad.'"

It was a man in a dark coat. He was carrying his hat in his hand. His hair was reddish-brown. There were flakes of snow on his coat and in his hair. Anne was afraid to look at him for fear the others would see him. She bowed her head. Reverend Sprague bent and scooped up a handful of dirt from the edge of the grave. "'Unto the mercy of Almighty God, our heavenly Father, we commend the soul of our brother departed and commit his body to the ground, earth to earth—'" He stopped, still holding the handful of earth.

Anne looked up. The man was much closer, walking rapidly between the graves. Victoria's father looked up. His face went gray.

"'Unto the mercy of Almighty God we commend the soul of our brother departed,'" Reverend Sprague read, and stopped again, and stared.

Victoria's father put his arm around Victoria. Victoria looked up. The man began to run toward them, waving his hat in the air.

"No," Anne said. With the toe of her boot she kicked at the dirt heaped around the grave. The dislodged clumps of dirt clattered on the coffin. Reverend Sprague looked at her, his face red and angry. He thinks I murdered Elliott, Anne thought despairingly, but I didn't. She clenched the useless key inside her muff and looked down at the forgotten coffin. I tried, Victoria. For your sake. For all our sakes. I tried to murder Elliott.

Victoria gave a strangled cry and began to run, her father close behind her. Reverend Sprague closed his book with an angry slap. "Roger!" Victoria cried, and threw her arms around his neck. Anne looked up.

Victoria's father slapped him on the back again and again. Victoria kissed him and cried. She took his large hand in her small gloved one and led him over to meet Anne. "This is my brother!" she said happily. "Roger, this is Miss Lawrence, who has been so kind to me."

He shook Anne's hand.

"We heard your ship was lost," she said.

"It was," he said, and looked past her at the open grave.

Anne stood outside the door of the choir room with the key in her hand until her fingers became stiff with cold and she could hardly put the key in the lock.

There was no one in the church. Reverend Sprague had gone home with Victoria and her father and brother to tea. "Please come," Victoria had said to Anne. "I do so want you and Roger to be friends." She had squeezed Anne's gloved hand and hurried off through the snow. It was nearly dusk. The snow had begun falling heavily by the time they finished burying Elliott's body. Reverend Sprague had read the service for the burial of the dead straight through to the end, and then they had stood, heads bowed against the snow, while old Mr. Finn filled in the grave. Then they had gone to tea and Anne had come back here to the church.

She turned the key in the lock. The rattling sound of the key seemed to be followed by an echo of itself, and she thought for a fleeting second of Elliott on the other side of the door, his hand already on the knob, ready to hurtle past her. Then she opened the door.

There was no one there. She knew it before she lit the candle. There had been no one there all week except herself. Her smallheeled footprints stood out clearly in the dust. The pew where Elliott had sat was thick with undisturbed dust, and in one corner of it lay the comforter she had brought him.

The toe of her foot hit against something on the floor, half under the pew. She bent to look. The packets of food, untouched in their brown paper wrappings, lay where Elliott had hidden them. A mouse had nibbled the string on one of them, and it lay spilled open, the piece of ham, the russet apple, the crumbling slice of cake she had brought him that first night. A schoolboy's picnic, Anne thought, and left the parcels where they were for Reverend Sprague to find and think whatever it was he would think about the footprints, the candle, the scattered food.

Let him think the worst, Anne thought. After all, it's true. I have murdered Elliott. It was getting very cold in the room. "I must go to tea at Victoria's," she said, and blew out the candle. By the dim light from the hall she picked up the comforter and folded it over her arm. She dropped the key on the floor and left the door open behind her.

─┤ • • • ├─

"So there I was, all alone," Roger said, "in the middle of a rough sea, my shirt frozen to my back, not one of my shipmates in sight, when what should I spy but the whaling boat." He paused expectantly.

Anne pulled the comforter around her shoulders and leaned forward over the fire to warm her hands.

"Would you like some tea?" Victoria said kindly. "Roger, we're eager to hear your story, but we must get poor Anne warmed up. I'm afraid she got a dreadful chill at the cemetery."

"I'm feeling much warmer now, thank you," Anne said, but she didn't refuse the tea. She wrapped her hands around the warmth of the thin china cup. Roger left his story to jab clumsily at the fire with the poker.

"Now then," Victoria said when the coals had roared up into new flames, "you may tell us the rest of your story, Roger."

Roger still squatted by the hearth, holding the poker loosely in his rough, windburned hands.

"There's nothing else to tell," he said, looking up at Anne. "The oars were still in the whaling boat. I rowed for shore." He had gray eyes like Victoria's. His hair in the firelight was darker than hers and with a reddish cast to it. Almost as dark as Elliott's. "I walked to an inn and hired a horse. When I got here, they told me you were at the cemetery. I was afraid you'd given up hope and were burying me."

His smile was more open than Elliott's, and his eyes more kind. His windburned hands looked strong and full of life, but he held the poker clumsily, as if his hands were cold and he could not get a proper grip on it. Anne took the comforter from around her shoulders and put it across her knees.

"You haven't eaten a thing since you got home," Victoria said. "And after all that time in an open boat, I'd think you would be starving."

Roger put the poker down on the hearth and took the cup of tea his sister gave him in both hands. He held it steadily enough, but he did not drink any. "I ate at the inn where I hired the horse," he said.

"How did you say you found the horse?" Anne said, as if she had not heard them. She held out a slice of cake to him on a thin china plate.

"I borrowed it from the man at the inn. He gave me some clothes to wear, too. Mine were ruined, and I'd lost my boots in the water. I must have been a sorry sight, knocking at his door late at night. He looked as though he'd seen a ghost." He smiled at Anne, and his eyes were kinder than Elliott's had ever been. "So did all of you," he said. "I felt for a moment as if I'd come to my own funeral."

"No," Anne said, and smiled back at him, but she watched him steadily as he took the slice of cake, and waited for him to eat it.

# The Soul Selects Her Own Society:
## Invasion and Repulsion:
## A Chronological Reinterpretation
## Of Two of Emily
## Dickinson's Poems:
## A Wellsian Perspective

Until recently it was thought that Emily Dickinson's poetic output ended in 1886, the year she died. Poems 186B and 272?, however, suggest that not only did she write poems at a later date, but that she was involved in the "great and terrible events"[1] at the turn of the century.

The poems in question originally came to light in 1991,[2] while Nathan Fleece was working on his doctorate. Fleece, who found the poems[3] under a hedge in the Dickinsons' backyard, classified the poems as belonging to Dickinson's Early or Only Slightly Eccentric Period, but a recent examination of the works[4] has yielded up an entirely different interpretation of the circumstances under which the poems were written.

The sheets of paper on which the poems were written are charred around the edges, and that of Number 272? has a large round hole burnt in it. Martha Hodge-Banks claims that said charring and hole

---

1 For a full account, see H. G. Wells, *The War of the Worlds*, Oxford University Press, 1898.

2 The details of the discovery are recounted in *Desperation and Discovery: The Unusual Number of Lost Manuscripts Located by Doctoral Candidates*, by J. Marple, Reading Railway Press, 1993.

3 Actually a poem and a poem fragment consisting of a four-line stanza and a single word fragment* from the middle of the second stanza.

\* Or word. See later on in this paper.

4 While I was working on *my* dissertation.

were caused by "a pathetic attempt to age the paper and forgetting to watch the oven,"[5] but the large number of dashes makes it clear they were written by Dickinson, as well as the fact that the poems are almost totally indecipherable. Dickinson's unreadable handwriting has been authenticated by any number of scholars, including Elmo Spencer in *Emily Dickinson: Handwriting or Hieroglyphics,* and M. P. Cursive, who wrote, "Her a's look like c's, her e's look like 2's, and the whole thing looks like chicken scratches."[6]The charring seemed to indicate either that the poems had been written while smoking[7] or in the midst of some catastrophe, and I began examining the text for clues.

Fleece had deciphered Number 272? as beginning, "I never saw a friend—/I never saw a moom—," which made no sense at all,[8] and on closer examination I saw that the stanza actually read:

> "I never saw a fiend—
> I never saw a bomb—
> And yet of both of them I dreamed—
> While in the—dreamless tomb—"

a much more authentic translation, particularly in regard to the rhyme scheme. "Moom" and "tomb" actually rhyme, which is something Dickinson hardly ever did, preferring near-rhymes such as "mat/gate," "tune/sun," and "balm/hermaphrodite."

The second stanza was more difficult, as it occupied the area of the round hole, and the only readable portion was a group of four letters farther down that read "ulla."[9]

This was assumed by Fleece to be part of a longer word such as

---

5 Dr. Banks's assertion that "the paper was manufactured in 1990 and the ink was from a Flair tip pen," is merely airy speculation.*

* See "Carbon Dating Doesn't Prove Anything," by Jeremiah Habakkuk, in *Creation Science for Fun and Profit,* Golden Slippers Press, 1974.

6 The pathetic nature of her handwriting is also addressed in *Impetus to Reform: Emily Dickinson's Effect on the Palmer Method,* and in "Depth, Dolts, and Teeth: An Alternate Translation of Emily Dickinson's Death Poems," in which it is argued that Number 712 actually begins, "Because I could not stoop for darts," and recounts an arthritic evening at the local pub.

7 Dickinson is not known to have smoked, except during her Late or Downright Peculiar Period.

8 Of course, neither does, "How pomp surpassing ermine." Or, "A dew sufficed itself."

9 Or possibly "ciee." Or "vole."

"bullary" (a convocation of popes),[10] or possibly "dullard" or "hullabaloo."[11]

I, however, immediately recognized "ulla" as the word H. G. Wells had reported hearing the dying Martians utter, a sound he described as "a sobbing alternation of two notes[12]...a desolating cry."

"Ulla" was a clear reference to the 1900 invasion by the Martians, previously thought to have been confined to England, Missouri, and the University of Paris.[13] The poem fragment, along with 186B, clearly indicated that the Martians had landed in Amherst and that they had met Emily Dickinson.

At first glance, this seems an improbable scenario due to both the Martians' and Emily Dickinson's dispositions. Dickinson was a recluse who didn't meet anybody, preferring to hide upstairs when neighbors came to call and to float notes down on them.[14] Various theories have been advanced for her self-imposed hermitude, including Bright's Disease, an unhappy love affair, eye trouble, and bad skin. T. L. Mensa suggests the simpler theory that all the rest of the Amherstonians were morons.[15]

None of these explanations would have made it likely that she would like Martians any better than Amherstates, and there is the added difficulty that, having died in 1886, she would also have been badly decomposed.

The Martians present additional difficulties. The opposite of recluses, they were in the habit of arriving noisily, attracting reporters, and blasting at everybody in the vicinity. There is no record of their having landed in Amherst, though several inhabitants mention unusually loud thunderstorms in their diaries,[16] and Louisa May Alcott, in nearby Concord, wrote in her journal, "Wakened suddenly last night by a loud noise to the west. Couldn't get back to sleep for worrying. Should have had Jo marry

---

10 Unlikely, considering her Calvinist upbringing.

11 Or the Australian city, Ulladulla. Dickinson's poems are full of references to Australia. W. G. Mathilda has theorized from this that "the great love of Dickinson's life was neither Higginson nor Judge Lord, but Mel Gibson." See *Emily Dickinson: The Billabong Connection*, by C. Dundee, Outback Press, 1985.

12 See Rod McKuen.

13 Where Jules Verne was working on *his* doctorate.

14 The notes contained charming, often enigmatic sentiments such as, "Which shall it be–Geraniums or Tulips?" and "Go away–and Shut the door When–you Leave."

15 See *Halfwits and Imbeciles: Poetic Evidence of Emily Dickinson's Opinion of Her Neighbors*.

16 Virtually everyone in Amherst kept a diary, containing entries such as "Always knew she'd turn out to be a great poet," and "Full moon last night. Caught a glimpse of her out in her garden planting peas. Completely deranged."

Laurie. To Do: Write sequel in which Amy dies. Serve her right for burning manuscript."

There is also indirect evidence for the landing. Amherst, frequently confused with Lakehurst, was obviously the inspiration for Orson Welles's setting the radio version of *War of the Worlds* in New Jersey.[17] In addition, a number of the tombstones in West Cemetery are tilted at an angle, and, in some cases, have been knocked down, making it clear that the Martians landed not only in Amherst, but in West Cemetery, very near Dickinson's grave.

Wells describes the impact of the shell[18] as producing "a blinding glare of vivid green light" followed by "such a concussion as I have never heard before or since." He reports that the surrounding dirt "splashed," creating a deep pit and exposing drainpipes and house foundations. Such an impact in West Cemetery would have uprooted the surrounding coffins and broken them open, and the resultant light and noise clearly would have been enough to "wake the dead," including the slumbering Dickinson.

That she was thus awakened, and that she considered the event an invasion of her privacy, is made clear in the longer poem, Number 186B, of which the first stanza reads: "I scarce was settled in the grave—When came—unwelcome guests—Who pounded on my coffin lid—Intruders—in the dust—"[19]

Why the "unwelcome guests" did not hurt her,[20] in light of their usual behavior, and how she was able to vanquish them, are less apparent, and we must turn to H. G. Wells's account of the Martians for answers.

On landing, Wells tells us, the Martians were completely helpless due to Earth's greater gravity, and remained so until they were able to build their fighting machines. During this period they would have posed no threat to Dickinson except that of company.[21]

---

17 The inability of people to tell Orson Welles and H. G. Wells apart lends credence to Dickinson's opinion of humanity. (See footnote 15.)

18 Not the one at the beginning of the story, which everybody knows about, the one that practically landed on him in the middle of the book which everybody missed because they'd already turned off the radio and were out running up and down the streets screaming, "The end is here! The Martians are coming!"*

\* Thus proving Emily was right in her assessment of the populace.

19 See "Sound, Fury, and Frogs: Emily Dickinson's Seminal Influence on William Faulkner," by W. Snopes, Yoknapatawpha Press, 1955.

20 She was, of course, already dead, which meant the damage they could inflict was probably minimal.

21 Which she considered a considerable threat. "If the butcher boy should come now, I would jump into the flour barrel,"* she wrote in 1873.

\* If she was in the habit of doing this, it may account for her always appearing in white.

Secondly, they were basically big heads. Wells describes them as having eyes, a beak, some tentacles, and "a single large tympanic drum" at the back of the head which functioned as an ear. Wells theorized that the Martians were "descended from beings not unlike ourselves, by a gradual development of brain and hands...at the expense of the body." He concluded that, without the body's vulnerability and senses, the brain would become "selfish and cruel" and take up mathematics,[22] but Dickinson's effect on them suggests that the overenhanced development of their neocortexes had turned them instead into poets.

The fact that they picked off people with their heat-rays, sucked human blood, and spewed poisonous black smoke over entire counties, would seem to contraindicate poetic sensibility, but look how poets act. Take Shelley, for instance, who went off and left his first wife to drown herself in the Serpentine so he could marry a woman who wrote monster movies. Or Byron. The only people who had a kind word to say about him were his dogs.[23] Take Robert Frost.[24]

The Martians' identity as poets is corroborated by the fact that they landed seven shells in Great Britain, three in the Lake District,[25] and none at all in Liverpool. It may have determined their decision to land in Amherst.

But they had reckoned without Dickinson's determination and literary technique, as Number 186B makes clear.[26] Stanza Two reads:

> "I wrote a letter—to the fiends—
> And bade them all be—gone—
> In simple words—writ plain and clear—
> 'I want to be alone.'"

"Writ plain and clear" is obviously an exaggeration, but it is manifest that Dickinson wrote a note and delivered it to the Martians, as the next line makes even more evident: "They [indecipherable][27] it with an awed dismay—"

---

22 Particularly nonlinear differential equations.

23 See "Lord Byron's Don Juan: The Mastiff as Muse" by C. Harold.

24 He didn't like people either. See "Mending Wall," *The Complete Works*, Random House. Frost preferred barbed wire fences with spikes on top to walls.

25 See "Semiotic Subterfuge in Wordsworth's 'I Wandered Lonely as a Cloud': A Dialectic Approach," by N. Compos Mentis, Postmodern Press, 1984.

26 Sort of.

27 The word is either "read" or "heard" or possibly "pacemaker."

Dickinson may have read it aloud or floated the note down to them in their landing pit in her usual fashion, or she may have unscrewed the shell and tossed it in, like a hand grenade.

Whatever the method of delivery, however, the result was "awed dismay" and then retreat, as the next line indicates:

"They—promptly took—their leave—"

It has been argued that Dickinson would have had no access to writing implements in the graveyard, but this fails to take into consideration the Victorian lifestyle. Dickinson's burial attire was a white dress, and all Victorian dresses had pockets.[28]

During the funeral Emily's sister Lavinia placed two heliotropes in her sister's hand, whispering that they were for her to take to the Lord. She may also have slipped a pencil and some Post-its into the coffin, or Dickinson, in the habit of writing and distributing notes, may simply have planned ahead.[29]

In addition, grave poems[30] are a well-known part of literary tradition. Dante Gabriel Rossetti, in the throes of grief after the death of his beloved Elizabeth Siddell, entwined poems in her auburn hair as she lay in her coffin.[31]

However the writing implements came to be there, Dickinson obviously made prompt and effective use of them. She scribbled down several stanzas and sent them to the Martians, who were so distressed at them that they decided to abort their mission and return to Mars.

The exact cause of this deadly effect has been much debated, with several theories being advanced. Wells was convinced that microbes killed the Martians who landed in England, who had no defense against Earth's bacteria, but such bacteria would have taken several weeks to infect the Martians, and it was obviously Dickinson's poems which caused them to leave, not dysentery.

---

28 Also pleats, tucks, rucking, flounces, frills, ruffles, and passementerie.*
* See "Pockets as Political Statement: The Role of Clothing in Early Victorian Feminism," by E. and C. Pankhurst, Angry Women's Press, 1978.
29 A good writer is never without pencil and paper.*
* Or laptop.
30 See "Posthumous Poems" in *Literary Theories that Don't Hold Water*, by H. Houdini.
31 Two years later, no longer quite so grief-stricken and thinking of all that lovely money, he dug her up and got them back.*
* I told you poets behaved badly.

Spencer suggests that her illegible handwriting led the Martians to mis-read her message and take it as some sort of ultimatum. A. Huyfen argues that the advanced Martians, being good at punctuation, were appalled by her profligate use of dashes and random capitalizing of letters. S. W. Lubbock proposes the theory that they were unnerved by the fact that all of her poems can be sung to the tune of "The Yellow Rose of Texas."[32]

It seems obvious, however, that the most logical theory is that the Martians were wounded to the heart by Dickinson's use of near-rhymes, which all advanced civilizations rightly abhor. Number 186B contains two particularly egregious examples: "gone/alone" and "guests/dust," and the burnt hole in 272? may indicate something even worse.

The near-rhyme theory is corroborated by H. G. Wells's account of the damage done to London, a city in which Tennyson ruled supreme, and by an account of a near-landing in Ong, Nebraska, recorded by Muriel Addleson:

> We were having our weekly meeting of the Ong Ladies Lit-erary Society when there was a dreadful noise outside, a rushing sound like something falling off the Grange Hall. Henrietta Muddle was reading Emily Dickinson's "I Taste a Liquor Never Brewed," out loud, and we all raced to the window but couldn't see anything except a lot of dust,[33] so Henrietta started reading again and there was a big whoosh, and a big round metal thing like a cigar[34] rose straight up in the air and disappeared.

It is significant that the poem in question is Number 214, which rhymes[35] "pearl" and "alcohol."[36] Dickinson saved Amherst from

---

32 Try it. No, really. "Be-e-e-cause I could not stop for Death, He kindly stopped for me-e-e." See?*

 \* Not all of Dickinson's poems can be sung to "The Yellow Rose of Texas."\*

 \*\* Numbers 2, 18, and 1411 can be sung to "The Itsy-Bitsy Spider." Could her choice of tunes be a coded reference to the unfortunate Martian landing in Texas? See "Night of the Cooters," by Howard Waldrop.

33 Normal to Ong, Nebraska.

34 See Freud.

35 Sort of.

36 The near-rhyme theory also explains why Dickinson responded with such fierceness when Thomas Wentworth Higginson changed "pearl" to "jewel." She knew, as he could not, that the fate of the world might someday rest on her inability to rhyme.

Martian invasion and then, as she says in the final two lines of 186B, "rearranged" her "grassy bed—/And Turned—and went To sleep."

She does not explain how the poems got from the cemetery to the hedge, and we may never know for sure,[37] as we may never know whether she was being indomitably brave or merely crabby.

What we do know is that these poems, along with a number of her other poems,[38] document a heretofore unguessed-at Martian invasion. Poems 186B and 272?, therefore, should be reassigned to the Very Late or Deconstructionist Period, not only to give them their proper place as Dickinson's last and most significant poems, but also so that the full symbolism intended by Dickinson can be seen in their titles. The properly placed poems will be Numbers 1775 and 1776, respectively, a clear Dickinsonian reference to the Fourth of July,[39] and to the second Independence Day she brought about by banishing[40] the Martians from Amherst.

> NOTE: It is unfortunate that Wells didn't know about the deadly effect of near-rhymes. He could have grabbed a copy of the Poems, taken it to the landing pit, read a few choice lines of "The Bustle in a House," and saved everybody a lot of trouble.

---

37 For an intriguing possibility, see "The Literary Litterbug: Emily Dickinson's Note-Dropping as a Response to Thoreau's Environmentalism," P. Walden, *Transcendentalist Review*, 1990.

38 Number 187's "awful rivet" is clearly a reference to the Martian cylinder. Number 258's "There's a certain slant of light" echoes Wells's "blinding glare of green light," and its "affliction/Sent us of the air" obviously refers to the landing. Such allusions indicate that as many as fifty-five* of the poems were written at a later date than originally supposed, and that the entire chronology and numbering system of the poems needs to be considered.

  * Significantly enough, the age Emily Dickinson was when she died.

39 A holiday Dickinson did not celebrate because of its social nature, although she was spotted in 1881 lighting a cherry bomb on Mabel Dodd's porch and running away.*

  * Which may be why the Martian landing attracted so little attention. The Amherstodes may have assumed it was Em up to her old tricks again.

40 There is compelling evidence that the Martians, thwarted in New England, went to Long Island. This theory will be the subject of my next paper,* "The Green Light at the End of Daisy's Dock: Evidence of Martian Invasion in F. Scott Fitzgerald's *The Great Gatsby*."

  * I'm up for tenure.

—| *Epiphanies*

# Chance

On Wednesday Elizabeth's next-door neighbor came over. It was raining hard, but she had run across the yard without a raincoat or an umbrella, her hands jammed in her cardigan sweater pockets.

"Hi," she said breathlessly. "I live next door to you, and I just thought I'd pop in and say hi and see if you were getting settled in." She reached in one of the sweater pockets and pulled out a folded piece of paper. "I wrote down the name of our trash pickup. Your husband asked about it the other day."

She handed it to her. "Thank you," Elizabeth said. The young woman reminded her of Tib. Her hair was short and blond and brushed back in wings. Tib had worn hers like that when they were freshmen.

"Isn't this weather awful?" the young woman said. "It usually doesn't rain like this in the fall."

It had rained all fall when Elizabeth was a freshman. "Where's your raincoat?" Tib had asked her when she unpacked her clothes and hung them up in the dorm room.

Tib was little and pretty, the kind of girl who probably had dozens of dates, the kind of girl who brought all the right clothes to college. Elizabeth hadn't known what kind of clothes to bring. The brochure the college had sent the freshmen had said to bring sweaters and skirts for class, a suit for rush, a formal. It hadn't said anything about a raincoat.

"Do I need one?" Elizabeth had said.

"Well, it's raining right now if that's any indication," Tib had said.

"I thought it was starting to let up," the neighbor said, "but it's not. And it's so cold."

She shivered. Elizabeth saw that her cardigan was damp.

"I can turn the heat up," Elizabeth said.

"No, I can't stay. I know you're trying to get unpacked. I'm sorry you had to move in in all this rain. We usually have beautiful weather here in the fall." She smiled at Elizabeth. "Why am I telling you that? Your husband told me you went to school here. At the university."

"It wasn't a university back then. It was a state college."

"Oh, right. Has the campus changed a lot?"

601

Elizabeth went over and looked at the thermostat. It showed the temperature as sixty-eight, but it felt colder. She turned it up to seventy-five. "No," she said. "It's just the same."

"Listen, I can't stay," the young woman said. "And you've probably got a million things to do. I just came over to say hello and see if you'd like to come over tonight. I'm having a Tupperware party."

A Tupperware party, Elizabeth thought sadly. No wonder she reminds me of Tib.

"You don't have to come. And if you come you don't have to buy anything. It's not going to be a big party. Just a few friends of mine. I think it would be a good way for you to meet some of the neighbors. I'm really only having the party because I have this friend who's trying to get started selling Tupperware and..." She stopped and looked anxiously at Elizabeth, holding her arms against her chest for warmth.

"I used to have a friend who sold Tupperware," Elizabeth said.

"Oh, then you probably have tons of it."

The furnace came on with a deafening whoosh. "No," Elizabeth said. "I don't have any."

"Please come," the young woman had continued to say even on the front porch. "Not to buy anything. Just to meet everybody."

The rain was coming down hard again. She ran back across the lawn to her house, her arms wrapped tightly around her and her head down.

Elizabeth went back in the house and called Paul at his office.

"Is this really important, Elizabeth?" he said. "I'm supposed to meet with Dr. Brubaker in Admissions for lunch at noon, and I have a ton of paperwork."

"The girl next door invited me to a Tupperware party," Elizabeth said. "I didn't want to say yes if you had anything planned for tonight."

"A Tupperware party?!" he said. "I can't believe you called me about something like that. You know how busy I am. Did you put your application in at Carter?"

"I'm going over there right now," she said. "I was going to go this morning, but the..."

"Dr. Brubaker's here," he said, and hung up the phone.

Elizabeth stood by the phone a minute, thinking about Tib, and then put on her raincoat and walked over to the old campus.

"It's exactly the same as it was when we were freshmen," Tib had said when Elizabeth told her about Paul's new job. "I was up there last summer to get some transcripts, and I couldn't believe it. It was raining, and I swear the sidewalks were covered with exactly the same worms as they always were. Do you remember that yellow slicker you bought when you were a freshman?"

Tib had called Elizabeth from Denver when they came out to look for a house. "I read in the alumni news that Paul was the new assistant dean," she said as if nothing had ever happened. "The article didn't say anything about you, but I thought I'd call on the off-chance that you two were still married. I'm not." Tib had insisted on taking her to lunch in Latimer Square. She had let her hair grow out, and she was too thin. She ordered a peach daiquiri and told Elizabeth all about her divorce. "I found out Jim was screwing some little slut at the office," she had said, twirling the sprig of mint that had come with her drink, "and I couldn't take it. He couldn't see what I was upset about. 'So I fooled around, so what?' he told me. 'Everybody does it. When are you going to grow up?' I never should have married the creep, but you don't know you're ruining your life when you do it, do you?"

"No," Elizabeth said.

"I mean, look at you and Paul," she said. She talked faster than Elizabeth remembered, and when she called the waiter over to order another daiquiri, her voice shook a little. "Now that's a marriage I wouldn't have taken bets on, and you've been married, what? Fifteen years?"

"Seventeen," Elizabeth said.

"You know, I always thought you'd patch things up with Tupper," she said. "I wonder whatever became of him." The waiter brought the daiquiri and took the empty one away. She took the mint sprig out and laid it carefully on the tablecloth.

"Whatever became of Elizabeth and Tib, for that matter," she said.

The campus wasn't really just the same. They had added a wing onto Frasier and cut down most of the elms. It wasn't even really the campus anymore. The real campus was west and north of here, where there had been room for the new concrete classroom buildings and high-rise dorms. The music department was still in Frasier, and the PE department used the old gym in Gunter for women's sports, but most of the old classroom buildings and the small dorms at the south end of the campus were offices now. The library was now the administration building and Kepner belonged to the campus housing authority, but in the rain the campus looked the same.

The leaves were starting to fall, and the main walk was wet and covered with worms. Elizabeth picked her way among them, watching her feet and trying not to step on them. When she was a freshman, she had refused to walk on the sidewalks at all. She had ruined two pairs of flats that fall by cutting through the grass to get to her classes.

"You're a nut, you know that?" Tib had shouted, sprinting to catch up to her. "There are worms in the grass, too."

"I know, but I can't see them."

When there was no grass, she had insisted on walking in the middle of the street. That was how they had met Tupper. He almost ran them down with his bike.

It had been a Friday night. Elizabeth remembered that, because Tib was in her ROTC Angel Flight uniform, and after Tupper had swerved wildly to miss them, sending up great sprays of water and knocking his bike over, the first thing he said was, "Cripes! She's a cop!"

They had helped him pick up the plastic bags strewn all over the street. "What are these?" Tib had said, stooping because she couldn't bend over in her straight blue skirt and high heels.

"Tupperware," he said. "The latest thing. You girls wouldn't need a lettuce crisper, would you? They're great for keeping worms in."

Carter Hall looked just the same from the outside, ugly beige stone and glass brick. It had been the student union, but now it housed Financial Aid and Personnel. Inside it had been completely remodeled. Elizabeth couldn't even tell where the cafeteria had been.

"You can fill it out here if you want," the girl who gave her the application said, and gave her a pen. Elizabeth hung her coat over the back of a chair and sat down at a desk by a window. It felt chilly, though the window was steamy.

They had all gone to the student union for pizza. Elizabeth had hung her yellow slicker over the back of the booth. Tupper had pretended to wring out his jean jacket and draped it over the radiator. The window by the booth was so steamed up, they couldn't see out. Tib had written "I hate rain" on the window with her finger, and Tupper had told them how he was putting himself through college selling Tupperware.

"They're great for keeping cookies in," he said, hauling up a big pink box he called a cereal keeper. He put a piece of pizza inside and showed them how to put the lid on and burp. it. "There. It'll keep for weeks. Years. Come on. You need one. I'll bet your mothers send you cookies all the time."

He was a junior. He was tall and skinny, and when he put his damp jean jacket back on, the sleeves were too short, and his wrists stuck out. He had sat next to Tib on one side of the booth and Elizabeth had sat on the other. He had talked to Tib most of the evening, and when he was paying the check, he had bent toward Tib and whispered something to her. Elizabeth was sure he was asking her out on a date, but on the way home Tib had said, "You know what he wanted, don't you? Your telephone number."

Elizabeth stood up and put her coat back on. She gave the girl in the sweater and skirt back her pen. "I think I'll fill this out at home and bring it back."

"Sure," the girl said.

When Elizabeth went back outside, the rain had stopped. The trees were still dripping, big drops that splattered onto the wet walk. She walked up the wide center walk toward her old dorm, looking at her feet so she wouldn't step on any worms. The dorm had been converted into the university's infirmary. She stopped and stood a minute under the center window, looking up at the room that had been hers and Tib's.

Tupper had stood under the window and thrown pebbles up at it. Tib had opened the window and yelled, "You'd better stop throwing rocks, you..." Something hit her in the chest. "Oh, hi, Tupper," she said, and picked it up off the floor and handed it to Elizabeth. "It's for you," she said. It wasn't a pebble. It was a pink plastic gadget, one of the favors he passed out at his Tupperware parties.

"What's this supposed to be?" Elizabeth had said, leaning out of the window and waving it at him. It was raining. Tupper had the collar of his jean jacket turned up and he looked cold. The sidewalk around him was covered with pink plastic favors.

"A present," he said. "It's an egg separator."

"I don't have any eggs."

"Wear it around your neck then. We'll be officially scrambled."

"Or separated."

He grabbed at his chest with his free hand. "Never!" he said. "Want to come out in the worms with me? I've got some deliveries to make." He held up a clutch of plastic bags full of bowls and cereal keepers.

"I'll be right down," she had said, but she had stopped and found a ribbon to string the egg separator on before she went downstairs.

Elizabeth looked down at the sidewalk, but there were no plastic favors on the wet cement. There was a big puddle out by the curb, and a worm lay at the edge of it. It moved a little as she watched, in that horrid boneless way that she had always hated, and then lay still.

A girl brushed past her, walking fast. She stepped in the puddle, and Elizabeth took a half step back to avoid being splashed. The water in the puddle rippled and moved out in a wave. The worm went over the edge of the sidewalk and into the gutter.

Elizabeth looked up. The girl was already halfway down the center walk, late for class or angry or both. She was wearing an Angel Flight uniform and high heels, and her short blond hair was brushed back in wings along the sides of her garrison cap.

Elizabeth stepped off the curb into the street. The gutter was clogged with dead leaves and full of water. The worm lay at the bottom. She sat down on her heels, holding the application form in her right hand. The worm would drown, wouldn't it? That was what Tupper had told her. The reason they came out on the sidewalks when it rained was that their tunnels filled up with water, and they would drown if they didn't.

She stood up and looked down the central walk again, but the girl was gone, and there was nobody else on the campus. She stooped again and transferred the application to her other hand, and then reached in the icy water, and scooped up the worm in her cupped hand, thinking that as long as it didn't move she would be able to stand it, but as soon as her fingers touched the soft pink flesh, she dropped it and clenched her fist.

"I can't," Elizabeth said, rubbing her wet hand along the side of her raincoat, as if she could wipe off the memory of the worm's touch.

She took the application in both hands and dipped it into the water like a scoop. The paper went a little limp in the water, but she pushed it into the dirty, wet leaves and scooped the worm up and put it back on the sidewalk. It didn't move.

"And thank God they do come out on the sidewalks!" Tupper had said, walking her home in the middle of the street from his Tupperware deliveries. "You think they're disgusting lying there! What if they didn't come out on the sidewalks? What if they all stayed in their holes and drowned? Have you ever had to do mouth-to-mouth resuscitation on a worm?"

Elizabeth straightened up. The job application was wet and dirty. There was a brown smear where the worm had lain, and a dirty line across the top. She should throw it away and go back to Carter to get another one. She unfolded it and carefully separated the wet pages so they wouldn't stick together as they dried.

"I had first aid last semester, and we had to do mouth-to-mouth resuscitation in there," Tupper had said, standing in the middle of the street in front of her dorm. "What a great class! I sold twenty-two square rounds for snake-bite kits. Do you know how to do mouth-to-mouth resuscitation?"

"No."

"It's easy," Tupper had said, and put his hand on the back of her neck under her hair and kissed her, in the middle of the street in the rain.

The worm still hadn't moved. Elizabeth stood and watched it a little longer, feeling cold, and then went out in the middle of the street and walked home.

Paul didn't come home until after seven. Elizabeth had kept a casserole warm in the oven.

"I ate," he said. "I thought you'd be at your Tupperware party."

"I don't want to go," she said, reaching into the hot oven to get the casserole out. It was the first time she had felt warm all day.

"Brubaker's wife is going. I told him you'd be there, too. I want you to get to know her. Brubaker's got a lot of influence around here about who gets tenure."

She put the casserole on top of the stove and then stood there with the oven door half-open. "I went over to apply for a job today," she said, "and I saw this worm. It had fallen in the gutter and it was drowning and I picked it up and put it back on the sidewalk."

"And did you apply for the job or do you think you can make any money picking up worms?"

She had turned up the furnace when she got home and put the application on the vent, but it had wrinkled as it dried, and there was a big smear down the middle where the worm had lain. "No," she said. "I was going to; but when I was over on the campus, there was this worm lying on the sidewalk. A girl walked by and stepped in a puddle, and that was all it took. The worm was right on the edge, and when she stepped in the puddle, it made a kind of wave that pushed it over the edge. She didn't even know she'd done it."

"Is there a point to this story, or have you decided to stand here and talk until you've completely ruined my chance at tenure?" He shut off the oven and went into the living room. She followed him.

"All it took was somebody walking past and stepping in a puddle, and the worm's whole life was changed. Do you think things happen like that? That one little action can change your whole life forever?"

"What I think," he said, "is that you didn't want to move here in the first place, and so you are determined to sabotage my chances. You know what this move is costing us, but you won't go apply for a job. You know how important my getting tenure is, but you won't do anything to help. You won't even go to a goddamn Tupperware party!" He turned the thermostat down. "It's like an oven in here. You've got the heat turned up to seventy-five. What's the matter with you?"

"I was cold," Elizabeth said.

⊣ • • • ⊢

She was late to the Tupperware party. They were in the middle of a game where they told their name and something they liked that began with the same letter.

"My name's Sandy," an overweight woman in brown polyester pants and a rust print blouse was saying, "and I like sundaes." She pointed at Elizabeth's neighbor. "And you're Meg, and you like marshmallows, and you're Janice," she said, glaring at a woman in a pink suit with her hair teased and sprayed the way girls had worn it when Elizabeth was in college. "You're Janice and you like Jesus," she said, and moved rapidly on to the next person. "And you're Barbara and you like bananas."

She went all the way around the circle until she came to Elizabeth. She looked puzzled for a moment, and then said. "And you're Elizabeth, and you went to college here, didn't you?"

"Yes," she said.

"That doesn't begin with an *E*," the woman in the center said. Everyone laughed. "I'm Terry, and I like Tupperware," she said, and there was more laughter. "You got here late. Stand up and tell us your name and something you like."

"I'm Elizabeth," she said, still trying to place the woman in the brown slacks. Sandy. "And I like…" She couldn't think of anything with an *E*.

"Eggs," Sandy whispered loudly.

"And I like eggs," Elizabeth said, and sat back down.

"Great," Terry said. "Everybody else got a favor, so you get one, too." She handed Elizabeth a pink plastic egg separator.

"Somebody gave me one of those," she said.

"No problem," Terry said. She held out a shallow plastic box full of plastic toothbrush holders and grapefruit slicers. "You can put it back and take something else if you've already got one."

"No. I'll keep this." She knew she should say something good-natured and funny, in the spirit of things, but all she could think of was what she had said to Tupper when he gave it to her. "I'll treasure this always," she had told him. A month later she had thrown it away.

"I'll treasure it always," Elizabeth said, and everyone laughed.

They played another game, unscrambling words like "autumn" and "schooldays" and "leaf," and then Terry passed out order forms and pencils and showed them Tupperware.

It was cold in the house, even though Elizabeth's neighbor had a fire going in the fireplace, and after she had filled out her order form, Elizabeth went over and sat in front of the fire, looking at the plastic egg separator.

The woman in the brown pants came over, holding a coffee cup and a brownie on a napkin. "Hi, I'm Sandy Konkel. You don't remember me, do you?" she said. "I was an Alpha Phi. I pledged the year after you did."

Elizabeth looked earnestly at her, trying to remember her. She did not look like she had ever been an Alpha Phi. Her mustard-colored hair looked as if she had cut it herself. "I'm sorry, I…," Elizabeth said.

"That's okay," Sandy said. She sat down next to her. "I've changed a lot. I used to be skinny before I went to all these Tupperware parties and ate brownies. And I used to be a lot blonder. Well, actually, I never was any blonder, but I looked blonder, if you know what I mean. You look just the same. You were Elizabeth Wilson, right?"

Elizabeth nodded.

"I'm not really a whiz at remembering names," she said cheerfully, "but they stuck me with being alum rep this year. Could I come over tomorrow and get some info from you on what you're doing, who you're married to? Is your husband an alum, too?"

"No," Elizabeth said. She stretched her hands out over the fire, trying to warm them. "Do they still have Angel Flight at the college?"

"At the university, you mean," Sandy said, grinning. "It used to be a college. Gee, I don't know. They dropped the whole ROTC thing back in sixty-eight. I don't know if they ever reinstated it. I can find out. Were you in Angel Flight?"

"No," Elizabeth said.

"You know, now that I think about it, I don't think they did. They always had that big fall dance, and I don't remember them having it since....What was it called, the Autumn Something?"

"The Harvest Ball," Elizabeth said.

Thursday morning Elizabeth walked back over to the campus to get another job application. Paul had been late going to work. "Did you talk to Brubaker's wife?" he had said on his way out the door. Elizabeth had forgotten all about Mrs. Brubaker. She wondered which one she had been, Barbara who liked bananas or Meg who liked marshmallows.

"Yes," she said. "I told her how much you liked the university."

"Good. There's a faculty concert tomorrow night. Brubaker asked if we were going. I invited them over for coffee afterwards. Did you turn the heat up again?" he said. He looked at the thermostat and turned it down to sixty. "You had it turned up to eighty. I can hardly wait to see what our first gas bill is. The last thing I need is a two-hundred-dollar gas bill, Elizabeth. Do you realize what this move is costing us?"

"Yes," Elizabeth said. "I do."

She had turned the thermostat back up as soon as he left, but it didn't seem to do any good. She put on a sweater and her raincoat and walked over to the campus.

The rain had stopped sometime during the night, but the central walk was still wet. At the far end, a girl in a yellow slicker stepped up on the curb. She took a few steps on the sidewalk, her head bent, as if she were looking at something on the ground, and then cut across the wet grass toward Gunter.

Elizabeth went into Carter Hall. The girl who had helped her the day before was leaning over the counter, taking notes from a textbook. She was wearing a pleated skirt and sweater like Elizabeth had worn in college.

"The styles we wore have all come back," Tib had said when they had lunch together. "Those matching sweater-and-skirt sets and those horrible flats that we never could keep on our feet. And penny loafers." She was on her third peach daiquiri and her voice had gotten calmer with each one, so that she almost sounded like her old self. "And cocktail dresses! Do you remember that rust formal you had, with the scoop neck and the long skirt with the raised design? I always loved that dress. Do you remember that time you loaned it to me for the Angel Flight dance?"

"Yes," Elizabeth said, and picked up the bill.

Tib tried to stir her peach daiquiri with its mint sprig, but it slipped out of her fingers and sank to the bottom of the glass. "He really only took me to be nice."

"I know," Elizabeth had said. "Now how much do I owe? Six-fifty for the crepes and two for the wine cooler. Do they add on the tip here?"

"I need another job application," Elizabeth said to the girl.

"Sure thing." When the girl walked over to the files to get it, Elizabeth could see that she was wearing flat-heeled shoes like she had worn in college. Elizabeth thanked her and put the application in her purse.

She walked up past her dorm. The worm was still lying there. The sidewalk around it was almost dry, and the worm was a darker red than it should have been. "I should have put it in the grass," she said out loud. She knew it was dead, but she picked it up and put it in the grass anyway, so no one would step on it. It was cold to the touch.

—|••|—

Sandy Konkel came over in the afternoon wearing a gray polyester pantsuit. She had a wet high-school letter jacket over her head. "John loaned me his jacket," she said. "I wasn't going to wear a coat this morning, but John told me I was going to get drenched. Which I was."

"You might want to put it on," Elizabeth said. "I'm sorry it's so cold in here. I think there's something wrong with the furnace."

"I'm fine," Sandy said. "You know, I wrote that article on your husband being the new assistant dean, and I asked him about you, but he didn't say anything about your having gone to college here."

She had a thick notebook with her. She opened it at tabbed sections. "We might as well get this alum stuff out of the way first, and then we can talk. This alum-rep job is a real pain, but I must admit I get kind of a kick out of finding out what happened to everybody. Let's see," she said, thumbing through the sections. "Found, lost, hopelessly lost, deceased. I think you're one of the hopelessly lost. Right? Okay." She dug a pencil out of her purse. "You were Elizabeth Wilson."

"Yes," Elizabeth said. "I was." She had taken off her light sweater and put on a heavy wool one when she got home, but she was still cold. She rubbed her hands along her upper arms. "Would you like some coffee?"

"Sure," she said. She followed Elizabeth to the kitchen and asked her questions about Paul and his job and whether they had any children while Elizabeth made coffee and put out the cream and sugar and a plate of the cookies she had baked for after the concert.

"I'll read you some names off the hopelessly lost list, and if you know what happened to them, just stop me. Carolyn Waugh, Pam Callison, Linda Bohlender." She was several names past Cheryl Tibner before Elizabeth realized that was Tib.

"I saw Tib in Denver this summer," she said. "Her married name's Scates, but she's getting a divorce, and I don't know if she's going to go back to her maiden name or not."

"What's she doing?" Sandy said.

She's drinking too much, Elizabeth thought, and she let her hair grow out, and she's too thin. "She's working for a stockbroker," she said, and went to get the address Tib had given her. Sandy wrote it down and then flipped to the tabbed section marked "Found" and entered the name and address again.

"Would you like some more coffee, Mrs. Konkel?" Elizabeth said.

"You still don't remember me, do you?" Sandy said. She stood up and took off her jacket. She was wearing a short-sleeved gray knit shell underneath it. "I was Karen Zamora's roommate. Sondra Dickeson?"

Sondra Dickeson. She had had pale-blond hair that she wore in a pageboy, and a winter-white cashmere sweater and a matching white skirt with a kick pleat. She had worn it with black heels and a string of real pearls.

Sandy laughed. "You should see the expression on your face. You remember me now, don't you?"

"I'm sorry. I just didn't...I should have..."

"Listen, it's okay," she said. She took a sip of coffee. "At least you didn't say, 'How could you let yourself go like that?' like Janice Brubaker did." She bit into a cookie. "Well, aren't you going to ask me whatever became of Sondra Dickeson? It's a great story."

"What happened to her?" Elizabeth said. She felt suddenly colder. She poured herself another cup of coffee and sat back down, wrapping her hands around the cup for warmth.

Sandy finished the cookie and took another one. "Well, if you remember, I was kind of a snot in those days. I was going to this Sigma Chi dinner dance with Chuck Pagano. Do you remember him? Well, anyway, we were going to this dance clear out in the country somewhere, and he stopped the car and got all clutchy-grabby, and I got mad because he was messing up my hair and my makeup so I got out of the car. And he drove off. So there I was, standing in the middle of nowhere in a formal and high heels. I hadn't even grabbed my purse or anything, and it's getting dark, and Sondra Dickeson is such a snot that it never even occurs to her to walk back to town or try to find a phone or something. No, she just stands there like an idiot in her brocade formal and her orchid corsage and her dyed satin pumps and thinks, 'He can't do this to me. Who does he think he is?'"

She was talking about herself as if she had been another person, which Elizabeth supposed she had been, an ice-blond with a pageboy and a formal like the one Elizabeth had loaned Tib for the Harvest Ball, a rust satin bodice and a bell skirt out of sculptured rust brocade. After the dance Elizabeth had given it to the Salvation Army.

"Did Chuck come back?" she said.

"Yes," Sandy said, frowning, and then grinned. "But not soon enough. Anyway, it's almost dark and along comes this truck with no lights on, and this guy leans out and says, 'Hiya, gorgeous. Wanta ride?'" She smiled at her coffee cup as if she could still hear him saying it. "He was awful. His hair was down to his ears and his fingernails were black. He wiped his hand on his shirt and helped me up into the truck. He practically pulled my arm out of its socket, and then he said, 'I thought there for a minute I was going to have to go around behind and shove. You know, you're lucky I came along. I'm not usually out after dark on account of my lights being out, but I had a flat tire.'"

She's happy, Elizabeth thought, putting her hand over the top of her cup to try to warm herself with the steam.

"And he took me home and I thanked him and the next week he showed up at the Phi house and asked me out for a date, and I was so surprised that I went, and I married him, and we have four kids."

The furnace kicked on, and Elizabeth could feel the air coming out of the vent under the table, but it felt cold. "You went out with him?" she said.

"Hard to believe, isn't it? I mean, at that age all you can think about is your precious self. You're so worried about getting laughed at or getting hurt, you can't even see anybody else. When my sorority sister told me he was downstairs, all I could think of was how he must look, his hair all slicked back with water and cleaning those black fingernails with a penknife, and what everybody would say. I almost told her to tell him I wasn't there."

"What if you had done that?"

"I guess I'd still be Sondra Dickeson, the snot, a fate worse than death."

"A fate worse than death," Elizabeth said, almost to herself, but Sandy didn't hear her. She was plunging along, telling the story that she got to tell every time somebody new moved to town, and no wonder she liked being alum rep.

"My sorority sister said, 'He's really got intestinal fortitude coming here like this, thinking you'd go out with him,' and I thought about him, sitting down there being laughed at, being hurt, and I told my roommate to go to hell and went downstairs and that was that." She looked at the kitchen clock. "Good lord, is it that late? I'm going to have to go pick up the kids pretty soon." She ran her finger down the hopelessly lost list. "How about Dallas Tindall, May Matsumoto, Ralph DeArvill?"

"No," Elizabeth said. "Is Tupper Hofwalt on that list?"

"Hofwalt." She flipped several pages over. "Was Tupper his real name?"

"No. Phillip. But everybody called him Tupper because he sold Tupperware."

She looked up. "I remember him. He had a Tupperware party in our dorm when I was a freshman." She flipped back to the Found section and started paging through it.

He had talked Elizabeth and Tib into having a Tupperware party in the dorm. "As co-hostesses you'll be eligible to earn points toward a popcorn popper," he had said. "You don't have to do anything except come up with some refreshments, and your mothers are always sending you cookies, right? And I'll owe you guys a favor."

They had had the party in the dorm lounge. Tupper pinned the names of famous people on their backs, and they had to figure out who they were by asking questions about themselves.

Elizabeth was Twiggy. "Am I a girl?" she asked Tib.

"Yes."

"Am I pretty?"

"Yes," Tupper had said before Tib could answer.

After she guessed it, she went over and stooped down next to the coffee table where Tupper was setting up his display of plastic bowls. "Do you really think Twiggy's pretty?" she asked.

"Who said anything about Twiggy?" he said. "Listen, I wanted to tell you..."

"Am I alive?" Sharon Oberhausen demanded.

"I don't know," Elizabeth said. "Turn around so I can see who you are."

The sign on her back said Mick Jagger.

"It's hard to tell," Tupper said.

Tib was King Kong. It had taken her forever to figure it out. "Am I tall?" she asked.

"Compared to what?" Elizabeth had said.

She stuck her hands on her hips. "I don't know. The Empire State Building."

"Yes," Tupper said.

He had had a hard time getting them to stop talking so he could show them his butter keeper and cake taker and popsicle makers. While they were filling out their order forms, Sharon Oberhausen said to Tib, "Do you have a date yet for the Harvest Ball?"

"Yes," Tib said.

"I wish I did," Sharon said. She leaned across Tib. "Elizabeth, do you realize everybody in ROTC has to have a date or they put you on weekend duty? Who are you going with, Tib?"

"Listen, you guys," Tib said, "the more you buy, the better our chances at that popcorn popper, which we are willing to share."

They had bought a cake and chocolate-chip ice cream. Elizabeth cut the cake in the dorm's tiny kitchen while Tib dished it up.

"You didn't tell me you had a date to the Harvest Ball," Elizabeth said. "Who is it? That guy in your ed-psych class?"

"No." She dug into the ice cream with a plastic spoon. "Who?"

Tupper came into the kitchen with a catalog. "You're only twenty points away from a popcorn popper," he said. "You know what you girls need?" He folded back a page and pointed to a white plastic box. "An ice-cream keeper. Holds a half gallon of ice cream, and when you want some, all you do is slide this tab out"—he pointed to a flat rectangle of plastic—"and cut off a slice. No more digging around in it and getting your hands all messy."

Tib licked ice cream off her knuckles. "That's the best part."

"Get out of here, Tupper," Elizabeth said. "Tib's trying to tell me who's taking her to the Harvest Ball."

Tupper closed the catalog. "I am."

"Oh," Elizabeth said. Sharon stuck her head around the corner. "Tupper, when do we have to pay for this stuff?" she said. "And when do we get something to eat?"

Tupper said, "You pay before you eat," and went back out to the lounge.

Elizabeth drew the plastic knife across the top of the cake, making perfectly straight lines in the frosting. When she had the cake divided into squares, she cut the corner piece and put it on the paper plate next to the melting ice cream. "Do you have anything to wear?" she said. "You can borrow my rust formal."

Sandy was looking at her, the thick notebook opened almost to the last page. "How well did you know Tupper?" she said.

Elizabeth's coffee was ice cold, but she put her hand over it, as if to try to catch the steam. "Not very well. He used to date Tib."

"He's on my deceased list, Elizabeth. He killed himself five years ago."

⊣•••⊢

Paul didn't get home till after ten. Elizabeth was sitting on the couch wrapped in a blanket.

He went straight to the thermostat and turned it down. "How high do you have this thing turned up?" He squinted at it. "Eighty-five. Well, at least I don't have to worry about you freezing to death. Have you been sitting there like that all day?"

"The worm died," she said. "I didn't save it after all. I should have put it over on the grass."

"Ron Brubaker says there's an opening for a secretary in the dean's office. I told him you'd put in an application. You have, haven't you?"

"Yes," Elizabeth said. After Sandy left, she had taken the application out of her purse and sat down at the kitchen table to fill it out. She had had it nearly filled out before she realized it was a retirement fund withholding form.

"Sandy Konkel was here today," she said. "She met her husband on a dirt road. They were both there by chance. By chance. It wasn't even his route. Like the worm. Tib just walked by, she didn't even know she did it, but the worm was too near the edge, and it went over into the water and drowned." She started to cry. The tears felt cold running down her cheeks. "It drowned."

"What did you and Sandy Konkel do? Get out the cooking sherry and reminisce about old times?"

"Yes," she said. "Old times."

In the morning Elizabeth took back the retirement fund withholding form. It had rained off and on all night, and it had turned colder. There were patches of ice on the central walk.

"I had it almost all filled out before I realized what it was," she told the girl. A boy in a button-down shirt and khaki pants had been leaning on the counter when Elizabeth came in. The girl was turned away from the counter, filing papers.

"I don't know what you're so mad about," the boy had said, and then stopped and looked at Elizabeth. "You've got a customer," he said, and stepped away from the counter.

"All these dumb forms look alike," the girl said, handing the application to Elizabeth. She picked up a stack of books. "I've got a class. Did you need anything else?"

Elizabeth shook her head and stepped back so the boy could finish talking to her, but the girl didn't even look at him. She shoved the books into a backpack, slung it over her shoulder, and went out the door.

"Hey, wait a minute," the boy said, and started after her. By the time Elizabeth got outside, they were halfway up the walk. Elizabeth heard the boy say, "So I took her out once or twice. Is that a crime?"

The girl jerked the backpack out of his grip and started off down the walk toward Elizabeth's old dorm. In front of the dorm a girl in a yellow slicker was talking to another girl with short upswept blond hair. The girl in the slicker turned suddenly and started down the walk.

A boy went past Elizabeth on a bike, hitting her elbow and knocking the application out of her hand. She grabbed for it and got it before it landed on the walk.

"Sorry," he said without glancing back. He was wearing a jean jacket. Its sleeves were too short, and his bony wrists stuck out. He was steering the bike with one hand and holding a big plastic sack full of pink and green bowls in the other. That was what he had hit her with.

"Tupper," she said, and started to run after him.

She was down on the ice before she even knew she was going to fall, her hands splayed out against the sidewalk and one foot twisted under her. "Are you all right, ma'am?" the boy in the button-down shirt said. He knelt down in front of her so she couldn't see up the walk.

Tupper would call me "ma'am," too, she thought. He wouldn't even recognize me.

"You shouldn't try to run on this sidewalk. It's slicker than shit."

"I thought I saw somebody I knew."

He turned, balancing himself on the flat of one hand, and looked down the long walk. There was nobody there now. "What did they look like? Maybe I can still catch them."

"No," Elizabeth said. "He's long gone."

The girl came over. "Should I go call 911 or something?" she said.

"I don't know," he said to her, and then turned back to Elizabeth. "Can you stand up?" he said, and put his hand under her arm to help her. She tried to bring her foot out from its twisted position, but it wouldn't come. He tried again, from behind, both hands under her arms and hoisting her up, then holding her there by brute force till he could come around to her bad side. She leaned shamelessly against him, shivering.

"If you can get my books and this lady's purse, I think I can get her up to the infirmary," he said. "Do you think you can walk that far?"

"Yes," Elizabeth said, and put her arm around his neck. The girl picked up Elizabeth's purse and her job application.

"I used to go to school here. The central walk was heated back then." She couldn't put any weight on her foot at all. "Everything looks the same. Even the college kids. The girls wear skirts and sweaters just like we wore and those little flat shoes that never will stay on your feet, and the boys wear button-down shirts and jean jackets, and they look just like the boys I knew when I went here to school, and it isn't fair. I keep thinking I see people I used to know."

"I'll bet," the boy said politely. He shifted his weight, hefting her up so her arm was more firmly on his shoulder.

"I could maybe go get a wheelchair. I bet they'd loan me one," the girl said, sounding concerned.

"You know it can't be them, but it looks just like them, only you'll never see them again, never. You'll never even know what happened to them." She had thought she was getting hysterical, but instead her voice was getting softer and softer until her words seemed to fade away to nothing. She wondered if she had even said them aloud.

The boy got her up the stairs and into the infirmary.

"You shouldn't let them get away," she said.

"No," the boy said, and eased her onto the couch. "I guess you shouldn't."

"She slipped on the ice on the central walk," the girl told the receptionist. "I think maybe her ankle's broken. She's in a lot of pain." She came over to Elizabeth.

"I can stay with her," the boy said. "I know you've got a class."

She looked at her watch. "Yeah. Ed-psych. Are you sure you'll be all right?" she said to Elizabeth.

"I'm fine. Thank you for all your help, both of you."

"Do you have a way to get home?" the boy said.

"I'll call my husband to come and get me. There's really no reason for either of you to stay. I'm fine. Really."

"Okay," the boy said. He stood up. "Come on," he said to the girl. "I'll walk you to class and explain to old Harrigan that you were being an angel of mercy." He took the girl's arm, and she smiled up at him.

They left, and the receptionist brought Elizabeth a clipboard with some forms on it. "They were having a fight," Elizabeth said.

"Well, I'd say whatever it was about, it's over now."

"Yes," Elizabeth said. Because of me. Because I fell down on the ice. "I used to live in this dorm," Elizabeth said. "This was the lounge."

"Oh," the receptionist said. "I bet it's changed a lot since then."

"No," Elizabeth said. "It's just the same."

Where the reception desk was, there had been a table with a phone on it where they had checked in and out of the dorm, and along the far wall the couch that she and Tib had sat on at the Tupperware party. Tupper had been sitting on it in his tuxedo when she came down to go to the library.

The receptionist was looking at her. "I bet it hurts," she said.

"Yes," Elizabeth said.

She had planned to be at the library when Tupper came, but he was half an hour early. He stood up when he saw her on the stairs and said, "I tried to call you this afternoon. I wondered if you wanted to go study at the library tomorrow." He had brought Tib a corsage in a white box. He came over and stood at the foot of the stairs, holding the box in both hands.

"I'm studying at the library tonight," Elizabeth said, and walked down the stairs past him, afraid he would put his hand out to stop her, but they were full of the corsage box. "I don't think Tib's ready yet."

"I know. I came early because I wanted to talk to you."

"You'd better call her so she'll know you're here," she said, and walked out the door. She hadn't even checked out, which could have gotten her in trouble with the dorm mother. She found out later that Tib had done it for her.

The receptionist stood up. "I'm going to see if Dr. Larenson can't see you right now," she said. "You are obviously in a lot of pain."

Her ankle was sprained. The doctor wrapped it in an Ace bandage. Halfway through, the phone rang, and he left her sitting on the examining table with her foot propped up while he took the call.

The day after the dance Tupper had called her. "Tell him I'm not here," Elizabeth had told Tib.

"You tell him," Tib had said, and stuck the phone at her, and she had taken the receiver and said, "I don't want to talk to you, but Tib's here. I'm sure she does," and handed the phone back to Tib and walked out of the room. She was halfway across campus before Tib caught up with her.

It had turned colder in the night, and there was a sharp wind that blew the dead leaves across the grass. Tib had brought Elizabeth her coat.

"Thank you," Elizabeth said, and put it on.

"At least you're not totally stupid," Tib said. "Almost, though."

Elizabeth jammed her hands deep in the pockets. "What did Tupper have to say? Did he ask you out again? To one of his Tupperware parties?"

"He didn't ask me out. I asked him to the Harvest Ball because I needed a date. They put you on weekend duty if you didn't have a date, so I asked him. And then after I did it, I was afraid you wouldn't understand."

"Understand what?" Elizabeth said. "You can date whoever you want."

"I don't want to date Tupper, and you know it. If you don't stop acting this way, I'm going to get another roommate."

And she had said, without any idea how important little things like that could be, how hanging up a phone or having a flat tire or saying something could splash out in all directions and sweep you over the edge, she had said, "Maybe you'd better do just that."

They had lived in silence for two weeks. Sharon Oberhausen's roommate didn't come back after Thanksgiving, and Tib moved in with her until the end of the quarter. Then Elizabeth pledged Alpha Phi and moved into the sorority house.

The doctor came back and finished wrapping her ankle. "Do you have a ride home? I'm going to give you a pair of crutches. I don't want you walking on this any more than absolutely necessary."

"No, I'll call my husband." The doctor helped her off the table and onto the crutches. He walked back out to the waiting room and punched buttons on the phone so she could make an outside call.

She dialed her own number and told the ringing to come pick her up. "He'll be over in a minute," she told the receptionist. "I'll wait outside for him."

The receptionist helped her through the door and down the steps. She went back inside, and Elizabeth went out and stood on the curb, looking up at the middle window.

After Tupper took Tib to the Angel Flight dance, he had come and thrown things at her window. She would see them in the mornings when she went to class, plastic jar openers and grapefruit slicers and kitchen scrubber holders, scattered on the lawn and the sidewalk. She had never opened the window, and after a while he had stopped coming.

Elizabeth looked down at the grass. At first she couldn't find the worm. She parted the grass with the tip of her crutch, standing on her good foot. It was there, where she had put it, shrivelled now and darker red, almost black. It was covered with ice crystals.

Elizabeth looked in the front window at the receptionist. When she got up to go file Elizabeth's chart, Elizabeth crossed the street and walked home.

⊣ • • • ⊢

The walk home had made Elizabeth's ankle swell so badly, she could hardly move by the time Paul came home.

"What's the matter with you?" he said angrily. "Why didn't you call me?" He looked at his watch. "Now it's too late to call Brubaker. He and his wife were going to dinner. I suppose you don't feel like going to the concert."

"No," Elizabeth said. "I'll go."

He turned down the thermostat without looking at it. "What in the hell were you doing anyway?"

"I thought I saw a boy I used to know. I was trying to catch up to him."

"A boy you used to know?" Paul said disbelievingly. "In college? What's he doing here? Still waiting to graduate?"

"I don't know," Elizabeth said. She wondered if Sandy ever saw herself on the campus, dressed in the winter-white sweater and pearls, standing in front of her sorority house talking to Chuck Pagano. She's not there, Elizabeth thought. Sandy had not said, "Tell him I'm not here." She had not said, "Maybe you'd better just do that," and because of that and a flat tire, Sondra Dickeson isn't trapped on the campus, waiting to be rescued. Like they are.

"You don't even realize what this little move of yours has cost, do you?" Paul said. "Brubaker told me this afternoon he'd gotten you the job in the dean's office."

He took off the Ace bandage and looked at her ankle. She had gotten the bandage wet walking home. He went to look for another one. He came back carrying the wrinkled job application. "I found this in the bureau drawer. You told me you turned your application in."

"It fell in the gutter," she said.

"Why didn't you throw it away?"

"I thought it might be important," she said, and hobbled over on her crutches and took it away from him.

They were late to the concert because of her ankle, so they didn't get to sit with the Brubakers, but afterward they came over. Dr. Brubaker introduced his wife.

"I'm so sorry about this," Janice Brubaker said. "Ron's been telling them for years they should get that central walk fixed. It used to be heated." She was the woman Sandy had pointed at at the Tupperware party and said was Janice who loved Jesus. She was wearing a dark-red suit and had her hair teased into a bouffant, the way girls had worn their hair when Elizabeth was in college. "It was so nice of you to ask us over, but of course now with your ankle we understand."

"No," Elizabeth said. "We want you to come. I'm doing great, really. It's just a little sprain."

The Brubakers had to go to talk to someone backstage. Paul told the Brubakers how to get to their house and took Elizabeth outside. Because they were late, there hadn't been anyplace to park. Paul had had to park up by the infirmary. Elizabeth said she thought she could walk as far as the car, but it took them fifteen minutes to make it three fourths of the way up the walk.

"This is ridiculous," Paul said angrily, and strode off up the walk to get the car.

She hobbled slowly on up to the end of the walk and sat down on one of the cement benches that had been vents for the heating system. Elizabeth had worn a wool dress and her warmest coat, but she was still cold. She laid her crutches against the bench and looked across at her old dorm.

Someone was standing in front of the dorm, looking up at the middle window. He looked cold. He had his hands jammed in his jean-jacket pockets, and after a few minutes he pulled something out of one of the pockets and threw it at the window.

It's no good, Elizabeth thought, she won't come.

He had made one last attempt to talk to her. It was spring quarter. It had been raining again. The walk was covered with worms. Tib was wearing her Angel Flight uniform, and she looked cold.

Tib had stopped Elizabeth after she came out of the dorm and said, "I saw Tupper the other day. He asked about you, and I told him you were living in the Alpha Phi house."

"Oh," Elizabeth had said, and tried to walk past her, but Tib had kept her there, talking as if nothing had happened, as if they were still roommates. "I'm dating this guy in ROTC. Jim Scates. He's gorgeous!" she had said, as if they were still friends.

"I'm going to be late for class," she said. Tib glanced nervously down the walk, and Elizabeth looked, too, and saw Tupper bearing down on them on his bike. "Thanks a lot," she said angrily.

"He just wants to talk to you."

"About what? How he's taking you to the Alpha Sig dinner dance?" she had said, and turned and walked back into the dorm before he could catch up to her. He had called her on the dorm phone for nearly half an hour, but she hadn't answered, and after a while he had given up.

But he hadn't given up. He was still there, under her windows, throwing grapefruit slicers and egg separators at her, and she still, after all these years, wouldn't come to the window. He would stand there forever, and she would never, never come.

She stood up. The rubber tip of one of her crutches skidded on the ice under the bench, and she almost fell. She steadied herself against the hard cement bench.

Paul honked and pulled over beside the curb, his turn lights flashing. He got out of the car. "The Brubakers are already going to be there, for God's sake," he said. He took the crutches away from her and hurried her to the car, his hand jammed under her armpit. When they pulled away, the boy was still there, looking up at the window, waiting.

⊣•••⊢

The Brubakers were there, waiting in the driveway. Paul left her in the car while he unlocked the door. Dr. Brubaker opened the car door for her and tried to help her with her crutches. Janice kept saying, "Oh, really, we would have understood." They both stood back, looking helpless, while Elizabeth hobbled into the house.

Janice offered to make the coffee, and Elizabeth let her, sitting at the kitchen table, her coat still on. Paul had set out the cups and saucers and the plate of cookies before they left.

"You were at the Tupperware party, weren't you?" Janice said, opening the cupboards to look for the coffee filters. "I never really got a chance to meet you. I saw Sandy Konkel had her hooks in you."

"At the party you said you like Jesus," Elizabeth said. "Are you a Christian?"

Janice had been peeling off a paper filter. She stopped and looked hard at Elizabeth. "Yes," she said. "I am. You know, Sandy Konkel told me a Tupperware party was no place for religion, and I told her that any place was the place for a Christian witness. And I was right, because that witness spoke to you, didn't it, Elizabeth?"

"What if you did something, a long time ago, and you found out it had ruined everything?"

"'For behold your sin will find you out,'" Janice said, holding the coffeepot under the faucet.

"I'm not talking about sin," Elizabeth said. "I'm talking about little things that you wouldn't think would matter so much, like stepping in a puddle or having a fight with somebody. What if you drove off and left somebody standing in the road because you were mad, and it changed their whole life, it made them into a different person? Or what if you turned and walked away from somebody because your feelings were hurt or you wouldn't open your window, and because of that one little thing their whole lives were changed and now she drinks too much, and he killed himself, and you didn't even know you did it."

Janice had opened her purse and started to get out a Bible. She stopped with the Bible only half out of the purse and stared at Elizabeth. "You made somebody kill himself?"

"No," Elizabeth said. "I didn't make him kill himself and I didn't make her get a divorce, but if I hadn't turned and walked away from them that day, everything would have been different."

"Divorce?" Janice said.

"Sandy was right. When you're young all you think about is yourself. All I could think about was how much prettier she was and how she was the kind of girl who had dozens of dates, and when he asked her out, I thought that he'd liked her all along, and I was so hurt. I threw away the egg separator, I was so hurt, and that's why I wouldn't talk to him that day, but I didn't know it was so important! I didn't know there was a puddle there and it was going to sweep me over into the gutter."

Janice laid the Bible on the table. "I don't know what you've done, Elizabeth, but whatever it is, Our Lord can forgive you. I want to read you something." She opened the Bible at a cross-shaped bookmark. "'For God so loved the world that He gave his only begotten Son that whosoever believeth in Him should not perish, but have everlasting life.' Jesus, God's own son, died on a cross and rose again so we could be forgiven for our sins."

"What if he didn't?" Elizabeth said impatiently. "What if he just lay there in the tomb getting colder and colder, until ice crystals formed on him and he never knew if he'd saved them or not?"

"Is the coffee ready yet?" Paul said, coming into the kitchen with Dr. Brubaker. "Or did you womenfolk get to talking and forget all about it?"

"What if they were waiting here for Jesus to save them, they'd been waiting for him all those years and he didn't know it? He'd have to try to save them, wouldn't he? He couldn't just leave them there, standing in the cold looking up at her window? And maybe he couldn't. Maybe they'd get a divorce or kill themselves anyway." Her teeth had started to chatter. "Even if he did save them, he wouldn't be able to save himself. Because it was too late. He was already dead."

Paul moved around the table to her. Janice was paging through the Bible, looking frantically for the right scripture. Paul took hold of Elizabeth's arm, but she shook it off impatiently. "In Matthew we see that he was raised from the dead and is alive today. Right now," Janice said, sounding frightened. "And no matter what sin you have in your heart, he will forgive you if you accept him as your personal Savior."

Elizabeth brought her fist down hard on the table so that the plate of cookies shook. "I'm not talking about sin. I'm talking about opening a window. She stepped in the puddle and the worm went over the edge and drowned. I shouldn't have left it on the sidewalk." She hit the table with her fist again. Dr. Brubaker picked up the stack of coffee cups and put them on the counter, as if he were afraid she might start throwing them at the wall. "I should have put it in the grass."

Paul left for work without even having breakfast. Elizabeth's ankle had swollen up so badly she could hardly get her slippers on, but she got up and made the coffee. The filters were still lying on the counter where Janice Brubaker had left them.

"Weren't you satisfied that you'd ruined your chances for a job, you had to ruin mine, too?"

"I'm sorry about last night," she said. "I'm going to fill out my job application today and take it over to the campus. When my ankle heals..."

"It's supposed to warm up today," Paul said. "I turned the furnace off."

After he was gone, she filled out the application. She tried to erase the dark smear that the worm had left, but it wouldn't come out, and there was one question that she couldn't read. Her fingers were stiff with cold, and she had to stop and blow on them several times but she filled in as many questions as she could and folded it up and took it over to the campus.

The girl in the yellow slicker was standing at the end of the walk, talking to a girl in an Angel Flight uniform. She hobbled toward them with her head down, trying to hurry, listening for the sound of Tupper's bike.

"He asked about you," Tib said, and Elizabeth looked up.

She didn't look at all the way Elizabeth remembered her. She was a little overweight and not very pretty, the kind of girl who wouldn't have been able to get a date for the dance. Her short hair made her round face look even plumper. She looked hopeful and a little worried.

Don't worry, Elizabeth thought. I'm here. She didn't look at herself. She concentrated on getting up even with them at the right time.

"I told him you were living in the Alpha Phi house," Tib said.

"Oh," she heard her own voice, and under it the hum of a bicycle.

"I'm dating this guy in ROTC. He's absolutely gorgeous."

There was a pause, and then Elizabeth's voice said, "Thanks a lot," and Elizabeth pushed the rubber end of her crutch against a patch of ice and went down.

For a minute she couldn't see anything for the pain. "I've broken it," she thought, and clenched her fists to keep from screaming.

"Are you all right?" Tib said, kneeling in front of her so she couldn't see anything. No, not you! Not you! For a minute she was afraid that it hadn't worked, that the girl had turned and walked away. But after all, this was not a stranger but only herself, who was too kind to let a worm drown. She had only gone around to Elizabeth's other side, where she couldn't see her. "Did she break it?" she said. "Should I go call an ambulance or something?"

No. "No," Elizabeth said. "I'm fine. If you could just help me up."

The girl who had been Elizabeth Wilson put her books down on the cement bench and came and knelt down by Elizabeth. "I hope we don't collapse in a heap," she said, and smiled at Elizabeth. She was a pretty girl. I didn't know that either, Elizabeth thought, even when Tupper told me. She took hold of Elizabeth's arm and Tib took hold of the other.

"Tripping innocent passersby again, I see. How many times have I told you not to do that?" And here, finally, was Tupper. He had laid his bike flat in the grass and put his bag of Tupperware beside it.

Tib and the girl that had been herself let go and stepped back and he knelt beside her. "They're not bad girls, really. They just like to play practical jokes. But banana peels is going too far, girls," he said, so close she could feel his warm breath on her cheek. She turned to look at him, suddenly afraid that he would be different, too, but it was only Tupper, who she had loved all these years. He put his arm around her. "Now just put your arm around my neck, sweetheart. That's right. Elizabeth, come over here and atone for your sins by helping this pretty lady up."

She had already picked her books up and was holding them against her chest, looking angry and eager to get away. She looked at Tib, but Tib was picking up the crutches, stooping down in her high heels because she couldn't bend over in her Angel Flight skirt.

She put her books down again and came around to Elizabeth's other side to take hold of her arm, and Elizabeth grabbed for her hand instead and held it tightly so she couldn't get away. "I took her to the dance because she helped with the Tupperware party. I told her I owed her a favor," he said, and Elizabeth turned and looked at him.

He was not looking at her really. He was looking past her at the other Elizabeth, who would not answer the phone, who would not come to the window, but he seemed to be looking at her, and on his young remembered face there was a look of such naked, vulnerable love that it was like a blow.

"I told you so," Tib said. She laid the crutches against the bench.

"I'm sure this lady doesn't want to hear this," Elizabeth said.

"I was going to tell you at the party, but that idiot Sharon Oberhausen…"

Tib brought over the crutches. "After I asked him, I thought, 'What if she thinks I'm trying to steal her boyfriend?' and I got so worried I was afraid to tell you. I really only asked him to get out of weekend duty. I mean, I don't like him or anything."

Tupper grinned at Elizabeth. "I try to pay my debts, and this is the thanks I get. You wouldn't get mad at me if I took your roommate to a dance, would you?"

"I might," Elizabeth said. It was cold sitting on the cement. She was starting to shiver. "But I'd forgive you."

"You see that?" he said.

"I see," Elizabeth said disgustedly, but she was smiling at him now. "Don't you think we'd better get this innocent passerby up off the sidewalk before she freezes to death?"

"Upsy-daisy, sweetheart," Tupper said, and in one easy motion she was up and sitting on the stone bench.

"Thank you," she said. Her teeth were chattering with the cold.

Tupper knelt in front of her and examined her ankle. "It looks pretty swollen," he said. "Do you want us to call somebody?"

"No, my husband will be along any minute. I'll just sit here till he comes."

Tib fished Elizabeth's application out of the puddle. "I'm afraid it's ruined," she said.

"It doesn't matter."

Tupper picked up his bag of bowls. "Say," he said, "you wouldn't be interested in having a Tupperware party? As hostess, you could earn valuable points toward..."

"Tupper!" Tib said.

"Will you leave this poor lady alone?" Elizabeth said.

He held up the sack. "Only if you'll go with me to deliver my lettuce crispers to the Sigma Chi house."

"I'll go," Tib said. "There's this darling Sigma Chi I've been wanting to meet."

"And I'll go," Elizabeth said, putting her arm around Tib. "I don't trust the kind of boyfriend you find on your own. Jim Scates is a real creep. Didn't Sharon tell you what he did to Marilyn Reed?"

Tupper handed Elizabeth the sack of bowls while he stood his bike up. Elizabeth handed them to Tib.

"Are you sure you're all right?" Tupper said. "It's cold out here. You could wait for your husband in the student union."

She wished she could put her hand on his cheek just once. "I'll be fine," she said.

The three of them went down the walk toward Frasier, Tupper pushing the bike. When they got even with Carter Hall, they cut across the grass toward Frasier. She watched them until she couldn't see them anymore, and then sat there a while longer on the cold bench. She had hoped that something might happen, some sign that she had rescued them, but nothing happened. Her ankle didn't hurt anymore. It had stopped the minute Tupper touched it.

She continued to sit there. It seemed to her to be getting colder, though she had stopped shivering, and after a while she got up and walked home, leaving the crutches where they were.

It was cold in the house. Elizabeth turned the thermostat up and sat down at the kitchen table, still in her coat, waiting for the heat to come on. When it didn't, she remembered that Paul had turned the furnace off, and she went and got a blanket and wrapped up in it on the couch. Her ankle did not hurt at all, though it felt cold. When the phone rang, she could hardly move it. It took her several rings to make it to the phone.

"I thought you weren't going to answer," Paul said. "I made an appointment with a Dr. Jamieson for you this afternoon at three. He's a psychiatrist."

"Paul," she said. She was so cold it was hard to talk. 'I'm sorry."

"It's a little late for that, isn't it?" he said. "I told Dr. Brubaker you were on muscle relaxants for your ankle. I don't know whether he bought it or not." He hung up.

"Too late," Elizabeth said. She hung up the phone. The back of her hand was covered with ice crystals. "Paul," she tried to say, but her lips were stiff with cold, and no sound came out.

# At the Rialto

Seriousness of mind was a prerequisite for understanding
Newtonian physics. 1 am not convinced it is not a handicap
in understanding quantum theory.

> —Excerpt from Dr. Gedanken's keynote
> address to the1988 International Congress
> of Quantum Physicists Annual Meeting,
> Hollywood, California

I got to Hollywood around one-thirty and started trying to check into
the Rialto.

"Sorry, we don't have any rooms," the girl behind the desk said.
"We're all booked up with some science thing."

"I'm with the science thing," I said. "Dr. Ruth Baringer. I reserved
a double."

"There are a bunch of Republicans here, too, and a tour group from
Finland. They told me when I started work here that they got all these
movie people, but the only one so far was that guy who played the friend
of that other guy in that one movie. You're not a movie person, are you?"

"No," I said. "I'm with the science thing. Dr. Ruth Baringer. "

"My name's Tiffany," she said. "I'm not actually a hotel clerk at all.
I'm just working here to pay for my transcendental posture lessons. I'm
really a model-slash-actress."

"I'm a quantum physicist," I said, trying to get things back on track.
"The name is Ruth Baringer."

She messed with the computer for a minute. "I don't show a reservation for you."

"Maybe it's in Dr. Mendoza's name. I'm sharing a room with her."

She messed with the computer some more. "I don't show a reservation for her either. Are you sure you don't want the Disneyland Hotel? A lot of people get the two confused."

"I want the Rialto," I said, rummaging through my bag for my notebook. "I have a confirmation number. W-three-seven-four-two-oh."

She typed it in. "Are you Dr. Gedanken?" she asked.

"Excuse me," an elderly man said.

"I'll be right with you," Tiffany told him. "How long do you plan to stay with us, Dr. Gedanken?" she asked me.

"*Excuse* me," the man said, sounding desperate. He had bushy white hair and a dazed expression, as if he had just been through a horrific experience or had been trying to check into the Rialto.

He wasn't wearing any socks. I wondered if *he* was Dr. Gedanken. Dr. Gedanken was the main reason I'd decided to come to the meeting. I had missed his lecture on wave-particle duality last year, but I had read the text of it in the *ICQP Journal,* and it had actually seemed to make sense, which is more than you can say for most of quantum theory. He was giving the keynote address this year, and I was determined to hear it.

It wasn't Dr. Gedanken. "My name is Dr. Whedbee," the elderly man said. "You gave me the wrong room."

"All our rooms are pretty much the same," Tiffany said. "Except for how many beds they have in them and stuff."

"My room has a *person* in it!" he said. "Dr. Sleeth. From the University of Texas at Austin. She was changing her clothes." His hair seemed to get wilder as he spoke. "She thought I was a serial killer."

"And your name is Dr. Whedbee?" Tiffany asked, fooling with the computer again. "I don't show a reservation for you."

Dr. Whedbee began to cry. Tiffany got out a paper towel, wiped off the counter, and turned back to me. "May I help you?" she said.

> Thursday, 7:30-9 P.M. *Opening Ceremonies.* Dr. Halvard Onofrio, University of Maryland at College Park, will speak on the topic, "Doubts Surrounding the Heisenberg Uncertainty Principle." Ballroom.

I finally got my room at five, after Tiffany went off duty. Till then I sat around the lobby with Dr. Whedbee, listening to Abey Fields complain about Hollywood.

"What's wrong with Racine?" he said. "Why do we always have to go to these exotic places, like Hollywood? And St. Louis last year wasn't much better. The Institute Henri Poincaré people kept going off to see the arch and Busch Stadium."

"Speaking of St. Louis," Dr. Takumi said, "have you seen David yet?"

"No," I said.

"Oh, really?" she said. "Last year at the annual meeting you two were practically inseparable. Moonlight riverboat rides and all."

"What's on the programming tonight?" I said to Abey.

"David was just here," Dr. Takumi said. "He said to tell you he was going out to look at the stars in the sidewalk."

"That's exactly what I'm talking about," Abey said. "Riverboat rides and movie stars. What do those things have to do with quantum theory? Racine would have been an appropriate setting for a group of physicists. Not like this...this...do you realize we're practically across the street from Grauman's Chinese Theatre? And Hollywood Boulevard's where all those gangs hang out. If they catch you wearing red or blue, they'll—"

He stopped. "Is that Dr. Gedanken?" he asked, staring at the front desk.

I turned and looked. A short roundish man with a mustache was trying to check in. "No," I said. "That's Dr. Onofrio."

"Oh, yes," Abey said, consulting his program book. "He's speaking tonight at the opening ceremonies. On the Heisenberg uncertainty principle. Are you going?"

"I'm not sure," I said, which was supposed to be a joke, but Abey didn't laugh.

"I must meet Dr. Gedanken. He's just gotten funding for a new project."

I wondered what Dr. Gedanken's new project was—I would have loved to work with him.

"I'm hoping he'll come to my workshop on the wonderful world of quantum physics," Abey said, still watching the desk. Amazingly enough, Dr. Onofrio seemed to have gotten a key and was heading for the elevators. "I think his project has something to do with understanding quantum theory."

Well, that let me out. I didn't understand quantum theory at all. I sometimes had a sneaking suspicion nobody else did either, including Abey Fields, and that they just weren't willing to admit it.

I mean, an electron is a particle except it acts like a wave. In fact, a neutron acts like two waves and interferes with itself (or each other), and you can't really measure any of this stuff properly because of the Heisenberg uncertainty principle, and that isn't the worst of it. When you set up a Josephson junction to figure out what rules the electrons obey, they sneak past the barrier to the other side, and they don't seem to care much about the limits of the speed of light either, and Schrödinger's cat is neither alive nor dead till you open the box, and it all makes about as much sense as Tiffany's calling me Dr. Gedanken.

Which reminded me, I had promised to call Darlene and give her our room number. I didn't have a room number, but if I waited much longer she'd have left. She was flying to Denver to speak at CU and then coming on to Hollywood sometime tomorrow morning. I interrupted Abey in the middle of his telling me how beautiful Cleveland was in the winter and went to call her.

"I don't have a room yet," I said when she answered. "Should I leave a message on your answering machine or do you want to give me your number in Denver?"

"Never mind all that," Darlene said. "Have you seen David yet?"

> To illustrate the problems of the concept of wave function, Dr. Schrödinger imagines a cat being put into a box with a piece of uranium, a bottle of poison gas, and a Geiger counter. If a uranium nucleus disintegrates while the cat is in the box, it will release radiation, which will set off the Geiger counter and break the bottle of poison gas. It is impossible in quantum theory to predict whether a uranium nucleus will disintegrate while the cat is in the box, and only possible to calculate uranium's probable half-life; therefore, the cat is neither alive nor dead until we open the box.
> — From "The Wonderful World of Quantum Physics,"
> A seminar presented at the ICQP Annual Meeting
> by A. Fields, Ph.D., University of Nebraska at Wahoo

I completely forgot to warn Darlene about Tiffany, the model-slash-actress.

"What do you mean you're trying to avoid David?" she had asked me at least three times. "Why would you do a stupid thing like that?"

Because in St. Louis I ended up on a riverboat in the moonlight and didn't make it back until the conference was over.

"Because I want to attend the programming," I said the third time around, "Not a wax museum. I am a middle-aged woman."

"And David is a middle-aged man who, I might add, is absolutely charming."

"Charm is for quarks," I said, and hung up, feeling smug until I remembered I hadn't told her about Tiffany. I went back to the front desk, thinking maybe Dr. Onofrio's success signaled a change. Tiffany asked, "May I help you?" and left me standing there.

After a while I gave up and went back to the red-and-gold sofas.

"David was here again," Dr. Takumi said. "He said to tell you he was going to the wax museum."

"There *are* no wax museums in Racine," Abey said.

"What's the programming for tonight?" I said, taking Abey's program away from him.

"There's a mixer at six-thirty and the opening ceremonies in the ballroom and then some seminars." I read the descriptions of the seminars. There was one on the Josephson junction. Electrons were able to somehow tunnel through an insulated barrier even though they didn't have the required energy. Maybe I could somehow get a room without checking in.

"If we were in Racine," Abey said, looking at his watch, "we'd already be checked in and on our way to dinner."

Dr. Onofrio emerged from the elevator, still carrying his bags. He came over and sank down on the sofa next to Abey.

"Did they give you a room with a seminaked woman in it?" Dr. Whedbee asked.

"I don't know," Dr. Onofrio said. "I couldn't find it." He looked sadly at the key. "They gave me twelve eighty-two, but the room numbers go only up to seventy-five."

"I think I'll attend the seminar on chaos," I said.

> The most serious difficulty quantum theory faces today is not the inherent limitation of measurement capability or the EPR paradox. It is the lack of a paradigm. Quantum theory has no working model, no metaphor that properly defines it.
> — Excerpt from Dr. Gedanken's keynote address

I got to my room at six, after a brief skirmish with the bellboy-slash-actor, who couldn't remember where he'd stored my suitcase, and unpacked.

My clothes, which had been permanent press all the way from MIT, underwent a complete wave-function collapse the moment I opened my suitcase and came out looking like Schrödinger's almost-dead cat.

By the time I had called housekeeping for an iron, taken a bath, given up on the iron, and steamed a dress in the shower, I had missed the "Mixer with Munchies" and was half an hour late for Dr. Onofrio's opening remarks.

I opened the door to the ballroom as quietly as I could and slid inside. I had hoped they would be late getting started, but a man I didn't recognize was already introducing the speaker. "—and an inspiration to all of us in the field."

I dived for the nearest chair and sat down.

"Hi," David said. "I've been looking all over for you. Where were you?"

"Not at the wax museum," I whispered.

"You should have been," he whispered back. "It was great. They had John Wayne, Elvis, and Tiffany the model-slash-actress with the brain of a pea-slash-amoeba."

"Shh," I said.

"—the person we've all been waiting to hear, Dr. Ringgit Dinari."

"What happened to Dr. Onofrio?" I asked.

"Shhh," David said.

Dr. Dinari looked a lot like Dr. Onofrio. She was short, roundish, and mustached and was wearing a rainbow-striped caftan. "I will be your guide this evening into a strange new world," she said, "a world where all that you thought you knew, all common sense, all accepted wisdom, must be discarded. A world where all the rules have changed and it sometimes seems there are no rules at all."

She sounded just like Dr. Onofrio, too. He had given this same speech two years ago in Cincinnati. I wondered if he had undergone some strange transformation during his search for room 1282 and was now a woman.

"Before I go any further," Dr. Dinari said, "how many of you have already channeled?"

*Newtonian physics had as its model the machine. The metaphor of the machine, with its interrelated parts, its gears and wheels, its causes and effects, was what made it possible to think about Newtonian physics.*

*— Excerpt from Dr. Gedanken's keynote address*

"You *knew* we were in the wrong place," I hissed at David when we got out to the lobby.

When we stood up to leave, Dr. Dinari had extended her pudgy hand in its rainbow-striped sleeve and called out in a voice a lot like Charlton Heston's, "O Unbelievers! Leave not, for here only is reality!"

"Actually, channeling would explain a lot," David said, grinning.

"If the opening remarks aren't in the ballroom, where are they?"

"Beats me," he said. "Want to go see the Capitol Records building? It's shaped like a stack of records."

"I want to go to the opening remarks."

"The beacon on top blinks out 'Hollywood' in Morse code."

I went over to the front desk.

"Can I help you?" the clerk behind the desk said. "My name is Natalie, and I'm an—"

"Where is the ICQP meeting this evening?" I said.

"They're in the ballroom."

"I'll bet you didn't have any dinner," David said. "I'll buy you an ice-cream cone. There's this great place that has the ice-cream cone Ryan O'Neal bought for Tatum in *Paper Moon.*"

"A channeler's in the ballroom," I told Natalie. "I'm looking for the ICQP."

She fiddled with the computer. "I'm sorry. I don't show a reservation for them."

"How about Grauman's Chinese?" David said. "You want reality? You want Charlton Heston? You want to see quantum theory in action?" He grabbed my hands. "Come with me," he said seriously.

In St. Louis I had suffered a wave-function collapse a lot like what had happened to my clothes when I opened the suitcase. I had ended up on a riverboat halfway to New Orleans that time. It happened again, and the next thing I knew, I was walking around the courtyard of Grauman's Chinese, eating an ice-cream cone and trying to fit my feet into Myrna Loy's footprints.

She must have been a midget or had her feet bound as a child. So, apparently, had Debbie Reynolds, Dorothy Lamour, and Wallace Beery. The only footprints I came close to fitting were Donald Duck's.

"I see this as a map of the microcosm," David said, sweeping his hand over the slightly irregular pavement of printed and signed cement squares. "See, there are all these tracks. We know something's been here, and the prints are pretty much the same, only every once in a while you've got this"—he knelt down and pointed at the print of John Wayne's clenched fist—"and over here"—he walked toward the box office and pointed to the print of Betty Grable's leg—"and we can figure out the signatures, but what is this reference to 'Sid' that keeps popping up? And what does this mean?"

He pointed at Red Skelton's square. It said, "Thanks Sid We Dood It."

"You keep thinking you've found a pattern," David said, crossing over to the other side, "but Van Johnson's square is kind of sandwiched in here at an angle between Esther Williams and Cantinflas, and who the hell is May Robson? And why are all these squares over here empty?"

He had managed to maneuver me over behind the display of Academy Award winners. It was an accordionlike wrought-iron screen. I was in the fold between 1944 and 1945.

"And as if that isn't enough, you suddenly realize you're standing in the courtyard. You're not even in the theater."

"And that's what you think is happening in quantum theory?" I said weakly. I was backed up into Bing Crosby, who had won for Best Actor in *Going My Way*. "You think we're not in the theater yet?"

"I think we know as much about quantum theory as we can figure out about May Robson from her footprints," he said, putting his hand up to Ingrid Bergman's cheek (Best Actress, *Gaslight)* and blocking my escape. "I don't think we understand anything *about* quantum theory, not tunneling, not complementarity." He leaned toward me. "Not passion."

The best movie of 1945 was *Lost Weekend*. "Dr. Gedanken understands it," I said, disentangling myself from the Academy Award winners and David. "Did you know he's putting together a new research team for a big project on understanding quantum theory?"

"Yes," David said. "Want to see a movie?"

"There's a seminar on chaos at nine," I said, stepping over the Marx Brothers. "I have to get back."

"If it's chaos you want, you should stay right here," he said, stopping to look at Irene Dunne's handprints. "We could see the movie and then go have dinner. There's this place near Hollywood and Vine that has the mashed potatoes Richard Dreyfuss made into Devil's Tower in *Close Encounters*."

"I want to meet Dr. Gedanken," I said, making it safely to the sidewalk. I looked back at David. He had gone back to the other side of the courtyard and was looking at Roy Rogers's signature.

"Are you kidding? He doesn't understand it any better than we do."

"Well, at least he's trying."

"So am I. The problem is, how can one neutron interfere with itself, and why are there only two of Trigger's hoofprints here?"

"It's eight fifty-five," I said. "I am going to the chaos seminar."

"If you can find it," he said, getting down on one knee to look at the signature.

"I'll find it," I said grimly. He stood up and grinned at me, his hands in his pockets. "It's a great movie," he said.

It was happening again. I turned and practically ran across the street.

"*Benji IX* is showing," he shouted after me. "He accidentally exchanges bodies with a Siamese cat."

> Thursday, 9-10 P.M. "The Science of Chaos." I. Durcheinander, University of Leipzig. A seminar on the structure of chaos. Principles of chaos will be discussed, including the Butterfly Effect, fractals, and insolid billowing. Clara Bow Room.

I couldn't find the chaos seminar. The Clara Bow Room, where it was supposed to be, was empty. A meeting of vegetarians was next door in the Fatty Arbuckle Room, and all the other conference rooms were locked. The channeler was still in the ballroom. "Come!" she commanded when I opened the door. "Understanding awaits!" I went upstairs to bed.

I had forgotten to call Darlene. She would have left for Denver already, but I called her answering machine and told it the room number in case she picked up her messages. In the morning I would have to tell the front desk to give her a key. I went to bed.

I didn't sleep well. The air conditioner went off during the night, which meant I didn't have to steam my suit when I got up the next morning. I got dressed and went downstairs. The programming started at nine with Abey Fields's Wonderful World workshop in the Mary Pickford Room, a breakfast buffet in the ballroom, and a slide presentation on "Delayed Choice Experiments" in Cecil B. DeMille A on the mezzanine level.

The breakfast buffet sounded wonderful, even though it always turns out to be urn coffee and donuts. I hadn't had anything but an ice-cream cone since noon the day before, but if David was around, he would be somewhere close to the food, and I wanted to steer clear of him. Last night it had been Grauman's Chinese. Today I was likely to end up at Knotts' Berry Farm. I wasn't going to let that happen, even if he was charming.

It was pitch-dark inside Cecil B. DeMille A. Even the slide on the screen up front appeared to be black. "As you can see," Dr. Lvov said, "the laser pulse is already in motion before the experimenter sets up the wave or particle detector." He clicked to the next slide, which was dark gray. "We used a Mach-Zender interferometer with two mirrors and a particle detector. For the first series of tries we allowed the experimenter to decide which apparatus he would use by whatever method he wished. For the second series we used that most primitive of randomizers—"

He clicked again, to a white slide with black polka dots that gave off enough light for me to be able to spot an empty chair on the aisle ten rows up. I hurried to get to it before the slide changed, and sat down.

"—a pair of dice. Alley's experiments had shown us that when the particle detector was in place, the light was detected as a particle, and when the wave detector was in place, the light showed wavelike behavior, no matter when the choice of apparatus was made."

"Hi," David said. "You've missed five black slides, two gray ones, and a white with black polka dots."

"Shh," I said.

"In our two series, we hoped to ascertain whether the consciousness of the decision affected the outcome." Dr. Lvov clicked to another black slide. "As you can see, the graph shows no effective difference between the tries in which the experimenter chose the detection apparatus and those in which the apparatus was randomly chosen."

"You want to go get some breakfast?" David whispered.

"I already ate," I whispered back, and waited for my stomach to growl and give me away. It did.

"There's a great place down near Hollywood and Vine that has the waffles Katharine Hepburn made for Spencer Tracy in *Woman of the Year.*"

"Shh," I said.

"And after breakfast we could go to Frederick's of Hollywood and see the bra museum."

"Will you please be quiet? I can't hear."

"Or see," he said, but he subsided more or less for the remaining ninety-two black, gray, and polka-dotted slides.

Dr. Lvov turned on the lights and blinked smilingly at the audience. "Consciousness had no discernible effect on the results of the experiment. As one of my lab assistants put it, 'The little devil knows what you're going to do before you know it yourself.'"

This was apparently supposed to be a joke, but I didn't think it was very funny. I opened my program and tried to find something to go to that David wouldn't be caught dead at.

"Are you two going to breakfast?" Dr. Thibodeaux asked.

"Yes," David said.

"No," I said.

"Dr. Hotard and I wished to eat somewhere that is *vraiment* Hollywood."

"David knows just the place," I said. "He's been telling me about this great place where they have the grapefruit James Cagney shoved in Mae Clark's face in *Public Enemy.*"

Dr. Hotard hurried up, carrying a camera and four guidebooks. "And then perhaps you would show us Grauman's Chinese Theatre," he asked David.

"Of course he will," I said. "I'm sorry I can't go with you, but I promised Dr. Verikovsky I'd be at his lecture on Boolean logic. And after Grauman's Chinese, David can take you to the bra museum at Frederick's of Hollywood."

"And the Brown Derby?" Thibodeaux asked. "I have heard it is shaped like a *chapeau.*"

They dragged him off. I watched till they were safely out of the lobby and then ducked upstairs and into Dr Whedbee's lecture on information theory. Dr. Whedbee wasn't there.

"He went to find an overhead projector," Dr. Takumi said. She had half a donut on a paper plate in one hand and a styrofoam cup in the other.

"Did you get that at the breakfast brunch?" I asked.

"Yes. It was the last one. And they ran out of coffee right after I got there. You weren't in Abey Fields's thing, were you?" She set the coffee cup down and took a bite of the donut.

"No," I said, wondering if I should try to take her by surprise or just wrestle the donut away from her.

"You didn't miss anything. He raved the whole time about how we should have had the meeting in Racine." She popped the last piece of donut into her mouth. "Have you seen David yet?"

> Friday, 9-10 A.M. "The Eureka Experiment: A Slide Presentation." J. Lvov, Eureka College. Descriptions, results, and conclusions of Lvov's delayed conscious/randomed choice experiments. Cecil B. DeMille A.

Dr. Whedbee eventually came in carrying an overhead projector, the cord trailing behind him. He plugged it in. The light didn't go on.

"Here," Dr. Takumi said, handing me her plate and cup. "I have one of these at Caltech. It needs its fractal-basin boundaries adjusted." She whacked the side of the projector.

There weren't even any crumbs left of the donut. There was about a millimeter of coffee in the bottom of the cup. I was about to stoop to new depths when she hit it again. The light came on. "I learned that in the chaos seminar last night," she said, grabbing the cup away from me and draining it. "You should have been there. The Clara Bow Room was packed."

"I believe I'm ready to begin," Dr. Whedbee said. Dr. Takumi and I sat down. "Information is the transmission of meaning," Dr. Whedbee said. He wrote "meaning" or possibly "information" on the screen with a green Magic Marker. "When information is randomized, meaning cannot be transmitted, and we have a state of entropy." He wrote it under "meaning" with a red Magic Marker. His handwriting appeared to be completely illegible.

"States of entropy vary from low entropy, such as the mild static on your car radio, to high entropy, a state of complete disorder, of randomness and confusion, in which no information at all is being communicated."

Oh, my God, I thought. I forgot to tell the hotel about Darlene. The next time Dr. Whedbee bent over to inscribe hieroglyphics on the screen, I sneaked out and went down to the desk, hoping Tiffany hadn't come on duty yet. She had.

"May I help you?" she asked.

"I'm in room six-sixty-three," I said. "I'm sharing a room with Dr. Darlene Mendoza. She's coming in this morning, and she'll be needing a key."

"For what?" Tiffany said.

"To get into the room. I may be in one of the lectures when she gets here."

"Why doesn't she have a key?"

"Because she isn't here yet."

"I thought you said she was sharing a room with you."

"She *will* be sharing a room with me. Room six-sixty-three. Her name is Darlene Mendoza."

"And your name?" she asked, hands poised over the computer.

"Ruth Baringer."

"We don't show a reservation for you."

> *We have made impressive advances in quantum physics in the ninety years since Planck's constant, but they have by and large been advances in technology, not theory. We can make advances in theory only when we have a model we can visualize.*
> — Excerpt from Dr. Gedanken's keynote address

I high-entropied with Tiffany for awhile on the subjects of my not having a reservation and the air conditioning and then switched back suddenly to the problem of Darlene's key, in the hope of catching her off guard. It worked about as well as Alley's delayed-choice experiments.

In the middle of my attempting to explain that Darlene was not the air conditioning repairman, Abey Fields came up.

"Have you seen Dr. Gedanken?"

I shook my head.

"I was sure he'd come to my Wonderful World workshop, but he didn't, and the hotel says they can't find his reservation," he said, scanning the lobby. "I found out what his new project is, incidentally, and I'd be perfect for it. He's going to find a paradigm for quantum theory. Is that him?" he said, pointing at an elderly man getting in the elevator.

"I think that's Dr. Whedbee," I said, but he had already sprinted across the lobby to the elevator.

He nearly made it. The elevator slid to a close just as he got there. He pushed the elevator button several times to make the door open again, and when that didn't work, tried to readjust its fractal-basin boundaries. I turned back to the desk.

"May I help you?" Tiffany said.

"You may," I said. "My roommate, Darlene Mendoza, will be arriving some time this morning. She's a producer. She's here to cast the female lead in a new movie starring Robert Redford and Harrison Ford. When she gets here, give her her key. And fix the air conditioning."

"Yes, ma'am," she said.

> *The Josephson junction is designed so that electrons must obtain additional energy to surmount the energy barrier. It*

*was found, however, that some electrons simply tunnel, as Heinz Pagel put it, "right through the wall."*
— From "The Wonderful World of Quantum Physics," A. Fields, UNW

Abey had stopped banging on the elevator button and was trying to pry the elevator doors apart. I went out the side door and up to Hollywood Boulevard. David's restaurant was near Hollywood and Vine. I turned the other direction, toward Grauman's Chinese, and ducked into the first restaurant I saw.

"I'm Stephanie," the waitress said. "How many are there in your party?"

There was no one remotely in my vicinity. "Are you an actress-slash-model?" I asked her.

"Yes," she said. "I'm working here part-time to pay for my holistic hairstyling lessons."

"There's one of me," I said, holding up my forefinger to make it perfectly clear. "I want a table away from the window."

She led me to a table in front of the window, handed me a menu the size of the macrocosm, and put another one down across from me. "Our breakfast specials today are papaya stuffed with salmonberries and nasturtium/radicchio salad with a balsamic vinaigrette. I'll take your order when your other party arrives."

I stood the extra menu up so it hid me from the window, opened the other one, and read the breakfast entrees. They all seemed to have cilantro or lemongrass in their names. I wondered if "radicchio" could possibly be Californian for "donut."

"Hi," David said, grabbing the standing-up menu and sitting down. "The sea-urchin pâté looks good."

I was actually glad to see him. "How did you get here?" I asked.

"Tunneling," he said. "What exactly is extra-virgin olive oil?"

"I wanted a donut," I said pitifully.

He took my menu away from me, laid it on the table, and stood up. "There's a great place next door that's got the donut Clark Gable taught Claudette Colbert how to dunk in *It Happened One Night*."

The great place was probably out in Long Beach someplace, but I was too weak with hunger to resist him. I stood up. Stephanie hurried over.

"Will there be anything else?" she asked.

"We're leaving," David said.

"Okay, then," she said, tearing a check off her pad and slapping it down on the table. "I hope you enjoyed your breakfast."

*Finding such a paradigm is difficult, if not impossible. Due to Planck's constant the world we see is largely dominated by Newtonian mechanics. Particles are particles, waves are waves, and objects do not suddenly vanish through walls and reappear on the other side. It is only on the subatomic level that quantum effects dominate.*
— Excerpt from Dr. Gedanken's keynote address

The restaurant was next door to Grauman's Chinese, which made me a little nervous, but it had eggs and bacon and toast and orange juice and coffee. And donuts.

"I thought you were having breakfast with Dr. Thibodeaux and Dr. Hotard," I said, dunking one in my coffee. "What happened to them?"

"They went to Forest Lawn. Dr. Hotard wanted to see the church where Ronald Reagan got married."

"He got married at Forest Lawn?"

He took a bite of my donut. "In the Wee Kirk of the Heather. Did you know Forest Lawn's got the World's Largest Oil Painting Incorporating a Religious Theme?"

"So why didn't you go with them?"

"And miss the movie?" He grabbed both my hands across the table. "There's a matinee at two o'clock. Come with me."

I could feel things starting to collapse. "I have to get back," I said, trying to disentangle my hands. "There's a panel on the EPR paradox at two o'clock."

"There's another showing at five. And one at eight."

"Dr. Gedanken's giving the keynote address at eight."

"You know what the problem is?" he said, still holding on to my hands. "The problem is, it isn't really Grauman's Chinese Theatre, it's Mann's, so Sid isn't even around to ask. Like, why do some pairs like Joanne Woodward and Paul Newman share the same square and other pairs don't? Like Ginger Rogers and Fred Astaire?"

"You know what the problem is?" I said, wrenching my hands free. "The problem is you don't take anything seriously. This is a conference, but you don't care anything about the programming or hearing Dr.

Gedanken speak or trying to understand quantum theory!" I fumbled in my purse for some money for the check.

"I thought that was what we were talking about," David said, sounding surprised. "The problem is, where do these lion statues that guard the door fit in? And what about all those empty spaces?"

> Friday, 2-3 P.M. *Panel Discussion on the EPR Paradox.*
> I. Takumi, moderator, R. Iverson, L. S. Ping. A discussion of
> the latest research on singlet-state correlations, including
> nonlocal influences, the Calcutta proposal, and passion.
> Keystone Kops Room.

I went up to my room as soon as I got back to the Rialto to see if Darlene was there yet. She wasn't, and when I tried to call the desk, the phone wouldn't work. I went back down to the registration desk. There was no one there. I waited fifteen minutes and then went into the panel on the EPR paradox.

"The Einstein-Podolsky-Rosen paradox cannot be reconciled with quantum theory," Dr. Takumi was saying. "I don't care what the experiments seem to indicate. Two electrons at opposite ends of the universe can't affect each other simultaneously without destroying the entire theory of the space-time continuum."

She was right. Even if it was possible to find a model of quantum theory, what about the EPR paradox? If an experimenter measured one of a pair of electrons that had originally collided, it changed the cross-correlation of the other instantaneously, even if the electrons were lightyears apart. It was as if they were eternally linked by that one collision, sharing the same square forever, even if they were on opposite sides of the universe.

"If the electrons *communicated* instantaneously, I'd agree with you," Dr. Iverson said, "but they don't, they simply influence each other. Dr. Shimony defined this influence in his paper on passion, and my experiment clearly—"

I thought of David leaning over me between the best pictures of 1944 and 1945, saying, "I think we know as much about quantum theory as we do about May Robson from her footprints."

"You can't explain it away by inventing new terms," Dr. Takumi said.

"I completely disagree," Dr. Ping said. "Passion at a distance is not just an invented term. It's a demonstrated phenomenon."

It certainly is, I thought, thinking about David taking the macrocosmic menu out of the window and saying, "The sea-urchin pâté looks good." It didn't matter where the electron went after the collision. Even if it went in the opposite direction from Hollywood and Vine, even if it stood a menu in the window to hide it, the other electron would still come and rescue it from the radicchio and buy it a donut.

"A demonstrated phenomenon!" Dr. Takumi said. "Ha!" She banged her moderator's gavel for emphasis.

"Are you saying passion doesn't exist?" Dr. Ping said, getting very red in the face.

"I'm saying one measly experiment is hardly a demonstrated phenomenon."

"One measly experiment! I spent five years on this project!" Dr. Iverson said, shaking his fist at her. "I'll show you passion at a distance!"

"Try it, and I'll adjust your fractal-basin boundaries!" Dr. Takumi said, and hit him over the head with the gavel.

> Yet finding a paradigm is not impossible. Newtonian physics is not a machine. It simply shares some of the attributes of a machine. We must find a model somewhere in the visible world that shares the often bizarre attributes of quantum physics. Such a model, unlikely as it sounds, surely exists somewhere, and it is up to us to find it.
> — Excerpt from Dr. Gedanken's keynote address

I went up to my room before the police came. Darlene still wasn't there, and the phone and air conditioning still weren't working. I was really beginning to get worried. I walked up to Grauman's Chinese to find David, but he wasn't there. Dr. Whedbee and Dr. Sleeth were behind the Academy Award winners folding screen.

"You haven't seen David, have you?" I asked.

Dr. Whedbee removed his hand from Norma Shearer's cheek.

"He left," Dr. Sleeth said, disentangling herself from the Best Movie of 1929-30.

"He said he was going out to Forest Lawn," Dr. Whedbee said, trying to smooth down his bushy white hair.

"Have you seen Dr. Mendoza? She was supposed to get in this morning."

They hadn't seen her, and. neither had Drs. Hotard and Thibodeaux, who stopped me in the lobby and showed me a postcard of Aimee Semple McPherson's tomb. Tiffany had gone off duty. Natalie couldn't find my reservation. I went back up to the room to wait, thinking Darlene might call.

The air conditioning still wasn't fixed. I fanned myself with a Hollywood brochure and then opened it up and read it. There was a map of the courtyard of Grauman's Chinese on the back cover. Deborah Kerr and Yul Brynner didn't have a square together either, and Katharine Hepburn and Spencer Tracy weren't even on the map. She made him waffles in *Woman of the Year*, and they hadn't even given them a square. I wondered if Tiffany the model-slash-actress had been in charge of assigning the cement. I could see her looking blankly at Spencer Tracy and saying, "I don't show a reservation for you."

What exactly was a model-slash-actress? Did it mean she was a model *or* an actress or a model *and* an actress? She certainly wasn't a hotel clerk. Maybe electrons were the Tiffanys of the microcosm, and that explained their wave-slash-particle duality. Maybe they weren't really electrons at all. Maybe they were just working part-time at being electrons to pay for their singlet-state lessons.

Darlene still hadn't called by seven o'clock. I stopped fanning myself and tried to open a window. It wouldn't budge. The problem was, nobody knew anything about quantum theory. All we had to go on were a few colliding electrons that nobody could see and that couldn't be measured properly because of the Heisenberg uncertainty principle. And there was chaos to consider, and entropy, and all those empty spaces. We didn't even know who May Robson was.

At seven-thirty the phone rang. It was Darlene.

"What happened?" I said. "Where are you?"

"At the Beverly Wilshire."

"In Beverly Hills?"

"Yes. It's a long story. When I got to the Rialto, the hotel clerk, I think her name was Tiffany, told me you weren't there. She said they were booked solid with some science thing and had had to send the overflow to other hotels. She said you were at the Beverly Wilshire in room ten-twenty-seven. How's David?"

"Impossible," I said. "He's spent the whole conference looking at Deanna Durbin's footprints at Grauman's Chinese Theatre and trying to talk me into going to the movies."

"And are you going?"

"I can't. Dr. Gedanken's giving the keynote address in half an hour."

"He is?" Darlene said, sounding surprised. "Just a minute." There was a silence, and then she came back on and said, "I think you should go to the movies. David's one of the last two charming men in the universe."

"But he doesn't take quantum theory seriously. Dr. Gedanken is hiring a research team to design a paradigm, and David keeps talking about the beacon on top of the Capitol Records building."

"You know, he may be onto something there. I mean, seriousness was all right for Newtonian physics, but maybe quantum theory needs a different approach. Sid says—"

"Sid?"

"This guy who's taking me to the movies tonight. It's a long story. Tiffany gave me the wrong room number, and I walked in on this guy in his underwear. He's a quantum physicist. He was supposed to be staying at the Rialto, but Tiffany couldn't find his reservation."

> *The major implication of wave/particle duality is that an electron has no precise location. It exists in a superposition of probable locations. Only when the experimenter observes the electron does it "collapse" into a location.*
> — The Wonderful World of Quantum Physics,
> A. Fields, UNW

Forest Lawn closed at five o'clock. I looked it up in the Hollywood brochure after Darlene hung up. There was no telling where he might have gone: the Brown Derby or the La Brea Tar Pits or some great place near Hollywood and Vine that had the alfalfa sprouts John Hurt ate right before his chest exploded in *Alien*.

At least I knew where Dr. Gedanken was. I changed my clothes and got into the elevator, thinking about wave/particle duality and fractals and high-entropy states and delayed-choice experiments. The problem was, where could you find a paradigm that would make it possible to visualize quantum theory when you had to include Josephson junctions and passion and all those empty spaces? It wasn't possible. You had to have more to work with than a few footprints and the impression of Betty Grable's leg.

The elevator door opened, and Abey Fields pounced on me. "I've been looking all over for you," he said. "You haven't seen Dr. Gedanken, have you?"

"Isn't he in the ballroom?"

"No," he said. "He's already fifteen minutes late, and nobody's seen him. You have to sign this," he said, shoving a clipboard at me.

"What is it?"

"It's a petition." He grabbed it back from me. "'We the undersigned demand that annual meetings of the International Congress of Quantum Physicists henceforth be held in appropriate locations.' Like Racine," he added, shoving the clipboard at me again. "*Unlike* Hollywood."

Hollywood.

"Are you aware it took the average ICQP delegate two hours and thirty-six minutes to check in? They even sent some of the delegates to a hotel in Glendale."

"And Beverly Hills," I said absently. Hollywood. Bra museums and the Marx Brothers and gangs that would kill you if you wore red or blue and Tiffany-slash-Stephanie and the World's Largest Oil Painting Incorporating a Religious Theme.

"Beverly Hills," Abey muttered, pulling an automatic pencil out of his pocket protector and writing a note to himself. "I'm presenting the petition during Dr. Gedanken's speech. Well, go on, sign it," he said, handing me the pencil. "Unless you want the annual meeting to be here at the Rialto next year."

I handed the clipboard back to him. "I think from now on the annual meeting might be here every year," I said, and took off running for Grauman's Chinese.

> *When we have the paradigm, one that embraces both the logical and the nonsensical aspects of quantum theory, we will be able to look past the colliding electrons and the mathematics and see the microcosm in all its astonishing beauty.*
> — Excerpt from Dr. Gedanken's keynote address

"I want a ticket to *Benji IX*," I told the girl at the box office. Her name tag said, "Welcome to Hollywood. My name is Kimberly."

"Which theater?" she said.

"Grauman's Chinese," I said, thinking, This is no time for a high-entropy state.

"Which theater?"

I looked up at the marquee. *Benji IX* was showing in all three theaters, the huge main theater and the two smaller ones on either side. "They're doing audience-reaction surveys," Kimberly said. "Each theater has a different ending."

"Which one's in the main theater?"

"I don't know. I just work here part-time to pay for my organic breathing lessons."

"Do you have any dice?" I asked, and then realized I was going about this all wrong. This was quantum theory, not Newtonian. It didn't matter which theater I chose or which seat I sat down in. This was a delayed-choice experiment, and David was already in flight.

"The one with the happy ending," I said.

"Center theater," she said.

I walked past the stone lions and into the lobby. Rhonda Fleming and some Chinese wax figures were sitting inside a glass case next to the door to the restrooms. There was a huge painted screen behind the concessions stand. I bought a box of Raisinets, a tub of popcorn, and a box of jujubes and went inside the theater.

It was bigger than I had imagined. Rows and rows of empty red chairs curved between the huge pillars and up to the red curtains where the screen must be. The walls were covered with intricate drawings. I stood there, holding my jujubes and Raisinets and popcorn, staring at the chandelier overhead. It was an elaborate gold sunburst surrounded by silver dragons. I had never imagined it was anything like this.

The lights went down, and the red curtains opened, revealing an inner curtain like a veil across the screen. I went down the dark aisle and sat in one of the seats. "Hi," I said, and handed the Raisinets to David.

"Where have you been?" he said. "The movie's about to start."

"I know," I said. I leaned across him and handed Darlene her popcorn and Dr. Gedanken his jujubes. "I was working on the paradigm for quantum theory."

"And?" Dr. Gedanken said, opening jujubes.

"And you're both wrong," I said. "It isn't Grauman's Chinese. It isn't movies either, Dr. Gedanken."

"Sid," Dr. Gedanken said. "If we're all going to be on the same research team, I think we should use first names."

"If it isn't Grauman's Chinese or the movies, what is it?" Darlene asked, eating popcorn.

"It's Hollywood."

"Hollywood," Dr. Gedanken said thoughtfully.

"Hollywood," I said. "Stars in the sidewalk and buildings that look like stacks of records and hats, and radicchio and audience surveys and bra museums. And the movies. And Grauman's Chinese."

"And the Rialto," David said.

"Especially the Rialto."

"And the ICQP," Dr. Gedanken said.

I thought about Dr. Lvov's black and gray slides and the disappearing chaos seminar and Dr. Whedbee writing "meaning" or possibly "information" on the overhead projector. "And the ICQP," I said.

"Did Dr. Takumi really hit Dr. Iverson over the head with a gavel?" Darlene asked.

"Shh," David said. "I think the movie's starting." He took hold of my hand. Darlene settled back with her popcorn, and Dr. Gedanken put his feet up on the chair in front of him. The inner curtain opened, and the screen lit up.

# Epiphany

*"But pray ye that your flight be not in the winter, neither on the sabbath day."*

—Matthew 24:20

A little after three, it began to snow. It had looked like it was going to all the way through Pennsylvania, and had even spit a few flakes just before Youngstown, Ohio, but now it was snowing in earnest, thick flakes that were already covering the stiff dead grass on the median and getting thicker as he drove west.

And this is what you get for setting out in the middle of January, he thought, without checking the Weather Channel first. He hadn't checked anything. He had taken off his robe, packed a bag, gotten into his car, and taken off. Like a man fleeing a crime.

The congregation will think I've absconded with the money in the collection plate, he thought. Or worse. Hadn't there been a minister in the paper last month who'd run off to the Bahamas with the building fund and a blonde? They'll say, "I *thought* he acted strange in church this morning."

But they wouldn't know yet that he was gone. The Sunday night Mariners' Meeting had been cancelled, the elders' meeting wasn't till next week, and the interchurch ecumenical meeting wasn't till Thursday.

He was supposed to play chess with B.T. on Wednesday, but he could call him and move it. He would have to call when B.T. was at work and leave him a message on his voice mail. He couldn't risk talking to him—they had been friends too many years. B.T. would instantly know something was up. And he would be the last person to understand.

I'll call his voice mail and move our chess game to Thursday night after the ecumenical meeting, Mel thought. That will give me till Thursday.

He was kidding himself. The church secretary, Mrs. Bilderbeck, would miss him Monday morning when he didn't show up in the church office.

I'll call her and tell her I've got the flu, he thought. No, she would insist on bringing him over chicken soup and zinc lozenges. I'll tell her I've been called out of town for a few days on personal business.

She will immediately think the worst, he thought. She'll think I have cancer, or that I'm looking at another church. And anything they conclude, he thought, even embezzlement, would be easier for them to accept than the truth.

The snow was starting to stick on the highway, and the windshield was beginning to fog up. Mel turned on the defroster. A truck passed him, throwing up snow. It was full of gold-and-white Ferris wheel baskets. He had been seeing trucks like it all afternoon, carrying black Octopus cars and concession stands and lengths of roller-coaster track. He wondered what a carnival was doing in Ohio in the middle of January. And in this weather.

Maybe they were lost. Or maybe they suddenly had a vision telling them to head west, he thought grimly. Maybe they suddenly had a nervous breakdown in the middle of church. In the middle of their sermon.

He had scared the choir half to death. They had been sitting there, midway through the sermon, and thinking they had plenty of time before they had to find the recessional hymn, when he'd stopped cold, his hand still raised, in the middle of a sentence.

There had been silence for a full minute before the organist thought to play the intro, and then a frantic scramble for their bulletins and their hymnals, a frantic flipping of pages. They had straggled unevenly to their feet all the way through the first verse, singing and looking at him like he was crazy.

And were they right? Had he really had a vision or was it some kind of midlife crisis? Or psychotic episode?

He was a Presbyterian, not a Pentecostal. He did not have visions. The only time he had experienced anything remotely like this was when he was nineteen, and that hadn't been a vision. It had been a call to the ministry, and it had only sent him to seminary, not haring off to who knows where.

And this wasn't a vision either. He hadn't seen a burning bush or an angel. He hadn't seen anything. He had simply had an overwhelming conviction that what he was saying was true.

654

He wished he still had it, that he wasn't beginning to doubt it now that he was three hundred miles from home and in the middle of a snowstorm, that he wasn't beginning to think it had been some kind of self-induced hysteria, born out of his own wishful thinking and the fact that it was January.

He hated January. The church always looked cheerless and abandoned, with all the Christmas decorations taken down, the sanctuary dim and chilly in the gray winter light, Epiphany over and nothing to look forward to but Lent and taxes. And Good Friday. Attendance and the collection down, half the congregation out with the flu and the other half away on a winter cruise, those who were there looking abandoned, too, and like they wished they had somewhere to go.

That was why he had decided against his sermon on Christian duty and pulled an old one out of the files, a sermon on Jesus' promise that He would return. To get that abandoned look off their faces.

"This is the hardest time," he had said, "when Christmas is over, and the bills have all come due, and it seems like winter is never going to end and summer is never going to come. But Christ tells us that we 'know not when the master of the house cometh, at even, or at midnight, or at the cock-crowing, or in the morning,' and when he comes, we must be ready for him. He may come tomorrow or next year or a thousand years from now. He may already be here, right now. At this moment..."

And as he said it, he had had an overwhelming feeling that it was true, that He had already come, and he must go find Him.

But now he wondered if it was just the desire to be somewhere else, too, somewhere besides the cold, poinsettia-less sanctuary.

If so, you came the wrong way, he thought. It was freezing, and the windshield was starting to fog up. Mel kicked the defrost all the way up to high and swiped at the windshield with his gloved hand.

The snow was coming down much harder, and the wind was picking up. Mel switched on the radio to hear a weather report.

"...and in the last days, the Book of Revelation tells us," a voice said, "'there will be hail and fire mingled with blood.'"

He hoped that wasn't the weather report. He hit the scan button on the radio and listened as it cycled through the stations. "...for the latest on the scandal involving the President and..." the voice of Randy Travis, singing "Forever and Ever, Amen"..."hog futures at"..."and the disciples said, 'Lord, show us a sign....'"

A sign, that was what he needed, Mel thought, peering at the road. A sign that he was not crazy.

A semi roared past in a blinding blast of snow and exhaust. He leaned forward, trying to see the lines on the pavement, and another truck went by, full of orange-and-yellow bumper cars. Bumper cars. How appropriate. They were all going to be riding bumper cars if this snow kept up, Mel thought, watching the truck pull into the lane ahead of him. It fishtailed wildly as it did, and Mel put his foot on the brake, felt it skid, and lifted his foot off.

Well, he had asked for a sign, he thought, carefully slowing down, and this one couldn't be clearer if it was written in fiery letters: Go home! This was a crazy idea! You're going to be killed, and then what will the congregation think? Go home!

Which was easier said than done. He could scarcely see the road, let alone any exit signs, and the windshield was starting to ice up. He swiped at the window again.

He didn't dare pull over and stop—those semis would never see him—but he was going to have to. The defroster wasn't having any effect on the ice on the windshield, and neither were the windshield wipers.

He rolled down the window and leaned out, trying to grab the wiper and slap it against the windshield to shake the ice off. Snow stabbed his face, stinging it.

"All right, all right," he shouted into the wind. "I get the message!"

He rolled the window back up, shivering, and swiped at the inside of the windshield again. The only kind of sign he wanted now was an exit sign, but he couldn't see the side of the road.

If I'm *on* the road, he thought, trying to spot the shoulder, a telltale outline, but the whole world had disappeared into a featureless whiteness. And what would keep him from driving right off the road and into a ditch?

He leaned forward tensely, trying to spot something, anything, and thought he saw, far ahead, a light.

A yellow light, too high up for a taillight—a reflector on a motorcycle, maybe. That was impossible, there was no way a motorcycle could be out in this. One of those lights on the top corners of a semi.

If that was what it was, he couldn't see the other one, but the light was moving steadily in front of him, and he followed it, trying to keep pace.

The windshield wipers were icing up again. He rolled down the window, and in the process lost sight of the light. Or the road, he thought frightenedly. No, there was the light, still high up, but closer, and it wasn't a light, it was a whole cluster of them, round yellow bulbs in the shape of an arrow.

The arrow on top of a police car, he thought, telling you to change lanes. There must be some kind of accident up ahead. He strained forward, trying to make out flashing blue ambulance lights.

But the yellow arrow moved steadily ahead, and as he got closer, he saw that the arrow was pointed down at an angle. And that it was slowing. Mel slowed, too, focusing his whole attention on the road and on pumping his brakes to keep the car from skidding.

When he looked up again, the arrow had slowed nearly to a stop, and he could see it clearly. It was part of a lighted sign on the back of a truck. "Shooting Star" it said in a flowing script, and next to the arrow in neon pink, "Tickets."

The truck came to a complete stop, its turn light blinking, and then started up again, and in its headlights he caught a glimpse of snow-spattered red. A stop sign.

And this was an exit. He had followed the truck off the highway onto an exit without even knowing it.

And now he was hopefully following it into a town, he thought, clicking on his right-turn signal and turning after the truck, but in the moment he had hesitated, he had lost it. And the blowing snow was worse here than on the highway.

There was the yellow arrow again. No, what he saw was a Burger King crown. He pulled in, scraping the snow-covered curb, and saw that he was wrong again. It was a motel sign. "King's Rest," with a crown of sulfur-yellow bulbs.

He parked the car and got out, slipping in the snow, and started for the office, which had, thank goodness, a "Vacancy" sign in the same neon pink as the "Tickets" sign.

A little blue Honda pulled up beside him and a short, plump woman got out of it, winding a bright purple muffler around her head. "Thank goodness you knew where you were going," she said, pulling on a pair of turquoise mittens. "I couldn't see a thing except your taillights." She reached back into the Honda for a vivid green canvas bag. "Anybody who'd be on the roads in weather like this would have to be crazy, wouldn't they?"

And if the blizzard hadn't been sign enough, here was proof positive. "Yes," he said, although she had already gone inside the motel office, "they would."

He would check in, wait a few hours till the storm let up, and then start back. With luck he would be back home before Mrs. Bilderbeck got to the office tomorrow morning.

He went inside the office, where a balding man was handing the plump woman a room key and talking to someone on the phone.

"Another one," he said when Mel opened the door. "Yeah."

He hung up the phone and pushed a registration form and a pen at Mel. "Which way'd *you* come from?" he asked.

"East," Mel said.

The man shook his balding head. "You got here in the nick of time," he said to both of them. "They just closed all the roads east of here."

> *"And thus I saw the horses in the vision, and them that sat upon them."*
>
> —Revelation 9:17

In the morning, Mel called Mrs. Bilderbeck. "I won't be in today. I've been called out of town."

"Out of town?" Mrs. Bilderbeck said, interested.

"Yes. On personal business. I'll be gone most of the week."

"Oh, dear," she said, and Mel suddenly hoped that there was an emergency at the church, that Gus Uhank had had another stroke or Lottie Millar's mother had died, so that he would have to go back.

"I told Juan you'd be in," Mrs. Bilderbeck said. "He's putting the sanctuary Christmas decorations away, and he wanted to know if you want to save the star for next year. And the pilot light went out again. The church was *freezing* when I got here this morning."

"Was Juan able to get it relit?"

"Yes, but I think someone should look at it. What if it goes out on a Saturday night?"

"Call Jake Adams at A-1 Heating," he said. Jake was a deacon.

"A-1 Heating," she said slowly, as if she were writing it down. "What about the star? Are we going to use it again next year?"

Is there going to *be* a next year? Mel thought. "Whatever you think," he said.

"And what about the ecumenical meeting?" she asked. "Will you be back in time for that?"

"Yes," he said, afraid if he said "no," she would ask more questions.

"Is there a number where I can reach you?"

"No. I'll check in tomorrow." He hung up quickly, and then sat there on the bed, trying to decide whether to call B.T or not. He hadn't done anything major in the fifteen years they'd been friends without telling him, but Mel knew what he'd say. They'd met on the ecumenical committee, when the Unitarian chairman had decided that, to be truly ecumenical, they needed a resident atheist and Darwinian biologist. And, Mel suspected, an African-American.

It was the only good thing that had ever come out of the ecumenical committee. He and B.T had started by complaining about the idiocies of the ecumenical committee, which seemed bent on proving that denominations couldn't get along, progressed to playing chess and then to discussing religion and politics and disagreeing on both, and ended by becoming close friends.

I have to call him, Met thought, it's a betrayal of our friendship not to.

And tell him what? That he'd had a holy vision? That the Book of Revelation was coming literally true? It sounded crazy to Mel, let alone to B.T, who was a scientist, who didn't believe in the First Coming, let alone the Second. But if it *was* true, how could he not call him?

He dialed B.T.'s area code and then put down the receiver and went to check out.

The roads east were still closed. "You shouldn't have any trouble heading west, though," the balding man said, handing Mel his credit-card receipt. "The snow's supposed to let up by noon."

Mel hoped so. The interstate was snow-packed and unbelievably slick, and when Mel positioned himself behind a sand truck, a rock struck his windshield and made a ding.

At least there was hardly any traffic. There were only a few semis, and a navy-blue pickup with a bumper sticker that said "In case of the Rapture, this car will be unoccupied." There was no sign of the blue Honda or of the carnival. They had seen the light and were still at the King's Rest, sitting in the restaurant, drinking coffee. Or headed south for the winter.

He passed a snow-obscured sign that read "For Weather Info, Tune to AM 1410."

He did. "...and in the last days Christ Himself will appear," an evangelist, possibly the one from yesterday, or a different one—they all had the same accent, the same intonation—said. "The Book of Revelation tells us He will appear riding a white horse and leading a mighty army of the righteous against the Antichrist in that last great battle of Armageddon. And the unbelievers—the fornicators and the baby-murderers—will be flung into the bottomless pit."

The ultimate "Wait till your father gets home," threat, Mel thought.

"And how do I know these things are coming?" the radio said. "I'll *tell* you how. The Lord came to me in a dream, and He said, 'These shall be the signs of my coming. There will be wars and rumors of wars.' Iraq, my friends, that's what he's talking about. The sun's face will be covered, and the godless will prosper. Look around you. Who do you see prospering? Abortion doctors and homosexuals and godless atheists. But when Christ comes, they will be punished. He's told me so. The Lord spoke to me, just like he spoke to Moses, just like he spoke to Isaiah...."

He switched off the radio, but it didn't do any good. Because this was what had been bothering him ever since he started out. How did he know his vision wasn't just like some radio evangelist's?

Because his is born out of hatred, bigotry, and revenge, Mel thought. God no more spoke to him than did the man in the moon.

And how do you know He spoke to you? Because it *felt* real? The voices telling the bomber to destroy the abortion clinic felt real, too. Emotion isn't proof. Signs aren't evidence. "Do you have any outside confirmation?" he could hear B.T. saying skeptically.

The sun came out, and the glare off the white road, the white fields, was worse than the snow had been. He almost didn't see the truck off to the side. Its emergency flashers weren't on, and at first he thought it had just slid off the road, but as he went past, he saw it was one of the carnival trucks with its hood up and steam coming out. A young man in a denim jacket was standing next to it, hooking his thumb for a ride.

I should stop, Mel thought, but he was already past, and picking up hitchhikers was dangerous. He had found that out when he'd preached a sermon on the Good Samaritan last year. "Let us not be like the Levite or the Pharisee who passes by the stranded motorist, the injured victim," he had told his congregation. "Let us be like the Samaritan, who stopped and helped."

It had seemed like a perfectly harmless sermon topic, and he had been totally unprepared for the uproar that ensued. "I cannot believe you told people to pick up hitchhikers!" Dan Crosby had raged. "If one of my daughters ends up raped, I'm holding you responsible."

"What were you thinking of?" Mrs. Bilderbeck had said, hanging up after fending off Mable Jenkins. "On CNN last week there was a story about somebody who stopped to help a couple who was out of gas, and they cut off his head."

He had had to issue a retraction the next Sunday, saying that women had no business helping anyone (which had made Mamie Rollet mad, for feminist reasons) and that the best thing for everyone else to do was to alert the state patrol on their cell phones and let them take care of it, unless they knew the person, although somehow he couldn't imagine the Good Samaritan with a cell phone.

There was a median crossing up ahead, but it was marked with a sign that read "Authorized Vehicles Only." And if I get my head cut off, he thought, the congregation will have no sympathy at all.

But it was threatening to snow again, and the green interstate sign up ahead said "Wayside, 28 Mi." And the carnival had been his Good Samaritan last night.

"'Inasmuch as ye have done it unto one of the least of these, you have done it unto me,'" he murmured, and turned into the median crossing and onto the eastbound side of the highway, and started back.

The truck was still there, though he couldn't see the driver. Good, he thought, looking for a place to cross. Some other Samaritan's picked him up. But when he pulled up behind the truck, the man got out of the truck's cab and started over to the car, his hands jammed into his denim jacket. Mel began to feel sorry he'd stopped. The man had a ragged scar across his forehead, and his hair was lank and greasy.

He slouched over to the side of the car, and Mel saw that he was much younger than he'd looked at first. He's just a kid, Mel thought.

Yeah, well, so was Billy the Kid, he reminded himself. And Andrew Cunanan.

Mel leaned across and pulled down the passenger window. "What's the trouble?"

The kid leaned down to talk to him. "Died," he said, and grinned.

"Do you need a lift into town?" he asked, and the kid immediately opened the car door, keeping his right hand in his jacket pocket. Where the gun is, Mel thought.

The kid slid in and shut the door, still using only one hand. When they find me robbed and murdered, they'll be convinced I was involved in some kind of drug deal, Mel thought. He started the car.

"Man, it was cold out there," the kid said, taking his right hand out of his pocket and rubbing his hands together. "I been waiting forever."

Mel kicked the heater over to high, and the kid leaned forward and held his hands in front of the vent. There was a peace sign tattooed on the back of one of them and a fierce-looking lion on the other. Both looked like they'd been done by hand.

The kid rubbed his hands together, wincing, and Mel took another look. His hands were red with cold and between the tattoo lines there were ugly white splotches. The kid started rubbing them again.

"Don't—" Mel said, putting out his hand unthinkingly to stop him. "That looks like frostbite. Don't rub it. You're supposed to…" he said, and then couldn't remember. Put them in warm water? Wrap them up? "They're supposed to warm up slowly," he said finally.

"You mean like by warming 'em up in front of a heater?" the kid said, holding his hands in front of the vent again. He put up his hand and touched the ding in the windshield. "That's gonna spread," he said.

His hand looked even worse now that it was warming up. The sickly white splotches stood out starkly against the rest of his skin.

Mel took off his gloves, switching hands on the steering wheel and using his teeth to get the second one off. "Here," he said, handing them to the kid. "These are insulated."

The kid looked at him for a minute and then put them on.

"You should get your hands looked at," Mel said. "I can take you to the emergency room when we get to town."

"I'll be okay," the kid said. "You get used to being cold, working a carny."

"What's a carnival doing here in the middle of winter, anyway?" Mel asked.

"Best time," the kid said. "Catches 'em by surprise. What're you doin' out here?"

He wondered what the kid would say if he told him. "I'm a minister," he said instead.

"A preacher, huh?" he said. "You believe in the Second Coming?"

"The Second Coming" Mel gasped, caught off-guard.

"Yeah, we had a preacher come to the carny the other day telling us

Jesus was coming back and was gonna punish everybody for hanging him on the cross, knock down the mountains, burn the whole planet up. You believe all that's gonna happen?"

"No," Mel said. "I don't think Jesus is coming back to punish anybody."

"The preacher said it was all right there in the Bible."

"There are lots of things in the Bible. They don't always turn out to mean what you thought they did."

The kid nodded sagely. "Like the Siamese twins."

"Siamese twins?" Mel said, unable to remember any Siamese twins in the Bible.

"Yeah, like this one carny up in Fargo. It had a big sign saying 'See the Siamese twins,' and everybody pays a buck, thinking they're gonna see two people hooked together. And when they get there it's a cage with two Siamese kittens in it. Like that."

"Not exactly," Mel said. "The prophecies aren't a scam to cheat people, they're—"

"What about Roswell? The alien autopsy and all that. You think that's a scam, too?"

Well, there was some outside confirmation for you. Mel was in a class with scam artists and UFO nuts.

"After what happened the first time, I don't know if I'd wanta come back or not," the kid said, and it took Mel a minute to realize he was talking about Christ. "If I did, I'd wear some kind of disguise or something."

Like the last time, Mel thought, when He came disguised as a baby.

The kid was still preoccupied with the ding. "There's stuff you could do to keep it from spreading for a little while," he said, "but it's still gonna spread. There ain't nothing that can stop it." He pointed out the window at a sign. "Wayside, exit 1 mile."

Mel pulled off and into a Total station, apparently all there was to Wayside. The kid opened the door and started to take off the gloves.

"Keep them," Mel said. "Do you want me to wait till you find out if they've got a tow truck?"

The kid shook his head. "I'll call Pete." He reached into the pocket of the denim jacket and handed Mel three orange cardboard tickets. They were marked "Admit One Free."

"It's a ticket to the show ,"the kid said. "We got a triple Ferris wheel, three wheels one inside the other. And a great roller coaster. The Comet."

Mel splayed the tickets apart. "There are three tickets here."

"Bring your friends," the kid said, slapped the car door, and ambled off toward the gas station.

Bring your friends.

Mel got back on the highway. It was getting dark. He hoped the next exit wasn't as far, or as uninhabited, as this one.

Bring your friends. I should have told B.T, he thought, even though he would have said, Don't go, you're crazy, let me recommend a good psychiatrist.

"I still should have told him," he said out loud, and was as certain of it as he had been of what he should do in that moment in the church. And now he had cut himself off from B.T not only by hundreds of miles of closed highways and "icy and snow-packed conditions," but by his deception, his failure to tell him.

The next exit didn't even have a gas station, and the one after that nothing but a Dairy Queen. It was nearly eight by the time he got to Zion Center and a Holiday Inn.

He walked straight in, not even stopping to get his luggage out of the trunk, and across the lobby toward the phones.

"Hello!" The short plump woman he'd seen the night before waylaid him. "Here we are again, orphans of the storm. Weren't the roads awful?" she said cheerfully. "I almost went off in the ditch twice. My little Honda doesn't have four-wheel drive, and—"

"Excuse me," Mel interrupted her. "I have a phone call I *have* to make."

"You can't," she said, still cheerfully. "The lines are down."

"Down?"

"Because of the storm. I tried to call my sister just now, and the clerk told me the phone's been out all day. I don't know what she's going to think when she doesn't hear from me. I promised *faithfully* that I'd call her every night and tell her where I was and that I'd gotten there safely."

He couldn't call B.T. Or get to him. "Excuse me," he said, and started back across the lobby to the registration desk.

"Has the interstate going east opened up yet?" he asked the girl behind the counter.

She shook her head. "It's still closed between Malcolm and Iowa City. Ground blizzards," she said. "Will you be checking in, sir? How many are there in your party?"

"Two," a voice said.

Mel turned. And there, leaning against the end of the registration desk, was B.T.

*"And there appeared another wonder in heaven, and behold a great red dragon."*
                                                    —Revelation 12:3

For a moment he couldn't speak for the joy, the relief he felt. He clutched the check-out counter, vaguely aware that the girl behind the counter was saying something.

"What are you doing here?" he said finally.

B.T. smiled his slow checkmate smile. "Aren't I the one who should be asking that?"

And now that he was here, he would have to tell him. Mel felt the relief turn into resentment. "I thought the roads were closed," he said.

"I didn't come that way," B.T. said.

"And how would you like to pay for that, sir?" the clerk said, and Mel knew she had asked him before.

"Credit card," he said, fumbling for his wallet.

"License number?" the clerk asked.

"I flew to Omaha and rented a car," B.T. said.

Mel handed her his MasterCard. "TY 804."

"State?"

"Pennsylvania." He looked at B.T. "How did you find me?"

"'License number?'" B.T. said, mimicking the clerk. "'Will you be putting this on your credit card, sir?' If you've got a computer, it's the easiest thing in the world to find someone these days, especially if they're using that." He gestured at the MasterCard the clerk was handing back to Mel.

She handed him a folder. "Your room number is written inside, sir. It's not on the key for security purposes," the clerk said, as if his room number weren't in the computer, too. B.T. probably already knew it.

"You still haven't answered my question," B.T. said. "What are you doing here?"

"I have to go get my suitcase," Mel said, and walked past him and out to the parking lot and his car. He opened the trunk.

B.T. reached past him and picked up Mel's suitcase, as if taking it into custody.

"How did you know I was missing?" Mel asked, but he already knew the answer to that. "Mrs. Bilderbeck sent you."

B.T. nodded. "She said she was worried about you, that you'd called and something was seriously wrong. She said she knew because you hadn't tried to get out of the ecumenical meeting on Thursday. She said you always tried to get out of it."

They say it's the little mistakes that trip criminals up, Mel thought.

"She said she thought you were sick and were going to see a specialist," B.T. said, his black face gray with worry. "Out of town, so nobody in the congregation would find out about it. A brain tumor, she said." He shifted the suitcase to his other hand. "Do you have a brain tumor?"

A brain tumor. That would be a nice, convenient explanation. When Ivor Sorenson had had a brain tumor, he had stood up during the offertory, convinced there was an ostrich sitting in the pew next to him.

"*Are* you sick?" B.T. said.

"No."

"But it is something serious."

"It's freezing out here," Mel said. "Let's discuss this inside."

B.T. didn't move. "Whatever it is, no matter how bad it is, you can tell me."

"All right. Fine. 'For ye know neither the day nor the hour wherein the Son of Man cometh.' Matthew 25:13," Mel said. "I had a revelation. About the Second Coming. I think He's here already, that the Second Coming's already happened."

Whatever B.T. had imagined—terminal illness or embezzlement or some other, worse crime—it obviously wasn't as bad as this. His face went even grayer. "The Second Coming," he said. "Of Christ?"

"Yes," Mel said. He told him what had happened during the sermon Sunday. "I scared the choir half out of their wits," he said.

B.T. nodded. "Mrs. Bilderbeck told me. She said you stopped in the middle of a sentence and just stood there, staring into space with your hand up to your forehead. That's why she thought you had a brain tumor. How long did this...vision last?"

"It wasn't a vision," Mel said. "It was a revelation, a conviction... an epiphany."

"An epiphany," B.T. said in a flat, expressionless voice. "And it told you He was here? In Zion Center?"

"No," Mel said. "I don't know where He is."

"You don't know where He is," B.T. repeated. "You just got in your car and started driving?"

"West," Mel said. "I knew He was somewhere west."

"Somewhere west," B.T. said softly. He rubbed his hand over his mouth.

"Why don't you say it?" Mel said. He slammed the trunk shut. "You think I'm crazy."

"I think we're both crazy," he said, "standing out here in the snow, fighting. Have you had supper?"

"No," Mel said.

"Neither have I," B.T. said. He took Mel's arm. "Let's go get some dinner."

"And a dose of antidepressants? A nice straitjacket?"

"I was thinking steak," B.T. said, and tried to smile. "Isn't that what they eat here in Iowa?"

"Corn," Mel said.

> *"And when I looked, behold...the appearance of the wheels was as the colour of a beryl stone and...as if a wheel had been in the midst of a wheel."*
> —Jeremiah 10:9-10

Neither corn nor steak was on the menu, which had the Holiday Inn star on the front, and they were out of nearly everything else. "Because of the interstate being closed," the waitress said. "We've got chicken teriyaki and beef chow mein."

They ordered the chow mein and coffee, and the waitress left. Mel braced himself for more questions, but B.T. only asked, "How were the roads today?" and told him about the problems he'd had getting a flight and a rental car. "Chicago O'Hare was shut down because of a winter storm," he said, "*and* Denver *and* Kansas City. I had to fly into Albuquerque and then up to Omaha."

"I'm sorry you had to go to all that trouble," Mel said.

"I was worried about you."

The waitress arrived with their chow mein, which came with mashed potatoes and gravy and green beans.

"Interesting," B.T. said, poking at the gravy. He made a half-hearted attempt at the chow mein, and then pushed the plate away.

"There's something I don't understand," he said. "The Second Coming is when Christ returns, right? I thought He was supposed to appear in the clouds in a blaze of glory, complete with trumpets and angel choirs."

Mel nodded.

"Then how can He already be here without anybody knowing?"

"I don't know," Mel said. "I don't understand any of this any more than you do. I just know He's here."

"But you don't know where."

"No. I thought when I got out here there would be a sign."

"A sign," B.T. said.

"Yes," Mel said, getting angry all over again. "You know. A burning bush, a pillar of fire, a star. A *sign*."

He must have been shouting. The waitress came scurrying over with the check. "Are you through with this?" she said, looking at the plates of half-eaten food.

"Yes," Mel said. "We're through."

"You can pay at the register," the waitress said, and scurried away with their plates.

"Look," B.T. said, "the brain's a very complicated thing. An alteration in brain chemistry—are you on any medications? Sometimes medications can cause people to hear voices or—"

Mel picked up the check and stood, reaching for his wallet. "It wasn't a voice."

He put down money for a tip and went over to the cash register.

"You said it was a strong feeling," B.T. said after Mel had paid. "Sometimes endorphins can—nothing like this has ever happened to you before, has it?"

Mel walked out into the lobby. "Yes," he said, and turned to face B.T. "It happened once before."

"When?" B.T. said, his face gray again.

"When I was nineteen. I was in college, studying pre-law. I went to church with a girlfriend, and the minister gave a hellfire-and-brimstone sermon on the evils of dancing and associating with anyone who did. He said Jesus said it was wrong to associate with nonbelievers, that they would corrupt and contaminate you. Jesus, who spent all His time with lowlifes, tax collectors and prostitutes and lepers! And all of a sudden I had this overwhelming feeling, this—"

"Epiphany," B.T. said.

"That I had to do something, that I had to fight him and all the other ministers like him. I stood up and walked out in the middle of the sermon," Mel said, remembering, "and went home and applied to seminary."

B.T. rubbed his hand across his mouth. "And the epiphany you had yesterday was the same as that one?"

"Yes."

"Reverend Abrams?" a woman's voice said.

Mel turned. The short plump woman who'd been on the phone and at the motel the night before was hurrying toward them, lugging her bright green tote bag.

"Who's that?" B.T. said.

Mel shook his head, wondering how she knew his name.

She came up to them. "Oh, Reverend Abrams," she said breathlessly, "I wanted to thank you—I'm Cassie Hunter, by the way." She stuck out a plump, beringed hand.

"How do you do?" Mel said, shaking it. "This is Dr. Bernard Thomas, and I'm Mel Abrams."

She nodded. "I heard the desk clerk say your name. I didn't thank you the other night for saving my life."

"Saving your life?" B.T. said, looking at Mel.

"There was this awful whiteout," Cassie said. "You couldn't see the road at all, and if it hadn't been for the taillights on Reverend Abrams's car, I'd have ended up in a ditch."

Mel shook his head. "You shouldn't thank me. You should thank the driver of the carnival truck I was following. He saved both of us."

"I *saw* those carnival trucks," Cassie said. "I wondered what a carnival was doing in Iowa in the middle of winter." She laughed, a bright, chirpy laugh. "Of course, you're probably wondering what a retired English teacher is doing in Iowa in the middle of winter. Of course, for that matter, what are you doing in Iowa in the middle of winter?"

"We're on our way to a religious meeting," B.T. said before Mel could answer.

"Really? I've been visiting famous writers' birthplaces," she said. "Everyone back home thinks I'm *crazy*; but except for the last few days, the weather's been *fine*. Oh, and I wanted to tell you, I just talked to the clerk, and she thinks the phones will be working again by tomorrow morning, so you should be able to make your call."

She rummaged in her voluminous tote bag and came up with a room-key folder. "Well, anyway, I just wanted to thank you. It was nice meeting you," she said to B.T, and bustled off across the lobby toward the coffee shop.

"Who were you trying to call?" B.T. asked.

"You," Mel said bitterly. "I realized I owed it to you to tell you, even if you did think 1 was crazy."

B.T. didn't say anything.

"That is what you think, isn't it?" Mel said. "Why don't you just say it? You think I'm crazy."

"All right. I think you're crazy," B.T. said, and then continued angrily, "Well, what do you expect me to say? You take off in the middle of a blizzard, you don't tell anyone where you're going, because you saw the Second Coming in a vision?"

"It wasn't—"

"Oh, right. It wasn't a vision. You had an epiphany. So did the woman in *The Globe* last week who saw the Virgin Mary on her refrigerator. So did the Heaven's Gate people. Are you telling me *they're* not crazy?"

"No," Mel said, and started down the hall to his room.

"For fifteen years you've raved about faith healers and cults and preachers who claim they've got a direct line to God being frauds," B.T. said, following him, "and now you suddenly believe in it?"

He kept walking. "No."

"But you're telling me I'm supposed to believe in your revelation because it's different, because this is the real thing."

"I'm not telling you anything," Met said, turning to face him. "You're the one who came out here and demanded to know what I was doing. I told you. You got what you came for. Now you can go back and tell Mrs. Bilderbeck I don't have a brain tumor, it's a chemical imbalance."

"And what do you intend to do? Drive west until you fall off the Santa Monica pier?"

"I intend to find Him," Mel said.

B.T. opened his mouth as if to say something and then shut it and stormed off down the hall.

Mel stood there, watching him till a door slammed, down the hall.

Bring your friends, Mel thought. Bring your friends.

*"For now we see through a glass darkly, but then face to face."*

—I Corinthians 13:12

"I intend to find Him," Mel had said, and was glad B.T. hadn't shouted back "How?" because he had no idea.

He had not had a sign, which meant that the answer must be somewhere else. Mel sat down on the bed, opened the drawer of the bedside table, and got out the Gideon Bible.

He propped the pillows up against the headboard and leaned back against them and opened the Bible to the Book of Revelation.

The radio evangelists made it sound like the story of the Second Coming was a single narrative, but it was actually a hodgepodge of isolated scriptures—Matthew 24 and sections of Isaiah and Daniel, verses out of Second Thessalonians and John and Joel, stray ravings from Revelation and Jeremiah, all thrown together by the evangelists as if the authors were writing at the same time. If they were even writing about the same thing.

And the references were full of contradictions. A trumpet would sound, and Christ would come in the clouds of heaven with power and great glory. Or on a white horse, leading an army of a hundred and forty-four thousand. Or like a thief in the night. There would be earthquakes and pestilences and a star falling out of heaven. Or a dragon would come up out of the sea, or four great beasts with the heads of a lion and a bear and a leopard and eagles' wings. Or darkness would cover the earth.

But in all the assorted prophecies there were no locations mentioned. Joel talked about a desolate wilderness and Jeremiah about a wasteland, but not about where they were. Luke said the faithful would come "from the east, and from the west, and from the north" to the kingdom of God, but neglected to say where it was located.

The only place mentioned by name in all the prophecies was Armageddon. But Armageddon (or Har-Magedon or 'Ar Himdah) was a word that appeared only once in the Scriptures and whose meaning was not known, a word that might be Hebrew or Greek or something else altogether, that might mean "level" or "valley plain" or "place of desire."

Mel remembered from seminary that some scholars thought it referred to the plain in front of Mt. Megiddo, the site of a battle between Israel and Sisera the Canaanite. But there was no Mt. Megiddo on ancient or modern maps. It could be anywhere.

He put on his shoes and his coat and went out to the parking lot to get his road atlas out of the car.

B.T. was leaning against the trunk.

"How long have you been out here?" Mel asked, but the answer was obvious. B.T.'s dark face was pinched with cold, and his hands were jammed into his pockets like the carnival kid's had been.

"I've been thinking," he said, his voice shivering with the cold. "I don't have to be back until Thursday, and I can fly out of Denver just as easily as out of Omaha. If we drive as far as Denver together, it'll give us more time—"

"For you to talk me out of this," Mel said, and then was sorry when he saw the expression on B.T.'s face.

"For us to talk," B.T. said. "For me to figure this—epiphany—out."

"All right," Mel said. "As far as Denver." He opened the car door. "You can come inside now. I'm not going anywhere till morning." He leaned inside the car and got the atlas. "It's a good thing I came out for this. You didn't actually intend to stand out here all night, did you?"

He nodded, his teeth chattering. "You're not the only one who's crazy."

> "By hearing ye shall hear, and shall not understand, and seeing ye shall see and shall not perceive."
> —Matthew 13:14

There wasn't a Hertz rental car agency in Zion Center. "The nearest one's in Redfield," B.T. said unhappily.

"I'll meet you there," Mel said.

"Will you?" B.T. said. "You won't take off on your own?"

"No," Mel said.

"What if you see a sign?"

"If I see a burning bush, I'll pull off on the side and let you know," Mel said dryly. "We can caravan if you want."

"Fine," B.T. said. "I'll follow you."

"I don't know where the rental place is."

"I'll pull ahead of you once we get to Redfield," B.T. said, and got into his rental car. "It's the second exit. What are the roads supposed to be like?"

"Icy. Snow-packed. But the weather report said clear."

Mel got into his car. The kid from the carnival had been right. The ding had started to spread, raying out in three long cracks and one short one.

He led the way over to the interstate, being careful to signal lane changes and not to get too far ahead, so B.T. wouldn't think he was trying to escape.

The carnival must have stayed the night in Zion Center, too. He passed a truck carrying the Tilt-a-Whirl and one full of stacked, slanted mirrors for, Mel assumed, the Hall of Mirrors. A Blazer roared past him with the bumper sticker "When the Rapture comes, I'm outta here!"

As soon as he was on the interstate, he turned on the radio. "...and snow-packed. Partly cloudy becoming clear by midmorning. Interstate 80 between Victor and Davenport is closed, also U.S. 35 and State Highway 218. Partly cloudy skies, clearing by midmorning. The following schools are closed: Edgewater, Bennett, Olathe, Oskaloosa, Vinton, Shellsburg...."

Mel twisted the knob.

"...but the Second Coming is not something we believers have to be afraid of," the evangelist, this one with a Texas accent, said, "for the Book of Revelation tells us that Christ will protect us from the final tribulation, and when He comes to power we will dwell with Him in His Holy City, which shines with jewels and precious stones, and we will drink from living fountains of water. The lion shall lie down with the lamb, and there...be...more—"

The evangelist sputtered into static and then out of range, which was just as well because Mel was heading into fog and needed to give his whole attention to his driving.

The fog got worse, descending like a smothering blanket. Mel turned on his lights. They didn't help at all, but Mel hoped B.T. would be able to see his taillights the way Cassie had. He couldn't see anything beyond a few yards in front of him. And if he had wanted a sign of his mental state, this was certainly appropriate.

"God has told us His will in no uncertain terms," the radio evangelist thundered, coming suddenly back into range. "There can't be any question about it."

But he had dozens of questions. There had been no Megiddo on the map of Nebraska last night. Or of Kansas or Colorado or New Mexico, and nothing in all the prophecies about location except a reference to the New Jerusalem, and there was no New Jerusalem on the map either.

"And how do I know the Second Coming is at hand?" the evangelist roared, suddenly back in range. "Because the Bible tells us so. It tells us *how* He is coming and when!"

And that wasn't true either. "Ye know neither the day nor the hour wherein the Son of man cometh," Matthew had written, and Luke, "The Son of man cometh at an hour when ye think not," and even Revelation, "I will come on thee as a thief, and thou shalt not know what hour I will come." It was the only thing they were all agreed on.

"The signs are *all* around us," the evangelist shouted. "They're as plain as the nose on your face! Air pollution, liberals outlawing school prayer, wickedness! Why, anybody'd have to be *blind* not to recognize them! Open your eyes and see!"

"All I see is fog," Mel said, turning on the defrost and wiping his sleeve across the windshield, but it wasn't the windshield. It was the world, which had vanished completely in the whiteness.

He nearly missed the turnoff to Redfield. Luckily, the fog was less dense in town, and they were able to find not only the rental car place, but the local Tastee-Freez. Mel went over to get some lunch to take with them while B.T. checked the car in.

It was full of farmers, all talking about the weather. "Damned meterologists," one of them, redfaced and wearing a John Deere cap and earmuffs, grumbled. "Said it was supposed to be clear."

"It is clear," another one in a down vest said. "He just didn't say *where*. You get up above that fog, say thirty thousand feet, and it's clear as a bell."

"Number six," the woman behind the counter called.

Mel went up to the counter and paid. There was a fluorescent green poster for the carnival taped up on the wall beside the counter. "Come have the time of your life!" it read. "Thrills, chills, excitement!"

Chills is right, Mel thought, thinking of how cold being up in a Ferris wheel in this fog would be.

It was an old sign. "Littletown, Dec. 24," it read. "Ft. Dodge, Dec. 28. Cairo, Dec. 30."

B.T. was already in the car when Mel got back with their hamburgers and coffee. He handed him the sack and got back on the highway.

That was a mistake. The fog was so thick he couldn't even take a hand off the wheel to hold the hamburger B.T. offered him. "I'll eat it later," he said, leaning forward and squinting as if that would make things clearer. "You go ahead and eat, and we'll switch places in a couple of exits."

But there were no exits, or Mel couldn't see them in the fog, and after twenty miles of it, he had B.T. hand him his coffee, now stone cold, and took a couple of sips.

"I've been looking at the Second Coming scientifically," B.T. said. "'A great mountain burning with fire was cast into the sea and the third part of the sea became blood.'"

Mel glanced over. B.T. was reading from a black leather Bible. "Where'd you get that?" he asked.

"It was in the hotel room," B.T. said.

"You *stole* a Gideon Bible?" Mel said.

"They put them there for people who need them. And I'd say we qualify. 'There was a great earthquake, and the sun became black as sackcloth of hair and the moon became as blood. And the stars of heaven fell into the earth. And every mountain and island were moved out of their places.'

"All these things are supposed to happen along with the Second Coming," B.T. said. "Earthquakes, wars and rumors of wars, pestilence, locusts." He leafed through the flimsy pages. "'And there arose a smoke out of the pit, as the smoke of a great furnace, and the sun and the air were darkened. And there came out of the smoke locusts upon the earth.'"

He shut the Bible. "All right, earthquakes happen all the time, and there have been wars and rumors of wars for the last ten thousand years, and I guess this—'and the stars shall fall from the sky'—could refer to meteors. But there's no sign of any of these other things. No locusts, no bottomless pit opening up, no 'third part of trees and grass were burnt up and a third part of the creatures which were in the sea died.'"

"Nuclear war," Mel said.

"What?"

"According to the evangelists, that's supposed to refer to nuclear war," Mel said. "And before that, to the Communist threat. Or fluoridation of water. Or anything else they disapprove of."

"Well, whatever it stands for, no bottomless pit has opened up lately or we would have seen it on CNN. And volcanoes don't cause locust swarms. Mel," he said seriously, "let's say your experience was a real epiphany. Couldn't you have misinterpreted what it meant?"

And for a split second, Mel almost had it. The key to where He was and what was going to happen. The key to all of it.

"Couldn't it have been about something else?" B.T. said. "Something besides the Second Coming?"

No, Mel thought, trying to hang on to the insight, it *was* the Second Coming, but—it was gone. Whatever it was, he'd lost it.

He stared blindly ahead at the fog, trying to remember what had triggered it. B.T. had said, "Couldn't you have misunderstood what it meant?" No, that wasn't right. "Couldn't you—"

"What is it?" B.T. was pointing through the windshield. "What is that? Up ahead?"

"I don't see anything," Mel said, straining ahead. He couldn't see anything but fog. "What was it?"

"I don't know. I just saw a glimpse of lights."

"Are you sure?" Mel said. There was nothing there but whiteness.

"There it is again," B.T. said, pointing. "Didn't you see it? Yellow flashing lights. There must be an accident. You'd better slow down."

Mel was already barely creeping along, but he slowed further, still unable to see anything. "Was it on our side of the highway?"

"Yes…I don't know," B.T. said, leaning forward. "I don't see it now. But I'm sure it was there."

Mel crawled forward squinting into the whiteness. "Could it have been a truck? The carnival truck had a yellow arrow," he said, and saw the lights.

And they were definitely not a sign for a carnival ride. They filled the road just ahead, flashing yellow and red and blue, all out of synch with each other. Police cars or fire trucks or ambulances. Definitely an accident. He pumped the brakes, hoping whoever was behind him could see his taillights, and slowed to a stop.

A patrolman appeared out of the fog, holding up his hand in the sign for "stop." He was wearing a yellow poncho and a clear plastic cover over his brown hat.

Mel rolled his window down, and the patrolman leaned in to talk to them. "Road up ahead's closed. You need to get off at this exit."

"Exit?" Mel said, looking to the right. He could just make out a green outline in the fog.

"It's right there, up about a hundred yards," the patrolman said, pointing into nothingness. "We'll come tell you when it's open again."

"Are you closing it because of the weather?" B.T. asked.

The patrolman shook his head. "Accident," he said. "Big mess. It'll be a while." He motioned them off to the right.

Mel felt his way to the exit and off the highway. At least it had a truck stop instead of just a gas station. He and B.T. parked and went into the restaurant.

It was jammed. Every booth, every seat at the counter was full. Mel and B.T. sat down at the last unoccupied table, and it immediately became clear why it had been unoccupied. The draft when the door opened made B.T., who had just taken his coat off, put it back on and then zip it up.

Mel had expected everyone to be angry about the delay, but the waitresses and customers all seemed to be in a holiday mood. Truckers leaned across the backs of the booths to talk to each other, laughing, and the waitresses, carrying pots of coffee, were smiling. One of them had, inexplicably, a plastic kewpie doll stuck in her beehive hairdo.

The door opened again, sending an Arctic blast across their table, and a paramedic came in and went up to the counter to talk to the waitress. "...accident..." Mel heard him say and shake his head, "...carnival truck..."

Mel went over. "Excuse me," he said. "I heard you say something about a carnival truck. Is that what had the accident?"

"Disaster is more like it," the paramedic said, shaking his head. "Took a turn too sharp and lost his whole load. And don't ask me what a carnival's doing up here in the middle of winter."

"Was the driver hurt?" Mel asked anxiously.

"Hurt? Hell, no. Not a scratch. But that road's going to be closed the rest of the day." He pulled a bamboo Chinese finger trap out of his pocket and handed it to Mel. "Truck was carrying all the prizes and stuff for the midway The whole road's covered in stuffed animals and baseballs. And you can't even see to clean 'em up."

Mel went back to the table and told B.T. what had happened.

"We could go south and pick up Highway 33," B.T. said, consulting the road atlas.

"No, you can't," the waitress, appearing with two pots of coffee, said. "It's closed. Fog. So's 15 north." She poured coffee into their cups. "You're not going anywhere."

The draft hit them again, and the waitress glanced over at the door. "Hey! Don't just stand there—shut the door!"

Mel looked toward the door. Cassie was standing there, wearing a bulky orange sweater that made her look even rounder, and scanning the restaurant for an empty booth. She was carrying a red dinosaur under one arm and her bright green tote bag over the other.

"Cassie!" Mel called to her, and she smiled and came over.

"Put your dinosaur down and join us," B.T. said.

"It's not a dinosaur," she said, setting it on the table. "It's a dragon. See?" she said, pointing to two pieces of red felt on its back. "Wings."

"Where'd you get it?" Mel said.

"The driver of the truck that spilled them gave it to me," she said. "I'd better call my sister before she hears about this on the news," she said, looking around the restaurant. "Do you think the phones are working?"

B.T. pointed at a sign that said "Phones," and she left.

She was back instantly. "There's a line," she said, and sat down. The waitress came by again with coffee and menus, and they ordered pie, and then Cassie went to check the phones again.

"There's still a line," she said, coming back. "My sister will have a fit when she hears about this. She already thinks I'm crazy. And out there in that fog today I thought so, too. I wish my grandmother had never looked up verses in the Bible."

"The Bible?" Mel said.

She waved her hand dismissively. "It's a long story."

"We seem to have plenty of time," B.T. said.

"Well," she said, settling herself. "I'm an English teacher—*was* an English teacher—and the school board offered this early-retirement bonus that was too good to turn down, so I retired in June, but I didn't know what I wanted to do. I'd always wanted to travel, but I hate traveling alone, and I didn't know where I wanted to go. So I got on the sub list—our district has a terrible time getting subs, and there's been all this flu."

It is going to be a long story, Mel thought. He picked up the finger trap and idly stuck his finger into one end. B.T. leaned back in his chair.

"Well, anyway I was subbing for Carla Sewell, who teaches sophomore lit, *Julius Caesar,* and I couldn't remember the speech about our fate being in the stars, dear Brutus."

Mel stuck a forefinger into the other side of the finger trap.

"So I was looking it up, but I read the page number wrong, so when I looked it up, it wasn't *Julius Caesar,* it was *Twelfth Night.*"

Mel stretched the finger trap experimentally. It tightened on his fingers.

"'Westward, ho!' it said," Cassie said, "and sitting there, reading it, I had this epiphany."

"Epiphany?" Mel said, yanking his fingers apart.

"Epiphany?" B.T. said.

"I'm sorry," Cassie said. "I keep thinking I'm still an English teacher. Epiphany is a literary term for a revelation, a sudden understanding, like in James Joyce's *The Dubliners*. The word comes from—"

"The story of the wise men," Mel said.

"Yes," she said delightedly, and Mel half-expected her to announce that he had gotten an A. "Epiphany is the word for their arrival at the manger."

And there it was again. The feeling that he knew where Christ was. The wise men's arrival at the manger. James Joyce.

"When I read the words 'Westward, ho!'" Cassie was saying, "I thought, that means me. I have to go west. Something important is going to happen." She looked from one to the other. "You probably think I'm crazy, doing something because of a line in *Bartlett's Quotations*. But whenever my grandmother had an important decision to make, she used to close her eyes and open her Bible and point at a Scripture, and when she opened her eyes, whatever the Scripture said to do, she'd do it. And, after all, *Bartlett's* is the Bible of English teachers. So I tried it. I closed the book and my eyes and picked a quotation at random, and it said, 'Come, my friends, 'tis not too late to seek a newer world.'"

"Tennyson," Mel said.

She nodded. "So here I am."

"And has something important happened?" B.T. asked.

"Not yet," she said, sounding completely unconcerned. "But it's going to happen soon—I'm sure of it. And in the meantime, I'm seeing all these wonderful sights. I went to Gene Stratton Porter's cabin in Geneva, and the house where Mark Twain grew up in Hannibal, Missouri, and Sherwood Anderson's museum."

She looked at Mel. "Struggling against it doesn't work," she said, pushing her index fingers together, and Mel realized he was struggling vainly to free his fingers from the finger trap. "You have to push them together."

There was a blast of icy air and a patrolman wearing three pink plastic leis around his neck and carrying a spotted plush leopard came in.

"Road's open," he said, and there was a general scramble for coats. "It's still real foggy out there," he said, raising his voice, "so don't get carried away."

Mel freed himself from the finger trap and helped Cassie into her coat while B.T. paid the bill. "Do you want to follow us?" he asked.

"No," she said, "I'm going to try to call my sister again, and if she's heard about this accident, it'll take forever. You go on."

B.T. came back from paying, and they went out to the car, which had acquired a thin, rock-hard coating of ice. Mel, chipping at the windshield with the scraper, started a new offshoot in the rapidly spreading crack.

They got back on the interstate. The fog was thicker than ever. Mel peered through it, looking at objects dimly visible at the sides of the road. The debris from the accident—baseballs and plastic leis and Coke bottles. Stuffed animals and kewpie dolls littered the median, looking in the fog like the casualties of some great battle.

"I suppose you consider this the sign you were looking for," B.T. said.

"What?" Mel said.

"Cassie's so-called epiphany. You can read anything you want into random quotations," B.T. said. "You realize that, don't you? It's like reading your horoscope. Or a fortune cookie."

"The Devil can quote scripture to his own ends," Mel murmured.

"Exactly" B.T. said, opening the Gideon Bible and closing his eyes. "Look," he said "Psalm 115, verse 5. 'Eyes have they, but they see not.' Obviously a reference to the fog.'"

He flipped to another page and stabbed his finger at it. "'Thou shalt not eat any abominable thing.' Oh, dear, we shouldn't have ordered that pie. You can make them mean anything. And you heard her, she'd retired, she liked to travel, she was obviously looking for an excuse to go somewhere. And her epiphany only said something important was going to happen. It didn't say a word about the Second Coming."

"It told her to go west," Mel said, trying to remember exactly what she had said. She had been looking for a speech from *Julius Caesar* and had stumbled on *Twelfth Night* instead. Twelfth night. Epiphany.

"How many times is the word 'west' mentioned in *Bartlett's Quotations?*" B.T. said. "A hundred? 'Oh, young Lochinvar is come out of the west'? 'Go west, young man'? 'One flew east, one flew west, one flew over the cuckoo's nest'?" He shut the Bible. "I'm sorry," he said. "It's just—" He turned and looked out his window at nothing. "It looks like it might be breaking up."

It wasn't. The fog thinned a little, swirling away from the car in little eddies, and then descended again, more smothering than ever.

"Suppose you do find Him? What do you do then?" B.T. said. "Bow down and worship Him? Give Him frankincense and myrrh?"

"Help Him," Mel said.

"Help Him what? Separate the sheep from the goats? Fight the battle of Armageddon?"

"I don't know," Mel said. "Maybe."

"You really think there's going to be a battle between good and evil?"

"There's always a battle between good and evil," Mel said. "Look at the first time He came. He hadn't been on earth a week before Herod's men were out looking for Him. They murdered every baby and two-year-old in Bethlehem, trying to kill Him."

And thirty-three years later they succeeded, Mel thought. Only killing couldn't stop Him. Nothing could stop Him.

Who had said that? The kid from the carnival, talking about the windshield. "Nothing can stop it. There's stuff you could do to keep it from spreading for a while, but it's still going to spread. There ain't nothing that can stop it."

He felt a flicker of the feeling again. Something about the kid from the carnival. What had he been talking about before that? Siamese twins. And Roswell. No. Something else.

He tried to think what Cassie had said at the truck stop. Something about the wise men arriving at the manger. And not struggling. "You have to push them together," she had said.

It stayed tantalizingly out of reach, as elusive as a road sign glimpsed in the fog.

B.T. reached forward and flicked on the radio. "Foggy tonight, and colder," it said. "In the teens for eastern Nebraska, down in the..." it faded to static. B.T. twisted the knob.

"And do you know what will happen to us when Jesus comes?" an evangelist shouted, "The Book of Revelation tells us we will be tormented with fire and brimstone, unless we repent now; before it's too late!"

"A little fire and brimstone would be welcome right about now," B.T. said, reaching forward to turn the heater up to high.

"There's a blanket in the backseat," Mel said, and B.T. reached back and wrapped himself up in it.

"We will be scorched with fire," the radio said, "and the smoke of our torment will rise up forever and ever."

B.T. leaned his head against the doorjamb. "Just so it's warm," he murmured and closed his eyes.

"But that's not all that will happen to us if we do not repent," the evangelist said, "if we do not take Jesus as our personal Savior. The Book of Revelation tells us in Chapter 14 that we will be cast into the winepress of God's wrath and be *trodden* in it till our blood covers the ground for a thousand *miles!* And don't fool yourselves, that day is coming *soon!* The signs are all around us! Wait till your father gets home."

Mel switched it off, but it was too late. The evangelist had hit it, the problem Mel had been trying to avoid since that moment in the sanctuary.

I don't believe it, he had thought when he'd heard the minister talking about Jesus forbidding believers to associate with outcasts. And he had thought it again when he heard the radio evangelist that first day talking about Christ coming to get revenge.

"I don't believe it," he thought, and when B.T. stirred in his corner, he realized he had spoken aloud.

"I don't believe it," he murmured. God had so loved the world, He had sent His only begotten Son to live among men, to be a helpless baby and a little boy and a young man, had sent Him to be cold and confused, angry and overjoyed. "To share our common lot," the Nicene Creed said. To undergo and understand and forgive. "Father, forgive them," He had said, with nails driven through His hands, and when they had arrested Him, he had made the disciples put away their weapons. He had healed the soldier's ear Peter had cut off.

He would never, *never* come back in a blaze of wrath and revenge, slaughtering enemies, tormenting unbelievers, wreaking fire and pestilence and famine on them. Never.

And how can I believe in a revelation about the Second Coming, he thought, when I don't believe in the Second Coming?

But the epiphany wasn't about the Second Coming, he thought. He hadn't seen earthquakes or Armageddon or Christ coming in a blaze of clouds and glory. He's already here, he had thought, now, and had set out to find Him, to look for a sign.

But there aren't any, he thought, and saw one off in the mist. "Prairie Home 5, Denver 468."

Denver. They would be there tomorrow night. And B.T. would want him to fly home with him.

Unless I figure out the key Mel thought. Unless I'm given a sign. Or unless the roads are closed.

> *"And, lo, the star which they saw in the east, went before them...."*
>
> —Matthew 2:9

"They should be open," the woman at the Wayfarer Motel said. The Holiday Inn and the Super 8 and the Innkeeper had all been full up, and the Wayfarer had only one room left. "There's supposed to be fog in the morning, and then it's supposed to be nice all the way till Sunday."

"What about the roads east?" B.T. asked.

"No problem," she said.

The Wayfarer didn't have a coffee shop. They ate supper at the Village Inn on the other end of town. As they were leaving, they ran into Cassie in the parking lot.

"Oh, good," she said. "I was afraid I wouldn't have a chance to say goodbye."

"Goodbye?" Mel said.

"I'm heading south tomorrow to Red Cloud. When I consulted Bartlett's, it said, 'Winter lies too long in country towns.'"

"Oh?" Mel said, wondering what this had to do with going south.

"Willa Cather," Cassie said. *"My Ántonia.* I didn't understand it either, so I tried the Gideon Bible in my hotel, it's so nice of them to leave them there, and it was Exodus 13:21, 'And the Lord went before them by day in a pillar of a cloud, to lead the way; and by night in a pillar of fire.'"

She smiled expectantly at them. "Pillar of fire. Red Cloud. Willa Cather's museum is in Red Cloud."

They said goodbye to her and went back to the motel. B.T. sat down on his bed and took his laptop out of his suitcase. "I've got some e-mail I've got to answer," he said.

And send? Mel wondered. "Dear Mrs. Bilderbeck, we'll be in Denver tomorrow. Am hoping to persuade Mel to come home with me. Have straitjacket ready."

Mel sat down in the room's only chair with the Rand McNally and looked at the map of Nebraska, searching for a town named Megiddo or New Jerusalem. There was Red Cloud, down near the southern border of

Nebraska. Pillar of fire. Why couldn't he have had a nice straightforward sign like that? A pillar of smoke by day and a pillar of fire by night. Or a star.

But Moses had wandered around in the wilderness for forty years following said pillar. And the star hadn't led the wise men to Bethlehem. It had led them straight into King Herod's arms. They hadn't had a clue where the newborn Christ was. "Where is He that is born king of the Jews?" they'd asked Herod.

"Where is He?" Mel murmured, and B.T. glanced up from his laptop and then back down at it again, typing steadily.

Mel turned to the map of Colorado. Beulah. Bonanza. Firstview.

"Even if your—epiphany—was real," B.T. had asked him this afternoon, "couldn't you have misinterpreted what it means?"

Well, if he had, he wouldn't have been the first one. The Bible was full of people who had misinterpreted prophecies. "Dogs have compassed me; the assembly of the wicked have enclosed me," the Scriptures said, "they pierced my hands and my feet." But nobody saw the Crucifixion coming. Or the Resurrection.

His own disciples didn't recognize Him. Easter Sunday they walked all the way to Emmaus with Him without figuring out who He was, and even when He told them, Thomas refused to believe Him and demanded to see the scars of the nails in His hands.

They had never recognized Him. Isaiah had plainly predicted a virgin who would bring forth a child "out of the root of Jesse," a child who would redeem Israel. But nobody had thought that meant a baby in a stable.

They had thought he was talking about a warrior, a king who would raise an army and drive the hated foreigners out of their country, a hero on a white horse who would vanquish their enemies and set them free. And He had, but not in the way they expected.

Nobody had expected Him to be a poor itinerant preacher from an obscure family, with no college degree and no military training, a nobody. Even the wise men had expected Him to be royalty. "Where is the *king* whose star we have seen in the east?" they had asked Herod.

And Herod had promptly sent soldiers out to search for a usurper, a threat to his throne.

They had been looking for the wrong thing. And maybe B.T.'s right, maybe I am, too, and that's the answer. The Second Coming isn't going to be battles and earthquakes and falling stars, and Revelation means something else, like the prophecies of the Messiah.

Or maybe it wasn't the Second Coming, and Christ was here only in a symbolic sense, in the poor, the hungry, in those in need of help. "As ye have done this unto the least of these—"

"Maybe the Second Coming really is here," B.T. said from the bed. "Look at this."

He turned the laptop around so Mel could see the screen. "Watch, therefore," it read, "for ye know neither the day nor the hour wherein the Son of man cometh."

"It's a website," B.T. said. "www.watchman."

"It probably belongs to one of the radio evangelists," Mel said.

"I don't think so," B.T. said. He hit a key, and a new screen came up. It was full of entries.

"Meteor, 12-23, 4 mi. NNW Raton."

"Examined area. 12-28. No sign."

"Weather Channel 11-2, 9:15 a.m. PST. Reference to unusual cloud formations."

"Latitude and longitude? Need location."

"8.6 mi. WNW Prescott AZ 11-4."

"Denver Post 914P8C2—Headline: 'Unusually high lightning activity strikes Carson National Forest. MT2427.'"

"What do you think that stands for?" B.T. said, pointing at the string of letters and numbers.

"Matthew 24, verse 27," Mel said. "'For the lightning cometh out of the west and shineth even unto the east, so shall also the coming of the Son of man be.'"

B.T. nodded and scrolled the screen down.

"Triple lightning strike. 7-11, Platteville, CO. Nov. 28. Two injured."

"Lightning storm, Dec. 4, Truth or Consequences."

"What about that one?" B.T. said, pointing at "Truth or Consequences."

"It's a town in southern New Mexico," Mel said.

"Oh." He scrolled the screen down some more.

"Falling star, 12-30, 2 mi. W of U.S. State Hwy 191, west of Bozeman, mile marker 161."

"Coma patient recovery, Yale—New Haven Hosp. Connection?"

"Negative. Too far east."

"Possible sighting Nevada."

"Need location."

Need location. "'Go search diligently for the young child,'" Mel murmured, "'and when ye have found him, bring me word again, that I may come and worship him.'"

"What?" B.T. said.

"It's what Herod said when the wise men told him about the star." He stared at the screen:

"L.A. Times Jan 2 P5C1. Fish die-off. RV89?"

"Possible sighting. Old Faithful, Yellowstone Nat'l Pk, Jan. 2."

And over and over again:

"Need location."

"Need location."

"Need location."

"They obviously think the Second Coming's happened," B.T. said, staring at the screen.

"Or aliens have landed at Roswell," Mel said. He pointed to the convenience store entry. "Or Elvis is back."

"Maybe," B.T. said, staring at the screen.

Mel went back to looking at the maps. Barren Rock. Deadwood. Last Chance.

Need location, he thought. Maybe he and Cassie and whoever had written "Too far east" on the website had all misinterpreted the message, and it was not "west" but "West."

He turned to the gazetteer in the back. West. Westwood Hills, Kansas. Westville, Oklahoma. West Hollywood, California. Westview. Westgate. Westmont. There was a Westwood Hills in Kansas. Colorado had a Westcliffe, a Western Hills, and a Westminster. Neither Arizona nor New Mexico had any Wests. Nevada didn't either. Nebraska had a West Point.

West Point. Maybe it wasn't even in the west. Maybe it was West Orange, New Jersey, or West Palm Beach. Or West Berlin.

He shut the atlas and looked over at B.T. He had dozed off, his face tired and worried-looking even in sleep. His laptop was on his chest, and the Gideon Bible he had stolen from the Holiday Inn lay beside him.

Mel shut the laptop off and quietly closed it. B.T. didn't move. Mel picked up the Bible.

The answer had to be in the Scriptures. He opened the Bible to Matthew. "Then if any man shall say unto you, Lo, here is Christ, or there; believe it not."

He read on. Disasters and devastation and tribulation, as the prophets had spoken.

The prophets. He found Isaiah. "Hear ye indeed but understand not; and see ye indeed but perceive not."

He shut the Bible. All right, he thought, standing it on its spine on his hand. Let's have a sign here. I'm running out of time.

He opened his eyes. His finger was on I Samuel 23, verse 14. "And Saul sought him every day, but God delivered him not into his hand."

> *"For all these things must come to pass, but the end is not yet."*
> —Matthew 24:6

All the roads were open, and, from Grand Island, clear and dry, and the fog had lifted a little.

"With roads like this, we ought to be in Denver by tonight," B.T. said.

Yes, Mel thought, finishing what B.T. had said, if you fly back with me, we could be there in time for the ecumenical meeting. Nobody'd ever have to know he'd been gone, except Mrs. Bilderbeck, and he could tell her he'd been offered a job by another church, but had decided not to take it, which was true.

"It just didn't work out," he would tell Mrs. Bilderbeck, and she would be so overjoyed that he wasn't leaving, she wouldn't even ask for details.

And he could go back to doing sermons and giving the choir plenty of warning, storing the star, and keeping the pilot light going, as if nothing had happened.

"Exit 312" a green interstate sign up ahead said. "Hastings, 18. Red Cloud, 57."

He wondered if Cassie was already at Willa Cather's house, convinced she had been led there by *Bartlett's Quotations.*

Cassie had no trouble finding signs—she saw them everywhere. And maybe they are everywhere, and I'm just not seeing them. Maybe Hastings is a sign, and the truck full of mirrors, and those stuffed toys all over the road. Maybe that Chinese fingertrap I got stuck in yesterday was—

"Look," B.T. said. "Wasn't that Cassie's car?"

"Where?" Mel said, craning his neck around.

"In that ditch back there."

This time Mel didn't wait for an "Authorized Vehicles Only" crossing. He plunged into the snowy median and back along the other side of the highway, still unable to see anything.

"There," B.T. said, pointing, and he turned onto the median.

He had crossed both lanes and was onto the shoulder before he saw the Honda, halfway down a steep ditch and tilted at an awkward angle. He couldn't see anyone in the driver's seat.

B.T. was out of the car before Mel got the car stopped and plunging down the snowy bank, with Mel behind him. B.T. wrenched the car door open.

Cassie's green tote bag was on the floor of the passenger seat. B.T. peered into the backseat. "She's not here," he said unnecessarily

"Cassie!" Mel called. He ran around the front of the car, though she couldn't have been thrown out. The door would have been open if she'd been thrown out. "Cassie!"

"Here," a faint voice said, and Mel looked down the slope. Cassie lay at the bottom in tall dry weeds.

"She's down here," he said, and half-walked, half-slid down the ravine.

She was lying on her back with her leg bent under her. "I think it's broken," she said to Mel.

"Go flag a semi down," Mel said to B.T., who'd appeared above them. "Have them call an ambulance."

B.T. disappeared, and Mel turned back to Cassie. "How long have you been here?" he asked her, pulling off his overcoat and tucking it around her.

"I don't know," she said, shivering. "There was a patch of ice. I didn't think anybody'd see the car, so I got out to climb up to the road, and that's when I slipped. My leg's broken, isn't it?"

At that angle, it had to be. "I think it probably is," Mel said.

She turned her face away in the dry weeds. "My sister was right."

Mel took off his jacket, rolled it up, and put it under her head. "We'll have an ambulance here for you in no time."

"She told me I was crazy," Cassie said, still not looking at Mel, "and this proves it, doesn't it? And she didn't even know about the epiphany." She turned and looked at Mel. "Only it wasn't an epiphany. Just low estrogen levels."

"Conserve your strength," he said, and looked anxiously up the slope.

Cassie grabbed at his hand. "I lied to you. I wasn't offered early retirement. I asked for it. I was so sure 'Westward ho!' meant something. I sold my house and took out all my savings."

Her hand was red with cold. Mel wished he had taken his gloves back when the kid from the carnival offered them. He took her icy hand between his own and held it tightly.

"I was so *sure*," she said.

"Mel," B.T. called from above them. "I've had four semis go by without stopping. I think it's the color." He pointed to his black face. "You need to come up and try."

"I'll be right there," Mel called back up to him. "I'll be right back," he said to Cassie.

"No," she said, clutching his hand. "Don't you see? It didn't mean anything. It was nothing but menopause, like my sister said. She tried to tell me, but I wouldn't listen."

"Cassie," Mel said, gently releasing her hand, "we need to get you out of here and into town to a hospital. You can tell me all about it then."

"There's nothing to tell," she said, and let go of his hand.

"Come on, there's another truck coming," B.T. called down, and Mel started up the slope. "No, never mind," B.T. said. "The cavalry's here," he said, and, amazingly, he laughed.

There was a screech of hydraulic brakes. Mel scrambled up the rest of the way. A truck was stopping. It was one of the carnival's, loaded with merry-go-round horses, white and black and palomino, with red-and-gold saddles and jeweled bridles. B.T. was already running toward the cab, asking, "Do you have a CB?"

"Yeah," the driver said, and came around the back of the truck. It was the kid Mel had picked up, still wearing the gloves he had given him.

"We need an ambulance," Mel said. "There's a lady hurt here."

"Sure thing," the kid said, and disappeared back around the truck.

Met skidded back down the slope to Cassie. "He's calling an ambulance," he said to her.

She nodded uninterestedly.

"They're on their way," the kid called down from above them. He went over to the Honda, B.T. following, and stuck his head under the back of it. He walked all around it, squatting next to the far wheels, and then disappeared back up the slope again.

"He says his truck doesn't have a tow rope," B.T. said, coming back to report, "and he doesn't think he could get the car out anyway, so he's calling a tow truck."

Mel nodded. "I saw a sign that said the next town was only ten miles. They'll have you in out of the cold before you know it."

She didn't answer. Mel wondered if perhaps she was going into shock. "Cassie," he said, taking her hands again and rubbing them in spite of what he'd told the kid about frostbite. "We were so surprised to see your car," he said just to be saying something, to get her to talk. "We thought you were going down to Red Cloud. What made you change your mind?"

*"Bartlett's,"* she said bitterly "When I was putting my tote bag in the car, it fell out onto the parking lot, and when I picked it up, the first thing I read was from William Blake. 'Turn away no more,' it said. I thought it meant I shouldn't turn south to Red Cloud, that I should keep going west. Can you imagine anybody being that stupid?"

Yes, Mel thought.

The ambulance pulled up, sirens and yellow lights blazing, and two paramedics leaped out with a stretcher, skidded down the slope to where Cassie was, and began maneuvering her expertly onto it.

Mel went over to B.T. "You go in with her in the ambulance," he said, "and I'll wait here for the tow truck."

"Are you sure?" B.T. said. "I can wait here."

"No," Mel said. "I'll follow the tow truck to the garage and find out what I can about her car. Then I'll meet you at the hospital. What time's the earliest flight home from Denver tomorrow?"

"Flight?" B.T. said. "No. I'm not going home without you."

"You won't have to," Mel said. "What time's the earliest flight?"

"I don't understand—"

"Or we can drive back. If we take turns driving we can be back in time for the ecumenical meeting."

"But—" B.T. said bewilderedly.

"I wanted a sign. Well, I got it," he said, waving his arm at Cassie, at her car. "I don't have to be hit over the head to get the message. I'm out here in the middle of nowhere in the middle of winter on a fool's errand."

"What about the epiphany?"

"It was a hallucination, a seizure, a temporary hormonal imbalance."

"And what about your call to the ministry?" B.T. said. "Was that a hallucination, too? What about Cassie?"

"The Devil can quote Scripture, remember?" Mel said bitterly. "And *Bartlett's Quotations*."

"Can you give us a hand here?" one of the paramedics called. They had Cassie on the stretcher and were ready to carry it up the slope.

"Coming," Mel said, and started toward them.

B.T. took his arm. "What about the others who are looking for Him? The watchman website?"

"UFO nuts," Mel said, and went over to the stretcher. "It doesn't mean anything."

Cassie lay under a gray blanket, her head turned to the side, the way it had been when Mel found her.

"Are you all right?" B.T. taking hold of the other side of the stretcher, asked.

"No," she said, and a tear wobbled down her plump cheek. "I'm sorry I put you to all this trouble."

The kid from the carnival took hold of the front of the stretcher. "Things aren't always as bad as they look," he said, patting the blanket. "I saw a guy fall off the top of the Ferris wheel once, and he wasn't even hurt."

Cassie shook her head. "It was a mistake. I shouldn't have come."

"Don't say that," B.T. said. "You got to see Mark Twain's house. And Gene Stratton Porter's."

She turned her face away. "What good are they? I'm not even an English teacher anymore."

Things might not have been as bad as they looked for the guy who fell off the Ferris wheel, but they were even worse than they looked when it came to the snowy slope and getting Cassie up it. By the time they got her into the ambulance, her face was as gray as the blanket and twisted with pain. The paramedics began hooking her up to a blood-pressure cuff and an IV.

"I'll meet you at the hospital," Mel said. "You can call Mrs. Bilderbeck and tell her we're coming."

"What if the roads are closed?" B.T. said.

"You heard the clerk last night. Clear both directions." He looked at

B.T. "I thought this was what you wanted, for me to come to my senses, to admit I was crazy."

B.T. looked unhappy. "Animals don't always leave tracks," he said. "I learned that five years ago banding deer for a Lyme disease project. Sometimes they leave all sorts of sign, other times they're invisible."

The paramedics were shutting the doors. "Wait," he said. "I'm going with her."

He clambered up into the back of the ambulance. "Do you know the only way you can tell for sure the deer are there?"

Mel shook his head.

"By the wolves," he said.

> *"Therefore the Lord himself shall give you a sign…"*
> —Isaiah 7:14

It took nearly an hour for the tow truck to get there. Mel waited in his car with the heater running for a while and then got out and went over to stare at Cassie's Honda.

Wolves, B.T. had said. Predators. "'For wheresoever the carcass is,'" he quoted, "'there will the eagles be gathered together.' MT2428."

"The Devil can quote Scripture," he said aloud, and got back into the car.

The crack in the windshield had split again, splaying out in two new directions from the center. A definite sign.

You've had dozens of signs, he thought. Blizzards, road closures, icy and snow-packed conditions. You just chose to ignore them.

"Why, anybody'd have to be *blind* not to recognize them," the radio evangelist had said, and that was what he had been, willfully blind, pretending the yellow arrow, the roads closing behind him, were signs he was going in the right direction, that Cassie's "Westward, ho!" was outside confirmation.

"It didn't mean anything," he said.

It was getting dark by the time the tow truck finally got there, and pitch black by the time they got Cassie's Honda pulled up the slope.

And that was a sign, too, Mel thought, following the tow truck. Like the fog and the carnival truck jackknifed across the highway and the "No Vacancy" signs on the motels. All of them flashing the same message. It was a mistake. Give up. Go home.

The tow truck had gotten far ahead of him. He stepped on the gas, but a very slow pickup pulled in front of him, and an even slower recreation vehicle was blocking the right lane. By the time he got to the gas station, the mechanic was already sliding out from under the Honda and shaking his head.

"Snapped an axle and did in the transmission," he said, wiping his hands on a greasy rag. "Cost at least fifteen hundred to fix it, and I doubt if it's worth half that." He patted the hood sympathetically. "I'm afraid it's the end of the road."

The end of the road. All right, all right, Mel thought, I get the message.

"So what do you want to do?" the mechanic asked.

Give up, Mel thought. Come to my senses. Go home. "It's not my car," he said. "I'll have to ask the owner. She's in the hospital right now."

"She hurt bad?"

Mel remembered her lying there in the weeds, saying, "It didn't mean anything."

"No," he lied.

"Tell her I can do an estimate on a new axle and a new transmission if she wants," the mechanic said reluctantly, "but if I was her I'd take the insurance and start over."

"I'll tell her," Mel said. He opened the trunk and took out her suitcase, and then went around to the passenger side to get her green bag out of the backseat.

There was a bright yellow flyer rolled up and jammed in the door handle. Mel unrolled it. It was a flyer from the carnival. The kid must have stuck it there, Mel thought, smiling in spite of himself.

There was a drawing of a trumpet at the top, with "Come one, come all!" issuing from the mouth of it.

Underneath that, there was a drawing of the triple Ferris wheel, and scattered in boxes across the page, "Marvel at the Living Fountains," "Ride the Sea Dragon!," "Popcorn, Snow Cones, Cotton Candy!," "See a Lion and a Lamb in a Single Cage!"

He stared at the flyer.

"Tell her if she wants to sell it for parts," the mechanic said, "I can give her four hundred."

A lion and a lamb. Wheels within wheels. "For the Lamb shall lead them unto living fountains of waters."

"What's that you're reading?" the mechanic said, coming around the car.

A midway with stuffed animals for prizes—bears and lions and red dragons—and a ride called the Shooting Star, a hall of mirrors. "For now we see in a glass darkly but then we shall see face to face."

The mechanic peered over his shoulder. "Oh, an ad for that crazy carnival," he said. "Yeah, I got a sign for it in the window."

A sign. "For behold, I give you a sign." And the sign was just what it said, a sign. Like the Siamese twins. Like the peace sign on the back of the kid's hand. "For unto us a son is given, and his name shall be called Wonderful, Counsellor, the Prince of Peace." On the kid's scarred hand.

"If she wants an estimate, tell her it'll take some time," the mechanic said, but Mel wasn't listening. He was gazing blindly at the flyer. "Peer into the Bottomless Pit!" it said. "Ride the Merry-Go-Round!"

"And thus I saw the horses in the vision," Mel murmured, "and them that sat upon them." He started to laugh.

The mechanic frowned at him. "It ain't funny," he said. "This car's a real mess. So what do you think she'll want to do?"

"Go to a carnival," Mel said, and ran to get in his car.

> *"And there shall be no night there; and they need no candle, neither light of the sun..."*
>
> —Revelation 22:15

The hospital was a three-story brick building. Mel parked in front of the emergency entrance and went in.

"May I help you?" the admitting nurse asked.

"Yes," he said, "I'm looking for—" and then stopped. Behind the desk was a sign for the carnival with dates at the bottom. "Crown Point, Dec. 14" it read. "Gresham, Jan. 13th, Empyrean, Jan. 15."

"May I help you, sir?" the nurse said again, and Mel turned to ask her where Empyrean was, but she wasn't talking to him. She was asking two men in navy-blue suits.

"Yes," the taller one said, "we're starting a hospital outreach, ministering to people who are in the hospital far from home. Do you have any patients here from out of town?"

The nurse looked doubtful. "I'm afraid we're not allowed to give out information about patients."

"Of course, I understand," the man said, opening his Bible. "We don't want to violate anyone's privacy. We'd just like to be able to say a few words of comfort, like the Good Samaritan."

"I'm not supposed to…" the nurse said.

"We understand," the shorter man said. "Will you join us in a moment of prayer? Precious Lord, we seek—"

The door opened, and as they all turned to look at a boy with a bleeding forehead, Mel slipped down the hall and up the stairs.

Where would they have taken her? he wondered, peering into rooms with open doors. Did a hospital this small even have separate wards, or were all the patients jumbled together?

She wasn't on the first floor. He hurried up the stairs to the second, keeping an eye out for the men in the navy-blue suits. They didn't know her name yet, but they would soon. Even if they couldn't get it out of the admitting nurse, Cassie would have given them her health-insurance card. It would all be in the computer. *Where* would they have taken her? X-ray, he thought.

"Can you tell me how to get to X-ray?" he asked a middle-aged woman in a pink uniform.

"Third floor," she said, and pointed toward the elevator.

Mel thanked her, and as soon as she was out of sight, he took the stairs two at a time.

Cassie wasn't in X-ray. Mel started to look for a technician to ask and then saw B.T. down at the end of the hall.

"Good news," B.T. said as he hurried up to him. "It's not broken. She's got a sprained knee."

"Where is she?" Mel asked, taking B.T.'s arm.

"Three-oh-eight," B.T. said, and Mel propelled him into the room and shut the door behind them.

Cassie, in a white hospital gown, was lying in the far bed, her head turned away from them as it had been in the frozen weeds. She looked pale and listless.

"She called her sister," B.T. said, looking anxiously at her. "She's on her way down from Minnesota to get her."

"She told me I was lucky I hadn't gotten into worse trouble than a sprained knee," Cassie said, turning to look at Mel. "How's my car?"

"A dead loss," Mel said stepping up to the head of the bed. "But it doesn't matter. We—"

"You're right," she said, and turned her head on the pillow. "It doesn't matter. I've come to my senses. I'm going home." She smiled wanly at

Mel. "I'm just sorry you had to go to all this trouble for me, but at least it won't be for much longer. My sister should be here tomorrow night, and the hospital is keeping me overnight for observation, so you two don't have to stay. You can go to your religious meeting."

"We lied to you," Mel said. "We're not on our way to a religious meeting," and realized they were. "You aren't the only one who had an epiphany."

"I'm not?" she said, and pushed herself partway up against the pillows.

"No. I got a message to go west, too," Mel said. "You were right. Something important is going to happen, and we want you to come with us."

B.T. cut in, "You know where He is?"

"I know where He's going to be," Mel said. "B.T., I want you to go get the road atlas and look up a town called Empyrean and see where it is."

"I know where it is," Cassie said, and sat up all the way. "It's in Dante."

They both looked at her, and she said, half-apologetically, "I'm an English teacher, remember? It's the highest circle of Paradise. The Holy City of God."

"I doubt if that's going to be in Rand McNally," B.T. said.

"It doesn't matter," Mel said. "We'll be able to find it by the lights. But we've got to get her out of here first. Cassie, do you think you can walk if we help you?"

"Yes." She flung the covers off and began edging her bandaged knee toward the side of the bed. "My clothes are in the closet there."

Mel helped her hobble to the closet.

"I'll go check her out," B.T. said, and went out.

Cassie pulled her dress off the hanger and began unzipping it. Mel turned his back and went over to the door to look out. There was no sign of the two men.

"Can you help me get my boots on?" Cassie said, hobbling over to the chair. "My knee's feeling a lot better," she said, lowering herself into the chair. "It hardly hurts at all." Mel knelt and eased her feet into her fur-edged boots.

B.T. came in. "There are two men down at the admissions desk," he said, out of breath, "trying to find out what room she's in."

"Who are they?" Cassie asked.

"Herod's men," Mel said. "It'll have to be the fire escape. Can you manage that?"

She nodded. Mel helped her to her feet and went and got her coat. He and B.T. helped her into it, and each took an arm and helped her to the door, opening it cautiously and looking both ways down the hall, and then over to the fire escape.

"I should call my sister," Cassie said, "and tell her I've changed my mind."

"We'll stop at a gas station," B.T. said, opening the door fully and looking both ways again. "Okay," he said, and they went down the hall, through the emergency exit door, and onto the fire escape.

"You go bring the car around," B.T. said, and Mel clattered down the metal mesh steps and ducked across the parking lot to the car.

The emergency-room door opened and two men stood in its light for a moment, talking to someone.

Mel jammed the key into the ignition, switched it on, and pulled the car around to the side of the hospital, where B.T. and Cassie were working their way down the last steps.

"Come on," he said, grabbing Cassie under the arm, "hurry," and hustled her across to the car.

A siren blared. "Hurry," Mel said, yanking the door open and pushing her into the backseat, slamming the door shut. B.T. ran around to the other side.

The siren came abruptly closer and then cut off, and Mel, reaching for the door handle, looked back toward the entrance. An ambulance pulled in, red and yellow lights flashing, and the two men in the door reached forward and took a stretcher off the back.

And this is crazy, Mel thought. Nobody's after us. But they would be, as soon as the nurse saw Cassie was missing, and if not then, as soon as Cassie's sister got there. "I saw two men push a woman into a car and then go peeling out of here," one of the interns unloading that stretcher would say. "It looked like they were kidnapping her." And how would they explain to the police that they were looking for the City of God?

"This is insane," Mel started to say, reaching for the door handle.

There was a flyer wedged in it. Mel unrolled it and read it by the parking lot's vapor light. "Hurry, hurry, hurry! Step right up to the Greatest Show on Earth!" it read in letters of gold. "Wonders, Marvels, Mysteries Revealed!"

Mel got into the car and handed the flyer to B.T. "Ready?" he asked.

"Let's go," Cassie said, and leaned forward to point at the front door. Two men in navy-blue suits were running down the front steps.

"Keep down," Mel said, and peeled out of the parking lot. He turned south, drove a block, turned onto a side street, pulled up to the curb, switched off the lights, and waited, watching in his rearview mirror until a navy-blue car roared past them going south.

He started the car and drove two blocks without lights on and then circled back to the highway and headed north. Five miles out of town, he turned east on a gravel road, drove till it ended, turned south, and then east again, and north onto a dirt road. There was no one behind them.

"Okay" he said, and B.T. and Cassie sat up.

"Where are we?" Cassie asked.

"I have no idea," Mel said. He turned east again and then south on the first paved road he came to.

"Where are we going?" B.T. asked.

"I don't know that either. But I know what we're looking for." He waited till a beat-up pickup truck full of kids passed them and then pulled over to the side of the road and switched on the dome light.

"Where's your laptop?" he asked B.T.

"Right here," B.T. said, opening it up and switching it on.

"All right," Mel said, holding the flyer up to the light. "They were in Omaha on January fourth, Palmyra on the ninth, and Beatrice on the tenth." He concentrated, trying to remember the dates on the sign in the hospital.

"Beatrice," Cassie murmured. "That's in Dante, too."

"The carnival was in Crown Point on December fourteenth," Mel went on, trying to remember the dates on the sign in the hospital, "and Gresham on January thirteenth."

"The carnival?" B.T. said. "We're looking for a carnival?"

"Yes," Mel said. "Cassie, have you got your *Bartlett's Quotations?*"

"Yes," she said, and began rummaging in the emerald-green tote bag.

"I saw them between Pittsburgh and Youngstown on Sunday," Mel said to B.T., who had started typing, "and in Wayside, Iowa, on Monday."

"And the truck spill was at Seward," B.T. said, tapping keys.

"What have you got, Cassie?" Mel said, looking in the rearview mirror.

She had her finger on an open page. "It's Christina Rossetti," she said. "'Will the day's journey take the whole long day? From morn to night, my friend.'"

"They're skipping all over the map," B.T. said, turning the laptop so Mel could see the screen. It was a maze of connecting lines.

"Can you tell what general direction they're headed?" Mel asked.

"Yes," B.T. said. "West."

"West," Mel repeated. Of course. He started the car again and turned west on the first road they came to.

There were no cars at all, and only a few scattered lights, a farm and a grain elevator, and a radio tower. Mel drove steadily west across the flat, snowy landscape, looking for the distant glittering lights of the carnival.

The sky turned navy blue and then gray, and they stopped to get gas and call Cassie's sister.

"Use my calling card," B.T. said, handing it to Cassie. "They're not looking for me yet. How much cash do we have?"

Cassie had sixty and another two hundred in traveler's checks. Mel had a hundred sixty-eight. "What did you do?" B.T. asked. "Rob the collection plate?"

Mel called Mrs. Bilderbeck. "I won't be back in time for the services on Sunday," he told her. "Call Reverend Davidson and ask if he'll fill in. And tell the ecumenical meeting to read John 3:16-18 for a devotion."

"Are you sure you're all right?" Mrs. Bilderbeck asked. "There were some men here looking for you yesterday."

Mel gripped the receiver. "What did you tell them?"

"I didn't like the looks of them, so I told them you were at a ministerial alliance meeting in Boston."

"You're wonderful," Mel said, and started to hang up.

"Oh, wait, what about the furnace?" Mrs. Bilderbeck said. "What if the pilot light goes out again?"

"It won't," Mel said. "Nothing can put it out."

He hung up and handed the phone and the calling card to Cassie. She called her sister, who had a car phone, and told her not to come, that she was fine, her knee hadn't been sprained after all, just twisted.

"And I think it must have been," she said to Mel, walking back to the car. "See? I'm not limping at all."

B.T. had bought juice and doughnuts and a large bag of potato chips. They ate them while Mel drove, going south across the interstate and down to Highway 34.

The sun came up and glittered off metal silos and onto the starshaped crack in the windshield. Mel squinted against its brilliance. They drove slowly through McCook and Sharon Springs and Maranatha, looking for flyers on telephone poles and in store windows, calling out the towns and dates to B.T., who added them to the ones on his laptop.

Trucks passed them, none of them carrying Tilt-a-Whirls or concession stands, and Cassie consulted *Bartlett's* again. "A cold coming we had of it," it said. "Just the worst time of the year."

"T. S. Eliot," Cassie said wonderingly. "'Journey of the Magi.'"

They stopped for gas again, and B.T. drove while Mel napped. It began to get dark. B.T. and Mel changed places, and Cassie got in front, moving stiffly.

"Is your knee hurting again?" Mel asked.

"No," Cassie said. "It doesn't hurt at all. I've just been sitting in the car too long," she said. "At least it's not camels. Can you imagine what that must have been like?"

Yes, Mel thought, I can. I'll bet everyone thought they were crazy. Including them.

It got very dark. They continued west, through Glorieta and Gilead and Beulah Center, searching for multicolored lights glimmering in a cold field, a spinning Ferris wheel and the smell of cotton candy, listening for the screams of the roller coaster and the music of a merry-go-round.

And the star went before them.